A Special Gift For You

To: Mum / Nanny
Lots of Love

Happy
Mothers
Day
xx

From: Robert, Debbie
& Butta xxx

A Mother's Gift

Josephine Cox was born in Blackburn, one of ten children. At the age of sixteen, Josephine met and married her husband Ken, and had two sons. When the boys started school, she decided to go to college and eventually gained a place at Cambridge University. She was unable to take this up as it would have meant living away from home, but she went into teaching – and started to write her first full-length novel. She won the 'Superwoman of Great Britain' Award, for which her family had secretly entered her, at the same time as her novel was accepted for publication. Her strong, gritty stories are taken from the tapestry of life. Josephine says, 'I could never imagine a single day without writing. It's been that way since as far back as I can remember.'

Visit www.josephinecox.com to find out more information about Josephine.

Also by Josephine Cox

JOSEPHINE COX

A Mother's Gift

TWO CLASSIC NOVELS
THE JOURNEY AND JOURNEY'S END

Josephine Cox

HarperCollins*Publishers*

Harper
An imprint of HarperCollins*Publishers*
The News Building
1 London Bridge Street
London SE1 9GF

www.harpercollins.co.uk

Published by HarperCollins*Publishers* 2016
1

A catalogue record for this book is
available from the British Library

ISBN: 9780008171551

Printed and bound in Great Britain by Clays Ltd, St Ives plc

MIX
Paper from
responsible sources
FSC **FSC™ C007454**
www.fsc.org

To my Ken, as always

To my ever loyal readers...

And to those who have not yet discovered the magic of holding a beloved book in your hands and heart, as you travel through the twists and turns of my characters' adventure...

I started writing the first of these two books over ten years ago, but the characters and their tale have stayed with me so strongly ever since that I am delighted to be presenting you with an anniversary edition of the complete set of books that makes up this haunting story.

It is the story of a devoted mother, Lucy Baker, and a good man. Their love for those they care most deeply about is immensely strong, but our lonely man is determined to commit a brave and sorry act that will inevitably destroy him.

Because he believes it to be right, he feels that he has no choice...

Meanwhile, despite the hardships and disappointments of her own life, Lucy has so much love in her heart, not least a mother's love. It is her inherent goodness that drives her to right the wrongs of the past, even if it means breaking a promise she has kept for many long years.

And so we find ourselves asking whether anyone in this tragic situation come out a winner, and will Lucy eventually find the happiness she so richly deserves?

These characters are real, as all my characters are to me. They walk and live, and open their hearts to you. They are much the same as we all are, travelling through our lives with hope, *and the belief that in the end all will be well. Sadly though, our hopes and dreams might fade away, or alternatively they will actually come to fruition. But whichever way your life might turn out, it is your life, and through your dreams and strong beliefs, it will carry you through, and the great and wonderful experiences will lift your spirits.*

There will surely be sadness, and tears, and a cruel dashing of your hopes – yet we struggle on, because we have to. Because deep down in the human spirit breathes a well of hope and believe that in the end it will all come right, one way or another.

We are duty bound to walk through our lives with dignity, belief and goodness as much as we can, because there is no other way but forward.

Just like Lucy, keep a strong heart and a deep well of strong belief in yourself so that you have it in you to rise above all the bad things that life will surely test you with. In this story, you will understand, how joy can overcome sadness. You will understand how love can turn around even the most painful experiences. And how family – the ones we find ourselves in, and the ones that we choose to make – is the most important gift of all.

I am so glad to be sharing this special story with you, and I hope it stays with you as it has stayed with me.

With all my love,

Josephine Cox

THE JOURNEY

CONTENTS

PART ONE

~

January, 1952

The Sad Woman

CHAPTER ONE

Salford, Bedfordshire

H E HAD SEEN them twice before, and each time his curiosity was aroused. Arm-in-arm, the two women would come softly into the churchyard, place their flowers, and linger awhile before leaving in the same discreet manner in which they had arrived.

Today, as his bumbling black Labrador Chuck tugged on the lead, the dog's nostrils twitching at the secret scent of rabbits in the churchyard, the women came again. He tried not to seem interested, but the moment they walked through the gate and passed him by, he could not stop himself from sneaking a glance. They acknowledged him with a polite nod of the head, then moved on, intent about their business. It was almost as if he was not there.

In her own way, each of the women was beautiful. The taller of the two, who looked about fifty, had long chestnut-brown hair, grey in places, tied back with a ribbon, and lovely golden-brown eyes, a smart though ample figure and softly rounded features. Today, the bouquet of evergreens cradled in her arm seemed to accentuate her beauty; though it was not a virgin beauty, for the crippling seasons of time and emotion were deeply etched in her face.

She walked with a stick, long and slender with bone handle

and silver-capped toe. It was obvious that she was crippled in some slight way, though this did not detract from her air of dignity and sense of purpose. With her sombre bearing and her carefully-measured steps, she made a striking figure.

He knew they were headed for the same headstone, where he himself had paused many times. In the shape of a cross, the headstone was small and nondescript, yet the words written there were so powerful, they raised that humble stone above all others. The words, carved deep, read:

BARNEY DAVIDSON

1890–1933

A MAN OF COURAGE.
HE MADE THE GREATEST
SACRIFICE OF ALL.

Having read the inscription and been intrigued by it, Ben knew it off by heart. It had set his thoughts alight with all manner of questions. What had this man done to deserve such an accolade? What did the words mean? And who had ordered them to be inscribed? Somehow, he didn't think it had anything to do with the heroism of war. This Barney Davidson would have been twenty-four when World War One broke out – and no doubt the young man had played his part – but he had died well before the second lot.

His attention was drawn to the two women.

With such tenderness that it took him aback, the older one stroked the tips of her fingers over the dead man's name. Her voice broke with pride as she murmured, 'Oh, my dearest Barney.' In that moment when she lifted her gaze to the heavens, her brown eyes glittered with tears. So much pain, he thought. So much emotion.

He sensed that, somewhere deep inside, she carried a

terrible burden. What was that old saying? 'The eyes are the mirror of the soul.' He wondered what sorrowful secrets were hers.

The man's discreet gaze went now to the younger woman. Smaller, with a neat, if slightly plump figure, her fair hair was bobbed to the shoulders, and even from where he stood, he could see that her pretty eyes were the deepest shade of blue lavender. He imagined that normally, those eyes were quick to smile – but not today. Today her concerned gaze was trained on the older woman.

The two visitors were sensibly dressed. Like himself, each wore a long coat and sturdy shoes, for the weather had been foul of late, and in places the ground underfoot was treacherous.

In the early hours of this January Sunday in 1952, ditches and paths had run high with the melting remnants of a heavy snowfall. By midday the wind had heightened and now, judging by the darkening skies, it seemed a new storm was gathering.

'Here, Chuck. Here, boy!' he said in a harsh whisper, and tugged on the leash, quickly bringing the dog to heel. In a burst of affection, the animal jumped up and licked him, nearly sending him flying. Recovering, he patted the dog, then set off for the lych-gate and home.

He was only a few strides away from Barney Davidson's tomb when the women left it and began walking on, merely an arm's reach in front of him. Slowing his step, he continued to follow, the dog plodding obediently at his side.

They were almost at the gate when the older woman's stick slipped in the mud and she fell heavily, seeming to twist her leg as she did so.

When her young companion cried out and immediately began struggling to bring her upright, he ran forward. 'Please ... let me help?' Sliding his two hands under the

5

older one's arms, he gently hoisted her up. When she seemed steady, he let go, recovered her walking stick and handed it to her. 'No real harm done, I hope?' he said politely.

'Thank you.' Her dark eyes appraised him. 'As you can see, I'm not as agile as I once was.'

A softer voice interrupted. 'Yes, thank you, Mr . . . ?' The young woman frowned. 'How can we thank you properly, when we don't know your name?'

His warm gaze enveloped her pretty face. 'The name's Ben,' he revealed. 'Benjamin Morris.' Holding out his hand in greeting, he was pleasantly surprised and thrilled when she put her small hand in his. Surprised, because he found her grip firm and strong, as though she worked with her hands in some way. Thrilled because she seemed to hold on just that moment longer than necessary.

Having witnessed his reaction, the older woman gave a pleasant laugh. 'My daughter Mary has a strong grip for a little one, don't you think?'

Mary tried to explain. 'It comes from gardening,' she said shyly. 'A few years ago our old gardener retired, and rather than take on someone new, I persuaded Mother to let me have a go at the job.' Her face flushed with pleasure. 'It's hard work, mind, but I love every minute of it.'

'Mary is a worker, all right,' her mother declared. 'When she's not up to her eyes in the garden, she works five days a week in her flower-shop in Leighton Buzzard, and whenever the chance arises, she's out and about delivering the flowers herself, driving the shop-van.' Tutting, she finished quietly, 'I don't know where she finds the energy!'

'A busy lady then?' Ben looked down into that bright lively face and wondered why she was not married. 'And may I ask what you do in this garden of yours?'

It was the mother who answered. 'She spends every spare

minute she's got in it, that's what she does!' From the reproachful glance she gave Mary, it was apparent that she thought her daughter should be enjoying her life and doing other things while she was still young. 'She grows all our own produce,' she said proudly, 'and she's completely rede-signed the garden, made it into a little paradise with delight-ful walkways and colourful blossom round every corner, except,' she glanced at the ominous skies, 'of course, on days like this.'

'Then it sounds like time well spent,' Ben commented. He wondered why it was that Mary spent every spare minute in the garden. Did she never go out? Was she never ap-proached by men who would like to enjoy her company? She was such a fetching little thing, *he* certainly wouldn't mind the opportunity to get to know her better.

'Oh, but the garden is so lovely!' That was the mother talking again. 'She's even managed to carve out a number of little nooky holes – quiet places where you can escape the weather and enjoy your own company.'

The younger woman's soft voice intervened. 'I just thought it would be nice to have a quiet place where you could hide from the rest of the world.' Blushing under her mother's lavish praise, Mary made an effort to divert atten-tion from herself. 'Do you like gardening, Mr Morris?'

For a long moment he gazed down on her, his heart turning over like never before. 'Why would you want to hide from the rest of the world?' he asked, ignoring her question.

Mary had not expected him to answer with a question of his own. 'Isn't that what we all sometimes need?' she asked cagily.

He wasn't sure how to respond to that, so he didn't. Instead he went back to her original question. 'I farm,' he answered lamely. 'I'm afraid there isn't a great deal of leisurely time left for gardening, or much else.'

Her smile was appreciative. 'In a way, farming could be called gardening, only on a larger scale . . . don't you think?'

'If you say so.' When those lavender-blue eyes beamed as they did now, her whole face seemed to light up.

'Well, I never!' With a quick, mischievous smile on her face, the older woman reminded them, 'There's me badly injured, and you two exchanging pleasantries as if I wasn't even here.'

The pair of them were mortified. 'Whatever am I thinking of!' Ben exclaimed. 'I'm so sorry.' He had been so occupied with the daughter, he had neglected the mother, and he was ashamed.

'I must get Mother home.' With her eyes still on Ben, Mary shifted closer to the older lady. 'I don't know what I would have done if you hadn't been here just now.'

She had seen this stranger before, striding down the streets of Salford with his faithful dog in tow as she drove past in her van. Discreetly taking stock of him now that he was here, close beside her, she liked what she saw. Handsome, of manly build, with dark, expressive eyes, he seemed to be taken with her, and it was strange, but she felt oddly drawn to him.

'I'm glad to have been of help.' He wondered how he could sound so calm with his heart thumping fifteen to the dozen.

He glanced at the older woman and caught the glint in her smiling eyes; he realised she was taking everything in. He gestured at her ankle. 'From the look of it, I don't think you've broken anything.'

She nodded. 'It's probably just a sprain. Once I get home and put my feet up, I'll be right as rain.'

'It's best you don't put too much weight on that foot.' Pointing across the fields, to the rambling, white-washed house in the distance, he informed them, 'Far Crest Farm, that's where I live. I'll help you up there, shall I, to take a look at the ankle and see what can be done.'

Sensing their reluctance, he quickly added, 'Or, if you'd prefer, I could nip up and get my car and take you home. It's only a few minutes to the farmhouse.'

The older woman thanked him. 'Don't think I'm not grateful.' She had a natural friendliness in her manner that warmed him to her. 'But I'll be well taken care of. Look there?' Gesturing to the long dark car that waited by the kerbside outside the church, she revealed, 'I have a car and driver waiting.'

Flustered, Ben apologised. 'Oh, I'm sorry. I didn't realise . . .'

'How could you?' Her smile deepened. 'I might be a frail old biddy walking with the aid of a stick, but as you see, I'm not short of a bob or two.'

Ben smiled. 'You don't strike me as a frail old biddy,' he remarked, holding open the lych-gate for the two women to pass through it. 'In fact, I imagine if anyone got on the wrong side of you, they might rue the day.'

The girl Mary had to smile at his comment. 'You're absolutely right. What you see is not always what you get.' She gave her mother a curious glance. 'Still waters run deep, isn't that what they say?'

The older woman nodded but said nothing, though her gaze roamed back to the headstone, and the name *Barney*.

He had been a man amongst men, she thought. A man of such bravery it made her humble. Even now after all these years her heart wept for him, and for the unbearable torment he had endured, all in the name of love.

'Oh, look! Here comes Adam now.' As the driver approached to help her down the pavement, she reached out and shook Ben by the hand. 'You've been very kind, Mr Morris. Thank you again.'

Leaning on the arm of her driver, she set off for the comfort of the big car, calling as she went, 'By the way, my name is Lucy.' She had taken a liking to this young fella me lad and, from the look on her daughter's face, she suspected Mary had done the same.

'Goodbye then,' Ben replied. 'Take care of yourself.'

'Not goodbye,' Mary said hopefully. 'I'm sure our paths will cross again.'

He smiled into her eyes. There was so much he would have liked to say, but not now. Maybe not ever, he thought sadly.

In a moment the women were gone, and he felt lonely, as never before. Retracing his footsteps to the simple headstone, he read out the inscription. *'He made the greatest sacrifice of all . . .'*

The words burned in his soul. 'Barney Davidson . . .' he mused aloud. 'Lucy's husband, maybe? Her brother?' Somehow he didn't think so. His curiosity heightened. 'What great sacrifice did you make, Barney?' he wondered.

Deep in thought, he almost leaped out of his skin when a quiet voice said over his shoulder, 'Barney was Lucy's husband – died soon after they moved here. And as for the inscription . . . I've wondered that myself, many a time.'

Swinging round, Ben came face to face with the new vicar, the Reverend Michael Gray. 'Oh, it's you, Vicar!' He greeted the older man with a sheepish grin. 'I don't usually make a habit of talking to myself,' he explained, 'but I must admit, I *am* curious.'

'You know what they say about a man who talks to himself?' In his late fifties, balding and bespectacled, Mike Gray had the hang-dog look of a man with the weight of the world on his shoulders. And yet his smile was heavenly.

When he began walking towards the gate, Ben went with him. 'As you know, I've only been here a matter of a few months,' the vicar went on to remind him, 'but like you, I'm intrigued by that grave.'

'Maybe you should ask the ladies?' Ben suggested. 'I'm sure they wouldn't mind it coming from you – I mean, you being their vicar here at Saint Andrew's.'

Mike Gray shook his head. 'There have been times when I was sorely tempted to ask,' he confessed, and slid a finger round to loosen his dog-collar. 'Then I felt I might be intruding, so I thought it best to wait, at least until I know them a little better. They've been worshipping here for around twenty years, I believe. But of course, the war has occupied everyone's thoughts, and that tombstone is old history now.'

'You're probably right,' Ben replied. 'All the same, it's a curious thing, an inscription like that.'

'Yes. As you say, a curious thing.' The Reverend paused to stroke Chuck's glossy head. 'Our man obviously did something out of the ordinary.' His features crinkled into a wry little smile. 'It's to be hoped we might all of us aspire to great things before we're called.' Raising his gaze to the skies, he gave a long, deep sigh. 'Sadly, a lot of poor devils had to be heroes in the war, whether they wanted to, or not. The truth of it is, most of us simply do not have greatness in us.'

By the time they reached the gate, the men had covered every possibility. 'Maybe he saved a life by forfeiting his own?' Ben speculated.

'Mmm.' The vicar nodded. 'Or he may have shown true bravery during the Great War. Certainly his age suggests he could well have been called up to serve his country.'

Ben considered that. 'Could be.'

Pausing in his stride, Mike Gray glanced back towards the headstone, now dim in the failing light. 'Whatever that inscription means,' he declared soundly, 'we can assume that our Barney Davidson was a remarkable man.'

Hearing a scuffle behind a great yew that stood near the vestry, Chuck suddenly slipped his lead and raced off. While Ben called him back, the vicar had spotted a dark object lying on the ground. He stooped to pick it up. 'Well, I never!' He wiped off the smears of dirt and dampness with the cuff of his sleeve.

A knowing smile creased his face. 'This must belong to one of our ladies,' he said. 'Maybe, if you were to return this, you might be privileged to discover the true nature of that inscription?'

'Mary's mother must have dropped it when she fell over earlier. I would gladly deliver the handbag.' Ben recalled the young woman and those pretty lavender-blue eyes. It would be good to see her again, he thought. 'Only I don't know where they live.'

'Couldn't be easier. They live at Knudsden House – you must know the place,' the Reverend Gray prompted. 'I recall admiring it when I came into the village for the first time. It's that big Edwardian house, with the large, beautifully kept gardens. You can't miss it.'

Ben *had* seen the place. An architect by training, he took a keen interest in the buildings around him. 'Of course!' he cried. 'It's the one set back from the lane, behind tall iron gates.' He shook his head in disbelief. 'I would never have guessed they lived there.' Somehow, despite the elegant walking stick, and the chauffeur-driven car, he had pictured the women living in a large rambling cottage, with thatched roof and roses growing at the door.

The vicar remarked thoughtfully, 'According to my house-keeper, Knudsden house used to belong to the village squire; he passed on some twenty years ago, and the house was put up for sale.'

Taking a moment to recall his housekeeper's exact words, he went on, 'It was then bought by Mr Davidson and his wife. Their daughter Mary was just an infant at the time. They were a family who preferred to keep themselves very much to themselves.'

There was a silence as Ben digested all of this information.

The vicar added thoughtfully, 'For a long time they rarely ventured out. In recent years though, they have concerned themselves more with the community, and have given generously to any good cause; the daughter with her time and labour, and the mother with cash donations.'

'Hmh! For someone who knows very little about the family, you seem to have gathered a fair amount of information.'

'So I have.' The vicar had surprised himself. 'Don't forget, I have my spies,' he said wryly. 'My housekeeper comes from a long line of gossips who've lived in this village since time began, so it goes without saying that what she doesn't know isn't worth knowing. Mind, the dead are good at keeping secrets – and even she doesn't know the answer to the mystery of that inscription.'

When the Labrador bounded up, Ben grabbed his lead and wound it around his wrist. He shivered. The temperature had dropped, almost while they were talking.

'And what about the daughter?' Ben asked. 'Did she attend the village school?'

'No. Mary was educated at home. A tutor arrived each morning and departed every afternoon.' The vicar's voice dropped to a whisper. 'It must have been a very lonely life for a little girl.'

Ben was thinking the very same, and his heart went out to her. 'So, as far as you know, she never made friends?'

'From what I'm given to understand, the daughter has no close friends, but she does get on very well with the two women who help them out. Elsie Langton does a bit of housekeeping. Her married daughter Rona works in the flower-shop. Mary is closer to Rona, which is understandable when they're at the shop together most days.'

Ben had heard the name. 'Is that the same Langton who keeps the smithy on the farm adjoining mine?'

'That's the father. He doesn't own the farm, I know that much, but he makes a reasonable living, what with his smithy and the market-gardening. The Langton family are closer to the Davidsons than anyone else in the village.'

'What about the man who drives for them?'

Again, the vicar was able to satisfy his curiosity. 'Adam Chives is an old friend of Mrs Davidson's who comes from Liverpool. He's a quiet, well-liked man who lives in the cottage next to the big house.' He passed the handbag to Ben. 'I really must stop chatting and be on my way. I'll leave this with you, shall I?'

'I won't be able to return it straight away.' Ben took the handbag from him. 'I've got hungry animals to be fed.'

'Of course. I understand.' Having worked all his adult life in rural parishes, the vicar was familiar with the way of things. 'The animals don't know or care what day it is, they still need tending.' He gave a knowing nod. 'Much like my own flock, eh?'

Ben examined the handbag; it was an expensive-looking leather one. 'I wonder we didn't notice this on the ground before,' he remarked. 'I mean, you could hardly miss it, could you?'

The vicar agreed, but just then he spotted a small, round person calling his attention from the lane. 'That's Betty . . . my housekeeper,' he groaned. 'No doubt she's landed herself in another crisis. Last week she broke the new vacuum cleaner; the week before that she let the bathroom sink overflow and nearly flooded the Vicarage.'

He rolled his eyes heavenward. 'The Lord only knows what kind of chaos she's been up to now!'

He waved a hand to let her know he was on his way. 'I'd best go,' he grumbled, 'before the house comes tumbling down round our ears!' His good-natured laugh told Ben he would probably forgive the housekeeper her latest mishap.

'What about the handbag?' Ben called after Mike Gray. 'What if it doesn't belong to them?'

'Then it will belong to someone else, I suppose,' the man turned and answered. 'But we won't know until you ask, will we? Just take the handbag with you. You can return it to Knudsden House, after you've seen to your animals.'

His wink was meaningful. 'Besides, I saw you and young Mary chatting, and if you don't mind me saying, I thought you made a right handsome pair. I'm sure she would be very pleased if you turned up on her front doorstep.'

Then he was away, rushing down the lane with a sense of urgency, following the small round person tripping on in front, shouting over her shoulder and seeming frantic about something or another.

Smiling to himself, Ben went on his way. A vicar's life wasn't as dull as he'd imagined. Then he thought about Mary, and his mood softened. The vicar was right: he and the girl *had* got on very well, though whether she really would be pleased to see him turn up on her doorstep was another matter altogether.

Away from the church-grounds and into open country-side, he set the dog loose. 'And don't go splashing through the brook!' he called after the big animal. 'I haven't got time to give you a bath today.' He had more important things to do. Uppermost in his mind was the proposed visit to Knudsden House.

Striding across the field, he kept a wary eye on the dog; when the Labrador took off after a rabbit, he called him back. 'Here, Chuck! Good boy.'

On his master's call, Chuck came bounding back, but was

soon off again at the sight of another dog being set loose across the field. Seeing the reason for his pet's excitement, Ben let him have his head, smiling at the sight of Chuck canoodling with the smaller, prettier animal. 'Casanova! Chase anything in a skirt, so you would,' he said aloud.

Covering the ground at a fast pace, he drew his coat tighter about him; the wind was getting up, the skies were darkening and the smell of storm was strong in the air. He called the dog to heel, but by now he was nowhere in sight. 'Chuck! Here, boy!' He scoured the landscape, and called again, but the dog was gone.

Ben was nearly home now. Quickening his steps, he made for the top of the rise. From there he had the world at his feet, and the dog in his sights. 'C'mon, fella!' But Chuck was too engrossed in dancing after his fancy piece. With a sterner voice Ben caught his attention. 'Here, boy!' he bellowed.

With ears pricked and head bent to the wind, the dog raced up the hill and was soon close to heel. A few minutes later the two of them were hurrying down the path to the farmhouse.

~

'I'm off now, Mr Morris.' The old man came through the field gate and clicked it shut. 'I shan't be sorry to get home,' he told Ben. 'It's turned real chilly all of a sudden.' Taking off his flat cap, he scratched his head and looked up to the skies. 'I reckon it's blowing up a real nasty storm.'

Ben agreed. 'You're right,' he observed. 'Mind how you go and I'll see you tomorrow.'

When Ben bought the farm, old Les had been part and parcel of the place. Ben had never regretted agreeing to keep him on because he was hardworking and reliable, a real treasure; besides which he had a cheery wife to keep, and a lazy good-for-nothing grandson, who showed up from time to time looking for a handout, and though he was more trouble than he was worth, poor old Les never turned him away.

'I've stripped the tree-branches and brought them down,' Les informed him now. 'You'll find them all stood up at the back of the barn, ready for chopping. By the time you've finished, there'll be enough to keep the whole of Salford in firewood. Oh, and I've levelled that back field just as you asked – though you'll need a new axle for the tractor. If you ask me it won't last above another month at best.'

Quick to agree, Ben put a proposition to the old fella. 'I think it's time we had a new tractor altogether. What would you say to that, eh?'

The old man's face lit up. 'I'd say that were a blooming good idea!'

'Right then. We'll make arrangements to go and look at a few. Now get off home, Les, and take a well-earned rest.'

'I could stay and help you with the animals if you like?' From the moment he had shaken Ben's hand, Les had recognised the good in him. His first impressions had proved right, for Ben was fair-minded, caring and generous, and though he had never worked on the land before he bought Far Crest Farm, he had taken to it like a duck to water.

'The missus won't mind,' Les persisted. 'Just say the word and I'll be right behind you. We'll have that lot fed in no time at all.'

Ben shook his head. 'Thanks all the same, but I can manage well enough on my own.'

'I'm not past it yet, I'll have you know,' the old man argued. 'And it weren't my fault that the boar took against me.'

'I know you're not past it. And I also know it wasn't your fault that the boar took against you. But he did, and you were almost killed, and I'm not prepared to take that chance again.'

Ben didn't want to hurt the old man's feelings, but if he hadn't managed to distract the boar that day, Les would have been killed for sure. As it was, he suffered a broken leg and had been left with a slight limp. Ben still felt guilty. 'Look, we've gone over all this time and again, and I won't change my mind,' he said gently, then: 'Besides, don't you think you do enough round here already?'

'I could do more, if only you'd let me.'

'There's no need, Les. The arrangement we have works very well. We do the ploughing and sowing between us. I keep the hedges down, you bring in the old branches, and I chop them up. With the help of casual work when the harvest is got in, this little farm runs like clockwork, so let's not spoil a good thing, eh?'

The old man shrugged. 'If you say so, Mr Morris.'

'I do, but don't think I'm not grateful for the offer. I'll let you into a secret, shall I? I enjoy feeding the animals.' He grinned. 'They've begun to think I'm their mummy.'

The old man laughed. 'You certainly have a way with 'em, I'll say that for yer.' He pulled the neb of his cap down over his forehead. 'If yer sure then, I'd best make tracks. I expect the missus will have the tea on the table and the kettle already singing away.'

Before they parted, Ben assured him quietly, 'Les – you do know I could never manage this place without you?'

That brought a smile to the old farmhand's face, for he was well aware of how Ben Morris had bypassed younger, stronger men in order to keep him in work. 'You're a good man, Mr Morris, God bless you.' With that he was quickly gone, away down the path, off to the village, and home to his darling woman.

⌒

For the next couple of hours, Ben was kept busy. He had a tried and tested feeding routine; despite this, it was not only a dirty job but a time-consuming one, too. There were two hundred chickens in the hen-house; twenty fat porkers in the pig-pens; the same number of milking cows in the small barn, and a small flock of thirty sheep in the big barn.

Feeding them all took between two and three hours in the morning and the same at night, and when they were let loose in the fields, all the barns and sheds had to be mucked out, ready for when the weather turned and the animals were brought back in again.

As he went inside the farmhouse, Ben gave a sigh of relief. He had fallen in love with the place the moment he set foot through the door. It was like a calm after the storm, a haven where he could lick his wounds and grow strong again.

The year leading up to the move had been the worst of his life. After leaving the RAF, in which he had served for three years after his training, he had gone back to his career as an architect. When the company went bust through financial mismanagement and shortages of some basic materials, he took out a loan to start up his own business. Sadly, it never really took off. He sold the premises at a loss, and found work with the local council, but hated every minute of it. His wife grew distant because there were no longer the funds to maintain the kind of life she wanted. Then his lively, darling daughter Abbie, by then aged eighteen, moved out of the family home and he had missed her terribly.

He hoped he and his wife Pauline would grow closer, and he believed this was happening – until he caught her in bed with his best friend, Peter. There had been a long and unpleasant period when he didn't know which way to turn. His daughter had been his salvation, but she had already forged a life of her own; she shared a flat with two other girls and had a good job, working for a tea-importer in London. Thankfully, the break-up of her parents' marriage had not seemed to interfere too much with all that.

The divorce had been a messy business, and the only ones to come out of it winning were the lawyers. Still, Ben was determined not to slide into bitterness, because what was done was done, and there was no turning back for either of them.

When it was over, he and his wife were left with enough from the sale of their family home to start again. She had gone to live abroad with her new husband, while Ben chose a completely different way of life. He was happy enough now. Perhaps happier, in a strange way, than he had ever been.

Taking a deep invigorating sigh, he looked around the farmhouse. There was a warm feel of history in this delight-ful little place. He could not deny it had its disadvantages, though they were small compared to the joy he had found here. The whisper of a smile crossed his features as he recalled the number of times he'd banged his head on the low cross-beams, and the wood-burning stoves caused more dust and dirt than he could ever have envisaged. The small windows were draughty, and when the wind drove the rain, it came right through the framework to soak the walls. The flagstone floors were sunk and broken in places and even in the height of summer there was a dampness in the air that got right into the bones. This was his first winter in the cottage, and once the better weather arrived, he knew he would have to put in many a long hour working on the house in between his other responsibilities.

Yet in spite of all that, he would not have changed one single thing.

As always, he went straight to the kitchen, where he turned on the gas stove, filled the kettle and set it for boiling. 'Now then, Chuck.' Going to the pantry, he took out a lamb chop and dropped it into the dog's bowl. 'You chew on that while I see who's been writing to me.'

Returning to the dresser, he picked up the mail which had lain there since yesterday. There was a bill for animal feed, a card reminding him to return an overdue book to the local library, and a white envelope with a tuppenny stamp and a small pink flower drawn in the corner.

'We know who this is from, don't we, eh?' He cocked an eye at the dog, who was far too busy enjoying his treat to worry about what the postman had brought.

Ben took out the letter and unfolded it, his eyes scanning the words and his heart warming as he read them aloud:

Dear Dad,

I've managed to get time off at last, so if it's OK with you, I plan to visit for a few days. It's been too long since we had a real heart-to-heart, don't you think? I'm not sure which day I'll turn up, but it'll either be next Sunday or Monday. If that doesn't fit in with your plans, you'll have to let me know a suitable date. If I don't hear from you, I'll assume it's all right to arrive sometime on one of those days. I'm really looking forward to seeing you. Meanwhile, take care of yourself,

Your loving daughter,
Abbie xxx

Folding the letter, he slipped it back into the envelope before dropping it onto the dresser.

'You'll need to look to your laurels,' he told the dog with a wag of his finger. 'Abbie's coming to stay, and when she's about, no one gets any peace!' His daughter was noisy, untidy and could be the most irritating creature in the world.

More than a week of her company and he would likely be pulling his hair out. But oh, how he was looking forward to seeing her.

He was so excited that he cut his finger when making himself a cheese sandwich, and then found he could only nibble at it, though he swigged down three cups of tea and ravished the jam-tart made especially for him by Les's wife. In fact, she'd made him a whole bagful only the day before yesterday, and this was the last one. 'Sorry, matey,' he told the dog who had demolished his chop and was begging for a crumb. 'You've had your tea. This is mine, and besides, there isn't enough here to share.' Nevertheless, he was still shamed into throwing him a bite.

With the jam-tart all gone and the teapot emptied, Ben put on his work-clothes and with the dog at his heels, made his way to the yard where he unlocked the feed room. Here he laid out three large galvanised buckets; one for the chickens; one for the sheep and another for the pigs. That done, he lifted the lids from three of the drums and scooping out several sizeable helpings of food from each of them in turn, he filled the buckets to brimming.

Taking up the buckets, two in one hand and one in the other, he made his way over to the big barn. Knowing exactly when feed-time was, the sheep were already crowded round the food-troughs. On sight of him, they began pushing and shoving their way forwards. 'Get back! BACK, I SAY!'

Fighting his way through the bleating animals, he partway filled the various troughs, then leaving the sheep to sort themselves out, he climbed the ladder to the hayloft, where he threw down four slices of hay, making certain that they landed far enough apart for everyone to get a fair share without too much argument.

Afterwards, he stood at the barn door for a minute or two. Satisfied that the sheep were all feeding and seeming content, he went outside to the tap, filled the bucket with water, returned inside and emptied it into the two water-troughs. 'That should keep you going for a while,' he told them. 'Come the morning, I might let you loose in the fields.'

It was always a pleasure to set them free, for sheep were not indoor animals. Small-minded and built to eat, it was in their nature to nibble the pastures, get caught up in brambles and go lame at every opportunity.

With the sheep fed and set up for the night, he tramped off to the undercover pig-pens. Here he went through the same procedure, but with a different and coarser food, for pigs were gluttons and required bulk. Ben was always wary when surrounded by the porkers. Weighing upwards of half a ton each, they were capable of doing a man some consider-able damage if he got in their way.

The boars in particular were an angry sort when penned, as old Les was quick to point out to Ben at the first opportu-nity. 'I once knew a man whose prize boar drove his tusks clean through the poor chap's thighbone; crippled him for life, it did. So don't go messin' with them big buggers, 'cause if they don't get yer with their tusks, they'll have yer over and trample yer underfoot!' Les did not have to tell Ben twice. It was ironic that poor Les himself came a cropper soon after he'd issued that warning.

With the pigs happily burying their snouts in the troughs, Ben attended to the other animals; first the cows, then the chickens.

The cows were housed in the smaller of the two barns. The area had been divided up to provide eight large pens on one side and six on the other, with a birthing pen at the far corner. The beasts had more than enough room and as long as they were fed and watered and clean underfoot, they saw out the winter in comfort; though once the worst of the weather was over they, too, were always happy to be let loose in the fields.

The spacious chicken-house was a vast, open area, which gave the chickens ample room to run. At night they would either roost in the lower beams, or retire to the many small wooden houses set along either side of the walls. Sadly, some of the chickens fell prey to the odd fox who dared to burrow under the wire, which was dug in and around the entire perimeter. Thankfully it had not happened just lately, and Les kept a wary eye out for weak links in the netting.

A long while later, Ben made his weary way back to the farmhouse. At the door he kicked off his boots and overalls before going through to the parlour.

First, he made himself a cup of well-earned tea, then it was off upstairs for a much-needed bath. He'd lit the geyser to heat up the water long since. 'I can't be going to see the ladies smelling of pig manure and chicken-muck,' he told the dog, who simply rolled over, gave a long, shuddering yawn and fell into a deep sleep.

In the bathroom he turned on the taps and let the bath fill while he stripped off. A few moments later he slithered under the water and lay there for awhile, luxuriating in the warmth and thinking of young Mary, with whose pretty lavender-blue eyes and the way her mouth turned up at the corners when she smiled . . .

CHAPTER TWO

AT EIGHT O'CLOCK that evening, Ben arrived at the front door of Knudsden House. Standing on the top step of the little flight of stairs, he fidgeted nervously before reaching up and knocking briskly.

The door opened and Mary stood before him. His breath caught. Divested of her heavy winter coat, she was wearing a lilac-coloured twinset and a pretty knee-length skirt. The light from the hall and from her, too, dazzled him.

Fumbling, he brought out the bag from where he'd been hiding it under his coat. 'I found this,' he said jerkily.

'It's my mother's! Thank you.'

The women had discovered the loss of the handbag once they'd arrived home. Fortunately, Mary had her own front-door key and could let them in. Adam had offered to go and look for it, after searching the car and not finding it, but Lucy had said no, not to worry. She felt far too unwell for any fuss, and the bag would turn up somehow. People round here were honest men and women.

'Won't you come in?' Mary asked now. 'I expect Mother will want to thank you herself.'

Accepting her invitation without hesitation, Ben followed her through to the drawing room. 'Is your mother all right? I mean, has she suffered any ill-effects from the fall?'

'She *says* she's all right. With Mother, you're never really sure.'

When Mary turned to smile at him, Ben felt foolish; like a shy young boy on his first date instead of a forty-year-old man of the world.

For what seemed the longest moment, she continued to gaze on him, her quiet smile reaching deep into his senses. Suddenly the smile fell away and, slowing her step, she confided in him.

'The truth is, since she fell in the churchyard, she hasn't seemed well at all,' she whispered. 'I'm worried about her.' Before she inched open the door, she confessed, 'I wanted to call Dr Nolan, but she won't hear of it.' A sigh escaped her lips. 'She's so independent – and stubborn like you wouldn't believe. But I'm half tempted to call the doctor anyway.'

'There's no use you whispering, my girl!' Lucy called out from the inner room. 'I can hear every word, and there'll be no doctor coming into this house!'

On entering the room, Mary was told in no uncertain terms, 'If I needed a doctor – *which I don't* – there is only one I would agree to seeing, and he's living out his retirement in Liverpool. So we'll have no more talk of doctors. Are you listening to me, Mary?'

Reluctantly, the girl nodded. 'Mr Morris found your bag in the churchyard. He's brought it back. I thought you might want to thank him yourself.'

'Mmm.' Her reproachful gaze rested on her daughter for a second or two before switching to Ben. 'I love my daughter dearly, but she will fuss.'

'Only because she's worried about you, I'm sure.'

While he spoke, Ben was aware of how the room reflected Lucy's personality. There was the solid furniture, reliable and stalwart, and then there was the colour and vibrancy in the curtains and the rugs. On following Mary into the room, he had felt her life all about him, in the lavish bright paintings on the walls, and the many figures, sculpted in china and pewter – some in the throes of embrace, others dancing, with arms in the air and feet atwirl.

They reminded him of Lucy herself; mature in beauty, yet very much alive.

'She's no need to worry,' Lucy snapped. 'I'm fit as a fiddle, thank goodness – always have been.' Her thoughts went back to her youth, to the time she'd gone astray, and the consequences that followed. Good times and bad, when life was lived to the full, when friends helped you through and nothing seemed to matter. *And then there was Barney.*

Her heart grew sore at the thought of that wonderful man.

Mentally shaking herself, she told Ben, 'That's two kindnesses you've shown me in one day. So thank you again, young man.'

'It was the vicar who found it,' Ben explained. 'I simply offered to return it.' He liked being called 'young man', though in truth, he was only about twelve years younger than Lucy, and indeed, had a grown-up daughter of his own. His feelings for Mary, however, were definitely not those of a father.

When he turned to smile at Mary, Lucy was quick to see the spark between them. 'I dare say that's because you wanted to see my Mary again.' Her face crinkled into that same mischievous smile he had seen at the churchyard. 'Taken a liking to her, have you?' When she gave a naughty wink, he couldn't help but grin, despite his bashfulness.

'Mother!' Mary's face went a bright shade of pink. 'What a thing to say! Don't embarrass Mr Morris. I'm sure he was thinking no such thing.'

But Lucy took no notice. Addressing Ben, she put him on the spot. 'Tell the truth and shame the devil, Mr Morris. You volunteered to return my bag because you hoped to catch a glimpse of Mary, isn't that the truth?'

Ben laughed out loud. 'Do you always see through people so easily?' It was strange, he thought, how easy he felt in her presence. 'Yes, you're right. I *was* hoping I might see her again.'

'There! I knew it!' Clapping her hands together with excitement, the older woman said triumphantly, 'I knew he'd taken to you, Mary – didn't I say so? And here you are – you haven't even asked our guest if he'd like to join us for supper. Shame on you, my girl!'

'Shame on *you*, Mother, for embarrassing us both like that.' Even though she was elated by Ben's admission that he had been hoping for a glimpse of her, Mary was so mortified she wanted the floor to open up and swallow her. Whatever would Ben think of her now? She hoped he would refuse the offer of supper and make some excuse to leave straight away.

Lucy's instincts were meanwhile telling her that here was a good man, a fine husband for her daughter, if he were free. She had little doubt but that these two could make a fine, happy life together. Yes! Should anything untoward happen to herself in the near future, Ben Morris was the very man to take good care of Mary, for he reminded her of Barney, in his smile and his manner.

Lately, she had been feeling very low in spirits and health, and Mary's future had come to concern her deeply. Although Ben must be twice her daughter's age, and would have his own story to tell about his life and the reasons for his arrival in Salford, he seemed a kind and honourable man. She had already noted the hint of sadness in his eyes, and his beautiful artistic hands, not yet roughened by farmwork. It was time to find out more about him. She would start with the most important question.

'Are you married?'

'REALLY, MOTHER!' Horrified, Mary sprang forward. 'One minute you invite Mr Morgan to supper, and the next you're quizzing him about his private life. I'm sure he won't stay a minute longer than he has to – and who would blame him?'

Over the past few years, there had been several young chaps who had shown an interest in her; to her dismay, Lucy had systematically sent them all packing. Yet there were good reasons for this: not one of them was good enough for her, Lucy said grimly, and had been proved right when each one had eventually shown his true colours.

'Nonsense! I mean no harm. I'm just being my usual, nosy self,' Lucy replied with a stay of her hand. 'Besides, I should be old enough now to speak my mind without offending anyone. I'm quite sure our Mr Morris won't mind. After all, we need to know the calibre of the man who's crossed our path twice today.'

Addressing Ben she asked pointedly, 'Are you offended by my questions?'

Ben shook his head. 'I was married and now I'm divorced,' he said quietly. 'Not the most pleasant experience of my life, I have to admit.'

'And have you children?'

'A daughter . . . Abbie.'

'And where is she?'

'Abbie lives in London, where she shares a flat with other young working people. I miss her, but she is due to come down to Far Crest Farm next week to spend a few days with me.'

'That's enough, Mother!' Stepping forward as though to protect Ben, Mary told him, 'You're welcome to stay to supper, but you can leave right now if you want to, and I wouldn't blame you. You see, Mother won't stop asking questions until she knows everything about you.' Mary so much wanted him to stay, but it had to be his choice.

'That's OK. I might even ask a few questions of my own, later,' he said.

Lucy laughed out loud. 'Now then, young man. Will you stay or will you run?'

'I'll stay.' His mind was already made up. 'Thank you very much. Should I go home and change for the occasion?' He had an idea that Lucy Davidson might be a stickler for protocol.

He was wrong. 'You look decent enough to me, so you can put that silly idea out of your head,' she said. 'It won't take Mary long to rustle up a meal for the three of us. Meanwhile, just make yourself at home.'

'If you say so.' It was a strange thing, but her brisk, authoritative manner was not offputting to him. His instincts told him it was all an act on her part. 'I'm grateful to you both.' When he and Mary exchanged smiles, Lucy was thrilled. The more she saw of Ben, the more she liked and trusted him. He was the one for her daughter; she was sure of it.

So it was settled.

Ben considered himself fortunate to be sharing an evening with Mary and her mother. He liked Lucy, she was a rare character. Though it was Mary at the forefront of his thoughts. For some inexplicable reason, the young woman had captured his imagination – and possibly his heart, though it was much too early to tell, he thought warily.

He had been in love before, and it had turned out to be a heartache.

After that crippling experience with Pauline, he was not ready to throw himself in at the deep end with anyone.

CHAPTER THREE

MARY PEERED OUT into the garden from the big bay window. Its light spilled out onto the lawn, where Ben was carefully picking his way along the path, looking at her handiwork.

'You don't need to send for Elsie,' she told her mother. 'I'm a poor thing if I can't organise a simple dinner for three.'

'I know that,' Lucy retorted. 'It's just that I want you and Ben to get to know each other, and you can't do that if you're in the kitchen cooking, can you?'

'Oh Mam, you're a devil, you are!' Mary couldn't help but smile. 'I know what you're up to, and I think you've embarrassed him enough, without trying to throw us together. If he likes me and I like him, then things might happen naturally, and if they don't, they don't.' Though she hoped they would, for she had not met a man like Ben before. He seemed so mature beside her former boyfriends.

'And do you?'

'Do I what?'

Lucy groaned. 'BEN! Do you like him?'

'I'd be a fool to tell you if I did.' Mary shook her head. 'Think whatever you want,' she said casually. 'You will anyway.' Her mother was the rarest and most wonderful of characters. She never missed a trick. When Lucy Davidson was around, there was no use trying to keep secrets.

'Where is he now?' Curious, Lucy stretched her neck to see out of the window. 'He's not escaped, has he? You've not frightened him off, I hope.'

Mary laughed at that. 'No! He wanted to see what I'd been doing to the garden, that's all.'

Lucy tutted. 'Silly girl! Don't you know anything?' Sometimes she despaired of her, and at other times she was proud of Mary – and proud of herself – because it meant that she had raised an intelligent, trusting girl who saw the good in everyone.

'What are you getting at, Mother?'

'It's fairly obvious, isn't it? He wanted *you* to go with him. Oh, dearie me!'

Mary would not admit it to her mother, but she had been sorely tempted to join Ben in the garden. However, there wasn't enough time. If the women had been on their own, a bowl of soup and slice of cold apple-pie would have done them proud for supper, but having invited Ben to join them, they had to do better than that. Mary was planning to cook some pork chops, and serve them with mashed potatoes and homemade pickle.

'You forget, I've a dinner to cook,' she answered. 'There'll be time enough later for us all to get to know each other.'

A familiar tap on the living-room door curtailed their conversation. Hurrying to the door, Mary drew it open. 'Hello, Adam,' she said, and hugged him. These past years, the small man had been like a father to her although, like the gent he was, Adam had always kept his distance.

Lucy's face lit up. 'Adam, come in. *Come in!*' Dismissing Mary with a wave of her hand, she reminded her, 'I thought you were away to start supper?'

'I was . . . I am.' Looking from Adam to her mother, the

girl couldn't help but wonder what was going on. Whenever her mother wanted her out of the way like this, there was usually something brewing. But then she was always involved in some scheme or another, bless her heart. It was what kept her going.

'Go on then,' Lucy reprimanded her. 'Adam and I have business to discuss, so be off with you.' She had been unable to speak to him privately earlier, when he'd driven her and Mary to the churchyard, and now she wanted a quiet word with him.

'She doesn't change, does she, Adam?' Mary groaned light-heartedly. 'Same old bully as ever.'

Adam's fond gaze bathed the older woman. 'She'll never change,' he said softly. 'Thank God.' The same age as Lucy, he had stayed with her through thick and thin, and every inch of the way he had loved and adored her from afar. Lucy knew it, yet she never said. She felt a lot of affection for him too. But it was not the same deep, driving passion she'd had for Barney. That kind of love happened only once in a lifetime.

And yet in her deepest heart, though he had taken good care of her and showed her nothing but kindness, she knew that Barney had *not* loved her back in the same way. How could he, when his own dearest love was thousands of miles away, probably still yearning for her darling Barney and suffering bitter-sweet thoughts of this wonderful man, whom she had adored more than any other, and who for reasons she might never know, had broken her heart and her life.

It had been a tragedy; a cruel and sorry business that only the gods could have prevented – at least, that was what Barney always claimed.

'I'm sorry I had to use the key to let myself in,' Adam explained. 'I did knock a few times, but no one answered. You obviously didn't hear me.'

'No need to apologise,' Lucy chided. 'The key was given so you could use it whenever necessary. It was necessary on this occasion, so we'll hear no more about it.'

'It's no wonder we didn't hear you at the door,' Mary remarked good-naturedly. 'Mother was too busy having a go at me, laying down the law and trying to fit me up with a man who was kind enough to return her handbag.'

'Dear, dear!' With an aside wink, Adam tutted loudly. 'Interfering again, is she? Mind you, I can't say I blame her.'

With her sound and wary experience of men, Lucy could tell the wheat from the chaff. Mary, on the other hand, was more trusting and less worldly-wise. The lass was not what you might call beautiful, but she was a good-looking young woman all the same, with a heart of gold and a great deal to offer. Adam had no doubt but that she would make some man a loving and loyal wife one of these days.

~

With Mary gone, Lucy bade Adam sit in the chair opposite her. 'Have you done what I asked?' she said in a low voice.

He nodded. 'I have. I drove straight up to Liverpool early yesterday and went to see him at his house.'

Lucy gave a long, deep sigh. 'Thank you. I knew I could rely on you.' Her eyes clouded with tears, she asked next, 'What did he say?'

Adam was reluctant to disappoint her. 'He was surprised to hear from me. I mean, it's been a good few years, hasn't it?'

She nodded. 'Nigh on twenty, plus there's been the war and all. And is he well?'

'None too bad, yes.'

'What was his answer?'

The man had no choice but to relay the truth. 'Sorry, Lucy. Much as he would love to see you again, he can't visit. At least not yet.'

Lucy was dismayed at the news. 'Oh Adam, why not?' Disappointment shook her voice. 'Why can't he come down here?'

Adam explained: 'He's been ill for some time, see – bronchitis and some sort of complication, like pleurisy. He's only now beginning to come through it. He's not as young as he used to be, think on. None of us are.'

Lucy nodded her understanding. 'He can't help being ill, I suppose,' she said.

'But he sends his regards and says you're to take care of yourself, and he promises to come and visit at the first opportunity.' Fishing in his pocket, Adam handed her an envelope. 'He asked me to give you this.'

Taking the envelope, Lucy tore it open and took out the letter, which she read aloud:

My dearest Lucy,

How wonderful to hear from you, after all these long years. I hope you are well, and that you're being your usual self . . . living life to the full, the brave young woman I remember from my days as a doctor.

I don't need to tell you how sorry I was to hear about Barney's death. Like you, I will never forget him, or what he did. When he begged me to keep his secret, I wrestled with my conscience but God help me, I could not refuse him.

Over the years, I have often thought of Barney, and his impossible situation, but I have never regretted doing what I did; nor I imagine did he.

Take care of yourself, Lucy my dear, and when I'm well enough, I promise I will come and visit. It will be just the tonic I need, I'm sure.

May I say, I was most pleased and surprised to see Adam Chives; your dear friend who, as I understand it, is never far from your side . . . as ever.

Best wishes. May God bless you both,
Raymond Lucas

Lying back in the chair, Lucy closed her eyes. For a long moment she remained silent.

'Lucy!' Adam knew she was bitterly disappointed. 'He *will* visit – he said so, and as I recall, he was always a man of his word.'

'I know.' She opened her eyes, which were bright with tears. 'Poor Raymond. I don't doubt he's had his own fair share of problems, but oh, it would have been so good to see him.' She paused, suddenly exhausted. 'Jamie . . .' she whispered.

Concerned, Adam touched her on the hand. 'Are you all right, lass?'

'It's brought everything back, that's all.' Needing to re-assure him, she gave her brightest smile, and for the briefest moment he saw her as she had been all those years ago – young and vibrant; hardworking and so generous of heart.

'So tell me, Lucy, what was the real reason behind your need to see him?'

'What d'you mean?' Lucy demanded.

Adam knew she could be wily. 'What I mean is this: are you ill and not telling?'

'If I was ill, you'd soon know about it,' she lied. Carefully choosing her words, she went on, 'You remember how it was all those years ago, don't you?'

'Of course I remember.' Looking away, he saw it all in his mind's eye. He had often wondered whether, if he had been put through the same test as Barney, he could have been as strong. 'I remember it all,' he whispered. 'How could I forget?'

'And you recall what a valued friend Dr Lucas was?' Her voice shook. Oh, the memories! She swallowed hard and went on: 'I just thought it might be nice to renew an old friendship.'

The truth was, Lucy had other reasons for wanting him here, but she didn't want to worry anyone. Not yet. Although the doctors hereabouts were fine, experienced men, she could not bring herself to trust them for something this serious. If there was one man who *would* tell her the truth, it was Raymond Lucas.

'I'm getting older, Adam. As each day passes, the memories become more vivid.' She drew herself up. 'I need to thank Dr Lucas for what he did. I want to see him, that's all . . . before it's too late.'

Alarmed, the little man looked her in the eye. 'Are you sure there's something you're not telling me?'

'Such as what?'

Dismissing her question he asked, 'What exactly did Dr Nolan say to you when he saw you at the surgery last week?'

She tutted. 'I've already told you. He said I needed to slow down. That I was exhausted.'

'And that's all? Nothing else?'

Tutting again, Lucy snapped, 'Stop fretting! I've already told you, I'm fit as a fiddle – for an old 'un anyway.' She chuckled, 'If they want rid of me, they'll have to shoot me first.'

There was a lengthy silence, charged with things unsaid. The bond between them was deep.

Even though the passage of their lives was already well run, there was nothing Adam Chives wanted more than to make Lucy Davidson his wife. He longed to take care of her, spoil her, hold her tight when she was sad and laugh with her when she was happy. To be there when she went to sleep and waiting beside her when she awoke; to share every precious moment of her life. That was all he had wanted for a long, long time.

Lucy knew it had been on the tip of his tongue to propose to her. She recognised the signs, the twinkle in his eye and the ache in his voice, and she had to disappoint him yet again. 'I don't want you worrying about me, old friend. You just need to remember, I'm no longer a spring chicken – and the same goes for you.' Sometimes her bones ached until she thought they would seize up altogether, and on occasions, when she had walked with her stick too far, her fingers curled round the handle and would not let go.

Reaching out, she took hold of his hand. 'I'm a lucky woman to have such a friend – the very best friend any woman could ever have.' Except for Barney, she thought. But then he had been more than a friend. He had been everything to her: friend, hero, lover, soulmate and confidant. All the men in the world rolled into one could never replace her beloved Barney.

Yet she owed this dear man so much. 'I could never have got through these past years without you.' She squeezed his hand fondly. 'You have to believe that.'

Gazing at her, his heart flooding with all kinds of emotions, he said gruffly, 'You know I'll always be here for you, whenever you need me.'

His heartfelt promise touched her deeply. 'Oh, Adam! So many secrets,' she murmured regretfully, 'so much pain. Whatever I do, I can't bring him back. I can't make it all better. Sometimes, when I'm in my bed with the sleep lying heavy on me, the awful memories come flooding back, and I think about Barney's loved ones.' She lowered her gaze. 'I *should* tell them, shouldn't I?'

Adam sighed deeply. 'You must follow your heart on that one, Lucy, my lass. I can't advise. No one can.'

'If only I knew whether it would make matters better or worse.' Her voice broke. 'God help me, old friend, I don't know what to do.'

'You should ask yourself: if you *were* to tell them, would it be to ease their burden . . . or your own?'

Lucy had already asked herself that same question many times. 'I don't think anything could ease my burden,' she answered thoughtfully, 'but it pains me badly, to think they may never know what sort of man he really was.'

Sometimes the weight of it all was unbearable. 'For the rest of their lives, they'll remember what happened; they'll think of it and the bitterness will rise. They can never see the truth. They'll see it the way Barney wanted them to see it.' She gulped back the threatening tears. 'That's a terrible thing, you know, Adam. It isn't fair to them, and it isn't fair to Barney.'

Weighing it up in his mind, Adam slowly nodded his head. 'You must do what your heart tells you, my darling,' he reiterated kindly. 'Like I say, no one can advise you on that, though once the truth is out, there'll be no going back. You do realise that, don't you?'

'Only too well.' The words sailed out on a long, quiet sigh. 'What would it do to them? Would they blame themselves? Would they blame *me* . . . or Barney? And could they ever find it in their hearts to forgive?'

With both her hands she grabbed him by the arm, as though clinging to him for support. 'God help me, Adam, if I make the wrong decision, they could be hurt beyond belief. And that wouldn't be right, because none of it was their doing.'

'What about Mary?' Having seen her grow up, he had great affection for Lucy's daughter. 'Will you tell *her*?'

'She will have to know at some stage.' Lucy had been giving it some thought for a long time now. 'I've agonised about what it would do to her if she learned the real truth about her daddy, but I've always known there would come a day when I would have to tell her the whole story.'

A look of pride flashed in her eyes. 'Mary is strong. What she learns will come as a shock to her, yes, but I truly believe that in the end, she might just be the one to hold it all together.'

For a moment, the two of them sat and held hands, united. Then, breaking the moment, Lucy let go and looked mischievously at Adam.

'Before I let you go, will you do me another favour?'

'Of course!'

'Knock on Elsie Langton's door and ask her if she wouldn't mind coming back to prepare a meal for three.'

He chuckled. 'You old fox! You've got it all planned, haven't you?'

'Well, the two of them will never get together with him in the garden freezing half to death and her in the kitchen getting all hot and bothered. It's up to us old ones to show them the way.' She gave him a little push. 'Go on then! Fetch yon Elsie back and tell her she'll be paid double time for the pleasure.'

Standing up, he looked down on her with admiration. 'Consider it done,' he said.

She waved her hand impatiently. 'Get a move on, then! Don't stand there until Mary's up to her neck in potato peelings and cabbage. A whiff of that and our Prince Charming will be gone for good!'

Adam laughed out loud. 'Mary's right. You really are all kinds of a bully.' With that he went away at a smart pace, chuckling and jingling the keys to the big car.

Then he wondered once more about the real reason she

had wanted to see Dr Lucas, and his heart sank. God forbid that anything should happen to her, for the world would be a darker place without his Lucy.

~

Reaching the smithy, Adam parked the big black car and walked up the footpath to the front door. Knowing how Charlie Langton was a bit deaf, he made a fist and knocked soundly on the door.

'Gawd Almighty!' Having rushed to see who was at his door, Elsie Langton's husband was none too pleased to learn the reason for this late visit.

'Can't you buggers look after yerselves for five minutes!' An old Lancastrian who had moved down south many years back, Charlie had lost none of his accent, and even less of his attitude. But he was harmless enough and there had never been such a dedicated blacksmith; besides which he always gave sweets to the children and was straightforward to deal with. You always knew where you were with Charlie, and after a while, folks had come to respect and like him.

Calling him inside he told Adam, 'The poor lass never stops! She's rushed in from the big 'ouse, got the dinner on the table, gulped hers down, and now she's upstairs changing the bedclothes.'

An ordinary man with ordinary needs, Charlie suffered from a nervous twitch in his left eye whenever things got too much for him. The more agitated he grew, the more his eye twitched, and it was twitching now like never before. 'Bloody folks wi' money . . . think yer can do what yer like wi' such as us!'

Being used to his ways, Adam took no offence. 'I haven't got any money,' he said loudly, 'and you know as well as I do that the Davidsons always do their best by this village.'

Charlie snorted and turning round, he informed Adam, 'Aye well, that's as mebbe, but I might like to 'ave the wife to mesel' now an' then. You buggers up at the 'ouse want to think o' that.' He gave the smaller man a shrivelling glance. 'Besides, I might be a bit deaf, but I've still got one good ear, so there's no need to shout like a damned fishwife.'

To Adam's amusement, Charlie grumbled all the way down the passage. 'She'll not want to come back, and I wouldn't blame 'er neither! If it were up to me, she'd be in the chair warming her feet by the fireside, but she'll not listen to me, so I'll not waste me time.'

Arriving at the bottom of the stairs, he raised his voice. 'ELSIE! It's the man from the big 'ouse to see yer!' Giving Adam a scathing glance with the steady eye, he bawled again, 'WANT BLOOD, THEY DO! YOU'D BEST COME AN' SEE TO 'IM, 'CAUSE I'VE OTHER THINGS TO BE DOING.'

Within minutes there was a flurry of activity from the upper level, swiftly followed by the sound of footsteps coming down the stairs. 'What's to do?' Round and homely, and looking flummoxed, it was Elsie. 'Oh, Adam!' Her first thought was for Lucy. 'She's not fallen over again, has she?'

'No,' he reassured her, 'it's nothing like that. She just wondered if you might be able to come back with me and help cook a meal and clear it up afterwards.' Raising his eyebrows in intimate fashion, he explained, 'She's got a visitor – yon chappie from Far Crest Farm – and he seems to have taken a real shine to Mary, and —'

Before he could finish, she gave a knowing wink. 'I see. And she wants me in the kitchen, so's the two of them can spend some time together, is that it?'

He smiled with relief. 'You know her almost as well as I do, Elsie, and yes, that's the general idea.'

'And does Mary know what her mother's up to?'

'Well, she doesn't know I've been to fetch you, if that's what you mean. She's in the kitchen as we speak, preparing the evening meal. I tell you what though, Elsie, she does seem to get on very well with the fellow in question.'

Elsie was delighted. 'In that case, how can I say no? Mary is a lovely young woman and deserves a good man to take care of her. Is this man a decent sort? Only I've not met him to speak to. We exchanged pleasantries as we passed in the lane once, but he didn't linger, 'cause he was off on one of his long walks. Every morning come rain or shine, he's away across the fields with that dog of his.'

From his chair by the fireside, Charlie had seen their lips moving but heard not a single word. 'What's he saying?' he asked irritably. 'What's going on now?'

'Nothing for you to worry about,' his wife told him sharply. 'I'm off to do an extra shift for Mrs Davidson, that's all.'

'Oh aye, I gathered that much. An' how long will yer be?'

'A couple of hours at the most, I reckon.'

He sat bolt upright in the chair. 'Don't forget to tell the buggers yer want double time!'

'Lucy will give me that without asking,' Elsie replied. 'She's a good woman.'

'An' what am I supposed to do while yer gone?' The old smith looked like a sulky child.

Elsie chuckled at that. 'You can do what you always do, whether I'm here or not.'

'Oh aye, an' what's that?'

'Hmh! As if you need telling. You can lie back and snore, or listen to the news on the wireless and swear at the bits you don't care for. An' if that fails, there's always your precious crossword.'

He gave her a fond smile. 'Cheeky bugger! Come 'ere an' give us a kiss afore yer go.'

Adam thought this was all wonderful. The Langtons didn't have much in the way of luxuries, but they were content, and obviously still in love after all their years together. It was what he wanted for him and Lucy. But it wouldn't happen, and deep down he had always known that.

With the kiss deposited and her coat on ready to go, Elsie was almost at the front door when Charlie came after her. 'I'll get yer bike for yer, lass.'

'No need, thank you, pet. I'm sure Adam will run me there, and fetch me back when I'm finished.'

'Oh no, he won't! I'm not 'aving that,' her husband retorted. 'I'm not letting every Tom Dick nor Harry run yer about. For all I know he might be a shocking driver. Like as not he'll get yer killed. *Then* where would I be?'

'Hey! I'm a good driver! I take Mrs Davidson and her daughter all over the place, as well you know.'

Charlie was having none of it. 'I don't give a bugger what yer get up to wi' other folks. Yer not driving my Elsie, an' that's an end to it.'

Climbing down the steps, he hurried to where Elsie had leaned her bike against the wall on her return home earlier. Taking it by the handlebars, he walked it back to Elsie and thrust it at her. 'For me, lass,' he pleaded. 'Do it for me, 'cause it would mek me feel content, to know yer were safe, on yer bike,' he sneered at the black car, ''stead o' being rattled about in that there ve'ickle.'

Put like that, Elsie could not refuse him. 'The trouble with you, Charlie, is that you refuse to catch up with the times. All you know is horses and bicycles.'

'Aye, an' that's all I *need* to know, an' all!' His parting words were for Adam and his shiny, new car. ''Orses will be 'ere long after then noisy damned things 'ave 'ad their day.'

'All right, I'll go on my bike,' Elsie assured him. 'Now you get back inside and put your feet up by the fire. I'll not be long.'

With that she set off on her treasured steed through the chilly evening air, with Adam following in the car and feeling like a right fool; though he had to smile at what he thought was a comical situation.

CHAPTER FOUR

THE FIRST MARY knew about the arrangement was when Elsie marched into the kitchen. 'Right then, miss, you get off and see to your visitor while I crack on with the meal.' She cast an experienced eye over the preparations. 'Well now! You've already done the vegetables and got the meat sizzling away in the oven. There's not all that much left for me to do, is there, bar serve it and clear it all away. I'll make a nice drop of gravy, shall I?'

Caught unawares, Mary asked her, 'This is Mother's doing, isn't it? She sent for you. Poor Elsie, I'm sorry for all the trouble you've been put to. Wouldn't you rather be at home with your Charlie?'

'No. I'd rather be here, cooking for you and earning double time, than listening to my old man snoring his head off.'

'All right then,' Mary conceded, 'but only on one condition.'

'What's that?'

'Put a plateful out for yourself. There'll be more than enough, and if there's any left over, take it home to Charlie.'

'I will, thank you.'

Mary gave her a hug. 'Thank *you*, Elsie. I won't forget this.' Washing her hands and patting her hair, she asked the woman shyly, 'Do I look respectable?'

'You look lovely.' Elsie had always thought Lucy's daughter had something special. Though she wasn't beautiful, she had a spark about her . . . soft, shining eyes of the loveliest shade, and a kind of warmth that endeared you to her. 'Go on, miss . . . go and rescue your young man. I'll have supper on the table in twenty minutes.'

Mary found Ben in the summerhouse. All the lights were on, and he was sitting in one of the easy chairs, deep in thought. 'Hiding from my mother, are you?' Her smile lit up the evening.

Having been miles away, reflecting on his disastrous marriage and the years he'd wasted, Ben was mortified. 'What must you both think of me?' he said. 'I'm invited to supper and here I am, lounging in the summerhouse. I only meant to be a few minutes but lost track of time.' On his feet now, he smiled down on her. 'It's your fault, you know.'

'Oh, and why's that?' It was strange, Mary thought, how she felt as though she'd known him all her life.

He gestured towards the garden. 'Your mother's right. You've done wonders with the garden . . . it's just beautiful. So many lovely hidden places.' It wasn't hard to imagine what a feast of life and colour it would be in the height of summer. 'If you wanted to, you could lose yourself forever here.'

'And do you want to lose yourself?' Just now when she came upon him unexpectedly, she had seen the sadness in his eyes, and it touched her deeply.

It took a few seconds for him to answer. There was so much he could have told her, but that was all gone now, water under the bridge as they say. Besides, if he didn't let go of the past, how could he ever have a future? Turning to her, he recalled, 'It was you who said there are times when we all need to hide from the world.'

Her blue eyes shone with mischief. 'And here was I, thinking you were hiding from Mother!'

He chuckled heartily. For a moment he studied her upturned face, the full plumpness of her lips, the small straight nose and smiling eyes, and he felt a rush of contentment. If he let himself go, he could love this woman, he thought. But *if* he let himself go, he could lose his heart and be hurt, *again.*

He looked towards the house. 'Have you come to fetch me?'

She nodded her head. 'Dinner will be ready soon.'

'Do we still have a few minutes?'

She nodded her head again.

Taking her by the hand, he asked light-heartedly, 'Would you care to join me?' Leading her to the bench, he sat her down. 'Welcome to Paradise.'

For a little while they sat and talked and laughed, and when she gave a long, trembling shiver, he dared to put his arm round her shoulders, and like Ben, she was afraid, of her feelings, and of the future.

Suddenly their private idyll was shattered, when a homely figure came rushing round the corner, calling out: 'Supper's ready. Your mammy says you're to come in out of the cold.' Elsie chuckled merrily. 'I'm to tell you, she doesn't mind you canoodling out here, but she doesn't want you catching pneumonia, and if I can't persuade you back into the house, she'll be out here and she'll chase you both inside with her walking stick. What's more, I've made a big jug of creamy custard, and I'd like Mr Morris to enjoy my apple-pie while it's hot. It's a deep-dish pie, stuffed with best cooking apples and covered in pastry that'll melt in your mouth. It's only reheated, mind, but I made it fresh yesterday.'

Ben's stomach rumbled. 'Sounds wonderful.'

'I'm not one for singing my own praises,' Elsie declared self-righteously, 'but I do make the best apple-pie in the whole of Bedfordshire, and woe betide them as says any different.'

~

The evening was a great success.

The pork chops were succulent, and the vegetables done to a turn, and just as she'd promised, Elsie's apple-pie was the best Ben had ever tasted. Lucy had produced a bottle of wine and drank more than the others put together. She also did most of the talking. She told Ben about her hometown of Liverpool and got carried away with the memories – *though there was one particular memory she did not divulge.*

'What did you love most about Liverpool?' Ben asked, intrigued by her stories.

'Oh, the docks, and the Mersey of course!' Taking another sip of her red wine, Lucy savoured it for a moment, rolling it round her tongue and smacking her lips, like a dog after a bone.

Ben was ashamed to admit it, but he'd never seen the Mersey.

'Maybe you'd think she was nothing out of the ordinary – just another river flowing away to the sea,' Lucy speculated, 'but to the ones who've lived and worked alongside her for most of their lives, she's very special. She changes, y'see – from day to day she's never the same. She has moods just like us . . . dark moods, quiet moods . . . and after a while you get to know her, and you can't help but be affected, in a kind of magical way.'

She gave a long, nostalgic sigh. 'If you've never seen the early morning Mersey when she's covered in mist, or stood beside her when the moonlight dances on the water and brings it alive, then your life is sadly lacking.'

'I can see I'll have to take myself up there at the first opportunity,' he said obediently.

'Quite right!' Lucy applauded. 'Make sure you do!'

While Lucy and Ben chatted, Mary thought it amazing how well they got on together. But then, right from the start, she had felt comfortable with him. Maybe it was because he was older than her? Ben was so easy and natural, it would be hard not to feel at home in his company.

'Do you mind if I ask you something?' With her engaging manner and interesting tales, Lucy had commandeered him, though he hoped that he and Mary would make up for lost time together later.

'Go ahead, young man. Ask away.'

'Well, I was just thinking . . . if you were so happy in Liverpool, why would you ever want to leave?'

Suddenly the air was thick with silence, and Ben immediately wished he had never asked. But then his hostess answered and her manner was curiously sombre. 'Life sometimes gives us problems that we aren't equipped to deal with. So we run away . . . like the cowards we are.'

Ben was mortified. 'Oh look, I'm sorry. I seem to have opened up old wounds.' She had that same look about her that he had seen in the churchyard; a look of resignation, a sadness that was almost tangible.

Lucy, too, was mortified, for she had let them both see through her armour, and now she was afraid. 'It's all right,' she assured him hurriedly. 'I did love Liverpool. I still do, but I can't go back.' Her voice stiffened. 'I could never go back.'

Mary had never heard her mother talk in that way, and it worried her. From a child, she had known there was something in her mother's past that played strongly on her mind. Her own memories were unreliable; her early childhood often seemed tantalisingly out of reach. With Ben having opened a door to which she herself had never had access, secrets might come out and at last she would know what it was that haunted her mother so.

Turning to Ben she confessed, 'You're not the only one never to have seen the Mersey. I was born in Liverpool yet I can't recall anything about it.' She glanced at Lucy. 'Time and again, I've offered to go back with Mother, but we never have, and now I'm beginning to think we never will.'

Lucy smiled. 'Oh, you'll see Liverpool,' she promised. 'Maybe not with me, but you'll go down the Mersey and know the wonder that I knew as a young woman. Curiosity will get the better of you and one day, you will go back, I'm sure of it.'

Mary asked her outright. 'And if I really wanted you to come with me, would you?'

Lucy shook her head. 'No.'

'Why not?' In spite of her mother's emphatic answer, Mary felt she might yet uncover the truth; until her hopes were dashed with Lucy's firm reply.

'Because I'm too old now. Travelling tires me, as you well know.' She laughed as she told Ben, 'We went to London on the train. Dear me! What a trial. All that climbing in and out, up and down. You wouldn't believe the traffic in the streets there, and folks rushing about as though it was the end of the world ... It was all too much for me.' Sighing, she finished, 'No, my travelling days are well and truly at an end.'

With dinner over, they retired to the cosy sitting room. Here, although the hour was growing late, they chatted on; among other things they talked of the introduction in America of the first colour television. 'The mind boggles!' Lucy declared. 'Colour television, indeed! Whatever next?' She herself thought the wireless was sufficient – why would you need one of those big, ugly television sets?

Mostly they talked about the grave illness of King George. 'He has been a good King,' Ben said. 'He'll be sadly missed.'

Mary had her say and it was this. 'You're right. He will

be missed, but his daughter Elizabeth will make a wonder-ful Queen.' And without hesitation, the other two readily agreed.

'Right!' After tapping on the door, Elsie showed her face. 'I'll be off now. I've washed the dinner things and cleared them away. I'll see you in the morning.'

'Thank you, Elsie.' Lucy was fond of that dear woman. 'Off you go and put your feet up.'

Elsie chuckled. 'Hmh! Chance would be a fine thing.'

Mary excused herself and saw Elsie out. When she returned to the sitting room, she saw how tired her mother seemed. 'I think it's time you went to bed,' she said affec-tionately.

'Nonsense!' Lucy was bone-tired, though she would never admit it. 'I'm getting to know our new friend,' she said. 'The more I learn about him, the more I like him.'

Ben laughed. 'I'm flattered,' he told her, 'but I have to agree with your daughter, and then there's that business of you falling and hurting yourself in the churchyard. It's been a long, heavy day and no one would blame you if you wanted to rest now.'

He had noticed how every now and then she would close her eyes and relax into the chair, and occasionally she would fitfully rub her hands together, as though fighting some inner demon.

'I see!' Looking from one to the other, Lucy smiled wickedly. 'Trying to get rid of the old biddy so the two of you can be alone – is that it?' Mary smiled, but in fact, she had been concerned about her mother these past months. She seemed to have grown frail, and less mobile, though she would not hear of seeing a specialist.

Changing the subject completely, Lucy told Mary, 'I think I'm ready for a nice cup of tea. What about you, Ben?'

'Sounds good to me, thank you,' he said, swallowing a

yawn. It was high time he was in bed, too. The animals would be waiting to be fed at dawn.

'Go on, then! Get the kettle on, Mary, before we all die of thirst, and don't bring the teapot, there's a good girl . . . too much fuss and ceremony. Just pour three cups, that'll do.'

Frustrated at her mother's insistence on referring to her as 'child' or 'girl', Mary groaned. 'All right, Mother, I'm on my way.' Turning to Ben she confirmed, 'One sugar and a little milk, isn't it?' She had remembered when Elsie brought him tea earlier.

'That's it, yes. Thank you.' He was surprised and pleased that she'd remembered.

'There you are!' Lucy chipped in. 'Already she knows how you like your tea. That's the sign of a good wife, wouldn't you say, Ben?'

'I'd say your daughter has a good memory,' he answered, and that was as far as he would go.

No sooner had Mary departed for the kitchen than Lucy was quizzing him again. 'You do like her, don't you?'

He had got used to her directness and thought it refreshing, but now and then she would ask a question that took him off guard. 'I do like her, yes.' What else could he say, when he had been drawn to Mary as to no other woman since his divorce.

Lucy seemed to be reading his thoughts. 'I know I can be impertinent, and I know what you must think of me, but I do worry for my daughter, and when I see how well the two of you get on, I can't help but wonder if she's found her man at last . . .' Her voice trailed away and her eyes slowly closed.

For a moment Ben thought she had fallen asleep, but then she suddenly straightened herself up in the chair and asked him another question. 'Do you think you'll ever get back with your ex-wife?'

Ben shook his head. 'It was a long and messy business, and now it's over, and so is our relationship.'

'And the girl?'

'You mean Abbie, my daughter?'

'Yes. How does she feel about you and her mother splitting up?'

To Ben, the question was like a stab below the belt, but he answered it all the same. 'It was hard for her – hard for all of us. In the end it was all for the best.'

'And is she an only child?'

'She is, yes.'

'Would you like more children?'

Ben smiled, a long, lazy smile. 'You mean, if I ever got married again?'

Lucy nodded. 'Of course! When you and Mary get married, I want a whole horde of grandchildren.' She grew wistful. 'A boy, especially. It would be wonderful to cuddle a little boy.'

At that moment, Mary returned with the tray. 'Here we are!' Setting it on the coffee-table, she handed each of them a mug and pointed to the plate of chocolate slices. 'Help yourselves,' she told them.

Over the next half-hour, the conversation centred on Ben and his farming.

'So you've found a new way of life, is that it?' Lucy was ever inquisitive.

'It's certainly a very different world from the one I knew,' Ben answered. 'As you said yourself, London is busy and demanding. I used to get up at seven, struggle into the office . . .' He had expected her to interrupt, and she did.

'What work did you do?'

'I'm an architect by trade.'

Lucy was impressed. 'And were you good at it?'

'Yes – or so I'm told.'

54

'And was it your own business?'

'It was, but I eventually went back to work for the local council in my home town.'

'Mmm.' She glanced at Mary, who was trying desperately to bring that particular conversation to a halt. 'So you're not short of a bob or two then?'

'Mother, please! No more questions, or I'm sure Ben will never want to set foot in this house ever again.'

Lucy addressed Ben. '*Have* you had enough of my questions?'

He gave her a half-smile. 'Look, I'll make you a deal. I'll tell you all I think you should know, and then there'll be no more need of questions.'

Lucy agreed. 'So, you were saying . . . you got up at seven and struggled into work.'

'That's right. Then I worked until eight or nine at night and struggled home again.'

'Hmh! It's no wonder your marriage broke up.'

'MOTHER!' Mary gave her a warning glance.

Lucy closed her mouth and listened.

Curiously relieved that he was finding it easier to talk about his troubles, Ben went on, 'One night I got home and found my wife in bed with my ex-partner, Peter. Apparently they'd been having an affair for almost a year.' He gave a sad little smile. 'So, you could be right. Working all those hours probably was the reason for my marriage break-up.'

Lucy couldn't help but make a comment. 'I hope you leathered him good and proper?'

'Oh, I was tempted, but it would have solved nothing. My wife wanted out, and I said yes.' Dropping his gaze to the floor he said in a small voice, 'I think the love had long gone, on both sides. By the way, you were right, Lucy. I am worth a bob or two. But that means little when your whole life has been turned upside down. I didn't want to stay in

London, so I packed a few things and set off. I looked far and wide before I found this lovely part of the world, and now I'm settled and content.'

He laughed. 'I'm a farmer and proud of it. These days I'm up in the fields checking my sheep at five in the morning, and often fall into bed just before midnight, but I've never been happier in my whole life.'

He paused to reflect before ending lightheartedly, 'So there you are!' He smiled. 'I hope that's told you enough to be going on with?'

His hostess gave a long, contented sigh. 'Even *I* am satisfied with that,' she said. 'Thank you, lad. It's been a lovely day today, all due to our having met you. And now, I really must go up the wooden hill to Bedfordshire!'

CHAPTER FIVE

IT WAS STRIKING eleven when Lucy announced she was ready for her bed. As she got out of her chair, Mary handed her the walking stick and Ben hurried to open the drawing-room door for her. 'I'll take you up, Mother,' Mary offered.

'No, you won't!' Waving her stick at Mary, she ordered, 'You stay here with Ben. I'm perfectly capable of taking myself up the stairs to bed without your help.'

Knowing how stubborn her mother could be, Mary did not argue, but walked on with her to the bottom of the stairs. 'Leave me be, lass!' Lucy was growing agitated. 'Don't make me out to be a useless old biddy who can't even climb a few stairs.'

In fact, if truth be told, Lucy was beginning to feel the worse for wear. The wine, and the long evening, and her fall in the churchyard, had all caught up with her. Halfway up the stairs, she suddenly took a dizzy spell; aware that the two of them were watching from the foot of the stairs, she clung onto the banister and braved it out. 'Go on, be off with you!' she complained impatiently. 'You're making me nervous.'

Regaining her composure, she set off again, but when the dizziness returned with a vengeance, it seemed as though the treads were moving beneath her feet and the whole flight of stairs was spinning round. As she felt herself falling, she could only think of Barney . . . *and them.*

Mary's voice lifted her senses. 'It's all right, Mother, I'm here.' She had run up the stairs to catch Lucy's crumpling figure. For a moment, she staggered; her mother a dead weight in her arms.

Mary was glad to let Ben take over. Sweeping Lucy into his arms, he followed Mary's directions and took Lucy straight into her bedroom, where he laid her on the bed.

'Please, Ben, run and tell Adam what's happened, will you? He lives in the cottage at the side of the house – you can't miss it.' Mary wondered how she could sound so calm, when her insides were in turmoil.

By this time Lucy was shifting in and out of consciousness.

'Tell him what's happened,' the girl said. 'He'll know what to do.' Lately, she and Adam had been so worried about Lucy that they were ready for any event.

Startling them both, Lucy took hold of Mary's cuff. 'No ambulance . . . no doctor,' she pleaded. 'Promise me!' And she was so agitated, Mary could do no other than promise.

In a quiet voice so her mother would not hear, Mary spoke to Ben. 'Tell Adam . . . no ambulance, but he's to fetch Dr Nolan as quick as he can.'

Ben was already across the room. 'Don't worry.' Though from the pallor of Lucy's skin and the laboured breathing, he knew Mary had cause to be anxious.

Although it was midnight now, and the whole village was asleep, Adam was still up and dressed. On hearing the news, the little man was beside himself with worry. 'I knew something like this would happen,' he said as he bolted out of the door. 'I could see it coming, but like the stubborn devil she is, she would never admit she was ill.'

Climbing into the big black car, he asked of Ben, 'Go back to Mary. Tell her I'll be as quick as I can.'

He was as good as his word. No sooner had Ben returned to the house where Mary had got Lucy into bed and was now bathing her face with cool water than Adam came rushing in with the doctor in tow.

Somewhat revived, Lucy was determined to fight him off. 'I told you, I don't need a doctor. GET AWAY FROM ME!'

Dr Nolan was equally adamant. 'You won't get rid of me so easily this time, Lucy.' Having suffered her temper once or twice before, he had finally learned how to handle her.

Turning to Adam and Mary, he told them, 'She might co-operate more readily if you were to wait downstairs.'

Reluctantly they did as he asked, and as they went they could hear Lucy ordering him out of the house. 'Just leave me be! I'm not ill!'

The pair lingered on the stairs. 'Sounds like she's getting her second wind,' Adam joked, then glanced at Mary, his eyes swimming with tears. 'Do you think she'll be all right?' he asked the dear girl beside him, his voice choked.

The little man had never been afraid of anything, but losing Lucy filled him with terror. For the past twenty years and more, he had seen life through her eyes, laughed with her, cried with her, and through it all, he had loved her from afar.

The ironic thing was, in the same way that he had loved her, Lucy had loved Barney. Yet Adam consoled himself with the belief that she had a different, special kind of love for him. It was that which kept him close to her, and always would.

'I hope so.' Mary's thoughts were on a par with his. She felt sick to her stomach. 'She's fought with poor Dr Nolan before and sent him packing,' she reminded him, crying even as she joked. 'But this time, he's as worried about her as we are.'

Each wondering what the outcome of this night would be, they continued down the stairs in silence.

They were still silent and sombre as they came into the drawing room. 'How is she?' Ben had not known Lucy long, but already she had won a place in his heart.

'We'll know soon enough,' Mary said quietly. She lingered at the door, her eyes searching the upper levels. *Dear God, let her be all right,* she prayed. *Don't take her from me yet.* Somewhere in the back of her mind she had always known there would come a day when she would lose the light of her life. But not yet, dear Lord. Not for many a year to come.

The waiting seemed to go on forever, until at last the doctor walked briskly into the room. 'She's sleeping now,' he told them all. 'I've given her a sedative.' His long thin face broke into a weary smile. 'She's hard work,' he said, 'but I got the better of her in the end.'

'What's wrong with her?' Mary cared nothing for his smile.

The smile fading, he took a moment to consider his answer. 'I can't be sure . . . I'd like to take a blood sample and have some tests done in the hospital labs.'

'What sort of tests?'

'Well,' he answered cautiously, 'she's unusually tired, and complaining of breathlessness: this could point to anaemia. She seems to have little strength.' The smile crept back again. 'Though she did manage to fight me off once or twice.'

Knowing how all three of them were hanging on his every word, he continued on a more serious note, 'I'm a little concerned about her heart and blood pressure, but I can't be sure about anything until we do those tests. For that I'll need her to come into hospital overnight.'

At the mention of hospital, Adam turned pale. 'But she will be all right, won't she?'

Careful how he answered, Dr Nolan momentarily lowered

his gaze. Lucy Davidson was a legend in this hamlet; despite her reclusive nature, she had made many friends and as far as he knew, no enemies. She was generous, funny, honest and outspoken, and he understood why these good people should be so concerned. However, at the moment, he could only make a guess at her underlying condition. She was ill, though. There was no denying that.

'Had she not worked herself into a state, I would have admitted her to hospital tonight,' he said. 'As it is, and because she's calmer now, there'll be nothing lost if we leave her till morning. She needs plenty of rest. Let her sleep, that's the best medicine for now. I'll be back first thing.'

'But *will* she be all right?' Like Adam, Mary was desperately seeking reassurance.

'We can only wait and see.' He chose his words wisely. 'I would rather not speculate, though I won't deny that your mother is ill,' he said kindly. 'She's very weak and, as you saw for yourself, her breathing was laboured.'

Before they could question him further, he put up a staying hand. 'Once we get her into hospital, we'll know more.'

As he left, he said, 'You may look in on her, of course . . . I would want you to do that. But she must *not* be disturbed. Rest is the best thing for her just now.'

With the doctor gone, the mood was solemn. Ben felt as though he was intruding, but when he suggested leaving, Mary persuaded him to stay awhile. 'I'll go and check on Mother. Adam can put the kettle on, if he doesn't mind?' The little man nodded his agreement and set off for the kitchen. Mary then turned to address Ben. 'We can all keep each other company for a while, unless you really want to leave?'

She thought of how he had come here to Knudsden House in good faith, to return her mother's bag, and had been quizzed relentlessly about his personal life; on top of that he had been made to think he was duty bound to ask her out one evening. Any other man would have been long gone, but she truly hoped he would stay; his presence gave her so much comfort.

'I'll stay as long as you like.' Ben did not hesitate. 'There's nothing urgent waiting at home.' He had only offered to leave out of consideration, and was delighted that she felt need of him.

'I won't be long.' While Ben went to join Adam in the kitchen, Mary ran upstairs and crept into her mother's bedroom. She gazed down on Lucy's sleeping face. In the gentle light from the bedside lamp, her mother looked so much younger; her skin was clear and smooth as alabaster, and her lashes lay like spiders' legs over the slight curve of her cheeks. Her long hair was loose about her shoulders and her wide, pretty mouth was ever so slightly turned up at the corners as in a half-smile.

Reaching down, Mary laid her own hand over that of her mother. She could feel the warm softness of her skin, and beneath the tip of her fingers, the blood running through Lucy's veins. Holding hands was not something she and her mother did all that often, so she felt privileged, and oddly humbled.

Choking back the emotion, she slid her mother's hand beneath the sheets and covered it over. She then stroked her fingers through the long greying strands of hair where they lay nestled on the pillow like silken threads; so soft in her fingers.

She gazed long on Lucy's face, her eyes following every feature, every shadow and shape, and all the while she wondered about her mother, and about her father. What had transpired before she was born? What was the secret that she had always known existed? And why had she never been told of her parents' true past?

Her heart turning with emotion and the questions burning bright in her mind, she kissed the sleeping woman and made her way back downstairs to the men. Adam had brewed the tea and was busy pouring it out. 'She's sleeping well,' Mary told them, gratefully accepting the cup that was handed to her. 'I don't think I've ever seen her looking so peaceful.'

'Thank God for that.' Adam knew what a restless soul Lucy was, and unlike Mary he knew the reason why. 'It will do her the world of good to sleep through the night.' His voice fell until it was almost inaudible. 'If she's in a deep sleep, maybe she won't be plagued by the bad dreams.'

'What bad dreams?' Mary had heard his quiet words and they bothered her. 'Mother never told me about any dreams.'

Silently cursing himself, the little man tried to dismiss his remark. 'Oh, it's nothing,' he lied. 'I recall how she once told me she'd had a bad dream, that's all.'

Mary wasn't satisfied. 'You said she was plagued. That doesn't sound like one bad dream to me.' She knew Adam had known her parents long before she was born, and now she realised he was part of the secret she had never been privileged to share. 'Is there something you're not telling me?'

Sensing something too deep for his understanding, Ben wisely changed the subject. 'The fire's almost out. Shall I put more logs on?'

Relieved that the moment was broken, Adam turned to him. 'I think it might be a good idea,' he said, and to Mary, 'if that's all right with you?'

Having believed that she was on the verge of a long-awaited peep into the past, Mary now felt cheated. 'Yes,' she answered, 'best keep the fire alive. I for one won't be going to bed tonight.'

Adam was horrified. 'You must get your sleep,' he told her. 'I'll stay here and keep a check on your mother. I promise to wake you if needs be.'

Mary looked at Ben. A man of few words, he had such quiet strength. 'Will you stay?'

He smiled on her, a slow, easy smile that filled her heart and made her feel safe. 'Of course. Adam's right, though. Your mother will need you to be bright and alert tomorrow. You'll sleep better in your bed.'

Mary would not hear of it. 'I'm staying here with you two. Three pairs of ears are better than one, and we can take it in turns to check in on her. Look – there are two big sofas and a deep armchair. We can all snatch a moment's sleep when we grow tired.'

She smiled from one to the other. 'Meanwhile, we'll drink our tea and talk.' She paused. 'The time will soon pass.'

~

While Ben and Mary sipped their tea and chatted about things other than the one which pressed on their minds, Adam became increasingly agitated. By referring to Lucy's nightmares, he had almost betrayed his long-held loyalty to her. *'Mary must never know . . . promise me you won't ever tell.'* That had been Lucy's request to him, and though he had done everything possible for the woman he cherished, he had managed to avoid making an actual promise not to tell.

Somewhere deep in his soul, he truly believed that one day, Mary would have to know the truth of what had happened; not least because she herself was part of that fascinating, devastating story, for without it, she would never have been born.

Discreetly watching him, Mary saw how Adam was pacing the floor, faster and faster, until it seemed he would go crazy.

She saw the panic in his face and the way he was rolling his fists together, much like her own mother did when anxious. And she knew, without a shadow of doubt, that old secrets were tearing Adam and her mother apart.

While she watched him, Ben was watching her. And just as she had seen the anguish and pain in Adam's eyes, he saw the very same in hers. Without a word he took her hand in his and, when she swung her gaze to him, he stroked her face, fleetingly. 'Your mother will be fine,' he whispered. 'You have to believe that.'

Mary acknowledged him with an unsure nod of the head. She wanted him to hold her, and kiss her, and be the safe haven she craved; for in that moment she had never felt so alone in the whole of her life.

Suddenly, Adam was standing before them. 'I thought I heard a noise – I'm sure it came from upstairs. Please, lass . . . will you check on your mother again? See if she's all right?'

Mary didn't need asking twice. She was on her feet and out of the room before he'd finished speaking. While she was running up the stairs, Ben grew concerned for Adam. Taking the little man by the shoulders, he sat him in the armchair. 'Here, sit down . . . before you fall down.' And when Adam was seated, head low in his hands and his whole body trembling, Ben dashed off to the kitchen and brought him back a glass of water. 'Drink this . . . it'll help calm you.'

By the time Adam had swilled down every last drop of the cool water, Mary had returned. 'Mother is fast asleep,' she told them. 'She hasn't moved, except to pull down the covers a little.' Lucy never did like being too warm, even in her sleep.

Adam grabbed her hand. 'Are you sure she's all right?'

'Yes, I'm sure.' Mary squeezed his hand comfortingly. 'Like the doctor said . . . she's sleeping soundly.'

And then Adam was weeping, quietly at first, until the sobs racked his body, and when he looked up at them he was like a man haunted. 'I couldn't bear it if anything happened to your mam,' he said brokenly. 'I love her, d'you see? I have loved her for a long, long time . . . and always will till the day I die, and even after that.'

Mary sat on the edge of the sofa, opposite Adam and next to Ben, but she did not let go of Adam's hand.

'Do you think I don't know how much you love her?' she asked tenderly. 'I've known it since I was very small. I've seen the way you look at her, and I've heard you whisper her name . . . talking to her when you thought she couldn't hear. But *I* heard, and I know how much you adore her.'

She had a question. 'Why did she not love you back in the same way?'

Adam was curiously hurt by her question, though he understood it well enough. 'She *did* love me . . . she still *does*!'

'Yes, I know that, but why did she not love you *in the same way?*'

He smiled painfully at that, a sad, lonely smile that made her feel guilty. 'We can't always choose whom we love,' he answered wisely. 'I didn't choose to fall head over heels in love with Lucy, any more than she chose to fall head over heels in love with your daddy.'

He gave a long, rippling sigh. 'And who could blame her for that? Y'see, Barney Davidson was a very special man. Not because he was handsome or rich, or even because he was exceptional in ways we mere mortals might understand.' His eyes shone with admiration. 'No! He was *more* than that. He was deep, and kind . . .' Hesitating, he gave a shrug. 'Sometimes, words alone can never describe someone.'

'Please, Adam, will you try to describe him for me? No one ever talks about him.'

Adam was shocked to see the tears running down her face and once again, was tempted to tell her everything. 'You never knew him, did you, lass – not really?' he murmured. 'You were only a wee thing when we lost him. He was my dear, dear friend . . . the best pal a man could ever have, and I loved him for it.'

Afraid of losing the moment again, Mary persisted. 'Please, tell me what you know, what you and Mother have always kept from me.' Her voice broke. 'I will never rest until I know what happened, and don't tell me there was nothing untoward in my parents' lives, because in here . . .' she tapped the cradle of her heart '. . . I know there was.'

Deeply moved, he looked into those lovely, tearful eyes. 'Your mother should never have kept it from you,' he conceded gruffly. 'I've always known she was wrong about that. I told her you had every right to know, that you were Barney's child through and through. But she was afraid . . . always afraid.'

'Afraid of what?' Mary gave a sigh of relief. At last she was getting nearer to the truth.

'I can't tell.' He looked from her to Ben. 'I made a promise. NO!' He shook his head. 'I never did make that promise. I thought it would be wrong, d'you see? I told her, "Mary will have to know everything one day" . . .' His words trailed away.

'Adam?' The girl's voice penetrated his deeper thoughts. 'That day is here and now. And you're right: I *have* to know, so tell me . . . please.'

Snatching his hand from her grip, Adam scrambled out of the chair. He paced the floor awhile, then took a moment to stare out of the window at the night, but he said nothing for what seemed an age. Then he walked to the door, opened it and went out, and from the room they could see him standing at the foot of the stairs looking up. His lips were moving, but they could not hear what he was saying.

Mary went to get off the sofa, but Ben reached out and, with a gentle pressure of his hand, held her there. 'Best to leave him,' he whispered. 'Give him time.' And, knowing Ben was right, she remained still until the little fellow came back into the room.

~

Upstairs, Lucy thought she heard something. A voice. *His voice.* Half-asleep, her brain numbed by the sedative, she called out his name. 'Barney!' Her voice, and her heart broke, and she could speak no more.

Restless as always, she turned. Forcing open her eyes, and summoning every last ounce of strength, she stretched out her hand, and felt the hard edge of the bedside drawer . . . Inching it open, she took out a long metal biscuit-box and drew it to her chest, where it lay while she caught her breath and recovered her strength.

A moment later she had opened the lid and dipping her fingers inside, she lifted out a photograph and a long envelope, yellow with age and worn at the corners from where she had opened it many times over the years.

Holding the photograph close to the halo of light from the bedside lamp, Lucy could hardly see it for the tears that stung from her eyes and ran unheeded down her face. 'Oh Barney, dear Barney!' The sobbing was velvet-soft. No one heard. No one knew. No one *ever* knew.

For nearly twenty years, she had kept his face alive in her heart and soul, but now, as her senses swam from the effects of the sedative, when she saw him smiling up at her from the photograph, it was as though he was real: the slight film of moisture on his lips, the pinkness of his tongue, just visible behind those beautiful white teeth, and the eyes, soulfully blue, and so sad beneath the smile; yet the smile, and the eyes, were so alive they twinkled.

It was almost as though Barney was here in the room with her.

The sick woman took a moment to rest, before in a less emotional state, she studied the familiar and much-loved features: the shock of rich brown hair, those mesmerising blue eyes – not lavender-blue like Mary's, but darkest blue, like the ocean depths. And the mouth, with its full bottom lip. The wonderful smile was a reflection of Barney's naturally joyful soul; through good times and bad, his smile was like a ray of sunshine.

As he smiled at her now, Lucy could hear him singing; Barney loved to sing when he worked. She could hear him so clearly, his voice lifted in song and carried on the breeze from the fields to her kitchen. He never sang any song in particular. And when he wasn't singing, he would whistle.

Barney was one of those rare people who, without realising it, could raise your spirits and make you feel good; even at your lowest ebb.

Lucy's heart grew quiet. Times had come when Barney's song was not so lilting nor his smile quite so convincing, and there had been other times, though they were few, when she had caught him sobbing his heart out. She knew then, that he was thinking of past events. And with every moment of anguish he suffered, she suffered it with him, and her love grew all the stronger.

Over their short time together, Barney became her very life. He was her and she was him. They were one. Together they would see it through, and nothing would ever tear them apart. But it did. Death claimed him much too soon!

And when she lost him, her own life, too, would have been over but for Mary, and Mary was a part of Barney. She saw him every time Mary smiled or sang, or chided her.

And she loved that dear child with the same all-consuming love that she had felt for Barney. It was Mary who had been her saviour; Mary who was like her daddy in so many ways; Mary who had brought her untold joy.

Adam had long believed that Mary should be told about the events which took place before she was born. But Lucy thought differently. The little girl was an innocent and must be protected, and so she was never told.

But what of the other innocents? Dear God above! *WHAT OF THEM?*

Weary now, she dropped her hands and the photograph fell onto the eiderdown. Too weak to raise her head, she felt about until it was safe in her grasp again, and then with slow, trembling fingers, she laid it down beside her.

Unfolding the letter from inside the envelope, she held it up where she could see it in the light from the bedside lamp. She remembered receiving this, one dark damp day in her little cottage up north, and knew that only the truth could put things right. She had read the letter so many times, she knew every word by heart. She whispered them now, the sentences etched in her soul for all time:

To Lucy Baker,

It pains us to put pen to paper, but we must. Word has come to us here that you are now living with our father and have a child by him. Because of what you have done, we feel only hatred towards you. Hatred and disgust! Lucy, you betrayed us! We thought you were our friend, our sister. We all trusted you, especially our mother, but you were a viper in our midst.

The day we left, we vowed we would never be back, and that vow remains strong as ever. We just want you to know what you and our father have done to all of us; and to our mother most of all.

You helped to ruin our lives. You are a wicked, evil woman, and if there is any justice in the world, there will come a day when you will both pay for what you did. We pray with all our hearts for that day to come.

We don't need to sign our names. You know them already.

We are Thomas, Ronald and Susan Davidson.

We are your conscience.

Lucy shakily folded the letter away. 'Such hatred!' she sighed. Her heart ached for those young people . . . for them and their poor mother, because of all their suffering. But they didn't know the truth. THEY DIDN'T KNOW! How could they?

Carefully, she replaced Barney's photograph into the biscuit-box, then the letter into its envelope. 'What am I to do, love?' she whispered. 'You said they must never know, but I feel I *must* tell them, even if it will be too much for them to bear. It is time to put things right, if God will grant me the time I need.'

Then weariness closed in and the sedative claimed her. But the dreams remained. Awake or asleep, the dreams were never far away.

～

Adam went over to the fireplace and stood there for a while, his arms reaching up to either side of the mantelpiece, and his head bowed. 'I'm not sure if it's my place to tell you,' he murmured.

Mary felt instinctively that she ought not to speak. If he was wrestling with his conscience, then she must not influence him either way. So she waited, and hoped, and in a while he turned round, looked at them both, and slowly made his way back to them. 'I think Barney would want you to know,' he told Mary heavily. 'I reckon you're right, lass, the time *is* here.' The haunted look had finally left his eyes.

'So, will you tell me now?' Her mouth had gone dry; she could barely say the words.

He nodded.

'And will you tell me *everything*?'

Mary knew this was it. At long last she was to cross that threshold which, though it had never affected the deep love between herself and Lucy, had always been present between them. Excitement and fear mingled as she sensed the door opening to her, that secret door which had been too long closed, and she had no doubts that something wondrous waited beyond.

'I don't know if I'm doing right or wrong, but I believe the truth is long overdue,' Adam answered. 'Though I may live to regret it, and Lucy may not thank me for going against her wishes, yes, I'll tell you everything, sweetheart. I promise I won't leave anything out.'

Ben hastily prepared to leave. 'This is private family business,' he said. 'I have no right to be here.'

Neither Adam nor Mary would hear of it. 'Please, Ben, I want you to stay,' Mary told him, and Adam gave a nod of approval. 'I believe you should *both* hear what I have to tell,' he said.

The little man had a deep-down instinct that these two were made for each other. In the same inevitable way that Barney was woven into Mary's past, Ben was destined to be part of her future. He had seen her look at Ben in the same way her mother had looked at Barney, and tonight in Ben, he had caught a glimpse of his dear friend. Something told him he was witnessing the start of another deep and special love, and he knew that Ben truly belonged here.

And so he settled in his chair and cast his mind back over the years. Drawing on his memory, he mentally relived the story; of Lucy and Barney, and of course the others who did not, and could not, see the truth of what was happening before their eyes.

But Adam had seen, and it had scarred him forever. Just as it had scarred Lucy, and the others; though to this day, those others had not learned the truth of what happened, and maybe they never would. *Maybe the hatred and the pain would always be paramount.*

Adam thought that was a sad thing, because the tragedy that had taken place all those years ago, had given birth to something glorious.

~

As the night thickened and the story unfolded, Mary and Ben were in turn shocked and uplifted, and the more they heard, the more they began to realise that their lives would never again be the same.

During the telling, Adam was at times joyful, then tearful, and when he recalled the awful sacrifice Barney had made, his eyes filled with pain. But above all, he was proud to be telling Barney's story.

Because, in his deepest heart, he believed it to be one of the most powerful love stories of all time.

PART TWO

~

Summer, 1930

Lucy's Story

CHAPTER SIX

T HE SUMMER OF 1930 was proving to be one of the most glorious on record, as if to compensate in some way for the misery of mass unemployment on Merseyside. Today, 25 May, the docklands were almost deserted but the narrow, meandering backstreets were as busy as ever. Young children played; scabby dogs lounged in cool, shadowy corners; floral-pinnied women in turbans busied themselves whitestoning their front doorsteps, pausing only for a snippet of gossip as a neighbour passed by; and having emptied gallons of milk from churn to jug, the milkman was on his lazy way home, the wheels of his cart clattering a tune on the cobbles . . . *clickety-clack, clickety clack, drink your milk and I'll be back* . . . the children made up the song and as he passed by, they ran after him chanting the words, skipping away once he'd turned the corner.

Back down in the docks, sailors disembarked, glad to come ashore after being at sea for many months. Placards everywhere gave out the news: *British Aviator Amy Johnson flies from London to Australia in nineteen and a half days.*

'There you go, boyo.' The tall, bony man with the unkempt beard had been at sea for too long, and now at last, he was done with it. 'While we've been conquering the seven seas, that brave lady's been conquering the skies.'

'Hmh!' The younger man was rough in looks and rough in nature. 'I'd rather her than me, up there all alone. I never have been able to stand my own company.'

The older man laughed. 'That's because you're a miserable bugger, and I should know, being the unfortunate that had the next bunk to you.'

'What d'you mean? We got on all right, didn't we?'

'That's true – but only because when you're on a ship in the middle of the ocean, you've either to get on with your shipmates, or jump off the ship. And I for one didn't fancy being the sharks' next meal.'

'So where are you off to now?'

'Home to South Wales, thank God. What about you? Where might *you* be headed?'

A crafty smile flickered over the younger man's features. 'I've a woman to see.'

'A woman, eh?' The other man knew of Edward Trent's liking for the ladies, because he'd witnessed it many a time in port. 'So, she's *another* one you left behind, is she?'

'Whether I left her behind or not, she'll still be waiting for me.'

'You're an arrogant devil, I'll give you that.'

'I might stay this time . . . make an honest woman of her,' Trent boasted.

The older man laughed out loud at the idea. 'Never!'

'Ah, but this one's different. She's full of fun, a real stunner. Moreover, she'll do anything for me.' He preened himself. 'A man could do worse than settle down with a woman like Lucy Baker.'

'Well, good luck to you then, boyo. As for me, I'm away to my beloved Wales. No more sailing the world's oceans for me. I'm finished with all that.'

'So, what will you do? There's mass unemployment, you

know. It may not be much of a picnic in your part of the world, matey.'

'That won't bother me.' The older man took a deep, gratifying breath, and when he released it, the answer came with it. 'I've not made up my mind yet, but what I do know is this: I'll spend my days as I please, tending my bit of land and fishing, and not be driven by money and command. I've worked hard and saved my wages, and God willing, you'll not see me again.' With that he threw his kitbag over his shoulder and strode off, with never a look back.

Watching him go, the other man laughed under his breath. 'That's what they all say,' he sneered, 'and you're no different from the rest.' Dark-haired, dark-eyed and with a heart to match, Edward Trent was a regular Jack the Lad who fancied he should please every woman he came across, and he had done just that, in every port across the world.

We're *both* going fishing, he thought as he walked on. I'll leave you to catch the ones with the tails, Taffy Evans, while I settle for the others – the ones that pretend to fight you off when all they really want is for you to catch 'em and show 'em a good time.

As he left the docks and headed towards the nearest lodging-house, he had only one woman on his mind; a young and spritely thing, with long flowing hair and a smile that could melt a man's heart from a mile off. 'You're a lucky girl, Lucy Baker!' he chuckled. He hoped she'd kept her looks and taken care of herself, because Eddie boy was on his way!

He called her up in his mind and smiled. Even after two years away and countless other women, he'd still got a soft spot for her. She'd been a virgin when they'd met, a hard-working shop girl, still living with her parents, and she'd fallen for him hook, line and sinker. Who knows, if she treated him right, he might even consider putting a ring on her finger. Somehow, she had got to him, where the others hadn't. Maybe it was her innocence and loyalty – things in short supply among the women he usually had dealings with.

He squared his shoulders and marched on. That doesn't mean to say I'll be staying for sure, he thought. Oh no! Like the man said, there are plenty of fish in the sea, and half the fun is catching them, then throwing them back for another day.

An hour and a half later, he had drunk a pint, had a strip-down wash and bedded the landlord's daughter, twice. And now he was on a bus, headed for Kitchener Street, a mile or so from the docklands – number 14. He checked his notebook and scanned the many names there. Yes, that was it – Lucy Baker at number 14, Kitchener Street, Liverpool.

'Will that be a return ticket, or one way?' The conductor had his ticket-machine at the ready.

'I might be coming back, or I might not.' Edward liked to hedge his bets, especially as he didn't quite know what awaited him. 'I'll have a return ticket, if you please.'

'Return it is.' Turning the handle on his machine, the conductor ran the ticket off. 'That'll be tuppence ha'penny.'

Twenty minutes later, the arrogant young seaman was strolling down Kitchener Street, checking the door numbers as he went. 'Here we are!' He had remembered the street as being long, with every house looking the same; narrow doors and white-stoned steps, and netted curtains up at the windows. But yes, this was the one – halfway down and look-ing exactly as he remembered. He rapped hard with the knocker.

After a couple of minutes, a plump, red-faced woman flung open the door. 'What the devil d'you think you're playing at?' she demanded angrily. 'I'm not deaf but I will be if you keep rattling the door like that?'

'I'm looking for Lucy Baker.' He'd forgotten that familiar

lilt of the Liverpudlian tongue; it was a comforting sound to a man who had travelled a hostile world.

'The Bakers don't live here no more.' Leaning forward, the red-faced woman looked up and down the street. Content that she would not be overheard, she confided, 'There was a bit of a to-do in the family, if you know what I mean.' And seeing that he did *not* know, she went on, 'Ted Baker – Lucy's father – he took another woman to his bed, d'yer see? Then his poor missus chucked him out, and rightly so if you ask me!'

'I don't need to know all the ins and outs,' he told her irritably. 'I just need to find Lucy.'

'I'm coming to that. When Lucy's dad was thrown out, he moved in with his new woman – went to live on York Street, they did – and good riddance to 'em! This house became vacant, and me an' my Eric moved in. Been here a while now.'

'So Lucy went with her father, is that what you're saying?'

'Did I say that?' She liked to tell her story properly, and wasn't finished yet. 'Well, soon after she gave him the old heave-ho, his missus upped sticks and buggered off and nobody knows where she went.'

'So where is Lucy?' Frustration rose in him. 'What happened to her?'

'Oh, aye, you might well ask!'

'I *am* asking, and I'd be obliged if you'd give me an answer.' Trent had no patience with folks like this, especially after the travelling. He'd come a long way to get here, and no doubt he'd be going a long way back, sooner or later. So, there was no time to be wasting.

'All I can say is, it's a good job Lucy was the only child.' Folding her fat little sausage arms, the woman rattled on: 'Y'see, her mam had such terrible trouble bearing a child. Lost four of 'em over the years, she did, an' as if that isn't enough to be putting up with, 'er scoundrel of a husband ends up in some other woman's bed. Shame on him, that's what I say!'

'That's enough o' the chatter, lady! All I want is the where-abouts of Lucy.' Another minute and he might end up stran-gling the old biddy.

Not one to be bullied, she declared sharply, 'Hold yer 'orses. I were just getting to that!'

'For Chrissake, woman, get on with it, then! Where the bloody hell is she?' When he now took a step forward, the red-faced woman took a step back.

'She's moved in wi' Bridget.'

'Who the hell's Bridget?'

The fat little woman gave a wicked grin. '*Everybody* knows Bridget!'

'Well, here's one who doesn't.' When he took another step forward, she took another step back. 'I couldn't give a toss about Bridget. Just tell me where my girlfriend is, and I'll trouble you no more.'

'All right! All right! There's no need to get aeryated. I already told you, I were coming to that.'

When he glared at her, she nervously cleared her throat and hurriedly explained, 'Bridget is a woman well-known in these parts . . . particularly by the *men*, do you get my drift? Oh yes, she might be generous with her favours, but she charges well enough, and so do her girls, though o' course we ain't supposed to know about what goes on in that place. The bizzies'll put her away if she's found out, an' none of us would want to be responsible for putting Bridget away, nor any of her girls neither.'

She took a well-deserved breath. 'For all her wrongdoings, she's gorra good heart, has Bridget, and she'll help anybody in trouble. Lives along Viaduct Street, number twenty-three. You'll find Lucy there.'

On seeing the question in his eyes, she quickly assured

him, 'No, she's not one of Bridget's girls. Lucy Baker is a stray lamb. She met up with a no-good fella who promised her the world then cleared off to sea, and then she had nowhere to go when her mam and dad split up, so Bridget took her in. Y'see, as I told you . . . Bridget's gorra soft heart and likes to help such folks.'

As he hurried away, she called after him. 'Hey! There's summat I forgot to tell you!'

Edward was not in the mood for listening, however. 'Silly old fool!' he muttered, and ignoring her, he walked on.

Seeing him march away all the quicker, the woman shrugged her fat little shoulders. 'Don't listen then,' she told his back. 'It won't matter to me. Anyway, I expect you'll find out soon enough.' The thought of him being caught unawares made her smile – until she recalled how he had nearly banged her door down and then stared at her so threateningly. Her hackles were up.

Shaking her fist after him, she yelled, 'And don't come bothering me again, Sonny Jim! I were busy at the wash-tub when you came pounding on my door with your damned questions. It's no fun washing blankets, but you wouldn't know about that, would you, eh? Oh no! You men with your damned questions. Go on! Bugger off and don't come back!'

When he turned to scowl at her, she slammed shut the door and scampered back to her wash-tub, grumbling as she went. 'If Lucy Baker gives that fella so much as the time o' day, she wants her head examining!' she muttered to herself.

~

When Edward Trent reached Bridget's house, he knocked on the door with the same force that he had used in Kitchener Street. 'You don't need to knock.' The woman who opened the door was in her late twenties, tall and slender, with a shock of dark hair and over-painted features. 'We don't stand on ceremony here.' She ushered him inside. 'It's down the passage and first left.'

He went first and she followed at a quickening pace. It wasn't often the younger men came to visit, and this one was handsome into the bargain, if a bit surly.

As she came into the room she quietly closed the door behind her. 'The other girls are out,' she confided. 'Mandy's having her hair done and Sandra's got a day off. So I'm afraid you'll have to make do with me. I'm Lynette.'

His frown became a smile. 'You think I'm a client, is that it?'

The young woman shrugged. 'I hope you are,' she replied. Giving him a knowing wink, she went on in silken tones, 'You make a nice change. We normally get the older men here – the blokes who don't get treated right by their own women ... at least, that's what they tell us.' She chuckled. 'So, what's your reason for being here? Wifey kicked you out, has she?'

Thinking that here was too good a chance to miss, he led her on. 'And what if she has?'

'Well, I dare say I'd have to cheer you up then, wouldn't I?' As she spoke, she walked over to him and slowly, tantalisingly, began to undo the flies on his trousers.

'Did I say you could do that?' He was enjoying every minute.

'I'm sorry. Was I supposed to ask?'

'Not now.' Taking her blouse by the shoulders he ripped it clean off her back. 'It's too late to turn back now.' Leaning forward he kissed her neck, then wiped his tongue along her throat. 'If you're game, then so am I.'

For the next fifteen minutes they played and touched and he took her without feeling or shame, with an insatiable hunger, and in the same aggressive manner that he might sink his teeth into a fat lamb chop or swill back a tankard of ale.

Afterwards, while she was dressing, he threw a few coins on the bed. 'That's for your trouble.' He threw down another. 'And that's for what you're about to do.'

'And what might that be?' This time, Lynette was not so sure of herself. He had been unexpectedly rough and slightly cruel, and she was right to be wary.

'Fetch Lucy Baker to me.' He wagged a finger in warning. 'One word to her about what we've just done, though, and your pretty face won't be so pretty any more.'

Astonished that Lucy would know such a man, she told him, 'Lucy isn't here.'

She had hardly finished when he caught her by the throat. 'You'd best not be lying to me!' he hissed.

'I'm not lying.' Fearful, she began to struggle. 'She skivvies at the squire's house, Haskell Hall – all the way over in Comberton village. She's there now. Let me go, please. I'm telling you the truth.'

Throwing her on to the bed, he stood over her. 'What time will she be back?'

'I'm not sure. Five, maybe six o'clock. She likes to work long hours. She needs the money for—'

'Shut your mouth!' Taking hold of her he yanked her up and held her close, kissing her mouth, her hair, her eyelids. 'How do I get there?' His voice resembled the soft, deadly hiss of a snake.

Cringing at his touch, she told him, 'Across the fields at the end of this road towards the water-tower.'

'How far?'

'Take the bridle-path, alongside the brook, towards the village of Comberton-by-Weir. It's sign-posted. Head for the hilltop, and you won't go wrong. Once past Overhill Farm, go down the other side and you'll find the squire's house half a mile on. It's called Haskell Hall. You can't miss it – a big old house with great trees lining the way up to the entrance. It's about a mile and a half in all.'

Throwing her aside he scowled. 'Ah, well. I suppose I've come this far, another mile or two will seem like nothing.'

Before he left he warned her again. 'We had our fun and that's an end to it. But one word to anybody, especially to Lucy, and you'll rue the day. D'you understand me?'

Fearing for her life, Lynette nodded. 'I won't say anything.'

'Good girl.' For an unbearable moment he stared her out. 'I expect I'll see you when we get back.' Grabbing her hair in a bunch between his thick strong fingers, he drew her head back and kissed her throat. 'Oh look, you're starting to bruise.' With a devious grin, he screwed a straightened finger into her forehead until she winced. 'Not a word!' he whispered. Then he went on his way, whistling merrily as he strode briskly down the pavement.

So far it had been a good day, he thought smugly.

Seeing Lucy would be the icing on the cake.

~

Back at Bridget's house, the woman herself had arrived; large-boned, with her mass of fiery hair and eyes green as a cat's in the dark, she was as Irish as the Blarney Stone, filling the front parlour with her presence. She was astonished to find one of her young people in tears. 'Hey now!' She dropped her bag into the nearest chair.

'Aw, will ye look at that!' she exclaimed. 'You'll have eyes like split walnuts if you don't stop the bawling, so ye will.' Sensing a man was involved, she demanded to know, 'Who was he? What did the swine do to you?' She banged her fist on the dresser. 'Sure, I'll have the bloody head off his shoulders if he's messed you up.' And by the ample size of her, she was well capable of carrying out her threat.

'It's got nothing to do with any bloke.' Afraid to reveal the truth, the young woman lied convincingly. 'It's just that I've had this awful toothache all day and it's giving me some gyp.'

Bridget relaxed. 'If that's all, you'd best get yourself a drop of the hard stuff out of the dresser. That should see you through the night, and if you're no better in the morning, you can take yourself off to the dentist. All right?'

'All right.' Lynette gave a sigh of relief. 'Oh, and there *was* a man here . . . not a client or anything like that,' she added quickly.

Bridget was disappointed. 'Pity. So what did he want?'

'He was looking for Lucy.'

'Was he now? And did you tell him where to find her?'

'Yes. I told him she was working over at the squire's house. He's gone there now, to meet up with her.'

'Mmm.' Bridget did not like the sound of it. 'And what did he look like, this fella?'

The young woman shrugged, her bottom lip turning down as she pretended to recall his features; while in truth she would never forget them. 'Rough-looking, I suppose, but handsome all the same.'

'That doesn't tell me much, does it? A description like that could fit anybody.' Bridget threw herself into the chair opposite. 'Come on, Lynette – what else?'

'Well, he had a weathered face as though he'd been in the sun a lot, and he was carrying a kitbag.' As the images burned deeper into her mind, her speech quickened, as though she wanted it all said and done with as swiftly as possible. 'He was dark-haired and he had this look about him – a real mean, peevish kind of look. I tell you what, Bridget, I wouldn't like to be Lucy if she's got deep in with that kinda fella. No, I certainly would not!'

Bridget was curious. 'For someone who's got a bad tooth-ache, you seem to have found enough time to get a real good look at him.'

'Well, o' course I did, because he stood on the doorstep and wouldn't go until I told him where Lucy was.'

'What, you mean he got nasty?'

'No, I don't mean that at all.' She had not forgotten his parting threat. 'He wanted to know where she was, and at first I wasn't sure whether to tell him, then he stood his ground and I had no choice.'

'So you told him, and he went?'

'That's right. I had to get rid of him. To tell you the truth, I didn't like the look of him.' Involuntarily, she shuddered.

'I see.' Bridget detected a great deal of fear in Lynette's manner. 'He sounds like a nasty piece of work,' she said quietly. 'You sure that's not why you were crying just now?'

'No!' Leaping out of the chair, Lynette laid the palm of her hand over her mouth. 'It's this damned tooth. It's driving me crazy.'

Bridget got out of her chair and wrapped her arms about the girl. 'You're to fetch a drop of whisky out of the cup-board, then get yourself off to bed. Come down later, when you're feeling better. A good night's sleep, then it's the dentist for you first thing in the morning.'

Before Lynette left the room, Bridget had one more ques-tion. 'This man . . . was he a sailor, d'you think?'

'He could well have been a matelot,' the girl said. 'He did have a tattoo – oh, and sailors do have kitbags, don't they?'

Bridget was quiet for a minute, as though she had just remembered who he was. 'Dark, with a mean kind of a look, you say. Mmm.' Then, her tone brisk, she told the young woman, 'All right, darlin', don't worry. Get off and take care of yourself. I'm sure Lucy will tell me all about it when she gets back.'

A few minutes later, with Lynette off to her bed, and the other girls not yet back, Bridget went through to the kitchen, where the young housekeeper, Tillie, having heard her come in earlier, was already pouring Bridget a cup of tea. 'Thought you might be ready for this,' she said, pushing it along the table to where Bridget had pulled up a chair and sat down. 'Had a good shopping trip?'

Having been thrown out of house and home by a violent stepfather these four years past, Tillie Salter had found a welcome at Bridget's house of pleasure. At seventeen, innocent and plain-looking as the day was long, there was never any intention to recruit her into the 'business'; so she was given a roof over her head and paid a wage to cook and clean and generally look after number 23, Viaduct Street, leaving Bridget free to keep a tight rein on her business, count her money, take care of her girls, and shop to her heart's content.

During the four years she had been there, Tillie Salter had loved every minute, and had come to look on Bridget as a surrogate mother. Bridget was her idol – her hero and her friend. She might run a brothel, but she was discreet in her dealings, she looked after her girls well, and had a heart of gold. So those who knew of her business said nothing, and those who thought she was a woman who had come into money legitimately, chatted with her in the street, and saw her as a kind soul, with a happy personality.

Moreover, she seemed ever ready to listen to their problems when others would not.

Bridget thanked her for the tea. She removed her light jacket and fanned her rosy face. 'You've no idea of the crowds,' she groaned. 'Pushing you this way and that . . . treading on your toes and thinking it's your fault and not theirs. Jesus, Mary and Joseph! What is it about shopping that makes martyrs of us poor women?'

Bringing her own tea, Tillie sat at the other side of the table. 'But you love it, don't you?' she said shyly. 'You love the noise and bustle, and spending your money across the counter. And I bet you went down the docks, dreaming of your homeland across the water.'

Bridget squeezed her hand. 'Ah, you know me too well, so ye do.' She gave a deep-down sigh. 'Aw, Tillie, there are times when I really do miss my Ireland.'

Tillie loved to hear the stories of Bridget's upbringing in Kilkenny. 'Tell me again, what do you miss most?' she asked eagerly.

Bridget was pleased to answer. 'I miss the rolling valleys and the way the sun goes down behind the hills of an evening. I miss my folks and I miss other people – like the old fella that used to sit outside the pub of an evening and play his accordion, so the people would throw a generous handful of coins into his cap as they sauntered by.'

'What else, Bridget?' Tillie persisted. 'Tell me what else.'

Bridget laughed. 'How many times must I tell you, before you're satisfied? I shall have to be careful, so I will, or you'll be up and off and across the water one of these foine days, so ye will!'

'Just tell me about the music, and the dancing,' Tillie urged, her grey eyes bright with anticipation in her homely young face.

'Ah, the dancing!' Rolling her eyes, Bridget leaned back in her chair; she could see and hear the festivities in her mind and her heart ached. 'I remember the fair in Appleby, when the horsemen would come from all over Ireland and even across the Atlantic from 'Merica, just to show their horses and traps and watch the goings-on. And if somebody took a liking to one of their best horses, they'd offer a price and when the haggling was done, they'd do the spitting of the handshake and the deal was agreed.'

Tillie cringed. 'Ugh! I don't think I'd want anybody spitting on *my* hand!' She hid her hands behind her back as if to protect them.

Bridget roared with laughter. 'It's the way things are done, so it is,' she said. 'Sure it's been that way for a hundred years and more, and likely it'll be that way for many more years to come!'

Caught up in the housekeeper's excitement, Bridget continued, 'When the deals are all done, the men go down to the pub and celebrate, drinking and singing and dancing, too – and oh, the good crack they have!' She threw out her arms with sheer joy. 'I'm telling you, Tillie me darlin', it is pure magic, so it is.'

'And what about the dancing, Bridget? Tell me about that!'

Bridget leaned forward. 'Sometimes it would be one couple on the floor and everybody watching, and when their feet got a-tapping and their hands got a-clapping and they couldn't watch no longer, they'd all link arms, so they would. Then they would all dance in a line, every one of them in tune with the other – feet crossing and jumping, and going high in the air as though they were one, and the tapping and the rhythm, and the noise against the boards . . .'

Her voice rose higher and higher and soon her own feet were a-tapping and her hands a-clapping, and, 'Sure, there's no magic in the world like an Irish jig!'

Suddenly she was calling for Tillie to clap a tune, and when the girl started, Bridget leaped to her feet and holding her skirt high, she began kicking out to the sound of the clapping. And soon the clapping got faster and faster and Bridget danced and laughed and it wasn't long before she fell into the chair, face bright red and aglow with delight. 'Come on!' she told Tillie. 'Get up and I'll show you how to do it.'

But before Tillie could do so, the sound of a child crying brought the laughter to an end. 'Oh, the poor little divil, we've woke him, so we have!'

Quickly now she ran through to the cot and took the child out – a healthy-looking little chap with a chubby face, startled from his afternoon nap by all the tapping and the clapping and the laughter that rang through the house.

'Ah, sure he's a bonny little fella, so he is,' Bridget cooed, and soon he was quiet on her lap, his mouth open like a fish at feeding time and his small hand stroking her blouse as he woke up properly.

'Will ye look at him,' she laughed tenderly. She handed the child to Tillie. 'Best get his supper ready, me darling,' she suggested. 'Then you might take him upstairs for his bath. It'll soon be his bedtime, so it will.'

Tillie put him in his high chair and there he sat, quiet as a mouse, chewing on his knuckles and watching Bridget as she gazed down on him. 'I can't believe how he's grown,' she declared. 'How old is he exactly?' She was never a one for figures – unless it was a strong man with a gorgeous arse and broad shoulders.

Tillie looked round from buttering his fingers of freshly-baked bread. She added some little squares of cheese for Jamie to nibble on while she cooked his soft-boiled egg. 'He's a year and six months old,' she enlightened Bridget. 'A real little boy now, no longer a baby.' She chuckled girlishly. 'He walked along the sofa-edge yesterday, and his fat little legs went all bandy.'

Bridget laughed. 'If he keeps on like that, it won't be long before he's off to work with his pack on his back,' she teased.

The women were tender with the little lad, as he had been born with one of his legs shorter than the other, and found it hard to balance. Bridget studied the child's features. Unlike his mammy, whose eyes were golden-brown, he had the darkest eyes; his hair, though, was the same colour as hers – the shiny rich brown of ripe chestnuts.

Like his mammy, the child had that same quick smile and infectious laughter; though these last two years Lucy had not laughed overmuch, because she was lonely and sad, though as with every deep emotion, she tried hard not to show it. But Bridget knew, and she wondered now about the man who had come to her door. 'There was a man here today,' she told Tillie, who had returned with the egg-cup and spoon, and a small beaker of milk for the child.

'I know.' Tillie was as discreet as ever. 'I heard him knocking the door down. He was determined to be heard.'

'Lynette answered the door, didn't she?' Bridget wondered if Tillie knew more than she was saying.

'Yes, I was changing this one's napkin. The others were out. They're still out, as far as I know.' She held the beaker-lip to Jamie's mouth again, cautioning him when he snatched at it and almost sent it flying. 'Why?'

Bridget thought a moment, then in a quiet voice she told Tillie, 'Lynette described him to me.'

'Did she?' The girl wiped the child's mouth and put the beaker to the floor. 'I didn't see him.' But she had heard him. She had heard *them*. Yet she never spoke of what she heard in this house. Bridget had given her a roof over her head and she never questioned or judged what went on here.

Bridget was quiet for a time, then she spoke, again in a quiet voice as though she was deep in thought. 'I've a feeling it's *him*!'

Tillie had spooned a helping of yolk into the child's mouth, but it was now all over his face, so she was wiping him with the flannel she had in her pocket. She looked up at Bridget's statement. 'Who?'

'Edward Trent – the baby's father. I think Lucy told you

how things started with him. He followed her home from Wavertree Park one day and was all over her, the bad bugger. Had his way with her, promised the earth then cleared off about three months later. After that, her parents split up and she lost her home. Fat lot of good her so-called boyfriend was then, eh?'

Having finished the feeding, Tillie lifted the child out onto her lap. 'Crikey!' Her eyes grew wide as saucers. 'I thought he'd upped and gone to sea. Got fed up wi' working on the docks, didn't he? An' he ain't never been in touch since.'

'That's right – and good shuts to him. But bad pennies have a way of turning up again. And he was a bad penny if ever there was one – though she never saw it.'

'She loved him, that's why.' Lucy had spoken long and deep to Tillie about her sweetheart, the father of her child. 'He was good to her, wasn't he?'

'Not all the time.' Bridget's expression hardened. 'I reckon he used to hit her – oh, not so's you'd notice from the outside, but he hurt her all the same. Even her mam an' dad warned her against him. She couldn't see what he was truly like, though. She loved him, y'see? She *still* loves him, even after he buggered off and left her with child.'

Bridget was afraid for Lucy. Afraid of why Edward Trent had come back. What was he after? As far as she was concerned, the man was no good, and never would be.

'He never even wrote to her, did he?' Tillie had not forgiven him for doing that to her friend. Poor Lucy had been frantic for a long while, not knowing which way to turn, wanting to tell him about his son once Jamie was born, but with no idea how to contact him.

Bridget didn't answer because her thoughts were miles away. What's he up to? she mused silently. Why is he here after all this time?

It seemed the very same question was crossing young Tillie's mind. 'Why do *you* think he's come back?' she said apprehensively.

Her employer shrugged. 'Who knows?' She recalled what Lynette had told her. 'He came looking for her, that's for sure. And he's gone to find her as we speak.'

She sighed. 'I only hope Lucy has enough sense not to be taken in by him a second time.'

CHAPTER SEVEN

UNAWARE OF DEVELOPMENTS at home, Lucy drove her energy into the last task of the day. 'Almost done now,' she told the curious magpie who had been watching her for the past ten minutes or so. 'Another few good wallops, and there won't be a speck of dust left.'

Raising the beater, she brought it down against the rug so hard that it danced on the clothes-line; another good hard wallop, and the dust flew in all directions, not as much as when she had first brought the rug out, but enough to give her a coughing fit, and send the startled magpie off to the skies.

'Cowardly creature!' she called after it. 'Mind, if I had wings, I'd be off too.' Oh, and she would an' all! Away above the chimney-tops ever so high, she would raise her head and flap her wings fast and furious until she was across the oceans, then she'd keep going until she reached some tropical paradise. But she wouldn't go alone, oh no. Wherever she went, she would take her darling son with her.

From the office window upstairs, the tall, elegant woman watched Lucy as she worked; the squire's secretary could hear Lucy's voice raised in song, but that wasn't unusual, because during her working day, whether inside or out, Lucy's melodious singing could be heard all over Haskell

Hall. 'You're a good soul, Lucy Baker,' Miss McGuire murmured, putting down her fountain-pen. 'Hardworking and happy as the day is long.'

As she watched Lucy hoist the rug from the line and drop it to the ground, she was taken by surprise when the girl suddenly looked up to see her there. 'I won't be long,' she called out. 'I'm finished just now.'

Lucy quickened her steps towards the house, the hot breeze playing with the hem of her skirt, her feet bare as the day she was born; with the rug carried in her arms, like a mother might carry a bairn, she made a fetching sight.

When a moment or two later, Lucy burst into the kitchen, Miss McGuire was waiting for her. 'For the life of me, Lucy, I don't know why you beat the rug when you could use that new vacuum cleaner. It *was* bought to suck up the dirt and dust from the floor, after all, and to save the staff here from heavy work.'

'I *do* use it,' Lucy protested, 'but it's not very good. Sometimes things get stuck in it and it won't work, and then old Jake has to see to it, and while he's doing that I still have to beat the rugs.' She prodded the one in her arms. 'This one is no good at all. It's got long fringes and they go flying up into the workings and then it's the devil's own job to free them. It's much quicker just to give it a sound beating on the clothes-line.'

The squire's secretary tended to agree, but did not say so. Instead she looked down at Lucy's bare feet. Small and neat, they were covered in a film of dust, and there was the tiniest leaf sticking out between the toes. 'Never mind the rug,' she retorted. 'Perhaps you'd like to tell me why you aren't wearing your boots?' Exasperated at the times she had asked the young woman to always wear her boots for fear of hurting herself on the harsh ground, she groaned. 'Just look at your poor feet, Lucy . . . covered in dust and picking up all the debris from the ground. One of these days you're bound to get an injury. I've asked you so many times to wear your work-boots, I'm worn out with it.'

Lucy looked down at her feet. 'I'm a mucky pup, I know,' she conceded, wiggling her toes to be rid of the leaf, 'but I feel so uncomfortable with the boots on. I'm sorry, Miss McGuire. I'll try to wear them, I promise.'

'And how many times have you said that?' The secretary rolled her eyes. 'And how many times have I seen you running about in your bare feet? It isn't as though you're a child, Lucy. You're a grown woman of nearly thirty, for heaven's sake, and you have a little one to think of. What would happen if something fell on your feet and broke them? How would you go on then, eh?'

'I know, and I'm really sorry,' Lucy repeated. 'I promise I'll try to keep the shoes on.' Lucy hated wearing shoes of any kind, almost as much as she hated cold porridge.

'Mind you do then.' The secretary was a kindly sort. She had little to do with the housekeeper's staff here at the Hall, but she had always had a soft spot for Lucy.

'Anyway, enough of this. It's time you went home,' she told Lucy now. 'There hasn't been a day in the past fortnight when you've left on time.'

'That's 'cause I like to finish all my work before I go,' Lucy explained.

'I know that, all too well,' came the reply. 'But you must leave time for yourself . . . and the child.' The secretary tried hard not to be shocked by the young woman's situation as an unmarried mother. The squire never listened to gossip so he remained ignorant of Jamie's existence; however, some of the other staff were aware of her status and shunned Lucy because of it.

'Oh, I do!' Lucy answered eagerly. 'When I'm not working here, I spend every passing minute with him.' A look of sheer joy lit her face. 'You can't know how much I love him. No one can.'

Dorothy was fond enough of Lucy to tell her, 'I'm sure I *do* know how much you love him. All I'm saying is this: it's no wonder you still haven't found a man to take care of you and the child, what with you working all hours, and here you are already twenty-nine years of age. Most young women are safely married and settled in their own home at that age.' This didn't apply to her either, she acknowledged sadly.

When she saw the downcast look on Lucy's face she was mortified. 'I've spoken out of turn, my dear. I didn't mean to be cruel. It's just that you're such a lovely young woman and I do care what happens to you. I'd hate to think you were destined to spend your life all alone.'

'It's all right, Miss McGuire, I don't mind.' But she did, and now her thoughts were filled with memories of a dark-eyed man who had quickly come into her life and filled her days with fun, and then just as quickly gone out of her life, without so much as a how's your father!

But she had not forgotten him. She never would. Especially when he'd left her with child, and it had caused so much trouble at home that she was made to leave in disgrace – and soon after, her mother and father split up and went their separate ways. And now she had no family at all, save for her little boy, who was everything to her.

'Go on then! Be off with you, before the housekeeper finds you another job to do. And don't worry. I'll let her know you've gone.'

The woman's voice invaded her thoughts, and when she looked up, the kindly secretary was already on her way down the long corridor.

Dragging the rug through the kitchen, Lucy got it to the drawing room, where she rolled it out before the big fireplace. 'All done for another day.' Sometimes Lucy sang, and sometimes like now, she talked to herself, and then there was the time when she got caught dancing on the sofa-table and almost got her marching orders from the housekeeper.

It was the same at home. Often Bridget would say, 'For the love of God, will ye sit still and be quiet!' But she couldn't. There was too much life in her, and it wasn't her fault.

Without wasting any more time, Lucy ran to the cupboard where her two pairs of shoes were lined up: black lace-up boots for work, and daintier shoes with ankle-straps for going home in. Taking out the ankle-strap shoes, she put them on and, flicking her long hair out of her eyes, she hurried out of the back door, her voice raised in song and her feet skipping as she went.

By the kennels at the side of the house, Lucy stopped to pet the hounds. She had a marvellous way with animals; whenever they had the chance, the squire's hounds would follow her everywhere, and while everyone else would stay clear of the bull in its pen, Lucy could often be seen defying instructions to lean over the gate and stroke its nose.

Lucy was halfway down the hill when she stopped to take off her shoes. The grass looked so warm, lush and inviting in the evening heat. Tying the ankle-straps together, she slung the shoes over her shoulder and went on in bare feet.

She was almost at the brook when she saw the figure of a man coming towards her. It wasn't the squire, or he'd have his dogs with him, and it wasn't Barney Davidson from Overhill Farm, because he was smaller-built.

She often spoke with Barney when he was out on the hills with his sheep or doing other work on the land. She liked him; he had a kind, caring manner, and was easy to talk with. In fact, if he wasn't married and she wasn't still completely infatuated with Edward, she could have fallen for him herself.

While Lucy grew increasingly curious about the man approaching from the bottom of the hill, he was also straining his eyes to see if it really was Lucy drawing ever closer, though when he saw that familiar wave of long hair flowing in the breeze and the cheeky swagger of her long limbs, he knew it was her and began to run. 'LUCY!' The wind carried his voice across the valley. 'LUCY BAKER, IT'S ME! IT'S YOUR SWEETHEART COME HOME!'

Hearing the voice, but unable to decipher the words, Lucy stopped and stared. With the sun directly in her face she couldn't see his features. But she saw the long, confident strides as he ran to her, and when he dropped the kitbag from his back, there was something disturbingly familiar about the way he moved. Slowly but surely, realisation dawned. 'Edward? My Edward?' She whispered his name; was it really him? Excitement coursed through her, but she didn't call out or run forward. She didn't dare trust her own judgement.

By the time he got close enough for her to recognise him, she took to her heels and ran to meet him. When he caught her in his arms and swung her high in the air, she laughed and cried with sheer joy. 'Oh Edward, I thought I'd never see you again!' She looked into his dark eyes and thought she would never again be so happy.

'I told you I'd be back.' Breathless, he set her down. 'I've never forgotten you, Lucy. Every day, every minute we've been apart, I've thought of this day.'

Caught up in the excitement of the moment, he kissed her long and hard, and held the kiss until Lucy thought she would suffocate.

'Stop!' Flattening her hands against his chest she remembered how he had walked out on her. 'What makes you think you can waltz back into my life and just pick up where you left off? You signed up and sailed away without a by your leave, and now you're back with the same damned cheek of it!'

Lucy had not forgotten the humiliation, the pain of it all, and then the despair. It had been a bad business for her, and then she found out she was with child and had to suffer in silence until she could hide the secret no longer. Her pregnancy – which caused a great scandal in the neighbourhood – created rows and repercussions between her parents, and in the end she witnessed the break-up of her family, and that was as much Edward's fault as her own.

For a long time things had gone from bad to worse, and still she had hoped he might return. But he never did – until now. And though she was thrilled beyond words to see him, she couldn't help but chide him. 'You let me down good and proper, Edward Trent!'

When he now looked desolate, she instantly forgave him and taking off at the run, shouted, 'If you want me, you'll have to catch me!'

And catch her he did; on the little slope just above the stream. He threw himself bodily at her, and together the two of them went rolling down the hill, until they landed up right next to the brook. She cupped a handful of water and chucked it at him while he lay helpless with laughter.

'You're a bloody lunatic!' he screeched, and she couldn't speak for spluttering. Her heart was leaping about inside her like a crazy thing: after all this time, when she had given up any hope of ever seeing him again, *Edward Trent was back.*

It was too wonderful for words. Her baby's father was home to make a proper life for them. They would be a family at last, and if Lucy could have jumped over the moon right then and there, she would have done.

Wrapping his strong sailor's arms about her slim waist, he inched her towards the soft rich grass that lined the stream's edge, and right there, with the clean, fresh water lapping over their bare feet, he laid her down and took her with a kind of animal hunger; not tenderly, not gently or cruelly, but the only way he knew how, driven by lust and the overriding greed to be satisfied. This was his third partner of the day, his fourth coupling, and for a little while, his passion subsided.

'That was so good, Lucy,' he said hoarsely. 'You don't know how long I've waited to be with you like that.'

But Lucy had not yet heard the words she yearned to hear. 'Do you love me?' she asked hesitantly. '*Really* love me?' Somehow she couldn't be sure, even now.

He laughed. 'That's a silly question.' And then, as though to dismiss the thought, he kissed her mouth. 'Didn't I just show you how much I love you?'

Lucy drew away. 'But you didn't *say* it. All the time we were making love, you never once said you loved me.'

'I did! I'm sure I did.' Bloody women, he thought. Are they never satisfied?

'Say it now.' Lucy needed convincing.

'What? Say *what?*' Anger trembled in his voice.

'That you love me . . . say it!'

'Jesus, but you're a persistent bugger.' Suddenly amused, he grinned down on her. 'But then you always were a spirited devil. It's what I liked most about you.'

'Say it then.' Melting to him, Lucy traced his lips with the tip of her finger. 'If you don't say it, I'll know you're not serious about us.'

Twice he opened his mouth to say it, but telling a woman that he loved her did not come easy, mainly because his idea of love and hers were not the same. Where she might think of something precious to them both – a sharing, giving emotion, with a deep-down need to build a life together – he was a cold, selfish man who saw his own needs to be of paramount importance.

103

Now, as he looked into that small, upturned face with the appealing brown eyes and the sunlight dancing off her long unkempt hair, he had to appease her. 'Silly bitch, o' course I love you!' Snatching her to him, he held her there for what seemed an age; until she drew away, to divulge a secret which shocked him to the core.

'Edward, I've got something to tell you.' She was so nervous, she could feel herself trembling.

He kissed her again. 'Have you, now. Well then, you'd best tell me, hadn't you?'

She nodded. 'When you were here before . . .' She hesitated, not knowing whether he would be pleased or angry. Yet, if they were to be married and start their own home together, he would have to know, and so she told him in a rush. 'We have a son, Edward. His name is Jamie, and oh, he's so beautiful.' As she gabbled on, intent on getting it off her chest, she did not see how the light in his eyes had dimmed, or the set of his jaw had hardened. 'He has such a look of you, and oh, just now he's beginning to learn to walk . . .'

She was silenced when he suddenly grabbed her by the shoulders. 'What are you saying, Lucy?' His hands dug into her skin, hurting her. 'A son? You're telling me that you have a child?'

'That's right, Edward – *we* have a child. He was born nine months to the day you went away. I had no idea that I was expecting. I wanted so much to let you know about him, but I couldn't, because I didn't know where you were.' Her voice faltered. 'I called him James – Jamie – after your middle name. Jamie Baker, he is – but now we can change it to Trent.'

Only a few minutes ago, her heart had been singing, but now she could see what a shock it was to him, and she was fearful.

'It'll be all right,' she gabbled. 'We'll get married and rent a little house and I'll work at Haskell Hall like now, and oh, Edward, it will be so wonderful . . .'

She paused, hope smiling in her eyes. 'It *will* be wonderful, won't it?'

The man didn't answer straight away. His mind was feverishly working. A child? A bastard to keep his feet tied to the ground while he broke his back working to keep him, *and her*. He didn't want that. Besides, how could he be sure it was his? He only had her word for it. For all he knew, he could be taking on another man's throwaway.

'Edward?' her small voice persisted. 'It will be all right, won't it?' Lucy had always realised that if he ever came back, the news would be a shock, but she had hoped that, in the end, he would be overjoyed to have a son.

'Of course, and why wouldn't it be?' His quick smile belied the rage inside. If she thought he was staying now, she'd soon find out different.

'And you're not angry?'

'Angry?' He held her close as though he would never let her go. 'How could I be angry? I won't deny it was a shock, but what man wouldn't be pleased to know he had a son waiting for him?'

Lucy was thrilled. 'We'll be a proper family, and I'll make you happy, I promise.' Even though there was still that little voice warning her to be wary, Lucy had to believe him.

'Where is he, this son of mine?'

'Back at Bridget's house. Oh Edward, she's been so good to us. Some people say she's the worst of the worst because she has girls who entertain, but she's a good woman. You'll see when you meet her. She has a helper by the name of Tillie who takes care of our son when I'm working . . .'

'I see.' He stopped her there. 'And you say she has girls who entertain?' He thought of Lynette, and smirked.

Lucy nodded earnestly. 'They're my friends. Bridget looks after them . . . like she looks after me.'

'Took them off the street, did she?'

'Something like that, yes.' Lucy didn't care for the way the conversation was going. 'But they're good girls . . . I mean, they're kind and thoughtful, and they've helped me through a bad time. When my parents found out about the baby, they went crazy. My mam wanted to send me to a woman in the back streets who does away with unwanted pregnancies, and my dad said she was callous, and that we should wait until you came back and he'd make sure it got sorted out.'

The memories had never gone away, though thanks to Bridget she had managed to push a lot of it to the back of her mind. Now though, it all came flooding back; the rows and upsets, and the terrible things that were said. Lucy had always thought her parents were happily married, when all the time they had just been 'rubbing along', as her mother had put it.

When she told them she was pregnant, it was as though she had lifted a lid they had each been struggling to keep shut, and all the venom came to the surface. 'Oh Edward, it was awful. In the end, they split up, and I found myself out on the streets. That was when Bridget took me in. She was at convent school with my mam, but she's as different from her as chalk from cheese.' Tears filled her eyes. 'Mam didn't want anything to do with me, or her grandchild, but Bridget's been both mother to me and granny to the bairn.'

Edward curled his lip at this description of a 'tart with a golden heart'. 'Well, you've no need to worry now,' he lied. 'I'm here and like your father said, it will all be sorted out.'

In reality he was already wondering where he'd dropped his kitbag, so he could go back and collect it and be gone like the wind out of here. If he'd had any feelings for her at all, they'd been suffocated by the news she'd given him. A bastard waiting to claim him for life, women who 'entertained' – and how could he be sure that Lucy herself had not 'entertained' some man or another, and that's how she came to be with child? Oh no! He might be a fool for a good-looking woman, but he was not fool enough to truss himself up like a chicken ready for the oven.

'Edward?' Lucy could see he was deep in thought. 'What's wrong?' She knew he was thinking of the news she had just given him.

'Oh, I'm sorry, sweetheart.' Scrambling to his feet, he took hold of her hand and pulled her up to him. 'I'll get my kitbag, then we'll walk back and you can introduce me to my son. Then we'll make plans. It's all going to be fine, Lucy.'

They got up and walked on, and she nestled in the curve of his arm, a spring in her step and a song in her heart. Edward was back. Everything would be fine now.

As they walked, Lucy was full of plans. 'We'll find a little house to rent with a good-sized garden, and we'll sit outside and watch our son playing, then of an evening, we can see the sun going down. Oh, sweetheart . . .' She looked at him and her heart was full. 'I'm so glad you're back.'

The man cared nothing for her dreaming. He had plans of his own, and they certainly didn't include sitting around in a garden and watching somebody else's kid playing. But he didn't want Lucy to know what he was thinking, so he said all the right things and convinced her that if that was what she wanted, then so did he. And Lucy believed him.

'Look!' Drawing his attention to the flock of sheep being driven to the brow of the hill, Lucy told him, 'There's Barney Davidson.'

As he turned to see, Lucy gave him a playful push and ran on. 'Race you to the lane!'

'You little sod!' She had caught him offguard, and he was thrilled. This was what spurred him on, a spirited woman fleeing and himself in full chase: and when he caught her, what fun it would be. 'Come on, Eddie boy,' he said to himself. 'Get after her. Leave her with another mouth to feed and happen she'll find some other poor bugger to take her on!'

For a moment he stood his ground and watched her running, bare-footed, with the pretty shoes dangling from her hand and her hair flowing behind, and the sound of her laughter exciting him – and he had a moment of weakness. For one dangerous, fleeting moment, he actually thought she might be worth staying for. But when fear took over, the moment was quickly gone.

Wickedness surged through him, and a sense of fun. There was no need to commit himself, not when he could have it all and walk away. Right now, Lucy wanted him to chase her and he would, and that was all right, because this was what he believed life was all about. Never mind responsibility. That was for other folks, not for a free-and-easy-living man like himself.

With a shout to let her know he was right behind, he set off at the run.

High on the hill, Barney saw the two of them careering across the field towards the stile; Lucy in front and going like the wind, and the man fast closing in.

He could hear the young woman's merry laughter and he smiled. 'Seems like she's found a bit of happiness,' he told Jess, his red-setter bitch, who trotted beside him, keeping an eye on the sheep. 'Lord knows, she deserves it after what she's been through.'

He knew Lucy because the two of them often chatted as she wended her way to work, and last winter, he had taken her along the lane in his cart because the hills were snow-covered. That was the very first time she had confided in him. After that, they had often walked the hills in the same direction, her going to and from the squire's house and himself to the outlying fields where he would check his flock.

As they got to know each other better, Lucy had confided in him more and more. Then one day when his lovely Vicky was walking with him, Lucy came along and joined them. The two women had got on so well that Vicky invited her up to Overhill Farm for tea, and it had been a very enjoyable evening.

'I don't know if that's the boy's father,' he told Jess as they strolled on, 'but even if it's not, Lucy seems content enough with him.'

Just then he heard a scream and on looking down again, he could see that Lucy had taken a tumble as she climbed the stile; he could see her lying among the big stones there and she didn't appear to be moving. 'Good God! Looks like she's hurt!' As he ran forward the dog bounded in front, ears pricked, sensing danger. Lucy wasn't getting up! What the hell was the bloke playing at? Cupping his hands, Barney called out: 'You there! Is she all right?'

As Barney drew nearer he could see how the man was standing still, looking down on Lucy and not making any move to help her. Suddenly he threw his kitbag over his shoulder and, with a backward glance at Barney, he began walking away, slowly at first then quickening his steps, and now with Barney less than fifty yards away, he bent his head, lengthened his stride and took off at speed. 'I can't help her, I've a ship waiting!' he yelled as he ran. 'I don't even know the woman.'

Barney had a choice; he could either go after the man and teach him a lesson he might never forget, or he could help Lucy, who was lying in a crooked position with her head oozing blood against a boulder.

His choice was no choice at all. He had to help Lucy. By now she was groaning; trying to move but seeming unable to.

Coming nearer, he began talking to her, soothing her as he fell to his knees beside her. 'It's all right, Lucy,' he said softly. 'You've taken a knock to the head, but you'll be fine, don't worry. I'll get you home to my Vicky. She'll know what to do.'

When Lucy gave no answer, he continued talking to her in a quiet voice, at the same time gently sliding his two arms under her slight form and collecting her to his chest. To him, she was but a feather in his arms, for he was a man possessed of strength that came from a lifetime labouring in the fields.

The movement disturbed her. With dazed vision she stared up at him, her shocked eyes looking into his. 'Where's Edward?' she asked brokenly, but her voice remained silent. Try as she might, she could not make her voice be heard. And now she closed her eyes and let herself drift. 'Edward?' Where was he?

'Lie quiet, Lucy.' Sensing her agitation, he guessed she was wondering about the cowardly man. 'I've got you now,' he told her. 'You'll have to trust me.' All the way home, he kept reassuring her, until she was limp and senseless in his arms.

Barney was a fit man who would have normally taken ten or fifteen minutes to reach his home from that particular spot, but Lucy was now a dead weight and with his every footstep she grew heavier in his arms, until home seemed a million miles away. 'Go in front, lass!' he called to the red-setter. 'Let her know I'm on my way.'

Vicky was taking in the washing when the dog came running up to nuzzle her legs. A small, golden-haired woman with soft grey eyes, she greeted the dog with a stroke of the head. 'What's the matter, girl, eh?' she laughed. Jess was a devil for the play and leaping at her now, even though she had an armful of clean clothes. 'No! Get off, you unruly hound.' The setter had run a long way at a fast pace and now her tongue was hanging out and slaver running from her jowls. Vicky feared she might drop the washing, and then: 'You'll slobber on the clothes, and I'll have to wash the blooming things all over again!'

When Jess continued to nuzzle her, Vicky dropped the clothes into the basket. Snatching it up into her arms, she chided the animal. 'What's got into you? Behave yourself!'

Now, as she turned, she caught sight of Barney out of the corner of her eye; a distance from the house and treading every step with care, he was carrying what she at first thought was a dead sheep. 'BARNEY!' Raising her voice, she ran forward. 'WHAT'S HAPPENED?'

Encouraged by the sight of home and his beloved, Barney hurried to her as fast as he could. 'It's Lucy,' he panted. 'She's taken a bad tumble. I reckon she needs a doctor and fast!'

Running before him, Vicky opened all the doors and in no time at all, Lucy was laid on the spare bed, with a blanket over her. 'You fetch the doctor,' Vicky instructed her husband. 'I'll get her out of these clothes and make her comfortable.'

And so, while Vicky set about helping Lucy, Barney rode into the village of Comberton on his bicycle to fetch the doctor.

By the time Vicky had bathed the wound on Lucy's head, changed her into one of her own nightgowns, and tucked her up in bed, Lucy was more alert, though still dizzy and not yet able to focus properly. 'Jamie!' Her first concern was for her son.

Vicky quietened her. 'He's fine,' she said. 'If you want, I'll ask Barney to go over and bring him to you, but for now, he's safe with Tillie, isn't he? She's taking good care of him.'

Subdued, Lucy cast her mind back to when she fell. 'I was running . . .' she tried to explain. 'Edward . . . he . . .' She raised her head a short distance from the pillow and dropped it again as though it was too heavy for her shoulders. 'He was behind me when I fell.' She tried to look into the room. 'Where is he?'

Vicky had no idea who this Edward was. 'I don't know,' she replied kindly. 'I expect he won't be far away.'

Lucy despaired. 'He's gone, hasn't he?' she whispered sadly. 'He's gone – and he's never coming back.' In her deepest heart she had always known he would be gone at the first opportunity, but she had so much wanted to be wrong. Her heart and her head had been at odds about Edward from the day he had set his sights on her. It was so hard to give up hope, to see things as they really were.

'I can't answer that,' Vicky answered softly. 'We'll find your Edward, I'm sure, the minute Barney comes back.'

However kindly her intention, Vicky's assurances gave Lucy small comfort. Desolate, she closed her eyes and let the sleep roll over her. He was gone. Edward was gone; and it had all been too good to be true. He hadn't even seen their son.

When Dr Lucas arrived he gave Lucy a swift yet thorough examination. 'There doesn't seem to be any lasting damage,' he concluded, 'though I would prefer her not to be too active, for at least a week.'

He handed Vicky a bottle of dark brown liquid. 'Bathe the wound in this morning and night, but it must not be covered . . . fresh air is the best thing. Light food, and a little exercise, but she must rest. A week of that, and I expect her to be good as new.' Having given his diagnosis and delivered the prescription, he bade them goodbye. 'You know where

I am if you should need me,' he declared, in that abrupt manner of any good doctor.

Afterwards, while Vicky went downstairs to put the kettle on, Barney told Lucy what the doctor had said. 'It might be best if you stay here with us for the week,' he suggested, and Lucy thanked him. 'If it isn't too much trouble?' she said tearfully.

'No trouble at all,' he promised. With a smile he added, 'With three offspring and yon Jess, I can't deny we're a noisy family at times, but I'll make sure you're not too disturbed. One of us'll nip over to the squire's tomorrow morning and let 'em know you've had a little accident so they won't expect to see you again for a few days, all right?'

Lucy thanked him again, and when he left her to rest, she cried until she thought her heart would break. Edward was gone, and with him, her own chance of a proper family. Her son would never know his father, and she would never experience the true happiness that she had witnessed between Barney and his Vicky.

Those two had something beautiful, a very special belonging that she could never even hope for.

CHAPTER EIGHT

I T WAS ONE of the happiest weeks Lucy had ever known. Having worked at the squire's house for some time now, she had come to know the countryside well, but she had never lived as close to nature as she had done this past week. She loved it all: the sound of the pigeons cooing at early morning, the dew glistening on the grass and the sun coming up over the hill, sending out warmth and light, and making the heart feel good. After a couple of days, her concussion had passed, but the kindly doctor advised her to stay where she was. Bridget and Tillie had brought Jamie up to Overhill Farm and enjoyed some country hospitality. Out here, the shortages and hardships of the townfolk had, to some extent, been kept at bay.

In the evening she could see the lake in the distance, shimmering and twinkling under the moonlight. It was all a new and wonderful experience and she found herself waking earlier than she had ever done. At 5 a.m. she would run to the window where she would see Barney's familiar figure as he went away to check his flock, the dog beside him and his master's merry whistle echoing through the quiet morning air.

Later, when she was pushing Jamie on the old swing in the orchard, it was a pleasure to see Barney and his sons as they worked the fields, always with the dog running behind, and the lovely Vicky, busy all the day long, collecting eggs, tending her washing, cleaning house and baking treats for her large, loving family; ever busy, ever noisy, just as Barney had promised.

Barney and Vicky had three children. Thomas, at seventeen, was a serious and hardworking young man. Like the others he was devoted to his father who, in his eyes, could do no wrong. A handsome fellow, with sincere eyes and dark hair, he burned with ambitions of one day owning his own farm, unlike Barney who managed Overhill Farm for the wealthy local landowner Leonard Maitland, who lived at The Manse, down in the village.

Along with his brother Ronnie, Tom helped Barney run the farm; the two sons did all the basic tasks, like feeding the many animals, collecting food from the supplier, taking produce to market and chopping trees, selling some wood and logging the rest for the home fires. In addition it was their responsibility to generally maintain the house and buildings.

Winter or summer, there was always work to be done, and come harvest it was all hands that could be spared.

At fifteen, Ronnie was two years younger than his brother. With wild fair hair and his father's blue eyes, he was accident-prone, fun-loving, sensitive, sincere and fiercely loyal. When he flirted outrageously, which was often, the girls fell at his feet. Though he loved his mother dearly, he was devoted to Barney, attempting to emulate him in everything he did.

Quiet and thoughtful, Susie was the only girl. Thirteen years of age and looking like a smaller replica of her mother, she adored her parents – especially Barney, who called her his 'little angel'.

Susie loved to do things for her daddy. She would polish his Sunday shoes before they all went to church; make daisy chains for him when they were picnicking, run and meet him when he came home of an evening. She would scold him when she thought he was not looking after himself and, except for when she was learning the art of hat-making under the scrutiny of an old eccentric by the name of Doris Dandy, over in Everton, she was never far from her daddy's side.

'I'd rather farm than make hats,' she told him once, and because he wanted her to acquire a regular skill that would stand her in good stead for the rest of her life, he would hear no more of such talk.

Lately, having become increasingly curious about the deeper things of the heart, Susie would often corner her daddy to discuss the mysteries and meaning of life. Sometimes out of his depth, Barney would talk and listen, and they would each learn from the other.

As for Lucy, in the short week she had lived under their roof, she had come to care deeply for Barney's family. Everyone who knew them had a good word to say for them. The love and support they all gave each other was wonderful to see; even when brothers and sister argued, that bond of togetherness never broke.

Witnessing family life at first hand made her own loss and disappointment all the more poignant. If only Edward had stayed, instead of running away again, she thought, maybe they could have had the same close family life. Yet in all her regrets, she did not hate him, though God knows she had tried hard enough to do so. She was bitter though; bitter and resentful of the fact that he could casually show up after all this time, only to turn her life upside down yet again. Thank goodness that the shock of the accident had brought on her monthly bleeding a week early. To have allowed Edward to make her pregnant *again* would have been a disaster.

Today was Lucy's last day with the Davidsons. While she got herself and her son ready, Vicky and her family were downstairs waiting for her to join them for the evening meal. 'I wish we could stay,' Lucy told the child as she fastened his blue jacket. 'It's been so lovely here. I'll miss it all so much.'

In reply, Jamie ran his little wooden engine over the floor making train sounds. He loved being read to and petted by the older children in Barney's family; in turn, they all adored the little chap and had spent many happy hours showing him all the farm animals. Like his mother, Jamie would miss all of this.

Lucy had been strong with every disappointment that life sent her way; Edward going off to sea; the discovery that she was with child, and having to tell her parents the truth; then her parents splitting up after weeks of rowing and fighting, and afterwards finding herself out on the streets.

And only a week ago, when Edward had come home, her hopes had soared only to be shattered again; and as though to add insult to injury he had run off and left her lying hurt, leaving Barney to take care of her. That was a cowardly thing he had done.

Through all of these events she had been strong. But now, as she prepared to leave Overhill Farm and the Davidsons, she felt so sad. It was one disappointment too many.

Now her stay was over, and when the meal was finished, Barney would take her back to Bridget's and life would resume exactly as it was before. She would rise early, leave her son in the care of little Tillie, and trudge through the fields to the squire's house, where she would work a hard day before trudging back again. She had never been afraid of work, but it was a lonely kind of life, and she missed her son. He was growing fast and she was losing out on his development.

No home of her own, working every hour God sent, and

no man to stand by her. Lucy thought it was not much of a life to look forward to. But that was the life she had been given and it was up to her to do the best she could with it. And she would, for what other choice did she have? She knew she should never have given in to Edward's wiles, should have kept herself pure for marriage, but somehow she'd never met the right man when all her schoolfriends did, and in her mid-twenties had felt like an elderly spinster. And oh – how Edward's caresses had thrilled her, and made her lose her head, heart, and virginity too. Oh well. It was true, the old saying that there was no use in crying over spilled milk – that was for sure. And now it was very unlikely that she would ever find a decent man who was willing to take both her and Jamie on . . .

As she walked into the homely kitchen, Lucy was astonished to see the family standing round the table, waiting for her; Ronnie, she noticed, had taken time to tame his unruly hair, Thomas gave her a welcoming wink, and Susie was quietly smiling.

Barney and his wife were standing together, he with his arm round her and she so content beside him. 'Come in, my love!' She ran to greet Lucy, and as she led her and Jamie across the room, she said, 'Look. I've made the table pretty for you.'

Overawed by what they had done, Lucy looked at the table and wiped away a tear. It was laid as if for a banquet. Normally the table was simply laid, with the meals already served on the plates. There was never any fuss or ceremony. Over dinner, everyone would get together, tuck into Vicky's home-cooking and talk about the day's events.

This evening, though, was extra special to all of them. There was an air of excitement which Lucy could not understand; especially when they knew she was unhappy about having to leave.

It was almost as though they were pleased at the prospect of having the house back to themselves. Yet even while the unfortunate thought crossed her mind, Lucy could not believe it. This past week, Barney and his family had done everything they could to make her feel like one of them, so why would they be relieved to see her go? No! She was wrong. All this fuss and excitement was their way of trying to make her feel better about it. That was it. This was their going-away present to her. They wanted her to leave on a good note. And, for their sake, she would smile and laugh, and they would never really know how wretched she felt.

'Well, Lucy?' Vicky nudged her elbow. 'What do you think to my table? They wouldn't let me do it on my own. Everybody helped and even then, we were worried we might not get it all finished before you came down.'

Draped in a long, flowing tablecloth of crimson, the big old table was set like Lucy had never seen it. There were candles in pretty holders; glasses with long stems and a twirl of napkin in each one. In the centre of the table stood platters laid with all manner of meats; there were bowls of steaming vegetables and a long dish of small crisply roasted potatoes – Lucy's favourites; there was also a wicker dish filled with freshly-baked rolls, whose aroma filled the room, and right in the middle, two bottles of Barney's homemade elderberry wine.

For what seemed an age, Lucy was speechless. 'Aw, Vicky. It's just ... beautiful!' Now, as the tears threatened, she let them fall before discreetly brushing them away. 'You shouldn't have gone to so much trouble.'

'It was no trouble at all.' Vicky slid an arm round her waist. 'It's our present to you,' she said, 'to show how much we love you, *and* this little one.' She tickled young Jamie under the chin, laughing as he gurgled with delight.

The child's response broke the atmosphere. Rushing

119

forward, Barney took Lucy by the arm. 'Tonight, you've been allocated my very own seat, at the head of the table.' And with no more ado he marched her there and sat her down. 'And as for this little chap . . .' Lifting the child out of her arms, he sat him in the homemade high chair, which had been finished only that afternoon, with sturdy legs and straps to hold the little fella safe.

'He can sit with the rest of us, like a grown-up,' Ronnie declared with pride. 'Father made the structure, Thomas made the legs, and I cut the leather straps to hold him in. We were still working on it up to half an hour since.' He groaned. 'In fact, if you'd come down that much earlier, the babby might be rolling on the floor, because we only had the one leg fixed to it, and that would never have supported the fat little lump!'

Everyone laughed, with Susie protesting that Lucy's Jamie was *not* 'a fat little lump'.

As always before the evening meal, Barney stood before his chair and said Grace. Being farmers and working closely with the land, they all understood how, with one dark mood, Nature could devastate a whole year's crop, and leave them desolate.

In all of Barney's experience that had only ever happened once, soon after he'd taken up the post of Farm Manager here. He had never forgotten. Nor had he forgotten to always give his thanks.

He gave his thanks now, 'For the food and warmth You send us. For bringing Lucy back to health, and keeping us all safe from harm.' Looking down on his wife, he stroked her hair. 'And for this wonderful woman You blessed me with. Thank You, Lord.' His words were spoken with such quiet gratitude that there seemed nothing more natural in the whole world. And in equally quiet voice, everyone echoed his thanks.

When Lucy looked up to see Vicky taking a discreet hold of Barney's hand, Lucy's heart was both sore and joyous. That small significant gesture between husband and wife was unseen by everyone else, but Lucy thought it the most touching thing she had ever been privileged to witness.

It was obvious that, even after more than twenty years wed, and three children into the bargain, Vicky and Barney still adored each other, as much as on the day they first met. Theirs was a deep, everlasting love, and one which Lucy sensed that neither she nor countless others would ever experience in their whole lives.

The meal was wonderful, and so was the company. They chatted and laughed and drank the wine, and when the child fell asleep in his chair, Barney lifted him out and made him comfortable on the sofa. 'Right!' Returning to the table, he told everyone to fill their glasses and raise them for a toast, and when that was done he stood for a moment looking from one to the other, until his gaze rested on Lucy. 'We would have liked you to stay here with us,' he said, and Lucy's heart rose, 'but as you know, your being here meant that Susie had to sleep downstairs on the couch, and though she didn't mind that . . .' he looked at Susie and she nodded in agreement '. . . it isn't a situation that could continue for any length of time.' He hesitated. 'You do understand, don't you, Lucy?'

Lucy understood, and even managed a bright smile. 'Of course I do,' she assured them. 'I never really expected that I could stay here. I'm just grateful for the time and help you all gave me. I'll never be able to thank you enough.'

Barney smiled at her. 'Look under your plate, lass.'

Lucy was confused. 'Under my plate?'

'That's what the man said!' That was Ronnie, being his usual comical self. But there was a certain twinkle in his eye. In fact, as Lucy glanced at each family member in turn, she saw a twinkle in *all* their eyes.

'Go on then, Lucy. Look and see what he's put there.' Susie was excitedly bouncing up and down in her chair.

Gingerly, Lucy lifted her plate and moving it aside, took out an envelope that was folded there. She opened the envelope and dipping her fingers inside, withdrew a large, shiny coin. 'A guinea!' Her eyes widened in astonishment. 'What's this for?'

Barney told her fondly, 'It's your first month's wages. Me and my Vicky have discussed it with the family, and we all agree there's enough work on this farm for all of us. When harvest comes there's no time to catch your breath; then there's the carting and stacking, and any number of other tasks that could do with another pair of hands . . . especially for Vicky, who's always rushed off her feet. This house is too much when she's needed outside. That's where you come in, Lucy. So, the job's yours, if you want it?'

In a minute Lucy was out of her chair; running round the table she threw her arms round Barney's neck. 'Oh Barney . . . all of you! You don't know what this means to me.' Going from one to another, she kissed and hugged them in turn. 'Instead of passing this house every morning, and trudging all the way on to the Hall, I'll be turning in at your gate.' The excitement was all too much. 'I'll be working with you all. Oh, it's wonderful!' She laughed through her tears. 'I can't believe it!' She was sure that no one apart from Dorothy would miss her at Haskell Hall.

At that moment there came a knock on the door. 'All right, matey, come on in.' Barney appeared to know who it was even before the door opened.

The door inched open and a man appeared; small of stature, with a kindly face and smiling eyes, he greeted everyone in turn. 'Hello, Lucy,' he finished. 'I hope you're fighting fit after your accident?'

Lucy was not surprised to see him. 'Hello, Adam,' she

answered. 'Yes, I'm well, thank you.' A kindly man in his early thirties, Adam Chives was well-known throughout the village of Comberton-by-Weir. In fact, there wasn't a single house that he had not been into at some time or another, for he was the local handyman, tried, trusted and greatly respected by one and all. Lucy always suspected that he had a soft spot for her, on the quiet. However, he was far too much of a gentleman to say anything.

'Come on then, m'laddo!' Barney held out his hand. 'I trust you've brought it with you?'

'I have,' came the proud reply. 'I've done everything you asked of me, and more besides.' He handed something to Barney, winked at Ronnie, and said, 'I expect there'll be a bonus in there somewhere for me, will there not?'

Barney took up the tease. 'There certainly will be – in the shape of a roast dinner with all the trimmings . . . if you want it, that is?'

Adam didn't need asking twice. 'That'll do me,' he told Vicky, who was chuckling at the pair of them. 'In fact, I could think of nothing else all the way here.'

'Right then! You sit down and fill your plate while I have a quiet word with Lucy.'

'Whatever you say.' In fact, Adam was already privy to the reason for Barney's need to talk with Lucy in private.

Adam had known Barney for many years; in their childhood they had learned the times-table together; ridden side by side across the fields on whatever horse they could borrow; shot rabbits for the pot, and later sat many a while on the porch, exchanging tales of when they were lads. They knew each other as well as any brothers might, and loved each other the same.

Leaving the others to chat, Barney rounded the table and taking Lucy by the hand, led her out to the back porch.

They sat on the bench and there, Barney spoke his mind. 'There's summat you need to think about.'

Lucy asked him what he meant. But she could never have imagined in her wildest dreams what he was about to say.

Barney continued, 'I know it's none of our business, but well . . . Me and Vicky have been talking and what we think is this: it's not good to bring a child up in a house of women – if you know what I mean?'

Lucy had no doubts. 'You mean women who entertain?'

Sucking in his lips he took a deep breath. Afraid she might have taken him wrong, he answered sincerely, 'It's not for me to judge other folks. All I'm saying is this: for little Jamie's sake, and yours, it won't be a bad thing when you move out of there.'

Lucy gave a wry little laugh. 'It's easier said than done.' She shrugged her shoulders. 'For a start, where would I go?'

He smiled. 'So, you would leave if you only had somewhere to go. Is that what you're telling me, Lucy?'

'Oh, yes.' Lucy was aware of her environment and knew as well as did Barney, that it was not a suitable place to raise a child. 'If I had somewhere to go, I'd leave – though I have to say, I would miss Bridget and the girls. They've been such good friends to me.'

'I know that,' he agreed. 'Haven't they visited you time and again since you've been here? And haven't I heard you laughing with them, when only hours before, you were fit for nothing? Believe me, Lucy, after you being so poorly, it did our heart good to hear you. Now then, lass, I want you to take this.' Opening his hand, he revealed a heavy iron key lying in his palm. 'Take it!' he urged. 'There's no rush. Just give it some thought and let me know what you decide.'

Lucy was confused. 'It's a key.'

He chuckled. 'Well, of course it's a key!'

'But where does it belong?'

'It belongs to the little cottage at the other end of the brook. The one where Leonard Maitland's gardener lived afore he threw him out for robbing him.'

Realisation began to dawn. 'What? You mean, the pretty one with the thatched roof and the little garden which runs right down to the brook edge?'

'Aye, that's the one.'

She took the key, which weighed heavy in her hand. 'So, this is the key to that cottage?'

Barney nodded affirmatively. 'That one opens the front door. I've another for the back. If you decide it's what you want, I'll let you have the other key an' all.'

The merest smile trembled on Lucy's mouth. 'But I don't fully understand. Why are you giving me this key?'

Smiling into her inquisitive eyes, he explained, 'The boss, Mr Maitland, and me had a little chat yesterday.'

'About me?'

'Sort of, yes. He was aware of your accident – you know how gossip flies around a village – and being the kindly gent he is, he took the time to ask after you. I told him the way things were, and he said if I thought it would help to offer you the vacant cottage, he wouldn't mind one bit; though he would expect you to give him half a day's work per week in lieu of rent . . . a bit of cleaning, that sort of thing. Besides, the cottage needed living in, that's what he said, or it would fall to rack and ruin. Y'see, his new gardener has his own cottage and has no need of this one. In fact, the boss had a mind to sell it off with a parcel of land, but he never got round to it. Moreover, he mentioned as how it's so tiny it wouldn't fetch much in the way of cash.'

He took a breath. 'To tellyou the truth, Lucy, the cottage is of small interest to Mr Maitland, so it's yours if you want it.'

Lucy gasped. 'I can't believe this is happening!' Thrilled

to her roots, she was astounded for the second time that evening. 'The cottage is mine? Really? Are you sure?'

Laughing out loud, Barney squeezed her hand. 'Well, aren't you the cloth ears,' he teased. 'Isn't that what I've just been saying?'

Lucy was speechless. And now the tears she had managed to hold back all day ran down her cheeks and all at once she was laughing and crying, and telling Barney, 'I haven't got a stick of furniture, but yes, oh, yes!' She was beside herself. 'We'll move in as soon as possible. Never mind a bed. We'll sleep on the floor if we have to.'

'There'll be no need of that. The cottage comes with its own furniture and such. Yon Adam has cleaned and aired the place all ready for you and young Jamie. All you'll want is new bedding and certain silly bits and pieces a woman needs to keep her happy. And you needn't worry about the bairn when you work the half-day for Mr Maitland, because Vicky's already said she'll be more than happy to keep an eye on him. And it goes without saying that when you're working here for the rest of the week, the bairn is welcome as the day is long.'

And so it was settled. Lucy would move in within the next few days, and while she was getting organised, Barney would make sure the garden was cleared and all was spick and span for her and the child.

~

A few days later, Lucy was saying her goodbyes in Viaduct Street. 'I'll never be able to thank you enough for what you've done for me.' Emotion thickened her voice as she threw her arms round Bridget and hugged her so hard, the poor woman had to wrench her off.

'Be Jaysus, will ye get offa me! Are ye trying to strangle

me or what?' Holding Lucy at arm's length, she looked into those sincere brown eyes and thought how much she would miss this young woman; with her impromptu singing and bright, happy presence, the house would be all the poorer for her not being there.

'I'm truly sorry to see ye go,' she told Lucy now, 'but I'm happy for you, so I am. You'll have your own front-door key and Jamie will have his own little room, and when me and the girls come a-calling, you'll have fresh-baked muffins ready for us, and a big pot o' tea waiting.' She gave a wink. 'Unless o' course you've a drop o' the good stuff hidden away in the cupboard for an old friend?'

With the sadness lifted, Lucy laughed out loud. 'Oi will,' she answered, mimicking Bridget's strong Irish accent. 'Sure Oi'll have a little bottle tucked away and ye can drink to your heart's content, so ye can.'

Bridget roared with laughter. 'Ye sound more like me than I do meself. Go on, ye little divil, be off wit' ye!' She gave her another hug, and craftily dropped a couple of coins into the palm of her hand. 'A little something to get ye started. Take care of yourself, m'darling,' she said softly, and before she might start blubbering herself, she sent Lucy on her way.

A few minutes later, along with her few belongings and the child on her knee, Lucy settled herself in Barney's wagon.

'Any regrets, lass?'

The young woman shook her head. 'Not a one.' The only regrets she had were old ones, and now they didn't seem to matter quite as much.

When he arrived at Bridget's house, Barney had greeted Bridget and the girls with his usual friendliness, and now he was leaving with Lucy beside him, he said his goodbyes with the same warmth, for that was his manner.

'All set, are we?' He had witnessed the emotional scene between Lucy and her friends, but like Lucy, he knew her leaving was all for the best.

'All set,' Lucy replied, a brief rush of sadness clouding her face.

'Then you'd best hold on tight because once I let this wild animal have its rein, there's no telling *where* we might end up!'

His little attempt at making her laugh worked wonders, because she laughed so hard she couldn't reply. Pleased with himself, he gave her a warming wink, gently slapped the horse's great wide rump to drive the bumbling animal forward, and told her in that quiet, no-nonsense manner, 'You did the right thing.'

And that was all he would ever again say on the matter.

As the shire ambled away down Viaduct Street, Lucy turned to look at the four women standing on the doorstep, and as they waved back, she blew a kiss. 'I'll miss you,' she murmured.

Barney glanced at her. 'There's your past and ahead is your future,' he said simply. Barney Davidson was known as a man of few words, but when he took a mind to speak, his few words said more than a vicar delivering a sermon.

As they meandered along, Lucy considered his wise words, and she knew he was right. After everything that had befallen her, this was the start of a new life, where she could put all the bad things behind her and start over again.

At long last, she had something to look forward to.

Once they were beyond the city roads and were heading towards Comberton, she watched Barney take the old briar-pipe and his baccy pouch from his waistcoat pocket; letting loose of the reins he gave the horse its head, and after carefully packing the pipe with the baccy he struck a match on the sole of his shoe and lit up. He then drew leisurely on the pipe, the twirls of smoke rising to slowly evaporate above his head.

Suddenly in the midst of his thinking, he turned to smile at Lucy in that comforting way of his. At the time, Barney's wonderful smile merely warmed her heart, though inevitably bonding her to him.

It was many years later when, looking back on that magical, intimate moment, with the child asleep and the two of them gently following the narrow country lanes, Barney contentedly smoking his pipe and the sound of the birds singing all around, Lucy realised she must have fallen hopelessly in love with him then – and she never even knew it.

Barney Davidson. A wise and kindly man who knew the earth as if it was his own; a man who had the heart of a lion and could protect the weak, that was Barney.

Just for now though, misinterpreting her deeper feelings, Lucy saw Barney only as a very dear friend. No more than that.

Yet, even though many a moon would shine before she came to realise the true depth of her feelings for him, Lucy already knew in her heart and soul, that she would never meet his like again.

CHAPTER NINE

THE WEEKS PASSED and already it was the end of July. Lucy and Jamie had settled in well to Mr Maitland's vacant cottage. It was almost as though they had lived there forever. Lucy was happier than she had ever been; every day was like a holiday. Her life was filled with new experiences and here in the countryside where she was a part of the greater picture, what had previously seemed to her like mountainous problems, now seemed almost trivial.

She counted herself fortunate to have such friends as the Davidsons; they were a joy to be with. Working or relaxing, every minute in their company drew her more and more into their family.

Sometimes on a Sunday evening, Bridget or one of the girls from Viaduct Street would visit, and they would sit and talk, and laugh to their hearts' content. Lucy made sure to keep a measure of the 'good stuff' hidden away for when Bridget came. 'Oh, you're a darling – what are ye?' Tipping up her glass and warming the cockles of her heart, Bridget would dance and sing and go home all the merrier.

As arranged, through the week Lucy worked with the Davidsons, and on Saturday morning she went up to Leonard Maitland's house, where she did the ironing and other jobs like cleaning his silver. After midday her work was done and the weekend was her own, to enjoy the cottage and play with her child.

Each day saw Jamie grow more and more sturdy; he now was very active and the fresh air was doing him a power of good. He loved his new family and had begun to talk in his own way to them all. Everyone loved the little toddler and enjoyed having him around the farm.

On this particular Saturday, Lucy was replacing the silver in the display cabinet, just about to finish her morning's work, when she heard voices in the next room. 'Sometimes I'm not sure I'm cut out to be a farmer's wife.'

'Hmh! I wish you'd told me that before I put an engagement ring on your finger.'

There followed a girlish peal of false laughter and the light-hearted suggestion, 'Oh, Lenny! Why don't you sell everything – this house, the land and cottages. We could move down to London – or go abroad! It would be so wonderful to travel. We could stay away for a whole year . . . see the world, do something exciting.'

There was a brief silence, then the woman demanded, 'Are you deliberately ignoring me?' Another silence, then in sterner voice: 'Leonard! Did you hear what I said?'

'I heard, and yes, I *am* deliberately ignoring you, Pat. We've had this same conversation so many times I'm beginning to tire of it.'

Only the thinness of a wall away, Lucy recognised the voices of Patricia Carstairs and Leonard Maitland. She tried hard not to listen and even softly sang to herself, but the voices grew louder and angrier, and she couldn't help but overhear every single word.

'Yes, and so am I tired of it!' Anger trembled in her voice. 'Whenever I take the trouble to drive over and see you, you've either got your head buried in paperwork, or you're out with your man discussing tractors or some such thing, or overseeing a delivery. Yesterday, and not for the first time, I came here to find you ensconced in your office with two other men, and even when you knew I was here, you just popped your head round the door and excused yourself. My God, Leonard! You didn't come out for a full hour, and I was made to hang around like a dog at its master's heels. These days, you hardly ever have time for me, and that is not how it should be. I should come first in your life and I don't. And I'm really fed up!'

'Then listen to what I'm saying.' Leonard sounded weary. He *was* weary – of her demands, of her chastising, and of her misguided belief that he, like her, had nothing better to do than socialise. 'I'm a farmer, Patricia . . . a busy man. You knew that when we met and you know it now. I can't change that. I *won't* change it.'

'But you don't actually farm, do you?' Her tone was cynical.

Leonard gave a dry, angry laugh. 'You just don't understand, do you?' he said. 'I may not often sit in the tractor, or plough in the seeds, or cut the corn when it's grown. But I'm a landowner and as such have certain responsibilities. I plan which seeds go into the ground, or which tractor suits the job best. I scour the country for the best price I might get for my harvest . . . There are a multitude of things that come with working the land. I monitor every single thing. I buy and sell, and treat my part of the job with respect.'

'But you have Barney Davidson. You sing his praises so often, I'm sure if you let him, he would take a lot more responsibility from your shoulders.'

There was another moment of silence; a moment when Lucy felt uncomfortable, for she could almost taste the atmosphere.

It seemed an age before, in a cutting voice, Leonard

Maitland spoke again. 'You will *never* understand, will you, Patricia? You don't even try to understand the implications of what I'm telling you. I bought this land because I needed to. If I didn't have land around me, I would simply suffocate. But land is not just for looking at, and when you take it on, you give yourself wholeheartedly to its well-being. You treat it like a living, breathing entity, because that's what it is. The land gives more than it takes, and it deserves to be cared for. But, like I say, you will never comprehend that, and I don't blame you for it.'

'I'm sorry, Lenny darling.' True or false, the voice and its owner seemed contrite. 'All I'm saying is, why not let Barney take over occasionally? After all, you've always said he knows the land as well as you do. I can't count the number of times you've remarked on how a capable man like Barney Davidson was meant to have his own farm, but that life had not treated him kindly enough.'

'Yes, Pat, and I meant it. But this is *my* land. *My* responsibility. Barney is my partner in a sense. He is my eyes and ears, and while I organise everything else, he farms, and that's all right, because he has the same love for the land that I do.'

'Oh Lenny.' The voice grew whining. 'I know how passionate you are about this place . . .'

'No, you don't.' Now he was calmer, wanting to explain. 'You live in town. You can have no idea of what it feels like to see the harvest being brought in, or to stride the fields on a winter's morning, when the snow lies deep in the ditches and the trees bend and dip with the weight.' His voice dropped. 'If you want us to marry, as I do, then you must accept that my work is important to me.'

'All right, my darling, but why can't we go away – for a month maybe?'

'We will,' he consoled her. 'Look, we're due to be married

next spring, and if it suits you, we can have a much longer honeymoon than planned. How's that?'

'And can I plan where we go?' She was a spoiled child.

'If you like, yes.'

'And money's no object?'

He gave a sigh. Did his fiancée not realise that most of the world was plunged into a financial crisis? 'It is our honeymoon after all,' he said resignedly.

'Oh, Lenny, it will be so wonderful!' Excitement coloured her voice. 'Then in the winter, can we go far away – to the South of France or even further afield? My London friends spent last winter in Sydney and they said it was the best time they ever had. Oh, it would be so nice to get right away. I do get so bored visiting the same old places.'

'You're a mystery to me.' A different emotion crept into his words. 'You're infuriating and selfish, and sometimes I wonder what I see in you. But fool that I am, I can't help but love you.'

'I'll remember that when you refuse me what I ask.'

'You will have to remember something else too.'

'For instance?'

'For instance, that being a landowner, I must bow to my duties here. There will always be times when I can't just take off at your every whim and fancy.'

There came that soft trill of laughter again. 'We shall have to see, won't we? Now I think you should give me a kiss, by way of apology.'

'Don't you think the apology should come from *you*?'

'Aw, Leonard! Does it really matter who apologises? Kiss me, and we'll forget we ever quarrelled.'

Silence reigned for a moment, when Lucy imagined they were in the throes of the 'apology'. Then came the sound of a door opening and closing, and when she glanced out of the window, Lucy saw them going arm-in-arm down the driveway to the long black car, recently chosen by Patricia Carstairs, paid for by Mr Maitland, and delivered only three days ago.

'Oh darling! Won't people be envious when they see us together in this!' was Patricia's parting remark as she climbed into the car.

Lucy watched them drive off; the woman slim, beautiful, and arrogant to the quick, while the gentleman was attentive and homely, a gentle giant of a man.

Lucy thought them quite unsuited. 'That one's trouble. He should drop her like a hot potato!' Closing the curtains, she pranced across the room on tippy-toe, emulating Patricia Carstairs, one hand on her hip, the other swanking by her side, mimicking the woman's voice to perfection. *'Oh darling! Won't people be envious when they see us together in this?'* She pitied the poor wretches who had no work and no money; to see a smart car passing by, occupied by that one with her nose in the air would be like a red rag to a bull.

Breaking into song, Lucy returned to her work, gave the large silver teapot another rub with the cloth, then with the greatest of care replaced it in the cabinet, where she shifted the silverware about until the display was pleasing to the eye.

She now closed the door, took up a clean cloth from her basket and giving the door-glass a good polish, gave a sigh of relief. 'All done for another week!'

A few minutes later, she was out of the house and running across the back lawns towards the fields. Now, as she rounded the brow of the hill, she heard the laughter from Barney's house. Pausing, she took off her shoes, set off at the run and before long was at the gate of Overhill farmhouse. 'Quick, Lucy!' Vicky was beckoning her. 'Hurry!'

When the young woman ran into the garden, she saw little Jamie standing with his back to the trunk of the apple tree, arms wide and laughing as only a child can laugh. 'He's trying to walk all the way over to us unaided,' Vicky told Lucy. 'Three times he's started off and three times he's fallen. I've stood him up again, but he loves this game, and he wants to carry on playing it.'

Lucy was delighted. Jamie was a good little walker now, but his gammy leg meant he often fell over. Falling to her knees, she opened her arms wide, coaxing the boy. 'Come to your mammy, sweetheart.'

He stopped giggling and stared at her, as though he might be giving it some thought. Then he looked up to excitedly point into the skies, at a hawk hovering nearby. 'Bird!' he shouted. 'Big bird.'

Arms still wide, Lucy took a step nearer. 'Look at me, Jamie. Come on, sweetheart.'

The child would have none of it. Completely ignoring her, he scoured the skies with his big bright eyes, one finger pointing as he slowly but surely slid downwards, his back seemingly glued to the tree.

'Stay there, Lucy!' Running forward, Vicky propped him up again. 'Try, sweetheart,' she urged the little man. Slowly she backed away, one hand up flat, as though it might dissuade him from sliding down again.

Standing next to Lucy, Vicky took a cooked sausage from the picnic hamper. 'Ooh – look what I've got.' She waved the sausage from side to side. 'If you want it, you'll have to come and get it.'

Lucy laughed. 'That's a wicked thing to do.'

Suddenly the child was interested. He licked his lips and raising his arms, made an effort to shuffle forward. 'He means it this time,' Vicky whispered. 'He'll do it now, you see if he doesn't.'

And he didn't, because when he spotted Barney appearing, he promptly sat down. 'Leave the little fella alone.' Still in his work-clothes, his cap pulled forward, Barney stood beside the two women and looking at the boy asked, 'What are they doing to you, eh?'

Lucy straightened up. 'We're trying to coax him to walk over here without falling over,' she answered. 'Vicky said he tried and failed three times.'

'Is that right?' The smile he gave Vicky spoke volumes; even when he wasn't saying he loved her, he still showed it – in his smile, in his eyes, in the way he always stood by her side – always there with her, even when he wasn't.

'Well, he looks proper fed up now, and no mistake. Poor little bugger, you've stuck him up against a tree and now he can't do nothing but sit down.' And that was exactly what Jamie had done. Sitting on the ground he was pulling the grass up and attempting to eat it.

'Go on then. Stand him up again, but this is the last attempt,' Barney insisted. 'Looks to me like he's had enough.' Tipping back his cap he stooped to one knee, and waited until Lucy had propped up the child. 'Right then, Jamie, old son.' Looking the child in the eye, he said quietly, 'You're to take no notice o' these women. They're like all women the world over – nag, nag, nag. Anybody'd think you'd only got a minute to learn the walking, when truth being, you've got all the time in the world.' He feigned a deep sigh. 'But if it's the only way you can get to sit down in peace and eat your sausage, then if I were you, I'd give it another go.'

He raised his arms and stretching them apart, he gave the boy a cheeky wink, quietly chattering to himself. 'It's up to you, son. You can either come and give Uncle Barney a cuddle, or you can refuse to budge an inch and sit down. Like I say, it's up to you. But you'd best be quick about it. I've been on the go since five o'clock this morning and every bone in my body aches. I need a cuppa tea and five minutes in the armchair to put me right, so come on ... walk on them fat little legs o' yourn. Do it for Barney, there's a good 'un.'

Vicky gave him a playful shove. 'Stop nattering to yourself. You have to raise your voice and talk clear, or he won't hear a word you're saying!'

In that moment, Lucy gave her a dig. 'Look at him, Vicky. Look at Jamie!'

Barney's 'nattering' seemed to have worked, for the child had stood himself up straight and was now pushing against the tree, trying to get started. Arms outstretched towards Barney, he took one faltering step, then another, then a third step. When he saw Barney making faces at him, he burst out laughing and almost lost his balance again.

A few minutes later, encouraged by the big man's coaxing, Jamie completed his walk across the orchard and fell into Barney's arms. 'Who's a champion then, eh?' After giving him a kiss and a bear hug, Barney swung him round to Lucy. 'There y'are. Now that he's walking so well, you'll need eyes in the back of your head, and serves you right, the pair of you.'

With that, he gave Vicky a knowing wink and strode off, still 'nattering' to himself. 'Poor little devil never had a chance. Women and their bullying – what's a man to do, eh?' But he wouldn't want to be without his Vicky for all the treasures in the world.

Thrilled at Jamie's performance, Lucy took him by the hand and the two of them slowly followed Vicky into the house. It was another special memory that Lucy would cherish forever.

While the child slept soundly after all his efforts, the three of them sat together in the kitchen, each with a cup of tea and a generous slice of homemade fruit-cake; Vicky and Lucy at the table and Barney in the armchair. Once or twice, Lucy caught the two of them discreetly exchanging glances, as though they shared something she ought to know about.

'Where's Susie?' Lucy had grown fond of Barney and Vicky's daughter, but she was hardly ever around. She was either out with her schoolfriends, or in town learning how to make hats.

'She's gone on a picnic with a group of friends.' Vicky worried about her young daughter. Though loving and giving, she seemed unsure of what she wanted to do with her life. Whenever Vicky spoke to Barney about her fears, he would tell her, 'Leave the child be, and she'll find her way soon enough.'

'There's something I've been meaning to ask you,' Vicky told Lucy after a while. 'It's been plaguing me for some time.'

Barney looked up at her remark. 'Then you'd best get it off your chest,' he urged. 'There's no use fretting about it.' He knew exactly what concerned Vicky, because it also concerned him, though not to the same degree.

'What is it?' For the first time in their company, Lucy felt uncomfortable. 'Is it something I've done, because if it is, I can't know if you don't tell me. Or is it that you can't have Jamie any more?'

If that was the worry playing on Vicky's mind, it would only mean the problem was shifted from her to Lucy, because Lucy had no one else, other than little Tillie, and she didn't really want the child to go back to Bridget's house.

'No, of course it isn't that!' Reaching across the table, Vicky patted the back of Lucy's hand. 'It isn't that at all. You know how much we love having the child. Good grief! I'd be lost without him now.'

Barney laughed as he remarked to Lucy, 'Now that he's walking so well, he can help Vicky peg the washing out. Give him another few months and I dare say he'll be out in that barn, chopping wood to his heart's content.'

'Shut up, you daftie!' Covering him with her smile, Vicky shook her head. 'We're talking serious here.'

Lucy was worried. 'What is it, Vicky? What's wrong?'

So, as kindly and quietly as possible, Vicky told her, 'I know it's not really my concern, and you can tell me to mind my own business if you like, only . . .' She gave a nervous little cough.

Barney intervened to save her. 'Spit it out, love. You've got Lucy thinking all sorts of terrible things.'

Taking a deep breath, Vicky said, 'It's just that . . . well, I've been wondering when you mean to have the boy baptised?' There! Now that it was said, she quickly picked up her cup of tea, took a great swig and nearly choked on it.

For a while, Lucy fell silent, and during the silence Barney and Vicky wondered anxiously whether she was angry or upset, or simply didn't want to speak about it because she considered it was none of their business.

Presently, obviously feeling emotional, Lucy told them, 'I've always meant to have Jamie baptised, only . . .' she paused to look at Barney, 'I kept waiting for his daddy to come home, hoping we might arrange for our son's christening together.' Her quick, bright smile belied the upheaval inside. 'Only when he came back and found out he had a son, he didn't want either of us.'

The humiliation was still heavy in her, and when it now showed in the threatening tears, Barney told her softly, 'You and Jamie are better off without him. It's all water under the bridge now, Lucy girl. Let it go, or it'll haunt you for life . . . you and the boy.'

Wise to the event, Vicky lifted Lucy's spirits. 'I've got an idea!' She went and stood beside Barney, from where she

addressed them both. 'Why don't we have a double celebration?'

Barney laughed at her enthusiasm. 'I'm sorry, love. You
can't baptise me. I'm already baptised.'

'No!' Tutting, Vicky returned to the table where she
excitedly told Lucy, 'We could have Jamie baptised on his
birthday. That way we'd have twice the reason to celebrate,
and twice the party. What d'you say, Lucy?'

Lucy thought it was an inspired idea. 'It's long overdue
and that shames me, but like you say, it's not too late, and
it would be a wonderful time to have him baptised . . . on
his second birthday.'

And so it was settled and the date in November put in the
diary. The two women agreed to go together to the church,
to make the arrangements, then take the rest of the day off
to go into Liverpool and do some shopping.

With a crafty glance at Barney, Vicky gave Lucy a wink.
'I'll need a new frock for the party,' she announced, running
her hands down her thighs. 'I might go into that new shop
on the corner of Victoria Street. I'm told they have some
lovely stuff there.' Patting her hair, she glanced in the
mantelpiece mirror. 'Oh, and I'll need a new hat for the
christening – an extra stylish one, with a little brim and a
big flower on the side.'

'You'd best get me one an' all,' Barney groaned. 'One
with the biggest brim you can find, so I can pull it over my
ears when you tell me the price of all this paraphernalia.'
With that he stretched out his legs, settled himself deep in
the chair and fell asleep.

~

With the preparations and the shopping, and all the work
in between, the next few weeks flew by; autumn soon arrived,

and with it came a revelation concerning Leonard Maitland that surprised even Lucy.

On the Sunday afternoon, Lucy was pushing Jamie in the box-swing which Barney had slung from the big oak tree in the cottage garden.

'We'll have to find a suitable christening gown for you,' she was telling the child as he laughed and clapped and kicked his fat little legs as he sailed through the air. 'I don't suppose I'll find a baby gown to fit you now,' she gave him another gentle push. 'You're a big boy into the bargain, so we might have to think of something else, though I want you dressed in white all the same, because when the man takes the pictures I want you to look beautiful.'

Pausing, she thought of Edward Trent and how he had abandoned his own son. 'When you're older I'll be able to tell you why I waited so long before I got you baptised.' She would tell him everything, but not with malice. After all, Edward was Jamie's father and much as she would like to, she could not change that.

Her thoughts deepened. Things could have been so different. They could have been a real family. Somehow she had known that would never be, but she had hoped, for their son's sake, that it might come about.

'Now that I know what he's really like, I never again want any part of him,' she murmured to herself. But Jamie must make up his own mind. If it's what he wanted when he was older, she would never stop him from seeing his daddy. Though she did not believe for one minute that Edward Trent would ever have the gall to show his face round these parts again.

When the swing slowed, the child began kicking his legs and shouting, 'More!' Lucy started pushing him again. 'All right. Just a few more minutes, then we'd best get you ready for bed,' she told him. 'You've had a busy day and by rights you should be worn out.' She wagged a finger. 'Barney was right. I do need eyes in the back of my head!'

'Talking to yourself, is it?' The husky voice was pleasantly familiar. 'Sure they lock ye away for less than that.'

'BRIDGET!' Turning to see her old friend coming across the garden, Lucy ran to meet her. Flinging her arms round the woman's waist, she gave her a bear hug. 'It's so good to see you.'

'Ye little lunatic, get offa me!' Laughingly shoving Lucy away, Bridget straightened her hat – a big black flowery thing with a long white feather. 'Haven't I told ye before, you're not to hug me so hard; I'm delicate as well ye know.'

She pointed to the child who was patiently sitting in his little box-swing. 'Enough o' this nonsense. I'll get meladdo out and we'll go inside for a drop o' the good stuff.' She gave a naughty wink. 'I expect you'll be wanting all the latest news.'

Without more ado, she went to the swing, drew the wooden bar back and lifted the child out. 'And as for you, young Jamie, I'll thank ye not to pee on me!' she warned. 'You ruined my skirt the last time, ye dirty little article!'

As she carried him away, he became fascinated with the feather in her hat, and when he began tugging at it, she promptly gave him to Lucy. 'Will ye look at that? Not content with having ruined one o' me best skirts, the little divil's after ruining me hat.'

Chuckling to herself, and delighted to suffer Bridget's complaining, Lucy took the child and followed her into the cottage. The Irishwoman was striding ahead, in charge as usual, looking grand and important in the dark straight skirt, cut to just below the knee, and the smart peplum jacket that accentuated her curves. The big flowery hat was perched at an angle on top of her fiery red hair, all twirled and tamed and secured beneath it – apart from the few wispy curls that had danced their way out.

'You look really nice,' Lucy complimented her sincerely. 'Is that a new two-piece?'

Bridget sailed on. 'New *and* expensive,' she replied over the shoulder. 'So you'll understand why I don't want it peed on?'

Lucy did understand. 'Is it bought for a special occasion then?'

'It certainly is! I have a gentleman collecting me any time now, so if you've anything you need to tell me, you'll have to be quick about it.'

With an important backward glance, she went on, 'I might tell ye, I've gone to a lot of trouble to get here. I caught a bus for the first time in ages and walked half a mile down the lane . . . dog's muck and horse-dung everywhere!' She glanced at her small-heeled shoes. 'I'll have you know, these were new only a few days since. This is the first time I've worn them. Now look at 'em! Whooh!' She had a whole gamut of wonderful expressions and the one she made now was priceless. 'I'll need to give 'em a shine before I leave.'

'Ah!' So this was the reason for the smart outfit and the new hat. 'You've got a new fella then?' Lucy teased. 'What's he like?'

Bridget touched the tip of her nose. 'You'll know soon enough,' she replied cagily. 'I'll tell you when I'm good and ready and not before.'

Bursting into the cottage with her usual flair, Bridget filled the room with her presence as always. She waited for Lucy to settle the child down for a nap before tea; he wriggled about for a while before falling fast and hard asleep. 'Good Lord above, will ye look at that? You've worn the child out, so ye have.' Now that he couldn't snatch at her feather, she leaned over and kissed him. 'He's such a wee, bonny thing.'

Though she loved children from a safe distance, Bridget was not cut out to be a mother and she made no secret of that. 'Making the child gives you pleasure,' she had been known to say with a twinkle in her eye. 'Raising them breaks your heart.'

Lucy went to the cupboard. 'Large or small?' she asked, the glass poised in the air.

'I'll have a large,' Bridget started, then, 'No! I'd best have a small.' A devious little grin shaped her handsome face. 'Sure, I've got to keep me wits about me today.'

As instructed, Lucy poured out a small measure of gin and brought it to her. 'Why? What's happening today then?' She handed her the glass and watched with amazement as Bridget took a delicate sip. It wasn't like her dear friend and benefactor to drink her gin sparingly. Normally, she would down one glass and be after another, before the first was hardly swallowed.

Bridget smacked her lips and looked up, and after taking another delicate sip, she smiled at Lucy with her magic green eyes and raising her eyebrows suggestively, said in a whisper, 'I've found the fella of my dreams, so I have.' The slightly smug expression on her face told it all.

'Have you now?' Lucy sat herself down. 'So, you really think he's the one?'

'Oh, he is. I just *know* he is!'

'Well, come on then. Who is he?'

Bridget opened her mouth to answer, then changed her mind. 'Get yourself a cuppa tea first – oh, and another o' these.' She held out her glass. 'I've a thirst come on me all of a sudden.' She shrugged her broad shoulders in that apologetic manner which Lucy knew only too well.

Lucy didn't argue, because she knew it would do no good. Instead, she took the glass, half-filled it and handed it back. 'You'd best make that last. Your fella might not approve of his woman being three sheets to the wind.'

Bridget took a ladylike sip. 'Why, ye cheeky young

heathen!' She then took another sip, this time longer. 'I'll be the best judge o' that, so I will!' She leaned forward in an intimate manner. 'I'm so glad you like the two-piece,' she said. 'I bought it special. I bought these special an' all.' Clambering out of the chair, she hoisted her skirt to display vast thighs, topped by the laciest pair of knickers Lucy had ever seen. 'Pure silk, I'll have ye know!' Bridget imparted, wide-eyed. 'Cost me a small fortune, so they did. Well – what d'ye think? D'ye like them? D'ye think *he'll* like them?'

Lucy was lost for words, and told Bridget so.

'Ah, go on and make the tea,' Bridget told her, disappointed. 'Sure, if he doesn't like them, he's not the fella I thought he was.'

Smiling to herself, Lucy retreated to the kitchen where she boiled the kettle and made the tea, then came back into the parlour with a plate of little fairy cakes. 'Have one of these,' she suggested. 'It'll soak up the gin.'

Bridget laughed aloud. 'So now you're telling me what to do, is it?' she spluttered. 'Seems to me you're getting above yourself, young woman.'

Seating herself in the other chair, Lucy leaned back, cup in hand and waiting. 'Well?'

Bridget frowned. 'Well what?'

'What's the latest news then?'

All in a rush as was her way, Bridget went over all the usual items of gossip. 'Little Tillie's gone off on a week's holiday to the Lake District. She fell out with her boyfriend a few days back and says she's finished with men forever, but she says that all the time and then she's off again, seeing some other lanky, pimply, no-good thing.' Taking a breath, she proceeded at a faster pace. 'I said to her, I said, "Will ye never learn, girl? The buggers are only after what's in your drawers," but will she listen? No, of course she won't!'

Lucy thought Tillie had done the right thing. 'The change

of scene will do her good. The Lakes are so beautiful. When she comes back, she can stay with me if she wants to.' Lucy had been through this all before with dear Tillie.

'What? Stay with you?' Bridget was horrified. 'She'll do no such thing! I need her back at the house, I do. While she's been gone, I've had to take on some useless woman from the other side of Liverpool.' She gave a long, agonising groan. 'I won't even tell you what a pain she is.' Rolling the palm of her hand across her forehead, she gave a trembling sigh. 'Sometimes I think I was born to be a martyr.'

'Oh Bridget, don't be so dramatic.' Wisely changing the subject, Lucy enquired, 'So tell me, what else is happening?'

Fast recovered, Bridget launched into the next snippet of news. 'I'm having a new bathroom fitted upstairs – all black marble and best cream carpet. Going posh, I am.' She gave that naughty wink again. 'That'll cost the clients a few bob more for their pleasure, I can tell ye.'

'And what else?'

'New curtains in the sitting room, o' course. And I'm considering whether to have the old Victorian fireplace out and get a new one fitted . . .'

Lucy listened patiently while Bridget outlined all the changes she was having made to the house. 'Like I say, it'll cost a bob or two, but no matter. It'll be the clients that pay, I'll make sure o' that.'

'And what news of the girls?'

Bridget took a long gulp of her gin. 'That's what I meant to tell you,' she said. 'Mandy's only gone and got herself pregnant . . .' Drawing breath she launched into the lecture. 'Time and again I've told them, "You must never let yourself get with child," but will they listen?' She gave a long, shivering shake of the head. 'Not at all! Now I know you wouldn't be without your Jamie for all the tea in China, the darlin', but you've got to admit, it's not the easiest thing in the world, is it, having a bairn without a ring on your finger? Anyway, our Mandy has decided to marry the fella in question, and now she's gone off to meet his family, would ye believe? Of course she won't tell them about her job, nor will her fiancé, who is a nice young man, I'll give him that. Nor will she let on that she's already with child or they'll immediately think she's a trollop, and she's not.'

She drew another, longer breath. 'Mandy's a good girl, always has been. To tell you the truth, her heart's never been in her work, so it might be as well that she's gone.'

Lucy was pleased. 'I hope she remembers to write.'

'I'm sure she will,' Bridget answered. 'But I don't really expect we'll see much of her again, because the fella is French, and that's where she's been whisked off to – a place called Montpellier.' She sighed. 'And there's me, left in the lurch, so I am.'

Lucy chuckled. 'You'll have to get your fella to comfort you then, won't you?' She had wanted to ask after the 'gent', and this was her chance.

'I'm sure he'll comfort me if I ask him,' came the confident answer. 'He's a real gentleman, bless his kind heart.' Bridget dredged her glass and held it up. 'Just a wee drop more?' she suggested. 'Be a friend. Send me on my way with a smile.'

Shaking her head and thinking how Bridget would never change, Lucy poured her another drink.

'Ah, but aren't you the *lovely* woman!' Bridget said, gulping down the gin.

When she again held out her glass, Lucy was adamant. '*No.* I won't be responsible for spoiling your date. If you want another drink, you'll have to get it yourself.'

'I wish you'd stop jumping to conclusions.' Bridget was suitably indignant. 'I'm only handing the glass back.'

It was just as well, because when she left half an hour later, her hat was tipsy on her head and her legs just the slightest bit wobbly. 'I'll see youse again,' she told Lucy. Then she lifted her skirt and clambered into the open-topped car.

Falling into the passenger seat, she plonked a smacker of a kiss on the man beside her; a 'gent' indeed, with his tailored moustache and cream-coloured blazer, he looked a right dapper. He also had red blood in his veins because having caught a glimpse of her knickers when she cocked a fine leg to climb into the car, he took the liberty of stroking his hand along her stockinged thigh, all the way up to the suspender, quickly removing it when he saw Lucy looking on with amusement.

She nodded a greeting to him and he nodded back. 'Hold onto your hat, my sweetie,' he told the blushing Bridget. 'We could get up to thirty miles an hour if I set my mind to it.'

He set off with a roar and a squeal, with Bridget laughing and screeching like a silly schoolgirl beside him.

Lucy held back the laughter until they were out of sight, then she collapsed in hysterics, mimicking Bridget as she was wont to do. Oh, how she hoped her friend could hold onto this one. He was an absolute treasure. Priceless!

Going inside, she wiped the tears from her eyes and made herself another cup of tea. Thirty miles an hour indeed! she thought, then said aloud, 'I don't know about holding onto your hat. If you ask me, it's not the *hat* you're in danger of losing so much as your pretty silk *knickers*!'

The laughter bubbled up again; the sight of well-upholstered Bridget in her wonky hat, flashing her lingerie, and the dandy-man goggle-eyed at this vision of heaven, was all too much for Lucy. She laughed so much that Jamie woke up!

But if Bridget was happy, she thought, picking her son up and hugging him, then so was she, because if it hadn't been for Bridget, she would have been lost, long since.

CHAPTER TEN

THE FOLLOWING DAY, Lucy's week started all over again. Rising early, she had her wash and got dressed; then she made her bed and collected the child from his cot.

With that done she sat him in his chair at the table, made his porridge and while he plastered his hands and face with that, she burned herself a piece of toast which she covered in Vicky's homemade strawberry jam. 'Your Auntie Vicky makes the best jam in the world,' she told the child, who was far too busy licking his chubby fingers to pay attention.

'I need you to be on your best behaviour,' she coaxed. 'There's work to be done in Long Field, harvesting the spuds, and it's a case of all hands to the deck. The crop is ready to be taken in, Barney says. The plants have died off and the soil is good and dry.'

This would be her first close experience of working on the land, and she was really looking forward to it.

She glanced at the mantelpiece clock. 'We need to be away from here by seven,' she took a great bite of her toast, 'so eat up, little fella, then I'll give you a drink and get you washed, and we'll be on our way.' Reaching over the table she tickled him under the chin, and the little boy giggled. 'Vicky said she would make up a picnic for when we stop to

eat. We'll have it down by the river, that's what she said –
and won't that be lovely, eh?'

In fact, life itself was so wonderful these days, she could
hardly believe her good fortune.

During the next half-hour, Lucy went about her chores;
she cleared and washed the breakfast things while Jamie
played, then took her son and washed him, made sure she
had everything they needed, then strapped him into his
pram and parked him outside on the path while she secured
the cottage behind her.

Taking the bridle path up to Overhill Farm, she found the
going hard; one minute she was pushing the pram and the
next she was pulling it, until her arms ached from shoulder to
wrist. But it was such a beautiful day, she didn't mind a bit.
Besides, little Jamie was in his element, laughing and chuckling, until he eventually fell asleep and all she could hear were
the birds singing and the river bubbling over the boulders.

As they came through the spinney, the terrain became
easier. Well-worn by travellers and locals alike, in parts the
meandering walkway was rough and bumpy underfoot, but
for the most part it was easy going. From the cottage to the
farm, it took exactly twenty minutes; Lucy had timed herself
on the first day.

'Vicky!' Waving as she approached the house, Lucy
saw Barney's wife hanging out the washing. 'I'm not too late,
am I?'

Waving back, Vicky took the wooden pegs out of her
mouth. 'The boys have already gone to the fields,' she
replied. 'Barney's taken Susie into town for her hat-making,
and he'll come back straight after. We won't be needed for
a little while yet.'

She was finished with the washing. 'My! You put me to
shame!' she exclaimed. 'You look lovely, Lucy. Bright and
fresh as a daisy.'

It was true. Lucy did look very fetching in the long dark skirt and loose white blouse, worn to work in the fields, and something about the way she had swept her hair back into a thick plait made her seem almost childlike. 'And look at me – hands red from rubbing the sheets in the dolly-tub, and hair all over the place. I must look terrible,' Vicky laughed ruefully.

'You don't look any such thing!' Lucy would have none of it. She looked at Vicky with her sunkissed hair and those wonderful expressive grey eyes, and all she saw was beauty and goodness. 'You always look lovely,' she said honestly. 'It's right what Barney says: you couldn't help but look pretty, even if you'd just come up from the coal-mines.'

Vicky laughed. 'That's my Barney,' she said. 'He looks at me through rose-coloured glasses and can't see the wood for the trees.'

'That's because he loves you.' Lucy wondered if she would ever find that kind of love. 'I've never known anyone love his woman, like Barney loves you.'

For a moment Vicky was silenced by Lucy's profound words. 'I love him the same way,' she quietly confessed. 'Sometimes it frightens me, the way Barney believes we'll always be together. The thing is, Lucy, when you're part of each other, like me and Barney, there can never be a happy ending. Someone is bound to be sad at the end of it all.'

When she looked up, there was a kind of desolation in her grey eyes. 'You see, when either of us is taken, the one left behind will be totally lost.'

Lucy was amazed at the depth of pain in Vicky's voice, in her eyes, in her whole demeanour. 'You're neither of you going anywhere!' she declared stoutly, in an attempt to break the moment. 'Not until you've made me enough strawberry jam to last me into old age, any road.'

The mood broke and Vicky laughed out loud. 'If you like it that much, you'd best take another jar from the pantry.' She then threw the pegs into her big basket and placing it under her arm, she put her other arm through Lucy's. 'Come on, you.' Her smile was content. 'The water's already hot in the kettle, it'll take but a minute to bring it back to the boil. We've time enough for a brew before we roll up our sleeves.'

In truth, both Vicky and Lucy had already had their sleeves rolled up these past two hours and more. All the same, it was nice to take time out for a cuppa and a chat, all girls together, and that was exactly what they did. 'Bridget came to see me yesterday,' Lucy imparted, grinning at the memory. 'You should have seen her, all done up in a new outfit and a hat like you could never imagine.'

Vicky took a gulp of her tea. 'Got herself a fancy man, has she?' Vicky was a broadminded woman who respected Bridget for her kindness, and welcomed her, when other townsfolk looked down their noses at her.

'Seems like that.'

While they drank their tea and Jamie slept on, Lucy relayed the gossip and the two of them hoped that Bridget had found a man who would take care of her, for she was a good-hearted woman and not as young as she used to be.

Twenty minutes later, with both tea and gossip done, they set about the daily chores; Lucy seeing to the bathroom upstairs and making up the beds with fresh-laundered linen while Jamie 'helped' her, and Vicky tackling the work down-stairs.

Some short time later, with the house all spick and span, they made their way to the fields, where Barney and his sons were already halfway down the potato field. Armed with light forks, each of them raised up the secret treasure of the potatoes, hidden beneath the rich soil. They were beauties

– no sign of rot or infestation – and Barney was delighted. A bumper crop might cheer Mr Maitland who had been looking very preoccupied of late.

'RONNIE!' Barney's voice could be heard shouting instructions to the younger of his two sons. 'Stop messing about and get on with it.' With the work piling up, Barney was in no mood for frivolous behaviour. 'We've the rest of this field to do yet!'

Unlike his father and brother Tom, Ronnie, free-spirited and happy-go-lucky, was too easily distracted. He would collect the potatoes in the barrow lined with sacking, then wheel it to the barn, where the crop was stored in the dark and cool, and on the way back, he'd lark about, talking to the horse in the next field and playing tricks on his brother.

'He's a good lad,' Vicky remarked tolerantly as she and Lucy made their way to the men. 'But he still has a lot of growing up to do yet.'

Thrilled to be here, Lucy soaked up the atmosphere. Her attention drawn every which way, she took it all in: Barney's familiar figure bent over the long trench; the sunlight bouncing off the tines of the men's forks; the seemingly endless skies, and the bright warm sunshine. Here, now, it was as though she and Jamie and Barney's family were the only people in the whole wide world.

'Fine crop of spuds this year.' Having worked many seasons alongside Barney, Vicky spoke from experience.

As Barney took his turn with the barrow, he shouted, 'Are you here to watch, or work?' He went away laughing. 'You're no good to me if all you've come to do is admire the scenery.'

'Cheeky devil!' Vicky yelled after him. 'Another remark like that and you can do the spuds on your own, 'cause we'd rather be in Liverpool, strolling round the shops!'

Vicky and Barney could bandy insults without getting offended. It was part of their deep knowledge of each other.

The hours passed too quickly and every experience was new to Lucy. Working and laughing, stumbling in the trenches and clambering up again, getting into a rhythm with the digging, with the sun on her face and the cooling breeze a welcome relief. She wanted this day never to end.

'I'll be glad when we stop for a break.' Vicky paused to wipe the sweat from her brow. 'I'm all in.' She stroked Jamie's hair as he squealed, pointing excitedly to a worm. They were surrounded by birds, swooping down as the tubers were revealed.

A short time later and aching through every bone, Barney paused to stretch his limbs. Taking out his pocket-watch he glanced at the time. 'Good Lord! Why didn't somebody tell me it was nearly one o'clock?'

To everyone's relief he called for a break, at the same time taking the opportunity to slide his arm round his wife's waist and give her a resounding kiss. 'I'm proud of the three of you,' he told Vicky, Lucy and Jamie. 'I might even go so far as to say you're as good as the men . . .' At that moment he saw Ronnie throw himself down some way off, to lie flat under a tree. 'And maybe better than most,' he added with a light-hearted groan.

Ronnie was the first to answer. 'Not bad,' he said airily. 'It took Lucy a while to get the hang of it, but she got there in the end.'

'They did well.' Thomas gave his dad a knowing wink. 'In fact, they did so well, I reckon us men should go home and leave them to it. Come on, Jamie.'

'You mind we don't leave *you three* to it.' Vicky rose to their teasing. 'Here.' She thrust a greaseproof pack of sand-wiches at each of them. 'These should quieten you down.'

Everyone took off their sacking aprons and quickly sluiced their hands with water from a big enamel pitcher, before sitting down and unwrapping their lunch.

The break, though short, was a pleasure, not only because they were famished and the thick sandwiches filled with cheese, ham and pickle were delicious, but because the company was pleasant and the day glorious. 'What about you, Lucy?' Barney addressed Lucy who had fed the child and was now preparing his drink. 'Have you enjoyed your first-hand experience of market-gardening?'

'It's tiring,' Lucy admitted. 'I don't think I've ever ached so much in all my life, but oh yes, Barney, I can't tell you how much I've enjoyed it.' She cuddled the child. 'Jamie's enjoyed it too,' she said fondly. 'Though he didn't like being strapped in his pram for most of the time.'

'Well, I'm proud of you,' Barney said, and without hesitation the others echoed his sentiments.

With the food all gone, Ronnie and his brother went for a quick dip in the river, to wash the dust and grime from their backs. 'Don't be long,' Barney called after them. 'We'll need to work till dark as it is.'

Shortly afterwards, Vicky followed with the plates and cutlery. 'I'll give these a rinse in the water,' she told Lucy. 'I don't fancy the flies plaguing us all the way home.'

Left alone with Lucy and the child, who had dozed off, Barney helped to clear the picnic things away. 'How are things,' he enquired, 'really?'

'Things are fine, thank you, Barney.' Though she had good friends in Bridget and the girls, Barney and Vicky were the only people she could really talk to; especially Barney. He had such a way with him, naturally attentive and caring, that Lucy felt she could tell him anything.

'So, did you do the right thing in moving out to the cottage?' Looking tired and worn, he leaned against the tree.

'It was the best thing I ever did, and it's all thanks to you and your family,' she answered.

Taking a rag out of his trouser pocket, Barney wiped the sweat from his face. 'And you're content, are you, working at the house with Vicky, and labouring in the fields under an Indian summer sun?' he grinned. 'Seems to me, we've thrown you in at the deep end.'

Lucy smiled. 'Oh Barney, I'm more than content. I don't know how I can ever thank you both.'

'No thanks necessary,' he answered softly. 'Just to see you smile like that, and know you're settled – that's more than enough.' Barney looked down on her and thought what a lovely woman she was.

'You and Vicky, you can't know what you've done for me,' Lucy persisted. 'I've never been so happy.'

'It's only right that you should be happy.' In a fit of coughing, he turned away, scarlet in the face. Lucy passed him a cup of water. When the coughing fit passed, he addressed her again, his voice still a little hoarse. 'You worked well today, lass.' He didn't look round. 'I want you to know how much I appreciate that.'

'Barney, can I talk to you?'

The young woman's anxious voice caused him to swing round. 'Of course you can. What is it?'

Hesitating, she shrugged her shoulders. 'It's nothing – I'm sorry.' Suddenly it seemed foolish to voice what was in her mind.

Concerned, he came to kneel beside her. 'Come on, tell me, love. What's wrong?'

Lucy looked at him, at his strong, kind face and the endearing look in his eyes and she opened her heart to him. 'I'm afraid, Barney . . . so afraid.'

'What d'you mean? What have you to be afraid of?' His expression hardened. 'That bugger Trent isn't back again, is he, because if he's bothering you . . .'

Lucy shook her head. 'No, he's not back – at least not

that I know of.' She gave a wry little smile, her heart sinking at the memory. 'After the cowardly way he ran, I shouldn't think he'll ever show his face round here again.'

'So what are you afraid of?'

In a small voice she told him, 'It might sound silly to you, Barney, but I feel I'm *too* happy, and I'm afraid because something is bound to go wrong, I just know it is.'

'Aw, Lucy girl! Come here to me.' Taking her in his arms, he held her close. 'Nothing will go wrong. I won't let it – *Vicky* won't let it. The worst is over for you now. We've got you safe with us.' He held her at arm's length. 'Promise me, Lucy, that whenever you're feeling worried you'll talk to me or Vicky. Promise me you won't ever be afraid to share what's on your mind.'

Her heart full, Lucy slowly nodded her head.

'That's my girl.' He rumpled her hair, and let her go.

~

A few minutes later, at Barney's suggestion, she left the child with him and made her way to the river. Here, she dropped to her knees and washed her grubby neck and face. Her fingernails were grimed with mud; she'd deal with them later.

She was shaking the river-drops from her hands when she heard a noise some way further along the river. She turned her head and there, where the weir rushed down and tumbled amongst the larger boulders, she saw Thomas and Ronnie clamber out of the water, their muscular well-toned bodies magnificently naked.

Until that moment, she had seen them as merely Barney and Vicky's two young sons: Thomas, serious and deep-thinking, and Ronnie a bit crazy – a daredevil ready to have a go at anything.

Now she saw them as men in their own right, and it came as a bit of a shock to her senses.

Climbing to where they had laid their clothes, Tom and Ronnie took up their shirts and began drying themselves while, blushing to the roots of her hair, Lucy took flight and did not stop running until she was back to base.

It was the very first time she had ever seen a man stripped off; even when Edward Trent had made love to her, it was a case of undoing his trouser-buttons and lifting her skirt. A virgin when she had met him at the age of twenty-seven, in many ways Lucy was still sexually inexperienced. She had only known brief couplings with Edward, which had heated her blood and brought her a child, but the richness and depth of married physical love was unknown territory.

She knew now that what she had experienced was not lovemaking in the way it should have been; it was pure lust and nothing more, and she felt ashamed at having thought it was ever anything else.

As she neared her son, still sleeping in his pram, she was amazed to find that there was no sign of Barney. She stood a moment, eyes scouring the area. That was strange. She hadn't thought that Barney would ever go off and leave Jamie on his own.

Suddenly she could hear him, or at least she could hear something, because the harsh, rasping sounds were not human. They were more like the cries of some unfortunate animal caught in a trap.

Leaving Jamie, she cautiously followed the sounds, and there, doubled up against the side of the tractor, was Barney. Obviously in pain and fighting for breath, he looked a frightful sight. Lucy ran to him. 'Barney – what in God's name is wrong?'

Breathless and exhausted, he couldn't speak, but when he looked her in the eye, she saw the anguish there and her heart turned somersaults. 'Don't . . . tell . . . Vicky,' he gasped.

Lucy gave no answer. Instead she held him until he was fully recovered, at which point he repeated his plea. 'Lucy . . . you mustn't tell Vicky about this. She'll only worry, and it's unnecessary.'

Lucy wasn't too sure about that. 'But you're ill!' she told him gently. 'You couldn't breathe – could hardly stand up on your own two feet!' Seeing him like that had given her a scare. 'You're wrong, Barney,' she told him. 'Vicky *should* know about this.' When she saw the look of panic on his face, she assured him, 'All right, I won't tell her. But you must.'

'There's no need!' Barney was recovering his strength now. 'I'm not ill. It's something to do with handling the tubers. They don't agree with me. Summat about them gets in and clogs up my lungs, hampers my breathing and makes me feel bad. It comes on quickly and goes away the same. Like I say, there's nothing to worry about. Right now, lass, let's get back to yon bairn. I'm sorry I left him, pet – didn't want to wake him, see?'

'All right, Barney, if you're sure.' She could see how agitated he had got when he believed she might tell the family.

'Look at me, Lucy.' Raising his arms, Barney let his hands fall to her shoulders, his smile quick and confident. 'You can see for yourself, I'm right as rain now. It was a coughing fit, that's all it was. I won't have Vicky or anyone else worrying about something and nothing.'

Lucy didn't argue. In fact, she was amazed at how quickly he had recovered. One minute he had looked so ill, she feared for his life, and the next he seemed fine. 'You're sure you're all right?'

He nodded. 'Like I said, right as rain.'

Believing she might have over-reacted, Lucy took him at his word. Besides, though his colour wasn't fully returned, he did seem fine now.

Barney called her attention to the three approaching figures; the two sons in front, obviously not aware that their mother was some distance behind. 'Remember,' he urged. 'Not a word.'

While they were looking across the field, they saw the figure of a man standing beneath the dipping boughs of a tree. 'It's the boss, come to keep an eye on us,' Barney said jokingly.

So, while Leonard Maitland watched the family, Barney and Lucy watched him. 'What the devil's he up to?' Like Lucy, Barney was intrigued.

'I expect he's been out for a long walk and is taking a rest in the shade,' she answered.

Barney laughed. 'He may well be,' he remarked, adding tongue-in-cheek, 'He's also taking a long, leisurely look at my woman.' Thrusting his hands into his pockets he seemed a proud man. 'I should've told him,' he said casually.

'Told him what?' It had not occurred to Lucy that Leonard Maitland was watching Vicky in particular, but now she could see that while he rested from the heat, Leonard Maitland did in fact seem more preoccupied with Vicky who, unaware of his interest, walked on, the plates cradled in her arms and with eyes only for Barney.

Like the cat that got the cream, Barney wore a smile from ear to ear. 'I should have warned him,' he said. 'Every man that's ever clapped eyes on my Vicky has fallen head over heels in love with her.' His eyes shone with joy as he watched her drawing nearer. 'And all she ever wanted were *me* . . . a farmworker who owns nothing and never will.'

His eyes widened with a rush of astonishment. 'What she ever saw in me, I'll never know.' His voice dropping to a whisper, he spoke as though to himself. 'I just thank the Lord for bringing the two of us together.'

As always, whenever she witnessed the love between these two people, Lucy was humbled. She saw the adoration in Barney's eyes and the joy in Vicky's face as she waved to him.

Vicky may have been aware of Leonard Maitland or she may not. But it was Barney she was looking at. *Barney*, her man, her everything. She was one side of the coin; he was the other.

'Look! He's going now.' Lucy brought his attention to Leonard Maitland's retreating figure.

Barney made no comment just then, but he noticed how Leonard Maitland continually glanced back at Vicky. And who could blame him, Barney thought as he brought his own tender gaze to the kind, caring woman he adored.

Vicky always looked lovely, he thought, but today she was especially beautiful with the breeze playing round the hem of her skirt, lifting it and twirling it, her golden hair blown gently back from her happy face, oh and that smile. Even now after all these years, he could hardly believe that Vicky was his wife. From the moment he had first seen her, he wanted no other. And he never would, for the kind of love they shared came only once in a lifetime.

Shortly afterwards, Barney's mate Adam arrived. 'I've finished thatching Widow Mason's porch,' he told Barney, 'so I wondered if you might have use for another pair of hands?'

Barney thanked him. 'The more the merrier, matey,' he said, and his pal threw off his jacket and got to work.

Tired and sweating under the hot sun, Lucy soon forgot Leonard Maitland and his seeming infatuation with Vicky. Barney, however, for good reason kept it quietly at the back of his mind.

~

Leonard Maitland needed a drink.

Having hurried home, tired and hot, he had rushed in, closed the door to shut out the world, and was now helping himself to a small whisky. 'God knows what they must have thought!' he muttered, gulping down the drink. 'Me standing there, gawping at another man's wife like some lovesick fool!'

Deep in thought, he wandered across the room, images of Vicky filling his mind: running, tripping, laughing, she was the essence of womanhood. Yet he had other, more urgent things to think about. A few days ago, he had received a letter from America, to do with his late grandfather's estate in Boston, Massachusetts. It seemed he might have to fight to retain the old man's house and lands. Things were happening which could send it either way. If it went one particular way, it could mean him selling up in this country and making a new life over there. Leonard had spent months at a time in his youth with his maternal grandfather, Farley Kemp, on the thousand-acre farm. He loved it out there – although his English heritage meant that he loved it here, too, east of the Mersey.

He considered for a moment. If he went to America, would he take Patricia with him? And what of Barney and his family . . . and Vicky? Leonard might be well-off financially, but he didn't have endless funds. The last thing he wanted to do was put Barney out of work, but he might not be able to avoid it.

If he had to, he'd fight tooth and nail to keep it all together. But there were things happening out there which could mean he had little choice. If it went one particular way, it could mean his having to sell up in England and make a new life in Boston, America.

He considered the prospect for a moment. He would almost welcome the challenge. It would mean he could keep his grandfather's beautiful house and vast estates. He had worked his way up from a farm-labourer to create one of the most successful businesses in Boston. Besides that, it was a wonderful home, warm and welcoming, filled with happiness and contentment, the kind of which he'd never really known.

The memories still came flooding back. When he was a child, the highlight of his year was going to see his grandparents. Those amazing weeks when he was there were the happiest of his life. His grandfather would take him across the estate; sometimes on the back of his horse and later Leonard would ride alongside him on a pony, and oh, what adventures they'd get up to . . . racing each other across the headlands; climbing trees or riding to the top of a hill, so his grandfather could show him the house and lands from a distance, and even then they could never see the horizons of what belonged to him . . . lands that were loved and tended, houses and homesteads nestling in the valleys, and cattle by the hundreds; all this, all painstakingly, lovingly forged out of nothing, with only the strength of his own two hands and the heart of a lion.

He closed his eyes, his emotions in turmoil. When his grandfather lost his wife, he lost all sense of purpose, and now everything he worked so hard for was at risk.

Going to the armchair, Leonard sat down and gazed into space for what seemed an age. He gathered his thoughts and knew what he must do. He wouldn't let it be lost. He couldn't let them take it. He didn't have so much here to fight for, but he could try and save his grandfather's dream, and given the chance, that's what he'd do! Getting out of the chair, he smiled, at ease with himself. 'I think it's time I had a new life, a new direction. There is little to hold me here. I've gone as far as I can go, and now it's time to face up to a new challenge.'

Dipping into his pocket, he took out a long, official-looking envelope with an American stamp. Unfolding the letter he began to read:

Dear Mr Maitland,

I am pleased to inform you that certain matters relating to the estate of your grandfather, the late Mr Farley Kemp, are now settled. However, several important issues remain which demand your urgent attention. As you are the only surviving relative of the deceased, it is imperative that you contact me as soon as possible, with a view to visiting these offices, in order that these issues can be dealt with.

As you must be aware, time is of the essence, and the situation requires that you be here in person.

I look forward to hearing from you at your earliest opportunity.

Yours sincerely,

Justin Lovatt, Attorney-at-Law

Leonard knew the letter word for word, for hadn't he read it umpteen times since receiving it? Tomorrow, he must make arrangements to travel.

'What's that you're reading?' Patricia's voice shocked him, invading his thoughts.

'Pat! Good God – I didn't hear you come in.' He swiftly folded the letter and slid it into his pocket. He hadn't heard the taxi pull up in the driveway.

Crossing the room, she slid her arm through his. 'Is it something I should know about, darling?'

He gave a nervous laugh. 'Why would you think that?'

'Because just now when I came in, you looked so worried, and as I'm soon to be your wife, I should know what is bothering you.'

'Really?' He tested her. 'And if I were to tell you that

165

I might have to make a difficult choice – a life-changing choice – what would you say to that?'

'It would depend.'

'Why's that?'

Growing flustered, she dislodged herself from his embrace. 'Well, for all I know it might change *my* life, and I don't know that I would be too keen on that.'

'Not even if it meant you and I would be together? Isn't that all that matters when a man and woman are in love?'

Something in his manner, in the way he was looking at her, made her nervous. 'No,' she answered defensively. 'Being in love *isn't* all that matters. What matters is that we both should be happy.'

'Yes,' he agreed, although he felt her resistance and was unnerved. 'But what if the choice I have to make is not really a choice at all, but something I feel obliged to do?'

She considered that for a moment, then like a child who wasn't sure of how to respond, she used her wiles and going to him, slid an arm round his waist. 'I think you had best tell me what you were reading, just now,' she wheedled.

'I'd rather not, Patricia. It isn't altogether settled, and it may not come to anything anyway.'

'Hmh! You're not about to do anything that would make me unhappy, are you, my darling?' she pleaded prettily. 'I mean, you will let me have my say in this choice of yours, won't you?'

Holding her at arm's length, he answered wisely, 'Of course you will have a say. But, like I said, there may not even be any choice to make. I won't know that, until I return from America.'

'*America?*' At once she was all smiles, confident that she would be going with him. 'I knew if I kept on at you long enough, you would take me away, but *America!*' She laughed excitedly. 'What an adventure that will be! When do we leave?'

Seeing her pleasure, Leonard was half-tempted to take her with him. He thought that if she saw the vast and beautiful land outside Charlestown and the sprawling house his grandfather had built over the years, she might grow to like the prospect of moving there. But commonsense prevailed, and he said merely, 'I'm sorry, Pat, but I shall be tending to important business. I can't take you with me this time. It's deuced inconvenient as it is, leaving Comberton at this time of the year.'

'Oh, come on, Leonard! What business do you need to tend that means I can't come along? We are to be married after all, aren't we?'

'Of course we are, but I simply can't take you, not this time. Look, when I get back, I promise we'll see about a weekend in Paris – would that suit you?'

'No, it would not.' Giving him a frosty look, she turned on her heel and stalked towards the door. 'I have shopping to do in Manchester. I imagine I'll be gone for at least four hours. That should give you plenty of time to decide whether I come with you or not.'

When he heard the front door slam, Leonard walked to the window, from where he could see Patricia climb into the taxi. She did not look back, but somehow that did not concern him.

Instead, he took out the letter and read it through again.

'No, Patricia,' he said aloud. 'I won't take you with me.' His mind was made up. The reason he was going to America was too important. This wasn't just about him and Patricia.

Thrusting his hands into his pockets he began to pace the room, his thoughts and loyalties all churned up. The decision was something he had to make by himself. If it turned out that there was, after all, no choice to make, then so be it. But if it came to a head, then he had to think of others who would inevitably be affected.

The people who had been loyal to him over the years, these were the people uppermost in his mind right now. He thought of Barney, that good man, and his heart was sore. Then he thought of Vicky, of maybe never seeing her again, and the prospect was unbearable. He found himself searching for a way that would allow him to take the Davidsons with him, but at the moment that seemed quite unrealistic.

His thoughts then flew ahead, and his heart sank. Whatever the outcome of his visit across the Atlantic, there was still Patricia.

And so far he had not decided what to do about her.

CHAPTER ELEVEN

'YOU'RE THIRTY-NINE years of age and you still have the body of a young girl.' Having climbed into bed, Barney leaned on his elbow and watched his wife undress. It wasn't often she undressed in front of him; for some reason she preferred the light out, and whenever he came upon her naked, she would blush and hide, and scamper into bed. 'You need never be ashamed of your body,' he told her now. 'You should be proud.' His voice dropped to the softest whisper. 'You're very beautiful, Vicky. You always were.'

Having finished brushing her hair, she slithered into bed beside him. 'I'm not beautiful,' she protested, though with a smile. 'You only think that, because you love me . . . like I think you're handsome, because I love *you.*'

Tenderly he placed a finger over her lips. 'No,' then with his other hand he stroked a stray lock of hair from her eyes. 'You really are a lovely-looking woman, my darling. You may not see it, but I do, and so does every other man who looks on you.'

'Stop it, Barney.' She went rosy with pleasure. 'What will you say when I'm old and toothless, and bent like a willow tree?'

His answer was to take her in his arms and hold her as close as any man could hold the one he loved. 'None of that would matter,' he answered honestly, 'because you will always be beautiful to me.'

In the halo of moonlight shining in through the window, she could see in his eyes the depth of his love for her, and she was deeply moved. 'I love you so much,' she said, her voice breaking. 'I love our children and I love the life we lead, but it would not be the same without you.'

He could feel the tension in her body, and he was shocked. 'Hey!' Lifting himself up, he looked into her sad face and was afraid – not for himself, but for her. 'You mustn't talk like that. We have each other and, God willing, we'll have each other for many years to come.'

'Do you promise?' she whispered. 'Do you promise never to leave me?'

Barney saw the tears rising in her pretty eyes, and was deeply moved when one plump, watery tear spilled over her cheek. 'I can't promise,' he answered, wiping away the tear with the tip of his thumb.

'Why not?'

'You know why not,' he chided gently. 'We none of us can see what the future holds.'

She tightened her grip on him. 'You have to promise me, Barney.'

'What's wrong?' Kissing her on the mouth, he wondered why she should ask him such a thing. 'Why do you insist, when you know a promise of that kind is impossible?' Fear squeezed his heart. Had she heard him in a coughing fit? Did she know how ill he had been feeling of late? Had Lucy told her about that day in the field, when she found him gasping for breath? And now Vicky was asking him to make a promise of this kind. He couldn't do it. Nor could he voice his fears.

'Promise me, Barney,' she entreated. 'Say you will never leave me, then I'll be content.'

Gazing into her quiet eyes, in the space of a single heart-beat he saw his whole life there, and somehow suddenly, the fear he had felt began to ebb away. 'I promise,' he murmured. 'If it's in my power to be with you forever, then I will.'

'There! That wasn't so hard, was it?' She smiled, and for no reason he could fathom, he was a man at peace with himself.

Cradling her face in his hands he kissed her long and passionately, and she responded with the nakedness of her body against his, rhythmically pushing against him then pulling away, until he rolled her beneath him and placing a gentle hand round each of her legs, he drew them apart.

There was no need of words; there was nothing to say that had not already been said a thousand times.

Wrapped around each other, they made such wonderful love; not as they had done many times before, with tenderness, but with a wild passion and a desperate, painful hunger that drove them into each other – almost as though they intended never to be separated.

And then it was over, when their bodies were aching and vibrant and the life-juices still flowing, they held onto each other. For the rest of their lives they would remember this night; when for the first and last time they made love as never before, and Vicky drew from Barney a promise which, he knew in his lonely heart, he could never keep.

∼

Two days later, on a fine, breezy morning, Leonard Maitland boarded a liner for America.

'I'll be away for some time.' An hour before setting off for the docks, he had called Barney to his office at The Manse. 'I'm leaving you in charge as always, and should you encounter any problems, though I don't imagine you will, you do know who to contact?'

'Yes, I do, sir, thank you. I have his name and address.' As ever, Barney was well organised.

'Good man! As I already explained, the agent knows as much about my affairs as I do, and he's well-placed to contact me in any event. I've arranged for the house to be taken care of, so there is no need for you to concern yourself about that. On the whole, I don't envisage any problems.'

'Thank you for your trust.' Over the years Barney had come to like and respect this man who was his employer. 'Rest assured I'll do my best to keep the farm running smoothly.'

'I know you will,' Leonard declared. 'You took excellent care of my interests when I was last in Boston. And now I must get off. I have a long journey ahead of me.'

Barney walked with him to the taxi, Leonard carrying his bag and briefcase, and Barney following with his portmanteau. 'Have a safe voyage,' he said as Leonard climbed into the vehicle. 'I hope your trip goes well.'

'Oh, so do I, Barney!' Leonard declared. 'So do I!' Gesturing for the driver to move out, Leonard caught sight of Vicky as she walked towards the river. He couldn't take his eyes off her. If only Patricia was more like her, he thought, he would be a much happier man.

Seeing the taxi, Vicky waved, her face wreathed in a smile.

His heart warmed and with her face in his mind, Leonard took the smile with him, all the way to Boston, USA.

~

'Well, it seems Mr Maitland went away at the right time.' The whole family were gathered round for Sunday dinner – a grand affair with the table sagging beneath the weight of a partly-sliced beef-joint, a ham shank ready for the carving, various deep dishes of crisp-roasted and boiled potatoes, cabbage, carrots, and a pile of Yorkshire puddings the like of which Lucy had never seen before.

There were also two large boats of meat-gravy and a dish of homemade horseradish sauce, a particular favourite of Lucy's.

'What makes you say that, Dad?' That was Susie, seated next to him and already helping herself to a slice of beef.

'Because the weather's on the change,' Barney explained. 'Once the cold wind starts coming in from the north, you can expect to see winter on its tail.'

Vicky tapped the back of Susie's hand. 'Don't start eating yet.'

She gave Barney a reminding nod, and he immediately roved his gaze across each person at the table in turn; when they were suitably attentive, he folded his hands together, bowed his head and started Grace. 'We thank the good Lord for a healthy harvest, and for the food we are about to eat. God bless friends and family.' He looked up, and already the dishes and plates of food were being passed round.

'Well!' Vicky tutted. 'That was a short Grace.'

'No matter,' her husband replied, shovelling a heap of cabbage onto his plate. 'It was sincere, and we're good and ready to eat the fruits of our labour while they're still hot.'

'Why *has* Mr Maitland gone to America?' Susie was curious.

Barney passed Lucy the potatoes and gave his daughter one of his impatient looks. 'You must have asked that question a hundred times or more,' he chided. 'The answer is the same as it was before – we don't know. What's more, it's none of our business.'

Still she persisted. 'It must be something important, because that's twice he's been this year.'

Rolling her eyes, Vicky smiled at Lucy, a smile that said, 'Wait until your son starts asking questions and you don't have the answers to give, it'll drive you crazy.'

'Well?' Susie was like a dog with a bone.

'Well, *what*?' Thomas asked, his mouth full of part-chewed meat.

'Don't speak with your mouth full!' Vicky reprimanded. 'We none of us want to see what you're eating, thank you.'

Lucy loved having Sunday lunch with the Davidsons. This was a real family, with arguments and conflicting opinions, and questions without answers, and even half-chewed mouthfuls of meat. 'I think Susie's right,' she said, glancing at the girl. 'Mr Maitland must have important business to tend, or he wouldn't have gone away again so soon.' She hastily rescued a potato that was about to fall on the floor from Jamie's teaspoon. The little boy was quite good at feeding himself now, but he was staring goggle-eyed at Tom's antics and wasn't paying attention. Lucy hoisted him straight. He was sitting on the high chair they had made him, and was in his element.

'But why did he go the first time?' Susie played with her Yorkshire pudding, spinning it on the end of her fork and nibbling at the crusty bits.

'Hey!' Ronnie leaned towards her. 'If you don't want that bit of pud, I'll have it.' Having already demolished three, he still had an appetite like a lion.

'You will not pass food from plate to plate!' Vicky declared, getting out of her chair. 'There are half a dozen more in the oven. I'll fetch them.' Which she did, with Ronnie stealing one away on the prongs of his fork before she even got to the table.

As Vicky sat down to resume her meal, Barney was explaining to his daughter, 'You see, sweetheart, we didn't make a big thing of it at the time, so you probably didn't know, but

Mr Maitland's old grandfather passed away earlier in the year, and he had to go out and see to things.'

Susie was indignant. 'Why didn't you tell me?' she asked petulantly. 'I'm not a baby to be protected.'

'I know that,' Barney apologised. 'But it isn't the sort of thing you like to talk about, is it?'

Susie shrugged her slim shoulders. 'It doesn't bother me.'

Ronnie intervened. 'So why did you cry your eyes out when your pet rat passed away?'

'That was different.' Susie's eyes filled with tears. 'Bobby was my friend.'

'Of course he was, and of course you cried.' Barney gave Ronnie a warning glance, before returning his attention to his daughter. 'Mr Maitland was upset about his grandfather too. Only when it's a person, there are things to be done . . . legal documents, matters o' that kind. That was why he went to America last time. As to why he's gone *this* time, I don't really know, but I suspect it might have something to do with his grandfather's estate. Y'see, Mr Maitland was brought up in Boston. He spent most of his youth there after his parents died, and from what he told me, he loved every minute.'

Having finished his first course, and patiently waiting for his pudding, Thomas addressed his father. 'From what I remember, you said his grandfather had hundreds of acres of land and a great, sprawling farmhouse?'

'That's right,' Barney replied, setting his knife and fork together and letting out a long sigh of satisfaction.

Ronnie spoke up. 'I've often wondered why he would leave the place if he loved it that much.'

'For an adventure?' That was Lucy. 'I've always wanted to see the world. Maybe Mr Maitland felt the same when he was younger, so when he got the chance, he took it?'

That sparked another question from Ronnie. 'How old is he now?' he asked Barney.

'I'm not exactly sure.' Barney cast his mind back to when Leonard Maitland had confided many things in him. 'He's not much older than me – forty-three, forty-four maybe.'

'Crumbs!' Susie groaned. 'That's ancient.'

While Lucy laughed, Vicky feigned indignation. 'Hey, young lady! I'll have you know, me and your father are still young at heart.'

Barney laughed out loud. 'We've aching limbs, a bad back and corns on our feet, but like your mammy says, we're still young at heart.'

Everyone laughed, including Jamie, which made them laugh more. The jam pudding and custard was served by Susie and her mother, and afterwards there was the luxury of a Sunday glass of homemade wine each; all except for Susie, who moaned and complained and still got only a quarter of a glass. 'Just enough to wet your whistle,' Barney advised firmly. 'Give it another year and if you're lucky, you might be allowed *half* a glass.'

When the meal was over and the women were clearing away, the men went for a tour of the farm, discussing their plans to prepare the fields for winter.

'There won't be too many more days like this,' Barney said, looking up at the cloudless skies. In a fleeting thought, he wondered how many more days *he* would have. So far he had managed to carry out his work without anyone suspecting the truth, but deep down in his soul he believed there was something badly wrong with him.

Lately, his only concern was the family. If anything happened to him, what in God's name would it do to Vicky? Dear Lord! It didn't bear thinking about, so he pushed the thoughts from his mind.

Maybe when all was said and done, there wasn't anything wrong that could not be put right, but the uncertainty was there, mainly because he still hadn't been back to the doctor.

On a different issue, yet with the bad thought ticking away in the back of his mind, he turned to his younger son, Ronnie. 'It's time you learned the farming inside out, son.'

'I already know the farming,' Ronnie argued. 'I've helped you since I were a little lad, Dad, just like our Tom. I've helped you bring in the harvest and led the sheep in for shearing, and I've walked that many times behind the hay-cart and made that many sheaves, I've lost count.'

Thomas intervened. 'Dad means *real* farming.'

Ronnie laughed. 'I thought that's what I'd been doing.'

'And you're right,' Barney agreed, 'but there's still much more for you both to learn.'

'Such as what?'

'Such as knowing the tractor inside out, every bit and bolt, how the engine works, how it should sound when running, and being able to put it right when it goes wrong. Then there are the implements, knowing which to use and when.' He went on, 'When the sheep are brought in for the shearing, you stay with them. You talk with the shearer and watch the job is done properly, and when he's not able to get here at the right time, you shear the blessed things yourself, or the maggots will eat them alive.'

'That's right!' Thomas exclaimed. 'The first time I saw a sheep with its back half-eaten, I didn't know what it was. I never knew maggots could get into the fleece and eat away the flesh.'

Ronnie's mouth fell open. 'God! That's awful!'

'So, that's another thing you've learned.' Barney took out his pipe and lighting up, began puffing away. 'They've to be dipped and they've to be sheared. It's a cycle and if it goes out of rhythm, something suffers somewhere along the way.'

He blew out a halo of smoke. 'You'll both make good farmers, if that's what you want. But there's still much to be learned. There's the wintering, and ordering of foodstuff, and keeping up with what's new. Then there's the paper-work, oh aye! Yon paperwork will keep you up till the early hours, and when that's done, it's time to get up for the milking.' He sighed deeply and pulled on his pipe. 'It's not like a job most other poor devils do – if they can get it – where you clock on in the morning and clock off again at night.'

He looked from one to the other. 'You work with the land and the animals; you're controlled by the seasons.' He smiled contentedly. 'It's hard work and by, it takes it out of you, but I swear to God you'll never find a better way of life.' Taking his pipe out, he paused, before saying in a serious voice, 'I can't tell either of you how to live your life and I wouldn't dream of doing that. It might be that you don't want to work for Mr Maitland and stay here in Comberton. You're both my sons and I'm proud of you, but you must spend your lives the way you see fit.'

'I've already decided what *I* want to do.' Thomas had been giving it some serious thought lately. 'At first I wasn't so sure, but now I am: I want to make farming my life. I want the kind of life you and Mother have had.'

Barney was thrilled. 'I'll not deny we've had a good life, me and your mother . . .'

Ronnie interrupted with a quiet smile. 'With many more years to come yet, eh, Dad?'

Taken aback by Ronnie's remark, Barney felt his heart turn over. 'Aye, lad, that's right . . . many more to come yet.' God willing, he thought. *God willing.*

'And I'm the same.' Like Thomas, Ronnie had missed the look of regret in his father's eye. 'I want to farm an' all. Winter or summer, it's a great way of life.'

Barney was filled with emotion, that his two sons had seen such contentment in his own life that they wanted the same for themselves. 'I'm glad,' he answered gratefully. 'It were allus my wish that the two of you would follow in my footsteps. But it had to be your decision, not mine.'

Just then, Lucy and Vicky arrived to join them, little Jamie toddling between them.

Barney grabbed hold of Vicky's free hand. 'Is there any o' that elderberry wine left over from dinner, sweetheart?'

'Half a bottle.' Vicky instinctively squeezed his hand. 'Why?'

His face beamed up at her. ' 'Cause we've summat to celebrate, that's why.' He gestured towards his sons. 'You and me have talked long and often, wondering whether the boys might take up the farming as a way of life, and tonight, they've given me their answer.'

When Barney's smile widened, Vicky gave a little squeal of excitement. 'Oh Barney! So they want to be farmers, like their dad?' With moist eyes and a smile hovering between tears and laughter, she ran to hug them. 'Oh, I'm so glad!' And now the tears came. 'We did think you might eventually decide to go out into the big, wide world and do summat different, but oh, we did hope . . .'

Ronnie held onto her a moment longer. 'If you're gonna start crying, we might have to change our minds. Stop it, Mam, you're scaring the little 'un.'

Laughing, she scooped Jamie up and said to Lucy, 'We'll go and get the kettle on, shall we, and dig out the wine again.'

'Good idea.' Lucy went up to the two young men and gave them each a kiss. 'It's wonderful news.'

Back in the big farmhouse kitchen, with everyone sitting comfortably, Barney filled the glasses and Vicky handed them round. 'A toast!' Barney raised his glass. 'To a fourth generation of the Davidson farmers.'

He thought with pride of his father and grandfather, and the ones who had gone before, all contented men who had lived well into their eighties. And now, his own two sons were to carry on the tradition.

His sense of pride was mingled with regret.

He couldn't help but wonder if he would ever see the next generation; his own grandchildren. That would be the greatest thing.

Somehow, though, his instinct told him that he was not destined to live the long life of his forefathers.

CHAPTER TWELVE

Leonard Maitland had spent several days trudging the many fine streets of Boston, going from one office to another, placating irate creditors and dealing with problems he had never envisaged. There was no chance for him to explore the city this time. As he strode along today, he thought how he would have loved to watch the Red Sox basketball team play at Fenway Park, as he had so often done with his grandfather, but there was no time, no time! His whole future depended on putting things right. Having studied everything with the lawyer executing the terms of Farley Kemp's Will, he had been kept so busy his feet had hardly touched the ground.

And now he was on his way to the lawyer's office to tie up all the loose ends.

'Go right in, sir.' Smart and efficient, the young woman behind reception had the sweetest smile. 'Mr Lovatt is expecting you.'

'Good to see you, Lenny. Please come in.' The big man with the horn-rimmed spectacles threw open the door of his inner office. 'I believe we're as ready as we'll ever be.'

Having been a respected lawyer in New York before the Wall Street Crash last year, Mr Lovatt's experience of matters relating to property was unsurpassed and, not surprisingly, his appointment book was invariably full.

Gesturing to the big leather armchair, he informed Leonard, 'I don't know about you, but I sure could use a cup of coffee. I'll order it while you make yourself comfortable.' With that, he pressed a button on his desk and said, 'Clara, a pot of coffee, please. Our client may also appreciate a few of those cookies your mom made – that is, if you have any left?' There was a pause, then, 'That's great!'

Returning his attention to Leonard, the lawyer took up a thick file and slid it across the desk to him. 'It's all there – names, addresses, the extent of debt and terms agreed.' He grinned smugly. 'We've covered a lot of ground, negotiated with the creditors, and now, with the meeting scheduled for tomorrow morning, the rest should be just a formality.'

Leonard nodded his appreciation. 'You've done all the back-breaking work, and it goes without saying, I'm very grateful.'

The big man settled back in his chair. 'As you know, I don't come cheap,' he said with a disarming smile. 'It's my job to know the enemy. Once you know what you're up against, you can prepare for battle.' He tapped his nose shrewdly. 'And win.'

Leonard was nervous, but he had done his homework and was ready. 'It's just unfortunate that it had to be this way.'

The big man also regretted the situation. 'Look, Lenny, with regard to your grandfather's Will, I'm real sorry it turned out like this.'

'It did come as a shock,' Leonard muttered, casting his gaze to the papers in front of him. 'I always thought that Farley was a wealthy man. He certainly always lived like one. He spoiled me rotten when my parents died, and he and Gramma Sophie came over to England to take me back with them.' A lump came into his throat. His parents had died when he was four, in an influenza epidemic in London. 'It shook me to the core when you told me he was in so much debt, he was on the brink of losing everything.'

When he looked up, his expression was pained. 'Why in God's name did he have to be so proud?' he said thickly. 'If only he had confided in me, I would have helped. Dear Lord, it must have troubled him so much!'

'I pleaded with him time and again to contact you,' the big attorney said sadly. 'I would have contacted you myself, but he absolutely forbade it.' He threw his arms out in a gesture of helplessness. 'All along, he insisted he had everything under control. I wasn't privy to all your grandfather's interests, so of course I took him at his word.'

Just then, a tap sounded on the door and in came the young woman called Clara with a tray containing a big pot of coffee, a jug of cream and a plate of delicious-looking biscuits. She poured them each a cup, and said with a smile, 'If there's anything else, you will let me know, won't you?'

The big man held out the plate. 'Cookie?'

Leonard took one. 'However could my grandfather have got so deep into gambling?' he mused aloud for the hundredth time, before drinking a sip of coffee and biting into the biscuit.

'You recall I told you about the two Irish brothers that Farley befriended?' the lawyer asked. 'How they came to work for him at the spread and turned up drunk one night, with a racehorse they'd won on the gambling. Your grandfather had been awful lonely these past few years, ever since he lost his wife. He found a welcome distraction at the racetrack, and he had a few lucky strikes before it all went wrong. You see, like all gamblers, he always believed the next big win was just around the corner.' He shrugged. 'An intelligent man like that . . . He wasn't the first to get in above his head and you can bet your bottom dollar he won't be the last. It's a sad thing, Lenny – but it happens.'

Deep down, if he was honest with himself, Leonard had not been too surprised at what the lawyer had told him. 'He always liked to place a bet on sporting events,' he admitted. 'I recall Grandmother lecturing him one time, but it was never a problem, not then anyway. And why in God's name did the banks let him get into so much debt?'

The attorney pointed to the file on his desk. 'As you've already seen, it wasn't only the banks, though they were by far the biggest creditors. Mr Kemp borrowed money from whoever would lend it, and no one refused, because they knew him as a respected and reliable man who ran one of the biggest homesteads in this part of Massachusetts. The Depression has affected everyone here in the States, as it has in your country, and these people want their loans repaying. They *need* that money, Lenny.'

'And now, if we can't agree a settlement, everything may have to be sold.' Leonard recalled the place where he had spent so many wonderful childhood years, and his face set grimly. 'I swear I'll behave honourably towards everyone who is owed money, but at the same time, I'll fight tooth and nail to keep the land.'

The other man heard the passion in his client's voice and saw how his fists instinctively clenched. 'We've done all we can,' he assured him. 'Tomorrow morning will tell us if it was enough.'

Despairing but not altogether without hope, Leonard returned to his hotel in Beacon Hill. So preoccupied was he, he hardly noticed the pretty cobblestoned streets and grand old townhouses that characterised this famed quarter of Boston. Feverishly, he went through his notes yet again, then packed them away into his briefcase. He glanced at the clock and, seeing how he had hours before he could sleep, slipped his jacket on and went out to find the nearest bar.

Ordering a beer, he went to sit at a table in the corner, where he thought ahead to the imminent, all-important meeting with the creditors. How would they react to his offer? Would they accept it as the best course open to them? Or would they insist that the Kemp estate be sold and the monies split between them?

Gulping down his beer, he felt nervous and worried.

What if it all went wrong?

What if the estate went to auction and was lost forever? Certainly he could never afford to bid for it.

What if this . . . what if that. His mind was in a whirl.

With so much at stake, tomorrow could not come quickly enough.

$\sim$

The following morning, Leonard climbed out of bed, weary from lack of sleep and eager to be on his way. He showered and shaved and put on a clean shirt and an expensive silk tie that Patricia had bought for him. Looking at his image in the mirror he shook his head. 'God Almighty, look at the state of you!' With dark circles under his eyes and wisps of unruly hair protruding from behind his ears, he presented a sorry picture. 'Leonard Maitland, you're a damned mess.'

Slicking back the clumps of hair, he fastened his jacket, straightened his tie and turned away. He was ready to do battle. And with that he went smartly out of the room.

Farley Kemp had borrowed money from many sources, but the largest slice of debt was owed to a major bank. The meeting was scheduled to take place there.

The doorman whistled up a cab. Handing him a dime for his trouble, Leonard climbed in and gave directions to the bank. Settling himself into his seat with the all-important documents on his lap, he peered out at the Boston streets, seeing nothing.

On arriving at his destination, he paid the cabbie and watched him drive away. For a long, pensive moment he stood on the sidewalk looking up at the building; an imposing structure with dark-suited businessmen arriving and departing through its doors. This was the place where his future would be decided.

As he came out of the elevator, he could hear them: the shuffle and bustle of many people in one room; the scraping of chairs and the pacing of footsteps; and as he opened the door to the offices, he could almost smell their anger.

Suddenly, a cloak of silence fell over the room as all eyes turned to look at him. Nervous and unsure, he nodded, his confident smile belying the turmoil inside.

'Very well, gentlemen.' Justin Lovatt took the chair. 'We're all here now, so we may as well get started.'

Everyone present made their way to the large oval table in the centre of the room. When they were seated, Leonard noted that some men were softly talking, while others sat in silence, looking angry and morose. All had but one purpose in mind: to get their money back.

When he had first entered the room, his eyes were instinctively drawn to a large, bespectacled man who, seeming to keep his distance from the others, was staring out of the window. It was he who now voiced what everyone else was thinking. 'Mr Lovatt, before you begin proceedings, can I just tell you this. All we want is to get back what we lent in good faith.' His voice was surprisingly calm and soft. 'We all have businesses to run, so let's get on with it.'

Two hours later, they were still 'getting on with it'.

An hour into the meeting, the men were on their feet, declaring with raised voices that they wanted every cent back and would not settle for half measures. No amount of persuasion from Justin Lovatt could convince them of any other way forward.

Deeply frustrated and losing hope, Leonard asked permission to speak. He was initially greeted with a hubbub of noise from enraged men who would not be pacified, but then the big, bespectacled man called for order. 'Let Farley Kemp's grandson speak,' he said firmly. 'He is not to blame for his grandfather's mismanagement, so give him a chance. We're getting nowhere like this.'

Standing up amongst them, Leonard looked round the table at the faces of these men whom his grandfather had known well; men who had trusted him to repay what they lent in good faith – and he felt ashamed.

Clearing his throat, he began to speak. 'Firstly, I want to say how I understand your anger. You trusted my grandfather and he let you down badly, and I apologise for that. I know that, despite the Crash, some of you could well afford to lose the money if you had to . . .' when they began loudly protesting, he put up his hand . . . 'please, if you will just let me have my say.' When they were again attentive, he went on, 'I'm not saying that you will or *should* lose any money. Of course you want your money back and rightly so. And there are those amongst you who *cannot* afford to lose what you lent. I know that and I'm here today to try and settle matters one way or another.'

He looked at the documents lying on the table before him, and a great sense of bitterness overwhelmed him. His grandfather's reputation was shattered forever; there was family honour at stake, and a debt to pay, and it was up to him to pacify these men who had put their trust in a man who had betrayed them and reneged on his debts.

What could he say to appease them? How could he put things right?

He was so deep in his reverie that he had not realised how long his lapse of concentration was; until he heard them shifting impatiently in their seats, and their exchanged whispers as they grew restless.

'See here, Mr Maitland: have you got our money or not – that's all we need to know.' That was the sallow-faced, grey-suited man on the far end.

'That's right!' another voice joined in. 'Have you brought our money from England?'

'No!' he answered truthfully. Strong and clear, his stark words echoed across the room, effectively silencing everyone. 'I have money for you, yes, but it isn't what you might have hoped.'

'What in hell does *that* mean?'

The voices began to rise. 'If you're here to waste our time, we might as well leave now.'

'All we want is our money back, God dammit.'

'Gentlemen, this is the situation,' Leonard quickly explained. 'I have a farm in England, which I can sell tomorrow – and I will. But it won't make enough to clear all the debts. Since I've been here I've raised as much money as I can, but even with the sale of my own farm, it still isn't sufficient to cover the total sums owed.' Before they could start protesting again, he went swiftly on. 'I've gone through everything with Mr Lovatt here, and we've calculated that you will get back seventy per cent of what's owed —'

'Seventy per cent!' The voices began again. 'What the hell use is that?'

'We won't settle for less than what we're owed! Plus interest!'

'So, this is all a waste of our time? You got us here under false pretences. Jesus! You're no better than your grandfather!'

The rage threatened to erupt.

At this point Justin Lovatt stood up and called for quiet. 'Mr Maitland has come a long way, and gone to a lot of trouble to try and sort out his family's debts, which are not – I repeat *not* – of his making. I believe you are all men enough to appreciate what he's been trying to do. The least you can do now is give him a fair hearing.'

Something in his words seemed to calm them and with all eyes on Leonard they listened to what he had to say.

He told them how he could do no more than he had already done, and that, 'If you wait for the Kemp estate to go to action, you may well end up with even less than I'm offering you now. You have copies in front of you, show-ing the proof that I am in a position to deliver seventy per cent of what you lent out. It's signed, sealed and can be delivered. With an auction, you can never be sure; it all depends on the day and how many people want the property, or can afford it. As you know to your cost, the value of the property has been badly affected by the slump in the world economy.'

'He's right.' One man who so far had remained silent spoke out. 'The farmstead is still a valuable asset, and sold to the right buyer, we may get lucky. But if there aren't enough buyers to force up the price . . .' He raised his palms in a gesture of surrender. 'Like the man said – we could end up worse off.'

Seeing how the tide might turn in their favour, Justin Lovatt intervened. 'Mr Maitland and I will leave the room for a while. You all have copies of the documents in front of you, which will verify what's been put forward: seventy per cent of what you are owed, without uncertainty, and without prejudice. Read the documents, and if you're in favour of accepting, we'll make it watertight in your favour.'

He paused, before going on in sombre voice, 'If, however, you decide to take your chances at auction, then so be it.

The meeting will end right there.' With that he summoned Leonard to go with him, and together they departed the room.

In the outer hall, Leonard voiced his concern. 'There are a few in there who would rather wait and see what happens at the auction,' he said. 'And who knows, maybe the estate will bring in more than enough to pay them off.'

'All we can do is wait and see. The decision is in their hands and we have no choice but to abide by it.' As a lawyer Justin was philosophical. He had seen it all before and there was no telling which way it would go.

~

They had been waiting an hour and a half before the nondescript man in the grey suit came out to tell them, 'We've come to a decision . . . of sorts.'

As they followed him to the boardroom, Leonard looked at Justin and mouthed the words, ' "Of sorts"?' Justin shook his head, meaning that he didn't quite know what that meant either.

When they entered the room, it was instantly apparent that the men were more at ease; the big man actually smiled at them as they walked to their places. 'We've looked through all the documents,' he began, and it was obvious they had elected him to be spokesman, 'and I'm afraid we still want our pound of flesh.'

Leonard's heart sank, then rose again at his next words. 'We accept your offer – but with certain conditions.' He looked around the room, making sure everyone was still of the same mind. When he received the nods, he went on, 'No one here is prepared to accept any less than the full figure they are owed.'

Leonard's heart sank again.

The big man continued, 'To that end, we *will* accept the offer, but with a legal proviso that the remaining thirty per cent is paid within a period of two years. So there you have it. That is our unanimous decision. Accept it, or we'll take our chances at the auction.'

Realising it had come as a shock to Leonard, Justin spoke on his behalf. 'You all know my part in this,' he reminded them. 'The decision does not rest with me. I can't say whether Mr Maitland can or cannot comply with what you ask. All I can say is, he and I need to talk. I request that you give us twenty-four hours to consider.'

A hush came over the room and all eyes turned to Leonard.

Head bent and heart heavy, he was lost. He frantically sought a way out and could see none. He had been prepared to sell his farm in England and borrow money on top of that, in order to keep his beloved grandfather's homestead in the family, where it belonged, but now he saw it all slipping away. To consent to this would cripple him financially.

A sense of urgency galvanised his thoughts. You only get one precious moment which can change the course of your life forever. This was his moment. If he let it go now, he knew there would never be another.

Looking up, he saw them all anxiously waiting for his response.

A kind of madness took hold of him. Straightening his shoulders, he thanked Justin then turned to sweep his gaze across the sea of faces all intent on him; his eyes falling on the big man last. 'I accept your offer,' he said simply. 'One way or another, you will all get your money.'

There was a brief silence, then a cheer went up. The relief in the air was palpable.

The big man came over to Leonard and asked if he could

shake him by the hand. 'Farley would have been proud of you,' he said quietly. 'Good luck.'

~

The next day, as he boarded the liner which would take him home to England, Leonard wondered if he had done the right thing. Even now he wasn't sure how he might repay the debt he had inherited from his grandfather. Yet he had given his word. The money was pledged and somehow, he would find a way.

Once upon a time, the Farley Kemp holdings had been a thriving, lucrative business – and it could become so again. Especially if he was to bring Barney across the Atlantic. They worked well together, he and his Farm Manager. If anyone could help him rebuild the estate and restore the place to its former glory, it was Barney Davidson. And the thought of having Vicky close at hand was wonderful. He had dreaded saying goodbye to her.

With that in mind, Leonard locked his cabin door and made his way to the nearest bar, where he ordered a large whisky. 'I've earned it,' he told the barman. 'I've just taken the biggest gamble of my life!'

CHAPTER THIRTEEN

Having informed Patricia of the date he would return, Leonard half-expected her to be waiting for him when he disembarked at Liverpool. Unfortunately, she was nowhere to be seen, even though he lingered for almost an hour, walking up and down searching every avenue in case he should miss her.

Finally he hailed a taxi and, bitterly disappointed, travelled back alone. He knew the house would be clean and tidy, thanks to his daily woman, Mrs Riley, who ran the place and used Lucy Baker on a Saturday to do any extra jobs. But it would be cold and lonely, too.

Arriving at The Manse he paid the driver and went inside; where the warm, earthy aroma of fresh bread filled his nostrils and took him straight to the kitchen. 'Why, it's young Lucy!' He was astonished to see her, sleeves rolled up, taking a crusty-baked loaf out of the oven.

'Welcome home, Mr Maitland,' she said with a shy smile. 'Vicky offered to look after Jamie so I could nip in and make you some supper, after your long journey. There's mushroom soup to go with the bread. I didn't think you'd want anything too heavy, so late in the day. Oh, and I've lit a fire downstairs and one in your bedroom. I hope that's all right?' She looked anxious.

He smiled. 'It's more than all right – it's a wonderful welcome. Thank you, my dear, for being so very thoughtful.' More thoughtful than his so-called fiancée, he thought.

Lucy took off her pinny and went to get her coat and hat. 'Don't slice the bread while it's still warm,' she urged. 'It'll only squash up and you won't get a clean slice.'

'I'll let it cool,' he promised. 'Now go home and get some rest.' All he wanted was to be alone, put his feet up, eat from a tray and enjoy a strong drink. 'There's a chill in the air.' He held Lucy's coat open for her. 'It was cold in Boston, too.'

'Good night, Mr Maitland. It's good to see you back.' Lucy hoped she wasn't being too familiar. She was rather in awe of Leonard.

He smiled. 'It's lovely to be home,' he told her.

By ten o'clock that evening, Leonard had bathed and changed, eaten three slices of the best bread he had ever tasted, dipped into a sizeable bowl of hot, thick mushroom soup; the whole lot washed down by two cups of tea and a tot of best whisky.

God, it was good to be back by his own fireside. Yawning, he was thinking about going to bed when a moment later, he was taken by surprise when the door opened and in walked Patricia, done up in all her finery and looking especially beautiful.

Purring like a kitten she wrapped herself round him. 'You smell delicious,' she whispered, caressing him and deeply arousing him. 'I've missed you, my darling.'

Summoning all his courage, he drew away. 'Did you now?' he asked cynically. 'So, why did you forget to meet me at the docks?'

She gave a long, impatient sigh. 'I didn't forget,' she answered rather petulantly. 'It was just . . . well, I went shopping. I wanted to look my very best when you saw me. It got late, and by the time I reached the dock, you must have already left.'

'So, you would rather go shopping than come and meet me, is that it?'

Her expression hardened. '*No* – but does it really matter? I'm here now, aren't I?'

Having moved away when she saw he was angry, she now came at him again, her avaricious eyes appraising his body and her roving hands touching him in all the right spots. 'I'm really sorry.' She put her lips to his ears and softly blew. 'I've missed you . . . I want you so much.'

He wanted her too. All the while he had been in Boston he had wondered if he should end his engagement the minute he got home. But now, when she was close like this, and his need was pressing, he had little control. He was a man, with a man's hunger, and here she was, a beautiful woman, his fiancée, freely offering herself to him.

So, he took her hand and walked her to the foot of the stairs, where he swept her into his arms and carried her up to his bedroom, lit and warmed by the fire Lucy had set earlier.

He carried her inside and closed the door behind them.

And they did not come out until morning.

$\sim$

It was eight-thirty the next morning when he took Patricia home to her parents' grand house on the other side of Liverpool. 'I'll see you later,' she told him. 'We can talk more about your trip to Boston then. I'm sure Daddy will loan you all the money you need, then there will be no need to sell Overhill Farm. Or you could still sell it and start a different business – nothing to do with farming. I think that would be a good idea, don't you?'

'I've already said, I don't want you discussing my business with your father,' Leonard said tightly.

'Why ever not?'

'For reasons you would not understand.' This woman was suffocating him.

'All right, but I think you're being selfish.'

Dear God. 'Like you said, I'll see you later.' He couldn't trust himself to say anything else at that moment.

As he watched her go inside, he thought, The more you open your mouth, the more I realise we will never be suited.

At that moment in time, Leonard was not only concerned about his relationship with Patricia. There was Barney and his entire family to think of now. How would they take the news that the farm was being sold from under them? And what would Barney's answer be, when Leonard asked him to come with him to America? And even if Barney agreed, what of Vicky and the three children? Would they be prepared to leave behind everything they knew?

Only now when he was home, did Leonard come to realise how huge a step he was taking, giving up his life here, moving back to the States, taking up his grandfather's crumbling business and starting it again from scratch, already deep in debt.

In the end, for whatever reason, he was now embarking on a lonely, daunting journey.

~

Early the following morning, Leonard drove into Liverpool. As always, the city was a busy, vibrant place, despite the serious problems of poverty and unemployment.

When he found the address he was looking for, Leonard drew into the kerb and parked. A sign hanging above the offices read:

W.H. Brewer & Son
Land Agents

Leonard had dealt before with the tall, whiskery-faced man inside, who greeted him now with: 'Ah, good morning, Mr Maitland. How can I help you, sir?' He pulled out a chair in his office for Leonard to sit on.

Mr Brewer was always very polite, particularly with a man of Mr Maitland's admirable character. Moreover, Leonard was a good customer, having piece by piece expanded his landholding until it was now some 400 acres in total.

While shaking hands he informed Leonard, 'If you've come looking for land, I'm afraid there is absolutely nothing at the moment. Investing in land is being seen as a reliable option these days; we have it one minute and it's gone the next. Oh – and the prices are on the up and up all the while.'

Leonard could hardly conceal his delight. He had been basing his own valuation of the land on rather pessimistic calculations. 'This is good news for me,' he answered, 'because I'm here to sell my entire holding.'

The other man was visibly shocked. '*Everything? Are you sure?*' he asked. 'The farm and the house and outbuildings, too?'

'Everything,' Leonard confirmed, 'although I haven't yet decided what to do about my old gardener's cottage.'

'Really?' The agent was intrigued. 'From what I can recall, it's little more than a ruin?'

Leonard nodded. 'Well yes, it is, and I've done nothing to it since he's been left these past years. It's a tiny place, with only one bedroom, and a scullery a man can hardly turn about in. I'm sorry to say it's been left to the elements; the little garden is shamefully overgrown, and the whole place is somewhat tumbledown. But I may have a mind to hang on to it so I'd appreciate it if you would exclude it from the sale.'

'What about Barney Davidson's cottage?' The agent knew how Leonard valued Barney and his sons.

'Hopefully, he won't be needing the cottage,' came the reply. 'I have other, more rewarding plans for him and his family.'

Thoughtfully, Mr Brewer stroked his finger along his beard. 'I should think we could get a substantial amount for that lot,' came the welcome answer. 'In fact, I could sell it tomorrow to a gentleman who has been searching for a property such as yours. But it would be best if we trod extra carefully on this one,' he said sagely. 'Of course I shall inform the gentleman straight away, but I will also inform some of my other clients, who might be interested in acquiring smaller parcels of land rather than the whole.'

Leonard knew only too well that buyers' ambitions were always dictated by the amount of capital they could raise. He thought of his own circumstances. If he had been able to pay off his grandfather's debts without selling his own land, he would not be in this office today.

'Sometimes, for whatever reason, a man may have more need of a smaller parcel of land,' the agent went on. 'But this can work well in our favour.'

He explained. 'We could sell off say, three hundred acres either in a single lot, or if you preferred, we could separate it into smaller units. That would leave one hundred acres with the house – which is a small farm in itself. This way, the sale will attract more money, or at the very least it will create competition, which will return a far more handsome price than if we went straight to the gentleman in question and sold him the entire holding.'

Leonard liked the idea. 'Let them fight it out between them – is that what you're saying?'

The Land Agent's smile was positively wicked. 'Of course, let them fight it out. And why not?'

So they got down to facts and figures, and when the meeting was over, Leonard dared to hope that if all went well, he might even be able to pay the US creditors every single dollar they were owed.

With that in mind, he got back into his car and drove straight to Overhill Farm, where he found Vicky standing on a box, singing to herself and cleaning the kitchen windows. When he saw her, he slowed down, his mood brightening even further at the sight of the small, familiar figure, her long silken hair gently lifted by the cool breeze. And now as she stretched on tiptoe to reach the upper part of the panes, his eyes were drawn to her slim, shapely ankles and calves. 'You're a lucky man, Barney Davidson,' he whispered, and now, as she turned to look straight at him, his heart did a dance inside his chest so he could hardly breathe.

'Morning, Vicky.' His voice gave nothing away as he climbed out of the car and went towards her. 'I wonder if I might have a word with Barney. Is he around?'

'Sorry, Mr Maitland, he's out in Top Field,' she said, preparing to clamber off the box. She was taken by surprise when Leonard reached his hands round her waist and lifted her down without effort. 'He's checking the sheep,' she said, her face flushing pink. 'I can fetch him if you like?'

'No, it's all right,' Leonard said. 'Best not disturb him at his work. What I have to say can wait until this evening.'

'Are you sure? It won't take above five minutes for me to fetch him. I can settle you with a cup of tea before I go?' Vicky's curiosity was heightened; it wasn't often the boss came down here to talk in the middle of the day.

'No, no,' he told her. 'It's fine. But will you please tell him I called by, and that I have business to discuss with him.' He paused, not wanting to alarm her. 'If you wouldn't mind,

Vicky, I'd like you to be there as well. In fact, what I have to say might concern all of you.'

Seeing her expression of concern, he quickly added, 'I'd rather not discuss it now, but I'll be here at about eight. Will you have finished your evening meal by then?'

'Well, yes, but – what is it, Mr Maitland? What's wrong? It all seems very serious.'

'You're not to worry,' he said gently. 'We'll talk this evening, then. Goodbye for now.' Quickly, before she could ask any more questions, he climbed into the car and drove off, leaving Vicky in a quandary.

'Is everything all right?' Lucy had seen Leonard leave and now, with Vicky seeming deep in thought, her happy singing silenced and the window-cloth hanging forgotten in her hand, she grew alarmed.

'He told me not to worry,' Vicky answered, 'but it's odd all the same.' She raised her gaze to Lucy. 'Mr Maitland says he has business to discuss with me and Barney.' Picking up her bucket she dumped the cloth in it and walked to the kitchen door. 'It all seems very serious to me,' she told Lucy. 'He's coming back tonight, after we've had our supper.'

'Crikey!' Lucy had become as close to this family as if she was born to it, and what affected them, was bound to affect her. 'What d'you reckon it could be, to fetch him out here at this time of day? And you say he's coming back again tonight . . .'

There was something not right here, Lucy thought. Something was brewing and like Vicky she, too, was afraid.

Her friend began pacing the kitchen floor. 'I'm not sure what to do, Lucy,' she said. 'Should I go and tell Barney now, or should I simply get on with my work and tell him when he comes home?'

'Do you want my opinion?' Lucy asked.

'Of course!'

'Do what you just said – wait till Barney gets home. Let's have a cup of tea and a sandwich like we allus do at this time of day, then we'll get on with our work and leave Barney to do the same. Tell him tonight, but not until after he's had his dinner, because if you tell him before, he'll be so worried he won't eat.'

'You're right, lass,' Vicky agreed. 'That's what we'll do.'

While Lucy went to fetch Jamie from his nap, Vicky put the kettle on. Dear God, was there some sort of trouble in store? Just now, when everything was going so well, she prayed their lives were not about to be disrupted.

In the sitting room, where Lucy was lifting the child from the pram, she had that same sense of dread. 'Mr Maitland's been here,' she told little Jamie. 'It seems he's got business to discuss with Barney and Vicky. I can't imagine what it could be, but it's important enough for him to come back and talk with them tonight.' She tutted. 'I just hope it isn't bad news.'

She kissed his head and sat him on the little enamel potty for a minute or two chiding herself for thinking the worst. For all she knew, it might even be good news. And keeping that in mind, she took the little boy to join Vicky, who was just laying the table for the three of them.

As she dragged the high chair across to the table, Lucy commented, 'Happen Mr Maitland is right and you shouldn't worry. I mean, it might be good news he's bringing to-night. There's no reason why it should be anything bad, is there?'

'No, there isn't!' Vicky's face lit in a smile. 'You could be right, lass – it might be good news.' The woman was glad of Lucy's encouraging words. 'It could be something to do with buying another tractor, mebbe, or he might even be sending in the workmen to put a new roof on this place. Lord knows, it's been leaking long enough.' She gave a comical little laugh. 'Barney's repaired it so many times it's beginning to look like a patchwork quilt.'

Going off to the scullery, she reappeared with a tray containing a pot of tea and four chunky ham-and-chutney sandwiches, together with a dish of soup for the child and an apple.

Vicky took a hearty bite out of her sandwich. She chatted and laughed with the little boy and his mother, but all the while at the back of her mind was Leonard's visit.

Lucy liked to think the best.

Vicky thought the worst.

She also thought of that unexpected moment when their employer had put his hands round her waist and lifted her effortlessly to the ground . . . 'Leonard Maitland is a kind man,' she told Lucy now, unable to leave the subject for long. 'I can't imagine he's about to bring us bad news.'

'Huh!' Lucy spooned a helping of soup into her son's mouth. 'It's that woman he's chosen to be his wife who's the bad news. The poor man came all the way back from his long journey, and there wasn't anyone with him. Don't you think she should have met him off his ship? No, if you ask me, he'll have a life of hell if he ever puts a ring on that one's finger.'

'I hope not,' Vicky answered quietly. 'He's such a lovely man, he deserves a good marriage.'

'Like you and your Barney,' Lucy said. 'But not every marriage can be as good as yours, you know.'

'I've been fortunate,' Vicky said wistfully. 'Oh Lucy, I love him so much! I don't know what I'd do without him. God did a wonderful thing, when He brought me and my Barney together.'

Not for the first time, Lucy wondered if she would ever know that same kind of love. 'I wonder what Edward Trent is doing now?' she said.

'Do you care?' Vicky was surprised to hear the girl mention that man's name.

Lucy shook her head. 'No. To tell you the truth, I don't know how I could ever have thought I loved him in the first place.'

'Well, at least he gave you little Jamie.' Vicky had come to love the child as if he was her own.

Lucy gazed fondly at her son. 'I know it's a sad thing to say, but I hope he grows up, never knowing his father.'

Vicky saw the bitterness in Lucy's face and deliberately changed the subject. 'Uh-oh – look at the time,' she said. 'Let's finish the chores, and after that, you and young James should get yourselves home before it starts getting dark. Besides, you must be bone-tired. What with cleaning all the upstairs windows and changing every bed in the house, you've done two days' work in one. I honestly don't know how I ever managed before you came to join us. Thank you, love.'

'Are you sure?' It was true – Lucy *was* exhausted and there was nothing she wanted more right now than to go home for a well-earned rest. However, seeing how worried Vicky was, she offered, 'I don't mind staying to help prepare the evening meal. I'm sure Barney or one of the boys would run me home.'

Vicky shook her head. 'Don't think I'm not grateful,' she told Lucy, 'but I'm best off working. By the time I've got the supper ready, Barney should be home. Soonever he's eaten, I'll tell him how Mr Maitland's coming by to visit.'

As she helped clear away the crockery, she added, almost to herself, 'I can't wait to know what business he has that he couldn't discuss with me – especially as he said he wants me there when he talks with Barney.'

A short time later, Lucy left, holding the little boy by his hand. It wasn't far to walk back to the cottage. She often left the pram at Overhill Farm. 'I hope everything goes all right,' she told Vicky. 'If you need me, you know where I am.'

~

At eight-thirty, Mr Maitland arrived. Welcoming him into the house, Barney took him straight through to the sitting room. 'Vicky tells me that this matter you need to talk through might affect us all.'

'That's right, Barney.' Leonard glanced round the room. 'Your children not here then?'

Barney explained, 'My sons have gone to meet friends in Liverpool and Susie is taking extra tuition on the hat-making. There is no need for them to be here. If you're bringing bad news, it's best that me and Vicky know first. That way we can talk to the young 'uns ourselves.'

'I understand.' Leonard had no way of knowing how all this might affect Barney's children. Even if Barney accepted his offer, the children might not.

'You'd best sit down.' Barney gestured to the armchair, while he and Vicky sat side-by-side on the sofa. 'I might tell you, I've been on pins since Vicky told me.'

Leonard sat down. He looked at the pair of them seated there, fine, kind-hearted people, hardworking as the day was long, and his heart sank within him. 'I have to tell you both . . .' he began. Then: 'This has not been the easiest day of my life.'

Barney looked him in the eye. 'So, it *is* bad news then?'

'I suppose it all depends on how you see it.' Leonard chose his words carefully as he went on, 'I've come here tonight, firstly to explain the outcome of my trip to Boston, and secondly, to ask something of you both.'

He took a deep invigorating breath. 'What I have to tell you has been playing on my mind these past weeks. It will be a relief to have it out in the open. I'm not like you, Barney,' he said kindly. 'I've always struggled to make friends.' He smiled shyly. 'In fact, I'd go so far as to say that you two are the nearest to friends that I've got. I have no family – no wife or children to talk things over with, so when I have problems, they often weigh heavy on my mind.'

When Barney seemed about to speak, he gestured for him to stop. 'I don't want you to say anything just yet, Barney. As you already know, I was summoned to Boston in order to learn the terms and conditions of my grandfather's Will, and to tie up any loose ends out there.'

He looked away momentarily as though in shame, and went on in a low voice: 'It was a great shock for me to learn that my grandfather had taken up gambling and was up to his neck in debt when he died, with all his land and properties on the point of being sold from under him.'

At the gasp of disbelief from Barney and Vicky, he got swiftly to the point. 'It means two things,' he said, 'and each of them will affect you and your family, in at least one way that I can see.'

He went on in great detail, telling them how it had all come about, how he had worked every waking moment to save what he could. There had been sacrifices made, and his own future, as well as theirs, was now hanging in the balance. 'I'm sorry to tell you that I have no option but to sell both The Manse and Overhill Farm.' There was no other way to say it but straight out.

Rendered speechless by the news, Barney stood up and with haggard eyes, he looked first at Leonard, and then at Vicky. His face white as chalk, he reached out for his wife's hand. Deeply concerned, she could only leave it to the men and hope they might salvage something worthwhile from this nightmare.

Leonard would have given almost anything to remove the look of devastation on Barney's face. 'If there had been any other way, you know I would have taken it,' he said helplessly, and wondered if there had been any kinder way he could have broken the news.

He plunged on. 'I have many business contacts in the farming world, and I'm sure I can get you a place locally, if it's what you want. Oh, I know it will never be the same because you've been here all these years, but you only have to say the word and I'll find something – you know I will.'

Barney nodded. 'Thank you for that,' he said quietly, 'but you're right – it's small compensation. I've been here so long, it's as if I've lived here all my life. My children have never known anything else.'

Leonard had one more thing to say before he left. 'There is one other option . . .'

Pre-empting his words, Barney interrupted, 'If you're offering me first refusal of the farm, there is no way on God's earth I could ever buy it. I'm not a man of money, I never have been. I've lived content year to year, raising my family and tending the land—'

Leonard stopped him. 'It's not that, Barney. I know you haven't the means to buy this farm, otherwise it would be yours. What I'm asking of you now needs even more commitment from you, and your family.'

'What do you mean?' Barney was puzzled. 'What is it you're asking?'

Leonard glanced at Vicky; sad-faced and twining her fingers together in her lap, she was obviously deeply disturbed by events.

'I've managed to save my grandfather's estate,' he began. 'It took some doing and I've never been in so much debt in my entire life, but I couldn't let it go without doing my damnedest to keep it.'

'I'm pleased for you, Mr Maitland.' Barney was magnanimous in his own disappointment. 'I know how much you loved that place. You've talked about it that many times, I almost feel I know it myself.'

'That's excellent!' Barney's remarks took Leonard naturally into his proposition. 'How would you like to see it, Barney – you and your family?' He looked again at Vicky, who was intent on his every word.

While Barney was momentarily taken aback, it was she who replied. 'What exactly do you mean?'

In tender, persuasive tones he told her what he had in mind. 'It's my dearest wish for all of you to come with me. I would like Barney and your sons to help me run the farm, and for yourself to take charge of the house. As for young Susie, there are any number of milliners in Boston – it's a very smart place – who will teach her the trade, if that's what she really wants.'

With the two of them shocked into silence, he leaned forward, hands on his knees and his eyes pleading with them each in turn. 'Barney . . . Vicky, please think about it. It would mean so much to me, if you would agree.'

When Barney spoke now, it was with a surge of emotion that trembled in his voice. 'But why?' he asked. 'Why would you want me and my family, when you could employ the best that money could buy?'

In Barney's face, Leonard could see the tiniest glimmer of hope. 'Oh Barney, don't you know that *you're* the best there is! That's why I want you – because I know the calibre of you, and I know that the homestead would be in good hands.'

He grew tremendously excited. 'Not only would I be taking the very best, but I'd be taking with me people I consider to be my friends . . . good people whom I've known for many a year.' He actually laughed out loud. 'Oh, you can't imagine what it's like over there. In Massachusetts, there's so much sky, you think it goes on forever! And the land . . . You could ride for half a day before you reach its borders. Boston itself is the capital – three hundred years old and full of history. Not everything in America is like Charlie Chaplin, you know!' He chuckled merrily.

By now he was on his feet. 'Say you'll come. Please, talk to your family. Tell them how it will be. You'll have a house twice the size of this one, and a garden to lose yourself in. There's an orchard – yes, it's overgrown now, but we'll soon get it round. Please! Say you'll accept this challenge. I won't let you down, and if after a while you're not happy there, I'll pay for you to come back, *and* I'll find you a house and work into the bargain. What d'you say? Barney . . . Vicky? Will you come?'

Suddenly Barney was laughing; the look of joy on Vicky's face urged him on. A moment later he was shaking Leonard by the hand. 'If the family are all in agreement, then our answer is yes, oh YES!' In the space of a moment his despair was replaced by a sense of joy.

In the excitement that followed, Vicky kissed Barney and then she kissed Leonard, and he was overjoyed.

'Talk to your sons and Susie,' he said. 'Tell them how wonderful a life it will be.'

Barney promised he would. 'Such an opportunity!' he declared. 'A new start – a new life. I can't thank you enough,' he told Leonard. 'It's the most amazing thing!'

A short time later, Leonard hurried away to collect Patricia. Behind him he could hear the Davidsons' old phonograph belting out some Dixieland jazz, and through the window as he drove off, he saw Barney take Vicky into his arms and wing her across the room. He smiled for them, the smile fading as he thought ahead to his meeting with his fiancée. Would it ever be like that with him and Patricia?

In subdued mood, he answered his own question: no. He couldn't see it somehow.

Screeching the car to a halt, he did a three-point turn and took the lane that would lead him home.

When he arrived at The Manse, he was surprised to find Patricia already there, emerging from a taxi. Once inside the house, she turned to him and said, 'Look here, Lenny. I've decided I can't come with you to America, so if you want me for your wife, you will just have to forget your foolhardy plan.'

'And is your mind absolutely made up?' he asked quietly.

'It is.'

'Then you don't give me any choice, Patricia.'

'What's that supposed to mean?'

'It means our engagement is over. I know now that we can never make a future together.'

'You can't say that! You're not thinking straight.'

When he continued to stand his ground, even when she nuzzled him and tried her usual wiles, she took a step back and eyed him with suspicion. 'There's another woman, isn't there?' Her eyeballs stood out like two glittering marbles. 'You've been cheating on me. American, is she? Met her over there, did you?' With every accusation her voice rose until now it was at screaming pitch.

'There is no other woman,' he answered steadily. 'Like I said, I can no longer see us in a future together. We want different things, Pat. That's the truth of it.'

In a swift and spiteful move that caught him unawares, she brought her hand across his face, leaving her fingernail marks down the side of his cheek. 'YOU BASTARD!' Still spitting obscenities, she stormed down the steps and marched off at breakneck speed towards the village.

Breathing a deep sigh of relief, Leonard felt as though a great burden was lifted from his shoulders. 'I'm truly sorry it turned out this way,' he muttered after her; and he really was.

Softly, he repeated her angry words. 'There's another woman, isn't there?' He smiled. 'Yes, Patricia, there is another woman. But she isn't American. In fact, she's only an arm's reach from here.'

He knew now, without any doubt, that he was head over heels in love with Vicky. However, just as the relationship between himself and Patricia could never evolve, nor could the one between himself and Vicky – but for very different reasons.

PART THREE

~

Onset of Winter, 1930

A Choice for Barney

CHAPTER FOURTEEN

AFTER THEIR PARENTS' euphoria, the Davidson children reacted to Leonard's offer in different ways.

'I'd rather stay here,' Susie said, in confrontational mood.

'Look, love, I've already told you. We *can't* stay here,' Barney explained for the third time. 'Mr Maitland has been forced to sell this farm to help pay off his grandfather's debts.'

'Listen to your father, sweetheart.' Vicky despaired. 'Whether we like it or not, this farm is being sold. It isn't Mr Maitland's fault, and it isn't our fault. It's the circumstances we all find ourselves in. We would all love to stay here, but we can't, and so we have to accept things the way they are.'

Unlike Susie, Thomas was thrilled at the news. 'You're being right selfish,' he told his younger sister now. 'The fact is, we're left with three choices. Either we take work in the Liverpool area, or we move away and hope something turns up that will suit everybody. Or we accept Mr Maitland's generous offer and be thankful. Think about it, Susie! AMERICA! There are many girls your age who would give their right arm for the chance we've been offered!'

'They can have it then!' Kicking the rug at her feet, Susie folded her arms and slumped into a chair. 'Because I don't want to go.'

Gesturing for the others to leave the room, Barney went and sat on the arm of her chair. 'What is it that worries you?' he asked gently. 'Is it because you'll be leaving your friends behind? If it is, you can always keep in touch. You can write to each other and later, maybe, they can even come and visit.'

'How can they?' Now the tears were falling. 'America is the other side of the world!'

'Naw . . . you've got that wrong, pet.' Sliding his arm round her shoulders, he drew her close. 'I won't deny it is a long way,' he coaxed, 'but it's not the end of the world. Look at Mr Maitland – he's gone over and come back twice this year, hasn't he?'

Susie looked up, her eyes swimming with tears. 'I'm frightened, Daddy.'

It cut him to the quick to see his daughter upset like this. 'There's nothing to be frightened of.' Barney put his hand under her chin and raised her face to his. 'Do you think me and your mammy would want to take you, if we thought you'd come to any harm?' He smiled his reassurance. 'Trust me, we'll take good care of you, my darling.'

Kissing the top of her head, he drew her closer. 'When you've seen the ships going away, how many times have you said to me that you'd love to be on one of them? Well, now you can!'

Looking up, she gave a shaky smile. 'I didn't think it could ever really happen.'

'Well, now it has. Look, we can sail off to America and try to make a new life, and if it doesn't work out, Mr Maitland has promised to pay our fare back. But we have to give it a chance, because everybody is so excited to be going, and like Thomas said, it's a wonderful, once-in-a-lifetime opportunity. And later, when we've saved enough money, we can come back for a visit. Would you like that?' With the tip of his finger he wiped away the tears that quivered on the end of her lashes.

'I think so.' At last a brighter smile. 'Yes, Daddy, I'd like that.'

Barney nodded. 'Then that's what we'll aim for – saving enough money between us to come back for a visit.'

'Do you promise?'

He hesitated, that small grain of dark instinct holding him back. 'I promise I'll do my very best.'

'So will I,' she said eagerly. 'You said Mr Maitland told you I could get work with one of the hat-shops, and they would teach me the trade?'

'Yes. That's what the man said all right.' Barney was relieved to see a glimmer of enthusiasm. It would break his heart to force her into something that made her desperately unhappy.

'Maybe one day, I might have my own shop in Boston?'

Barney laughed. 'You might at that,' he said. 'Work hard and save, and who knows what the future holds?' For *all* of us, he added silently. He only hoped his health would hold up through the trials and thrills that lay ahead.

Having placed herself where they could not see her, Vicky watched from the doorway. Deeply moved by Barney's understanding of his daughter's fears she had wiped away a tear or two, but now that she could see how Barney had somehow managed to dispel Susie's fears, she crept quietly away.

Once Susie had run off to tell Vicky how she meant to have her own shop in America, Barney let himself slide down into the chair, where for a time he sat, lost in thought and deeply disturbed. Giving a long, shivering sigh, he instinctively placed a hand on his heart. 'No, Susie lass, none of us knows what the future holds.' A dark premonition rippled through his soul.

He was startled when his wife came rushing in. 'Barney

Davidson, you could charm the birds right out of the trees!'
She threw herself into his lap. 'One minute she's refusing
to go, and now she's full of dreams. Somehow she's got the
idea into her head that she's going to own a string of shops,
right across America!'

Barney smiled contentedly. 'Let her dream,' he murmured, drawing her into his embrace. 'If we don't have
dreams, how can they ever come true?' His own dream had
come true, the day he met this darling woman.

Content to be silent, husband and wife sat awhile together.
It was a moment of quietness in a love that was both deep
and fulfilling; one of those rare and precious moments that
each of them would cherish to the end of their days.

~

The following morning, when Lucy was told the news by an
emotional Vicky, she didn't know whether to be thrilled for
the Davidsons, or sad for herself. 'It's a wonderful opportunity,' she said, suppressing her fears. 'You must go, Vicky,
you and Barney, and the family.'

While Vicky was explaining how it all came about, Barney
strolled into the kitchen. 'Hello, Lucy, love. Vicky's told you
then?' He had been concerned as to how the young woman
might take the news.

She ran to hug him. 'I'm so excited for you!' she told him
sincerely. 'But I'll miss you all so very much.' The tears were
close but she would not let them be seen, not now, not
when these good folk were so looking forward to their new
adventure. 'Whatever will I do without you?' At the back of
her mind she couldn't help but wonder where she and her
boy might live.

'We'll miss you too – dreadfully.' Vicky looked at Jamie
and her lips quivered. She hugged him, then opened the

kitchen cupboard so he could sit and play with the saucepans and wooden spoons.

'Well, I'll tell you one thing, Lucy girl.' Barney sat her down. 'You won't need to worry about being out of work. I've just come from giving our answer to the boss, and I've spoken to him about you. He says you'll have work with whoever buys the farm, he'll make sure it's written into the contract of sale.'

It was a great relief to Lucy. 'Oh Barney, how can I ever thank you?' She felt quite weak at the knees. Without a job and a home, she and Jamie would be in dire straits.

'Don't thank me,' he protested. 'Thank the boss, and thank the fella who's buying the farm. It's good news all round. The Land Agent has already been out this morning to tell him he's got a buyer, a gent who's been looking for such a property as this, and because he means to grab this place afore anybody else, and prevent it being split up and sold off he's offered fifty guineas above the asking price.'

Vicky was amazed. 'Good Lord! And did Mr Maitland accept it?'

'He most certainly did.' He gave an aside wink to Vicky, who was thrilled to hear Lucy would not be put out of work. 'What's more . . .' Barney's smile grew wider as he looked at the two women in turn, '. . . Mr Maitland says Lucy can stay in the cottage,' he told them, '. . . it's because he's got such a good price, and I'm to tell you straight off, he's not selling the cottage with the farm. Because it's such a tiny place with so much that needs doing, it has little or no value so neither Mr Maitland nor the agent could see it as making any difference to the value of the overall holding. It's all been agreed.'

Unable to keep the news any longer, he blurted it out with a shout of triumph. 'It's *yours*, Lucy girl!' he laughed with the sheer joy of it.

He drew in a long breath and blowing it out through his

nose he took hold of Lucy by the shoulders, his voice lower, more intimate. 'Now then, what have you to say to that, eh?'

For the moment Lucy could say nothing because not only had the news rocked her to the roots, but she was completely lost for words.

Instead she stared at Barney with big shocked eyes, her lips quivering, and her heart pounding ten to the dozen. 'I can't . . . believe it,' the words stumbled out. 'The cottage . . . is it really *mine?*'

'That's right, Lucy girl . . . it's yours. Mr Maitland says to tell you he'll be along to see you shortly, and that you're not to worry, because everything will be done legal.'

'This calls for another celebration!' Rushing to the cupboard, Vicky took out the best glasses and a bottle of her homemade wine.

Barney raised his glass. 'To our new life – and to Lucy, our dear friend who, along with young Jamie here, will never again be without a roof over her head.'

It was the most bitter-sweet emotion for Lucy. She found it hard to believe her own good fortune, but while she was thanking the Good Lord, she paused again to think of how it would be when Barney and his family were gone.

Even in the midst of her joy, the thought of losing them forever was a sad, lonely thought.

~

'Are you all right, Barney?' It was two o'clock in the morning when Vicky woke to find herself alone in bed. Half-asleep and bleary-eyed she rolled sideways, looking towards the window, where Barney's shadowy figure was just visible in the dim light. 'What's wrong, pet, can't you sleep?'

Still breathless from the chest pains which had woken him, Barney sshed her. 'Go back to sleep, love.'

'I can't. Not until you come back into bed.'

In the past weeks, Barney had learned to hide his pain and put on a brave face; it had become like second nature to him. Taking a deep breath, he painted on a smile and managing the few paces to the bed, he climbed in. 'Now will you go to sleep?' He wriggled down the bed, avoiding touching her, having stood at the window for some time, he had become chilled.

Instinctively, she turned and wrapped her arm around the girth of his belly. 'Brrr!' she shivered. 'You're freezing! How long have you been stood there at the window?'

'Not long,' he lied. 'Now go to sleep.'

Worry marbled her voice. 'Are you all right?'

'I'm fine.'

'Are you worried about moving to Boston? Is that what woke you?'

'No. I think it was a touch of indigestion.' Before she could protest, he added, 'I ate a bite from a cooking apple, and you know how sour they are.'

'You shouldn't eat them, then!'

'I know, but they looked so tempting.'

There was a groan. 'Barney Davidson, will you never learn?'

'Go to sleep now, Vicky. It's only three a.m.'

'And are you really not worried about moving to Boston?'

'No, why should I be?'

'No reason. I just wondered, that's all.'

'Are *you* worried, sweetheart? You can tell me if you are.'

There came a sigh. 'I would tell you if I was worried, but I'm not. To tell you the truth, I'm really excited! Oh, I know there are things and people here that I'll miss, but who wouldn't look forward to a brand new start? And like you said, it's not the end of the world. Oh Barney! It will be such an adventure, and the children are all looking forward to a new life there . . . even our Susie, thanks to you.' She gave him a squeeze. 'You're such an understanding father, Barney. That little chat you had with her did all the good in the world.'

In that quiet, opportune moment Barney might have confided in her; he might have confessed how he had been suffering such pain of late, and how sometimes he could hardly stand up straight for the cramp in his chest. But when he turned to her, Vicky had rolled over onto her back and was fast asleep.

Barney did not sleep though. Instead he waited a while, then he slipped out of bed again and slumped into the chair, where he remained head in hands and his heart pounding, until the sun peeped over the horizon, then he got quietly back into bed.

Even then he did not sleep, but planned his day. This morning, he had to call in on Adam. He had promised to lend his old pal a helping hand with the tractor he was working on. Afterwards, he would go and see Dr Lucas and tell him his troubles. Who knows? he thought hopefully. It might even turn out that he was worrying about nothing at all.

Finally he slipped into a shallow, unsettled slumber, where he dreamed of ships sailing away and his family always just out of reach, and when he woke with a start, Vicky was already out of bed and dressing. 'Wake up, Sleepyhead,' she teased him. 'It's time to start the day.'

As she went out of the room, she called over her shoulder, 'By the time you get downstairs, I'll have the ham and eggs on your plate ready and waiting.'

As always, Vicky was as good as her word.

Twenty minutes later, the whole family was tucking into one of Vicky's renowned and substantial cooked breakfasts.

Thankfully, the endless chatter pushed Barney's worries to the back of his mind; while enjoying a generous helping of Vicky's speciality, he took a discreet look around the table. There were Ronnie and Thomas, arguing as usual, this time about which one of them might beat the other in a horse-race. 'You're even frightened to jump the brook at the narrow end,' Ronnie tormented his brother, 'but not me! I'm not afraid to jump my horse over anything.'

'That's only because you've got the best horse,' his brother replied. 'You ride the mare, and she has the heart of a lion. You know how scared of water the stallion is.'

Ronnie sniggered. 'It's not the stallion that's scared, it's you!'

Thomas put down his knife and fork. 'Right, little brother! What about a race – across the wide end of the brook and up to the far end of Down Field?'

'What? Not likely! You've got to be out of your mind. Down Field is full of potholes.'

Whereupon Vicky cautioned them, and the subject was dropped.

Barney loved family mealtimes, when everyone sat down together and talked, when laughter and noise and arguments happened, and you felt as though you belonged to something very special.

He watched Vicky forking the two extra ham slices onto Ronnie's plate and smiled to himself. She was the bedrock of this family. She was his first reason for living.

His gaze wandered to Susie, and his smile became a burst of laughter. 'What in God's name is that on your head?'

'She thinks it's about to rain,' Ronnie teased.

'No!' Thomas had another idea. 'She's worried the ceiling might fall in, that's what it is.'

Indignant, Susie defended her new creation. 'It's my new design,' she explained. 'Miss Dandy said I should take home this material and make a hat, the like of which has never been seen before.'

'Is that so?' Trying his damnedest not to laugh, Barney looked at the hat; it was a sickly green, with a white feather sticking out of the top and a brim so wide that Susie's little face was almost hidden. He tried to think of something constructive to say, and came out with: 'Well, *I've* never seen anything like it before, and I don't suppose anyone else has.'

'So do you think she'll be pleased?'

'Well . . .' He huffed and puffed, and didn't know quite what to say. 'I just think she'll be amazed!'

'Flabbergasted, more like!' Ronnie commented.

'You've done well.' As always, Thomas was supportive. 'Not everyone could make a hat like that.'

Suddenly Vicky was rocking in her chair, helpless with laughter, tears running down her face. 'Oh, darling girl.' She couldn't speak for laughing. 'It's the most comical hat I've ever seen.'

Open-mouthed, everyone stared at her. 'MUM!' Thomas was shocked. Barney could hardly believe his eyes and Susie was close to tears. Ronnie, however, like his mammy could see the humour in what was the worst example of hat-making there could ever be. His face began to crumple and then he hooted and now he was laughing so hard he was bent double over the table.

'You're horrible!' Hurt, Susie stared from one to the other. 'It took me half the night to make this!' But in that moment when she got up to storm off, the hat fell over her eyes and she couldn't see where she was going.

In a moment the place was in uproar, with everyone shrieking with laughter; and now even Susie saw the funny side. 'I bet you lot couldn't make a hat like this!' she spluttered, and they all agreed wholeheartedly.

The meal ended as always, with good humour, and a short discussion as to what part each man would play in the day's labours. 'Right! I'll leave you to it then,' Barney said. As he went out, Lucy came in. 'Morning, lass.' Like the rest of the Davidson clan, he had a real soft spot for her.

'Morning, Barney!' Before Lucy had even got her coat off, Vicky had poured her a cup of tea and was already taking Jamie's coat and leggings off.

Barney gave Lucy a cheery parting wink and went merrily on his way, while behind him, Susie lost no time in telling Lucy how cruel they had all been about her beloved hat.

∼

Taking the horse and cart, Barney went to Casey's Farm by way of the back lanes. He had arranged to meet Adam there, to help him repair the tractor. A small, nondescript place, the farm was situated some three miles away.

As they ambled along, Barney talked to the old shire-horse as usual. 'Don't you go taking off at a gallop!' he warned him, even though at thirty years old, the elderly horse did not have a gallop left in him. Content to be with his master, he pricked up his ears and listened to what Barney had to say, and understood not a single word.

On approaching the track that led to Casey's Farm, Barney spied his friend about to slide under the tractor. 'Adam, hang on a minute!' he bawled. When the little man appeared not to have heard him, he shouted again, this time louder. 'ADAM! WAIT A MINUTE!'

This time, Adam heard. Scrambling to his feet, he waited for Barney to bring the horse and cart to a halt. 'You're late,' he grumbled. 'I expected you half an hour since.'

Barney jumped down from the cart. 'What the devil d'you think you're doing! You know how dangerous it is to be getting underneath a tractor without anyone else about.'

'Old Casey needs this oil leak plugged before he can

use the tractor,' Adam explained. 'And being as he's got mountains o' stuff to shift before the weather turns, he needs it right now.'

'In that case, first we'll get it jacked up proper, afore somebody gets hurt. If we get a move on, it shouldn't take above an hour. Besides, I've an appointment this morning and I don't want to be late.'

They completed the task within the hour and now, all that was left was for Adam to tidy away the tools and such. 'Leave it to me now, Barney. I'll finish up later, after you've gone off to your appointment,' Adam told him. 'The old fella's left the kitchen open for us to get a drink and a wash, so we'll away in, eh?' He led the way. 'I appreciate you helping me out on this one,' he said as they went along. 'I'd never have done it on my own.'

'It's no trouble.' These two were always there for each other, and it had been that way for many years. 'That's what friends are for.'

Washed and thirsty, Barney sat himself at the table while Adam mashed the tea.

'You look tired, matey.' Adam put the teapot on the table, together with a plate of sandwiches. 'Mrs Casey made these afore she went to the shops,' he explained. 'The Caseys are not a bad old couple, but if you ask me, it's time he called it a day. He doesn't walk so good these days, and his sight isn't what it was, but he still refuses to retire gracefully.' Seating himself in the chair, he passed the bowl of sugar to Barney. 'He's much like you – work is his life. I dare say he'll not stop till he drops!'

When Barney seemed to be deep in thought, his friend delivered a torrent of questions. 'What's wrong? Didn't you sleep well? Are you worrying about the move – is that it?'

Curious, he studied Barney's face and thought he had never seen him so worried. 'You've changed your mind about going and you don't know how to tell them. I'm right, aren't I? You don't want to go after all?'

Barney smiled. 'You're so wrong, Adam.' Unbeknownst to anyone, Barney had a drastic plan, and though it would shatter his life, Barney believed in his heart that it was the best option for his family. 'Think about it,' he urged. 'I have the most wonderful wife a man could ever hope for, a daughter who already has ambitions, and two fine sons with farming in their blood, but what is there here for them?'

'The same as what there's allus been.' Adam was a simple man with simple means. It didn't take much to make him happy; a good friend, a day's honest work, his own little place to come home to, and a warm smile from Lucy . . . though there wasn't a waking minute, when he didn't wish it could be more.

Unlike Barney, he had no family to rely on him, and so he did not have the same responsibilities, whereas Barney's family was his entire world. There was no doubt in anyone's mind but that he would lay down his life for them.

'It's a hard cruel world out there,' Barney replied. 'England is beautiful. It's our home and we love it, we always will. But everybody knows the bigger opportunities are out there in America.' Barney's instincts told him that his children would make it big in America.

He smiled, a painful, wistful smile that betrayed his own regret at not being able to share in his beloved family's once-in-a-lifetime adventure. 'I can see it all now,' he murmured. 'My two boys, riding across their own land . . . with my Vicky watching from the house . . .' He looked up, the pride alive in his face. 'Oh, Adam! I know they can do it. Given the opportunity, I just know they'll grasp it with both hands.' His excitement heightened. 'I can see it! I can feel it in my bones!'

'I know you want the best for them, Barney, and so you

should . . .' Adam had a gut feeling there was something going on in Barney's mind, something other than what he was telling. 'But, don't you think it's a big step to take? Uprooting yourselves to sail away to a strange land when there's always a chance they might make it good here?'

Barney slowly shook his head. 'I've worked hard all my life,' he answered sombrely. 'I've brought scrubland back to life, I've toiled every godsent hour until my hands bled and my knuckles were raw. I've sown the seeds and reaped the harvest, but nothing was mine. I did everything a man could be asked, but I never made enough money to buy even a square foot of land to call my own . . . to look out across the fields and say this is mine, this is what I've given my life for.'

He paused, his mind going back over the years. 'It's allus been the man in the big house who's been able to do that.'

He gave a long heartfelt sigh. 'Nothing's changed. There's no magic formula that says my boys will do any better than me, even though they'll work the same hours and give the same blood and sweat.'

'But, Barney, don't you think they'll be content just to work the land alongside their dad?'

Even though he could see Barney's reasoning for going away to make a new life, he so much wanted him to stay. But that was selfish, and he felt ashamed.

Barney tried to explain. 'You might well be right, old friend,' he conceded. 'They *are* content to be working alongside me, but for how long, eh? There'll come a day when they'll need to strike out on their own. That's when they'll realise like me, that nothing is for nothing. All they have is the wages I pay them, and Lord knows that's poor enough. What chance have they got of owning their own farm? The way things are, they'll be old and grey and still working somebody else's land. What kind of a future is that for two strapping lads who have it in them to do better?'

In the face of Barney's explanation, Adam was convinced but saddened. 'All I can see is the way the three of you work . . . a well-balanced team, strong together, all pulling the same way, and all the while seeming to know what the other is thinking.' He nodded his head. 'Happen I don't see the true picture after all.'

Barney corrected him. 'NO! You do see the true picture, and it's a wonderful way of life. But can't you hear what I'm telling you? None of it belongs to us and it never will . . . not the land nor the cattle, not even the roof over our heads. There have been many times when I've dreamed of going to America . . . who hasn't? And now, we've been given an opportunity that may never come again.'

He went on quietly, 'I have little money . . . certainly not enough to buy my own land. So if we stayed, I'd be forever a tenant farmer, with no chance of ever owning my own farm, and that being the case there will be nothing for my sons to build on. Oh, yes, I accept that they might move on and somehow, sometime in the far distant future they just might get as far as owning something or another. But I can never be certain of that, and neither can they. As for Susie, if she's ever to fulfil her ambitions, she'll need all the help she can get because sometimes talent and skill isn't enough. She needs opportunities to show what she can do; money to put her through the right kind of college, and then the means to ease her into her own little business.'

He paused, thinking of Vicky and their children, and his heart swelled with pride. 'I want them to have every chance,' he murmured. 'I want them to see something of this beautiful world we live in. I want them to have every opportunity to make a wonderful life, and because of the generosity of one man, they've been offered the best chance they'll ever have . . . a new life, a bigger sky, new horizons and the way forward to make something of themselves.' His eyes shone with love. 'They're so excited. They want the challenge.' His voice dropped to a whisper. 'Who am I to deny them that?'

Adam's tone changed to one of admiration. 'You're right, old friend, but it's a big step for anybody to be taking, and I'll tell you this . . . I'll miss you all like the very devil, but I do envy you. You're a brave man, Barney, I'll say that. There's many of us who would love the same challenge, but some of us are forever dreamers while others, like yourself, have the courage to give it a go.' He saw the sadness in Barney's eyes. 'All the same, it's worrying you, isn't it?'

Barney shook his head. 'No, Adam.' He took a sip of his tea. 'It's not *that* that's been worrying me, well, not for the reasons you might think anyway.'

'Hmh! If's not that, what is it then?'

Barney paused, his expression serious as he caught Adam's curious glance. 'What I'm about to tell you now, Adam . . . you're not to repeat it to a living soul, d'you understand?'

Concerned, Adam replaced his biscuit onto the plate. 'I've never been one to spread folks' business,' he chided, 'especially when it's an old friend confiding in me. You should know that by now, Barney.'

Barney was mortified. 'I'm sorry, Adam. It's just that, I've not told anybody else, and I won't. When I leave here, I'm seeing the doctor. I've not told Vicky, and I don't want her to know . . . whatever the outcome.'

Now, as Adam began to grasp the seriousness of the situation, he gulped so hard, his Adam's apple felt like a brick in his throat. 'I think you'd best explain what you mean by that,' he said.

Barney felt such relief that he had been able to confide in someone, and as it was Adam, he knew his secret would go no further. 'I'm sorry to put you in this situation,' he said, 'only I had to talk to somebody.'

Deeply worried, the other man brushed aside his apology. 'What is it, Barney old mate? What's wrong?'

Barney didn't want to frighten Adam unnecessarily, but on the other hand, should anything untoward come of his visit to the doctor, he needed someone outside the family to be in full possession of the facts. 'I reckon as how there's summat wrong wi' me,' he began quietly. 'Summat the doctors can't put right.'

Adam was visibly shocked. 'God Almighty, Barney, whatever makes you say a thing like that?'

Barney explained. 'For some months now, I've been getting these crippling pains in my chest. Sometimes I can hardly breathe, and other times I'm as sick as a dog at the slightest thing. I'm allus tired, but I can't ever get a good night's sleep. It's summat serious, Adam, I know it is.'

'And why are you so sure about that?' His pal would have none of it. 'You're no doctor, to say it's summat serious that they can't put right. Good God, Barney, it could be any number o' things.'

A glimmer of hope fluttered through Barney. 'What could it be then?'

'Well, *I* don't know, do I?' Adam replied irritably. 'Like yourself, I'm no doctor. All I know is, you shouldn't go jumping to conclusions. It could be a simple little thing that can easily be dealt with.'

'Such as what?'

'Well, such as a bad bout of indigestion. I get it all the time – it nigh doubles me up, but it's nothing to worry about. Then there's the nature of your work; you're out all hours in all weathers, and how many times have I seen you lying on the damp ground, under a machine, or hanging on the edge of a ladder reaching for this or that, then another time you'll be stacking hay up to the ceiling in the barn. Jesus! You're allus up to summat, stretching your body to its limit and not giving a thought to the consequences.'

He wagged a finger. 'You know as well as I do, there's many a farmer gone crippled because of his work and the changing weather.'

'I know that, but it's not the same thing at all.'

'Like as not you've overstretched a chest-muscle, or you might even have fractured a rib. That's been known to happen afore now and not been discovered for many a week – by which time it's got worse.'

Barney's hopes rose. 'You're right. I didn't think of all that.'

'No, you didn't,' Adam confirmed. 'You were too busy thinking the worst instead.'

'So, do you reckon I should still see the doctor?'

'It wouldn't hurt, not now that you've made the appointment.'

Barney nodded. 'I'm glad I told you, Adam.'

'So am I.' The other man, though, was secretly worried. 'You'd best mek tracks, lad. Soonest done is soonest mended.'

A few minutes later, Barney was ready to set off. 'I'll call in and see you at home on my way back,' he told Adam. 'Let you know what Dr Lucas says.'

His old friend waved him off. 'You do that,' he advised. 'And stop your worriting!'

Long after Barney was out of sight, Adam stood at the door, mulling over what Barney had told him: pains in his chest, being sick, sleeping badly and at times hardly able to breathe. He had assured Barney it could be any number of minor things, but deep down he had to consider that it could be really serious – far more serious than he had led the other man to believe. He was frightened for his pal.

So frightened for him that he downed tools there and

then and made his way home, intending to wait for Barney to let him know what Dr Lucas had to say.

~

Expecting his appointment to last some fifteen minutes or less, Barney was in Dr Lucas's surgery for a whole hour and a half.

Having been pummelled about and then quizzed for what seemed an age, Barney dressed behind the screens and came out to stand before the man's desk. 'What's the verdict then, Doctor?' he asked. He needed to know, but was dreading the answer. Not for nothing had Raymond Lucas called in his colleague from the other consulting room, and each in turn had examined Barney yet again; in quiet tones discussing his condition while he quickly dressed.

The doctor smiled. 'Sit down, Mr Davidson.' His quick smile was not a reassuring one; instead, to Barney it seemed more of a consoling smile, and sure enough with his next words he confirmed Barney's suspicions. 'I'm afraid it's not good news.'

Suppressing the fear inside him, Barney asked tremulously, 'It's my heart, isn't it?'

Dr Lucas slowly nodded. 'I'm sorry.' Quickly adding, 'But it's not all bad news. With proper medication and rest, you could go on for years yet.'

Shocked to the soul, Barney interrupted him. 'What you're saying is, if I stop work and spend the rest of my life doing nothing, then I might live a few years more?'

'Well, I'm not suggesting you should do *nothing*. I'm saying you will have to take things a lot easier. No more building haystacks, or driving in the sheep on a frosty winter's morning. You have a damaged heart. It isn't functioning as it should and that's a dangerous thing, especially for an active man such as yourself, whose very livelihood depends on him using his strength to carry out his work.'

A note of impatience marbled his advice. 'From now on, you must be sensible in everything you do, and I cannot emphasise that strongly enough.'

Barney wasn't listening. By now he was seeing the future in his own mind, and what he saw was more crippling than anything he had so far endured. 'Tell me, Dr Lucas . . .' he paused, hoping against hope that he might receive the answer he needed. 'Is there anything you can do to repair the damage?'

The doctor shook his head. 'I'm afraid the damage seems to be quite considerable. The breathlessness, the pain and sickness . . . it all has to do with the heart not doing its work. As far as we can tell, there is little that can be done, except to give you the advice I've just given, and for you to follow it to the letter.' He bent his head to his desk and taking out a notepad, began scribbling furiously. 'I can carry out any number of tests and no doubt get a fuller picture. But the heart is a complex organ and often it can be more dangerous to interfere with it, than to leave it alone.'

Looking up, he added in a serious voice, 'My opinion and that of my colleague is for us to treat the symptoms, and for you to do your part . . . follow my advice, and take the medicine prescribed. That way, it's certainly possible that you may enjoy a few more good years.'

Handing Barney the folded paper, he told him, 'I've made an appointment for you to be admitted into the Infirmary first thing in the morning.' His smile was sympathetic. 'I'm sorry the news was not what you might have expected, Mr Davidson, but we'll do the best we can – as indeed *you* must.'

Barney was devastated.

In a kind of half-drunken stupor he left the surgery and made his way to the horse and cart, which he had tethered outside. Without his usual greeting to the old horse, he climbed aboard, took up the reins and clicking the horse away, sat back on his slatted wooden bench and turned his thoughts to Vicky and the family.

As he left the village behind and came into the open countryside, he stopped the horse in its tracks, and climbing down off the bench, stood at the top of the valley, from where he could see the whole world.

He stood for a long time, his mind numbed and his heart sore, and when the doctor's words flooded back . . . *It's possible you may enjoy a few good years* . . . he lifted his face to the skies and with the tears streaming down his face, he accused that Great Master somewhere in the heavens: 'Every step of my life I've always trusted You, and now when my life seems to be taking a turn for the better, You snatch it away.' Anger roared through him. 'WHAT TERRIBLE THING DID I DO TO DESERVE THIS?' Sobbing, he fell to the ground.

In his mind's eye he could see Vicky, and his children. He saw the joy in their eyes and the excitement in their voices as they spoke of their imminent new life in Boston, and it was as though a knife was twisting his soul.

Sobered by the prospect of telling them, he climbed back onto the cart, but he did not take up the reins. Instead he sat hunched and desolate, without hope; without a future.

～

Adam was sitting on the doorstep smoking his pipe when he saw Barney coming up the lane. 'At last!' He had almost given him up. Knocking out his pipe on the porch column, he laid it beside his empty beer mug and ran out to meet his old friend. 'Where've you been? You've been gone an age,' he told him as Barney wearily climbed down. 'I thought you were never coming back.'

Half an hour later, the dreadful news imparted and shared, tears shed and dried, and a pint pot of beer swallowed, Barney turned to Adam and confided his chief worry.

'How on earth can I go off to farm in Boston when I'm in this state, fit for nowt? I can't see myself sitting about like an old-timer, gazing across the land, watching while the others work their fingers to the bone.'

When his voice broke, it took a moment to compose himself before he could go on. 'I couldn't do that to them, Adam, and I won't do it to myself. I think I've known these past few months that my time on earth is short, but it's so hard to think of leaving Vicky and our children. But I'll have to! Dear Lord, somehow I'll have to.'

When he now turned to look at Adam, the latter saw the sorrow in his eyes and the bitterness in the hard edge of his mouth. 'You above all people know I can't do it,' Barney confided. 'I can't *not* bring in the harvest or go out in the tractor when the earth is just waking, seeing the dew sparkle like jewels on the ground and the night creatures running before me as I plough the furrows.'

As he spoke his eyes lit up. 'The joy of my life is bringing in the sheep, collecting the apples from the branches where Vicky can't reach, tending the land from first light to darkness. It's in my nature, it's in my blood, Adam – you know that! If I can't do it, my life might just as well be over.'

As he stood up to leave, Barney placed a hand on Adam's shoulder. 'This is just between you and me, old friend,' he said quietly. 'No one else need ever know.'

Slumped forward, shocked by Barney's news, Adam was lost for words. There was no man on this earth could change Barney's mind once it was made up.

He knew Barney better than most, apart from Vicky who knew him like she knew herself. And he was aware that, whatever Barney decided to do, he would not embark on it without a great deal of thought and much agonising.

Fixing his gaze on the clumps of mud he had earlier walked onto the path, Adam nodded. 'I shall be here if you need me,' he said simply.

It was little enough, he thought. But at a time like this, God help him, what else could he do?

CHAPTER FIFTEEN

Throughout the following week, Barney carried on as usual, though sometimes when he was out in the fields alone, he would take time to rest, not because he wanted to, but because he was tired, and ill, and stubborn as he had ever been.

He had always loved the onset of winter, with the crisp clean air coming up the valley to pinch his face and make him feel alive, but on this particular day he found it all too much. His whole body ached, and for the first time in an age, he had felt the need to wear an overcoat.

'Things aren't the same, are they, old fella?' He wrapped his arms round the thick hairy neck of his four-legged pal. 'I thought I had years to go yet. I'm not old, only in my mid-forties, and I still have ambition in me. I thought I might be going on the greatest adventure of my life, taking the whole family to America and starting all over again. But I'm useless now, and growing more useless by the day.'

His voice carried a sense of irony. 'In horse years, you must be as old as the hills.' He gave a wry little laugh. 'But summat tells me you'll still be here, long after I've gone.'

Drawing away, he went to the back of the cart and took down a nosebag of hay. After he'd tied it round the horse's ears, he walked to the top of the hill, where he stood and

236

gazed around him, imprinting that familiar, magnificent panorama in his mind, in case he might never see it again.

Lost in memories and regret, he did not hear the footsteps drawing closer. 'Hello, Barney. Vicky told me where I might find you.'

Startled, Barney swung round to find Dr Lucas there. 'I was out walking,' he told Barney. 'Being that it was on my way, I thought I'd call in at Overhill Farm and have a little chat with you, but you'd already gone.' He glanced at the cart, which was loaded down with branches, half-trees and all manner of debris, and wagging a finger at Barney, he said, 'I sincerely hope someone helped you on with that load?'

Barney didn't answer. His mind was still with the doctor's greeting, and he was horrified. 'You say you've been to the house?'

'I called in, yes.'

'You haven't told Vicky anything, have you? She doesn't know yet.'

'No, Barney. I haven't told anyone. You specifically asked me not to betray your confidence, and I won't. I can't.' Raymond Lucas knew how badly Barney had taken the news – and who could blame him? 'It's you I'm concerned about. Twice now, over the course of the past week, I've seen you from a distance, standing up here, on the edge of this very hill.' He frowned. 'Today, I thought I might come and chat awhile.'

Barney couldn't help but chuckle. 'You thought I might throw myself over the edge, is that it?'

Dr Lucas shook his head. 'I would never think that of you, Barney. Whatever obstacle life puts in your way, I know you'll face it head on.' He smiled. 'Given the same disturbing news, some people might well throw themselves over the edge. But not you.'

Looking down, Barney nodded. 'Don't think I haven't considered it,' he said truthfully, kicking the ground. 'Because I have.'

The other man said nothing. Instead, he walked back to the cart with Barney, and listened to what he had to say.

'It's the family I fear for,' Barney confided. 'I don't know how to prepare them. I know I should tell them, but I don't want them to know. We've allus been close – too close, mebbe, because that makes it all the more painful. As for my Vicky . . .' He sighed heavily. 'She's been my reason for living ever since the day I first saw her.'

When his voice began to waver, he stopped, composed himself and when he was ready he looked up at Dr Lucas. 'I've searched my heart and I've turned every which way, to think of how I might break the news. Then I imagine what it will do to them, and I can't . . . I just can't do it!'

They walked on in silence for a moment, the doctor filled with sadness, and Barney hurting like he had never hurt before. 'I'm not sure yet how to deal with it all, but I will,' he said softly, as though talking to himself. *I'll find a way!*'

Not for the first time, Raymond Lucas felt helpless. In latter years, there had been significant strides forward in medicine, but as yet, there was no way to renew a heart that was damaged beyond repair. 'I'm sorry, Barney. I hope you know that.'

Barney slowly nodded his head. 'So am I,' he said, and then he had a question. 'If I had come into the Infirmary like you wanted, could you have made me healthy again? Would I have come home, being able to do all the things I've allus done?'

The other man shook his head decisively. 'No.'

Barney smiled. 'Thank you. That's what I thought.'

Dr Lucas had heard the exciting news, about how the

Davidson family were off to America. 'Have you decided what to do about Mr Maitland, and his offer of taking you all to Boston?'

'I'm working on it.' Barney climbed onto the cart, took up the reins and reminded the other man about his promise. 'Don't you worry your head about that,' he said firmly, but not disrespectfully. 'It's my business and I'll deal with it my way. Your part is to say nothing. That's our agreement as I understand it. Am I right, Dr Lucas?'

'Yes, you are, Barney. But you mustn't leave it too late before you tell them. It would not be fair – not to you, or to them.'

That said, he waved goodbye and took the path to the forest, while Barney went the long way round, through the valley and down by the river.

He wasn't ready to go home just yet.

He had a lot to think about.

~

By the time he got back to the farmhouse, Barney was his usual self. 'What's all this then?' The dining-table was piled high with all manner of things – clothes and papers and odds and ends he had never seen before; even a leather football he had bought years back to teach his young sons the game.

'I'm clearing out what we won't be taking to Boston with us.' Flicking the dust from her hair, Vicky gave a muffled sneeze. 'You would not believe the things that have turned up,' she chuckled. 'I even found that cowboy hat you wore to the first barn-dance we ever gave.'

Grabbing the hat from the table, Lucy plopped it on Barney's head. 'It suits you,' she laughed. 'You should wear it when you're bringing in the sheep.'

'Why don't I wear it to the celebrations?' he suggested cheerfully.

'Great idea!' Smiling, she turned to Lucy. 'I'm glad you decided to have the child christened the day *before* his second birthday.' Having both celebrations on the same day would have been too much.

Lucy was looking forward to it all. 'There you are, Barney,' she cried. 'Two parties in one. You'll never have a better excuse to wear that hat.'

Barney took it off and placed it on the pile. 'Look at this!' Certain articles had slid to the floor and there wasn't a single spare inch on the table. 'It looks like a rag-shop in here,' he said jokingly. He picked up a pair of trousers some two sizes too big for him now. 'I hope you're not expecting me to wear these an' all,' he said, making a face.

'I might, if you don't stop complaining,' Vicky answered with a click of the tongue.

Seeing the garments and artefacts piled high on the table was like the remnants of their lives together, and it shook him deeply. 'Why you felt the need to clear out wardrobes and such just yet, I'll never know,' he declared. 'The ship doesn't sail until the sixth of November . . . that's still well over two weeks away.' If things had been different he might have been helping but now, it was too frightening how fast the days were rushing by.

'That's not long,' Vicky argued. 'Not when I need to sort every drawer and cupboard, throw some stuff away, give some to the church for the needy, and get the rest washed and ironed to come with us. It can't all be done in five minutes.'

'Vicky's right.' Lucy had been helping all morning and still they had hardly started. 'Then there's the whole house to be gone over – floors so well-scrubbed you could eat your bacon and eggs off them, cupboards washed and lined with fresh newspaper, and every window-pane polished to a brilliant shine . . .'

'And that's only the *inside!*' Vicky was beginning to panic. 'You men haven't got a clue, have you?'

'I've got a thirst though.' Barney made his way to the kettle. 'I expect you could both do with a cuppa?'

'You two sit yourselves down.' Bringing him back, Lucy sat him in the chair. 'I'll mash the tea.'

Tired and weary, Barney didn't argue. 'I wouldn't mind a piece o' that fruit-cake, if there's any left?'

There was, and when Lucy brought it in along with the tea, Barney wolfed it down. 'By!' He washed it down with a gulp of hot tea. 'I reckon my girl is the best cook in the whole world,' he said, smacking Vicky's bottom as she walked by.

'Enough o' that, Barney Davidson,' she reprimanded. But there was a twinkle in her eye, and the twitch of a smile on her lips as she turned away.

'I wouldn't mind another piece o' cake if you're going to the kitchen?' he called out hopefully.

'I am going to the kitchen,' she called back, 'but it's no cake for you.'

'Aw – why's that?'

' 'Cause your dinner will soon be on the table, that's why.'

For the next few moments while Vicky was clattering about in the kitchen, Barney and Lucy sat together as they often did, talking and planning and wondering what the future held.

'I'll really miss you, Barney,' Lucy told him shyly. 'I know I shouldn't say it, not when you're all so excited and looking forward to it, but sometimes I wish Mr Maitland had never asked you.' She was instantly mortified. 'Oh, that's a terrible thing to say! I'm sorry, Barney, really I am.' She almost hero-worshipped this man, and didn't want him to think badly of her.

Instead, he said kindly, 'I wish you were coming too, you and young Jamie. You're part of the family now. As you know, I even asked Mr Maitland if there might be a place for you, but he's already altered the contract of sale on your account.'

Lucy understood. 'He's done a generous thing in leaving me secure with a job and a home. You're not to concern yourself about me,' she said. 'I'll be fine. I've got Bridget, and I've got little Jamie, and to tell you the truth, I've never been happier – though it will take some getting used to, not having you Davidsons just up the road.'

Reaching forward, she slid her hands over his. 'I'm really glad for you, Barney ... all of you. It's wonderful what's happening!' She allowed herself a little daydream. 'I don't know anybody who's gone to start a new life in America.' Feeling the warmth of his hands through hers, she drew away.

It was strange, the way she sometimes felt a thrill when he looked at her; and unforgivable, how she had come to think of Barney as more than a friend.

Just then, Barney felt the pain beginning in his chest. When he tried to take a deep breath it sounded like a strangled cough, and now the pain was spreading, like two mighty hands squeezing the life from him. Bending forward, he got out of the chair, his face drained and his mouth half-open as though he was having difficulty breathing.

'My God, what's wrong?' Lucy was quickly on her feet and helping him. She would have shouted for Vicky, but Barney gave her a warning glance.

As quickly as he could before Vicky came back into the room, he brushed past Lucy and stumbled outside. Frightened by what she had witnessed, Lucy ran after him; thankfully, Vicky neither heard nor saw them as they went out through the front door.

Lucy found Barney in the wood-shed; leaning over the pile of stripped saplings, he was still gasping for breath, but seemed to be recovering by the minute. 'I'm sorry, lass.' He afforded her a smile as she came rushing in. 'It were a raisin or summat out o' the fruit-cake. Went down the wrong way, I reckon.'

'Don't lie to me, Barney,' she warned him. 'I've seen you like this before. You're ill, aren't you? Tell me, Barney . . . what's wrong? What's happening to you?' Fear struck at her heart. She could just about cope with the idea of him going to America, but if anything bad should happen to him . . . no! The prospect was unthinkable.

'It's summat and nowt,' he wheezed, trying to sound casual. 'It's just an upset. It comes and goes.' Another spasm gripped him and he gasped.

'Have you seen the doctor?'

'I have, yes. And if you don't believe me, ask Adam Chives.' A thought occurred to him; he must remember to warn his pal not to let Lucy know the truth. 'You mustn't mention any of this to Vicky,' he wheezed. 'She's got enough on her plate at the minute, without worrying about me.'

Lucy came closer. 'You're not lying to me, are you?'

Barney appeared shocked. 'Good God, woman! Why would I do that, eh?' He stretched his arms out either side, inviting her to, 'Look at me, Lucy. I'm fit and strong, and like I said, it were summat and nowt.' Taking her by the arm he turned her round and walked her back to the house. 'Any minute now there'll be a houseful. Happen you'd best give Vicky a helping hand with the dinner, eh?'

Over dinner, Lucy watched Barney closely; he laughed and chatted and played with young Jamie and she began to wonder whether she'd imagined it all. In the end she gave up the worrying and joined in the excited chatter about the forthcoming adventure.

'I mean to be a millionaire before I'm thirty,' Thomas declared.

'Not before me,' Susie butted in. 'Miss Dandy showed me a map. She thinks I could have at least ten shops in Boston, before I start on New York.'

'Lucy, will you dance with me at the party?' Ronnie asked. 'I've been let down and now I've nobody to partner me.'

'Well, thank you, I'd be honoured, sir.' Lucy laughed. She was thrilled. It was a long time since anyone had whisked her round the dance-floor. She thought of Edward Trent with a familiar flash of anger. All along she had loved him, and all along he had told her how much he loved her back. Like a fool she had believed him, and he let her down badly.

Now, though, because of what he had done when she lay injured, she could walk by him in the street and not even turn a hair. Gently, unconsciously, she fingered the scar by her hairline where she had smashed her head against a rock.

'That reminds me!' Barney had completely forgotten. 'First thing tomorrow, I need the pair of you lads to help me set out that wooden floor in the barn. It hasn't been used since me and your mam had our twentieth wedding anniversary. With all the invites that have gone out, I've an idea we might need to make a couple or more extra squares.'

The excitement mounted. 'Christenings, birthdays and sailing off to a new land . . . whatever next!' Vicky raised her wine-glass for the umpteenth time. 'To the future!' And everyone drank heartily.

Everyone except Barney, who touched the wine against his lips and pretended to drink; Lucy, who saw him do it, wondered if he was hiding something after all.

In that worrying moment he glanced up and smiled at her; and the smile was so beautiful and easy, it took her breath away. She smiled back and raised her glass. 'All right,

Barney?' She mouthed the words. He nodded, raised his glass and took a sip. Soon he was laughing, and all seemed well.

~

The christening went even better than planned.

The sun came out to brighten the day and the service was simple, yet awe-inspiring. Even when the sacred water was poured over his forehead, Jamie did not flinch. He seemed to enjoy the whole thing.

Barney picked him up and held him; Bridget and Adam swore to be godparents, and the child was blessed.

'Now, how d'you feel about it?' Barney asked afterwards, and Lucy told him she felt it had been the right thing to do.

Vicky said he was now a child of God, and they drank to his future.

Then, in all the excitement, Jamie wet his pants. Lucy changed him and he promptly fell asleep, exhausted from being the centre of attention, while family and friends held a simple little lunch. 'We've still got the birthday party tomorrow to look forward to,' Ronnie said, and Susie ran upstairs to check that nothing had happened to the pretty dress Vicky had bought her for the occasion.

Later that afternoon, Adam was tidying up his porch when he caught sight of someone going across the headland. Convinced it was Barney, he put on his coat and climbed the hill towards him.

When he got to the spot where he thought he had seen Barney,' there was nothing there, not a bird or a rabbit, or anything, save for the winter-chill that swept across the land when evening came.

'That's funny!' Adam was sure he'd seen someone up there. Cupping his mouth, he called against the wind.

'BARNEY! Where the devil are you!' but there was no answer.

Puzzled, he made his way back to Casey's Farm. 'I could have sworn . . .' He shook his head. 'Adam Chives, you must be losing your marbles.' But then, he chided himself, was it surprising he'd begun to imagine things, when his best and only real friend in the world had told him he would probably not live to see another Christmas?

Further down the hill, the figure remained hidden until Adam had gone on his way, then furtively it emerged, to continue along the path in the direction of Overhill Farm.

~

The two Davidson boys were in the barn and had been for the past hour. 'No, no!' Barney rushed forward, just in time to stop Ronnie from laying the section too close to the corner. 'You need to leave room for the dancing,' he said. 'If you take it too far into the corner, there'll be no space for folks to swing about.'

Ronnie laughed at that. 'Oh, so you do intend we'll all be swinging about, do you?'

'I hope so!' Thomas brought forward another two sections. 'I'm bringing the prettiest girl ever, and I'd be real disappointed if we weren't able to dance!' He winked at Ronnie who told him he was fortunate, because so far, he himself didn't have a partner.

'You've got Lucy,' Barney reminded him. 'And if you think she can't dance then you'd best think again, because from what me and your mammy have seen, she can cut a rug along wi' the best of 'em!'

In fact, he had often caught Lucy when she was playing the gramophone and dancing on her own across the parlour. 'What's more,' he added, 'she's a fine-looking young woman.

You should be proud she's agreed to dance the evening away with you, my lad.'

'How many more sections do you think I need to make?' Thomas had been making wooden-slatted squares all morning, and now it seemed his father was right and there wouldn't be enough of a dance-floor to cope with all the folks that were invited.

Barney walked the area with him. 'We'll need it right up to there,' he said, pointing to the barn wall. 'That's where the food will be. Then it needs taking to within three feet of the far end. That's where the benches will be set out, and folks can sit if they're not dancing.' He scratched his chin and mentally calculated. 'I reckon if you could make another two, that should do it.'

As Thomas went back outside, Barney informed Ronnie, 'That's your job when once you've finished laying the floor. We'll need at least four long benches for folks to sit on.'

'I like the way you say "we",' Ronnie quipped. 'I haven't seen you lift a single thing yet, Dad!'

'Cheeky young divil!' Barney wagged a friendly finger. 'Some of us have more to do than prepare for a barn-dance. There's plenty of other work wants seeing to.'

Just lately, Barney had found it increasingly necessary to delegate the work he was physically incapable of doing. Thankfully, so far he had managed to hoodwink everybody. 'Stop your moaning and get on with it, you young scoundrel. And be quick about it. Afore we know where we are, tomorrow will be here and so will all the folks.'

By the time evening came the barn was ready, with colourful trimmings hanging from the rafters, a long table set up to hold the food and a whole wall of benches to accommodate weary bottoms. Much to Barney's delight, the makeshift dance-floor was not only a job to be proud of, but large enough for the dancing of many partygoers. 'You've done a grand job,' he told his sons. 'I couldn't have done better myself.'

Ronnie reminded him that the tables for the guests to eat at were not yet put up. 'There'll be time enough to root them out tomorrow,' his father said. 'If I remember rightly, the fold-up tables are buried under all kinds of rubbish at the back end of the wood-shed.'

It was gone nine by the time Barney and his sons returned to the house. 'That's us done for the night,' he told Vicky who, together with Lucy, was still taking trays of pork pies out of the oven. 'It's over to you now, girls.' He was concerned at the late hour. 'It might be best if Lucy and the child stayed the night,' he suggested to Vicky. 'She looks fair worn out – you both do. Leave it all now, and get up early in the morning. The party doesn't start till evening. There'll be plenty of time to finish off whatever needs doing.'

'I've already asked Lucy to stay.' With the back of her flour-speckled hand, Vicky wiped away a wisp of hair. 'Bless him, little Jamie's fell asleep hours ago . . . Lucy's just about to go up.'

Bone-tired and ready for her bed, Lucy washed her hands at the pot sink, said her good nights and climbed the stairs to be with her child.

After checking little Jamie she stood for a while at the window, looking at the night sky and thinking how strange life could be. One minute she was footloose and fancy free; then along came Edward Trent, who promised her the world, made her with child then cleared off; then back he strolled into her life, fooled her into thinking he'd mended his ways and was ready to make her his wife and give his son a name, when he ran away again – in the most cowardly fashion yet.

Somewhere along the way, her life had gone very wrong, and now here she was, without a husband and Jamie without a daddy, and in a couple of weeks' time, her dear friends would sail away and she would be left here alone.

She worried about Barney. No matter how hard he tried to reassure her that things were fine with him, Lucy could not rid herself of a niggling doubt. Was he ill? Or was it, as he said, 'summat and nowt'?

Too weary and weighed down with regrets to make sense of it all, she undressed and, climbing into bed, drew the child to her. It was only a matter of minutes before she, too, fell asleep.

CHAPTER SIXTEEN

WHEN, AFTER A fitful few hours Lucy woke, it was to hear the stairs creak as someone crept down them. Darting to the door, she inched it open and saw Vicky on her way down to the kitchen. She turned to see Lucy and hissed, 'Go back to bed! It's only half past five. I'll call you in an hour.' With that she continued on tiptoe down the stairs.

Lucy went into the bathroom, had a wash at the basin and quickly got herself dressed. A look to make sure that Jamie was still deep asleep, and then she was down the stairs and after Vicky.

'I thought I told you to go back to bed?' Vicky already had the mixing bowl out and the flour jar in her hand. 'You could have had another hour's sleep.'

Grabbing a pinafore, Lucy wrapped it round her. 'While you're doing the scones, I'll make the apple-pies,' she said, and before Vicky could answer, she was inside the pantry, collecting together all the ingredients.

Over an hour later the men came downstairs, followed by a very sleepy Susie; the pleasant aroma of baking filled the air and Barney commented on the array of goodies covering the dresser. 'By! There's a table fit for a king,' he said, licking his lips at the pies, cakes, scones and joints of meat ready for the slicing.

Vicky scrutinised him. 'Are you all right, love?'

' 'Course I'm all right.' Barney's heart turned somersaults. 'Why wouldn't I be?' He had suffered another bad night, pacing the floor half the time or propped up against the pillow, massaging the ache in his chest.

'No reason.' Vicky shrugged her shoulders. 'You seemed restless, that's all.'

'How d'you mean?'

'Well, you shifted about a lot, turning this way and that.'

'So, did I disturb you?' He was afraid she might have seen him pacing the floor.

Vicky chuckled. 'You know me,' she answered. 'Once I'm out, it would take an earthquake to wake me. No, you didn't disturb me,' she assured him. 'It's just that when I got out of bed to visit the bathroom, you seemed a bit unsettled.'

'I expect I was dreaming of all the things that could go wrong with this party.' He looked round. 'Where's the birthday boy?'

'Still fast asleep.' Lucy poked her head out from the pantry. 'So don't you go waking him.'

'And don't you go worrying about things going wrong with the party!' Vicky advised. 'Because everything is in hand. It's all been checked and double-checked; Jamie's presents are all wrapped and ready, the birthday cake is setting and will be perfect for cutting tonight, the trimmings are up and the barn is all ready . . . or so you say!'

'It is!' Ronnie grumbled, falling into the room. 'Apart from a few finishing touches which'll only take a few minutes.' Hunched in his chair, unshaven, unwashed and with his hair standing on end, he looked like he'd been fished out of the river.

'Right!' Clapping her hands together to release a flurry of flour, Vicky went to the tap and filled the kettle which she then put on the stove. 'Lucy! A dozen rashers of bacon and a bowl of eggs, if you please. We've a hungry mob waiting to be fed.'

'I'll have three eggs if they're going.' That was Thomas, bleary-eyed and yawning.

'God Almighty! Look at the state of the pair of you!' Vicky laughed. 'I hope you can both manage to recover for tonight.' She did a little jig on the spot. ''Cause your mammy's expecting you to give her a dance or two!'

Lucy saw how Barney's strained face lit in a smile at his wife's antics. 'There you go, Vicky.' Placing the eggs and bacon on the side, she peeped again at Barney, and suddenly in that one precious moment, there was not another soul in the room but herself, and him.

~

At 6.30 p.m. the first partygoer arrived. 'I'm a bit early,' Adam apologised. 'Only I thought there might be summat I could do to help.' In truth he had wanted a quiet talk with Barney.

'You'd best come wi' me.'

Barney guessed the reason for his early arrival. 'We'll check the barn and see if I've forgotten anything.' In his grey corduroy trousers, best blue shirt, and with his unruly hair tamed to a shine, Barney looked good.

'The ladies are upstairs titivating theirselves and the boys are in the kitchen picking at the food.' He chuckled. 'If Vicky catches them, they'll wish they'd never been born.'

As they strolled to the barn, Adam asked, 'How are you feeling, matey?'

'If you mean am I looking forward to the party,' Barney replied, 'the answer's yes. If you mean have I accepted what's gone on with me . . .' He shrugged his shoulders. 'What choice have I got, old friend?'

Saddened to his heart, Adam nodded. 'And what will you do about America?' He was reluctant to interfere but knew the dilemma Barney faced. 'There'll come a point when you have to tell the family.'

'I'm dealing with it.'

Adam sighed. 'Remember, you're not on your own, Barney,' he said softly. 'I'm here for you. Any time you want me, I'll be here.' When the tears filled his eyes he blinked them away.

'I know.' Throwing an arm round the little man's shoulders, Barney walked him to the barn, where he threw open the door. 'Well, what d'you think?'

Adam was mesmerised. The barn was festooned with colour from one end to the other: paper chains and streamers hung across the roof and down the walls, and in between, strategically hung so as to be safe, were a dozen long lanterns, all lit and twinkling. The benches were set out; the food table was dressed in a long pink cloth, and the dance-floor stretched away as far as the eye could see.

'It's like Wonderland!' Adam marvelled and Barney laughed. They went inside and walked round the floor. Then Susie came running in. 'Mam says you're to come and help carry the food,' she said, and ran out again.

For the next half-hour it was mayhem, with everyone trotting backwards and forwards with plates and dishes of food, cutlery and jugs, dodging each other and making a second and third trip, and when the long table was filled to bursting, the guests started arriving: the butcher and his wife; Doris Dandy from Everton, various villagers and others who had known the Davidsons for many years.

Jamie was getting very over-excited; dressed in his best clothes and overwhelmed by all the noises and strange faces. Lucy let him enjoy himself for a half-hour or so, then she popped back to the farmhouse with him and put him to bed, waiting until he had fallen asleep before returning to the festivities.

Leonard Maitland arrived alone, his attention instantly drawn to Vicky, who looked very fetching in her new cream-coloured skirt and pink lace blouse, with her hair loosely looped up on top of her head, and long wispy strands curling round her face. She was a picture of loveliness.

There were two neighbouring farmers and their entire families, and finally, arriving in a flurry of excitement with one of her new girls trailing in her wake, Bridget came waltzing through the doors. 'Jaysus, Mary and Joseph, will ye look at this! It's like heaven come to earth!' she screeched with excitement.

A moment later, taking the young woman aside, she reminded her, 'You're not here to enjoy yourself.' She kept her voice low. 'Sure, haven't I suffered the bad atmosphere in the house these past few days, the pair of youse, fighting and arguing like two alley cats! I've only brought you here tonight so I can keep an eye on you, while the other one calms down.'

She wagged a warning finger. 'Watch your tongue and keep yourself to yourself, Brenda. I don't want ye messing with the men tonight.' She edged closer until they were eyeball to eyeball. 'I swear, if I so much as see you look at a fella, I'll thrash the arse off ye, so I will!'

Wisely, the young woman backed off. 'What am I supposed to say if anybody comes talking to me?'

'Oh, you'll think o' something, I'm sure.' Bridget gave her a gentle shove. 'Now be off and fetch me a glass o' that wine they're handing out.'

With everybody safe inside and a glass of best homemade wine in their hand, Barney stood on the chair and welcomed them all. 'This is really a triple celebration,' he said, winking at his wife. 'Not only is it to mark little Jamie's birthday and christening although the little chap in question has gone to his bed, but as most of you will already know, the Davidson family are away to start a new life in America.'

Pausing for breath, he thought about the imminent journey, and his secret heart was heavy. 'It's good to see you all here,' he finished. 'And now let's have a toast – to Jamie . . . and America!' There was an almighty cheer. 'To Jamie and America!'

'God bless you and your family, Barney, and all the luck in the world. It's no more than you deserve.' The glasses were raised again, and when they were empty, Vicky and Lucy and Susie were on hand to fill them up again.

While the toasts were given, Dr Lucas stood at the back of the barn and raised his glass along with everyone else. But, with the exception of Barney and Adam, he was the only one who knew that Barney might never be going to America. And if that was the case, then his family would not be going either.

It wasn't long before the music started, in the form of old Victor and his accordion and beside him, the blacksmith, who could not only shoe a horse in record time but could also play a mean flute. Between the two of them, they played a merry tune and soonever the music struck up, the partygoers flocked to the dance-floor and let themselves go.

'Would you look there!' Barney nudged Lucy, gesturing across the dance-floor to where the butcher was swinging his wife round on the edge of his podgy arm. 'I reckon he must think she's a side o' beef,' Barney joked, 'the way he's chucking her about!'

Lucy's attention was caught elsewhere. 'It didn't take Leonard long to get Vicky on the dance-floor,' she remarked, and when Barney looked across he was taken by the manner in which his boss held Vicky, close and tight, as though he did not want to let her go.

The smallest surge of jealousy rippled through him. 'Come on, lass, let's show 'em how to do it!' Grabbing her by the arm he ran her onto the dance-floor, and when the music suddenly changed to a waltz, he slid his arm round her waist and bent her to him. 'You look lovely,' he whispered in her ear. 'I meant to tell you that soonever I saw you, all dressed up like a princess, with your pretty eyes shining.'

Lucy laughed. 'Why, thank you, sir, and you don't look bad yourself either.'

Secretly, she was thrilled to be in his arms, and as he moved her slowly round the dance-floor, she closed her eyes and imagined he was her real partner; having brought her to the dance, later, when it was over, he would take her home again. On the doorstep he would kiss her good night, and she would go to bed and dream of him.

She laughed as Barney swung her round again. She knew it would end, but it didn't matter. Tomorrow was reality. But tonight was a memory she would keep forever.

While dancing with Lucy, Barney kept an eye on Vicky. Looking up at Leonard, she was talking, seemingly unaware that he might be holding her too close, or that he wasn't listening to a word she was saying. Instead he was looking into her eyes, discreetly content to be holding the woman he loved.

Barney saw all this and now, as Vicky turned to smile at him, he smiled back and winked; pleased when his wife blew him a conspiratorial kiss.

Barney laughed with Lucy, and swung her round like a young man with his sweetheart, yet all the while he was thinking of the future, and his lovely Vicky. He knew how devastating the news of his illness would be to the family, and to her, and he would have done anything on God's earth not to have to tell her. If only there was a way, he thought. If only he could somehow save his family from the pain and anguish they were bound to suffer.

In the darkness of his mind, an idea was growing; an idea which, in the fullness of time, would come to fruition and shape their destiny.

~

During the evening, Lucy would return to the farmhouse every so often; an old dear from the village was there, keeping an eye on little Jamie. 'He's the same as he was when you came in half an hour since.' A widow these many years, old Meg now filled her life with looking after other people's children. 'He's sleeping,' she told Lucy with a toothless grin. 'You go and enjoy the party, dear, and leave me to my knitting. Your little lad is safe enough with me.'

After going upstairs to check Jamie, Lucy gave the old woman a grateful kiss and returned to the party.

Outside in the shadows, Edward Trent emerged from his hiding-place and crept stealthily towards the barn. Placing himself where he would not be seen, he peered in through the window.

He saw Barney's son, Ronnie, hand-in-hand with Lucy as he led her onto the floor. The two of them danced wildly to the rhythmic sound of the accordion, Ronnie playing the fool and Lucy laughing at his antics while he flirted outrageously with her.

When the music stopped and Lucy was making her way back to the table with Ronnie, his brother Tom came on the scene and grabbing Lucy, he led her back onto the dance-floor. The music changed to a slower tempo, and soon she was moving effortlessly round in his arms, chatting and smiling, and seeming at peace with herself.

Edward saw all this and the rage inside him knew no

bounds. Thrusting his fists against the window it seemed for one moment that he might smash it from its frame. Then the music stopped and everyone was clapping, and when in that moment a woman turned towards him, he ducked down and disappeared into the shadows again.

'What d'you think you're doing?' Ronnie demanded light-heartedly of his brother. 'Stealing my woman from under my very nose?'

'I rescued her,' Thomas answered, stuffing a piece of pork pie into his mouth. 'I could see she was fed up dancing with a four-footed idiot, so I thought I'd show her what a real partner could do.'

Lucy giggled. 'Stop it, you two,' she said. 'I'm having a wonderful evening. You're both good dancers and you know it!'

'Ah, you're just saying that.' Ronnie searched the table for another chunk of fruit-cake. 'I bet you're really in agony from the number of times he's trodden on your toes.'

At half past midnight the evening came to an end.

As they left, everyone said what a wonderful time they'd had, and how good the food was, and how they would be so sorry to see the Davidson family leaving.

Standing side-by-side at the door as they saw everyone out, Barney and Vicky thanked them all in turn.

'I'll see youse out and about before you sail away, so I will!' Having downed more booze than she was capable of holding, Bridget was four sheets to the wind. 'Oops!' Laughing raucously, she hobbled out to the waiting car, clutching hold of her companion, her jacket stained with wine and her hitherto beautifully coiffured hair looking as if it had been through a wind-tunnel.

Behind her, Barney and Vicky walked arm-in-arm back to the house with Lucy and Susie, who had danced with her friends until her feet ached.

'Leave all that till the morrow,' Barney told his sons, who had a mind to start clearing away the furniture. As it was, he left them sitting on the barn floor, finishing off their drink and deep in conversation. 'D'you think they're worried about going to America?' Barney asked Vicky.

'Not a bit of it!' she declared. 'They're very excited, like the rest of us. In fact, Thomas said he would be broken-hearted if Leonard Maitland suddenly changed his mind and said we couldn't go after all.'

Her words did not help Barney. Instead he felt as though his own heart might break, because very soon he would have no choice but to confess the truth of his illness. And the more he thought of it, the more he dreaded the day.

Inside the house, they found old Meg fast asleep in her chair, with the knitting on her lap and snoring like a good 'un. Barney chuckled. 'We'll have to wake her,' he said. 'The old dear needs her bed.'

Vicky gently shook her, and when she woke it was with a start that frightened them all and sent her knitting clattering to the floor. 'What's up? What d'you want?' With big eyes she stared at them. 'Oh, it's you.' Her mouth opened in a toothless grin. 'I thought for a minute it was me old man come back to haunt me.'

'Come on, my old darling, it's time you were tucked up in bed.' Barney helped her out of the chair, Vicky went to fetch her hat and coat and Lucy paid her for the night.

Ronnie came rushing in. 'Your son's here,' he told her, and her old face lit from ear to ear. 'He's a good lad,' she said. 'He does look after his old mammy.'

No sooner had she been helped into the car than she was fast asleep. 'Salt of the earth,' her son told Barney with a proud smile. 'Never stops . . . allus on the go. She's in her seventies now, but I reckon I'll be worn out long afore she is.'

After Meg had gone, Jamie woke up and started crying. Lucy ran upstairs and came down with him in her arms. 'Oh dear, he's wet the bed. I am sorry. I've put the sheets in the pail to soak and I'll rinse them through tomorrow. The mattress is still dry – thanks to your old rubber sheet. Look – I think we'd best go home.'

'If you want to stay I'm sure we'll find something suitable to wrap his little bottom in,' Vicky said. 'And there's plenty o' clean sheets – you know where they are.'

Lucy thanked her but thought it might be best if she took Jamie home and saw to him there. 'It's been a very long couple of days and he'll rest easier tucked up in his own cot.'

'We'll see you tomorrow then,' Vicky told her, while Barney went to fetch his big coat.

Ten minutes later, wrapped against the cold night air, she and Barney set off with the child, who by now had nodded off again. 'I don't know how to thank you,' Lucy told Barney.

'Thank me? What for?' He hoisted Jamie higher in his arms.

'For giving Jamie the party.'

'It was a pleasure,' Barney answered. 'And don't forget, it was also to mark our going to America.'

Something in his tone caused Lucy to ask, 'And is that what you really want, Barney, to go to America?'

The man chose his words carefully, not least because Lucy had already voiced her concern about his health. 'O' course I want to go! Why wouldn't I?'

Lucy gave him a sideways glance; in the moonlight he looked incredibly pale, and there was a quietness about him that wasn't natural. Twice during the evening she had seen a kind of sorrow in his face that worried her.

'What's wrong with you, Barney?' she asked quietly. 'And don't fob me off with untruths. I've come to know you fairly well, and I've a feeling there's something up. What is it? You can trust me – you know that, don't you?'

Barney didn't answer, nor did he look at her. Instead he kicked irritably at the roadway. 'It's high time somebody did summat about these damned ruts in the lane,' he grumbled. 'Last week, old Ted Foggarty's horse caught its fetlock in one and had to be put down!'

Lucy persisted. 'Talk to me, Barney.'

'I *am* talking.' He gave her a cursory glance.

'I haven't said anything to Vicky and I won't, but I know there's something wrong,' Lucy repeated. 'Bridget told me she saw you going into the doctor's surgery some time back.'

Turning to look at her, he said, 'I won't hear any more of this nonsense, Lucy. Yes, I won't deny I went to see the doctor, but only because I was feeling run down. I've been under the weather recently and I thought it might be a good idea to go and get some tonic.'

'And did he prescribe some?' Lucy was slightly relieved but still left with the feeling that he was not telling all.

'He did, and I've been taking it religiously.'

'And is it working?'

Barney was feeling trapped. 'Well, you've not seen me being other than fine, have you?'

Lucy shook her head. 'No.' Enough was enough. Barney was getting grouchy. 'But I'm not always looking in your direction, am I?'

Barney laughed it off. 'I should hope not!'

When they reached Lucy's cottage, he helped her inside with her bag and the child. A few minutes later, he and Lucy emerged from the front door. 'Good night, Lucy girl,' Barney said, and yawned long and hard. As always, he kissed her on the cheek. 'See you the morrow.'

'Good night, Barney.' She waved him off down the lane, and afterwards went back inside, her face still burning from the touch of his lips. It was a sad thing, she thought, to love a man who belonged to your best friend. But love him she did, and try as she might, she could not change that.

Neither Barney nor Lucy had seen Edward Trent hiding in the shadows, watching and waiting. When Lucy was kissed good night, he was shaken by the look of love on her face as she waved Barney off. And his heart was black with jealousy.

Having had a run of bad luck of late, he had heard through the grapevine how Lucy had been given a cottage to live in and regular work. With no sailings available and with nowhere to live, Trent had thought to foist himself onto Lucy by persuading her that he loved her and the child. Once he'd got his feet under the table, he'd plan his next move, while Lucy worked to bring in the wages and he worked to spend them.

The thing that shocked him now was that, having come back with purely selfish motives, he had seen Lucy in other men's arms and realised he still had deep feelings for her. She belonged to him, by God. He'd taken her virginity, and by rights she was his, and the mother of his son – not that he could even remember the brat's name.

Inside the cottage, Lucy quickly washed the child with a drop of warm water, talking to him as she did so. 'This is our home, Jamie. It might be small and cramped, but now that Barney's mended the roof and fitted new doors, and me and Vicky have polished the entire place till it shines, it might not be the poshest place in the world, but it's cosy enough for me and you.' In fact she loved its every nook and cranny.

'It was a good party,' she said, slipping on his pyjamas. 'Barney and Vicky gave it just for you.' She recalled what Barney had said. 'And it was to say goodbye to their friends as well, because soon they will be off to a new life across the water.'

Pushing the heartache to the back of her mind, she told the child, 'You're christened now, sweetheart.' She kissed his sleepy face. 'It's wonderful, isn't it? You have your name written down in the book for everyone to see.'

When she tickled him he chuckled and squealed, and she took him in her arms, hugging him as if she would never let him go. 'You're Mammy's big boy,' she said. 'We'll soon be losing the best friends we've ever had, so we'll need to look after each other, you and me, eh?'

'Not when I'm around to take care of you.'

'EDWARD!' Even before she turned, Lucy knew the voice, she knew the man, and could hardly believe he was standing right here in her house.

'You should always lock your door at night.' His slow, dangerous smile enveloped her. 'You never know *who's* lurking about.'

'What do you want?' Instinctively, she held the child closer. When he took a step nearer, Lucy stepped back.

'I want *you*, Lucy.'

She had been afraid, but now she was over the first shock, she was angry. 'You didn't want me when you ran off, leaving me unconscious, like the coward you are!'

Cunning as a fox, he momentarily bowed his head as though with shame. 'That's why I'm back,' he lied, his eyes sad with regret. 'I did behave like a coward, and I want to make it up to you.'

'I don't believe you!' Standing tall and defiant, Lucy looked him in the eye. 'I've made a life for myself, Edward, and I'm happier than I've been in years. There is no place here for you now.'

'Please, Lucy, don't say that,' he whined. 'It took a lot of courage for me to come here after what I did.' He glanced around the room, thinking it warm and cosy; a far cry from the dives where he'd been holed up of late. 'We could have a good life together,' he went on. 'You've already got work up at the farmhouse, and I'll find a job, I promise. We've got to give it a go.'

When he saw her expression he grabbed her roughly by the arm. 'Aw, look, Lucy. We were always good together, you know that!'

'You used me!' Shaking him off, she told him in a quiet, trembling voice, 'You lied to me all along, and when I needed you more than ever, you ran off.' She stared at him, wondering what she had ever seen in him. 'We don't need you, Edward. We don't want you here. Please go. Leave us alone.'

He was desperate now. 'I love you, Lucy, it's why I keep coming back. I've always loved you. I didn't realise it until now.' Darting forward, he grabbed her by the arm. 'I had you, and I threw you away,' he said angrily. 'But I've got you back now and I don't intend to let you go.' Cupping her face in the palms of his hands, he whispered earnestly, 'I know I did wrong, but I do love you, Lucy. You've got to believe me.' And he did love her, as much as a man like him could ever love anyone.

'Get off me!' Lucy's instincts told her that at long last he might be telling the truth, but it was too late. Edward Trent no longer meant anything to her. Thankfully she was over him now, and could see him for the selfish, vicious man he had always been. 'I don't want you here, now get out!' She put Jamie down and tried to distract him with a toy while she hissed, 'Go on! Get out of my house!'

Realising she meant every word, Edward shook his head and smiled. 'I'm not going anywhere,' he said softly. 'Not without you.'

Afraid now, Lucy had to think hard. She had to be rid of him, but how? Suddenly an idea came to her. 'For a long time I hoped and prayed you might come back,' she lied, 'but you didn't. So I had to make a life for me and little

Jamie, and now I'm going away to America. We're leaving soon, Edward – it's all arranged.' She added as an after-thought to appease him, 'I'll write to you. Give me an address, and I promise I'll write as soon as we get there.'

Visibly shocked, he took a step back. *'America!'* Looking into her eyes he gave her a shaky smile. 'I don't believe you.'

'It's true.' She was desperate to make him believe. 'Why would I lie? If you were hanging about outside, you must have seen Barney Davidson bring me home. There's been a big party up at Overhill Farm to say goodbye to all the friends and neighbours. Mr Maitland has sold up here, and we're all going with him to help run his farm in Boston, Massachusetts. If you don't believe me, ask anyone. It's common knowledge round here!'

'You little bitch!' Without warning he tore the child from her, and over the sound of his terrified cries, he said calmly: 'You're not going anywhere, with Mr Maitland or anyone else. You're coming with me. We're getting right away from here. I'll find us lodgings in London. Somehow we'll man-age. We'll be all right together, you and me . . . and him.' Though he had acknowledged his love for Lucy, he had little feeling for the child; so far he had not spoken to Jamie, or even looked at him.

'No, Edward! There was a time when I would have walked to the ends of the earth for you, but not any more. You see, I don't love you.' The calmness in her voice belied the tur-moil inside. 'Now give me my son.' Reaching to collect little Jamie, who by now was screaming hysterically, she did not expect what happened next. Raising his hand, Trent brought it down hard against her temple and sent her reeling across the room.

'I must be out of my mind to want you back,' he snapped. 'Dancing and laughing, and flirting with every man in sight. You're nothing but a trollop!'

Hurt and dazed, she dragged herself up by the chair; somewhere in the chaos of her mind she heard Jamie crying. 'Give me back my son!' she said hoarsely.

'Want the brat back, do you?' He gave a low, grating laugh that sent shivers through her. 'You can have him . . . but you'll have to take me as well.'

Lucy was frantic. 'Please, Edward, it wouldn't work between us. All I want is to be left in peace.'

Clambering up against the chair, she went sprawling again when he thrust his booted foot into her side. 'You don't seem to understand what I'm saying,' he growled. 'You either come with me now, or I'm taking him with me, and you'll never see him again. So, what's it to be?'

Terrified that he might carry out his threat, Lucy was tempted to give in and let him stay – anything to have little Jamie safely back in her arms. But what then? He might rape her – get her with child again! Her flesh shuddered at the thought of his touch. He was repulsive to her. Anyway, he would soon discover that it was a trick on her part, and then his rage would know no bounds. What would happen to her and Jamie then?

'*Well?*' He stood over her, his face dark with loathing.

Lucy looked at her son, still sobbing with fear. She turned her gaze on Edward and begged, 'Don't hurt him, please. If you want to stay, you can stay, and we'll talk again in the morning.'

When she saw the look in his eyes she knew it wasn't enough. 'Please, Edward, you're asking me to give up everything I know and love, to go away with you. I'm not saying no, but I'm not saying yes either. Give me time to think about it; you owe me that much.' She held out her arms. 'And now . . . *give me the child.*'

~

As he cut across towards the river on his way back home, Barney thought his world was a beautiful place, when the moon was full and round and the skies speckled with a myriad of twinkling stars. All along the chilly hedgerows he could hear the night animals scurrying about, and in the distance, the unique sound of a barn owl. 'You made something wonderful when You made this earth,' he murmured, his gaze roving the heavens. There was such peace and beauty on God's earth, and he felt deeply privileged to be a part of it.

Then, suddenly, Barney was made to stop in his tracks. 'What's that?' From somewhere close he could hear the sounds of human voices raised in anger. Turning this way and that, he tried to pinpoint where the voices were coming from, but it was difficult; the tumbling of water from the weir diverted his senses.

There it was again! His attention was drawn back, towards the high bend in the river, not too far from Lucy's cottage. It sounded as if somebody was in trouble! Quickly now, he made his way back, pausing every now and then to catch his breath, and taking off again when a child's wail shattered the night air.

As he came round by way of the spinney, he saw a figure running in the moonlight; he was carrying something – what was it? A sack ... a child? Dear Lord, it was a child! And coming up behind him was a woman, running and stumbling, and all the while calling out for the man to stop.

When he recognised her, he was horrified. 'Lucy?' He couldn't believe his eyes. The woman was Lucy, and the child must be little Jamie ... but the man – who was he? His name appeared in Barney's mind like a lit beacon. EDWARD TRENT! It had to be!

'*Lucy!*'

Quickening his steps to a run, time and again Barney called out her name, but Lucy didn't hear. They were too close to that part of the river where the water tumbled over the rise and thundered down into the basin beneath.

Gasping for breath, his chest afire, Barney took off again to gradually close the gap between them. He saw how, on reaching the river, Lucy launched herself at Trent. There was a struggle during which, with one backward swipe of his burly arm, Trent knocked her down.

At the top of the rise, Barney had to stop again. He bent his head low, and with his hands on his knees, he took some long deep breaths, and after a moment or two, slowly regained his composure. When he set off again, he could see Edward Trent. With the child under his arm, he was using the moonlight to illuminate his way across the most dangerous part of the river – a line of big boulders straddling the water. Doggedly pursuing him, out of her mind with fear, Lucy was yelling for him to give her the child. Jamie was frantically struggling in the man's arms, making the situation even more dangerous.

When Trent ignored her pleas, she followed, slipping and sliding across the slimy boulders towards the far bank.

'No, Lucy, come back!'

When Barney yelled out, in a part of this nightmare Lucy heard, but she kept on going, because Edward Trent had her baby, and she would follow him to Hell if needs be.

By the time Barney came to the river, Lucy and Edward Trent were locked in a fierce struggle on the rocks above the weir, with the terrorised child screaming hysterically.

Desperate to get Lucy and her son out of there and with no thought for his own safety, Barney ran slithering over the boulders. Taking hold of her, he tried to get her to safety, but she wouldn't listen; all she knew was that her baby was in terrible danger. When driven by desperation she foolishly made a grab for the child, Trent lost his footing, and to her horror Lucy went with him.

Wading through the water to get to them, Barney saw Trent scrambling towards the shore and when, with the saturated clothes clinging to her body, Lucy went after him, Barney warned her to stay back. 'Leave him to me, Lucy!' He bellowed a warning. 'You're putting the child in more danger!' But with reason long gone, she took no heed.

Everything happened so quickly there was nothing Barney or anyone else could have done. Going against Barney's advice, Lucy made another grab for the child. As she caught him safely in her arms, Trent missed his footing and fell into Lucy, who then lost her balance – and in seconds the fast-flowing river snatched Jamie from her arms and whirled him away in its embrace.

Lucy made a brave effort to rescue her son, but not being a strong swimmer she was buffeted against every obstacle, as her son got washed further away.

Ahead of her, Barney got to the child first, but it was already too late. The force of water that had snatched him away and carried him downriver, had wedged him between two half-submerged rocks.

When Barney found him, the water was swirling over his face, and there was nothing he could do.

Desolate and bedraggled, he took the drowned child into his arms and waded upriver, to where Lucy was making her way towards them.

At first she began shouting for joy. 'You've got him!' She laughed out loud. 'Oh Barney, you've got him!' Her heart soared at the sight of her boy, safe in Barney's arms.

With tears streaming down his solemn face, Barney looked into her eyes and slowly shook his head.

When Lucy saw the expression on his face, it was as if the world had come to an end; there were no words to describe the horror that tore through her. For the longest, deepest moment, the silence in that place was awesome.

As she tenderly took her baby from him, Lucy thought she would never again in her life know such pain.

Half-blinded by her tears, she gazed on that small, still face and her heart-wrenching cry echoed across the valley, shaking the night and striking fear into the cowardly heart of Edward Trent, who by now was already some distance away.

CHAPTER SEVENTEEN

L IKE EVERYONE ELSE in Comberton-by-Weir and far
beyond, Leonard Maitland was deeply shocked by the
events of that night.

When Jamie Baker was laid to his rest, Leonard had been
there for Lucy, along with her friends and neighbours; for
with her parents split up and out of touch, with no thought
or care for their little grandson, since he had been born –
and died – out of wedlock, poor little mite, Lucy had no real
family to help her through.

The service was very emotional, and afterwards, when
everyone gathered at Overhill Farm, the air was thick with
disbelief. No one there could recall anything of such a tragic
nature happening in their lifetime.

In the dark days that followed, Lucy withdrew into herself;
by day she wandered restlessly over the fields and hills, as
though searching for her lost child, and at night she headed
blindly for Barney's house, where he and Vicky and the
children were waiting to give support and comfort. They,
too, missed the little boy and were heartbroken.

On this chilly day, with the date of departure fast
approaching, Lucy and Barney prepared to visit Leonard
Maitland. 'Lucy, love, are you sure you know what you're
doing?' Barney had worried about Lucy's decision and

had done all he could to change her mind, without success.

He tried again to dissuade her, but she was adamant. 'You and your family have been kindness itself,' Lucy told him, 'but soon you'll all be gone away. I have to take charge of my own life now.' Her voice broke. 'You know how much I love the cottage, Barney, but I could never go back there, not without my little angel.' Taking a moment to compose herself, she said in a whisper, 'How can I ever forgive myself, Barney?'

'Whatever d'you mean?' But he knew well enough what she meant, for hadn't he told her time and again that she was wrong?

'I know you will never admit it, Barney, but it *was* all my fault.' Gulping back the tears, she went over that awful night in her mind. 'If I'd only listened to you and kept back, you would have saved Jamie, I know you would . . .' When emotion overtook her, she crumpled into him and he held her close against his heart, his two arms keeping her safe while she sobbed helplessly.

After a time, when she was quiet, they walked on, with Barney keeping his arm around her shoulders. 'Listen to me, Lucy love,' he said tenderly. 'What happened that night was no fault of yours. Evil took your baby, and the way things were, there was nothing more you or I could have done to prevent that terrible thing. We both tried our level best to save little Jamie, but it wasn't enough.'

He sighed from deep within. 'Sometimes, sweetheart, there are greater powers in force than we could ever hope to understand.'

Gently bringing her to a halt, he turned her round to face him. Looking into her reddened stricken eyes, he said emotionally, 'I'm so proud of you, Lucy. We all are. You've come through what will probably be the worst time of your entire life, and you've already begun to make decisions.' He smiled wryly. 'I don't agree with the decision about moving back to Bridget's, but it's your life, and you have to do what you feel is right.'

Lucy gave a little gulp. 'The truth is, I don't know what's right any more,' she confessed tearfully. 'All I know is that I have to make a new start, and before I can go forwards, I need to go backwards.'

Even in her sorrow, she noted the change in Barney; the trauma of that night had made him look so terribly ill. Raising her hand, she laid it on the side of his dear face as though comforting *him.* 'You mustn't upset yourself on my account,' she pleaded. 'You look so worn and tired, and I don't want to be a burden on you.'

Afraid that she might see how truly ill he was, he laid his hand over hers and, moving it from his face, held it tightly as they walked on. 'You could never be a burden to us,' he said gruffly. 'We love you like family, you know that.'

Lucy smiled wistfully. 'I know, and I love you for it, but I won't always have you to lean on. I have to try and get my life together, if I can.'

'You will.' He was sure of it. 'But I'm not happy about this business today.'

'It will be all right,' Lucy assured him.

But he was far from satisfied.

∽

Some twenty minutes later, in Leonard Maitland's study, the pair of them explained what Lucy had decided, and like Barney, Leonard disagreed with her. 'Of course it's your decision, my dear, but is it wise to return to your friend Bridget's house? Don't get me wrong, she's charming and kind, and I know she's been the best of friends to you, but she runs a bad house, Lucy. If you want my opinion, I don't think that's the right place for you to be.'

'It's the *only* place for me to be,' Lucy answered. 'Since she took me in, and right up until I moved into your cottage, she was like a mother to me. We understand each other, and I know that when Barney and his family leave, she will be my rock. She's been kind enough to ask me if I want to stay with her, and I've accepted.'

'Well then, if your mind is made up, I have to ask if you will do something for me?'

'If I can, I will,' Lucy readily agreed.

On arriving, she had placed the keys to the cottage on his table. He now took them up and held them out to her. 'Please take these back. I gave you the cottage to live in, with a secured tenancy, and though you may not want it at this moment in time, you may be glad of it later, when you're able to think more clearly about your future and security.'

When she hesitated, he lifted her hand and placed the keys on her palm. 'Take them, Lucy. If you can't go in yet, that's fine, but there may come a day when you find comfort there. Whether you like it or not, the cottage is yours to live in, legal and binding.'

With her hand still stretched out, Lucy remained unsure until, taking a step forward, Barney closed her fingers around the keys and pressed her arm to her side. 'Mr Maitland's right,' he told her gruffly. 'There might come a time when you need that cottage.'

It was a moment before Lucy responded, and then she threw her arms round a startled but delighted Leonard Maitland. 'Thank you,' she whispered, her eyes bright and sad, and her heart so sore she could hardly bear it. She had come dangerously close to being lost forever, but these kind, caring folks had brought her back from the brink of despair.

Maybe after all, there was a future for her. Time alone would tell.

On the way back, feeling unwell, Barney stopped several times on the pretence of watching a hare or seeing 'summat running through the spinney'. Lucy saw nothing of what he pointed out, so deep in thought, she took him at his word.

'I'm so glad Mr Maitland managed to delay our voyage and the signing of the sale for another two weeks.' Having recovered for a while, Barney strolled beside her. 'He's a thoughtful sort, don't you think?'

Lucy agreed. 'You've all done more than enough for me, and now I've prepared myself for you all to be leaving soon. An extra two weeks won't change that, will it?'

'Mebbe not, Lucy love, but Mr Maitland is a real gentleman. He explained the circumstances to his solicitor, and out of respect for you, they've managed to hold it back, but only for the short term.' He had other reasons for being grateful that the leaving would be delayed. 'Vicky will be pleased when I tell her. She's been that worried about you.'

When a short time later they relayed the news to Vicky, she was thrilled. 'At least now we'll have a little more time together and it will help you get used to the idea of us going. What's more, I can satisfy myself that you're properly settled before we leave.'

While they carried on talking, Barney excused himself. 'I've a few things to tend to,' he said, hurrying away before Vicky could question him too closely.

Dodging anyone who knew him, Barney made his way to the village and Dr Lucas's afternoon surgery. There was no one else there, and he was quickly shown in. 'I trust you're here to tell me you're now ready to admit yourself for the tests?' Having asked Barney several times to agree to go into the Infirmary, Dr Lucas never gave up hope that his patient would at last change his mind.

Barney, however, soon shattered the man's expectations. 'If I came in for the tests, would it improve matters in any way?'

'I can't promise that.' He was the kind of doctor who answered straightforward questions with straightforward answers. 'As I've already explained, your heart is badly diseased, but we can't tell how badly until we investigate further.' Having already observed Barney's laboured breathing and the grey pallor of his skin, he was deeply concerned. 'I hope you realise how serious your condition is?'

'I'm beginning to.' Barney was truthful. 'I've noticed how quickly I get tired of late, and sometimes it hurts to breathe.' He gave a bright smile. 'But I'm still here and I'm still fighting, so it can't be all that bad, can it?'

Giving no answer, but taking the stethoscope from around his neck, the doctor asked Barney to go behind the screen and take off his shirt. A moment later, he gave Barney a thorough examination.

'Right! You can put your shirt back on now,' he said, walking away and perching himself on the edge of his desk. There was a look of apprehension on his face.

'Well?' Barney, too, was apprehensive. 'Is it worse?'

'Bad enough.' Looking directly at Barney he told him flatly, 'You're playing with fire, man.'

'In what way?'

'You haven't followed my instructions at all, have you?'

'Yes, I have,' Barney blustered. 'I'm taking the medication, just as you advised.'

'That's only part of it, and even that is only a short-term precaution until we know the extent of the damage. You haven't slowed up much in your work, and I've seen with my own eyes how you still slave away on the farm, even after I warned you not to exert yourself.'

Anger thickened his voice as he reprimanded his patient.

'Good God, man! Are you intent on killing yourself? Keep on the way you are, and I can't promise you'll be alive a year from now, or even less!'

Barney had known he was ill, but to have it spelled out like that, shocked him to the core. 'I'm a working man, Doctor,' he said quietly. 'I can't stop doing what I do; the cows won't milk themselves if I can't do it. My sons are a boon, but they need me with them a while yet.'

The doctor did not mince his words. 'If you continue to ignore my advice, they won't have you at all.'

'Then tell me this.' Barney was torn all ways. 'If I stopped working right now, and sat about like a cabbage in a patch, would that prolong my life by any great measure?'

The doctor carefully considered Barney's question before giving an honest if vague answer. 'As I told you before, we don't really know with these things. Your heart is in bad shape, and if you agreed to slow right down, that could well improve matters. I can't be more specific than that.'

Barney's courage was never as low as it was in that moment; he was afraid for himself, but more so for his beloved family. When he spoke now, his words were sure and final. 'There will be no hospital, and no tests,' he said gruffly. 'If I have a year, or less, then so be it.' Standing to leave, he smiled wearily. 'Thank you for all you've done.'

Dr Lucas had known Barney well, and it pained him to see his spirit so low. 'I'm very sorry,' he said. 'I only wish there was something more I could do.'

'There is.'

'Then name it.'

'Without me to drag them down, my family have the chance to start a new life, and nothing must spoil that.'

The doctor was astonished. 'What are you saying? Surely you don't still intend taking such a long and arduous journey?'

'That's for me to decide,' Barney replied firmly. 'All I'm asking of you is that what transpired between you and me goes no further.'

Dr Lucas nodded. 'I believe we've already agreed on that.'

'And do I have your word, as a gentleman?'

'As a gentleman and a doctor, yes.'

Barney shook him by the hand. 'Goodbye. I won't be coming to see you again.'

He left then, a wiser, sadder man. A man who knew what must be done, and had to find the courage to see it through.

CHAPTER EIGHTEEN

'EXCUSE ME, MISS ... I believe this is your stop.'
The bus conductor had noticed how Lucy was not watching the landmarks. Instead, she was sat deep in thought, in the far corner, sometimes looking out of the window, sometimes with her eyes closed. Now, staring ahead, she appeared to have no idea of her surroundings.

Startled by his concerned tap on the shoulder, Lucy thanked him and made her way to the platform. When the bus came to a halt, she quickly clambered off.

It had been comfortingly quiet on the bus, but now as she set off in the direction of the church, the noise and bustle of Liverpool was all around her; the clatter of horse and cart, the smell and sound of petrol-driven vehicles; the sight of rich women in furs, poor women in thin coats and men in suits, all going about their business. This was Friday, a day when people looked forward to their weekend and couldn't wait for the day to end. But for Lucy, since losing her child, every day seemed the same.

Leaving the mayhem behind, she came up the rise towards the church. The further from the centre she got, the more the wind seemed to swirl and blow. Beginning to shiver, Lucy drew her coat more tightly about her.

Taking the side path, she went along by the hedge and

into the churchyard; little Jamie's resting-place was to the right of the gate under the oak-tree. Lucy had chosen St Saviour's as she had come to Sunday school here as a child, and had happy memories of it. The church at Comberton now seemed tainted, somehow, with the evil of Edward Trent.

Removing a handkerchief from her coat-pocket she wiped it over the small cross, which was temporarily erected until a marble heart could be set there. After laying down the posy of pretty leaves, together with a small toy, she knelt down to tell Jamie how much she missed and loved him. As always, she imagined him in her mind; toddling in the garden and chuckling as she chased him, and the tears were never far away.

After a while, when the cold seemed to penetrate her bones, she said a heartfelt goodbye. 'I'll see you again soon, my darling.'

In the church, she lit a candle to guide her child on his way to Heaven, and when the flame flickered and danced to life, she remained there for some long time, asking questions of the Lord. What had she done that was so wicked He had to take her baby? What would she do now without him? Why had the police not caught Edward Trent and brought him to a harsh punishment? And finally, would He please take care of Barney and the Davidson family on their long journey to a new life?

A short time later, spent of emotion, Lucy made her way back to the bus-stop. As she clambered on the bus, she caught sight of Barney. Emerging from a public-house and somewhat unsteady on his feet, he had a woman clinging to his arm.

Laughing together, they set off down the street and were soon gone.

Falling into her seat, Lucy was riveted with shock. She had recognised the woman as being a close friend and colleague of Bridget's, and knowing the nature of her business, Lucy found it hard to understand what Barney was doing in her company. She suspected also, if his unsteady gait was anything to go by, that he had been drinking. That in itself was astonishing, because as far as Lucy knew, Barney enjoyed the occasional glass of something only when the occasion demanded.

Convincing herself that there must be an innocent explanation, she vowed to ask him next time they met.

On arriving home, she went into the kitchen to make herself a cup of tea. 'Make one for me while you're at it.' Bridget almost fell into the room. 'I've been trudging round the shops for hours and I've got a throat like sandpaper.'

She threw down a heap of bags and sitting herself at the table, she told Lucy, 'I've left the girls searching for new outfits. They've bagged a lucrative job for next week, escorting some London businessmen about town. Lord knows, if we're to put the business on a more respectable footing, they'll need to look their best.'

With her mind still on Barney and the woman, Lucy heard not a word. 'Three sugars, isn't it?' she asked, beginning to spoon it out of the bag.

'Best make it four,' the woman advised. 'I'm shattered, so I am!'

When Lucy placed her cup and saucer before her, Bridget noticed how preoccupied she seemed. 'What's wrong wit' you? You've got a face like a wet weekend.'

'Nothing.' Lucy sat down with her tea and took a sip of it.

'Aw now, don't give me that.' The big Irishwoman wagged a finger. 'I've known you long enough to spot when something is wrong, so out with it! What's on your mind?'

Hesitating for a second or two, Lucy told her, 'I've just seen Barney Davidson coming out of a pub, and he was drunk . . . or near as dammit.'

281

'I see.' Bridget raised her cup to her mouth and took a long slurp. 'And ye are sure it was Barney ye saw?'

'I'm certain.'

Bridget peered at her over the rim of her cup. 'Was he alone?'

'No. He was with a woman.' She hesitated to say it was one of Bridget's friends.

'I see.'

When Bridget next spoke, it was to give Lucy a warning. 'Don't get mixed up in what you don't understand,' she cautioned. 'What Barney does or doesn't do is none of our business.'

From Bridget's reaction, Lucy suspected she knew more than she was saying. As the realisation dawned, she confronted her. 'You knew all about it, didn't you?' she demanded. 'You knew Barney was drinking and womanising. Don't deny it, because I can see it in your face!'

'All right, yes, I did. In fact, I'm told it's been going on for some time, and now it seems he doesn't give a bugger who sees him! But I didn't think it was my place to tittle-tattle. If Barney Davidson has a problem, he'll deal with it. Doesn't he always?' Not wishing to be drawn onto dangerous ground, Bridget quickly drank up her tea, took her shopping and went upstairs with it. 'I'll see youse later,' she called back.

Unable to get Barney out of her mind, Lucy vowed to visit the Davidsons that evening. 'I've got to go and see him,' she muttered as she helped Tillie to peel the potatoes for dinner. 'I need to ask him outright.' She knew him well enough to do that.

Barney had been preying on her mind a great deal of late; behaving strangely, going away for hours on his own, and now this. In the beginning, she had thought it might be the trauma of what had happened that night, but drinking in a public-house with such a woman; arm-in-arm in the street and laughing as if he didn't give a damn who saw him . . . this was not the Barney she knew and loved. In the wake of Jamie's death, her embarrassingly romantic feelings towards him had vanished; but now they had resurfaced and she couldn't help it, he was never out of her thoughts. It was getting to the stage where she was afraid to look Vicky in the eye, in case her friend read the truth on her face.

Later that evening, when dinner was over and the kitchen at 23, Viaduct Street was spick and span, Lucy put on her hat and coat and set off for Overhill Farm.

As she went up the path to the front door she heard raised voices and the sound of a door slamming. Suddenly, the front door was flung open and Susie came rushing out, straight into Lucy's arms. 'Oh Lucy! Ronnie and Daddy are saying bad things to each other, and they won't stop . . .' She began to sob uncontrollably.

Lucy held her close. 'Ssh, don't worry, it'll be all right,' but she could still hear the two men inside, and now Thomas's voice, pleading with them to stop arguing. A moment later, the door opened and Vicky emerged, looking distraught as she searched for Susie. On seeing Lucy she was visibly relieved. 'Oh, dear God, Lucy, I don't know what to do. It's like my whole world's falling apart.'

Trembling and distressed, she took Susie by the shoulders. 'Run inside, sweetheart, and fetch our coats.' Calming herself for the girl's sake, she suggested with a shaky smile, 'We'll go for a little walk, eh, you, me and Lucy? When we come back, happen it'll all have sorted itself out, eh?'

Relieved to see her mammy smiling and comforted by her words, Susie ran to get their coats. 'What's happening?' Lucy asked worriedly. 'Is it Barney?' In her troubled mind she could still see him and the woman.

'Yes.' Vicky shook her head. 'There's something very

wrong,' she said. 'Barney's been so odd of late – wandering off and not coming back till all hours. He's not been sleeping easy, and sometimes when I wake in the middle of the night, I look out of the window and he's pacing the yard like a trapped animal. He's suddenly got the devil of a temper on him, too, snapping and snarling and jumping down our throats at the slightest thing; he even smacked Susie last night because she came downstairs crying after having a bad dream. It's not like him, Lucy. He's always been such a loving man.'

She took a long, weary breath. 'And now, Ronnie swears he saw Barney in Liverpool today . . . "arm-in-arm with a trollop", he says, and he swears that the pair of 'em were drunk.'

With raw eyes she looked into Lucy's face as though searching for some kind of reassurance. 'I didn't believe it of him, Lucy. "It couldn't have been your father" – that's what I told Ronnie. "He would never do such a thing".' Her voice broke. 'But to be honest, Lucy, somewhere in the back of my mind, God forgive me, because of the way Barney's been behaving, I'm half-inclined to believe what Ronnie saw.'

When Susie returned and they had on their coats and scarves, the three of them wandered away to the spinney; these days they were reluctant to go near the river, because of the bad memories.

Lucy made no mention of the fact that, like Ronnie, she too had seen Barney on the streets drunk and laughing with a woman. Instead she told Vicky, 'I've an idea Barney might still be suffering the effects of that night. It was a terrible thing for him to witness. Grief and shock can affect us all in different ways,' she said in a low voice. God knows, she herself was half-demented with it. 'Maybe Barney is not able to deal with the horror of what happened?'

Vicky had already considered that. 'Of course he suffers

from remembering, as we all do.' She reached out to squeeze Lucy's hand. 'But it's more than that,' she went on sombrely. 'Now I think about it, I've seen a few changes happening in Barney, long before that night. He's been getting more preoccupied and distant, as though he's always got something on his mind, and none of us are a part of it.'

She shrugged. 'He's been working so hard – pushing himself until he hurts. It's as if he's trying to prove something. He's changed, Lucy, and now it's got so I can hardly recognise him as the man I married.'

In spite of her determination not to let young Susie see her upset, Vicky began to cry, softly at first, and when she could no longer hold it back, the crying became wrenching sobs that tore her apart. 'I'm sorry,' she kept saying. 'I'm so, so sorry.' For the first time in her married life, she did not know how to deal with Barney.

Running to her, Susie threw her arms round Vicky's waist; in a choked voice she told her, 'Don't cry, Mammy, it's all right. Please don't cry.' The normal roles of mother and child were reversed, and Vicky was ashamed.

After a time they walked on; Lucy lost in her own thoughts, Vicky also quiet now, and Susie with her hand clutched in her mammy's.

All three were thinking of Barney. Lucy was determined to get him alone and have a heart-to-heart with him; Vicky wondered how she could win back the man she loved; and her frightened daughter silently brooded over the night's event, her heart alive with all manner of emotion – and shockingly, even the smallest beginnings of hatred towards the father she adored.

When they got back to the house, despite the cold, Ronnie was seated on the garden bench. With his head down and his hands over the back of his neck, he did not hear them approach.

'Ronnie?' Going immediately to him, Vicky put her arm around his shoulders. 'What are you doing out here in the cold?'

Ronnie looked up. In the half-light from the windows she could see that he'd been crying. 'What is it, love?' She sat beside him. 'What's happened?'

For a long anxious moment, Ronnie gave no answer. Instead he glanced back at the house, then he looked at his mother and the tears ran down his face. 'That man in there,' he whispered brokenly. 'I don't even know who he is any more.'

Rising to Barney's defence, Vicky told him firmly, 'Whatever he says or does, and whatever you may think of him just now, he is still your father!'

Ronnie shook his head. 'No, he's not. I know my father like I know myself, and that man in there is a stranger.'

Vicky understood but was horrified all the same. 'Your father is ill,' she said lamely. 'He doesn't seem to understand how he's hurting us. Barney is a good man. He's stood by all of us at one time or another, and now it's our turn to stand by him.'

Scrambling to his feet, Ronnie looked down on her in amazement. 'How can you say that?' he demanded. 'I saw him with my own eyes! He was drunk in the street, in the company of a woman like *that* . . . They went away laughing – laughing at *you*, Mother! He's not only cheating on you, but he's doing it openly. He gets himself drunk and then he comes home arguing and causing trouble in the family.'

His voice shook with rage. 'You can stand by him if you like, but I won't! I can't forgive him.'

Seeing her brother stride off angrily into the night, Susie wailed, 'Stop him, Mammy. STOP HIM!'

Grabbing her close, Vicky held her tight. 'I can't,' she said, 'but he'll be back. You'll see, sweetheart, Ronnie will be back.' In her heart though, she could not be certain of that.

'Do you want me to go?' Having witnessed the distress in this close-knit family, Lucy was afraid for them all, including Barney. She wanted to stay but sensed that Vicky needed to be alone with her family.

Vicky nodded. 'I'm sorry, Lucy,' she apologised. 'I'll get Thomas to see you home.' Because the night was cold and because she had great affection for Lucy, she invited her to come inside first.

She led the way, with Susie at her side and Lucy following.

When she walked into the sitting room, Lucy was shocked at the sight of Barney. Unkempt and unshaven, he sat in the armchair, his shirt undone to the chest and his head lolling sideways. Lucy thought he looked ill and quietly said so to Vicky.

Thomas had been standing before the fire, his eyes alive with anger as he stared at his father. 'He's not ill.' He spat out the words. 'He's drunk!'

'I'll deal with your father.' Taking hold of him by the arm, Vicky led him away. 'I need you to take Lucy home in the trap.'

Thomas nodded. 'Will you be all right?'

'I'll be fine,' she answered with a smile. 'Oh, and take Susie with you.' When the girl protested, she told her gently, 'Lucy would like that, wouldn't you, lass?'

Realising Vicky's intent, Lucy nodded. 'Yes, I would.' Addressing Susie she told her, 'I need to know all about the new clothes you and Mammy have bought for the journey to America.'

At Lucy's remark, Thomas gave a grunt. 'That's if we ever go!'

Susie gave a cry. 'We *are* going, aren't we, Mammy?'

Vicky nodded. 'That's the plan, sweetheart.' Though her

heart was breaking, she smiled her brightest. 'In just over a week's time we'll be boarding the ship for America.' She gave Barney a sideways glance. *'All of us!'*

On the way back to Viaduct Street, Thomas sat hunched on the driving seat, quiet and morose. He had only ever seen his father drunk once, and that was when his friend Adam had brought back some strong homemade cider to mark his birthday. It was a memorable night, which ended in laughter and good humour. This time it was different. And in all his life, Thomas had never felt so helpless.

~

Over the next few days, Barney's hitherto good name deteriorated further. 'Cheating on his good wife,' people tutted. 'Carrying on wi' all kinds, and drinking himself into a stupor every chance he gets.'

'I hear he stayed out all night a while back.' Even on the bus they tittle-tattled about him. 'Lord knows what that family's going through, and them supposed to be leaving for America any day now.'

Seated behind the two gossiping women, Lucy could not wait to get off at her stop; though as she passed them she commented loudly on 'folks who can't help but gossip, even when they don't have a clue what they're talking about'!

As she hurried home, she wondered where it would all end.

Bridget was alone. 'The girls have gone on another one of these "business" appointments,' she said proudly. 'Sure, haven't we gone up in the world, don't you think?'

'Mmm.' Seating herself at the table, Lucy recalled what the women on the bus had said. 'I hear that Barney stayed out all night a while back. How on earth do folks find out so much so soon?'

Bridget plonked a cup of tea down on the table. 'What exactly are we talking about?'

Lucy told her about the two women and the conversation they were having. 'What on earth are we going to do about Barney?' she asked. 'I'm at my wit's end.' She gave Bridget a wary look. 'What if Vicky ever finds out he was here the night he went missing?'

'I won't tell if you won't,' Bridget replied. 'What was I supposed to do when he turned up, soaking wet and looking to come inside? He only slept the drink off while I dried his clothes, that's all.' With big eyes she chided Lucy. 'Should I have turned him away – is that what you're saying?'

Lucy shook her head. 'No, of course it's not.' All the same, she felt as though she was betraying Vicky by not telling her, and she told that to Bridget now.

Bridget was angry with her. 'Now look here, young lady! Sure the man himself pleaded with you not to tell where he was for most of the night. You did right not to say anything, and besides, didn't they have the holiest of rows and didn't she get angry and lock the door against him?'

'So I'm told, yes.'

'There y'are, then! Even if he'd gone home, he wouldn't have been able to get in. He'd have had to sleep on the garden bench, so he would!'

Once Bridget was in full sail there was no stopping her. 'I gave him a bed for the night and there's nothing to be ashamed of in that. You and I both know how hard I'm trying to get this house respectable. It may well have been a house of pleasure a while back, but things are changing.'

She bristled with pride. 'You'll notice I'm more of a businesswoman now, so ye will. What's more, little Tillie has taken to her new job of bookkeeper like a duck to water.' She gave a short whistle. 'I never knew she was so good at keeping proper accounts! And she's delighted with the shorter hours and the bigger wage-packet.'

Lucy had to smile. 'You always were ambitious,' she said fondly. 'And happen you're right about giving Barney a bed for the night. If he had upset Vicky so much that she locked the door against him, she might have done worse if he'd gone banging on the door in the middle of the night.'

Bridget beamed. 'Well, there y'are then. Sure, isn't that what I've been saying all along?' She had a question. 'Did ye manage to have a quiet word with him . . . about the womanising and the drinking?'

Lucy shook her head. 'I've tried time and again to get him on his own, but he always manages to dodge me.' This time she was determined. 'I've spoken with Adam. He's worried sick about Barney, but even he hasn't been able to talk any sense into him. Vicky and the boys will be up at Leonard Maitland's tonight. Apparently he's concerned about Barney and unsure about what's happening. He's asked the family to come and talk it through, so tonight, Barney will be on his own.'

Bridget was doubtful. 'Will Barney stay in, d'ye think? Or will he be off out with his floozy?'

Lucy tapped her nose by way of a confidence. 'It's all been arranged. Barney's agreed to see Adam, and being as he's let Adam down twice before, we're hoping that this time he'll keep his word and be at home when his old pal arrives.'

Bridget got the picture. 'But it won't be Adam who turns up, will it? It'll be you, is that right?'

Lucy confirmed that was the idea. 'Seeing as he keeps avoiding me, this seems to be the only way.'

'Well, I hope it works, because somebody needs to talk some sense into that foolhardy head of his,' Bridget declared. 'Sure, if anybody can do it, you can.'

Just then the girls came in, dressed in their new outfits

and looking like a million dollars. 'I've just spent a whole afternoon in one of the best hotels in Manchester.' Brenda's tall, willowy figure was wrapped in the most expensive coat with fur collar and deep fur-trimmed pockets.

'And I've been to the races.' Shorter and perfectly formed, Lynette was better suited to the small-brimmed hat and brown silk two-piece.

'I hope you both behaved like ladies?' Raising her eyebrows, Bridget gave them a warning glance.

On hearing how they had been paid handsomely for their escort duties, Bridget congratulated them. 'Sure if we keep on like this, we'll have to move to posher premises,' she joked. 'Now off upstairs wit' ye, and out of those expensive clothes. You'll need them again, I hope, so make sure you hang them up nice and neatly.'

Shortly after the girls had departed, Lucy excused herself. 'I'd best get ready,' she told Bridget.

'Off ye go then, and I wish ye well.' Her friend was concerned. 'It's a crying shame to see how Barney's hurting that poor family of his. If he doesn't come to his senses soon, there'll be no America for him, and no family to speak of neither.'

With all that preying on her mind, Lucy got washed and changed and made herself ready to meet Adam. Having lately acquired a little black Ford, he was to run her up to the end of the lane and wait there until she came out again.

She didn't have to wait long before the little car drew up outside number 23. 'What d'you think to it?' he asked proudly. 'Cost me an arm and a leg, but it was worth it.'

Lucy told him she thought it was handsome, and smiling from ear to ear he helped her climb on the running board and then get inside, before taking the starting handle and thrusting it into the front of the car. Perspiring from the effort, Adam drove up the street erratically, with the car lurching and bumping. 'I'm not quite used to it yet,' he apologised sheepishly. 'But I'll get us there – don't you worry about that.'

When they reached the end of the lane leading to Overhill Farm, they sat awhile. 'Have the family gone out yet, d'you think?' Adam was on pins.

'I'm not sure.' Lucy, too, was nervous. If she did get to see Barney on his own, what would she say? How could she convince him that what he was doing was tearing the family apart? What about the future? What about America, and the family so looking forward to it now? *And why was he doing this?* That was the main thing.

While they waited and watched, Lucy spoke her mind to Adam. 'I don't understand why Barney's suddenly started behaving like this,' she said. 'He's an intelligent man, compassionate and caring, and yet here he is, wantonly throwing away everything he cherishes.'

Adam had an idea, but he could not give her the answer. 'It's the strangest thing,' he said thoughtfully. 'I've known him a very long time, but I can never recall him acting the way he is now, hurting the ones he loves and seemingly hellbent on destroying himself. One minute he's all fired up at going to America, and now it's as though he has to destroy every chance they've got of starting a new life. I've tried to reason with him, but he just walks away. He won't listen to me.'

Reaching out, he took Lucy's hand into his. 'Happen he'll talk to you,' he said, patting the back of her hand. 'Happen *you'll* get through to him where I can't.' In the half-light he smiled on her, trying not to show the love he felt. She was his good friend, and he was not prepared to spoil that by speaking his heart.

Suspecting nothing of his true feelings, Lucy gave him a nudge. 'Here they are now,' she said. The family emerged from the house; Vicky and Susie first, then the two sons.

Huddled together, they set off on foot in the other direction, along the lane and on towards Leonard Maitland's house, The Manse. 'We'll give it another minute or so and then you'd best go in,' Adam said. 'D'you think he'll open the door to you?'

Lucy smiled secretly. Reaching into her handbag, she drew out the key to Overhill Farmhouse. 'I never thought to give this back after I stayed there once,' she told him. 'I knew it would be more polite to knock, but like you say, he might see me out of the window and be gone through the back door. So I shall just let myself in.' She did not like the idea of doing it, but saw no other way.

Climbing out of the car, Lucy softly closed the door and approached the house. She could see Barney through the window; slouched in his chair he was leaning forward, deep in thought and looking lost.

Concentrating on what she was doing, she slipped the key into the lock, opened the door and went inside; and because she did not want to alarm him, she deliberately made a noise as she came towards the sitting room.

'Who's there?' Barney's voice sailed through the house. 'Vicky! Is that you?'

When suddenly he was standing before her, his face fell with astonishment. 'Lucy! What the devil are you doing here? How did you get in?'

'Sorry if I frightened you.' When Lucy now took a step forward, Barney took a step back. 'Please, Barney. We need to talk.'

'I don't want to talk. Go away, and leave me be.' Seeing her there and knowing how, like the rest of his beloved family, she was worried out of her mind, he so much wanted to take her in his arms and open his heart to her. But if he did, then all of this would have been for nothing. 'How did you get in? Did Vicky let you in, is that it? Did she think you might get me to tell you things I can't tell her?' His eyes bright with tears, he lowered his sorry gaze to the floor.

'Vicky doesn't know I'm here,' she told him. 'Look! I still have my key.' She laid it on the coat-stand. 'There. I've returned it now.'

As she walked towards him, he barred her path, his shoulders squared tall and his face blank, with no expression. 'I don't need you here. I want you to go.'

Now, as Lucy stared him in the eye, he looked away, as though he could not bear to see the pain and anxiety in her face. 'I said I want you to leave. Now!'

Lucy refused. 'You'll have to throw me out, Barney.'

The man was in anguish; he wanted to tell her the truth, but he daren't. He *couldn't.*

'Talk to me, Barney.' Laying her hand on his arm, she thrilled at his nearness, but for now all she wanted was to make him at peace, to let him know that he was not on his own. 'Why are you doing all of this?' Her voice was like silk to his ears. 'You were always such a kind and loving man, concerned about other people's feelings. You're not a drunk, or a bad man. You're a worker and a fighter. You risked your own life to save my baby and you were my strength afterwards. Was it that night, Barney? Was it because of what happened to little Jamie?' Her voice broke. 'You said it yourself – there was nothing we could have done. It was too late, Barney . . . all too late.'

When she paused, choking back the pain of remembering, Barney looked up. He was so ashamed. 'How are you now, Lucy?' His voice was merely a whisper, but it came from the heart.

Looking up with bright eyes and a sorry smile, she told him, 'I'm coping, Barney. But I'm so worried about you . . . we all are. What is it? What's wrong? You have to let me help. You have to let *us all* help.'

She could sense that he was weakening, when suddenly the front door was pushed open and in walked a woman, tall and attractive, with wild hair and a ruddy complexion, and the smell of booze about her. 'You shouldn't leave your door open of a night-time,' she quipped. 'And who might this be, Barney? I know it's not your wife because you told me she'd be out with the family.'

'Jesus!' Thrusting Lucy aside he took hold of the woman by the arm. 'What the hell are you doing here, and drunk into the bargain!'

She smiled. 'I remembered you saying your family were going out and that I should come and pay a call on you if ever I was passing. Well, I might not have been passing, but I'm here now, and I've brought us some cheer.' Holding up a bottle of sherry, she taunted him with it. 'If you don't want to stay here, we can always go to my place. I've got a car outside.' Staggering sideways, she almost lost her balance. 'The driver is an old friend of mine . . .' she gave a wink '. . . if you know what I mean?'

About to throw her out into the night, Barney stopped himself. No! This might be his best chance. Just now, Lucy had almost got him to confide in her, and if his unwelcome visitor hadn't turned up, he might well had said things he regretted. And that would have been a disaster.

'She's the woman I saw you with in Liverpool.' Lucy was shocked and angry. 'Ask her to leave, Barney. She's tainting Vicky's lovely home.'

Enraged, the woman made a grab for her. Barney stepped between them. Turning on Lucy he sounded like a stranger. 'Good night, Lucy. I don't want to see you again. You can leave now.'

Lucy was taken aback. 'You don't mean that?'

He gave a slow, affirmative nod. 'Thank you for coming here tonight, but I don't need your help.'

Lucy could have argued with him, but there would have been no point. Instead she reached up and, placing her hands on his shoulders, she kissed him on the cheek. 'Think what you're doing, Barney,' she pleaded quietly. 'We all love you so much.'

For what seemed an age he looked at her, and just for the briefest moment she really believed he was listening. Then he took her by the arm and led her to the door, where he pushed her unceremoniously onto the outer step. One hard, appealing stare, and then he closed the door.

As she walked down the path, Lucy could hear their laughter. 'May God forgive you, Barney Davidson,' she whispered.

Climbing into the car she sat for a moment, unsure what to do.

'I saw the woman.' Adam's voice interrupted her thoughts. 'I wondered if I should come in, and then I thought it best not to.'

'If you'd come in, it would only have made matters worse.'

'What about the woman?'

Lucy shook her head. 'She's the one he's been seeing. He's got her in there now, and he's not in the mood for talking.' She turned to him, a sad little smile on her face. 'He almost confided in me,' she revealed. 'If that woman hadn't arrived, he would have talked, I know he would.'

They sat a moment longer; Adam feeling as though he should go in there and throw her out, and Lucy thinking how low Barney had sunk.

'What's wrong with him, Adam?' she asked now. 'Why is he doing this?'

Adam didn't know any more than she did, although a suspicion lurked at the back of his head. 'Maybe we didn't know him as well as we thought we did,' he answered thoughtfully. 'Or maybe he's pushed himself so hard, and then . . . your awful tragedy . . .' He paused, making sure he had not upset her. 'Who knows what it takes to turn a man like Barney?'

Lucy had to agree. 'We've tried,' she murmured. 'We couldn't have tried any harder. Maybe there'll be an opportunity later on.' She gave a deep sigh. 'I don't know any more.'

'Home then?'

When Lucy nodded, he started the engine, turned the car about, and went down the lane at a leisurely pace. They did not talk. For now, there was too much on their minds.

CHAPTER NINETEEN

LEONARD MAITLAND HAD welcomed the family into his home, and for a time they had enjoyed his hospitality. When the discussion turned serious, he asked Vicky outright, 'So, with the way things are at home, will you and the family still be able to come with me to Boston?'

Vicky looked at her sons, and her heart was breaking. 'I'm sure you know what's happened with Barney?'

Leonard nodded. 'I'm sorry.' He was more sorry than she would ever know, he thought, because if he was going to Boston without Barney, he would be going without Vicky. He knew that, even before she told him.

'I'm not sure if we'll be able to come or not,' Vicky said solemnly. 'We so much want to – in fact, we've all been so excited about it . . .'

She would have explained, but Ronnie blurted out: 'Tell him the truth, Mother! Tell him how we might have to give up the greatest adventure we're ever likely to have, and all because my father's turned into a drunk and a laughing stock.'

'That's enough!' Now, when Thomas put his hand over his brother's arm, Ronnie bent his head in shame. 'It's true though, isn't it?' Getting out of his chair, he strode across the room and ran out of The Manse into the night.

'Go after him, Tom. Take care of him.' Vicky was desolate. As Thomas went to look for his brother, she addressed Leonard with a degree of pride. 'I'm sorry we've caused you so much concern,' she said. 'If you have to look for someone else to help you with the farm in Boston, we will understand.'

Leonard stopped her there. 'Vicky, listen to me.' Coming to sit beside her, he spoke with real compassion. 'I fully understand what you must all be going through at this time, and I wouldn't dream of rushing into looking for anyone else.'

'Do you mean that?'

'Of course. We still have a little time. Until then, I'll assume that Barney is going through some sort of crisis; probably stemming from the idea that he should have saved the child and couldn't. He's a good man, and he did his best, that's all any of us can do.'

'Pray it will turn out all right,' Vicky said. Deep down she feared that Barney had gone so low he might never come back to her. 'All I'm saying is, I don't want you to be hampered in your plans, especially when you've been so good to us.'

Outside, Thomas had managed to calm his brother, and when Vicky came out with Susie, the four of them began their way back down the lane. 'It's all gone, hasn't it?' Ronnie was broken. 'Our happy family, our dream ... all of us wanting to go to America and start over – all gone.'

Quickening his steps he walked on in front. Thomas kept a close eye on him, while Vicky walked between him and Susie, wondering why her happy, safe little world had been so cruelly shattered.

$\sim$

Inside the house the woman was all over Barney. 'You're not very friendly tonight, are you?' Seated on his knee, she nibbled at his ear. 'C'mon. Want to make love, do you?'

Barney didn't answer. The touch of her skin against his was repugnant to him, and he could smell her boozy breath on his face. 'Best not,' he said. 'There's no telling what time the family will be back.' In his mind he could still see Lucy's downcast face. She had come here to help him, and he had turned her away. What kind of monster was he becoming?

Yet what choice did he have? This was the worst time of his life and he desperately needed his family by him. Instead, for their own sakes, he was deliberately alienating them.

When the door suddenly opened to admit his two sons, Barney was flustered; for a split second he wasn't sure what to do, but then he knew and with a sore heart he played his part well. 'Oh look!' Kissing the woman soundly on the mouth, he pointed to his family who, shocked and disgusted, were now gathered at the door. 'It's my precious family,' he laughed. 'Shall we ask them to leave? What d'you think?'

Brazen, the woman sniggered. 'A minute later and they might have caught you with your trousers off,' she said.

'Get out of my house!' White-faced, her fists clenched with rage, Vicky rushed towards the woman. 'Get out, or I swear to God, I won't be responsible for my actions!'

Realising he had tipped Vicky over the edge, Barney clambered to his feet. Taking hold of the woman he told her, 'You'd best go.'

'I want you to go with her.' Vicky spoke quietly, but the rage trembled in her voice. She did not look at Barney. She had seen enough. 'You've gone too far this time,' she told him. 'I don't want you near me any more.' The tears were rising, but she would not let them see.

He hesitated, hating himself, loving her so much it hurt. He wanted to take her in his arms and tell her it was all an act, that he had never stopped wanting her, that he would always love her.

But he couldn't do that. Instead, he looked at her and drank in her beauty, knowing he might never again hold her in his arms.

'You heard what she said. GET OUT!' Giving Barney a shove, Ronnie sent him sprawling towards the door.

Before Barney could recover, his sons took one arm each and bundled him out of the door; the woman with him.

'What kind of man are you?' Thomas was shocked to his soul by Barney's inexplicable behaviour. 'You must know what you're doing to us all. But it's done now! You can't hurt us any more. As far as we're concerned, the Barney Davidson we knew is gone forever.'

Outside in the cold, with the door to his own house closed against him, Barney was made to realise that at long last, he had earned the cold hatred of the family he adored. *Dear God, what had he done?* Not for the first time he questioned the wisdom of his own behaviour.

'Come on, handsome!' The woman grabbed hold of his arm. 'Never mind them. Let's find somewhere to bed down for the night.'

Angry with himself, angry with her, he thrust her away. 'Get out of my sight!'

'Well, yer miserable bugger, all I'm doing is trying to cheer yer up!'

Realising it wasn't her fault, Barney softened. 'You said you have a car waiting?'

'That's right.' She pointed to the small vehicle tucked into the lane. 'There it is.'

Barney took her by the arm and leading her to the car, told the driver, 'See she gets home safely, will you?'

The driver, a burly fellow wearing a trilby, gave him a nod. 'I got her here, and I'll get her back,' he said.

Barney helped her into the front seat, and watched them drive away. For a long time, he stood hidden by the window, watching as his sons comforted Vicky. Seeing her sob like that wrenched him apart.

Suddenly, Susie saw him there and running out, she grabbed up a handful of mud and threw it at him, catching him hard on the neck. 'I hate you!' Sobbing uncontrollably, she kept saying it over and over, throwing the mud and telling him, 'I hate you, I hate you . . .'

A moment later, Vicky appeared to put her arm round the girl's shoulders. 'Come away, sweetheart.' She looked at Barney, covered in mud, forlorn and haggard, and for a while it seemed she might go to him. But then she said brokenly, 'I don't know who you are any more.' Head bowed and with her daughter close, she walked away, and never once looked back.

Barney was a finished man. He saw the curtains close against him, and he remained there until he felt the cold reach right into his bones. Broken, he turned away, and walked on through the night, not knowing where he was going, not caring.

~

Having talked with Barney's family, Leonard Maitland set out for a walk across the heath, as he always did at this time of night. It was a sorry affair, he thought. Barney had a new life just for the taking, and now it all seemed to be thrown by the wayside. He couldn't know how fortunate he was, to have a lovely family and a wife like Vicky – so beautiful, hardworking and totally devoted. Leonard would have given anything for such a woman, and here was Barney, casting her aside, like the bloody fool he was!

He walked on; his usual route was to turn at the spinney

and come back by the river. Just then, he saw a figure sitting on the ground. Leonard could hardly believe his eyes. 'Barney Davidson! What in God's name d'you think you're doing, man?' Coming forward, he leaned down. 'Are you all right? Are you ill?' Sitting, arms folded with his back to a tree trunk, Barney was shivering uncontrollably.

Leonard went to help him up, visibly startled when Barney took hold of him. 'You have to listen,' Barney pleaded. 'You have to help me.'

'Of course I'll help you. What on earth are you doing out here? Come home with me. We'll soon get you warmed up and then I'll run you back to the farm. Heavens above, man, you're like ice!' Taking off his jacket he wrapped it round Barney's shoulders.

But Barney would not budge. 'You don't understand,' he mumbled. 'None of them understand.' Suddenly he was sobbing. 'I had to do it, y'see? I had to turn them against me, it was the only way. The booze, the women, the fighting – it was all an act. *I had to do it . . .*'

When the sobbing took hold and he could no longer speak, Leonard took him gently away.

'Come home with me,' he said compassionately. 'Whatever it is, we'll make it right. I promise.'

Half-supporting, half-carrying him, Leonard took Barney through the night, and when they reached The Manse he settled him on the sofa in front of a roaring fire. 'I'll get a blanket . . . keep you warm. Then I'll let your wife and family know that you're safe,' he told him.

Panicking, Barney stumbled from the sofa and taking hold of Leonard by the collar, he begged him not to tell them. 'I can never go with you, but the family can. They mustn't know about me. Nobody knows, except for Adam and the doctor, and they are duty bound not to tell.'

When he began fighting for breath and pleading with

Leonard not to tell, the older man calmed him. 'Very well, Barney, your secret is safe with me, but let me get the blanket, and a hot drink, then we'll sit and talk, you and me, with no one else to bother us. All right?' He was shocked and saddened by Barney's situation. Grey-faced and with his eyes all but sunk into his head, Barney looked more ill than Leonard could ever have imagined.

Barney nodded feverishly. 'All right, yes, but I need to ask you something . . .'

'You can ask anything you like,' Leonard promised. 'But not until I have you settled and warm.' Lifting Barney's legs he laid him back onto the cushions before going off to the kitchen. 'I'll be as quick as I can.'

He returned within minutes, carrying a tray with hot milk with whisky and biscuits, and under his arm a blanket. 'Here we are!' Setting the tray on the side table, he wrapped Barney in the blanket. 'Good! You've stopped shivering.' He was relieved to see that the man's colour was already returning.

Handing the mug to Barney, he warned him, 'Be careful, now . . . it's very hot.' But it was exactly what Barney needed. 'Now then.' Leonard sat in the armchair facing him. 'Are you ready to talk?'

Barney gave him a wary look. 'Can I trust you?'

Leonard assured him, 'I'm not one to betray a trust.'

Setting his mug of milk on the hearth, Barney threw back the blanket and edging his legs round so as to be sitting opposite Leonard, he sat quiet for a while, with the only sound the ticking of the clock. When he finally spoke it was to say in a low, secretive voice, 'I want you to take my wife and family to America.'

Leonard was curious. 'But isn't that what we have already decided? You and the boys are to help me run the farm, and Vicky is to run the house. I thought it was all agreed.' He paused. 'You've changed your mind – that's it, isn't it, Barney?' There was disgust in his voice. 'That's why you've been behaving in such a shocking way – because you've changed your mind and didn't have the guts to tell me. So you thought if you behaved badly enough, I wouldn't want you with me anyway?'

'I wish to God that was the way of things,' Barney said sadly. 'You asked me a moment ago if I was ill. Well, yes, I am ill . . . *very ill.* In fact, there isn't much time. The thing is, I'm concerned about Vicky, and my children. If they knew how desperately ill I am, they would never leave me, and I'm so afraid for them. I want you to take them with you, Mr Maitland. Make a good life for them, and I'll be forever in your debt.'

Leonard was shaking his head in disbelief. 'I don't understand. Are you asking me to take them, *without you?*'

'That's exactly what I'm asking.'

'For God's sake, man, what's going on in your head? Have you lost your mind altogether? For one thing, if you're so ill, you need your family more than ever. Vicky would never go without you. And there's another thing: I need *you,* Barney. No other man could help me put the farm back on its feet like you can.'

There was a long moment when Barney laid back on the sofa, eyes closed and wishing he was not having this conversation. However, he had no choice, not if his family were to have the chance of a new life in America.

Leaning forward he told Leonard, 'You're not listening to me. I want you to understand why I've been behaving the way I have. More than that, I need you to help me, or it will all have been for nothing.'

Realising how serious Barney was, Leonard remained silent, attentive to his Farm Manager's every word.

Barney told him everything: that his heart was fading and

that he could never recover. He had agonised over and again about how he might still give his family the chance of starting a new life without him, aware that if they were to suspect that he was seriously ill, they would never abandon him. He told Leonard of their great excitement and of his own despair because, 'Through no fault of my own, that wonderful opportunity you gave us has been snatched from me. But it must not be snatched from my wife and children. That's why I've behaved the way I have – to turn them against me – to make them hate me as they have never hated anyone.'

He paused again, unable for a moment to go on, and when he did, the tears spilled over. 'I know you love my Vicky,' he said. When Leonard made to protest, Barney put up a staying hand. 'Please don't deny it. I've known for some long time that you love her. I've seen the way you watch her when she's in the field. I saw how you danced with her at our party, with love in your eyes and the tender touch of a man with the woman he loves. She has the children, but she will need you more than you know. You're a good man, Mr Maitland. Take her, and look after her, I beg you. I will ask Adam to write to you and let you know when it's all over, so you can marry my lovely Vicky in the fullness of time.'

He had one more thing to say, because now his strength was depleted. 'I'm not strong any more, but my sons are. I can't help you bring the farm back to life, but they can. I've taught them everything I know. Give them their dream, I beg you! Take them away, and never in your life tell them about our conversation this night.'

Exhausted, he lay back on the cushions. 'You have to promise me this, or the bad things I've done will all have been for nothing.'

Leonard had been devastated by Barney's terrible news, and now this request had him in turmoil. 'You're asking too much of me, Barney.' With his head bowed low, he searched for the right words. 'How can I take a man's family across the Atlantic and leave him behind to . . .' He couldn't even bring himself to say it. 'How can I possibly do that?'

'You can do it, Mr Maitland, because if you don't, they'll remain here, with no home and no one to guide them. God knows, I'll be gone soon enough, and it's more than I can bear. I'm asking you to help me. Who else can I turn to? You offered them a new life, a journey the like of which they will never know again. It's up to you.' His voice weak, he pleaded for the last time: 'Surely you won't refuse me? Think of Vicky. Think of her, alone and unprotected. No, Mr Maitland, you can't refuse me this.'

For a time, Leonard paced the floor, back and forth, up and down, occasionally stopping to shake his head and turn the matter over and over in his mind.

Presently, he came to sit in the armchair. 'What will happen to you, Barney?' he asked worriedly. 'Who will take care of you?'

The sick man did not hesitate. 'Lucy will be there when I need her, I'm sure.'

Leonard gave a long, deep sigh. 'I don't know, Barney, I just don't know. You're ill, you need your family about you. *You need Vicky* . . . What would she say if she ever found out that I had taken her away when you needed her most?'

Barney looked at him then, a world of understanding in his eyes. 'Vicky must *never* know. None of them must know.'

Leonard was humbled. 'Do you really trust me that much?'

'I do, yes. I trust you never to tell, for as long as you live. I trust you to promise me and keep your promise. Will you do that for me, Mr Maitland? Will you promise to take them and look after them, and never betray me?'

Amazed at Barney's calm manner, Leonard observed him as never before; that ordinary man, with an extraordinary courage, and he was deeply humbled. 'I'm sorry, Barney,' he said harshly. 'I'm sorry for what's happened to you, and I'm sorry that your family will be losing the bravest man it's ever been my privilege to meet.'

'But will you promise all those things? *Will you?*'

Leonard got out of his chair and began pacing the floor again, his hand cupping his chin as he thought deeply about this unique situation. It was true that he loved Vicky, and it was true that he desperately needed men he could trust, like the Davidson youths, to help him restore his grandfather's farm to its former glory. Barney was the Farm Manager here, but his two fine sons were made in the same mould.

The promise weighed on his mind. How could he promise never to tell Vicky about Barney, to say that she ought to be worshipping the ground he walked on instead of rejecting him? Everything Barney had done – the bad things and the angry things, making them despise him while he was suffering so terribly – all of it had been done deliberately, so as to save his family a world of further pain and suffering.

Could he play his part in it, as Barney pleaded with him to do? And if he did, could he live his life, seeing Vicky and her sons every day; working alongside and getting to know them and keeping secret the amazing truth about their father? Was he that strong?

It seemed a wicked, deceitful thing, and yet it was what Barney wanted, what he craved: to see his family settled and safe – the only thing that could give him peace of mind and heart.

While Barney patiently waited, Leonard continued to pace, and when at last he came to rest, his mind was made up. 'All right, Barney, if it's in my power to grant you the peace of mind you seek, I promise to do as you ask.'

Visibly overwhelmed, Barney leaned back and closed his eyes. After a moment, his eyes shining with tears, he looked up at this man, and in a strong, quiet voice he told him,

'You can't know what you've done for me, my friend. You have my deepest gratitude. Whatever happens from now on, I know I can rest easy.'

On the pretext that his milk had gone cold, Barney asked Leonard if he wouldn't mind bringing him another glass. The man readily obliged, and while he was gone but a few minutes, he returned to find the front door open and Barney loping slowly along the lane, making his way through the darkness like a wounded animal.

At first, Leonard started out after him. But then he thought better of it. 'No doubt you have things to think about,' he whispered, closing the door. 'We *all* have much to think about now.'

CHAPTER TWENTY

I T WAS THE day before the Davidson family were due to
sail. The mood in the farmhouse was one of excitement,
though it was tempered with a sombre atmosphere. 'I never
thought I'd see the day when your father turned his back on
all of us.' Vicky had suffered sleepless nights since Barney's
departure from their lives.

Ronnie was unrepentant. 'I don't have a father any
more,' he declared angrily and, though his heart was sore
at the thought, Thomas also agreed. Too much had happened. There had been too many tears and too much soul-
searching, and now it was time to call an end to it.

'He's chosen his way, and now we have to choose ours.'
Going to his mother, Tom put his arms round her shoulders
and held her close. 'We'll look after you, Mother, me and
Ronnie and our Susie.'

Having gathered the last of her things to be laid out for
packing, Susie looked up at her brother's words. 'That's
right,' she said. 'We won't let you down, not like *he's* done!'
Shutting her father out of her life was the hardest thing
Susie had ever had to do, but now it was done, and though
there were regrets, there could be no turning back.

Ronnie looked on, morose and bitter. He had said all he
wanted to say on the matter of Barney Davidson, and now

he was concentrating on the exciting prospect of a long sea-journey, and at the end of it, a new life; a life in which there was no place for the man who had once been their beloved and respected father.

Although their mother assured them that everything was going to be all right and that they must not worry about her, inside she was broken up. Her love for Barney had never wavered, even through the terrible times when he had humiliated her, flaunted his women and driven her to the edge of sanity.

'Mr Maitland is coming for us early in the morning,' she reminded them. 'Make sure you pack everything you want to take. There'll be no coming back once we've gone.' The words stuck in her throat – *once we've gone.* How casual it sounded, when all the time this remarkable journey to America would be the most frightening step she would ever take, especially without her beloved Barney by her side.

'I need to get a few things in town,' she lied now. 'I won't be long. You all carry on with what you're doing and we'll go through everything when I get back.'

Ronnie walked with her to the door. 'It'll be all right, you know,' he said quietly. 'We will manage without him.'

Displaying a bright smile, she nodded. 'I know, son.'

'You still love him, don't you?'

The smile slid away and in its place came a bitter-sweet look of regret. 'Yes, I'll always love him,' she answered softly. 'And so will you . . . we all will.'

Feeling her pain, he took her in his arms.

Neither of them spoke again, and when Vicky drew away, he helped her on with her coat and opened the door for her. And when she went down the lane he stood there for what seemed an age. 'It's just the four of us now,' he murmured. 'We'll have to take care of each other.'

Vicky had already done all her shopping and was ready to

leave Liverpool forever. But she had to make one last desperate attempt to recover the Barney she knew, and rebuild the marriage in which she had found such great joy all these years.

With that in mind, she made her way to Bridget's house.

~

Lucy was in the sitting room talking with Barney when she heard the knock on the door. 'I bet that's Bridget, forgotten her keys again,' she told him. Having taken Lucy's advice these past few days, Barney was rested and feeling much better.

When she opened the door, Lucy was astonished and delighted to see Vicky standing there. 'Oh, Vicky! I'm so glad you came,' she told her. 'I was going to come and see you later on, to wish you well.' She stood aside. 'Come in. Please, come in.'

Vicky made no move. 'I wondered if you might be thinking of coming out to the house again.' Her tone was unfriendly. 'But you would not have been welcome today, any more than you were yesterday. You know how we feel about Barney staying here.' Her expression hardened. 'You're the last person I would have thought to keep my husband away from us.'

Lucy was about to reply, when Barney himself appeared. 'Lucy has nothing to do with it,' he told Vicky. 'I'm staying here with a woman friend.'

Vicky looked at him, at this stranger, unshaven and thinner than she remembered, and in his eyes there was a look she did not recognise. 'It's not too late,' she told him. 'You can still make amends.'

Now, as Barney gazed down on her tired face, he realised the pain she had suffered, and all because of him. His head swelled with love and he wanted so much to take her in his arms and tell her that he adored her still, and that his family meant more to him than anything else in the world.

Instead, his expression stiffened. 'Why would I want to make amends?' he asked cruelly. 'These days I have no worries or responsibility. I'm free to do what I want, go where I want, and I don't have to break my back working to keep a family.' His smile was wicked. 'I'm shot of all that rubbish. Yes!' He even managed to swagger a bit. 'I consider myself to be a fortunate man!'

For a moment, Vicky was at a loss as to what she could say. In the end she said nothing.

Instead she walked away and Barney fell back into the hallway, his hands covering his face. 'God help me!' he cried. 'How can I do it to her? How can I be so cruel?'

Lucy took him back into the sitting room. 'It's a terrible thing you're doing,' she said shakily, 'but you've gone so far down the road and now that you've told me the truth about how ill you are, I can see how it might be the only way to protect and secure your family, even if it means sending them away, hating you.'

She held him in her arms while he sobbed. 'But you're right, Barney. Even though what you're doing is terrible, not only for them, but for you as well, I do understand.'

He turned to her then, his eyes scarred with pain. 'So am I right, Lucy?' he asked. 'Am I right to do what I'm doing?'

It was some small compensation when she smiled on him, a smile that was filled with love and sorrow, and hope. 'Yes, Barney,' she said honestly. 'You're putting yourself through the worst nightmare, and at the end of it, you'll be left without family or peace. But yes, I do believe you're doing the right thing . . . *for them.*'

Not for himself, she thought. Not for this darling man,

who was making a sacrifice, the enormity of which she could not even begin to imagine.

'Thank you, Lucy, you're a good friend,' he murmured. 'So, you do think I'm doing the right thing.' His smile was content. 'That's all I needed to know.'

~

Early the following morning, Lucy walked with him to the quayside. From their vantage-point they watched as Barney's beloved family clambered aboard that great ship. To see them go without him was more crippling than anything he had ever endured. What he felt now, in that terrible moment, was the most desolate feeling in the world.

Aware that Barney must be watching them from some secret, lonely place, Leonard Maitland looked repeatedly over his shoulder for a glimpse of him. He did not spot him because, reluctant to let his family see him there, Barney was well hidden from view.

It was only when the ship began to move out, that Barney shifted his position, the better to watch as the big liner took his family further away from him. He gave a futile wave, but they didn't wave back. How could they?

From the deck, Vicky stretched her neck to see if he was there. When she could see no sign of him, she returned to her cabin and there she sobbed until she thought her heart would break.

A moment later, Susie came running into the cabin, excited about everything and, for the moment at least, seeming to forget about the man they were leaving behind.

'Come quick, come and see!' she cried. 'Mr Maitland's taking us all to the bridge!' Taking Vicky by the hand, she rushed her away.

As they ran, Vicky discreetly wiped her eyes. She was all

they had now. And unlike Barney, she would not let them down.

~

Later that day, when Barney was sleeping, Lucy asked Bridget to keep an eye on him. 'I'm going up to the cottage,' she said. 'I think Barney would be more comfortable there. It's been shut up since . . . Edward Trent came back.' She still could not bring herself to say what had actually happened. Even though most days she visited the churchyard, it still seemed like some kind of a nightmare to her – not real, not possible.

Bridget agreed with her, not least because she could see for herself how desperately ill Barney was and she imagined the kind of care he might need before he was back to strength. Yet she did not know the truth, that Barney had so little time left to live.

'I expect the cottage will want airing,' she told Lucy now. 'You'll need to light a fire, and there must be an inch of dust all over. Take what you want from the cleaning cupboard, and if there's anything else you need, let me know and I'll send one of the girls up with it.'

Lucy thanked her and as an afterthought she added, 'If it's all right with you, I'd like to keep the cleaning work; I will still need the wages.'

Bridget groaned. 'Ah, sure, who else would do it if you didn't? Tillie's gone above herself with the bookkeeping, and the girls think they're God's gift, so they wouldn't dream of spoiling their delicate hands. No, the work is yours, Lucy girl, for as long as you need it. Who else would I want in me house, tell me that?'

On leaving 23, Viaduct Street, every step Lucy took reminded her of Jamie, and Edward Trent. 'I won't let that monster ruin my life any more,' she muttered, nearing the cottage. 'I'll make a new life here, with Barney, and I'll care for him as long as he needs me.'

Opening the door to the cottage, she stood looking into the tiny sitting room. Her very first and only home of her own, it had been a bright, happy place, with its chintz curtains and pretty rugs, and the little seascapes hanging on the walls.

Swallowing a sob, she flung open the curtains and let the afternoon light flood in. Bridget was right, the whole place was covered in dust. It was covered in memories too. Memories of Vicky and her family; memories of Barney when he was fit and strong and life was wonderful, and Jamie was everywhere ... toddling around the house, holding her hand, so full of love and trust.

She wallowed in nostalgia and then she cried, and then she got on with the work. Within two hours there was a cheery fire in the grate, the furniture was shining and the place felt like home again. It was not the same as before – it could never be the same – but it was alive with memories she did not want ever to lose.

'We'll be happy here, Barney and me.' A sense of belonging came over her as she thought of that wonderful man.

'I'll look after you,' she murmured. 'We'll make use of every moment we have left. We'll walk and talk; we'll sit by the river and watch the birds come to drink, and in the evening we'll laze in the garden and watch the sunset. Such plans. Such love.'

A great sense of peace entered her soul. 'We'll be good for each other,' she told the walls. 'And maybe, even after all that's happened, life won't be so bad after all.'

Later that evening, however, Barney was not so easily persuaded. With his heart and soul dented by the savage hand Fate had dealt him, he wanted only to curl up in a corner and die, for he could see little future without his loved ones.

'No, Lucy.' The two of them had been given the privacy of Bridget's parlour. 'I can't move into the cottage with you. What would people say? Your reputation would be in tatters.'

'I don't care about my "reputation"!' Lucy argued. 'I only care about you.'

'Lucy, sweetheart, don't think I'm not grateful because I am, but the answer has to be no. I won't do that to you.'

Lucy was persistent. 'Please, Barney.'

Barney shook his head and said not another word. Lucy knew he would not be persuaded.

When she departed some half an hour later, he went to his bed to rest, while Lucy made her sorry way home. 'I want you to need me,' she murmured as she walked away. 'I need to care for you, Barney.'

But Barney was already sleeping. He was heart-weary, and for the moment there was only one thing on his fevered mind, and that was his family. 'God help me!' he cried. 'I'll never see them again . . . oh, dear God! Dear God!' When he slept he dreamed, and his dreams were soul-destroying.

～

Over the following weeks, Lucy visited every day. She and Barney sat in Bridget's parlour and talked. Occasionally she made him laugh and when he did, she knew it was the thinnest veneer over his hurting, but it was good to hear it all the same, and her heart soared with hope.

Maybe the doctors were wrong and Barney would get better. Maybe there was a future for the two of them – oh, not in the same way it had been with his Vicky, but in a warm, dependent way, with each filling a need for the other, because now they each knew what loneliness was.

All too soon, though, her hopes were shattered.

More and more Barney took to his bed, and though Bridget was a wonderful friend, she found it all too much. 'Much as I would like to, I can't run a business and take care of him,' she told Lucy. 'And there is no room for you here, you know that.' In a soft, caring voice she urged Lucy, 'He really needs to be where he'll get proper medical help.'

Lucy was at her wit's end. 'I won't let them take him away!' she protested. 'I couldn't bear it.'

With a plan forming in her mind, she went to Barney. 'Let me take you home with me?' she pleaded. 'Bridget has been wonderful, but now it's my turn.'

Weak though he was, Barney was still adamant. 'I know she's been wonderful, and I know she's finding things difficult just now. But I'm not totally bedridden,' he smiled, that old cheeky, mischievous smile. 'So don't write me off yet, my girl!'

'Come home with me, Barney. Let me take care of you . . . please.'

'So that's your plan, is it?' he asked. 'To "take care of me"?'

'Yes.'

'And you think I can't take care of myself?'

'I know you can, but for how long, Barney?'

Barney thought about that, because of late he had been growing weaker. 'And are you prepared to risk your reputation just to keep me from ending my days in a hospital bed?'

'You know I am!'

Barney gave that same wonderful smile. 'Then how can I refuse?'

'Oh, Barney!' Thrilled that they would be together at last, even though she did not fool herself it would be for long, Lucy threw her arms round his neck. 'You won't regret it, I promise.'

Barney laughed. 'If you don't stop suffocating me, I won't be around long enough to regret it,' he said.

Lucy let go with a look of horror. 'You mustn't say things like that,' she chided.

In serious voice he told her, 'And you mustn't pretend I'll be around forever, because I won't.'

Subdued, she nodded, the joy gone from her eyes. 'I know,' she whispered. 'But it will be so good to have you near for now.'

And so it was arranged, and surprisingly no one saw the move as anything other than Lucy looking after an old friend. Indeed, they admired her for it.

Over the coming months, Barney and Lucy spent almost every minute in each other's company. 'I'm so glad you persuaded me to come here,' he told her one night when they were seated by the fire. 'Being here with you has been a joy. I watch you sometimes when you're hanging out the washing, and I think of Vicky. I'm deeply humbled by the way you've become part of my life . . .' he smiled wryly, 'what's left of it. The doctor told me a year at the outset, maybe less, but lately I've found a new strength and it's all thanks to you, Lucy.'

'I'm glad.' Lucy had seen the way he had rallied since coming out to the countryside. 'But it's not me,' she said. 'It's the country air that suits you.'

Barney corrected her. 'It's not only that, Lucy,' he said softly. 'It's the peace and comfort I feel, just being here, with you.'

'I wish I could be Vicky,' Lucy answered. 'I wish I could get your family back for you.' If only she could restore his happiness and the family he adored, she would have given up every minute spent with him.

'You can't bring them back,' he murmured, 'and even if you could, I would not want you to. I hope they never know the way things are with me. That's why I sent them away . . . so they would find the new life they so looked forward to, and not be made to watch me suffer, or feel the anguish I feel.'

He reached out to take hold of her hand. 'You can't know how grateful I am to you,' he said. 'You've been the best friend anyone could ever have.'

'I wish you could . . .' Lucy's voice broke. 'I wish . . .'

She was about to say she wished he could love her as she loved him, but instead the tears began to fall, and before she realised, he was holding her in his arms, and when he kissed her, she could hardly believe it. 'I know what you wish for,' he soothed. 'I've seen it in your eyes and somehow I just know . . .' He cradled her face. 'You are the sweetest person, Lucy . . .'

The kiss was gentle. The lovemaking that followed was fumbled and tender, and Lucy gave herself to him with all her heart.

Afterwards, they held each other, and Lucy cried, and he comforted her. 'We belong together now, you and me,' he whispered. 'We could never be as Vicky and I were, but we're together, and that must mean something.' He smiled into her eyes. 'Do you understand what I'm saying?'

Lucy nodded. 'I think I've always loved you,' she said.

'And I've come to love you, but it's a very different love from what I feel for Vicky. Ours is a quiet, gentle love. But is it enough for you? Is it, Lucy?'

'Yes.' Lucy's heart was at peace. 'It's enough,' she whispered, nestling contentedly in his arms.

~

Over the coming weeks, Barney confounded the doctors by finding a new strength. Life was good; they took gentle strolls

through the countryside; they sat long in the garden, and
once a week they would go to the churchyard and lay a posy
on little Jamie's resting place. But in the back of their minds
there was always the fear of Barney's relapse, and the growing weakness in his limbs.

When Lucy found to her immense joy that she was carrying Barney's child, their happiness knew no bounds. But
Barney was adamant. 'We can't let it be known that you're
with child,' he said. 'That would only set tongues wagging. God knows they've already been busy enough, what
with me being here and the two of us living under the same
roof.'

It was true, Lucy thought. At first everyone had accepted
that she was merely caring for Barney. But now, after months
passing and the two of them being seen out together, the
gossip knew no end, and it was not pleasant.

'Look, Lucy, I have a small amount of money put by. Let's
move away . . . rent a place somewhere far off, where folks
won't point the finger at you or the child.'

It was just an idea, but Lucy was reluctant to leave the
area. 'You need to be near the doctors, you know,' she told
him. 'You don't want to be starting over with someone new
who doesn't know you like Dr Lucas. You're doing all right
for now. Please, Barney. don't take any risks.'

'But you will think about it, won't you, Lucy?' he urged.

And the more Lucy thought about it, the less she liked
the idea of moving Barney out of the area. He had Dr Lucas,
who knew him like an old friend, and the hospital close
enough to have him in quickly should it be needed. He had
his old friend Adam, who came to visit regularly, and others
who were concerned for his health.

But none of this bothered Barney. All he wanted was that
the child should not grow up where people pointed the
finger.

Lucy's immediate concern, however, was for Barney, and so, for the moment she tactfully let the matter slide.

When she told Bridget about the coming baby, and Barney's wish to move away, Bridget was thrilled and horrified at the same time. 'Oh, Lucy! I think it's wonderful that you and Barney have found each other. Even though he'll always pine for Vicky, at least he's found a measure of peace and happiness with you, and as for you, well, you're positively blooming!'

She observed Lucy's bright eyes and the spring in her step when she walked and her heart went out to her. 'I've always known you loved him,' she confided. 'Anyone with half an eye could see it.'

~

Some months later, the child, a girl, was born to Lucy and Barney. They called her Mary, after Barney's late mother. 'She's beautiful,' he said, the joy written on his face. 'I know I will never see her grow to a woman but, God willing, I might be here long enough to see her as a real little person.'

And he did, for though his illness was a terrible threat hanging over all of them, he saw little Mary when she began toddling, and when she gurgled her first word it was for him alone. 'LUCY! . . .' One fine morning, Barney greeted Lucy from the garden with tears in his eyes. 'She called me . . . "Daddy".' It was one of the most beautiful moments in his life, and Lucy thanked the good Lord for His mercy in letting Barney live long enough to experience the joy of it all.

But on Mary's second birthday, Barney took a turn for the worse. Confined to his bed for a week, he had time to consider his future, and that of his daughter and Lucy. 'It's time to leave here,' he told Lucy one evening when they sat by the fire. 'I don't want Mary to know what happened to Vicky and the family. I don't want her to think me some kind of monster to have sent them away without me. I made them hate me, Lucy, I made them think I was a drunk and a womaniser. What kind of thing is that for our daughter to hear? And hear it she will, because I'm certain everyone round here must know the truth. As soon as she can under-stand, Mary will hear it, and I don't want that. D'you hear me, sweetheart? I don't want her to know until she's old enough to understand the tittle-tattle and to be able to for-give me for it!'

Lucy gently replied, 'I'll tell her when the time is right. I'll tell her what a courageous and wonderful thing you did for love of your family. She'll understand.'

'But I want us to move, Lucy,' he pleaded. 'I know it's the right thing for Mary.' Barney could not be dissuaded, and when she gave it more thought, Lucy could see the wisdom of his reasoning. So, she spoke to agents and even wrote away as far as Bedfordshire.

Before Mary's third birthday, the cottage was sold. The same businessman who bought Leonard's farm wanted it to extend and then sell on with a minimum of five acres of pasture-land. He had competition from another source, and between them they sent the price up, enough for Barney and Lucy to secure a sizeable property further afield.

It wasn't long before her efforts paid off. She got news of a house some two hundred miles away in a small hamlet near the town of Bedford.

The house was of some substance, a 'proud and beautiful woman past her best' was how it had been described to her. Apparently the house had stood empty for many years and had gradually fallen into disrepair. Consequently it was going cheap for anyone who had the heart to bring it back to its former glory, and if not, then it was still habitable, with no apparent structural defects.

Because the journey would be too arduous for Barney, Lucy went with Adam to view the house. She fell instantly in love with it. There was also a small house in the grounds, that too brought to its knees by neglect and the elements. 'If I move with you and Barney, I could set up a business in the village.' Adam grew excited. 'Meantime, I could work on the house. I'm not a builder, but I do know how to use my hands.' The truth was, he could not bear the thought of being so far away from Lucy in her hour of need, especially when Barney's health seemed to be failing fast.

In truth, Lucy had seen Barney's health deteriorate so much of late, that even though he fervently assured her to the contrary, she feared he might not be strong enough for the move.

On Lucy's return, she thanked Bridget who had kindly stayed at the cottage with Barney while Lucy travelled south to view the house. 'So, what did you think of it?' Bridget was excited, though she would miss her dear friend. 'Was it as grand as they said?'

Lucy described the house in detail, its strong Edwardian features, the high ceilings and panelled walls, the long windows with panoramic views across open countryside. 'It could be beautiful,' Lucy told her. 'But it does need a lot of work, though Adam has come up with an idea.'

When Adam explained it to Barney, he was thrilled. 'That would be good,' he told him. 'I've been so concerned about Lucy and the child. I could rest easy if I knew you'd be around to keep an eye on things.'

So the deal was done and plans were quickly underway.

In a few weeks' time Barney, Lucy, Adam and Mary were away to pastures new; though for Barney it would never be a long adventure; they all knew that.

PART FOUR

~

Back to January, 1952

Mary and Ben

CHAPTER TWENTY-ONE

WHILE LUCY SLEPT upstairs, Adam Chives sat by the fire in Knudsden House, his mind going back over the years, and his heart both proud and sad. 'Barney and your mother lived in that cottage together for more than two years,' he told Mary, while Ben listened. 'The doctors had given him a year at the most, but Lucy brought him a degree of peace, and after a time they made a life together.' He smiled wistfully at the memory, for he had loved Lucy as much as she loved Barney. 'To this day, she has never stopped loving him.'

'You were born out of that love, Mary.' Lucy's quiet voice filled the room. 'You're so much like your father. You have the same beautiful eyes and the same gentle ways.'

'Lucy!' Adam was horrified. 'Dr Nolan said you were to stay in bed.'

'Nonsense, I'm perfectly all right,' she argued. 'There is nothing wrong with me, and I'm far from in my dotage, for heaven's sake! Doctors don't know everything. I've simply been overdoing it, that's all.'

Hobbling but determined, she came into the room where she stood beside Adam, her hand resting on his shoulder and her gaze bathing every inch of her daughter's face. 'Every time I look at you, I see Barney.'

Adam looked at Mary and he, too, saw Barney in her every

feature – softer and more feminine, yes – but strong and handsome too.

'I was there when you were born,' Adam said fondly. 'I waited in the sitting room with your father, while Dr Lucas was upstairs bringing you into the world. When he heard your first cry, Barney went up those stairs like he was born all over again. He took you in his arms and oh, he was such a proud, happy man.'

When Adam laid his hand over Lucy's, she hardly noticed, though deep down she derived a measure of comfort from his touch.

Deeply moved by everything she had heard, Mary went to Lucy and taking her mother gently over to the armchair, she sat her down. 'I never knew,' she said. 'I never dreamed that was the secret you kept from me all these years.' She had learned more about her father and her own background in one evening, than in all the years she was growing up. There was so much to think about. The revelation that she had three half-siblings in America, plus the sorrowful knowledge that her half-brother Jamie had died before her, was a huge shock to her system, and she knew that it would take a long, long time to come to terms with everything she had learned tonight.

Lucy was glad that Adam had chosen to tell the truth. 'It's been such a burden all this time,' she admitted now. 'But I gave my promise, d'you see? I gave my promise and I could never break it.'

Adam reassured her. 'You didn't break it,' he reminded her. 'It was me who thought Mary should be told. I've always thought it was her right to know.'

Lucy smiled. 'So you thought you'd tittle-tattle while I was laid up, did you?'

'I'm not sorry the truth is out,' he said stoutly. 'I'm only sorry if I've upset you.'

Lucy sighed. 'You did right, my old friend. You did right.' She turned to address Ben, who had been mesmerised by the whole story. 'What do you think of my darling Barney?' she asked. 'Do you think *he* was right in what he did?'

Lucy was testing him. In Ben she had seen something akin to Barney, but she needed reassuring.

Ben considered her question, and when he gave his answer, he gave it with a sense of wonder. 'In all my life, I've never heard of such a man,' he said. 'What he did was incredible. For the sake of his loved ones, he belittled and punished himself beyond endurance. I understand now what the inscription means. "He made the greatest sacrifice of all."'

Lucy asked him another question. 'In those circumstances, would you have done the same?'

Ben smiled inwardly. Already, because of what Adam had told of Lucy's strength of character, and because he had witnessed it for himself from the moment they met, Ben knew he was being tested, and he suspected her view of him would hinge on the kind of answer he gave.

'Well, young man?' As was her way, Lucy grew impatient.

Ben considered the question again, and when he answered it was as straight an answer as he could give. 'Any man would be prepared to do whatever was in his power to protect his loved ones,' he told her, 'but like a grain of sand or a drop of rain, each man is different. A man will be judged on his merit. Barney Davidson is the kind of man every other man would want to be, but I'm not Barney, nor could I ever be. All the same, I would hope that, given the same circumstances, I might find the courage and fortitude to do what he did. Other than that, I can't say.'

There was a moment while they reflected on his words, before Mary asked of her mother, 'What happened to my father? How did it end?'

Lucy gave a whimsical smile. 'It ended the way we always thought it might end,' she said. 'It was the most beautiful summer's evening. We were sitting in the garden watching the sun go down, when Barney turned to me and told me how much he had come to love me . . . but that he could never love me in the same way that he loved Vicky. She had been his life, while I had *become* his life, that's what he said.'

Lucy thought about Barney's words, just as she had done on that memorable night. 'I often wondered about that,' she said. 'I thought it a strange thing for him to say, and for a time I couldn't understand his meaning.'

Looking up at Mary, she took hold of her hand. 'After a while, I did understand. What he meant was that he and Vicky had grown together, learned together and knew each other's very thoughts . . .'

She paused. 'With me it was different. When Barney and I met, I simply became part of the family that was already Barney's; I was an outsider coming in. But then suddenly it was just the two of us, and we learned to know and love each other. Like Ben said just now, he could not be Barney . . . any more than I could be Vicky. We're all different and we touch each other's lives in different ways. But love is love, no matter which way you look at it.

'Thank you,' she said gravely, and he knew he had passed the test. 'Love *is* love, and that's what we had, me and Barney. We had such love to share, just talking and laughing and simply being together. And if I never have another day of contentment, I had more happiness in those years with Barney, than most women have in a lifetime.'

Suddenly, Lucy shivered. 'I'm tired now, my darling,' she told her daughter. 'Take me back to my bed?'

Mary took her upstairs and when Lucy was made comfortable, the young woman asked, 'Did you ever hear from Vicky, or the family?'

Lucy shook her head. 'No, never.' Fearing that Mary had too many questions to which she might not have the answers, Lucy told her, 'For reasons I hope you now understand, Barney did not want them to know about you.'

'So I have two brothers and a sister I may never see?' Though Mary had been deeply touched by the story of her father, she felt cheated somehow, filled with all kinds of regrets, regrets that she had never known him, and regrets that she was never told the truth. But now she knew it all, and it was as though a cloud was lifted from over her head. But what of the rest of her family?

'Will I ever meet them – Thomas and Ronnie, and my sister Susie?'

Lucy was not ready for this. 'Leave me now, love,' she said. 'Let me sleep.'

Quietly, Mary left. Tomorrow, when her mother was rested, she would ask again. And she would keep on asking, until Lucy agreed to reunite her with the family she had never known.

~

It was much later that Adam tapped on Lucy's bedroom door to check on her. Ben had gone home and Mary was in bed. Lucy herself was sitting up in bed, awake but at peace with herself.

'Ben is so much like Barney,' Lucy murmured. She had Barney strong in her mind tonight.

'Tell me something,' Adam asked. 'Do you think you will ever contact Vicky?'

'I made a promise never to tell them,' she sighed. 'You made that same promise.'

'I know, and I've always regretted it. I kept it when Barney was alive, and I've kept it all these years. I didn't even mention it when informing Mr Maitland of his death, as Barney requested in his last hours. But I've never felt comfortable about it, Lucy. I think they have a right to know why he did what he did, the same as Mary had a right to know. God only knows how they have suffered all these years.'

When she remained silent, he asked her again. '*Will* you tell them, Lucy? *Will* you contact Vicky?'

Unable to answer such a momentous question, Lucy thought fleetingly of her daughter and Ben, and her heart was glad. There was magic happening between those two.

'I love you, Lucy.' Adam's voice was so close to her ear, she felt his warm breath against her skin.

'I know.' She turned to smile on him. 'I've always known.'

'You never said.'

'Because there would have been no point and I might have hurt your feelings. You see, I didn't love you back.'

'Do you love me back now?'

'I think so.' She turned away. 'You realise I could never love you in the same way I loved Barney?'

'Will you marry me?'

'We're too long in the tooth for that nonsense,' she laughed. But secretly she felt quite excited. She had had two children by two very different men – one full of darkness and one full of light – and yet had never been married. Maybe that was the next experience that Fate had in store for her.

For now, the moment passed and they were quiet again.

'When you get in touch with Vicky,' Adam persisted, 'will you tell her what Barney did for them?' Taking Lucy by the shoulders, he turned her round to face him. 'I know Leonard Maitland gave you his address. You can get in touch if you want to,' he said. 'They won't have moved from the farm.'

Lucy patted the tip of her nose in a gesture of secrecy. 'I

might – and I might not.' Her smile grew mischievous. 'But that's another story altogether, don't you think?'

Adam knew that when Lucy was in this strange mood of hers, there was no reasoning with her. He kissed her then – not the kiss of a lover, but the kiss of someone who knew her well. 'Good night, Lucy.' Smiling resignedly, he shook his head. 'Sleep tight.'

For a while after he'd gone, she continued to gaze at the little photograph still lying on the eiderdown. It was the only picture she had of Barney, and it was her treasure. Taken on the day he took delivery of his new tractor, Barney stood beside it, a proud man, while Leonard Maitland recorded the moment forever.

Taking the photograph into her hands and looking down, she let herself be drawn back over the years, to summertimes and harvests, and picnics and laughter, when Jamie was always at her side and in her heart. Moving pictures in her mind; warm and real in her heart. They were glorious times with the Davidson family, all together and not a cloud in their sky.

'Happy days,' she murmured. 'But it's not the end, my darlings.'

Replacing the photograph, she glanced again towards the window, where outside, new love was beginning.

~

'Your father's story is the most remarkable I've ever heard.' Ben had been deeply shaken by the turn of this night's events, and if he lived to be a hundred, he would never forget this night nor the man who was Barney Davidson.

'I never knew,' Mary answered thoughtfully. 'All these years and I never knew.'

'Your mother said you looked like him.' Ben observed her

small pretty face, and he had an urge to take her in his arms. 'You have such a calmness about you, I can imagine you must also have inherited some of his character traits as well.'

Mary smiled. 'I hope so.'

'I'm glad we met.' Reaching out he took hold of her hand, and to his delight she did not draw it away. 'Do you think we might have a future together, you and me?'

Thrilled by his remark, her answer was to lean forward and kiss him. She looked into those dark, sincere eyes and at the strong set of his jaw and that air of confidence about him, and she thought of all that had passed long ago.

But that was not her life. This was her life, hers and Ben's, and suddenly, when she felt his loving arms about her, she knew it was where she belonged, with this man whom she hardly knew, and yet she felt as though she had known him forever.

'You still haven't answered me, Mary.' His voice was soft in her ear. 'You haven't said if you think we might have a future together?'

Turning her head, she looked up at him. 'Yes,' her smile was content, 'I really believe we might.'

Lucy saw it all. She saw them kiss, and she saw the tenderness in his embrace, and it made her think of Barney. 'I hope you find happiness together,' she whispered.

Wearied and content, Lucy climbed into bed. For a while she lay awake, her mind back there where it all took place. It had been an amazing adventure. But it was not yet over.

For now, though, it was time to reflect, and be thankful.

JOURNEY'S END

CONTENTS

PART ONE

~

Late March, 1954

The Telling

Salford, Bedfordshire

CHAPTER ONE

SHE WOKE WITH a cry. It was the same dream as before – the same place, the same faces, the same jolt of terror; real in her dream, real in her life. Would it never leave her be?

The sweat dripping down her temples and her whole body trembling, she clambered out of bed and went to the window, where for a moment she stood, regaining her composure, collecting her senses.

Drawing back the curtains, she peered into the darkness, thick and impenetrable, like the deepest recesses of her mind. Dismissing the nightmare, she returned to the question that tormented her.

Should she tell? Would it destroy lives and minds? Would they hate her or, as she desperately hoped, would they thank her? But then, why would they thank her when the news she had to reveal was so unbearably cruel?

'Dear God, give me the courage to do what's right,' she prayed.

Maybe it would be better if the truth was never told. Yet that would be the coward's way out, and she might be many things, but Lucy Baker was no coward.

She glanced at the clock; it was five minutes past three – another day beginning. Taking her robe from the back of the chair, she slipped into it and sat on the edge of the bed, where she remained for a time. She sighed, a long, broken sigh. 'Oh, my dearest Barney, my joy, my life.' There was a murmuring of guilt, but never regret. 'I loved you then, and I love you still.'

Barney had been her only true love, and it was a love all-consuming, all-powerful. There was no way to describe how much she missed him. No words. Only memories.

The smile slipped away and in its place came a look of hatred.

While Barney had brought her joy, *Edward Trent had brought her tragedy.*

'Edward Trent . . . *monster*!' Her mouth curled with loathing, she spat out his name as though it was tainted with poison. His wickedness had caused such pain; she would carry the burden of it for the rest of her days.

Lucy was no stranger to nightmares. A thousand times, she had awoken terrified and sobbing, reliving the night when Edward Trent had kidnapped her little son Jamie, and caused him to drown.

In the sorrowful years that followed, Trent had haunted her every waking and sleeping hour. In the daytime she would be in the middle of a mundane task, like washing the dishes or drawing the curtains, and suddenly he was gnawing at her mind until she could hardly think straight. Then at night came the dreams which left her breathless and shaking. Eventually, over the past twenty and more years, she had grown used to them. Like the hatred, they had become part of her life.

In the dreams it was always the same: the darkness, the water, and the chase . . . that unforgettable chase, ending in such horror.

This time though, the dream had been different. There was no frantic chase, no rushing water as it tumbled downstream, tugging at her ankles and throwing her off-balance; there wasn't even the soul-wrenching sound of her child crying. This dream was like nothing she had ever experienced.

She had seen only his face, that swarthy, handsome face, his mouth frozen in an easy smile. Unlike before, he was not threatening her, nor was he reaching out. There was only the smile. And those mesmerising eyes, utterly chilling. And the silence – eerie, absolute.

'Take a hold of yourself, Lucy,' she said aloud. Grabbing the crumpled corner of the bedsheet, she wiped the sweat from her face. 'It was just a dream. *He* can't hurt you any more.' So many times she had tried to convince herself of that. Even so, the fear never went away.

It never would.

~

In the adjoining room, in that lazy space between sleeping and waking, Mary lay in her bed and listened. She heard her mother open the curtains, and she heard her muffled footsteps as they paced the floor. The young woman did not attempt to go in: she knew that Lucy would not want that. Instead, for the next hour, she lay waiting, the only sound the ticking of the clock.

This was not the first time she had heard her mother agitated, unable to sleep. The first time was many years ago, when she was just an infant. The sound of Lucy sobbing had disturbed her deeply. In her childish manner, Mary had gone to comfort her, but her mother sent her away. Since then, whenever she heard her mother weeping in the night, Mary would keep vigil, desperately hoping it would not be too long before her mother went back to sleep; as she always did.

Mary had known there was some secret torment in her

mother's past; some fearful thing that touched all of their lives in some way – herself, her mother, and Adam, that dear kind man who had always been there to protect them.

Only recently, Adam had taken it upon himself to tell the truth of what happened all those years ago. In the telling, he had betrayed Lucy's trust and broken his vow to his old friend Barney. At the time he believed it was for the best. Now, he was not so sure.

Mary was shaken to her roots by the story he told. Even now it was not ended. There were others who had to know: the ones who had gone away; the ones who had never known the truth of Barney Davidson's sacrifice.

In Mary's far-off memories, she recalled her father, Barney, who had died when she was a tiny girl. He had been a special kind of man, frail in body but powerful in spirit. She recalled how he would sit her on his knee and create magic through his vivid fairytales; he made her laugh with his comical mimicry, and sometimes when she woke crying, he would hold her up to the window and show her the stars and describe the beauty and wonder of the world they lived in. He told her she must never be afraid, because there would always be someone looking over her.

She loved him so much, and then he was gone, and their lives were never the same again.

When she was satisfied that her mother had gone back to sleep, Mary turned over and relaxed. Tomorrow, there would be no mention of this night. Mother and daughter would smile and chat, and talk of everything else, and it would be as though the nightmare had never happened. Because that was how Lucy wanted it.

CHAPTER TWO

B Y HALF PAST eight, Lucy was out of her bed, washed and dressed and sprucing herself in the mirror. 'Not bad for an old 'un, if I say so myself!' Laying down the hairbrush, she ran her two hands through her short cap of greying hair, teased out a few stray curls and thought how, if it wasn't for the occasional lapse of memory and the age spots on the back of her hands, she could maybe pass for a young thing of fifty.

Sighing wistfully, she shook her head. 'Wish all you like, my girl,' she chided herself. 'It won't change the fact that you're past your prime, so stop fancying yourself in the mirror. Before you know it, the doctor will be here,' she frowned, 'not that you need him, because you don't – but it makes him feel wanted, so shift yourself, and be quick about it.'

She observed her image in the mirror. She did her best to keep what was left of her looks, but had not yet regained her strength since stumbling in the local churchyard a couple of years ago. The incident seemed to have sparked off a form of arthritis, but this was what you expected, wasn't it, at her age. You had to slow down, whether you wanted to, or not.

She gazed critically on herself; the skin was not as glowing as it used to be, and there appeared to be more of it which hung in little loose swathes round her neck, and there were lines round her eyes and mouth. But the small straight nose and heart shaped face were still pretty, and the blue eyes as bright as ever. She had never been a beauty, that much was true, but she'd been better off than most women because, even though it was for a cruelly short time, she had had the love of a man like Barney Davidson.

Thoughts of her beloved overwhelmed her. She knew that Barney had never loved her as he had loved his wife, Vicky. In the end, Lucy may have filled his heart, but it was only ever Vicky who filled his soul.

Lifting the photograph from the dresser, she gazed down on herself and Barney, and the infant girl in his arms. It was a cherished picture, taken only a few months before Barney was lost to her, and even then, when the illness ravaged him, the goodness of the man, and his absolute joy of life shone out of his face – still a handsome face for all that.

Lucy choked back a sob. They had had so little time together, yet she thanked God for every second. They had shared everything – the anguish of seeing his wife and children leave him; the guilt and tears afterwards; the companionship between him and Lucy that grew into a kind of loving contentment, then the sheer joy and pride when Mary was born to them.

Through all the ups and downs of every passing day, they never forgot the others: Leonard Maitland, a man who had gone away knowing the truth, even though it meant he would never again have peace of mind, and Vicky and the children who had sailed with him, estranged from Barney and in total ignorance of the price he had paid for their new lives in America.

Lucy recalled the day when they left. 'There was no other way, Barney,' she murmured now. 'No other way . . .'

The loud spluttering of a car engine brought her hurrying to the window. 'Adam!' The brightness of a spring day was startling, and the skies above were blue and cloudless. For late March, it was unusually warm. 'Adam, what's going on?' she called down.

Covered in muck and oil, Adam was standing before the car in the drive of Knudsden House. He had the bonnet up and the starter-handle lodged into position.

'The damned thing's been playing up again,' he called back, 'and now it's completely given up the ghost. I've done what I can, but I reckon she'll need a new engine.' Diving his head under the bonnet again, he fiddled with a few nuts and bolts, before returning to swing the handle for the umpteenth time. There was a shuddering and a spluttering, and a shout of victory when he thought he'd done the trick, but then the engine fell silent again. 'It's no good.' Defeated, he gave a shake of the head. 'There's no spark at all now.'

Lucy shouted down: 'Leave it! Come inside . . . Come on.'

His heart warmed by the invitation, Adam waved up to her. 'I'll be there in a minute.'

Closing the window, Lucy smiled to herself. No spark, eh? She hoped the day never came when they said that about her! Life might be a bit more of a challenge these days and her health was not as robust as she would have liked, but by God, she wasn't done yet. Not by any means!

By the time Adam showed his face at the kitchen door, both Lucy and Mary were seated at the table, Lucy enjoying her eggs and bacon, and Mary toying with her scrambled eggs. 'Look at the state of you!' Pointing to Adam's mucky face and hands, Lucy asked him sternly: 'Have you had your breakfast?'

'Not yet, no.' Because the car had been playing up the previous day, he'd got out of his bed early this morning to work on the engine. 'There was no time for breakfast,' he explained. 'Two hours I messed about with that blessed machine this morning.' He groaned. 'I honestly thought I'd fixed it!'

Lucy felt as though she had known him forever. A loyal friend to them both, Adam Chives had been part of her life with Barney, and after Barney was gone, he had seen her through a bad time and remained ever close. Lucy had often wondered why he never married, until some time ago he confessed to her that she had always been the only woman he had ever truly loved.

Time and again Adam had asked her to be his wife and time and again she had gently refused. But knowing how persistent he was, Lucy was in no doubt that some time in the not too distant future, he was bound to try again.

Taking a gulp of her tea, Lucy discreetly regarded him. Homely, well-built, with thick greying hair and kind expressive eyes, Adam was an ordinary kind of man, but with an extraordinary sense of loyalty. When he made a friend it was a friend for life and when he fell in love, it was with heart and soul.

Over the years, Lucy had prayed that he might find a woman who would bring him the happiness he deserved; though in the beginning she had never believed it was herself he needed.

When some years ago, she expressed her hope that he might find a good woman to share his life, he told her he wanted no other wife but her. And that he would always be there for her as long as she needed him.

His confession had touched Lucy deeply.

'Right then, if you go and wash up,' she told him now, 'I'll see to your breakfast.'

'Thank you, Lucy, but no thanks!' Hungry though he was, he didn't want her fussing over him. 'I don't like to put you to any trouble, especially when you've got the doctor coming this morning.'

Brushing aside his protests, Lucy took another long gulp of her tea, before pushing back her chair and standing up. 'Breakfast will be ready when you are,' she assured him. 'And don't worry about the doctor. I can handle him.' She laughed. 'He seems a bit nervous of me. No sooner is he in the door than he's itching to get out again.'

'I'm not surprised. Poor devil!' Adam chuckled. 'I've seen how you boss him about.'

'Only when he tries to tell me what to do!' she retorted. 'I know I'm not as young and foolhardy as I once was; my bones ache like the devil and there are times when I want to run and can only shuffle. Some days it's like going through a fog . . . one minute it's clear as a bell and I can go forward, then the next I can't find an easy way and have to slow down.'

She smiled into his eyes. 'So you see, Adam, the bad times come and go, but I'm not bedridden yet, thank God. If I'm tired I rest, and if I feel all right I'll do whatever I please.' She gave a wry little smile. 'Either way, I expect I'll pop my clogs soon enough.'

Rolling his eyes to the ceiling, Adam gave a boot-deep sigh. 'You can't be serious for one minute, can you? Whatever will we do with you, eh?' He knew what *he'd* like to do. He'd like to sweep her into his arms and carry her off. But you didn't do that with Lucy. She was stubborn and a law unto herself. But that was the nature of her, and he would not have it any other way.

'And don't leave the sink with a rim of oil round it neither!' Lucy's voice sailed across the kitchen.

'Right, boss.' Bowing slightly, Adam gave a mock-servile tug of his forelock. 'I'll make sure I leave it ready for inspection.'

11

Having put the plug in the sink and taken the kettle from the hob, he began pouring the warm water into an enamel bowl. Looking over his shoulder with a cheeky wink, he made Lucy smile.

Through all this good-natured banter, Mary had remained silent, but now she told Adam, 'Best do as you're told. You know she'll examine your hands back and front before you're allowed to sit down – oh, and don't forget to wash behind your ears, or you'll be made to stand in the corner.'

Lucy wagged a finger. 'Behave yourself, young lady. I may be getting on a bit, and you a grown woman now, but I'm still capable of clipping your ear.'

Mary chuckled. 'I'm sure you are!'

At the sink, Adam took a moment to think. Getting on a bit? In his mind's eye he could see Lucy Baker, as she then was, as a young woman running barefoot across the fields, her long flowing locks lifted by the breeze, and on her face a smile bright and warm as a sunny morning. Sometimes, before the world was wide awake, when he was out walking across the headlands, he would see her by the river, seated on a fallen log with her feet dipped into the water. He had loved her then and knew how, for the remainder of his life, he would never love another woman. What he felt for Lucy was a love that would endure forever.

'Nay, you're far too full of yourself to ever get old,' he said cheekily.

'Well, thank you, Adam,' Lucy replied. 'I shall take that as a back-handed compliment, shall I – though I think you are seeing me through rose-coloured spectacles.' Something in his voice and the look in his eyes told Lucy that he might be ready to ask her again if she would marry him, and just for the briefest moment, her heart seemed to turn over.

'They say beautiful women never really know they're

beautiful,' he added softly. 'I reckon that's true where you're concerned.'

'Get away with you, you old flatterer!' Strangely embarrassed, she took a forkful of leftover egg and popped it into her mouth, and astonished Mary by blushing bright pink.

Graciously refusing Mary's offer to cook Adam's breakfast instead, Lucy threw two more rashers of bacon and some mushrooms into the pan. In no time at all, they were sizzling away.

A few moments later, having finished washing at the sink and making sure he'd wiped it round afterwards, Adam seated himself at the table, where his breakfast was put in front of him. 'Cor! Look at that – a real feast.' He hadn't realised how truly hungry he was until the aroma of hot food flooded his nostrils.

'Thank you, Lucy.' He turned to Mary with a wink. 'Your mother's not only beautiful, she's a good cook into the bargain.'

Lucy thought one fine compliment was enough in a day. 'Food is for eating,' she said, placing a platter of toast before him. 'So stop chatting and get it down you, before it goes cold.'

Smiling to herself at the way these two seemed to fit together like a hand in a glove, Mary was already getting out of her chair. 'I'll make some fresh tea.' She knew how much Adam loved her mother, and she also suspected that, although she didn't yet realise it, her mother had come to love him back.

Leaving them to talk, she took her time making the tea, while occasionally glancing at the two of them, now deep in conversation and looking for all the world like any other husband and wife; though they were neither of them ordinary. They were special, at least to her.

A short time later, having set them up with a fresh pot of tea, Mary excused herself. 'Ben will be here soon,' she explained. 'We're going into Shefford to look at a new tractor.'

'A new tractor, eh?' Lucy was delighted at how her daughter's friendship with Ben Morris, the owner of Far Crest Farm, had grown into a close and loving relationship. It had been her dearest wish for Mary to find a man who cared deeply for her, and she truly believed Ben to be that man.

'Talk of the devil, here he is now.' Adam looked out of the window and drew their attention to the dark-haired, good-looking man on his way up the drive; with his tall capable build and long, easy strides, he looked like a man who could handle whatever obstacles life put in his way.

A few years ago, emotionally and mentally drained by the break-up of his marriage, Ben had decided to uproot himself and build a whole new way of life. It was not an easy decision, but when he eventually moved to the area of South Bedfordshire, he kept in close touch with his only child, Abbie, who had a secretarial job in London and shared a flat there with friends.

On first arriving in Salford, Ben, a former architect knew next to nothing about farming. But thanks to his practical nature, and learning as he went, he now had a comfortable income and a way of life he couldn't have possibly ever imagined. And he had never been happier.

After the trauma and deceit that caused the end of his marriage to Pauline, he had not wanted another deep relationship. But then he met Lucy's daughter, Mary, and had soon come to realise that not all women were the same. Where his wife had been dominant and deceitful, Mary was kind and caring; though she did have a fiery side. Last summer while they were strolling across the fields, they saw a man kicking his dog, and before Ben could intervene, Mary had snatched the dog away and confronted the man with a passion.

This incident had only served to convince Ben that he was a fortunate man, because here was a woman he could trust and respect. And he had come to love her so much, it frightened him.

'BEN!' Knocking on the window, Adam hoped to catch his attention, but the younger man was already out of ear-shot. 'Don't you two go running off before I've had a chance to see him,' he said to Mary as she hurried from the room, 'I want to ask the lad if he'll have a look at the car. There's nothing I don't know about tractors, but I'm jiggered if I can fathom out what's wrong with this blessed car!'

He frowned. 'It starts then it dies away, coughing and spluttering. Ben knows his way round engines. With a bit of luck, he'll be able to make more sense out of that damned vehicle than I can.'

'Hey!' Lucy's voice followed them. 'That's quite enough of that cursing, if you don't mind.'

Half-turning, Adam gave another tug of his forelock. 'Sorry, boss,' he said nervously. 'I'll not do it again.'

Chuckling heartily, Lucy returned to her tea.

A few minutes later, when she started to clear away, a feeling of total exhaustion overwhelmed her. Sudden pains shot down the back of her neck, and her spine felt as though it was being squeezed. This had happened before; thank-fully, the attack always passed, though lately the passing seemed to take longer.

Resting a moment to recover, she rolled up her sleeves and was soon up to the elbows in hot sudsy water. It was a hard thing to come to terms with, growing old, and she resented the years rolling away behind her. Life was too short, and love too fleeting.

She thought of Barney wistfully. She would never again hold his hand or experience that wonderful surge of joy as he slid his arm around her when she least expected it. Life could be so cruel. But she had Mary, and so she still had a part of Barney in her life.

Looking out of the window, she saw how content her daughter was. She saw Mary helping Ben off with his jacket, and she witnessed the way they briefly touched and held hands before he leaned into the car engine. They belonged together, Lucy had known that from the first minute she saw them together in St Andrew's churchyard all those months ago. That was why she had deliberately dropped her handbag there for Ben to find. When returning it to Lucy at her home, Knudsden House, he had met Mary again, and their romance had begun on that long, fateful night. And neither of them had ever suspected her part in it!

Ben reminded Lucy so much of Barney – oh, not in his physique, for Ben was taller and bigger-built than Barney and their colouring was different. But the essence of the man was the same; they each had a certain commanding presence. They smiled with their eyes and had that same kind of trustworthy, open nature.

Lucy's heart swelled with love as she gazed fondly on her daughter. Mary would never know how thankful she was that the girl had found someone she truly loved, and who loved her back in the same way.

She couldn't help but compare Mary and her sweetheart, to herself and Barney. She had loved her father in the same way the girl loved her Ben, deeply and without reservation.

She could see it all in her mind's eye – herself, Barney and Vicky, his true wife, soulmate, and the mother of his three other children. It was a devilish triangle, destined to torment them all, and Barney the unwilling centrepiece of a cruel game that no one could ever win.

She had often wondered what she could have done to save them all so much pain, and the answer was always the same: there was nothing. She could not have prevented what happened, at least not without hurting Barney, and she loved him so much she would gladly have died for him. God help her, she loved him still with every fibre of her being.

Her eyes swam with sadness as she followed Mary's every move. Oh, I don't fool myself, she thought, because even though for a glorious time we were together and you, my darling, were conceived out of love, your father was never really mine.

Barney *had* loved her, in his own way, but it was Vicky of whom he dreamed. Even after he had sent her away, she filled his heart and soul. Lucy had always understood: Barney and Vicky were made for each other, and Lucy could never take the other woman's place, nor would she want to. Vicky had been his first and only love . . . *just as you were mine,* she thought.

CHAPTER THREE

As LUCY CARRIED on rinsing the pots, dreaming quietly to herself, she heard Mary call out a greeting to someone. Lucy raised her gaze to see a familiar figure approaching up the path. 'Elsie!' Lucy was not expecting her so early.

Quickly now, she wiped her arms and rolled down her sleeves, and backing away from the sink, she sat at the table, for all the world as though she had been there all along.

As was her way, Elsie Langton burst in through the door like a wayward wind, her sharp eyes going straight to the sink, half-filled with sudsy water and the few plates resting on the wooden draining-board alongside.

'What's all this then?' she demanded, indignantly folding her arms. 'You've been washing up again, haven't yer? For heaven's sakes, can you never do as you're told and take it easy? What's more, I'd be obliged if you would stop doing my work. One fine day I'll come through that door and there you'll be, waiting with my pay packet and a "cheerio, how's yer father but I don't need yer any more". Then what will I do, eh? Tell me that if yer please!'

Lucy tutted impatiently. 'Don't talk so much nonsense, woman.' Clambering out of her chair, she confronted the little person with a sense of outrage. 'Anyway, who's in charge round here, you tell me that.'

As the bantering continued, Mary stood by the door, quietly amused. There was no harm in these fiery exchanges, she knew that. Her mother valued Elsie as part of the family. And as for the little woman herself, she was hardworking, funny and lovable, and totally devoted to Lucy; but when she had a bee in her bonnet she could be a real terrier.

'Out with it,' Elsie demanded grimly. 'What else have yer been up to? Sweeping the yard, taking down the curtains – what?'

With a measure of dignity, Lucy stood her ground. 'Just listen to yourself. You above all people should know I'm past doing those kind of things. Anyway, what if I *had* done everything you claim? It's my right. It's my house, isn't it?'

Exasperated, Elsie waggled her fat little head from side to side, which in turn wobbled the fat little shoulders. 'It's no use yer arguing with me,' she retorted. 'You had strict orders from the doctor . . . "gentle exercise and the occasional walk, as long as it's not too far", isn't that what the man said?'

Lucy glared at her. 'Good God, you make me sound like some poor old dog that needs to be put down!'

'Dearie, dearie me!' Elsie had a way of making you feel guilty even though you hadn't done anything wrong. 'If yer don't mind me saying, it's *you* that's talking nonsense now. My only concern is that you keep strong and healthy. I don't want to see you standing at the sink to wash the dishes, or turning the mattress, like you did the other day. And if I hadn't arrived in time when you were struggling to get the vacuum cleaner out of the cupboard under the stairs, like as not you'd have broke a limb. And only yesterday I caught you cleaning out the pantry. God give me strength, you're always meddling in places where you've no right to be. Cleaning, fetching and carrying is what *I'm* here for.'

When again she shook her head, her chubby little chops

shivered with irritation. 'It's why yer pay me, for goodness' sake!'

They both looked up as Mary stepped forward from the doorway. 'I'll make us a fresh pot of tea, shall I?' she suggested tactfully. 'That's if nobody has any objections?' Rona, Elsie's daughter, worked alongside Mary in her flower-shop in Leighton Buzzard, and the two young women were fast friends. She'd be sure to report the latest exchange to her!

Grateful for the intervention, Lucy gave a warm smile. 'Thank you, dear, that would be nice.'

But Elsie's feathers were still ruffled. 'I'll have two sugars in mine,' she snapped, 'and just a whisper of milk, if yer please. There's some Garibaldi biscuits in that tin. We're keeping the homemade ones for Doctor Nolan.' With that she took off her coat and hat and hung them up. 'Mean-while, I'd best make a start on cleaning the winders ... before somebody we all know takes a mind to do it herself!' With that she threw Lucy a withering glance and departed.

Lucy was left chuckling. 'Anybody would think I interfered with her daily routine.'

Mary turned with a wry little smile. 'You do.'

'Well, maybe I do, but I'm frightened that if I stop doing things, I might seize up altogether. Don't you know how hard it is for me to be still?'

'I think I know that more than anybody. Don't forget, I'm the one who has to live with you.'

'Do you think I should apologise to Elsie? She's such a treasure.'

'It wouldn't do any good if you did.'

'Why not?' Lucy had not expected an answer like that.

Coming to the table, Mary set the tray down. 'Because the pair of you will only be going at it hammer and tongs again tomorrow.'

Taken aback, Lucy stared up at Mary open-mouthed. 'Are we really that bad?'

'Worse!'

When the laughter carried outside to the men, they stopped work to look towards the kitchen. 'Something's tickled their funny-bones,' Ben remarked with a grin.

'Sounds like it,' Adam agreed; the merry laughter was infectious.

'That should do it.' Laying down the spanner, Ben asked Adam to start the car, and when it spluttered into life and seemed to run smoother than before, the older man gave a sigh of relief. 'Don't know how to thank you,' he said, and Ben told him he was only too pleased to have been able to help.

'I'd best get cleaned up, and take Mary to approve my new tractor.' Ben smiled at the prospect. 'After that, we've got the whole day to please ourselves what we do.'

Adam saw the gleam in Ben's eye and his heart warmed. 'You really love her, don't you?'

Ben's answer was instant and sincere. 'Like I've never loved anyone in my life,' he said. 'I can't recall what my life was like before she came along, and now I can't imagine a day without her.'

Suddenly, Mary was making her way towards them. Upstairs, hanging out of the window with her cloth, Elsie was shouting down to her, 'What were you two laughing about, eh?'

'It's Mum. You know what she's like.' Mary was still chuckling. 'She was saying how she'd best teach you your place, because you're getting too big for your boots.'

'Huh! It's the other way round, more like!'

When, a moment later, Elsie saw the doctor getting out of his car, she dropped her cloth into the bucket, ran to the landing and called down to Lucy, who quickly made her way upstairs, brushed her hair and sat nervously on the edge of the bed, waiting to greet him.

Though deep down she knew it was unfair, Lucy harboured a certain distrust of doctors. It had started when Barney fell ill and they could do nothing to help him. To Lucy's mind, doctors were all the same – authoritative and full of good advice, but as yet they had not managed to instil any degree of confidence in her. There was one exception and that was Dr Raymond Lucas, from her old home outside Liverpool. He had been a true and trusted friend, and even now Lucy valued his letters and friendship.

Interrupting her thoughts, the knock sounded on the door for the second time. 'Come in.' Like a rebellious child, Lucy remained seated.

The door inched open and a smiling face peeped in at her; with his cheeky grin and that ridiculous cap of thick brown hair, the doctor looked far younger than his early thirties. 'Am I all right to come in?' he asked gingerly. 'Or am I likely to get my head chopped off at dawn?' He knew Lucy well by now, and was aware that his visits were unpopular.

Lucy laughed and the atmosphere eased. 'I'm not that much of an ogre, am I?' she asked, shamefacedly.

'There are those who might argue the point.' Straightening his shoulders, he pushed open the door and sauntered in.

Lucy asked him pointedly, 'You're not about to put me through the grinder, are you?'

He took a deep breath. 'I'll do whatever's necessary to satisfy myself that you haven't been overdoing it.' He peeked at her with suspicion. 'And have you?'

'What?'

'Been overdoing it?'

'I don't think so.' Lucy hoped he would leave before

coming into contact with Elsie, who was certain to have her say on the matter.

'Mmm.' Slowly nodding his head, he made that peculiar sound that some doctors make when they're not quite sure what to say. 'Mmm . . . ah.'

'You don't believe me, do you?'

'I don't know what to think.' He ventured forward. 'And if I don't believe you, it's no one's fault but your own.'

'What do you mean by that?'

'I mean, I need you to be honest, but sometimes you tell me one thing and do another. How am I supposed to know if you're following my instructions when you won't tell me the truth?'

'Huh!' Lucy couldn't help but like him. 'So now I'm a liar, am I?'

Fearing he might have got on the wrong side of her, he suggested meekly, 'I'm sorry, Lucy, that is not what I meant at all. Perhaps we should forget the conversation so far and start again, what do you think?'

Lucy smiled her sweetest. 'I think that's an excellent idea.'

With a twinkle in his eye, he made the smallest bow and to Lucy's amusement, greeted her with a bright, 'Good morning, Mrs Davidson.'

'Good morning, Doctor Nolan.' Bright as a button, Lucy's quick smile betrayed her enjoyment. 'How very nice to see you,' she lied beautifully.

Placing the big black bag on the bedside table, Dr Nolan opened it and took out his stethoscope. 'And how are you today?'

'I'm fine, thank you, Doctor.' Unbuttoning the top of her blouse, Lucy prepared herself for the shock of the cold stethoscope against her skin.

'Have you anything to report?' he asked gently.

'No, nothing.' Sensing the game was over she replied in

serious tone, 'Everything is just the same as it was the last time you were here.' She was determined not to reveal how her arm still hurt like the devil after trying to shift that heavy cleaner out of the cupboard, for which Elsie had rightfully given her a scolding.

'So, no aches or pains then?' He proceeded to examine her, discreetly ignoring Lucy's visible shudder as the cold receptacle pressed against the flat of her chest.

Lucy shook her head. 'No more than usual,' she answered. 'There are times when my joints feel as though they've locked together, and other times when I feel I can carry the world.'

'No change there then?' he said, concentrating now on the job in hand of checking her blood pressure.

'Not really, no.' She laughed out loud. 'I was flattered this morning when Elsie accused me of being ambitious enough to take down curtains, and clean all the windows.' She rolled her eyes to the ceiling. 'Those days are long gone, more's the pity.'

Lucy remembered the time when she could throw a pitchfork of hay on top of a wagon, or carry an injured lamb on her shoulders, but that was in another life. If she could bring it all back, she would. But it was gone, all but in her sorry heart.

A few moments later, after a thorough examination, the doctor put away his instruments and closed the bag. 'It seems you're no better and no worse, so you must be following my instructions after all.'

Lucy smiled triumphantly. 'Isn't that what I told you, Doctor?'

'So it is,' he replied. 'So it is – but you need to remember you're not the young woman you once were and your joints aren't quite so flexible. I'm not saying you can't do certain things – of course you can – but you must take care not to aggravate your condition. And that includes getting all hot and bothered about things.'

'I won't.'

'Good.' He wrote out a prescription. 'Your blood pressure is slightly up. Take one of these each morning, and an hour's rest in the afternoon. Right?'

'Whatever you say. You're the doctor.'

'I'll call again in a few days to check your blood pressure, just to be sure.'

Glad that the examination was over, Lucy relaxed. 'Are you ready for tea and biscuits?'

'Need you ask?' It had become a ritual; a bit of a banter, then the examination, before tea and biscuits. He had come to look forward to it. 'That's the main reason I come to visit,' the young man teased. He picked up his black bag. 'A few quiet moments in that delightful kitchen of yours sets me up for the day.'

Inching herself off the bed, Lucy slipped her shoes on. 'You haven't forgotten how I like mine, have you?'

He shook his head. 'Strong, with a little milk and two sugars.'

'That's it.' She waved him away with a gesture. 'Off you go then. You make your way down, and I'll follow on.'

By the time Lucy arrived in the kitchen, the doctor was pouring out two cups of tea and had got out a plate of Elsie's home-baked shortbread. 'I can't stay long,' he told Lucy. 'I must check on Maggie Craig; she's not too far away from giving birth.'

Lucy tut-tutted. 'That's her eighth in as many years. If you ask me, it's not Maggie as wants checking on, it's her old man. Quickest way to help Maggie and cut your work down into the bargain, is to chop it off for him. That'll give every-one a rest, won't it?'

The doctor laughed. 'It's a bit drastic, don't you think?'

Lucy shrugged. 'He's a selfish bugger, though. If it was *him* having the babies, he wouldn't be so quick to make them.'

She thought of her dead son, little Jamie, drowned these past twenty years or more, and her heart was sore. 'Mind you,' she went on in a softer voice, 'there is nothing more magical than holding a child in your arms.'

The doctor looked up to see the sadness in her eyes; he had seen it before and had been curious. Not for the first time, he sensed there was something in Lucy's past that she was unable to let go. He might have asked, but the young man's instinct told him Lucy would not thank him for it. So he waited until the sadness had passed, and she was smiling at him, as though everything was all right in her world.

'I expect you have a busy day ahead of you, Doctor?'

'I have, yes.' Finishing his tea, he munched the last of his biscuit, and when he thought Lucy wasn't looking, he tucked one into his jacket pocket. 'I really must get on now,' he excused himself. 'Remember what I said, won't you?'

Lucy nodded. 'I will, yes. Thank you, Doctor, and mind you don't crush that biscuit to crumbs in your pocket. Here.' Taking a napkin from the drawer she gave it to him with a knowing little smile. 'Best wrap it up in that, eh?'

Looking like a little boy caught with his hand in the sweetie jar, Dr Nolan did as he was told, and went sheepishly on his way.

～

Through the window Lucy watched him leave and when he was gone her gaze fell on Mary, who was walking with Ben towards the house.

'We're away now, Mother.' Mary arrived to kiss Lucy cheerio. 'Ben's just washing the oil from his hands, then we're off to organise the tractor.'

Lucy laughed. 'And what do you know about tractors?'

Mary made a face. 'Nothing,' she admitted. 'I know about cutting grass, about fertilising the soil, growing flowers and vegetables, plants from seed and collecting eggs from the chickens to sell at market, but that's as far as my knowledge stretches.' She gave her mother a curious glance. 'What are you smiling at?'

Lucy's memories had never jaded. She could remember Overhill Farm in the little Wirral village of Comberton by Weir as if it was yesterday, with Barney and his sons ploughing and seeding, and harvest-time, when the world was aglow with sunshine and the fields yielded their bounty. Somehow, without even knowing it, she had come to learn quite a bit about tractors and the way they worked. 'I was just thinking,' she said vaguely.

'From the look on your face, they must be pleasant thoughts.' Mary had often seen that look on her mother's face, a look of yesteryear, sometimes sad, sometimes warm with joy, and not once had she ever felt a part of it. 'What were you thinking about?'

'Oh, things that happened before you were born.'

'What things?'

Lucy was wary now. Even though Mary knew something about the secrets of the past, Lucy found it hard to discuss every little detail. 'I was just remembering how much I seem to have learned about tractors, that's all.'

Mary was intrigued. 'You loved helping Daddy on the farm, didn't you?' How she wished she had been a part of it all. But not the heartache, not that.

Lucy didn't get a chance to answer because now Ben was in the room, unrolling his sleeves and preparing to leave. 'If you're ready, we'd best be off now,' he told Mary, and to Lucy he suggested, 'Would you like to come with us?'

Lucy was tempted. 'That's very kind,' she said, 'but you

don't want me limping along, acting the wallflower. Besides, I've got things to do. You two get off and enjoy yourselves. You can tell me all about it when you get back.'

All too soon the two of them were climbing into Ben's car, laughing and talking, and Lucy was thrilled to see them so happy and content. 'See that, Barney?' she murmured aloud. 'That was you and me, in the short time we had together.'

Ravaged by emotions and memories she found difficult to cope with, Lucy went back to her room, slipped out of her shoes and lay down on the bed. Her gaze fixed on the ceiling, eyes closed, bittersweet tears trickled down her face. 'I want you back,' she whispered. 'Oh Barney, even now, after twenty years, I still miss you so much. I want you back – and I know it will never happen.'

For a time her heart was unbearably heavy. When she was quiet at last, she went to the bathroom and washed her face. Afterwards, feeling fresher and more able to face another day, she went downstairs, where Elsie was covering a large pie with pastry. 'Steak and kidney pie and mash for dinner tonight,' she advised Lucy. 'I'll cover it with greaseproof paper and set it on the shelf in the pantry. Oh, and there's apple crumble for afterwards. Won't take a second for Mary to heat up the spuds with a knob of butter, and to boil up some custard.'

Lucy was astonished. 'Good grief!' She stared at the pie and then at Elsie. 'You've got your skates on this morning, haven't you?' She glanced about the kitchen, which by now was spick and span. 'Are you in a hurry or what?'

For a minute it seemed as though Elsie had not heard Lucy's question, because she continued cutting the edge of the pastry to a pattern, then carried the pie to the pantry. Now she was at the sink, slapping her hands together to rid them of the flour before washing them under the tap.

Lucy spoke again. 'Elsie! Did you hear what I said?'

'I did, yes, and there's no need to shout.'

'Well then, have the manners to answer.'

The woman turned. 'All right – then yes, I am in a hurry.'

'Why?'

'Things to do.' Elsie never used many words when a few would do.

'What things?'

Elsie carried on wiping the table. After replacing the table-cloth she looked Lucy in the eye. 'Very well, if you must know, I'm taking Charlie to have his eyes tested.'

Lucy was open-mouthed. 'Can't he take himself?'

'No.'

'Why not? He's a grown man with a tongue in his head, isn't he?'

'That's the trouble.'

'What?'

'The tongue in his head. Gift o' the gab – that's his prob-lem! If I'm not there to explain what's been going on, he'll convince the optician that he's fine. Then there'll be no spectacles and he'll carry on the same as before.'

'And what's wrong with that? Charlie is a fine blacksmith. Surely he doesn't need spectacles for shoeing horses?'

'Hmh! Shows how much *you* know.' Hands on hips, Elsie seemed ready for another fight. 'Last week, Ted Willis brought his old mare into the yard for re-shoeing and Charlie put the shoe on upside down; the poor animal went away limping worse than when Ted fetched her in. If Ted hadn't brought her back, she'd have gone lame for sure.'

Lucy thought the woman was being a bit harsh. 'Charlie doesn't often make a mistake like that. Does it really mean he wants marching off to the optician's?'

Elsie bristled. 'I think I'm the best judge of that, if yer please. And it weren't the only time he got it wrong neither.'

'Oh, you've always had a tendency to exaggerate,' Lucy scoffed.

Elsie was indignant. 'What about this then?' she demanded haughtily. 'A few days ago, Larry Barker brought his cart in for a new wheel to be put on, and when he came back to collect it, Charlie had only ruddy well changed the wrong wheel! Then the week afore *that*, I asked if he'd come into Bedford with me as I had a lot to carry home. We went round the shops and when we got back to the bus-stop there was a queue. When the bus arrived, blow me down if he didn't follow Maggie Craig on, grab her shopping-bags and sit himself beside her . . . The silly article thought he were sitting next to *me*. I wouldn't mind if she hadn't got a backside the size of the gasworks and a gob to match!'

At first, Lucy thought she ought not to laugh. Then she began to titter and suddenly the pair of them were laughing hysterically. 'Now you know why he needs the spectacles,' Elsie spluttered.

And Lucy had to agree.

'I've done all the chores for now,' Elsie said finally, wiping her eyes. 'See you same time tomorrow.'

As the little woman put on her coat, Lucy told her: 'Be gentle with him, won't you? I know what a bully you can be when the mood takes you.'

'Huh!' Elsie gave her a scornful glance. 'Look who's talking!' Off she went, shoulders high and head up, muttering to herself: 'Do this, do that . . . never satisfied unless she's interfering! Besides, what does she know about my Charlie?'

'Have you two been arguing again?' Adam stuck his head round the back door.

Lucy swung round. 'That woman's getting more difficult by the day,' she said. 'Does as she likes and won't listen to a word anyone says.'

Adam smiled. 'Like someone else we know then, eh?'

31

Lucy laughed. 'You're right. I do have too much to say at times.' Whenever she was in Adam's company she felt content. 'Is the car all right?'

'Running like silk.'

'So, you'll be away on your errands now, will you?'

'That was the plan,' he answered quietly. 'Go into Bedford and collect the curtains you ordered, then visit the Post Office and the baker's on the way back. Then I've the rest of the day to put the new shelves up in the outhouse.'

'How long will you be?'

'I can't say for certain. Sometimes the road gets busy, sometimes it isn't.' Sensing her loneliness, he asked, 'D'you want to come with me?'

Lucy shook her head. 'No.'

Adam knew Lucy's every mood, and at this moment he knew he should not leave her alone with her memories. 'There's nothing so urgent that it can't wait till later,' he said softly. 'I'll keep you company for a while – if you want me to, that is?'

The tears still moist in her eyes, Lucy looked up. 'Thank you, Adam, I'd like that,' she whispered. No one alive knew her better than Adam, she thought fondly.

Relief flooded through him. When Lucy was sad, he was sad. And he was always content to be with her even if only as a friend; though one day, God willing, she might come to see him through more loving eyes.

He went over and settled himself in the chair opposite. 'What's wrong?' he asked. 'And don't say nothing, because I know you too well.'

'What makes you think something's wrong?'

He smiled knowingly. 'You're thinking of Barney, aren't you?' His voice was kind.

Lucy nodded.

'And you've been crying, haven't you?'

She nodded again.

'D'you want to talk about it?'

Drawing a deep sigh, Lucy confessed: 'I can't stop wondering about Barney's other family . . . Vicky and the children. Lately I can't seem to get them out of my mind, wondering where they are, and if they're safe.' She gave a nervous smile. 'I won't always be here, Adam. I'm getting old. How could I go to my Maker, with such a weight of secrets in my heart?'

Adam gave a slow, knowing nod. 'I understand how you feel, because I, too, often think about the others. To be honest, Lucy, I'm not sure if it would be kinder for them to know how it all came about. Or would the truth ruin what small contentment they might have found?'

Adam's concerns echoed in Lucy's mind. 'If they are to be told, it's me who should do the telling. And like I say, I'm getting on now, and time is rushing by. I must soon decide one way or the other.'

The very thought of not having her around filled him with dread. 'Don't talk as though you're old and decrepit because you're not,' he urged. 'God willing, you and I have many more years to enjoy, before our time comes.'

For a moment Lucy reflected on his words, and as always Adam had brought a kind of quietness to her heart. 'I hope so,' she murmured. 'But I can't shut out the past, and I can't see a way forward.'

Adam felt the same, but his first instinct had always been to protect Lucy. 'All I'm saying is, don't torment yourself. For all our sakes, try and let it rest. For now at least.'

Driven by doubts and guilt, Lucy reminded him, 'Some time ago, you insisted that Mary was entitled to know the truth, and you were right. So, don't you think *they* should know it, too? You say we risk ruining any contentment they may have found, but what if all these years they've never known peace of mind? What if the children have grown into adulthood, still carrying all the pain and anger that drove them away. And what of young Susie? Dear God, she loved her father with all of her young heart.'

Lucy recalled the powerful bond between Barney and his daughter. 'I can't get her out of my mind. I see the two of them sitting on the swing in the orchard, talking and laughing . . . happy and content in each other's company. She was so young, Adam. She knew only what she saw and heard, and that was a shocking thing. She never knew how Barney was suffering . . . how much he adored her. Susie was his darling little girl, and she went away hating him . . .'

Her voice breaking with emotion, Lucy bowed her head. For a moment neither she nor Adam spoke, but when he reached out to lay his hand over hers, she grasped it tight, drew it to her face and held it there for a moment.

To Lucy the moment was immensely comforting. Adam was right. He knew her as no one else could. He had travelled the years with her and Barney, and when Barney was gone, he was her beacon of light through days of darkness.

Though he could never be Barney, Adam was a very special man.

When the moment was gone, she released his hand and raised her eyes to his. 'I try, but I can't stop thinking about them – Susie, the two boys and Vicky, that lovely gentle woman who did all she could for me and Jamie – treated us like her own family. You know how devoted she and Barney were to each other, how they lived their whole life around each other. What happened to them, to the children, was so cruel, Adam . . . so terrible!'

So many sunsets had come and gone since those days over twenty years ago, she thought. In her mind she cast her memory back to the time when she could run like the wind and her life was filled with sunshine and the joy of youth. But there had been pain too; such pain she had thought never to recover from it. But somehow life goes on and takes you with it, whether you want it to or not.

Later, when everything else was lost, she and Barney had known their own joy together, and though it was for such a short time, Lucy had thanked the Good Lord many times over.

After Barney had died from the heart disease that had destroyed his last few years on this earth, her life seemed desolate. But then Barney had left her with a new life: Mary, their daughter, had been her salvation. Along with her dear friend, Adam, that patient, endearing man to whom she owed so much.

'Sometimes I think I'm the luckiest woman in the world.' Speaking her thoughts in a whisper, she hardly even noticed that Adam was beside her.

'Lucy?' Adam's quiet voice invaded her thoughts. 'What are you thinking?'

She looked up at him, her quiet eyes bathing his face. 'I was just thinking how Barney and I had so little time together. The days went all too swiftly, and even when we were making love and Mary was conceived, I always knew it was Vicky he needed, and not me.' Her smile was bittersweet. 'I didn't mind, not really. I would rather have had that small part of him, than live all of my life without him.'

Adam had never heard Lucy talk of her relationship with Barney in that particular, intimate way. He felt embarrassed and humbled, yet proud that she felt able to impart such a confidence to him.

Suddenly she had his face cradled in her hands, her warm blue eyes hinting a smile. 'I'm sorry.'

Relaxed in her gaze, he asked, 'Why should you be sorry?'

'I've been insensitive . . . talking of private moments with Barney, when I know how you feel towards me.'

Adam did not want her to reproach herself, and so he led

her away from that place. 'Have you always known how much I love you?'

Lucy's smile was radiant. 'You were never very good at hiding it.'

'Did you think I was foolish?'

'Never! Besides, I always loved you back. But not in the way I loved Barney.'

Adam's face crumpled in a smile. 'It's an odd world,' he said. 'I love you; you loved Barney; and he loved Vicky. The eternal triangle.'

Letting go of him, Lucy sat back in her seat. 'We can't help the way we feel,' she answered.

With her touch still tingling on his skin, Adam waited a moment, before in a spurt of boldness he asked, 'Marry me?'

Momentarily taken aback, Lucy was about to answer, when he stopped her. 'You said just now you loved me, though I accept it could never be like it was with Barney. But I've never loved anyone else and never could. Think about it, Lucy. We're so good together. We can talk easily to each other . . .'

There was so much he wanted to say. 'We've known some wonderful times, Lucy,' he remarked thoughtfully. 'Some good, some bad. But we've lived through them together, always supporting each other. We make each other laugh, we're content and easy in each other's company. What more could we ask, at our time of life? And I'll always take care of you, Lucy. You know that.'

Lost for words, she took a moment to consider what he was saying. This was not the first time Adam had proposed, and she suspected it would not be the last. But this time there was a kind of desperation about his boldness, and it made her ashamed.

'Oh Lucy, I'm so sorry.' Wishing he had kept his silence,

Adam was concerned that he had turned her against him. 'Now I've spoiled everything, haven't I?'

Lucy put his fears to rest. 'No, you haven't, you darling man. We've always understood each other, and we've always been able to speak our minds. That will never change. You'll always be very special to me.'

'But you won't marry me?'

'I can't.'

'Never?'

Lucy had learned to count her life in minutes and weeks. 'Never is a long time.'

Sensing a kind of acceptance, Adam thought it wise to back away from the subject of marriage. 'I won't mention it again.'

Lucy chuckled. 'Yes, you will.'

'Do you want me to?'

Loth to mislead him, she made a suggestion. 'Why don't we just leave things as they are for now? When I have a change of mind, I'll be sure to tell you. Agreed?' She held out her hand for him to hold.

Adam was thrilled. Lucy had said, 'when I have a change of mind'.

That was his first real glimpse of hope. 'Agreed!' Reaching out, he took hold of her hand and kept it clasped in his for a moment longer than necessary, until Lucy gave him one of those reprimanding, twinkling looks that turned his toes up and set his old heart racing.

The conversation took another direction. 'Lucy . . .' He hesitated. 'Will you let me take you back?'

'*Back?*' She knew what he meant, but could not bring herself to acknowledge it. 'What do you mean?'

'Back there . . . to Jamie.' Before she could protest, he went on, 'For your own peace of mind, you must go back. Do you think I don't know how it haunts you? Sometimes, when your mind wanders, I know you're thinking of him, reliving that night, remembering every little detail. I feel your pain, Lucy. You need to be there. It isn't enough that you've arranged to have his grave looked after, and no, Bridget did not tell me about that. She didn't have to.'

Lucy felt the weight of his every word. 'Are you judging me?' she whispered.

Adam shook his head. 'I would never judge you, you know that,' he assured her. 'We all need to deal with things in different ways. I knew you could never come away and not have someone look after Jamie's resting-place. Bridget was the obvious choice; she's loyal and honest, and she thinks of you as family.'

Lucy gave a wistful smile. 'She's always been there for me, and now she's there for little Jamie. I owe her so much.'

'I know that. And it's a good arrangement, but it isn't the same, is it? Forgive me, Lucy, but anyone can pay weekly visits and place the flowers there, and I know Bridget is a long and loyal friend, but she is not his mother. *You* are.'

Pausing a moment, he then went on in softer tone, 'I know how, deep down, you long to go back. Let me take you, Lucy. Please! Let me do that much for you at least?'

'I can't!'

'Why not?'

For a long moment Lucy lapsed into silence, her mind alive with the past, then in a fearful voice she asked, 'What do you think happened to Edward Trent?'

Adam snorted with disgust. 'We can only hope and pray he's already got his comeuppance. A man like that must incur enemies and loathing wherever he goes.'

'Why do you think they never caught him after . . . after he . . .' Her voice broke.

'Because like all rats he knows all the dark places where he can scurry away and hide.'

'Do you think he's still alive?'

Adam shook his head. 'Who knows? If there's any justice, he'll be rotting in the fires of Hell where he belongs!'

When now, Lucy turned away, her face cold and set with loathing, he asked tenderly, 'Let me take you back, my darling. It might help to lay the ghosts.'

But Lucy would not be persuaded. 'I don't want to talk about it any more,' she replied quietly.

Realising that Lucy had put up the barriers and he had no chance of getting close, Adam departed, leaving her to ponder on what he'd said.

~

Strolling to the dresser, Lucy held Barney's photograph and for a time she looked at his familiar face, the strong set of his jaw, the light in those wonderful eyes, and the boyish, mischievous smile that played about his mouth. A sigh rippled through her body. So much to think about. So much guilt. And what about Vicky and the others? Should she write to them, or should she leave well alone?

The thought of revealing Barney's long-held secret was almost unbearable. Lucy asked him: 'How can I tell her how you put yourself through Hell, so she and your children could have peace of mind and security?'

She lingered a moment longer, tracing the profile of his face with the tip of her finger, and turning the whole idea over in her mind. 'If the truth *must* be told, I pray they will find the strength to deal with it,' she whispered.

As she walked away, Lucy turned back to the photo one last time. She thought of those on the other side of the Atlantic, and at last she knew what must be done. 'I know I will have to tell them, Barney,' she said out loud, 'and I know it will come as a terrible shock. If I had it in my power,

I would make it less painful for them.' Her heart sank. 'But it's not.'

Squaring her shoulders, she searched inside herself for an answer, but there was none. 'They would need to find the strength to live with it.' The smallest hint of bitterness shaped her words. *Just as we did, all those long years ago.'*

~

Outside, Elsie was chatting with the coalman, conveniently forgetting she was in a rush and making him chuckle as always. 'I saw you in front as you came down the lane,' she told him. 'I might have begged a lift only you were too far away.'

A bumbling, homely sort with a wonky shoulder got from years of carrying heavy bags, the coalman joked, 'So you don't mind your arse being covered in coaldust then?'

'Not really, no,' Elsie replied. 'I might tell yer, I've had worse than that in my time. But I've never had a ride in a coalcart.'

'An' would you enjoy two grown men fighting over yer?'

'Hmh? That'll be the day.'

'What would your Charlie say, if I let you sit on my cart?'

Elsie laughed. 'I've no idea, but I'm willing if you are.'

'I'd watch what you say if I were you.' The coalman gave a naughty wink. 'There's many a man might take advantage of a remark like that.'

'You behave yerself, Bert Peters!' Elsie chided. 'I'm too old in the tooth to be flirting with the likes of you – and besides, if I were to pounce on you now, you'd run a mile. Don't deny it!'

Bert roared with laughter. 'Aye, an' if you *were* to pounce on me now, I'd more likely collapse. I've carried that many bags o' coal today, me legs 'ave gone.'

Back in Knudsden House, Lucy heard their shrieks of

laughter echo across the valley, and couldn't help but smile. The world might be crumbling round your ears, she thought, but somehow, life went on.

Her thoughts returned to what Adam had said earlier, and her mind was made up.

Suddenly she knew what she must do. She looked up to the heavens, a deep yearning for peace flooding her heart. 'I will go back and face the demons,' she declared. 'Maybe then, I can find some kind of peace.'

It would not be easy, she knew that. It had been a lifetime since she had travelled that particular road. When she left that familiar and much-loved place, she left behind a wealth of laughter, sun-filled days and happiness. The pain she took with her, for it had never gone away.

Her train of thought turned to the monster who had snuffed out her baby's life.

'Edward Trent, may you rot in Hell for what you did! You murdered your own son!'

She had no idea where he was. After the tragedy he had fled into the darkness of the night, and was never heard of again.

Many times over the years, Lucy had prayed that, somehow, he had been made to pay for the evil thing he did.

In the beginning, the hatred had eaten into her very soul, but now as the years caught up with her, after World War Two had changed everybody's lives forever, she had learned not to let it rule her life. By contrast, with the passing of time, memories of Barney and the personal sacrifice he had made grew ever stronger; as did the need to put things right before it was too late.

She thought of how it had been, and her heart was sore. 'I'm going back, Barney,' she murmured. 'Then I'm going to tell it all, to try and bring a measure of peace to Vicky, and the children.'

First, though, there was someone she needed to see.

CHAPTER FOUR

T HE GOVERNOR WAS busy poring over official documents when the knock came on the door. 'Yes, who is it?'

The prison officer told him, 'I've got Carter with me now, sir.'

At once the Governor's face betrayed his repugnance. 'Right! Let's have him.'

Momentarily disappearing, the prison officer threw open the door and thrusting Edward Carter inside, positioned him before the desk. 'All right, Carter! Stand up straight!' he growled. Digging him in the back with the flat of his hand, he pushed the prisoner forward.

For a seemingly long time, the Governor remained in his seat, his head bent and his long bony finger flicking over the pages of his document. He neither spoke nor looked up.

When, beginning to tire, the prisoner lolled to one side, his hands sliding deep into his pockets, he was caught up short by another dig in the back, this time rougher and more meaningful.

Without raising his head, the Governor peered over his rimless spectacles. 'Remember where you are, Carter. Hands out of your pockets . . . NOW!' he ordered.

Wary of this new Governor, who had already proved

himself to be a harsh disciplinarian, the man quickly did as he was told. After all, he had secrets to hide. Moreover, he had almost served his time and did not want to jeopardise his date of release.

Intending to unnerve the prisoner, the Governor continued to stare at him, his observant gaze taking in every detail of the man: the strong, stocky build, the inherent arrogance, the thick shock of greying hair and the deeply-etched lines on the once-young and handsome face.

Here was a puzzle, he thought. Carter was a devious cunning sort, capable of anything, a man seemingly without a background; though if it was ever uncovered, it would probably betray him as an evil and merciless creature.

While the Governor studied the prisoner, the prisoner did the same in return. He observed the lank dark hair and the small beady eyes behind the spectacles; the long sinuous fingers now drumming on the desktop, racking his nerves and sending a ripple of murderous intent through his every sense. There were many men inside this prison he would like to strangle, but the greatest pleasure would come from feeling his hands round the Governor's slender white throat.

His train of thought was abruptly broken as the Governor smiled directly into his face. 'You'd like to kill me, wouldn't you, Carter?' he asked tantalisingly. 'You'd love to get your two big hands round my throat and squeeze the life out of me. I'm right, aren't I? You hate me so much you can taste it.'

Gulping so hard his Adam's apple bobbed up and down, the prisoner lowered his gaze, his thoughts going wild. Jesus! How did he know that? He must be a bloody mind-reader . . . but he was right. The prospect of choking him until he stopped breathing filled him with excitement.

The scraping of a chair told him the Governor was standing up. He could feel the coldness of his gaze as it fell on him. 'Look at me, Carter.' The sound of air being drawn through his nose was oddly loud in that warm, uncomfortable room. 'LOOK AT ME, I SAY!'

Carter looked up. 'Sir!'

The Governor came close, so close his smoke-stained breath fanned the prisoner's face. 'You broke both his legs, Carter.' The voice was almost tender. 'You went into the showers and broke both his legs. Why would you do a thing like that?'

The big man looked up. 'I didn't do it. I never touched him.'

'Liar!'

'No, sir. I'm no liar.'

'So you say.' The Governor put his hands behind his back and strolled about for a while, eventually coming up behind the prisoner. 'If *you* didn't do it, who did?'

'Don't know, sir. It pays to keep yourself to yourself in this place. All I know is, it weren't me.'

'You were seen.'

'No, sir. It weren't nothing to do with me.'

'There was a witness, Carter! You were seen . . . slithering into the space beside him. One minute he was washing, and the next he was writhing on the floor and you were gone.'

'No, sir!' As he glanced up, rage fired his eyes. If ever he found out who had grassed on him, he'd slit their throat without a second thought. 'Who was it, sir? Who lied about it being me?'

Silence fell, and in that moment the air was charged with a sense of danger. Eventually the Governor spoke, his voice so soft it was barely audible. 'Did I tell you to look up?'

The prisoner dropped his gaze. 'No, sir.'

'Did I give you permission to speak . . . to ask *me* questions?'

'No, sir.'

'Mmm.' The smaller man remained still for a moment, then he strolled round the room, and after a time he returned to stand before the prisoner. 'You were *seen*!'

Cursing himself for almost losing control, the prisoner gave no reply.

'You had an argument with him earlier. Later, you saw your opportunity, and you viciously broke both his legs.'

Slowly shaking his head, the prisoner remained silent.

'They say you threw him to the ground and stamped on his legs, so hard that they cracked under the weight. Did you do that, Carter? Did you?'

Sweating profusely, the prisoner looked up and in hesitant voice denied it yet again. 'No, sir. I swear it.'

'I see.' Anger and disappointment coloured the man's voice. 'This is not the first time you've been brought before me, Carter,' he snapped. 'Time and again you've caused trouble amongst the prisoners. You're a nasty, evil sort who belongs more in a cage than a prison.'

He took a step away, as though he suddenly could not bear to be near such low-life. 'I know you did this, Carter, I'd gamble my life on it. But you're such a devious devil, I can't prove it. Y'see, they're all too cowardly to come forward, but you already knew that, didn't you?'

He leaned forward, his face almost touching that of the prisoner. 'You may be off the hook on this one, but there will come a time when I get you bang to rights. So watch out, Carter, because from now on, you won't be able to scratch your backside without me knowing.'

Turning to the officer, he ordered briskly, 'All privileges stopped for the foreseeable future. Now get him out of my sight!'

With that the prisoner was dismissed, and when he was gone, the Governor sat at his desk, muttering under his breath, 'Nasty piece of work! No background, no past. It's as though he was never born.'

Taking off his glasses, he placed them on the desk and with both hands he wiped the sweat from his face. 'I wish I knew what made the bastard tick. If I knew that, I'd be able to finish him once and for all.'

Replacing his spectacles, he resumed his paperwork. But the leering face as it went out of the door burned in his mind, until a few minutes later, he had to stop work, go to the cabinet and taking out a bottle, pour himself a much-needed drink. There were times when he wondered if he really needed this job after all.

~

That evening, when the lights were out and only the narrow-est shaft of silver moonlight filtered through the window-bars, Edward Trent – for Carter was only an assumed name – lay in his bunk, his eyes closed and his mind full of thoughts about the woman he could not get out of his mind, and the child called Jamie, his one and only son, who was lying in a cold churchyard because of him.

'I don't suppose you've got a ciggie hid away somewhere, 'ave ye?' The voice with the Scots accent belonged to the man in the lower bunk; young and bold, he feared no one, except maybe the man above him, who was renowned for his quick temper and cruel punishment of anyone who set against him.

The answer was instant and sharp. 'If I had, what makes you think I'd give it to you?'

'Well, for one thing, I thought you might appreciate the way I kept my mouth shut when questioned by the Governor this morning.'

'You had a choice. I didn't ask you to keep quiet about that weasel in the shower.'

There was a low peal of laughter. 'What d'you take me for? What would have happened if I'd told them how I saw you go in, I heard him squeal, and then I heard the crunch of his bones? I also saw you come out and slink away. I knew what you'd done, all right. I could have shopped you if I'd wanted.'

'Why don't you then?' Hanging his upper end over the bedrail, Trent hissed at the young man, 'Go on! Call for the screw and tell him what you know, you Scottish nonce.'

'Oh yeah? And have both my legs broken tomorrow? No thanks. I'll settle for a ciggie.'

There was a pause while Trent stared down on the bold young man. Then he swung away, delved into the curve of the wall and a moment later threw down a hand-rolled cigarette. 'Two draws and no more,' he warned. 'If they get a whiff of smoke they'll be in here to search the place from top to bottom.' He gave a devious grin. 'It wouldn't do for them buggers to poke about where they're not wanted.'

The young man sat up. 'I need a light.'

Another moment and the match was thrown into his lap. 'Two draws and no more,' he was reminded.

Having struck the match on his shoe, the young man lit the cigarette. He took a deep, satisfying draw. Then: 'D'you mind if I ask you something?'

'I don't know till you ask me.'

'Have you ever killed anybody?' Taking a long smooth drag of the cigarette, the young fella looked up, startled when he was suddenly grasped round the neck and hoisted into the air. 'Woah, woah! I didnae mean nuthin'.'

He was hoisted almost to the top bunk, shaken hard, then dropped to the ground where he lay for a moment, choking on the smoke he already had in his throat. 'You're a damned lunatic!' he gasped. 'Isn't a man allowed to ask a question without the wind being knocked out of him?'

Above him the big man leered over the edge of his bunk. 'Twice,' he said softly. 'I killed twice; one was a thieving bastard who thought he could get one over on me . . .'

'Hmh!' Clambering up, the young man brushed the dust from his prison nightwear. 'He won't be thieving from you again then, will he, eh?'

'Too right he won't.' Lying back in his bunk, the big man was in a confiding mood, especially as he knew his cellmate was not the gabbing kind. 'I've got this temper, y'see? When folks rile me up the wrong way, I lash out. I can't help it.'

'Is that right?' No sooner had the young man taken another deep drag of the cigarette, than it was torn from his mouth. 'Jesus! You've ripped the skin offa my lips!'

'I said two draws. It's mine now.'

'Who was the other one?'

'What other one?'

'You said you'd killed twice.'

The answer was slow in coming. 'A child . . . I killed a child, but it was an accident.' Suddenly he was back there, the dark rage alive in him as it was then. 'The bastards should never have chased me! If they'd stayed back like I asked, it never would have happened. I knew she wouldn't come with me, so I took the kid, but she ran after me . . . the other man was coming upriver and I felt trapped. I didn't mean for it to happen. It was as much their fault as mine. *They should never have come after me!*' The last words were a howl.

'Whose kid was it?' The young man knew his cellmate was a bad lot, but a child! That was a terrible bad thing.

'It was mine.'

'Christ Almighty! You killed your own child?'

He might have said more but when two iron-like fists tightened round his head, he thought he too was about to die. 'All right! All right! It was an accident – I understand. Let go, you crazy bugger, let go of me!' In the second before the other man let go, the young Scotsman was sure his head would burst.

49

Trent went on, his voice thick with emotion: 'His mammy was the best woman I ever had. I didn't realise how much I loved her until I'd let her go, then she went off with some other man, and I couldn't get her back. She turned me away, told me she wanted nothing to do with me ever again.' Anger quivered in his voice. 'Have you any idea how that makes a man feel?'

For a time he was silent, reliving that night. 'I was crazy . . . out of my head. I grabbed the boy and carried him off, hoping she'd change her mind and come with me, but instead she went wild! She came after me and I panicked. She tried to snatch the boy and somehow it all went wrong. It was the river, y'see? The river took him away. It was Lucy's fault. If she'd agreed to make her life with me, it never would have happened.' His voice broke. 'I don't suppose Lucy will ever forgive me.'

'What happened to her?'

'I don't know. I ran as far away as I could . . . went back to sea for many a long year. When war broke out I was over in Canada – went to work in a logging camp for the duration. Didn't see why I should get a bullet in the arse from Hitler while I could avoid it.'

The other prisoner, who had been too young to fight, didn't think much of this attitude, having lost an elder brother and an uncle, both soldiers, in the war. However, he wisely kept silent, although something of his feelings came over when he asked: 'So, they didn't put you away then?'

'No.'

'And you got away with it?'

'Yes.'

'And the other one?'

'What other one?'

'The one that stole from you.'

'I was clever. After I'd killed him, I put him where he'd never be found. He was a nobody, a thief and vagabond; it was easy enough to take on his name. I made sure I stayed away long enough to build up my new identity.' Arrogant as ever he went on, 'Twenty year and more, I managed to stay out o' the limelight, then one night on shore leave in Liverpool I got drunk and picked a fight which ended up nasty, and got me sent down.'

'Is Edward Carter your real name?'

A moment, then: 'More questions, eh, Scotty?' Trent grew cautious. 'Sounds to me like I've said more than enough.'

'You're a lucky man. By rights you should have been hung from the neck for what you did.'

With amazing agility that belied his age, the big man swung himself down from the bunk, caught the young fella by the shirt-collar and yanked him to his feet. 'You should be honoured,' Trent growled. 'You're the only person I've ever confided in. Maybe it was a bad idea. Maybe you know too much for your own good.'

Tightening his grip, he drew the younger man closer still. 'Have I made a big mistake? For all I know, you might be the sort who would like to make a few bob out of what I've told you. Are you? Are you the gabby sort?'

Eyes wide with fear, the young man assured him, 'You know I'd never do a thing like that. I'd have to be some kind of a fool! I value my legs too much. I wouldn't want to be left crippled or worse, just 'cause I don't know how to keep my mouth shut.'

The big man hissed, 'What do you know about me?'

'Not a thing! Not a single thing!'

'Very wise.' Flinging him aside, Trent hoisted himself back on his bunk. A moment later the cigarette end was thrown down to the other prisoner. 'I often wonder about her.'

'Who?' Thankful to still have the use of his legs and

another couple of draws into the bargain, the young man was still shaking.

'Lucy Baker. She was the most exciting woman you could ever meet. She wasn't what you might call a beauty – not dazzling or glamorous or anything like that.'

'If she wasnae glamorous or beautiful, what attracted you to her?'

'Lucy was different somehow, hard to forget. She was childlike – pure and innocent, but mischievous, too. She was more alive than any other woman I've ever met. Her smile was more radiant than a summer's day, and when she laughed it turned your heart over. She was small and homely, with eyes that sang. They kinda latched onto you and wouldn't let go.'

'What happened to her?'

'I don't know.' He dreamed of her. 'She's older now, like me. I often wonder if she still has that magical quality, or whether she's all shrivelled and ugly. I've taken good care of myself over the years, but I can't tell what she looks like. I've still got this image in my mind . . . might be a shame to spoil it with the real thing.' He gave a wry little laugh. 'I daresay I'd be shocked if I were to see her now.'

'Have you ever been back . . . to that place?'

'No. I want to, though. I've always wanted to, only I might stir it all up. There was a bloke, Barney Davidson his name was. Likely as not if he saw me, he'd come after me. From what I recall, he wasn't a big man, but he had this bull-like strength about him. There's bound to be trouble. I don't know if I should risk being carted off and strung up for what happened that night.'

'So, you won't ever go back there then?'

The big man gave a gruff laugh. 'I've been thinking about it a lot lately. I just might decide to go there and find out if she's still around. First though, I have to keep my nose clean and get out of here.' He hung over the end of the bunk. 'But don't think I won't seek you out, if ever you open your mouth about what you heard here tonight.'

The young man handed back the tab end of the cigarette. 'I might be bold and reckless at times – it's what got me here in the first place. But I'm not wrong in the head. Your secret's safe with me, so you needn't worry.'

His cellmate gave a soft, sinister laugh. 'I don't intend to,' he replied confidently. 'I'd rather let *you* do the worrying.'

Long into the early hours, the young man lay awake to consider his companion's veiled warning. There was no doubt in his mind; if he ever talked of what was discussed this night, he would be made to pay a terrible price.

All the same he was intrigued by what he'd heard of the child and the woman; and how, even now after all this time, the big man was still besotted with her. This Lucy: she sounded like the woman every man needed in his life – not glamorous enough to attract other men, but with a special inner beauty that shone out.

What was she doing now? What did she look like? Was she shrivelled and ugly as Carter feared, or was she still the same magical person she had always been? Most of all, what were her feelings towards him? After all, indirectly or not, he had murdered her child.

One thing was certain. It was only the fear of capture for what he had done that had kept Carter away all this time.

Glancing up to make sure his cellmate was asleep, the Scotsman mulled over the story he'd been told. He muttered softly as though talking to Lucy direct, 'Seems to me, the madman still has a craving for you.'

Closing his eyes, he made the sign of the cross on himself. 'God help you, lady. I've got a feeling you're not rid of him yet!'

CHAPTER FIVE

'Do you want to help?' Emerging from the barn at Far Crest Farm, Ben made his way over to Mary, who was leaning on the fence. 'Look what I've found.' Holding out a pair of wellies he told her, 'They're a bit big, but I'm sure you'll manage.'

With his brown cords tucked into his own wellingtons and wearing a woolly polo-neck jumper under his knee-length coat, she thought he looked every inch the farmer. 'What? You want *me* to help round up the sheep?' she said nervously. 'I wouldn't have a clue how to start.'

He smiled patiently. 'And you never will if you don't let me show you how.' With the confidence of a man who was content with his lot, he came up beside her and slid an arm round her waist. In each other's company they were quiet and easy, lingering a moment to enjoy the feast of Nature spread out before them.

'This is the time of day I love the most.' Ben never failed to be amazed at how quickly he had forgotten the city life. His work and his heart were now firmly rooted here in Salford. 'There are three times in the day when I feel closer to the land,' he confided now. 'First thing in the morning when the world still sleeps and the dew is on the grass; the end of the day when the sun is going down and the sky is shot with colour; and now when it's turning midday, with the morning slipping into afternoon.'

Reaching across, he kissed Mary softly on the face. 'Before I met you, I was a lonely man,' he murmured in her ear. 'I watched the days change and pass, and with the ending of each one, I felt even lonelier. Because there was so much beauty around me, I learned to live with my loneliness and enjoy what I have here. But now I have you to share it all with, and I've never been happier, or more content.'

Taking her by the shoulders, he gently turned her round to face him. For a long moment he looked on her face, on those deep, lavender-blue eyes and the shock of thick fair hair that framed her pretty features. 'I love you,' he whispered. 'Now that I've got you, I never want to be without you.'

'If I have my way,' Mary teased him, 'I promise you will never be.' Her thoughts turned to her parents, Barney and Lucy. 'Sometimes though, I can't help but feel frightened,' she added.

Ben held her close. 'Frightened of what?'

'Of the way we are, you and me.'

'Why should you be frightened?'

'Because of my parents. They loved each other too, yet after a pitifully short time they were parted.' After years of waiting for the right man, Ben had brought her alive, and at the same time made her more afraid than she had ever been. 'I couldn't bear it if I lost you, Ben.'

Ben held her close. He understood her fears, for didn't he feel the very same? 'When you love someone,' the feel of her silky hair against his face was wonderful, 'you have to take each day as it comes and live it to the full. The truth is, you have two choices, my darling: on the one side, you have to accept that there can never be a happy ending for one or the other of you . . . unless somehow you were to leave this earth at one and the same time.'

Mary had not thought of it that way, but now she realised how starkly true that was. 'You said there were two choices?'

He nodded. 'On the other hand, you can choose never to commit yourself to anyone. But if you do that, you will never know what it's like to love someone the way your mother loved Barney, or the way we love each other.' He slowly shook his head. 'I wouldn't want to miss out on what we have now.'

Mary had no doubts either. 'I'd rather suffer pain and loneliness for part of my life, than never know what it was like to love you,' she told him.

Holding her at arm's length he was astonished to see the tears bright in her eyes. With the tip of his finger, he wiped them away. 'You and I have been very lucky because some-how, we found each other. So, for the moment let's just be grateful and, as I said, take each day as it comes.'

Having returned from his wanderings, Ben's faithful old Labrador Chuck ran to meet them, excitedly yapping. 'I think he's trying to tell us something,' Mary laughed.

Ben leaned down to pacify the animal. 'All right, all right! Calm yourself down.' Looking up to Mary he asked, 'So, are you willing to give it a go? Do you want to help with the sheep?'

Never having done it before, Mary took a moment to answer, but when she did, it was with enthusiasm. 'Very well. I'll give it a go.'

'I knew it!' Ben exclaimed. 'We'll make a farmer of you yet.'

~

As it turned out, Mary had never enjoyed herself so much. The dog was a master at rounding up the sheep. 'Gently now, boy!' Ben kept him under control so as not to send the sheep into a run, which could damage the pregnant ewes.

In no time at all, the flock were teased into the pen, ready for Ben and Mary to weed out the more heavily pregnant sheep and release the others.

With great care and tenderness, though never losing authority, Ben examined each and every one. The heavily-pregnant ewes were given over to Mary, who then led them into the smaller adjoining pen which ran behind the field-gate, while one by one the others were returned to graze the main field.

When the flock had been sorted, Ben and Mary took a breather. 'I'm proud of you,' Ben told Mary. 'You're a born farmer's wife.'

The twelve pregnant ewes were next ushered into the smaller paddock nearer to the homestead, where Ben could keep an eye on them. 'I think we've earned a break,' he yawned.

Mary agreed and the two of them made their way to the cottage, where they kicked off their boots, hung up their coats and washed the smell of sheep and muck off their hands.

Inside the cosy parlour, Ben soon had a cheery fire going, while in the kitchen Mary made the tea. She loved this pretty little place; with its low-beamed ceilings and big open stone fireplace, it was like a cottage you might find on a picture-postcard.

When the fire was roaring up the chimney and each of them had a warming drink, Ben sat in the armchair, while Mary curled up at his feet, her face aglow from the fire's heat, and a contented smile on her face.

When she lapsed into a long silence, Ben leaned over her shoulder. 'What's wrong, sweetheart?'

Mary shook her head. 'Nothing.'

But Ben knew different. 'Hey! This is me you're talking

to. Something's playing on your mind. If you're worried, I'd like to know.'

Reaching up, she took hold of his hand. 'I'm sorry, Ben.' She didn't want to spoil the moment, but she really did need to talk. 'It's something you said . . . about my parents. It's been a year since we were told, and I still can't take it all in – Barney sending his family away like that, making them hate him while all the time he was so ill, and in desperate need of them. And Mother, loving him like she did, when all the time he loved someone else.'

'That must have been so hard for her,' Ben remarked thoughtfully. 'To work all the day long with someone you love, and to know that he only has eyes for his wife . . . although that's exactly how it should be in a happy marriage.'

Mary had been thinking along the same lines. 'It must have been Hell for her. And yet she stayed, content enough just to be near him.'

'She and Barney were together in the end though,' Ben reminded her. 'And I for one am grateful for that, because if they hadn't, then you would never have been born, and I would never have known you.'

'What will she do, Ben? Will she ever bring herself to tell Barney's other family what happened? Or will she leave them to live out their lives, in ignorance?'

Trusting him implicitly, she opened her heart. 'I need to know where they are. I need to meet them and talk with them, about my father, and the way it was. I want them to know what he did for them . . . that he never stopped loving them, and that he sent them away because he didn't want them to lose the opportunity of a new life in Boston by finding out that he was terminally ill.'

Since Adam had confided the truth, Mary had thought about little else. 'Do you understand what I'm saying, Ben?

Do you think it's wrong for me to meet my other family . . . Thomas and Ronnie, and Susie? As for little Jamie, he was just a baby of two when he drowned, and Mum won't talk about him. I have to know my roots, where I came from. I want to go back there, to Liverpool where it all happened!'

Her voice broke. 'Oh Ben! If only I could remember clearly. Why won't she take me there? Is she trying to protect me? Is she afraid I'll be hurt by it all? But I'm hurting now, can't she see that? Why doesn't she understand that I desperately need to see where it all unfolded, if only to gain some peace of mind? I only know half the story and she won't talk to me about it. I need to stand in the fields where they worked; I have to walk by the river where they fought to save little Jamie. I have to see where he lies and make my own peace with him.'

Taking her in his arms, Ben quietened her. 'I know it's hard, but it's hard for your mother too. She lived through it, and now she's having to live with the consequences of it all. Give her time. It will take a lot of strength for her to face it all again, but your mother is a strong, determined woman. She *will* go back. She *will* show you where it all happened, I know she will. Be patient, my darling. She needs to be sure; when the time comes for her to face all those demons, she's bound to want you there beside her. Because you're hers and Barney's child, and because going back will be one of the hardest things she's ever had to do.'

The two of them talked a while longer, until his embrace tightened and the kisses grew more urgent, and soon, right there on the rug, they made love for the very first time. It was a joyful, fulfilling experience, a bonding of heart and body, when the love between them was forged even stronger.

Afterwards, with passion melted and bodies exhausted, they lay in the warm glow of the fire, thinking and dreaming of their future together. They didn't speak for a long time, because their hearts and minds were in harmony. There was no need for words.

After a time, while Mary was dressing, Ben ventured outside. A moment later, he was calling her. 'MARY! Quickly – come and see!'

Not knowing what to expect, she ran out to find him beckoning to her, his face alight with excitement.

'Look!' He pointed to one of the ewes. Head down, almost on her knees, and with the whole of her weight pressed against the fence, she was in labour, and seemingly oblivious to their presence.

The next few minutes were magical. Inch by inch, the newborn appeared. Bathed in fluid, the lamb wormed its way out until, with the slightest plop, it slid to the ground. For what seemed an age, the mother did not move. Instead she stood, head hanging, resting. Then suddenly she turned to her offspring and began licking away the slimy, covering membrane.

Moments later, the lamb stood up, its legs unsteady and its head seeming far too large for its tiny body. It gave itself a shake, fell over and struggled up again, and in an incredibly short time, it was searching out its mammy's teat.

Mary was thrilled. 'It's beautiful.'

'Have you never seen a lamb born before?' Ben had seen it many times now, and each time was just as wonderful as the last.

'I've never seen one actually being born,' Mary admitted. 'I've walked the fields at different times and I've seen the newborns playing and skipping, but I've never actually seen a ewe giving birth.'

'Have you ever touched a newborn lamb?'

'Never.'

'Would you like to?'

She was surprised. 'Won't the mother be hostile?'

Ben shook his head. 'No.'

'Then yes, I'd like that.'

They waited a while, until mother and newborn had bonded and the young one had its fill of milk. Then, with great care and talking to the mother as he went, Ben led Mary across the paddock.

He did not take the newborn straight away. Instead he gestured for Mary to be still; he murmured to the sheep that he was just as proud of her baby as she was, and that he meant no harm except to show her off and then return her. But the mother displayed little interest in them, and when he reached down to lift the newborn into his arms, she merely stood and watched, almost as though she knew he meant no harm.

At first, the little one struggled, but Ben secured the squirming bundle and holding it towards Mary, told her to smell its coat.

Nervously, Mary leaned towards the tiny creature and sniffed at its coat. 'It smells warm, and tangy . . . like fresh-made marmalade,' she laughed. 'Can I touch her?'

When he nodded, she reached out and stroked her fingers over its fleece; the sensation was like nothing she had ever experienced. Beneath her touch, the tight curls of fleece felt hard and wiry. She was amazed. 'I thought it would be *soft* to the touch,' she said in wonderment.

Before returning the lamb to its mother, Ben dipped a finger in the fluid which had cradled the newborn and was now lying in little pockets in the grass. He then wiped it over the back of the lamb and returned it to its anxious mother, who ran her tongue over its back before leading it away, contented.

Mary was curious. 'Why did you do that?'

Ben explained, 'Sometimes, a ewe will reject a lamb if she's not sure it's hers. We've both handled the lamb and we've left our smell on it. By wiping the fluid on its back, I made sure she could smell and recognise her newborn, so there would be no doubt in her mind.'

This had been a day that Mary would always remember. She had made love with her husband-to-be and witnessed the miracle of birth, almost as a sign of the babies that she might have, one day in the future. But for now, she was anxious to get home and talk with her mother. For the moment, there were other important issues that needed to be resolved.

~

Lucy saw them arrive. 'They're back now,' she told Adam, who had been polishing the car and was now enjoying the sandwich Lucy had brought him.

'Good!' Finishing his sandwich, he excused himself. 'I'll away and get out of these overalls.'

'Don't be long, will you?' Strange how with every passing day, Lucy needed him to be more a part of everything she did.

Adam was thrilled but doubtful. 'Are you sure you want me to stay?'

'Yes, Adam, I'm sure.' Lucy had no doubts. 'You've always been a part of all this.'

'Right then. I'll go and get washed up. Give me ten minutes or so. Oh, and thanks for the sandwich.' He handed her the plate. 'It was tasty as always, though a bit more pickle would not have come amiss.' With that he gave a mischievous wink and hurried away.

Lucy went outside and waited for her daughter and Ben to climb out of his car. 'You've had a delivery this morning,' she told her daughter. 'It's near the greenhouse.'

Mary, who was looking more beautiful than her mother

had ever seen her, had completely forgotten. 'What sort of a delivery?'

'A load of rotting manure,' Lucy groaned. 'Adam helped to fork it off the cart, and by God does it stink! I can even smell it from the kitchen.'

'You won't grumble when I've dug it into the ground to produce fat cabbages and juicy carrots,' Mary grinned. 'Anyway, we had another sort of delivery today, didn't we, Ben?'

Ben was absent-mindedly running the flat of his hand along the side of Lucy's car. 'Adam keeps this car beautiful,' he said. 'It's a credit to him.'

'Ben!' Mary gave him a nudge. 'I was just saying, we had another kind of delivery today, didn't we?'

'We certainly did . . . the first of the spring lambs decided to make an appearance,' he announced proudly. 'And we saw the whole thing, from birth to suckling.'

Mary eagerly imparted the bones of her little adventure. 'I stroked its coat. I always thought it would be soft and downy,' she told her mother excitedly, 'but it was harsh to the touch, and tight as a coiled spring.'

'I could have told you that,' Lucy teased. 'Your daddy once had a whole flock of sheep. Spring was always the best time, when the lambs were born and I could sit on the tree-stump by the edge of the woods and watch them frisking and leaping about.'

Before her memories could overwhelm her again, she announced briskly, 'Come inside. I have something to tell you.'

By the time they strolled to the kitchen door, Adam was already there, washed and changed and looking apprehensive. 'Hello, you two!' he greeted them. Stepping aside, he waited for the family to pass before following them across the hallway and into the drawing room.

When they were all seated – Ben and Mary on the sofa together, Adam in the leather armchair and Lucy in the matching chair beside him, she told them all, 'For a long time now, I've been toying with the idea of going back North.' As she went on, the nervousness disappeared and a calm strength emerged. 'It won't be an easy thing for me to do. There will be other people living in Barney's old house now, and strangers farming the land.'

She grew wistful, eyes downcast. 'The memories will still be there though, in the fields and the cottage. Memories that will never leave me . . . such joy and regret, and oh, the laughter we all shared.' Such laughter, such joy, friendship and the yearning for a man she believed could never be hers.

Swallowing hard, she looked up to see her daughter silently coaxing her to go on. Bracing herself, she cleared her throat and in a firm voice told them, 'A visit is long overdue, and now with time seeming to pass ever more quickly, I won't leave it any longer. I have a very old friend in Doctor Lucas, as I'm sure you're all aware of by now. He knows me well,' glancing at Adam, she instinctively reached out and took hold of his hand, 'almost as well as my good friend, Adam.'

Turning a deep shade of pink, Adam smiled. 'Doctor Lucas is a fine man,' he remarked. 'It will be good to see him again, I'm sure.'

Mary had a question for Lucy. 'Have you told him you're coming?'

'Not yet, no.'

'When do you intend going?'

Lucy shook her head. 'I'm not sure. I've only just made the decision. In a couple of weeks' time, maybe? I'll write to Doctor Lucas. There are any number of good hotels in the area.'

Mary had another question. 'Mother?'

'Yes, dear?'

'Can we come with you – me and Ben?'

Lucy quickly reassured her. 'I wouldn't dream of going back without you,' she said. 'When we left there, you were too young to remember what it was like . . .'

Nostalgia flooded her senses. 'I need to show you the fields where your daddy and the family worked alongside each other, and the cottage where we lived. I can't wait to see Bridget, either. From her letters, she's still full of life, with the dancing and the singing and the shameless flirting. She's married four men and dumped them all one after the other, and doesn't seem to have changed one bit. But oh, how wonderful it will be to see her again. I bet she's grown old disgracefully, and made a fortune out of everything she's ever touched.'

Ben was intrigued. 'Have you never met up in all this time?'

Lucy shook her head. 'Bridget's been too busy making her fortune, and until now, I've never really mustered enough courage to go back.' She laughed heartily. 'I wouldn't mind betting she looks exactly the same, and as far as I can tell, she's still up to her old tricks, wheeling and dealing, and playing havoc with the men.'

Caught up in Lucy's enthusiasm, Mary ran to sit on the arm of her mother's chair. 'Oh Mum, I'm longing to meet her! And I want to see it all – the fields and the cottage, and the river . . .'

She paused when Lucy looked at her through agonised eyes, almost as though her mother knew what was in her mind at that moment. 'Will you take me to see where he is, Mother?' Sliding a hand into Lucy's, Mary gently persisted, 'Will you take me to the churchyard where little Jamie lies?'

In her mind Lucy saw it all – that night, and the horror

– and thrusting it to the back of her mind, she avoided the question. 'So there you are, my dear,' she said brightly, and turning to Ben, she asked, 'You will come with us, won't you, Ben?'

Just as she had hoped, Ben did not hesitate. 'I'd like that. Thank you, Lucy.'

Lucy clapped her hands. 'Good! That's wonderful. I'm sure Adam will organise it all.' She winked at him. 'Of course, it would be nice to have a date for the wedding too, so we can start planning for that as well. Ben's daughter Abbie will make a beautiful bridesmaid, don't you think, Adam?'

Mary flung her two arms round her mother's neck. 'You're a conniving old biddy,' she chided, 'but I wouldn't swap you for the world.'

Lucy would not be deterred. 'Well, Ben? Is there soon to be a wedding or not?'

Delighting in Lucy's character, Ben promised, 'I think you should get your hat and outfit ready. I wouldn't be at all surprised if it didn't happen before too long, isn't that right, Mary?'

Mimicking her mother, the girl was a little coy. 'We'll have to wait and see, won't we?' With that, she took her leave. 'Who wants a cup of tea?'

For now, the discussion was over, but there was much to look forward to.

And much to fear.

CHAPTER SIX

B RIDGET HAD TAKEN flowers to the churchyard every
Saturday, and this Saturday was no different.

Twenty years ago, she had made a promise to a friend,
and though she had been many things in her life, some of
which she was not proud of, it was not in her nature to break
a promise.

Stooping to lay down the posy of white and yellow narcissi,
she dug into her pocket and took out a white envelope.
Then she held it up, almost as though she thought little
Jamie could see it. 'I had a letter from yer mammy this
morning,' she murmured in her soft Irish lilt. 'At long last,
she's coming to see us. What d'you think o' that, eh? Ah,
sure, it won't be easy for yer mammy . . . what with a family
in the cottage an' the river only a spit away, as if nothing
bad ever happened there. But we all know different, don't
we, eh?'

Drawing a deep breath through her nostrils, she blew it
out in a great sigh. 'Ah, but she's a brave woman, yer
mammy. After you were took, she went away with dear
Barney. She made a new life and though we've written time
and again, we've not clapped eyes on each other these many
years.'

When a dewdrop appeared on the end of her nose she

cuffed it away. 'There's a chill wind brewing,' she said. 'I'd best be going, or my knee will seize up again.' She chuckled. 'I'm not so young as I was, more's the pity, but I can't let the years get the better of me, 'cause once I do that, I'm finished.' She squared her shoulders. 'Inside, I'm still the young woman who fought and clawed her way to the top.'

After rearranging the posy in a nicer position, she clambered to her feet, groaning as she straightened up. 'The old bones are beginning to complain, but the mind's as quick as it ever was.' Bridget was thankful for the good health she enjoyed. It meant she could keep to her schedule and stay one step ahead of advancing years.

She rubbed her sore knees and for a moment was quiet in contemplation. 'In some ways it might be better if yer mammy never came back, poor wee thing,' she said, 'but then I wouldn't see her, would I? An' she wouldn't see *you*, an' that would be a terrible shame, especially when it's taken her so long to make this particular journey.'

The man's kindly voice startled her. 'You know what they say about people who talk to themselves?'

Swinging round, she almost fell over. 'Jaysus! I almost had a heart attack. What d'you want to creep up on me like that for?'

The man apologised. 'I wasn't creeping up on you,' he said. 'It's just that I've seen you so often down here, I thought I might come up and say hello.'

Slim and tidy, with a pleasant bearded face, something about him jogged Bridget's memory. 'Have I seen ye somewhere before?' she asked. 'You look familiar.'

He laughed at that. 'Isn't that what the men are supposed to say when they see a woman who takes their fancy?'

Bridget could see the funny side. 'Ah well now, it's not that I'm after taking your fancy,' she joked in return. 'I really do believe I've seen ye somewheres before.'

Offering the hand of friendship, he introduced himself. 'The name's Oliver Rogers.'

Bridget shook his hand. 'An' how d'you do then, Oliver Rogers.' Suddenly she was blushing to the roots of her hair. 'Ah, now I know where I've seen ye. That's it! You used to visit my old place . . . Gawd Almighty! Sure, that's more years ago than I care to remember.'

He laughed. 'You're right. It must be at least twenty-four years since I climbed the steps to spend an hour or so with one of your girls.'

Bridget nodded. 'If I remember aright, you always asked for Judy.'

'That's right, I did.' He seemed embarrassed. 'But only because she was the nearest to you I could get . . . same red hair and that wonderful bubbly nature. It was always you I wanted, Bridget. You were the loveliest of them all, but you were always just out of reach.'

Like a young schoolgirl on her first date, Bridget protested, 'Away with you! Why would you want me, when you could have the pick of my girls?'

He gazed at her for a moment, before answering softly, 'We can't help who we fall in love with, can we?'

For the first time in her life, Bridget was lost for words. When she did speak, her voice was alive with anger. 'Soft talk, is it? I expect you've found out that I've made it good and you want a slice of it. Well, aren't you the cunning blighter, eh? In love with me, you say? Hmh! I know what you're after, so I do.' She wagged a finger at him. 'I'm far too canny to fall for all that nonsense, so ye'd best be on yer way, before ye see a side to me you wouldn't like! Go on, be off with you! I've no wish to renew our acquaintance. What's more, I can't be wasting the day talking to the likes o' you. I'm a busy woman, so I am.'

With that she turned on her heel and went smartly down

the path, muttering to herself and cursing. 'Bloody maniac! Coming up behind me like that. Does he think I were born yesterday? Sure, I've worked hard to get where I am today. I started with nothing and fought my way up. Now I've got a good life and a healthy bank-balance, I'm not about to share it with some crafty, grasping old bugger!'

She stole a glance behind. Looking very sorry for himself, the man was standing right where she left him. 'Be Jaysus! I've a good mind to go back and smack him one, so I have.' She clenched her fist and thrust it into her pocket. 'Just let him try it again, that's all.'

'Bridget!' His voice followed her. 'I didn't mean to offend you. Come back . . . let's talk.'

'Sod off!'

'Please, Bridget! I'm sorry if I spoke out of turn.'

'Ye heathen! You'd best be gone, or ye *will* be sorry!'

'Don't go . . . BRIDGET!'

Ignoring his plea, Bridget climbed into her beloved Hillman Minx. Losing no time in case he might follow her, she shut the door and turned on the engine.

'Bloody cheek!' Stamping her foot on the clutch, she slammed the car into gear. Lurching forward, it jerked into a spasm and for a moment she almost lost control. 'Come on, come on!' She kicked on the accelerator and it took off at a crazy pace, throwing her back in the seat.

Oliver Rogers was right behind. When the car shot forward, with the wheels skidding and squealing, the hail of dust and muck thrown up from the hoggin-path covered him in a thick cloud. 'You're still a damned lunatic!' he yelled. But Bridget was already out of earshot.

He brushed himself down. 'That's my girl,' he chuckled. 'You might think I'm after your money, but nothing could be further from the truth.'

Walking the few steps to the large, sleek Humber, he

climbed in and watched as Bridget's car skidded and danced all the way down the road. 'You're a bit older, with a few more wrinkles and greying hair,' he nodded approvingly, 'but you're still the same lively little devil you always were.'

Slipping into gear he manoeuvred the vehicle onto the road. 'You're a right handful,' he laughed. 'That's what I like most about you. And that's why I mean to have you before we're both too old to enjoy what's left.'

~

Driving like one demented through the streets of Liverpool, Bridget had pedestrians leaping out of the way. 'Don't you swear at me!' she had snapped at an angry young couple who had the misfortune to step out in front of her, and now she didn't see the old dear who ran back to the pavement in fear for her life. 'Sorry, love, but ye should have the good sense to look where you're going!' Bridget tutted as the old woman waved her stick at her. 'Hmh! From the way she scooted up onto the pavement, she doesn't need that stick at all.'

As she slowed down a little, Bridget grinned to herself. 'I wouldn't mind betting she only carries it about to whack folks on the head,' she said aloud, and was still laughing as she pulled up outside an imposing office. Situated on a wide quiet street just a brisk walk from the city centre, it boasted her name above the entrance:

The Bridget Business Agency

Climbing out of her car, Bridget stood for a moment as she always did, filled with pride and a sense of accomplishment to see what she had achieved.

The Bridget Business Agency. Even now, after so many years, she could hardly believe that this imposing building was really hers, paid for lock, stock and barrel. 'You've done well, Bridget my girl,' she told herself. It was a far cry from that little house in Viaduct Street, with its poky rooms and second-hand furniture.

At one time, these offices had been two shops; one a man's tailor's and the other an ironmonger's; the upper floors provided spacious living accommodation.

Having outgrown her previous offices, and wanting to stay fairly central, Bridget bought the two shops and gutted them. She redesigned the building and filled it with the most expensive furniture, creating the air of discretion and professionalism that her clients preferred.

She had eight attractive young women working for her, and nowadays, the business was of a more respectable and lucrative nature. Most of the work was done over the telephone and through appointments, with the majority of clients being genuine businessmen needing escorts; though of course there was always the occasional gentleman who wanted a little more than that. After thoroughly vetting them, Bridget did occasionally turn a blind eye.

But that was the exception rather than the rule for she had built up an admirable reputation in Liverpool and protected her standing like a tiger protecting her cubs.

Making her way upstairs, Bridget burst into reception in her usual robust manner. 'Top o' the morning, Amy, me darling.' She strode across the room. 'You're looking pretty, I must say. Off out, are you?'

Middle-aged and still single, Amy had taken the place of Tillie Salter as Bridget's right-hand helper. With her baby-face and sad eyes that made a body want to hug her, she never over-dressed or went out of her way to show herself off; in fact, quite the contrary.

At home, she would wear anything and everything as long

as it felt comfortable. But while at work she was always smart and trim, with her hair tied back and her white shirt stiff and starched. But not this Saturday morning, for she had her hair washed and loose, and curled up at the ends, and she wore a soft blue blouse with a little daisy brooch on the lapel.

'Will ye look at you!' Bridget loved to tease her. 'Don't deny it – you've got a date, so ye have.'

'No, I haven't!'

'Why else would ye be done up all pretty, with yer eyes shining and a smile on yer little face?'

Amy blushed to the roots of her hair. 'You're imagining things, like you always do. I'm not going on a date.'

'Hey now!' Bridget wagged a finger. 'You might be in charge when I'm not here, but I'm the boss and I'm allowed to think and say what I like. So don't you forget it, young madam!'

In charge of the offices, Amy had been with her for a good while now. She was an excellent organiser and had a flair for figures – which had never been Bridget's strong point.

Amy explained, 'I thought I might go to the pictures this afternoon, that's all. It's a Norman Wisdom film.'

Bridget glanced at the clock. 'In that case, you'd best make tracks or you'll miss the matinée,' she told her. 'I should never have asked you to come in on a Saturday. It was unfair of me, so it was.'

'Don't worry about it,' Amy assured her. 'I didn't know myself about the film until I got out of bed this morning. When the postman told me that he was going to see it, I just thought it would make a nice treat for me too.'

Bridget chuckled. 'So, it was the postman put the sparkle in yer eye, was it?'

'No, it was not.'

'Ah, don't gimme that now. I've seen your postie and he's a fine body of a man, so he is.' She made a smiley face. 'It's him that's taking you to the pictures, is it?'

Pretending to tidy some papers, Amy looked away. 'He's not taking me,' she protested, 'though it's likely we could bump into each other . . .'

When Bridget opened her mouth to speak, Amy cautioned her, 'Don't leap to conclusions, because there's nothing going on, and that's an end to it.'

'Sure, I wasn't about to say anything at all.'

'Yes, you were. I saw it in your face.'

'Well, all right, yes, I was about to speak. But it was nothing to do with the postman.' She couldn't resist another little jibe. 'If you fancy a torrid affair on the quiet with him, who am I to judge?'

Ignoring her teasing, Amy asked, 'So, what were you about to tell me just now?'

Feigning indignation, Bridget pouted, 'Ah, sure, I've changed me mind. I'm not telling you now.'

Amy laughed. 'You're itching to tell me. So, come on. What is it?' Leaning over the desk, she folded her arms. 'I'm not doing any more work until you tell me.'

'So! Refusing to work now, is it?' Bridget was enjoying the little exchange. 'I hope ye realise, I could sack you for that.'

'But you won't.'

Bridget's smile grew wider. 'I got a letter this morning.'

'Oh? An old boyfriend, was it?' Amy knew how to turn tables.

'No, 'twas not!' Waving the letter under Amy's nose, she said, 'You'll never guess who it's from.'

'Aw, Bridget, stop teasing.' With sleight of hand, Amy tried to get at the letter, but Bridget was too quick for her.

'Don't be impatient.' She could be a real torment.

Amy tried another tack. 'Well, I'd best be going now. I've updated the appointment book. There's just a bit of filing to be done, but that can wait until Monday.' She began to turn away.

Horrified, Bridget grabbed hold of her arm. 'Aw, go on then,' she said, and thrust the letter at her. 'Open it, why don't ye?'

A moment later, Amy was clapping her hands and shrieking, 'Oh my God, it's Lucy! She's coming to see us!' Running round the desk she caught hold of Bridget and wouldn't let go. Then she was crying and laughing all at the same time. Tears of joy ran unheeded down her face.

'Behave yourself,' Bridget chided. 'Sure, I know you're thrilled and so am I, but will ye stop the damned bawling . . . oh, now will ye look at that! You're plastering snot all over the sleeve of me coat!'

Amy wiped her eyes with the back of her hand. 'I'm sorry,' she whimpered, 'but I can't believe it. All this time, Lucy kept her distance, not wanting to see us and not wanting to come back, and now she'll soon be here, and I can't believe it. Oh Bridget!'

'Hey!' Taking her by the shoulders, Bridget warned, 'Don't start bawling again, or I'll have you locked away somewheres, then you won't see her at all, will ye?'

Amy laughed at that. 'Oh, but isn't it wonderful?'

The other woman agreed. 'It is, yes – though I'm not sure why the sudden change of mind after all this time.'

Amy's eyes widened. 'You're right. She hasn't said why she's coming to see us. Oh no. You don't think she's poorly, do you – really poorly, I mean? Oh Bridget, I couldn't stand it if she was coming back to tell us that.'

Although the very same thought had initially occurred to Bridget, she immediately put Amy's mind at rest. 'Oh for heaven's sakes, will ye stop yer blathering! Think about it. If

Lucy was that ill, she wouldn't be travelling all this way to see us, would she, eh? Instead, I'm sure we'd be asked to go to *her.*'

Amy gave a sigh of relief. 'You're right. Oh, and it will be lovely to see her, won't it?'

Bridget smiled, that deep-down smile that spoke more than words. 'Yes. Now get off, or you'll miss the start of the picture, so ye will.'

While Amy went to fetch her coat, Bridget threw herself into the high-backed leather chair.

'I'm away now,' Amy said, then had a sudden thought. 'Lucy won't arrive today, will she?'

'O' course not. I only got the letter this morning. You read it yourself. She'll write again with a date to expect her. So, get off now, or you'll miss the postman.' She winked knowingly. 'And ye wouldn't want that now, would ye?'

'Bridget! You shouldn't be saying things like that. It could cause all manner of trouble if that kind of silly gossip got out.'

Bridget tutted. 'Oh. Married, is he?'

'No, he's not married, and as far as I know, he's not planning to, though from the sound of it you'd have us both marching down the aisle whether we want to or not.'

Bridget gave a naughty wink. 'Whatever gives you that idea?'

Amy shook her head in frustration. 'I'll see you later.' That said, she hurried out of the room.

'Wait on!' Behind her, Bridget gave a loud groan. 'Oh Amy, you little darlin', I don't want you to miss the Pathé News, but you couldn't fetch me a bowl of hot water, could ye? All that walking. Jaysus! Me feet are like two roasted chickens.'

Amy looked at her watch and gave a shrug. 'I don't suppose it will matter if I miss the first ten minutes.'

She returned to make Bridget more comfortable, though on delivering the bowl of hot water she gave her a lecture. 'You're too hard on yourself,' she chided. 'You do too much, always on the run, and frightening the life out of anybody who gets in the way of you and that mad machine. You need to remember, you're not getting any younger.'

Bridget was indignant. 'I didn't build this business by sitting on my backside,' she retorted. 'And because there's more competition ready to muscle in on me, I need to work at staying on top. I haven't got time to grow old, thank you very much, and I don't need reminding how I'm not getting any younger.'

Dipping her bare feet into the bowl, she gave a long, delicious sigh. 'As for my mad machine, that car is a godsend to me. It saves my legs and gives me the freedom I need.'

Leaning over, Amy gave her a peck on the cheek. 'I'm sorry,' she told her. 'I worry about you, that's all.' If she lost Bridget it would be like losing her best friend, and entire family.

'Well, there's no need.' Bridget dismissed this with a wave of her hand. 'Now, be off with ye.'

As she went, Amy remarked once more on Lucy's imminent visit. 'I can't wait to see her,' she said. 'I wonder if she's changed?'

'Well, o' course she's changed!' Bridget scoffed. 'We all have. We're older and slower, with wrinkles and greying hair.'

Amy laughed at that. 'Not *you*!' she called out as she went through the office. 'You have your hair dyed and slap enough make-up on to frighten the devil. And you're still as mad as a hatter.'

With that she closed the door and went on her way, leaving Bridget wondering about Lucy, and remembering how it was, before she went away. 'Aw, Lucy my old friend, you had it hard, so ye did. What with losing the bairn and then Barney, and ye never even told us about him until a year later. But I think I understand why you needed to shut us out.' She lounged deeper into the chair. 'You thought to save us any distress, and like a wounded animal, you needed a place to hide.'

She closed her eyes and gave up a heartfelt prayer. 'God willing, you maybe found a measure of peace, in your far-off hideaway.'

CHAPTER SEVEN

NORMALLY, ON A Sunday, Bridget would not see hide nor hair of Amy, and if by chance she did pop round to see her boss, it was never before midday. 'I like my extra hour or two in bed of a Sunday,' Amy would declare. And if truth be told, Bridget also enjoyed her bit of a lie-in.

But not today, because on this warm, bright Sunday in April, Lucy was coming to see them. 'What time do you think she'll arrive?' Amy was like a cat on hot bricks.

'Sit down and stop wearing out my floor, if ye please, and turn that blessed wireless off. I'm in no mood to listen to the Goons!' Bridget groaned. 'Like I've told ye for the umpteenth time, Lucy has a long way to travel. Who knows how long it might take. She'll be here when she arrives – no sooner, no later.'

In fact it was a quarter to four when Adam drove through the main streets of Liverpool; on this Sunday as on every other, the heart of the city was quiet, with only the odd window-shopper strolling about.

'All this time and nothing seems to have changed,' he remarked.

Adam had hardly got a word out of Lucy all the way up from Bedfordshire, and now as he tried hard to draw her into a conversation, he could only imagine the emotions raging through her. His own heart, too, was churning at seeing his familiar old hometown.

Loth to betray her feelings, Lucy was deeply moved at seeing all the familiar haunts. Greedy to keep and hold it forever, she took in everything; the church on the corner, the avenue of shops, the street-lamps, and even the kerbs and pavements worn down over the years by the feet of many, including Barney's and her own.

'You're wrong, Adam,' she answered quietly. 'It *has* changed. There was a time when I thought Liverpool would always belong to me. When I last walked down these streets, they were comforting and friendly, because Barney was still alive. If I was out shopping, he was always at the back of my mind, and I knew that when I got home he would be there, waiting for me – that warm, wonderful man.'

Yes, Liverpool was still here, she thought, and yes, it *looked* the same – the proud old buildings, the old cobbler's on the corner, and the tearooms where she and Vicky often took a rest from the shopping.

Even the pub where she had seen Barney and the street-woman on that dreadful day – that was still there. Everything looked the same, but it didn't feel the same, because now they were all gone – her darling boy Jamie, Barney, Vicky and the others.

It was gone four by the time they booked into the hotel. 'Do you want to rest before we do anything else?' Adam was concerned for her. 'We could give it an hour or so, before we go to Bridget's. I could order tea and sandwiches, and you could have half an hour or so in your room resting.'

'Are you tired, Adam?'

'Not really, no. We had an hour's stop. That was enough to refresh me.'

'Good!' Lucy was adamant. 'There'll be time enough for us to rest later. I really do need to see Bridget, and Amy, and . . .' She paused. 'Leave the porter to take up our bags, Adam. I'd like to go to Bridget's straight away.'

The porter was instructed and they climbed back into the car. 'Do you know where you're going?' Lucy asked. 'If I remember rightly, Duke Street is situated in the posh area along by the marketplace then second right, turning past the cinema.'

Adam laughed. 'Unless they've moved the streets, I know every twist and turn,' he assured her. 'We'll be there in a few minutes.'

Adam was as good as his word. In no time at all, they were turning into Duke Street; tree-lined and flanked with expensive houses. 'I'd forgotten how posh this area was,' he said.

As he drove slowly by, Adam carefully read the names and numbers of each house. Every one was different – some with high gates, others with no gates at all, but each one oozing money and affluence. 'Bridget wasn't exaggerating when she wrote and told you she was comfortably off,' he said.

Lucy smiled at his remark. 'I always knew Bridget would move up in the world,' she said proudly. 'This is all a far cry from the old place.'

~

Having been back and forth to the window this past hour and more, Bridget saw the car draw up and Adam get out of the driver's seat. At first she didn't recognise him, but then as he opened the rear door for Lucy, he looked towards the house and Bridget was sure. 'It's them!' Raising her voice she called Amy, who had been keeping vigil at the window but had now gone to sit by the fireside. 'AMY! It's them!'

Excited, Bridget hurried to the front door and flung it open, and there after all these years was her dear friend Lucy, still strong, still defiant against all odds. Even though she leaned on her walking-stick, there was a grim determination in her step as she began her way up the path.

Her hair that once hung thick and loose over her shoulders, was now gathered into a clip, and she appeared slimmer, her shoulders upright and straight. Over the years, Lucy had carried a great burden on those slim shoulders, but she had borne her troubles well, and never once had she leaned on others who would have helped if only she had asked.

Now, as she paused in her steps to look up, her eyes were warm and clear, shining with goodness.

'Hello, my darling Bridget.' The voice was Lucy's. The woman was the girl again, and the girl was the same, with this precious moment frozen in time. They were young again, and the years were as nothing.

Bridget had vowed not to cry or be emotional, but as she ran to meet her old friend, the tears flowed, and when she called Lucy's name her voice broke and faltered. 'Oh, Lucy . . .' Unable to speak any more, she snatched Lucy to her, and they held each other in a close embrace; it was the most magical moment. One brief moment, born out of tragedy and joy, and a friendship which from a distance had spanned a lifetime.

Adam stood by, a lump in his throat and his heart soaring. These two should never have been parted, he thought, but Lucy had done what she felt she must do, and now thank God, she was back.

With her arm secure round Lucy, Bridget opened her embrace to include him. 'Oh Adam, you don't know how wonderful it is to see you both.'

He went to them and they stood a moment, holding each

other as though they would never let go, and the pain in Lucy's heart was eased. This is right, she thought. This is how it should be.

When Amy came running down the steps, Lucy took her into her arms. 'Amy!' She kissed her face and smiled. 'You look taller, and smarter.' Amy had made a special effort to look good for Lucy. She had on a pretty cream-coloured jacket and brown skirt, her hair was especially bobbed and she had on a touch of lipstick.

'You look every inch the businesswoman.' Lucy had been told how Amy ran Bridget's business almost single-handed. 'But to me, you'll always be shy little Amy.'

Amy laughed. 'Not so shy now,' she said. 'And not so little, either. I've put on a few pounds since you last saw me.'

'Come inside.' Bridget led them onwards, Amy and Adam talking softly behind, with herself and Lucy in front. 'We're like two old soldiers,' Bridget joked tearfully. 'Back from the wars, licking our wounds and ready for the next battle.'

Lucy smiled at that. All my battles are done, she mused. But then she thought of Edward Trent, and her heart fell.

Inside the house, while Amy went to the kitchen, Bridget took Adam and Lucy on a tour; first stop was her large office overlooking the garden. 'This is the room where I enjoy a drop o' the good stuff, put me feet up and think o' the old days,' she confided. 'Back there I had a humble little place with a backyard and men who visited discreetly for pleasure, and now I have a house with beautiful gardens and a posh office, and I'm still in the same business of providing lovely girls for lonely men, only this time it's more business than pleasure.' She shrugged philosophically then confided, 'And would you believe, I'm making ten times the money.'

'I can see that.' Lucy was taken from room to room, in and out of five large bedrooms, all furnished in the latest style; two enormous bathrooms shaped in marble and glass, and then down the wide staircase into a drawing room with French doors leading out to a magnificent garden.

'You have a beautiful house, Bridget.' Lucy fell thankfully into the wide armchair; Adam sat close and when Amy brought in the tray of sandwiches and tea, the four of them reminisced about the past. 'Will you ever come back here to live?' Amy asked hopefully, and Lucy told her she would not; that though she had fond memories, the bad ones were still too real.

'Besides,' she said, 'I'm too old in the tooth to be moving house and starting over.'

Adam told them he felt the same. 'Liverpool will always be where my roots are,' he confessed, 'but my home is in the south . . .' no one missed the adoring glance he shot in Lucy's direction, '. . . with Lucy and her daughter.'

'And how is your daughter, Mary?' Bridget enquired of Lucy. 'Sure, I thought you were bringing her with you, and this young man of hers – Ben, isn't it?'

'They'll be along shortly,' Lucy promised. 'Mary called on us this morning before we set off and said how Ben's sheep had all started lambing. The pair of them were up all night, and the lambs were still coming when we left.'

'And do they know where to find us?'

Adam intervened. 'I copied out the directions you sent to Lucy,' he said. 'I'm sure they'll find you, no trouble.'

'Good!' Like Amy, Bridget was longing to see Lucy's daughter. 'Oh, I can't wait to meet her,' she told Lucy. 'When you took her from here, she was just a tiddler, so she was.'

There was something else Bridget wanted to know, but she wasn't quite sure how to broach it.

Anticipating the question, Lucy enlightened her. 'We didn't go to the churchyard,' she said quietly. 'If that's what you're wondering?'

Bridget nodded. 'You read my mind, pet. I was just after asking if you might have called there first.'

When emotion threatened to creep up on her, Lucy merely shook her head. The memories were vivid as always: after little Jamie's second birthday party on that joyous November night, Trent had appeared at her cottage, wanting her back, beseeching her to leave Liverpool with him. Then, when he realised that her love had turned to hate, he had snatched her child and disappeared into the night.

Mortally afraid for little Jamie, Lucy had pursued him, but he was like a madman fleeing through the pitch-dark fields. Stumbling and calling, she had gone after him, but he was always a distance away. And then he was crossing the river, carrying the child over the slippery boulders that straddled the water above the weir, now in full flood. Screaming hysterically, Lucy had followed him. And it was while grappling with him that Edward Trent began to lose his footing in the raging torrent.

It all happened so quickly. She pleaded with him to give her the child, but he was so crazed and evil there was no reasoning with him. Then Barney came out of the darkness and shouted for her to go back, to leave it to him, but instead, fearful for little Jamie, she followed her instincts and reached out for her baby. Then suddenly it all went wrong. In one frantic, desperate moment, she and Trent lost their footing, and their son was gone. And as the water carried him away, she prayed, like she had never prayed in her life before or since.

Caring nothing for his own life, Barney had gone after the child but it was all too late, and since that terrible moment when he had carried Jamie's lifeless body to her, she had blamed herself. If only she had listened to Barney when he told her to get back. If only she had not pursued Edward Trent, he might have returned her child safely. If only he had not made for the river . . . if only. *If only.* Dear God, would the heartache never end? And now here she was, where it all happened, and for her own peace of mind, she must visit little Jamie's last resting-place.

The prospect was unbearable to Lucy, and yet she desperately needed to stand where he lay, to speak with him and in her heart and mind to hold his hand and reassure him that she had not forgotten, that she still loved and remembered him and would do so until the day she followed.

So often she had mentally prepared herself for this day, when she would be with him, yet each time she had resisted. Because she knew how hard it would be, how devastated she would feel. But it was ever in her mind and heart. These past twenty years and more she had thought of little else.

'So, will ye go?' Soft and encouraging, Bridget's voice entered her consciousness.

Lucy nodded. 'You know I will.' Of that there was no question.

'Not today though, eh, Lucy?' Adam could see how tired she was. He above all others knew what an emotionally draining experience it would be when Lucy finally returned to her baby's resting-place. 'I think we should go back to the hotel and take it easy for the rest of the evening.'

As always, his only thought was for Lucy. 'I'll take you to the churchyard first thing in the morning, when you've had a good night's sleep. What do you say, Lucy? It's been a long journey. You need to take it easy now.'

Lucy took a while to answer. To the others, she appeared calm and controlled, while inside, her heart and mind were in turmoil. How could she go there? How could she not? Yet she must. She must! Oh, but where in the name of God would she find the strength?

Suddenly her heart was open and her mind at peace.

From Barney, she realised; that's where she would find the strength.

'You're right, Adam.' She smiled on him and his heart warmed. 'It might be best to leave it until morning.'

Bridget had a suggestion. 'I wouldn't mind betting ye haven't had a good meal all day, am I right?'

Up to now, Lucy had not felt hungry, but suddenly she was famished. 'Why don't we all have dinner at the hotel?' she suggested, perking up.

'Well, I never!' Bridget cried excitedly. 'You took the very words out of my mouth. It'll be my treat, so it will, and no arguments.'

Neither Adam nor Amy needed much persuasion and so it was arranged. 'You take yerselves off, and me and Amy will be there soonever we've painted our faces and put on our glad rags.'

At seven-thirty they gathered in the hotel bar. Having rested awhile, Lucy was now bathed and changed. She had on a black straight-skirted dress with blue collar and cuffs, and her hair was swept back into a loop and fastened with a daisy-chain pin. 'You look lovely!' Even if she was dressed in sacks, Adam would still think the same. In his eyes, Lucy was everything perfect.

All the same, Lucy was flattered. 'You don't look so bad yourself.' In his dark suit and pale green shirt, he made a handsome figure.

Amy and Bridget arrived on time; Amy looking young and fresh in a brown two-piece, Bridget painted to the eyeballs with dark rouge, crimson lipstick, and the smartest bright green two-piece. 'Don't tell me,' she laughed. 'I look like a leprechaun.' She cast a scathing glance at Amy. 'Sure, haven't I already been told that?' Doing a twirl she fished for compliments, and got them a-plenty.

Spending a few minutes in the bar for a pre-meal drink,

they were delighted when Mary and Ben came through the door. 'What a lovely surprise! You're just in time for dinner.' Lucy gave them each a hug before proudly presenting them to Amy and Bridget.

'Gawd love us!' Bridget wrapped herself round Mary and squeezed her so hard, Lucy warned her she'd have her eyeballs out. 'Look at her ... she's all grown up, so she is!' There was no stopping Bridget once she started. 'Oh, and isn't she like her daddy! Oh Lucy, I can't believe it.'

Becoming emotional, she was almost in tears, until Lucy told her firmly, 'Behave yourself, and let the young 'uns get ready for dinner.'

An hour later, they all went through to the dining room.

The evening was perfect, the food was done to a treat, and the conversation at different times both sparkling and nostalgic; with Bridget unable to take her eyes off Mary, and Mary content to see her mother's eyes shining with pleasure at being with her old friends.

Later, when they had a few minutes alone, she mentioned to Ben that tomorrow would be a difficult day for Lucy. 'God only knows how she'll cope when she goes to the churchyard and sees little Jamie's grave. It's bound to bring it all back with a vengeance.'

Ben had few doubts. 'Your mother will cope like she always does,' he assured her. 'She's the strongest, most determined woman I've ever met.' Looking down at Lucy's daughter, he observed the fine straight features and honest clear eyes, and his voice softened. 'And you, my lovely, are a chip off the old block!'

~

The next day started badly for Lucy. She had not slept well. She saw the dawn light the skies and she heard the first birdsong, and for a time, she sat gazing out the window, her mind shot with all manner of mayhem.

This morning she would see the little cottage given to her by Leonard Maitland, her employer up at The Manse in the village of Comberton by Weir. This was the cottage where she and Barney had lived for a while before moving down to Salford, the cottage where Mary had been conceived, in love, in anguish. The same cottage where she had spent several idyllic months with her young son, enjoying the countryside and the company of their friends, the Davidsons. The cottage where she had shed so many tears, mourning the loss of his bright presence. Bittersweet memories that would never leave her.

Oh, why ever had she come here to this place which she had deliberately shut out of her life for so long? How would she cope? How could she force herself to go through with it all? Had she made a terrible mistake?

All the yearning in the world could never bring back what she craved; her firstborn son, her youth, Barney's love – albeit a love that could never be as powerful and absorbing as hers was for him. It was all gone now. Time had rolled it away, out of sight but not out of mind. And some day, time would roll her away too, and Adam, and everything else she cherished.

It was a sobering thought, which made her even more appreciative and protective of the family she still had – Mary and Adam, and now Ben – and she still had her friends – friends she did not deserve, for hadn't she deliberately distanced herself from them all this time?

After washing and dressing, and feeling more settled in her mind, Lucy went downstairs, where Adam was already wait-ing. 'Sleep well, did you?' His wide smile was all-enveloping.

'Not too badly,' she lied. 'What I need more than anything right now, is a refreshing cup of tea and a plate of scrambled eggs on toast. That should set me up for the day.'

'Then you shall have it.' Holding out his arm he escorted her to the dining room, where they were led to a small round table by the window.

In no time at all, Lucy had her eggs and a handsome pot of tea, with the daintiest cup and saucer, and a jug of milk filled right to the top. 'Just what the doctor ordered,' she said, and Adam agreed, while eagerly tucking into a full and generous breakfast.

'Talking about doctors,' he remarked, 'when do you intend seeing old Doctor Lucas?'

Lucy had been thinking about that. 'Later,' she said. 'First of all, I'd like to show Mary the cottage where she was born, and the fields where her daddy and the rest of us broke our backs to bring in the harvest, but oh, Adam, they were such wonderful times, weren't they?'

'They certainly were.' His eyes dimmed with emotion. The memories were powerful, painful in their beauty. Reaching out, he laid his hand over hers. 'Wonderful times, yes,' he agreed. 'Sadly, long gone.'

He smiled encouragingly. 'But we're still here, you and me, and Mary, and soon, God willing, once she and Ben are wed, you might be a grandmother, and how would you like that, eh?'

Lucy smiled wistfully. 'Grandma Lucy. Who would ever have thought it, eh? That young wild creature running barefoot across the fields . . . a grandmother.'

Just then Mary and Ben showed at the door. Catching Mary's attention, Lucy gave a wave and the two of them came across.

'I slept like a log,' Mary said. 'I think the long drive must have tired me.'

Ben told her jokingly how he was the one who should be tired, because he had done all the driving.

The waiter came across and they ordered bacon and eggs for Ben, and toast for Mary.

Through breakfast they discussed plans for the day, and while Adam explained how Lucy wanted to take them to see the cottage and the fields, Lucy's courage began to falter; until Adam sensed her dilemma and winked at her in his usual cheeky manner.

The intimate gesture seemed to harden Lucy's determination. 'We'll go out to the cottage,' she declared. 'Then we'll visit the churchyard, and after that it's on to see Doctor Lucas.'

Lucy and Adam finished their breakfast and left Ben and Mary to finish theirs. 'We'll see you in the foyer in half an hour,' Lucy said. With that she took her leave, and Adam went with her up the staircase. When they reached Lucy's room, he excused himself. 'I'll see you downstairs in half an hour then.'

With that he hurried away, thinking how he would have preferred to be going into the room with her. But maybe that was for another day, when he had persuaded her into being his wife.

Some short time later, the four of them climbed into Ben's car; they drove away from the city of Liverpool and on, towards the outskirts and the open fields of Comberton. Lucy was apprehensive, but knew that she must not shirk from doing what she came here to do. Just once, that was all, and afterwards she would never visit the old places again.

Sitting in the back of the car with Adam beside her and her daughter and Ben in front, she felt strangely isolated, and so incredibly lonely, it was almost unbearable. Then Adam reached out and, tucking her hand into his, he shifted closer to her. His nearness, the touch of his hand and the way he looked at her, as if to say, 'You're not alone, we're all here with you,' gave Lucy a warm feeling.

In all her life, she had learned never to lean on anyone.

But now here she was, leaning on this dear man. And somehow it felt so natural.

Following Lucy and Adam's directions, Ben headed the car away from the main road. As they trailed the curve of the lanes, she was taken back to those far-off days when she worked in those same fields with Barney and his family.

'In here, Ben.' Excitement trembled her voice. 'Pull in here.' On the way over, Lucy had known every twist and turn, and now as they neared the cottage, her heart lurched as she recognised the meandering avenue of oak trees, and the orchard where little Jamie had so often played.

When the car was stationary, she climbed out; for a moment she stood by the gate, her hungry gaze taking it all in. Instinctively now, she went through the gate and following the very same path she had so often followed before, she climbed to the peak of the hill, her every step a trial.

Behind her, Mary prepared to get out of the car. 'Not yet.' Adam felt for Lucy and he knew she would need to be alone. 'Let's give your mother a few minutes, eh?'

Mary nodded, and so they stayed. They watched the small figure climbing and saw how her steps occasionally faltered.

At the top of the rise, Lucy stood tall and proud, her face turned towards the cottage and her gaze marking the spot for all time.

In her mind's eye she saw herself outside the cottage, laughing and playing with Jamie, swinging on the branch of the tree, and gathering fruit from the orchard. She saw Barney and Vicky, sitting on the swing-seat that Barney had created out of old rope and fallen trees, and then there was the party; the barn was still there, its roof sagging and the door hanging lopsided on its hinges. She could even hear the music and the dancing.

It was all there, caught in time forever. And she was content to have been a part of it all.

'It's still here, Barney,' she whispered. 'This wonderful place, that gave us all such happy times.' Rolling down her face and wetting her lips, the tears burned her skin. 'I came back, Barney,' she murmured. 'I came back.' Suddenly she was sobbing, unable to speak for the emotion raking her soul. With her hands over her face, she took the moment to feel his presence and when she looked up again, she was calmer. 'I came back to see if it all really happened,' she whispered, 'but I can never come back again, Barney. It's too much . . . too painful. I'll take it with me, but I know now, it's time to say goodbye.'

She gave a small, choking sob. 'I'll always love you, Barney, you know that, don't you?'

After a restful interlude, she looked up to find the others beside her. 'It's beautiful here.' Sliding her hand into Lucy's Mary admitted, 'The descriptions you gave were so lovely, I thought you might have exaggerated. But you didn't, because it's everything you said.' In her distant memory she felt a part of it, too, yet not in any detail. It was more a deep-down feeling of belonging.

And so they stayed awhile. Drenching her mind with images she had never forgotten, Lucy told them stories of how it was. Adam also had a few comical tales to tell.

'I remember when me and Barney were painting the out-side walls of the big barn. We ended up with more paint on us than on the walls . . . and another time he hosed out the pig-pen and didn't see me in the corner. Talk about a drowned rat!' Everyone roared, and then he added, 'It's a wonder I didn't go down with pneumonia!'

So many memories, alive as though they had happened only yesterday. 'Another time, he nearly killed me when he felled a big old tree that was rotting from the roots up. If Vicky hadn't called out, I'd have been flattened like a pan-cake on the ground.'

They talked and smiled and laughed out loud, and Lucy felt the anguish draining away. People often said that anticipating an event could sometimes be worse than the doing, and so far it seemed they were right, she thought. Instead of pain, the visit had brought a measure of joy.

After a while they walked on down to the river.

On the night they lost little Jamie, the river had been a raging torrent, but now it was unusually quiet, with the shimmering waters gently rolling over the boulders before leaping and dancing on their way down to the valley below.

In her mind, Lucy relived that awful night for the ten-thousandth time, right up to the sight of Barney walking towards her through the water, the tiny lifeless body in his arms and his desolate face preparing her for the worst. Dear God Almighty, how had she lived with it since? How could she go on living with it?

'Come away, my dear.' Lucy was startled by the touch of Adam's fingers as they closed gently round her arm. 'You've lingered enough,' he told her. 'Please, Lucy . . . come away now.'

Turning away from the waters, Lucy assured him she was fine, though at that moment, she wished she could be anywhere but here, in this particular place. It was not over yet, she thought. The next stage of her journey would be the worst.

~

The flowers that Bridget had taken to Jamie on Saturday morning were still fresh and colourful. Even from a distance, the yellow and white spring blooms brightened the little boy's grave.

As she walked through the churchyard, Lucy kept a steely determination not to break down.

In truth, it was Mary who broke down.

Having learned only a year or so ago about her baby brother, she was very emotional. 'You did wrong,' she said, rounding on Lucy, her voice shaking. 'You should have told me long ago. I had a right to know,' she sobbed. Though this trip had been an ordeal for her mother, it had proven difficult for her, too.

Before she could run away, Lucy took hold of her. 'I'm sorry, sweetheart,' she whispered. 'You're right, I should have told you about him – our little Jamie. But it was so hard. I couldn't bring myself to speak of it. I thought if I shut it all out it wouldn't hurt, but it did, and now *you're* hurting, and I won't forgive myself for that.'

For what seemed an age, Lucy held her daughter, as the scent of narcissi rose in the air and surrounded them like a prayer. She let her cry and cried with her, and afterwards, Ben came and took Mary away, while Lucy stayed with Jamie for a while longer. 'I'll always love you,' she murmured. 'As long as I live, I will never forget you. I had to come back, to see you one last time.' Wiping away a solitary tear, she then stroked her fingers tenderly over the name on the granite stone. 'My darling little boy, thank you for the joy you brought me.'

After a while she walked away; leaving the car and the others far behind she went to the edge of the churchyard, where she leaned on the fence and let her mind wander over the fields, as though drawing every memory to her, so that when she left this place it would come with her.

She didn't hear his footsteps as he came to stand beside her, nor at first did she realise he was there, until he spoke softly. 'I can't help you, Lucy, my darling. I want to help you . . . but I don't know how.'

His words touched her deeply. Turning to him, she smiled with all her heart. 'You *have* helped me, Adam,' she said. 'All these years you've been there for me.'

He was leaning on the fence, with his hands clasped before him, when suddenly she reached out and slid her hand into his. 'You're a remarkable man, Adam; kind and caring, always backing me up, always there for me.' She paused, searching for the right words, wanting to convey her feelings. 'The truth is, you mean far more to me than you could ever know.'

When it seemed he might speak, she put her finger over his lips. 'No, Adam, I need to tell you how I feel.' She took a deep breath. 'Coming here, seeing everything again, things I tried so hard to shut out for so long, has made me realise what a fortunate woman I've been, and still am. There have been two men in my life – Barney and you. Both good, unselfish men.'

After faltering a moment, she regained her composure. 'You know I could never love you in the same way I loved Barney, but lately I've come to realise just how much I do love you.' Her eyes told him all he needed to hear. 'Dear Adam, I couldn't bear it if I lost you.'

'You'll never lose me,' he promised. 'Because wherever you are, that's where I'll be.' He saw the tears shining in her eyes and he felt the honesty of her words, and he was the happiest man on God's earth. He ached for her to be his wife; he needed to know that she loved him that much. But his instincts told him that this was not the time nor the place. And so he kept his silence, slid a protective arm round her shoulders, and together they made their way back to the car.

Mary and Ben saw them coming. 'Look at the pair of them, like two sweethearts,' Ben remarked. 'Who knows? We might be having a double wedding, eh?'

Calmer now, Mary was thrilled to see how easy they were, talking and smiling and so comfortable in each other's company. 'Coming here must have made them realise how quickly time flies away and that we must take whatever chances life brings us. Those two were always meant for each other. At one time when I was small, I even thought Adam was my father. He was always around, always looking out for us.'

She paused. 'But there was always Barney. Mother made sure I knew my father, she spoke of him all the time, until I could see him clearly in my mind's eye; I felt as though I knew him as well as she did. There was never any other man for her. But Adam is special. He knew Barney like a brother. Then afterwards, when Mother was left alone, Adam was there; he has grown old with her, and with every year his love for her has become stronger. I know, because I saw it, every day of my life.'

Ben was intrigued. 'And now they're together here, putting the past to rest.'

Their story was amazing, he thought. And now, he too was a part of it, and proud to be so.

CHAPTER EIGHT

T HAT EVENING THEY paid a visit to Dr Raymond Lucas, their former local doctor of twenty years ago. He knew all of them – Barney and his family, Lucy and Adam. The old man was delighted to see them. 'Still the same pretty girl that went away,' he said, kissing Lucy on the cheek.

She laughed. 'You old flatterer, you. That girl is long gone. What you see before you is a woman past her prime, carrying a stick and aching from top to toe. I feel as if I've climbed mountains today,' she groaned. 'Oh, but it's so good to see you.' She thought he had not aged too well. His skin was creased and leathery, his hair almost all gone, and his shoulders had sagged, but his smile and friendly manner were the same.

'You already know Adam Chives?' She brought him forward. 'My dearest friend and confidant.'

The elderly physician shook hands with Adam. 'It's been a long time,' he said. 'I'm glad you brought her to see me . . . thank you.'

Adam chuckled. 'It's more a case of Lucy bringing *me*,' he declared. 'What Lucy wants, Lucy gets. But I'm so glad we're here. To my mind, this visit is long overdue.'

Drawing Mary forward, Lucy was proud to tell him, 'This is Mary . . . mine and Barney's daughter.'

The old man was visibly taken aback. 'Good heavens above! She has a definite look of him.' He held out his hand in friendship. 'You were a beautiful child and you've grown into a lovely woman. Your father would have been proud of you.'

Mary thanked him and linking her arm with Ben's she explained, 'This is Ben, my fiancé. We plan to wed very soon.'

'Then we must celebrate!' Tugging on the bell-rope by the fireplace, Dr Lucas summoned the housekeeper. 'Lizzie, are you able to squeeze another four in for dinner?'

Lizzie did not hesitate. 'Of course,' she replied indignantly. 'Don't I always make extra, and isn't there always enough of this or that in the pantry to conjure up a fine meal?' Large-boned and formidable, she gave the appearance of being an ogre, when in fact they discovered afterwards that she was a real gem, and that the doctor valued her above all else.

Lucy was horrified at the doctor's suggestion. 'We can't put you both to all that trouble, and besides, we're not dressed for a social occasion.'

Dr Lucas would hear none of it. 'You look all right to me,' he protested. 'You're here now and we've so much to talk about. There's a great deal I want to ask, and besides, I need to make the acquaintance of your daughter and her good fellow.'

And so it was settled.

Brushing aside Lucy and Mary's offer of help, Lizzie advised them firmly, 'I was a master cook in my time. Worked in a top hotel, I did! At times we were lucky if we got half an hour's notice to prepare food for upwards of sixty guests; hard work, but good training. Ever since then, I've always been prepared, never caught offguard, and if the spare food isn't eaten, it'll always warm up and do for another day.'

That understood, she marched out and set about preparing the meal.

'I've never dared to argue with her,' the doctor confided jokingly. 'And I don't mind telling you, she frightens the life out of me at times. But she's worth her weight in gold. A real treasure, she is.'

After making sure they were settled and comfortable in the drawing room, he poured them each a drink; a gin and tonic for Lucy, a glass of sherry for Mary, and a measure of whisky each for Ben and Adam.

'That'll warm the cockles of your hearts,' he remarked jovially.

For the next half hour they discussed anything and everything from the old days, content just to reminisce. At first the talk was light-hearted and there was much laughter. But then the talk grew serious, and the doctor recalled how, 'I was devastated when it was discovered that Barney was so ill. Of course, I couldn't tell anyone. Barney made me promise not to, but even so, I have an oath to my profession, so of course I couldn't tell . . . not even when I saw him falling apart.'

He sighed from his boots. 'What happened to Barney was tragic,' he muttered. 'In all my years as a doctor, I have never seen a man so hellbent on hiding his condition from his family; especially when he desperately needed them, more than at any other time in his entire life.'

He glanced at Lucy, who had been intently listening to him. 'I found his actions so hard to comprehend. I could understand why he was reluctant to tell them how ill he was until the last possible moment, but to make them hate him! To deliberately make them believe he was a drunk and a womaniser; to alienate himself from the family he doted on, so they would embark on a new life without him. Dear God! I can only imagine what that must have done to a man like

Barney . . . so in love with his wife, and doting on his children the way he did. Anyone could see how Barney's family were his entire world.'

He glanced at Mary. 'Your father was a remarkable man.'

'I'm beginning to realise that more and more.' Mary answered him softly, her thoughts taking her back to the daddy she remembered, the kindly man who would sit her on his knee and enthral her with magical tales.

An anger took hold of her. 'He needed them so much! Why didn't he tell them how ill he was? He should have told them. HE SHOULD HAVE TOLD THEM!'

'No, Mary.' Lucy calmed her. 'You're so wrong, my darling.' Lucy herself had often wondered why Barney did not put himself first, especially when he was so desperately ill. Deep down though, she knew he had done the right thing – for his family if not for himself. 'If he had told them how ill he was, they would have stayed. They would have seen him suffer the way I saw him suffer, day and night, hurting, fading away until he was like a helpless baby.'

She paused and swallowed, then went on in hushed tones: 'After they were gone, he was so lonely. He would have given anything for it not to have happened. He desperately needed Vicky and the children to be with him to the end, to support and help him, and lift his spirits when he was down.'

'Then why didn't he tell them?'

'Because he was a bigger man than that. He sent them away, out of love. He knew he was not able to go with them; that the opportunity had been cruelly snatched from him. But, by turning them against him, he gave them all their once-in-a-lifetime opportunity, a chance to go to America and build the kind of life they would never be able to find here.'

Adam intervened. 'I can't begin to imagine how he must have suffered, to see his beloved family sail away without him. Barney Davidson loved his family like no other man I know. Yet he made them believe that he didn't care for them any more – that he despised them. He wanted them to believe that he was rotten to the core, a drunkard who preferred the company of street-women to his own darling wife.'

He took another swig of his whisky. 'God only knows where a man could find the strength to do a thing like that.'

The talk now focused on Barney's family, with the doctor asking, 'His daughter Susie will be what . . .' He did a mental calculation, '. . . thirty-five, six?'

'Older, I think,' Lucy answered. 'Ronnie would be about thirty-nine, and Thomas, a couple of years older.' She shook her head in disbelief. 'It seems incredible. In my mind's eye I still see them as young people. I often wonder, if I saw them in the street, would I even recognise them?'

She thought of Barney's wife, that lovely, vivacious creature he adored, and her heart was sore. 'As for Vicky, she was a few years older than me.' Adding up the years, she was shocked. 'Good Lord! She must be well into her sixties by now.'

'Do you think they've made good, the way Barney hoped they would?' That was Mary's question.

Lucy pondered for a moment. 'Yes,' she answered. 'No doubt Susie will have gone on to be a designer of sorts. Thomas was always the shrewd businessman – there was a lot of Barney in Thomas. As for Ronnie, well, I wouldn't like to say. He was headstrong and never seemed to have a particular direction in his life, and after what happened with Barney and everything, I don't know. There was a lot of bitterness in the end. Who can tell how they all survived the trauma of what happened?'

Mary acknowledged her mother's words with a thoughtful

nod of the head. 'You're right,' she murmured. 'It doesn't bear thinking about.'

The old doctor remembered each family member with affection, but as he recalled, Barney's wife was an exceptionally delightful creature. 'Vicky has managed to survive intact, I believe. Marriage to Leonard Maitland has given her security and companionship.'

Lucy said stoutly, 'Yes, Vicky would have kept them all together. She was strong in nature, and very protective of them all. On that last day when she came to see Barney, it was to plead with him. Even after all he had done, she was ready to forgive him. But he played his part well. He sent her away, and that must have broken her heart; it certainly broke his. But, yes! I think somehow or another, Vicky would have kept them all going despite their problem.'

'You did know that Leonard Maitland was in love with Vicky?' the doctor said.

Lucy smiled. 'I think most people knew that – even Barney. He would tease Vicky about it. But it made no difference to either of them, because they had eyes only for each other.'

She imparted a secret she had kept for too long. 'One day, soon after Mary was born, Barney and I were sitting outside on the swing, when he spoke of Leonard. He told me how he had always known Leonard was a good man, that he had confided in Leonard and made him swear never to tell anyone the truth. He also said that he had asked Leonard to take care of Vicky, and marry her when he was dead, because he knew how much in love with her he was.'

Adam nodded. 'Knowing that Leonard had promised to take care of Vicky would have given Barney some peace of mind.'

During the course of the conversation, they touched on

most things. There was talk of Lucy writing to Vicky, and she said it was something she had to do, and very soon.

'One thing at a time though,' she said. 'Coming here has taken up all my energy. But I have it in mind to contact Vicky.' She looked at the old doctor. 'I haven't been able to write before, because I had no way of knowing where they were. But I have a sneaking feeling that you have their address. Am I right, Doctor Lucas?'

A shy little smile crept over his features. 'You've caught me out,' he admitted. 'I do have the address of Leonard's office in Boston. On the day he sailed for America, he said if there was anything that Barney needed, I was to let him know straightaway.'

He gave a long, drawn-out sigh. 'Of course, I never asked him for anything. Firstly because Barney would not have wanted me to, and secondly, because there was absolutely nothing that Leonard could have done for him. When all was said and done, I thought it best to cut away from them, for the family's sake, and because Barney had gone to such horrendous lengths to make sure they would not come back.'

'Would you mind giving me the address?'

'Not at all. I know exactly where I have it.' He struggled out of his chair and picked up his stick. 'In fact, I may as well find it now, and then we can simply enjoy our evening together.'

As he went from the room, Mary crossed to the window and peered out. 'Such an interesting garden,' she observed. 'I do love the conservatory.' Stroking her chin with the tips of her fingers, she mused aloud, 'I wonder if there might be space for us to have one built at home?'

When she beckoned for the others to come and see, Lucy and Ben made their way over to join her. Adam, however, had other ideas. Leaving the room, he stood a while in the hallway, listening intently. When he heard the doctor muttering and moaning, he followed the sound down the passage towards the old man's study, and tapped on the open door. 'Do you think we could have a word?' he asked as the doctor swung round to face him.

'But of course. Come in!'

Adam thought he had never seen such a chaotic room.

The study was piled high with boxes of old files and documents; boxes on the desks, boxes against the wall, and more boxes on top of the filing cabinet. 'I'm always meaning to set about tidying this place up,' the old man explained, 'but somehow, I never seem to get round to it. Lizzie kindly offered to sort it all out, but I can't let her loose on this little lot. The poor darling would not know what goes where, or how to decipher half of it. Besides, most of these are patients' private records. They need to be carefully gone through and meticulously filed, and that's my job.'

He carried on muttering as he threw boxes out of the way. Then: 'There it is!' Digging into one of the half-open desk-drawers, he waved a piece of paper in the air. 'I knew it wouldn't be far away.'

'I just need a minute of your time, if that's all right?' Adam thought that Raymond Lucas was more like an absent-minded professor than a doctor.

'Sorry!' He sat on the edge of the desk. 'You have my full attention now, so please fire away. What's on your mind?'

'May I close the door?'

Dr Lucas frowned. 'If you must, yes . . . close it.'

Adam quietly did so. 'It's just that I wouldn't want Lucy to overhear this.'

'Well, go on then, man! What is it?'

'It's just that, well, as you have the contact address for Leonard, I wondered if you might also have information regarding another ghost from the past.' He lowered his voice. 'Edward Trent . . . the man who caused little Jamie's drowning. Lucy still has nightmares about that. She doesn't know whether he's alive or dead, or even if he might turn up at any minute. So, if it turned out that somebody had finished him off, it would give us all some peace of mind.'

The old man understood immediately. 'That was a terrible thing and no mistake,' he said sombrely.

'So, have you any idea what happened to him?'

'No,' the doctor apologised. 'None whatsoever. It's a mystery to me why they never caught him, but then we knew him to be a cunning fox. Either he had an argument with some other lowlife and was left for dead in some dark, God-forsaken place, or he managed to get far enough away to escape the law.'

'So, God forbid, he could still be on the loose somewhere?' Adam was bitterly disappointed, because even though many years had passed, Edward Trent still cast a dark shadow over their lives.

Though Adam would never mention it to Lucy, not a day went by when he didn't fear for her safety. 'When Lucy rejected him that night, he seemed to lose his sanity. I would feel much safer if I knew where he was today. Somehow, I don't believe he's a man who would easily forget being rejected by a woman.' A thought occurred to him. 'I hope you never give out Lucy's address?'

The older man was wounded. 'Good God, man, what do you take me for? Haven't I kept her address safe these many years?'

Adam apologised. 'I'm sorry. It's just that I do worry about her. There's always the chance that he might come back and look for her.'

'I doubt that. He may be dangerous, but he's not mad. Even if he is still alive, why would he take a chance like that now?'

All the same, he understood Adam's concern. 'Let's hope we'll never see hide nor hair of him again, and Lucy can learn to forget.'

But Adam was unconvinced. 'She will *never* forget,' he murmured. 'And neither will I.'

CHAPTER NINE

LUCY HAD RETURNED home to Salford with the intention of writing to Vicky at the earliest opportunity.

Unsure of how to start, she took a moment to reflect.

Looking out across the garden of Knudsden House, her mind was alive with memories of her incredibly eventful life. Where had they gone, all those years? How did they fly away, without her even noticing?

Tears of regret burned her eyes. Fate was so cruel. She brought you joy, filled your heart with love and hope, then just when you were beginning to feel safe and content, you turned around and it had all been taken away from you.

Releasing a great sigh that seemed to move her very soul, she stood before the desk in the sitting room, her gaze falling to the blank page awaiting her, her voice whisper-soft as she spoke her thoughts aloud. 'Oh Vicky, I'm so sorry!'

Slowly shaking her head, she let her gaze momentarily drift to Barney's photograph. For a long, agonising moment she soaked the contours of his familiar features into her senses, the bright eyes, the winning smile, the wonderful energy in his face. Such a man, she thought. Such a joy.

She returned to his smile, though whilst his was sunny, her smile was sad. 'You should never have left me,' she chided. 'Oh, dear God, Barney! Look how long I waited to be with you . . . then suddenly one day when I wasn't looking, you were gone.'

When emotion threatened to overwhelm her, she sat herself down at the desk, and picked up her fountain pen.

Three times she started the letter, and three times she tore it up and threw the remnants in the waste-paper bin.

Leaning back in the chair she closed her eyes, let her mind reshape her thoughts and started again.

My dearest Vicky,

I know this letter and its contents will come as a shock to you, and for that I deeply apologise. But there is something you should know.

All those years ago, you left for America, wrongly believing that Barney had forsaken you. He made you think he did not love you or his children, that he wanted rid of you all. You must have been heartbroken. I can't even begin to imagine how desperately hard it was for you.

Sadly, Barney had a reason for wanting to make you believe he had turned bad. I knew the truth and I wanted to tell you, but I could not, until now . . .

Throwing down her pen, she snatched up this page, too, and tore it into the tiniest fragments. 'It's not right!' She was angry, with Vicky for not being here where she could explain face to face, with Barney for having created such a dilemma, and with herself for not being strong enough to do what she knew in her deepest heart must be done.

'Why can't I say the right things?' she asked herself. 'Why can't I say them in a way that won't cause her any more heartache?'

She gave a wry little laugh. Look at her – trying to protect Vicky, when what she really wanted to say was that, whatever

Barney had done or said, Vicky should have trusted and loved him enough to know that when everything bad was happening, she should have questioned it more. As his wife, Vicky should have known that being cruel or spiteful was *not* in Barney's nature.

Pushing the chair back, Lucy began to pace the room, her own heart beating fast in agitation. Vicky should never have left him! Never have doubted him! When he needed her, she should have been there for him. Instead, his wife had left him alone . . . deserted him and sailed to the other side of the world, just when he needed her the most.

After a time, anger and confusion subsided. She regained her composure and returned to sit at the desk, where she laid out a clean sheet of paper and began to write. 'It has to be done,' she murmured as she formulated her thoughts. 'Painful or not, Barney's family must be made aware of the truth.'

As she wrote, the years rolled away and memories sharpened into focus: of Barney, Vicky, their three lovely children and the times they all enjoyed together.

Though determined not to avoid what she now considered to be her duty, Lucy was later to recall writing that letter as one of the most painful episodes in her life.

~

The room was small. Smelling of new polish and aging leather, it had magnificent panelled walls and narrow high windows, and behind the long table, the four men talked amongst themselves in whispers.

Eventually one by one they straightened their shoulders and all raised their heads to look at Edward Trent; though of course he was known to them as Edward Carter.

'Pay attention, Carter,' the Governor snapped. 'We have

looked at the facts and examined your record here. Unfortunately, it seems you have excelled yourself in making trouble and undermining the discipline of this establishment.'

Grim-faced and unforgiving, the man who spoke recognised that he had a personal dislike of this particular prisoner; though it would jeopardise his own position if he was not seen to be impartial. 'In our view, and it is unanimous, your record is such that you should consider yourself fortunate not to have your sentence lengthened. You're a threat to every prisoner here; whenever there have been stabbings or punishment attacks, your name comes up time and again.'

His expression hardened. 'We know you're behind it, Carter, but you have such cunning that so far you've managed to escape blame.'

He finished with a dire warning. 'You're being watched, man. It's only a matter of time before you're caught red-handed.'

His stiff gaze rested on the prisoner a moment longer, before stamping the document with a flourish. 'Appeal denied!'

Instructing the officer to take him away, he was deeply shaken when at the door, the prisoner turned to stare at him, and in those brooding eyes, he saw a glimmer of pure evil.

With the prisoner gone and the room plunged into silence, he turned to the men around him. 'There goes a bad lot!'

'He deserves to be locked up for good,' said one. 'Two men scarred for life; another terrorised out of his mind, and another in hospital for three months. And we all know who's responsible.'

'Yes, but he's so devious,' said another. 'The other prisoners are in such fear, we've never been able to prove anything against him.'

114

The Governor had to agree with his colleagues. 'We all know he's the culprit, and so far we've managed to keep him detained. But I'm very much afraid there will come a time when we can't keep him under lock and key.' Anger coloured his voice. 'Unless he happens to slip up, or some brave man steps forward to point the finger.'

There was a lull in the conversation, during which every man there felt helpless.

When after a few moments someone spoke out, it was with deadly earnestness. 'So, what you're saying is, we may have to let him go, the next time he's brought before us?'

A quieter voice intervened. 'Even if he gets out, he'll be back soon enough. A man like that . . . it's only a matter of time before he kills.'

PART TWO

October, 1954

Barney's Family

Boston, Massachusetts

CHAPTER TEN

Late autumn in Boston was a time when the magnificent colours of the trees, which had created magic to the eye only a few weeks before, were already drifting away as their leaves fell, heralding the onset of winter. But in spite of all that, it was Mrs Vicky Maitland's favourite season.

'I always enjoy our evening walks alongside the water,' Vicky tucked her arm through her husband, Leonard's, 'but autumn is best. The trees may be shedding their leaves, but the beauty never fades.' She playfully kicked the leaves along under her feet. 'It's just different,' she mused. 'A quieter, deeper kind of beauty.'

Leonard smiled down on her. 'You see beauty in everything,' he said lovingly. 'But yes, I know what you mean – and you're right, as always.'

They strolled on for a time, eventually sitting down to rest where the overhanging branches of a giant tree dipped into the water.

For what seemed an age, not a word passed between them. Over the years they had grown so close, they almost knew what the other was thinking. And just now, in that moment, Vicky was thinking of another stretch of water, the Atlantic Ocean, and a journey that she would never forget. It seemed a lifetime ago when she and her children boarded the liner that would carry them away from their homeland forever.

She thought of Barney, and the way their marriage had ended. What he did had broken her heart. It had almost ruined one of their sons, made the other forever bitter, and taken away their daughter Susie's childhood. Each and every one of them had changed because of what Barney had done, and for that, Vicky could never forgive him.

In the beginning, there was deep shock, and a yearning to punish him for splitting the family asunder. But though she might blame him for the pain he had caused, Vicky could never stop loving him. Barney was her first and last real love. Nothing could ever change that.

Eventually, she forgave him for what he had done to her. But she could never forgive him for what he had done to the children – Susie in particular. She had been made to grow up before her time.

'A penny for them?' Leonard's voice cut across her thoughts.

'Oh Leonard, I'm sorry,' Vicky apologised. 'I was just thinking.'

'You were miles away.' Sliding an arm round her shoulders, he drew her to him. 'You were thinking of Barney again – I can always tell. But it's all right, my dear. I understand, I really do.'

Vicky felt ashamed. 'You're such a good man,' she muttered. 'I don't deserve you.'

'No, you don't,' he agreed, 'because you deserve the best – and in your eyes that will always be Barney Davidson. I don't pretend to match up to him, because I never will, nor would I want to. Yes, I know he caused you all such pain. But it's never the *bad* things we remember about the person we love. It's always the good times – the laughter and the joy.'

Pausing to gather his thoughts, he watched the rowboat go past. He saw some children running along the riverbank trying to keep up, and it made him smile. 'We do the best we can,' he said. 'We strive and struggle, yet sometimes it's not enough. We must never forget, Barney was very special. A strong, determined man, he was totally devoted to you and the children. You can't dismiss a man like that – and no one would expect you to, least of all me.'

In the deepest recesses of his mind, he recalled the night he had found Barney huddled by the tree trunk, desperately ill and almost out of his mind. That night, he had made a sacred promise to Barney, and for Vicky's sake he had kept that promise; though with every passing year, the burden of guilt weighed heavier.

Deeply moved by his quiet words, Vicky reached up to kiss him softly on the mouth. 'You know me so well,' she chided. 'I can never keep a secret from you.'

She needed to tell him something now – something she had never said before. 'What you say is true, Leonard – I do still love Barney, and I will love him to the day I die. But I love you, too. I love being your wife, and I love the way you took me and the children under your wing. You're kind and thoughtful, and I'm so glad you were there for us.' She moved closer to him. 'Have I been a good wife to you, Leonard?'

He squeezed her tenderly. 'You know you have.'

'I always knew you had a fancy for me,' she chuckled. 'Barney was the first to notice it, and he would tease me mercilessly. It's strange how things worked out,' she mused. 'Do you think some things are meant to be?'

'In what way, exactly?'

'You and me . . . do you think there really is something called Fate, which channels our lives into a particular direction?'

In answer, he took her by the elbows and stood her up. 'I'm certain there is,' he replied. 'I think it was Fate that made me get rid of that monstrous fiancée of mine; it was Fate that made me fall in love with you, and it was Fate that brought us here to this land of America, where I won your heart . . . not your soul because that belongs to Barney. But we're here together, safe and secure. And yes, I do believe we have Fate to thank for that.'

Vicky nodded. 'Or some almighty hand that guides us to our destiny.'

They resumed their stroll in silence.

After a time it was Vicky who spoke. 'Leonard?'

'Yes, my darling?'

'Will Ronnie ever come home to us?'

Leonard nodded his head. 'I hope so. He's already made a start by coming to work on the estate.'

'I really thought he would go to gaol after that last court hearing. Drunk in the road . . . cursing and fighting with the officers when they tried to arrest him. In some ways, you would think he was seventeen, not a man of nearly forty. Oh Leonard, I wish now that we had let him fight in the war, even though it would have broken my heart to see him go. It might have got rid of some of his demons.' Her heart turned over at the thought of it all. 'He carries such anger inside.'

'I know. But he does seem to be coping with life better these days. Perhaps he's turned the corner at long last.'

In his heart, Leonard held out small hope. Ronnie had always clung to his father; all his young life he had modelled himself on Barney, and after they were made to leave him behind, Ronnie never really got over it.

∼

'To hell with it!' Sliding out from underneath the tractor, Ronnie threw the wrench across the ground. 'The damned thing was rotten right through. It's snapped in half now and I can't shift it no way!'

Having stood patiently by while Ronnie tried to replace the bolt in the floor of the tractor, Thomas picked up the wrench. 'Don't get all worked up,' he told him sternly. 'You're always in too much of a hurry, that's your trouble.'

'Huh! Well, that's rich, I must say. I've been working at it for half an hour.'

Getting down to his knees, Thomas peered beneath the tractor. 'Ten minutes, not half an hour,' he reminded his brother. 'You've been at it for *ten* minutes, and in that time you've managed to cause chaos. You caught the fuel pipe and almost ripped it off in a panic, and now you've chopped the bolt off so there isn't enough left to grip hold of.' He gave a weary grin. 'Do me a favour, will you?' he asked light-heartedly.

Ronnie groaned. 'Now what?'

'While I'm under here, I want you to stay right where you are. Don't do anything! Don't try to help, and don't move, not even an inch. Do you think you could manage that?'

Ronnie had to smile. 'I reckon so,' he answered sheepishly. 'I'm sorry, Tom . . . bad night, worse morning. One o' them days, eh?'

Thomas crawled under the tractor. 'I know what you mean,' he remarked cynically. 'Since first light this morning you've been a right pain, moaning and groaning, dropping this and throwing that. To tell you the truth, I'd rather you stayed away when you're in one of those moods.'

'All right, all right! There's no need to keep on, dammit!' Kicking the tractor with the flat of his foot, Ronnie cursed under his breath when his foot began to throb. 'It's just that, well, these days, I've got things on my mind. I can't seem to concentrate.' A wry smile lifted the corners of his mouth. 'Everything I touch seems to go wrong.'

Thomas smiled up at him. 'You're a walking disaster,' he agreed. 'Now just remember to stay right where you are – at least until I get out from under here. That's all I'm asking.'

Ronnie nodded. 'Sure.'

'Oh, and by the way, what happened to that good-looking woman I saw you with at the park . . . Norma, wasn't it?'

Ronnie tutted. 'Nancy! Her name was *Nancy.*'

'OK, so what happened to Nancy?'

'It wasn't working out.'

Thomas slid out from under the tractor. 'What you mean is, she got fed up with your fiery moods and quick temper, and she dumped you. Am I right – *is* that what happened?'

'Something like that, yes.' Ronnie shrugged his shoulders. 'She went off with some wagon-driver. It doesn't bother me, though. She wasn't so perfect either, when it came right down to it. Truth is, I think I'm well out of that one.'

Tapping him on the shoulder with the wrench, Thomas warned his younger brother, 'One of these days you'll find somebody you really love. You'll drive her away with that raging temper of yours and live to regret it.'

'So what?' Ronnie gave the tractor another vicious kick. 'It wouldn't be the first thing I've lived to regret!' With a parting shot he strode off. 'Tell Mom I'm staying in town tonight.'

'Why don't you stay home, just this once?' Thomas asked angrily. 'You know that's what she wants.'

'Oh yeah?' Ronnie turned on him. 'Well, we don't always get what we want out of life, do we, eh? I wanted her to stay and work it out with Dad, but she refused. When we got here, I wanted her to go back and try again, but oh no! And when it was too late and we heard that Dad had died, it didn't take her long to marry Leonard, did it? All women are bitches, in my opinion.'

'It wasn't like that, and you know it!'

Grabbing him by the shirt-collar, Thomas reminded him, 'Leonard has been good to us. If it hadn't been for him, God only knows where we might have ended up. As for Mom, she was devastated when Dad did what he did . . . parading himself through the centre of Liverpool with tarts and drunks. And don't forget how he turned on her when she tried to reason with him! I'll never know why he changed like he did. But he did, and it hurt. It hurt us, and it hurt her more. Don't tell me she didn't try to rebuild the family, because she tried time and again, belittling herself for our sakes, but Dad was so far gone he didn't want to know! As for her marrying Leonard, what would you have her do, eh? Spend the rest of her life being lonely, brooding over what happened?'

He gave Ronnie a shake. 'Did you really want her to go back and beg Dad to change his mind? Did you want her to suffer another round of shame and rejection? Is that what you wanted? Is it?'

There were tears in both men's eyes.

Thomas, too, had been affected by leaving his father in Liverpool, but through it all he saw himself as the man of the family. With Susie and his mother in pieces and Ronnie getting involved with all manner of bad things, it was up to him to reassure the others, when all the time he was feeling heartbroken and bitter. He loved his father. But seeing him turn into a stranger had been devastating. To his dying day he would never understand why it happened the way it did. But it did, and they had to live with it – Ronnie included!

Suddenly, the younger man was crying, loud bitter sobs that shook Thomas to his roots. 'I didn't mean to blame her,' he wept. 'I know it wasn't her fault.'

Wrapping an arm round him, Thomas held him in a brotherly hug. 'Just remember, she did what she could,' he said quietly. 'She secured us a future, and I for one am glad she has somebody else to look out for her. Leonard is a good man, you know that.'

Ronnie didn't look up. Instead, he nodded his head. Then he turned and walked away.

Thomas watched him go. He saw the hunched shoulders and the dogged steps, and it tore him apart. 'Ronnie, come back . . . RONNIE!' Instead, Ronnie broke into a run. He ran down the dip and on towards the lane, where he jumped the five-bar gate, and was quickly gone.

Behind him, Thomas leaned against the barn door, his sorry gaze following Ronnie as he disappeared out of sight.

He was torn two ways. He knew how hard his younger brother had tried to stay out of trouble, and for a time he had managed it. He stayed home and worked the land with Thomas. He slotted back into the family fold and was even forging a friendship with Leonard. But like always, this period of peace was short-lived. Somehow he always drifted back to the bad ways, hanging out with ruffians on the wrong side of town, getting drunk in bars and causing mayhem wherever he went.

Seeing his brother so damaged, was deeply troubling to Thomas. There seemed no peace for him, no salvation. Inevitably his thoughts returned to the day they sailed out of Liverpool, when he had seen young Ronnie hiding behind a column on deck, looking back, tears in his eyes as he searched for the figure of his father; there was no sign of Barney, only the Mersey docks, getting smaller and smaller, until they disappeared altogether.

Time and again over the years he had tried to reach out to Ronnie, but when he was in one of his black moods, there was no reasoning with him.

The boy had gone, the man had emerged, but the heart was still raw with loss. And because Barney was not here to ease his pain, he blamed everyone else – his brother, his mother, and most of all, Leonard.

Susie was the only one he would talk to, because she knew how he felt. She, too, had gone through all the emotions, the bitterness and hatred, the longing and regrets. But over the years she had poured all her energy into work, and somehow had managed to come to terms with the upheaval that had turned all their lives upside down.

On seeing his mother return with Leonard, Thomas quickly went into the barn and resumed work on the tractor.

When he heard a noise at the barn door, he looked up to see his mother standing there. 'Is everything all right?' she asked worriedly. 'Was that Ronnie I saw running across the fields?'

Thomas told her that Ronnie had been helping him service the machines. 'He had to go,' he explained. 'Things to do, or so he said.'

Vicky came closer. 'Don't fob me off, young fella,' she said. 'Ronnie was running like the devil was on his heels. Something's wrong, I know it.' She saw the pain in her elder son's eyes and her heart sank. 'What's wrong this time? Where was he headed? Please, lad, tell me the truth.'

Thomas straightened his shoulders. 'He's gone,' he said simply.

'Gone where?'

'God knows.'

'Why did he go? WHY?'

'Who can tell?' Anger and frustration rippled through him. 'One minute he was working under the tractor, then we were talking and now he's gone, like you say . . . running as though the devil was on his heels.'

Vicky didn't need to ask but she did anyway. 'What exactly were you talking about?'

'Nothing in particular,' he said cautiously. 'This and that.'

'It was Barney, wasn't it?' Where Ronnie was concerned, her instincts were always right. 'You were talking about your father, and he got himself all aerated?'

Thomas was stuck for an answer. So many times he'd been caught in the middle, not wanting to hurt Ronnie, not wanting to hurt his mother. 'All right, yes, we were talking about Dad, or at least Ronnie was,' he said finally.

She nodded an acknowledgement. 'And he was blaming everyone. You, for not persuading me to go back and try to reunite the family, and Leonard for marrying me?'

'Look, Mom, Ronnie's got it all wrong. He took it bad when the family broke up.'

Vicky put up her hand to stop him. 'We *all* took it bad!' she reminded him. 'You, Susie, and me. We've *all* had to deal with it. Did you tell him that it was twenty years ago, and that he must learn to come to terms with it? Otherwise it will ruin him, and if it ruins him, it will ruin us too.' A thought crossed her mind. 'What else did he say?'

Thomas knew his mother would not let it go until she had the whole story. 'He said you should never have married Leonard,' he muttered, hating to say the words.

'I see.' She bowed her head. 'He still dislikes him, doesn't he?'

'No, I don't think he dislikes him. It's just that he sees him as having taken Dad's place.'

Vicky's quiet voice reflected her thoughts. 'He doesn't know how wrong he is. No one could ever take the place of Barney.'

His sorry eyes belied the bright smile on her face. 'Ronnie will be back,' she assured him. 'He needs us, just like we need him, so let's not worry too much, eh?'

As she walked away, the tears burned brightly in her sad eyes. In the curve of the lane she paused to look up at the skies; just then the clouds shifted and from somewhere deep in the Heavens, the sky was lit with a warm glow. 'Help him, Barney,' she pleaded. 'He's so bitter and unhappy, and he won't let any of us near. He's your son, my darling, and he's in turmoil. Help him, please.'

After a while she blinked back the tears and walked on.

She knew how Ronnie felt and she could not blame him. There were times when she, too, felt the pain and loneliness of not having Barney in their lives. Yes, she had made a new life with Leonard, and yes, she had her family around her. But every day, every minute something was missing. That something was Barney.

In the beginning she had often been tempted to go back, to make contact with him and talk it through, until she reminded herself that it was Barney himself who had made the choice; it was Barney who had broken all their hearts and sent them away; and it was Barney who had cruelly rejected her, time and again. For whatever reason, their happy life together had been poisoned for all time.

That was when the pain turned to anger, and she hardened herself to move on, away from the past and into the future.

For all their sakes, it had seemed the only way.

CHAPTER ELEVEN

SUNDAY-EVENING DINNER with the family had become a regular event. This Sunday was no different, except by the time Vicky had set the table ready for serving, Ronnie had still not shown up. 'He's deliberately staying away again, isn't he?' She was at her wits' end. 'He can't even bring himself to sit at the table once a week with his own family!'

Leonard had seen it all before and try as he might, he could not get through to Ronnie. 'I'm sorry, sweetheart, but you know what he's like. He'll either turn up or he won't. Either way there is little we can do. We can't frog-march him here.'

Vicky still blamed herself. 'If only he would talk to you, it might help.'

'No, it wouldn't.' Leonard shook his head. 'I've tried to be a father figure, but he's not having it. I can't force myself on him, sweetheart. It's got to come from him.'

Leonard had kept his promise to Barney. In all this time he had not once betrayed that amazing man. It frightened him that if they ever discovered he had known the truth all along, none of them would forgive him, least of all Vicky. So he remained silent; though there was not a minute in the day when he didn't feel the weight of that fateful promise he made to Barney.

There was an element of guilt, too. Through no fault of his own, Barney had lost everything – the family he cherished and his own precious life – while he, Leonard, had gained everything – a new life here in America on his grandfather Farley Kemp's huge farm, now restored to its former productivity and wealth, and most of all, he had Vicky.

He observed her now, her slim figure, the pretty hair that was once rich and golden with youth, now plaited back, the telling streaks of grey betraying her age. The handsome features were still strong, and just as he had done since the first moment he saw her, he loved her with every fibre of his being.

'With luck he'll turn up, there's still time.' Vicky set her younger son's place along with the others. 'I'd best get back to the kitchen, or the meat will be like charcoal.' Vicky had not changed from the woman she had been; always happiest when caring for the family.

'I don't know why you won't have a cook to do all that for you.' Leonard had tried in vain to persuade Vicky to have more help in the house. 'It's a big place for one woman to run by herself.'

'I don't run it by myself,' Vicky reminded him. 'I have Beth.'

'Yes, but she only comes in twice a week to do the bedrooms. You take care of the rest – polishing and cleaning, cooking and gardening. There's no end to it!'

'I'm a born housekeeper,' Vicky told him with a smile. 'Now, will you please stop nagging, and put the glasses out. The family will be here soon.' She glanced out the window. 'Ronnie too, I hope.'

It was eight-thirty when the family started arriving.

Thomas was the first, along with his wife. Tall and willowy, with bobbed black hair and dark eyes, Sheila was a stunning beauty, even at the age of forty. Married these sixteen years, she and Thomas lived close by, in a fine house they had designed themselves.

Unbeknownst to Thomas, who adored the ground she walked on, Sheila had indulged in several affairs, all of them brief and sordid. When the novelty wore off and the fun was over, she would pay off her sexual partners with a wad of money to keep their silence.

'Vicky, how are you?' Kissing her mother-in-law on the cheek, Sheila made a show of affection. 'You're looking wonderful as always.' She observed Vicky's long red dress and that ever-slim figure, and though Vicky was far older than her, with her best years behind her, she could not suppress a vicious surge of envy.

'Thank you, Sheila, I do the best with what I've got.' Vicky was always pleasant and friendly, but she had no illusions where her daughter-in-law was concerned. She had long entertained suspicions about the woman's fidelity, but that's all they were . . . suspicions. She so much wanted to believe that Thomas and his wife were truly happy together. Certainly Thomas was, and for that she must be grateful.

It had been a bitter disappointment that there were no grandchildren on the scene. It was probably too late for Thomas and Sheila, but there was still Ronnie; and though Susie was edging past the child-bearing years, there was time enough for her to become a mother. Having devoted all her time and effort to her business, Susie had yet to find the man she loved, but God willing, he was out there somewhere.

Like a caged cat looking for an escape route, Sheila glanced about the room, her eyes alighting on Leonard. 'Oh, there you are, Lenny,' she gushed. 'And how are you?'

Leonard got out of his chair to kiss her fleetingly on the cheek. 'I'm fine, thank you, Sheila.'

She traversed her gaze around the room. 'No Ronnie then?'

'Not yet, no.' Vicky showed no concern. 'But I'm sure he'll be here any minute.'

'Really?' Sheila's sly grin made Vicky clench her fists. 'You know very well he won't turn up,' she gloated. 'He never does.'

Thomas stepped in. 'Sheila! That's a hurtful thing to say.'

'Maybe, but it's true. He doesn't give a damn about anybody but himself, least of all his family.'

'Enough said!' Stepping forward, Vicky thrust a tea-towel into her hands. 'The roast potatoes need taking out of the oven. Would you mind, please?'

The two women stood eyeball to eyeball, the older one smiling calmly and the younger one silently seething, but she knew better than to show her resentment. 'Of course I don't mind,' she replied with a shrug. 'But I'm surprised you're so behind with the cooking, Vicky, honey. Normally you have the food all ready for serving.'

Turning on her heels she went away grumbling. 'I guess it don't matter that I've just painted my nails, and if the grease spills down my new expensive jacket, who is there to care?'

Vicky knew her daughter-in-law was goading her, but she did not retaliate. She had more important things on her mind than exchanging verbal blows with the spiteful Sheila. What she really wanted was for Ronnie to show his face. But she was not fooling herself. Sheila was right; he probably would not turn up, more's the pity.

~

A striking figure in a blue pencil skirt with matching bolero and cream-coloured blouse, Susie climbed the three flights of stairs to her brother's apartment in the heart of Boston.

As she climbed, she kept a wary eye about her. This was not the best of neighbourhoods.

Yet again the elevator was out of order, and on the stairs that wound up the outside of the building, a lone visitor was a prime target for the hopeless bums who frequented this area.

'Ronnie Davidson, you're a hopeless bugger!' she muttered as she traipsed upwards. 'Hiding in your room skulking – I'm fed up with it! You live in a slum, you think the world's against you, and you abandon your family at the drop of a hat. I won't have it, d'you hear? You're still my brother and God help me, I care about you . . . we all do.'

Tripping over an empty box flung across her path, she kicked it aside. 'You can moan and grumble all you like, but I don't intend to let you waste your life like this!'

Holding onto the handrail she followed the row of doors; damaged doors with broken windows, doors without any windows at all; doors that were kicked in and hanging on their hinges – and when she reached the door that had the name RONNIE painted on it in big, clumsy letters, she stopped, took a deep breath and knocked. 'Ronnie! It's me, Susie. Open up.'

After a few more determined knocks and a series of loud shouts through the letter-box, the door slowly inched open, to reveal Ronnie's unshaven face. 'I thought I told you never to come here,' he said in a surly voice. 'It's not safe for a woman on her own.'

Susie pushed past him into the sitting room. 'You know what they say: if the mountain won't come to Mohammed and all that?'

He glared at her. 'What d'you want, sis?'

'What do you *think* I want?'

'I won't know if you don't tell me.' Scratching his head, he sauntered across the room. 'Banging on the door, yelling through the letter-box like a crazy woman!'

Ignoring his rantings, Susie instructed him to get dressed.

'I am dressed!'

Shaking her head, she regarded his appearance: the shirt-tail hanging out, the crumpled trousers and the hair standing on end. 'I'm not taking you out to the spread looking like that,' she said. 'You've got ten minutes,' she warned. 'I want you washed and dressed and fit to sit at the table with ordinary human beings.'

'I'm not going to Mom's house.'

'You are!'

'No, I'm not. And there's nothing you can say that will make me change my mind.'

'All right then.' Hands on hips she gave it her best shot. 'What if I was to say that if you don't come with me now, I will never visit you again? I'll forget I ever had a brother called Ronnie, and when you need me – which you frequently do – I'll refuse to see you. I'll cut you out of my life and leave you to sulk and hide and feel sorry for yourself, and when they drag your worthless body out of here, with your clothes stuck to your back, your teeth all rotten and your hair all gone, I'll look the other way and make out I don't even know you. Now then, what d'you say to that?'

Ronnie burst out laughing. 'You're a lunatic!' But he loved her. When he didn't want his mother to know how deep he had sunk, and Thomas was driven to distraction, it was always Susie he turned to, always Susie who would sit for hours and listen to his sorry tale, and never judge or condemn. She simply came to his rescue, without question or reprimand. But not today. Today it seemed he had overstepped the mark with her.

Susie cocked a thumb towards the bathroom. 'I assume you have soap and water?'

'Somewhere, I suppose.'

'Then go wash!'

Ronnie was still laughing at her previous remark. 'I think I'd better,' he said. 'I don't want to end up being dragged out of here with my clothes glued to my back . . . no teeth, no hair . . . whatever would the neighbours say?' Then: 'You'd make a good horror-writer, sis. I have to say, you certainly paint a gruesome picture.'

Still chuckling, he made his way to the bathroom, where he ran the tap and stripped off, with the intention of making himself respectable.

While he was splashing and scrubbing, Susie's voice sailed in from the other room. 'This place is a disgrace! The holes in the carpet, if you can call it that, are filled with cigarette butts, the springs in the sofa are poking through, and the curtains are hanging by a thread.' There was a pause while she ran the tip of her finger along the window-sill. 'Dust an inch thick everywhere. Dirty socks in the corner. The place stinks to high heaven. How in God's name can you live in a dump like this?'

While she went about the room tidying everything away, Ronnie mimicked her in the bedroom, where he was sorting a decent pair of trousers from the pile on the bed. 'The place stinks . . . dirty socks, raggedy curtains, holes in the carpet.' He chuckled, 'I should think myself lucky to have a carpet – not everybody round here has that luxury.'

A moment later he burst out of the bedroom. 'Right then, kiddo, do I look human enough?' He made a handsome figure; tall and slim, with his thick mop of fair hair brushed back from his face, which was now shining clean and free of whiskers.

Susie approved of the new Ronnie. 'Where did you get the trousers from?'

'I've had them for ages, why?'

'They're too big.' Susie observed how the belt was too long to fit the buckle-prong into the holes, so it was wrapped round and round, with the tail end tucked into the pocket of his trousers.

'I've lost weight.' Thrusting his hands into the pockets, Ronnie looked set for a confrontation. 'So now you're about to have a go at me for that, are you? No doubt you'd rather have me fat and flabby with drooping jowls and a huge belly hanging over my belt.'

'Oh, don't be silly!'

'You're right, I am silly. Silly to think that somewhere in that hard heart of yours, you might find a snippet of praise for the effort I've made.'

'Is that the only belt you've got?'

''Fraid so.'

With time marching on, Susie was considering how she could rectify the situation. 'Have you by any chance got a pair of scissors?'

'Nope.'

'A sharp knife then?'

'Nope.'

'What do you use to cut your cheese?'

'I don't. I just take a bite whenever I feel the urge.'

'That's disgusting!'

'No, it's not.' He cocked his head. 'You should try it,' he advised. 'It tastes better when you tear off a chunk with your teeth.'

While he ranted on, teasing and taunting, Susie dug into her handbag. 'Got it!' Brandishing a pair of nail scissors, she advanced on him with a determined gleam in her eye.

'Hey!' Backing off, Ronnie demanded to know what she was about.

'Stand still, and stop your moaning!' Grabbing hold of him, she whipped the belt from his trousers and while he struggled to hold them up, she gouged a couple more holes in the belt. 'Here, try it now.'

He slid the belt round his waist and was delighted to find that it fitted snugly with the new holes. 'You're not just a pretty face, are you, sis?'

Snipping off the tag end of the belt, she stepped back to view her handiwork. 'There – that looks better.' Grabbing his jacket from the chair she threw it to him. 'We'd best get going, or we'll miss dinner altogether.'

He frowned. 'Do I have to come?'

Her answer was to drag him out of the door. 'If anybody needs a good meal inside him, it's you. So come on, move yourself, and when you get there don't sulk in a corner, and don't refuse the drink Leonard is bound to offer you.'

As they went down the fire-escape to the sidewalk she was still giving out her orders. '. . . And don't drink too much, or you'll only end up saying the wrong thing.'

'Gee, Suze, I never knew you were such a nag!'

'Get in the car.' In minutes she had him inside with the door shut, and after scrambling into the driver's seat she went off down the road at such a speed he hung on to his seat for dear life. 'Slow down, you're driving like a damned lunatic!'

'Rubbish! I'm only doing fifty miles an hour.'

'That's what I mean. I'm too young to die.'

The banter continued all the way out of town and on towards the big farmstead.

'If you get us there in one piece I'll eat my hat!' Ronnie promised.

'For God's sake, shut up and relax. I know what I'm doing.'

By the time they arrived, Vicky was about to serve the first course. Placing the tureen of soup on the table, she ran out to meet them. 'You decided to come after all. Oh Ronnie, I'm so pleased.'

'Your bullying daughter dragged me here,' he moaned.

'She also made me wash and shave, she cut off a chunk of my belt, and nearly killed us both on the way here.'

'Take no notice of him, Mom.' Kissing Vicky on the cheek, Susie explained, 'It wasn't my driving that made him a shivering wreck. He was already like that when I found him.'

Leonard was delighted to see Ronnie. 'Your mother was worried about you,' he said.

Ronnie never had much to say to Leonard, and tonight was no exception. Without replying, he addressed Vicky. 'There's no need for you to worry. I'm quite capable of taking care of myself.'

'I only wish that were true!' Vicky knew her children like she knew herself, and she never cared much for the way Ronnie deliberately excluded Leonard from any conversation. 'But I'm glad you're here, all the same. We all are, aren't we, Leonard?'

His stepfather smiled at Ronnie, a smile that said, 'Even if you don't accept me, I'll still be here whenever you need me.'

'I think Ronnie already knows,' he replied. 'I'm always glad to see him.'

Vicky gave Susie a grateful glance, discreetly thanking her for bringing Ronnie home, even if it was only for a short time. He was the stray sheep that had not yet found its way back to the fold.

'Right,' she announced, 'dinner's ready. There's pea and ham soup to start, thick and rich, the way you all like it.' It had been one of Barney's favourites.

～

The evening went just as Vicky had planned, with everyone together, all eager to catch up with the latest news and gossip. 'Now that we've managed to secure Baron's Farm, that will bring our holding up to close on a thousand acres of prime productive land.'

Leonard had been after the 200-acre farm for some long time, and now that he had secured it into the family holding, he was desperate to persuade Ronnie to come back and work with them. It was what he wanted and, more importantly, it would make Vicky a contented woman.

Vicky picked up immediately on his piece of news. Addressing Ronnie, she told him, 'Leonard has it in mind to renovate the old farmhouse. It's yours, if you want it.' Under the table she kept her fingers crossed, hoping he might leap at the chance. 'You know the place,' she reminded him. 'It's in a lovely spot, and you can be as isolated as you want. Please, Ronnie, we all want you to come home. Say you'll take it.'

All eyes were on Ronnie as he seemed to be considering the proposition. When at length he gave his answer, it was not the one Vicky wanted to hear, yet it was the one they all expected. 'Not yet, Mother.' He gave a determined shake of the head. 'I'm not ready. It's not that I don't want to, you know that.'

'So, what is it then?' Thomas was quick to lose his temper where Ronnie was concerned. 'You don't seem to know how lucky you are. Leonard is offering you a tidy house, and a chance to come back where you belong. At least give it a try. If it doesn't work out, then you've got choices.'

But Ronnie could not be persuaded. 'Like I said, I'm not ready. It's a wonderful offer and I appreciate the thought, but I can't be shackled. I need the freedom to work when I can and wander when the mood takes me.' He looked at his stepfather. 'Sorry, Leonard. Like I say, it's not that I don't appreciate the offer.'

While Susie had kept her silence, Sheila was bolder. 'You must be mad!' This was the first *she'd* heard of Baron's Farm being sold to Leonard. 'If it's not wanted, we'll take it, won't we, darling?' Snuggling up to Thomas she made cow eyes. 'We could really do something with that old place, and like Lenny says, it's in a lovely spot.'

Like everyone else, Thomas ignored her comment. He, more than most, knew how Sheila was never satisfied with what she had. To her, the grass was always greener on the other side.

'The house was not offered to us,' he said coolly, 'and even if it was, we don't need two houses. End of discussion.'

'The farmhouse is yours, whenever you're ready,' Leonard assured Ronnie. 'You're an important part of the family business, and we all want you with us, like I say . . . whenever you're ready. At the moment, the house is being totally renovated. The builders reckon it should be finished in about six months' time. Take it or leave it, but it's yours. The deeds will be in your name, and the keys put aside for when you decide to come and collect them. There's no pressure. It's entirely up to you.'

Ronnie thanked him sincerely, and now that the discussion was over and the mood had lightened, Susie had a thing or two to say. 'I wouldn't give him a choice,' she teased. 'I'd lock him up in the house until he came to his senses. Anywhere is better than that hellhole he lives in.'

Grinning, Ronnie shrugged his shoulders. 'It's *my* hellhole,' he objected. 'It's where I want to be . . . for now.'

Vicky had listened to all of this, and her heart ached for Barney's youngest son. Like the rest of them he was still hurting, but instead of getting on with life, he had immersed himself so deeply in the past, he just couldn't let go. All she could do was wait and pray, and hope that sometime soon, Ronnie would find peace in his heart and the need for his family about him. More than that, she could not do.

She now turned her attention to her daughter. 'And what's happening in the world of hats?'

Susie swallowed a forkful of potato. 'Well, I too have bought property – I acquired the old butcher's shop, and I'm already having plans drawn up to change it into a fashionable milliner's. It's in a good area, on a corner position, with two panoramic windows and huge floorspace. It's got great potential.'

'Well done, sis!' Thomas exclaimed. 'I'm proud of you.'

Everyone raised their glass in celebration, even Sheila, though her comment was a touch sarcastic. 'What will that be – your fifth shop now? Soon you'll own the whole of Boston and we won't be able to walk down any street without seeing your name in lights.'

Her face fell with Susie's second revelation of exciting news.

'You know I've been after that contract to supply the French house for the spring season?'

Ronnie groaned. 'We should do,' he said jovially. 'You've been harping on about it these past nine months! I told you then – the French have cracked it where hats and fashion are concerned. You've no chance. Might as well forget it, sis. This time you've lost out.'

'Ah, well that's where you're wrong!' Susie took delight in telling them all, 'I sent them half a dozen samples and they've all sold. I have now secured the contract to supply for the coming two seasons. There! I told you I'd get it and I have.'

Vicky leaped out of her chair. 'Oh Susie, you clever thing.'

Glasses were raised for the second time, and everyone congratulated her.

All but Sheila, who skulked in her chair, loathing Susie as never before. She envied the girl her dogged determination to succeed in business; she resented her natural talent and skills, and the warm caring nature she had been blessed with. But mostly she envied her natural prettiness; with her gently-rounded figure, childlike features and soft shining hair, Susie was attractive in an unassuming way. Yet in spite of the fact that she was no striking beauty, Susie had caught the eye of many an admirer. As yet though, none of them had captured her heart.

To her lazy, ungrateful sister-in-law, Susie appeared to have everything, when all *she* had was a husband who lacked imagination and ambition. From the start, the loyal, hard-working and generous Thomas had never been enough for her. He knew that and because he loved her, he reluctantly accepted it.

Grudgingly accepting that for now at least, Thomas was the best meal-ticket she had, Sheila raised her glass to show willing. 'Congratulations, Susie!' she cooed. 'I'm sure we all hope your luck will continue to hold out.'

No one missed the hidden meaning of her words, least of all Vicky.

'Thank you, Sheila,' she said sweetly. 'I, too, hope *my luck* holds out.' And she did, because even though she worked hard and long, there had to be a measure of luck to bring it all together.

Her business was thriving, yes, but she was often lonely, especially at night-time when the day's work was over and she could sit for a while before starting on the neverending paperwork. It was then, when she was relaxed and alone, that she would reflect on her hard-earned achievements and wish that somewhere along the way, she could have found someone to share her success with, to share her life and be there when she needed just to talk. Someone to come home to of a night; some kind and loving man who would help plan their future together.

But as yet, there was no sign of it, and Barney's older daughter was beginning to wonder if she would ever find her soulmate.

CHAPTER TWELVE

LEONARD MAITLAND SIPPED his wine and watched the family as they chatted, and he felt like a man blessed. Since coming back to Boston with Vicky and the children, he had known happiness of a kind he had never dreamed would be his.

Years ago, against his every instinct, he had made a promise to Barney that he would never reveal the real reason why Barney had deliberately driven his beloved family away. Through all the long years, even after Barney's death released him from that promise, and in spite of many times being tempted to confide in Vicky, he had remained silent.

Now, his greatest fear had come true. A few days ago, a letter from England had arrived at his office. Deeply unnerved, he had left it unopened, his mind in turmoil as to who might have sent it. The postmark was smudged and gave him no clues. He did not recognise the handwriting.

There were only three people who might be writing to him from England. One was his solicitor. Another was Raymond Lucas, who had known the truth and with whom, over the years, Leonard had exchanged letters, which of course he had hidden away for fear that Vicky or someone else might inadvertently come across them.

The only other person who might have reason to write to

him was Lucy Baker. She had been the closest to Barney after his family left.

In the early letters exchanged between himself and Dr Lucas, there had been much mention of Lucy, of how devotedly she had cared for Barney. He knew that some time after the family's departure, Lucy had borne Barney's child; the couple had moved away soon after.

Yet Lucy had not known this address, so how could she have written to him? Lately though, she had been in touch with Dr Lucas; he knew that much because in the last letter from the doctor, he had written of her visit to Liverpool. So, had the doctor given her this address – and, if so, why? What did she want with him?

In the mist of his thoughts, Leonard could hear the family laughing and talking, and his feelings were anguished. This was *his* family now, and had been for the past twenty years. Was Barney reaching out to take them from him? No! His imagination was running riot. Barney was gone. For their future security and happiness, Barney had willingly entrusted Vicky and the children to his care. So now they were his family, but the letter had made him fearful; was something about to happen that might take his loved ones from him? It was unthinkable. He couldn't lose them. He must not!

Instinctively, his hand went to the letter in his breast pocket, and his heart pounded.

'Are you all right, my love?' Vicky's voice filtered into his mind. 'I called you twice,' she said curiously. 'You were miles away.'

Mentally shaking off his thoughts, Leonard looked up. 'Sorry, darling. I must have dozed off.'

She glanced at the tumbler in his hand. 'How many glasses of wine did you have?'

'Three, I think.' In truth he'd had only one.

Vicky was horrified. 'Oh Leonard! You know how wine affects you . . . giving you such bad heartburn you can't sleep.'

Somewhere in the back of her mind she did not altogether believe him. She had not seen him take more than one glass of wine. Moreover, just now when she was calling him, he didn't appear to be asleep. Instead he seemed to be in deepest thought. 'Are you sure you're all right?' Although Barney was always with her, Leonard had earned a part of her heart, and she had come to love her second husband dearly.

'I'm fine now.' Getting out of the chair, he rested his head for a moment on her shoulder. 'Why were you calling me?'

'Susie wants to know if you would do her the honour of opening her new shop, when it's ready?'

Leonard was thrilled. 'Of course I will.' Raising his glance to the far side of the room, he saw Thomas and Ronnie talking, and over by the drinks cabinet, Sheila was helping herself to a measure of brandy. There was no sign of Susie. 'Where is she?'

'She must have gone outside,' Vicky said. Giving him a little push, she suggested, 'You'd best go and find her.'

Leonard found his stepdaughter seated on the bench by the pond. It was pitch black now, and the wind was freshening. 'Fancied a quiet spell on your own, did you?' Sitting down beside her, he took hold of her hand. 'Mom says you would like me to open your shop when it's ready.'

Susie smiled up at him. 'If you don't mind?'

Beaming from ear to ear, he said, 'Why ever would I mind? I'm flattered you've asked me, though I don't know what I've done to deserve the honour.'

'You saved me,' she murmured. 'When we came here, you saved us all.'

In the twilight Susie observed this man who had been their salvation, and a great surge of love filled her heart.

147

When she was just a child, frightened and confused, he had taken her under his wing, and where her beloved daddy had caused her pain, this kind and gentle man had healed the wounds, though the haunting memories could never be erased.

Leonard sensed her emotions. 'You're lonely, aren't you, sweetheart?'

She gave a wry little smile. 'Sort of. Sometimes.'

'You won't always be lonely,' he said assuredly. 'One day, sooner or later, there will be a certain someone for you, I just know it.'

She smiled at his words. 'Do you?'

He nodded. 'A bright young thing like you, I know you're not meant to live your life alone. There'll be someone some-where, just as lonely, looking for a lovely young woman like you to share his life. Fate will bring you together. You must believe that, my dear.'

They hugged for a moment, then he walked her back to the house.

One by one, the family left, until only he and Vicky remained. 'It's been a wonderful evening, don't you think?' she said dreamily.

Vicky began to clear away the dinner plates. 'And wasn't it nice to have Ronnie here? Just like old times.'

'I shouldn't pin too much on that,' her husband warned. 'Don't forget, it was Susie who dragged him here. And remember how he's twice tried to live in the family fold. It didn't work out for him then, so there's little reason to think it might work out a third time.'

'I live in hope,' Vicky answered confidently. 'I'm just relieved that Susie gets through to him, where no one else can.'

'Yes – but you mustn't be too disappointed if it doesn't happen.'

Brushing aside Vicky's protests, Leonard helped her clear away the dinner things, then helped to wash them up and put them away. Afterwards, while Vicky made him hot milk and honey to help him sleep, he sat up in the drawing room, listening to her moving around in the kitchen and pondering about the letter in his breast pocket. 'Should I open it?' he muttered. 'Or should I burn it?'

Sliding his fingers into his pocket he took out the letter and stared at it for a moment, his anxious eyes scanning the handwriting:

> *Mr Leonard Maitland,*
> *Office of Farming and Land Management*
> *Number 16, Roiter Place,*
> *Corner of Derwent and Launceston,*
> *BOSTON,*
> *U.S.A.*

Try as he might, he could not recognise the handwriting; it was not the hand of his solicitor, and certainly not the almost indecipherable scrawl of the doctor. In fact, he began to wonder whether he had got it altogether wrong in thinking it might be from Lucy.

With newfound confidence, he decided to take a peep inside. First though, he listened, making certain that Vicky was still busy at her tasks. Satisfied, he took the letter between his fingers and began to open it, almost leaping out of his skin when Vicky suddenly rushed in through the door.

'I've made a whole jug full,' she told him as he hurriedly thrust the open letter into his pocket. 'It's been such a hectic day, I thought a mug of honey and hot milk might help me sleep, too.' She placed the tray on the small table before him.

For a while they sat and talked, of Ronnie, and Thomas

149

and Susie. 'I'm proud of them all,' Vicky said. 'Thomas has taken to helping you manage the estate like a duck to water.' She cast her mind back, as she often did, more so as she grew older and the memories sharpened. 'Mind you, he had good training with his dad,' she said fondly. 'Though managing a small farm is different from managing a vast estate like this.'

Leonard nodded. 'It is,' he agreed. 'But when you get right down to it, the principle is the same: you plough the land, set the seeds, and reap the harvest.'

He gave a contented smile. 'I'm fortunate to have a man like Thomas working with me,' he admitted. 'I have good people in the office, but outside in the fields I can leave it all to Thomas and know everything will be taken care of. He works hand-in-hand with the office, orders the right machinery for the job, brings in the right mix of seed, and oversees the working of the land. He's good with the men, and has an instinct for the seasons. Moreover, he knows every machine inside out; there's nothing he can't fix and he's always ready to pass his knowledge on to the men. Matter of fact, I don't know what I'd do without him.'

After a while, Vicky shifted the conversation to Ronnie. 'I only wish that lad would settle down. He doesn't seem to have the heart for anything.'

Leonard was philosophical where his other stepson was concerned. 'He's still coming to terms with life's disappointments,' he said kindly. 'Give him time, he'll come round.'

'Do you really think so?'

'Yes, I do. Like Thomas, he's a good man.'

'Lonely though?'

'Well, yes, there is that. But some people like their own company.'

For different reasons, all of her children worried Vicky. There was Thomas working all hours God sent, with a wife who thought only of dressing herself up and trawling the most expensive shops. She wanted for nothing, she had a husband who doted on her, and still she wasn't satisfied and, if Vicky's instinct served her right, Sheila was in the throes of yet another affair. 'Sometimes, I wonder if Thomas ever suspects that his wife sees other men?' The words were not meant to be said out loud, but they just popped out.

Leonard was not surprised. 'So, you think the same as me, do you – that she's being unfaithful to him?'

'I'm convinced of it.' Vicky told him of her fears. 'I think she's had several affairs. If Thomas knows, he must love her so much, he can't bring himself to confront her in case he loses her – though if you ask me, that might be the best thing all round.'

'Well, I don't think she would leave him, whatever he said to her.'

'No, you're right!' she conceded angrily. 'Why *would* she leave him, when she has everything all her own way . . . a husband who adores her, money to fritter on clothes and fancy furniture, a house she helped to design. Anything she asks for she gets – holidays, jewellery – and on top of all that, whenever she fancies a fling, she just goes out and finds herself a man.'

Clenching her fists, she almost spat out the words. 'Sometimes, Leonard, I feel like pinning her against the wall and making her confess what she's been up to. I hate what she does to Thomas. I despise the way she takes advantage of him and gives so little in return!'

Seeing how upset she was becoming, Leonard reached out and closed his hand over hers. 'It's up to them,' he reminded her. 'They'll sort it out between them. One day, Thomas will wake up and realise what she is. When that happens, he'll deal with it in his own way.'

'Oh, I do hope so!'

'Trust me. For now, he's taking a beating, because he loves her. He probably knows what she's up to, but Thomas is nobody's fool. He won't put up with it forever.'

Regaining her composure, Vicky sighed. 'Susie's doing well, isn't she?'

He nodded. 'She's a born businesswoman.'

'Do you think she's lonely?'

'Maybe.'

Vicky was sad about that. 'The trouble is, she works such long hard hours, she never has time for a social life. So, she never meets anyone outside of work.'

'Well now.' Leonard had also given it a lot of thought. 'Maybe when she meets her man, it could be the very one she's been working alongside all the time. It's been known to happen.'

Vicky smiled. 'So, that could be any one of about ten.'

'There you go!' Somehow, Leonard always managed to say the right thing. 'She's got a healthy choice right there on her doorstep.'

The couple sat quiet and content for a time, their faces pink and warm in the heat from the cheery fire. In the background, the grandfather clock struck eleven, and Leonard began to nod off. 'Hey!' Vicky gave him a nudge. 'That milk and honey seems to be working well, but don't go to sleep yet,' she said. 'You lock up, and I'll put the guard in front of the fire. Then we'll away up the stairs and into bed.'

'You go,' he said. 'I'll be along shortly.' He needed to stay down for a while. He needed to think.

Vicky put the guard in front of the fire, gave him a kiss, and made her way upstairs. She thought nothing of him not going up with her. Often Leonard would work in his study long after she'd gone to sleep.

Upstairs, she made her way to the bathroom, while downstairs Leonard remained in the armchair, his hand spread over his jacket pocket where the letter was safely tucked away.

He wanted to open the letter and read it, but his every instinct once more urged him to throw it into the fire.

After a time, common sense took over. He knew he should read the letter, if only to make sure it contained nothing that could harm himself or his adopted family. And if it was a threat, he might need to deal with it as quickly as possible.

Taking out the letter he glanced towards the door; he could still hear Vicky pottering about in the bedroom upstairs. He got out of his chair and went across the room, where he quietly closed the door.

Returning to his chair, he sat a moment, the letter in his hand, his gaze mesmerised by the flames dancing in the coals. 'Come on, old man,' he chided himself. 'Open the damned thing and see who it's from!'

With trepidation he opened the letter, surprised to find another envelope inside, which was simply addressed to Vicky.

Unfolding the accompanying letter, he thought he might have recognised the sweeping scrawl, but that was not the case. Instead his fears were made tenfold by what was written there:

Dearest Leonard,

I hope you will not think badly of me for writing to you after all this time, but lately my conscience has been troubling me, so much so that I feel compelled to make contact with you.

I've spoken with Dr Lucas, who very reluctantly gave me your address in Boston, but please don't blame him for that. I can be very persuasive when needs must.

All I ask of you is that you give Vicky the enclosed letter. It tells of the tragic circumstances that made Barney send his family away. I know from Dr Lucas that you have faithfully kept the promise you made to Barney, and I respect you for that, as I realise what a heavy burden you have had to carry alone.

Now though, before the truth is lost forever, I believe it is time to tell Vicky and the family. If you give her my letter, in which I have written about Barney and the way it was, you will not be breaking your promise.

I could have addressed this letter to Vicky and sent it via your office; the doctor stopped short of giving me your home address. But I believe it is right for me to send the letter to you, and leave the choice to you and your conscience. If you decide not to give her the letter, I will of course accept your decision and I will never again contact either of you.

However, I am hoping that over the years you have been tempted to tell her, and was not able to because of your promise. This way, if you do give her the letter, it will be me who tells and your promise will remain intact.

I believe the time is right for Barney's family to learn that he never stopped loving them. For the remainder of his short life, he talked of them, and longed for them, and his heart remained broken up to the day he lost his fight to live.

I can imagine you reading this letter now, and being torn in two by it, and I am deeply sorry for that. You may pass the letter to Vicky, or you may dispose of it, and she will never know. Please, Leonard, don't be rash in your judgement.

We saw what happened, you and I, and we know what pain it caused both Barney and the family. Surely, in your heart you must accept that it is their right to be made aware of the facts.

I have enclosed my address here. Please let me know what you decide,

Yours, with fondest memories,

Lucy

Shaken by what he had just read, Leonard made no move for what seemed an age. After a while, he read the letter again, and again, until every word was burned into his mind. 'I can't tell her,' he murmured. 'How can I hurt her like that? How can I tell Barney's children that they deserted their father when he was so desperately ill?' A great burst of rage surged through him; slamming his fist on the arm of the chair he cried out, 'I CAN'T DO IT TO THEM! I WON'T! DO YOU HEAR ME, LUCY? I WON'T HURT THEM LIKE THAT!'

Taking the envelope addressed to Vicky, he crumpled it in his hand. When, emotionally broken, he bent his head and began to sob, the crumpled letter slipped from his grasp and fell to the ground, and as it did so, the door opened and there stood Vicky, alerted by his cries and looking shocked to see him so upset.

Before he could prepare himself, she had walked towards him, on the way recovering the crumpled envelope from the floor. 'What is it, Leonard?' she asked worriedly. 'I heard you cry out. What's wrong? Has something happened? Is it Ronnie?' Of all her children, it was always Ronnie she worried about the most.

Realising there was no way back, Leonard looked up with haggard eyes. 'I'm so sorry, my dear. So terribly sorry.' Holding out the letter, he pleaded forlornly, 'Read it. Read them both, and I hope you can find the generosity of heart to forgive me.'

Confused and anxious, she took the letter from him, and as she prepared to read it, he could see his whole life slipping away.

∼

As Vicky read Lucy's words, a sense of horror came over her. When she had finished reading, she looked at Leonard in disbelief, her face set like stone. She said not a word, and her expression gave nothing away.

She walked to the table, where she set down the letter addressed to herself and with slow, measured movements straightened the envelope so it was readable.

Leonard watched her open it and read the letter. With a broken cry, she leaned forward, hands on the table, eyes closed and her whole body seeming to tremble in shock. Lucy's words were emblazoned on her soul . . .

'he never stopped loving them . . . he talked of them, and longed for them, and his heart remained broken up to the day he lost his fight to live . . .'

Her pain was crippling. 'I didn't know,' she sobbed and gasped over and over. 'I didn't know, I didn't know. Dear God, we none of us knew!'

For one aching moment Leonard was tempted to go to her and hold her. But his instincts warned him against it. Instead he watched and prayed that she might understand the reason why he had deceived her for so long.

After a time she collected both letters and, without a glance at him, walked across the room and out of the door. Then she was gone, leaving him alone and afraid. 'What have I done?' he whispered. 'Dear God, what have I done?'

Afraid for her, afraid for the family, and for his part in their lives, he went after her.

As he came out onto the verandah, he saw her, some short distance down the garden, leaning against a tree, bent double as she sobbed his name. 'Why did you do it, Barney?' Her broken voice echoed in the still night air. 'Why did you send us away . . . why did you make us hate you, when all the time, all we ever wanted was to be with you?' The sobbing became uncontrollable. 'Oh Barney! Barney! Why didn't you tell me?'

'Vicky?' Unsure and anxious, Leonard approached her. 'Barney did it because he didn't want to hurt you. I made him a promise not to tell. I'm sorry it had to be this way. We'll get through this, you and me, and the children . . .'

He stopped in his tracks as she turned to look at him; in the light from the verandah he was shocked to see such raw anger on her face. As she spoke, slowly and with cold precision, he knew the hatred she felt for him. *You let me think bad things of him. You took me away, when he needed me most.'*

'No! Listen to me, Vicky. It wasn't what *I* wanted – it was Barney's wish. He made me promise. He did it to save you the pain of seeing him suffer. He knew what it would be like for you . . .'

Shaking her head, she gave the saddest smile. 'All that time, you knew, and you never told me, because if you had, you knew I would go back. And you didn't want that, did you?' Her damning words froze his heart. *'As long as I live, I will never forgive you.'*

Brushing by him, she returned to the house, packed an overnight bag, collected her car keys and passed him on her way out without a word or glance.

All she could see was Barney. At that moment he filled her heart and soul; there was no room for anyone else, especially the man who had kept her from him, when Barney desperately needed her.

As she drove away, Leonard called after her. She didn't hear him. Instead, all she could hear was Barney calling out to her; Barney in pain; Barney left behind, his entire family gone forever.

She needed to hold him, to tell him she was there, that

he was not alone. But it was too late. Barney was gone, and she had never had the chance to say a proper goodbye.

Another thought crossed her mind. The children! However was she to tell them this devastating news!

CHAPTER THIRTEEN

I T WAS 8.15 A.M., the morning of 4 January 1955.
The streets of Liverpool were still fairly quiet, some
shops were not yet open and only the keenest of shoppers
had braved the bitter cold, to catch the early sales bargains.

Warm and cosy inside the offices of Bridget's empire, Amy
and Bridget had been up since the early hours. On a day when
the offices were still closed and there was no one to interrupt
them, this was the perfect time for the two women to go
through the books and prepare them for the accountant.

Having already been ensconced in the office for almost
two hours, Bridget was ready for refreshment. Stretching
and groaning, she leaned away from the desk. 'I think we'll
down tools for a while, Amy me darling,' she said now. 'It's
been a long two hours, and the old bones are threatening
to seize up.'

Pushing the ledger away, she gave Amy one of her winning
smiles. 'I'm ready for a drink, so I am.'

'I couldn't agree more.' Getting out of her chair, Amy
began her way across the room. 'Fancy a nice cup of tea?'

Bridget was horrified. 'Have ye lost your mind? It's not
tea or coffee I'm needing. It's a drop o' the good stuff I'm
after. It's in the top drawer of the filing cabinet, same as
always. An' don't be sparing with it neither.'

When it came, Bridget took a tiny sip, then another longer one. 'Ah sure, there's nothing like a wee dram to warm the cockles,' she said, smacking her lips. 'Unless it's a randy man with a trim body and no clothes on.'

Grinning like the Cheshire Cat, she went on to tell the bemused Amy, 'Did I ever tell you about the time me and Oliver found a quiet spot in the countryside? Well now, he got to feeling frisky, so we climbed into the back of his car . . . and ye know there's not much room there at all.'

Amy couldn't help but chuckle. 'Honestly, when will you ever grow up? Don't you think you're too old to be rolling about in the back of a car?'

'You're right, and I won't be doing it again, I can promise ye that! Only the dear Lord knows how I ached from top to bottom for weeks after. But y'see, poor Oliver was so frustrated. He tried Gawd knows how many times to get his leg over, and well – you've never seen such a carry-on in all yer life! First off, he got his foot caught between the front seats, then he couldn't get it out . . .'

She could hardly talk for laughing. 'When I say that, I'm not just referring to his foot, though that was the divil of a problem, so it was. No, I mean he couldn't get his little pecker out neither, whichever way he turned.'

Amy tutted. 'It's a wonder you weren't arrested.'

'Ah, but that's not all.' Taking another healthy measure of her good Irish whiskey, Bridget got a fit of the giggles. 'When we realised it was no use, we got out of the car and laid on the grass. Within minutes we were fleeing for our lives, him with his trousers round his ankles, and me with me drawers in me hand.'

Amy could hardly contain her curiosity. 'What happened? Did the police come along and find you?'

'Oh no! It weren't the police. We were just getting down to business, if ye know what I mean, when we must have disturbed a nest of wasps. Sure I never ran so fast in all me life, and as for poor Oliver, he got bit twice on his dangly bits. Jaysus! They came after him like he was their next meal. And him screaming and shouting like a banshee. Never mind that I was falling behind and likely to be got any minute. As far as that bleddy coward was concerned, I could get stung to Hell and back!'

Amy almost fell off the chair laughing. 'I always knew you were mad as a hatter,' she roared. 'Whatever will you get up to next, I wonder?'

'Well, I can tell ye one thing. Next time he feels amorous, he can bugger off.'

'So, does that mean you've finished with him?'

'Oh no! Sure, I never said that. But it's the last time he manhandles me in the back seat of a car. And as for pulling up in the hedgerow and rollicking in the long grass, he can forget it.'

She took another helping of her drink. 'He can have his wicked way any time he wants, but I told him, I did. "I'm a lady with taste," I said. "From now on, it's a bed covered in silk sheets and a feather pillow under me, or it's nothing at all".'

'And what did he say?' Amy was enthralled.

'He liked the idea. Especially when he couldn't sit down for a week, seeing as his precious little bits were all full o' bumps and lumps.'

There was a flurry of laughter and more naughty talk, before the conversation ended and the two of them returned to their work.

Shortly after that, they had completed the accounts and having filed away the paperwork, began to pack up for the day.

'Isn't it tonight when Vicky arrives?' Amy recalled Bridget telling her as much earlier on.

Bridget nodded. 'Yes. She disembarked at Southampton last night, and will be in Salford by tea-time tonight.' With the effects of drink beginning to wear off, her face reflected the seriousness of Lucy's situation. 'It'll be a strange meeting, that's for sure,' she remarked thoughtfully. 'There's been a lot of water under the bridge since those two last met. Oh aye, they'll have a lot to talk about, so they will.'

'Do you think Vicky will be resentful?'

'In what way?'

'Because Lucy never told her about Barney?'

'Oh sure, there's bound to be resentment.' Of that Bridget had no doubt. 'According to what Lucy wrote me, on the night she discovered the letter to Leonard, Vicky walked out on him and she's never been back since. Cleared off for two whole months, that's what I've heard. But then she got in touch with Lucy, and today is the day they finally meet after all these years.'

She shuddered. 'I don't mind telling ye, it's thankful I am that it isn't me who has to explain why I didn't get in touch with Vicky long before now.'

Amy was torn two ways. 'Do you really think Lucy should have broken her word to Barney?'

Thinking deeply, Bridget took a moment to answer. 'For what it's worth, I believe Lucy did what she thought was right, for Barney's sake, and for the sake of the family. I mean, look now at the heartache and trouble that's been caused by the telling after all these years. Vicky's life seemingly in tatters, and Lucy riddled with guilt at having sent the letter. It's a tragedy, isn't it?'

Amy agreed wholeheartedly. 'I for one wouldn't want to be in Lucy's shoes when she meets up with Vicky.'

Bridget was momentarily preoccupied in thinking of Barney's children. 'Isn't it strange how Vicky never even mentioned the children when she contacted Lucy? She wrote of how she and Leonard had split up, but there wasn't one word on the three children.'

Amy's heart went out to Thomas, Ronnie and Susie. 'I know what it's like to see your family torn apart,' she said. 'It's a terrible thing – and those three had the added agony of being sent away believing their father was a drunk and a womaniser, a bully who thought nothing of hurting them every which way he could. And now, they discover that he was nothing of the sort, and that he loved them all along.'

'Whatever did they think when they learned how desperately ill he was?' Bridget mused. 'And that what he did, he did for the love of each and every one of them. He saved them from the pain and anguish of seeing him deteriorate with every passing day. Moreover, he secured them a decent future. If that isn't love and courage of a very special kind, I'm sure I don't know what is.'

They each reflected on that, and after a time they shut up shop and went their separate ways. 'And don't get up to any hanky-panky!' Amy quipped as she went.

'Away with ye,' Bridget replied haughtily. 'Why would I ever want to be doing that? Sure, I'm a woman in the sunset of me life, so I am.'

Amy laughed. 'Sunset nothing! You might have been around a long time, but you've not lost the come-on twinkle in the eye yet. Sixty going on sixteen, that's you.'

Bridget prided herself on keeping active and fit. 'You know what the secret is, don't you?' she said cagily.

'No, what's that?'

'When the hair goes grey and your face is so dry and wrinkled it resembles the sole of your shoe, you dip your hair in dye, pile on the make-up and go out and get your man. If ye think old and done with, you'll *be* old and done with. If ye think young and randy, you can hold off the years for as long as you like, and bugger them as thinks you're mutton dressed as lamb.'

As she got into the car she had another piece of advice for Amy. 'There's something else ye should know.'

'Oh yes, and what's that?'

'If you turn up late in the morning, you'll be sacked.'

With that daunting piece of news, she drove away, leaving Amy shaking her head. 'You should be locked up,' she muttered with a smile. 'A woman your age should be at home with her feet up and a shawl over her legs, but oh no, not our Bridget, she's got more important things to do. You defy old age, you scheme and fight and lie through your teeth to get what you want, and you show no mercy to anyone who tries to muscle in on your territory. The truth is, if you weren't running a legitimate business, you'd make a first-class villain.'

As she walked away, Amy thought to herself, I've a good mind to turn up late, just to see if you really would sack me. You're a bully and a slave-driver, and you make me tired, just watching you run around.

Bridget was like no one she had ever known. But, warts and all, she would not have her any other way.

At that moment some short distance down the street, Bridget was engaged in a heated exchange with the milkman. Having pulled up in front of her at the junction, his horse had taken the opportunity to dump a load of manure all over the road in front of her; in the process splashing the bonnet of her Hillman Minx. 'You filthy heathen!' Shaking her fist at the man, she told him in no uncertain terms, 'Look what your damned horse has done to me car. You should be put away, you and the horse along with ye!'

When the milkman took not the slightest notice, she roared off, making a most unladylike gesture as she went.

'Time was when old women stayed at home and waited on their menfolk!' shouted the milkman. 'But I don't imagine there's a fella this side of Australia that would take on a harridan like you!'

After making another rude gesture, Bridget wisely put a fair distance between herself and the milkman. She didn't want to cause too many upsets, especially with a policeman strolling nearby, and even more especially when she had never applied for a driving licence, nor ever had one granted.

Coming into the quieter part of town, her thoughts soon turned to Lucy, and the ordeal she was about to face. 'God bless you, Lucy girl,' she murmured. 'I hope it all goes well with you and Vicky.' Like Amy, she did not envy Lucy the task ahead of her.

~

Adam had been awake since the early hours.

Concerned about the arrival this evening of the woman he still looked on as Barney's wife, he decided to go across to Knudsden House and make sure Lucy was all right.

From the front window, Lucy saw him coming. She too had been awake since the early hours. 'Only a few hours to go,' she told him as he walked in the door. 'To tell you the truth, Adam, in my entire life I've never been so nervous.'

Occasionally stopping to glance at the mantel-clock, she paced up and down, back and forth, now pausing at the window and looking out on the bitter-cold January morning. 'I'm not sure if I've done the right thing. What if I've ruined all their lives?'

'You can't turn back the clock now, Lucy my dear, so don't torment yourself.' Adam had the same worries, but he did not want to convey that to Lucy. Instead he was doing his best to encourage her, because right now she was beginning to make herself ill.

'I can't help worrying,' Lucy argued. 'I've already caused a split between Vicky and Leonard. She said in her letter that I shouldn't blame myself, but if I'm not to blame, who is? After all, it was me who put the cat among the pigeons so to speak.'

'Look, Lucy, what you did was certainly not done out of malice. It was done out of concern: you thought they had a right to know. Well, I agree with that and so, it seems, does Vicky.'

Lucy was still not convinced. 'It might have been better though, if I had left well alone.'

'Ah, but in the end, my dear, the truth has a way of sneaking out. Who's to say Vicky or her children would never return home at some time in the future, even for a visit. They would find out then, wouldn't they? There can't be a single person in Liverpool who hasn't learned the sad story of Barney Davidson, and they would tell it to anyone, neighbour or stranger. No, Lucy, you did right. What happened between Vicky and Leonard is something aside, which only the two of them can sort out.'

Eager for peace of mind, Lucy nodded. 'Maybe you're right,' she conceded hesitantly. 'Maybe it would have come out sooner or later.'

'Are you ready to face her tonight?'

Lucy nodded. 'Ready as I'll ever be, I suppose.'

∾

Early that evening, the car was out and Lucy was waiting at the door as he arrived, looking smart and sophisticated in her high-necked cream-coloured jumper and skirt, with a coffee-coloured winter coat and dark shoes. Her greying hair was swept up in a loop of straying curls that framed her face, and she carried her best silver-topped stick; though she half-hid it in the folds of her coat. Even now she had a reluctance to show her slight handicap.

'You look lovely as ever,' Adam commented as he held open the door for her to climb into the back. Whenever he saw her, morning noon or night, it was always the same; his old heart would leap to his throat and he had to stop himself from taking her in his arms.

As they travelled through the country roads towards Bedford town and the railway station, Lucy wondered aloud, 'What will she look like, do you think?'

Adam glanced at her in the mirror. 'I'm sure I don't know,' he answered. 'She was lovely as a young woman, but not everybody stays as handsome as you.'

Lucy laughed. 'You old flatterer,' she said. 'Truly though, Adam, do you think we'll recognise her?'

'Don't know. Can't say.'

'Do you think she'll recognise *me*?'

'I think so. Your hair's a little greyer, you're slower of foot, and we all know you're not the young thing you once were, but then none of us are – Vicky included.'

Lucy had to smile. 'Well, thank you. Is that supposed to make me feel better?'

Adam made no apology. 'All that aside,' he said, 'you're still so vibrant and your features haven't changed all that much. You have the same slim figure and those wonderful, smiling eyes. I think she would have to be looking in the opposite direction not to recognise the Lucy Baker we all know and love.'

For the remainder of the journey, Lucy fell silent, with Adam frequently glancing in his rear-view mirror to make sure she was all right.

When at last they arrived at the station, he pulled up as

near to the entrance as he could. 'Do you want me to come with you?'

Lucy thanked him. 'Yes, I'd like that, Adam. But try if you can to keep a discreet distance when the train arrives. I don't want her to think we're there in force.'

Adam understood. 'Trust me,' he said. 'You won't even know I'm around. But if you want me, I'll be only a heartbeat away.'

Lucy gave him a friendly peck on the cheek. 'What would I do without you, eh?' Adam was always there when she needed someone to share her fears and dreams. More and more she had come to rely on him. And today was particularly unnerving, for she was about to meet Vicky again for the first time in many years; Vicky, the beautiful person whom Barney adored above all others, and who had been cruelly robbed of her chance to say goodbye to him. Vicky, who had welcomed young Lucy and her little Jamie into the very heart of her family, and shown them both nothing but kindness.

Adam was still pondering on her remark. 'What would you do without me, eh?' he mused aloud. 'Let me think now.' Feigning a frown, he told her, 'You'd have to find a careful new driver for a start. Then there'd be no one to fetch and carry for you, or collect your orders from the shops when you don't feel like being in a crowd. You'd have no one to boss about or moan and grumble at, and when you feel lonely, there'll be no one there to hold your hand.'

Lucy laughed. 'I've always got Mary.'

'Ah, but it's not the same. Think about it,' he urged. 'Here you have a big handsome man ready to answer your every call; a man who's besotted with you, ready to marry you at the drop of a hat, and on top of all that, he can make the best hot cocoa that's ever passed your lovely lips.'

'You're incorrigible,' Lucy chided.

'But you love me, don't you?'

'Course I do.'

'But not enough to marry me?'

'Behave yourself. Go and park the car, and I'll get the platform tickets.'

'Only if you say you'll think about letting me put a ring on your finger.'

'Go on with you!' Dismissing him with a wave of her hand, she walked away, the merest of smiles curving her mouth at the corners. She had long thought he would make a wonderful husband, though it would never do to tell him that.

One day he'll wear me down, she thought. One fine day, he'll ask me and I just might say yes.

But she couldn't see that day in sight for a very long time. Maybe never.

Waiting for Vicky's train to arrive from London was nerve-racking. Lucy had lost count of the number of times she had walked the entire length of the platform, looking this way, looking that way, shivering in the bitter cold and beginning to despair. 'Will the blessed train ever arrive?' she asked Adam. 'Maybe Vicky's changed her mind. Maybe she's decided not to come after all.'

Adam was more concerned about Lucy. 'Don't panic. The train isn't even due to arrive for another half hour,' he reminded her. 'Look! I want you to come along to the café and get a hot drink down you. It's perishing cold out here.'

'But what if we miss the train arriving? If we're not here waiting for her, she won't know what to do.'

'Listen to yourself,' he advised. 'We won't miss the train arriving, and even if we did, she's a grown woman, intelligent enough to get a taxi. She has your telephone number and address. So come on now, Lucy.' He gently cupped the palm of his hand beneath her elbow. 'Ten minutes, that's all, to get you warmed up and comfortable. I don't want you catching pneumonia.'

'Stop fussing, Adam!' Shaking him away, Lucy was adamant. 'I'm perfectly all right. You go if you like, but I'm not moving.'

Adam knew from old that once her mind was made up, there'd be no shifting her. 'I only wish Mary was here,' he grumbled. 'She'd make you go inside, and no mistake.'

Lucy shook her head. 'I wouldn't listen to Mary, any more than I'm listening to you,' she replied haughtily. 'I'm here to meet an old friend who's travelled many miles, all the way from America. I will not have her arriving in a strange place, all alone and me not there to greet her.'

All the same, at that moment in time she wished she was any place but here. Vicky had been robbed of precious time with Barney, while she herself had earned a measure of his love, and had even borne him a child. How would Vicky react to that? What would she think? Was she bitter? Did she blame Barney? Did she blame *her*? Lucy was so frantic, it was all she could do to restrain herself from turning tail and fleeing from the station.

Adam's voice resonated in her ear. 'Lucy Baker, will you stop fretting! Lord help me, I love you more with every day that passes. You're the most caring, considerate, aggravating woman I've ever come across.'

'And you're beginning to get on my nerves.'

'Let me bring you a hot drink then, and I'll not say another word – unless, of course, you want me to?'

'I *don't* want you to. But I'd very much appreciate that hot drink. Honestly, Adam, I can't imagine why you didn't think of it before, instead of causing such an almighty fuss about me leaving the platform!'

While Adam went to get the drinks, Lucy's anxious gaze

scanned the far-off track, hoping to see the train as it appeared down the line. 'What will I say?' she fretted. 'How will I greet her? We were close at one time, but it's been so long, I don't know how it will all turn out.'

Her nerves were jangling. In her mind she could see the old Vicky, pretty as a picture and lovely in nature. But what was she like now? Had she hardened over the years? Had she turned cold and resentful because of the shocking way her idyllic marriage had come to an end?

And what of the letter that had ended her *present* marriage? It was Lucy herself who had written it, and now she was beginning to regret it deeply. Maybe Adam was right after all. Maybe she should have let sleeping dogs lie.

Suddenly the shrill tones of the announcer came out of the loudspeaker: 'The ten forty-five from London St Pancras will be arriving at Platform Two in precisely ten minutes. There are no delays.'

～

On board the approaching train, a similar announcement was given over the air.

'Ten minutes!' Vicky had grown more nervous with every passing mile. With only two other passengers in her compartment, she had found a seat next to the window, and managed to collect her thoughts.

She had never been one for travelling. In all of her life she had only ever made two long journeys; the first had taken her away from everything she had ever known. The second was bringing her back.

At least when she sailed away from Liverpool, she had believed Barney to be alive and well, although it had come as a terrible shock to learn of his death, a mere three years later. Doctor Lucas had relayed the news to Leonard, who in turn gently told her and the children. Yet part of her, a very deep part was not surprised. How could her beloved Barney survive without her love, and without the love of his children? God knew, it had nearly killed her to be without him, and look at the effect on their three children.

She glanced out of the window at the darkening rural landscape. Nothing here was familiar, though the patchwork of fields and the occasional spinney reminded her of the fields up North where she had worked alongside Barney. This area of Bedfordshire should have been meaningless to her, but it was important now, because this was where her husband had spent his last days, with Lucy, and their daughter, Mary.

She was not surprised that Barney had turned to Lucy, for the latter was not only a lovely-natured person, but she had been a close friend of the family, and like all of them, Barney had a soft spot for her. But for Lucy and Barney to become lovers and conceive a child? That would never have crossed her mind in a million years. It was a bitter pill to swallow.

Yet for all that, she looked forward to seeing her, and strangely, she also looked forward to meeting Barney's other daughter. She wondered if Mary had a look of him, and if so, she would have a look of Susie, because Barney's first daughter was more like him in appearance than any of his other children.

Thinking about her children brought a degree of pain to Vicky. When she needed them most, they had not been ready to forgive.

Unable to deal with it for now, she closed her mind to them and forced herself to remember the days when she was with Barney, happy, carefree days which would never come again. It made her heart sore to think they had gone forever, but gone they were.

Her fretful thoughts were submerged into the rhythm of

the train wheels as they hurried along the track . . . *Clackety-clack, marches the army, clackety-clack, I love you Barney*. The sound of iron against iron merged with the hiss of steam and somehow it became a song in her heart, and the song created in her a soothing sensation.

~

Lucy was grateful for the cup of tea in a thick white mug that Adam had brought. 'Did you water the plants on your way here?' she quipped, staring into the cup. 'It's half-empty.'

'An accident,' Adam told her sheepishly. 'There were people pushing and shoving at the ticket-desk. I dodged past them, trying my best to keep out of their way . . .' He rolled his eyes. 'The truth is, this infant ran in front of me and I tripped over. But I managed to keep hold of the cups.'

Lucy was at once sympathetic. 'Are you all right? Did you hurt yourself?'

'No.' Having given Lucy one cup, Adam placed his own on the bench and brushed himself down. 'There was help at hand.'

He pointed to a child now climbing onto a platform bench, and with him was a woman the size of a ten-ton truck, arms like a navvy and a turban wrapped round her hair, tied so tight her eyes seemed to pop out. 'She picked me up,' he said with some embarrassment.

Just then the woman turned round and gave him a wonky smile. Adam smiled back, his face bright red as he frantically brushed the dirt and dust from his best trousers.

'That woman there? She was the one who picked you up?' Lucy's face crumpled. 'Her unruly infant knocked you down, and *she* picked you up?' In her mind she had this hilarious image of the elegant Adam going flying across the floor, arms in the air, and that enormous person who looked more like an all-in wrestler than a woman, manhandling him as he fought to keep the cups upright.

It was all too much. The laughter sparkled in her eyes and then Adam was giggling, and now as the woman sat herself on the bench, legs apart and bloomers showing, Lucy had to quickly walk to the waiting room where she erupted in a fit of laughter, tears streaming down her cheeks.

After a time, she managed to compose herself and return to Adam. 'I would have given anything to see it,' she told him.

'You're a wicked woman,' he told her, still laughing at himself, and she gave him a kiss for being so entertaining.

Now, as the train-whistle blew, Lucy's mind was focused once more on Vicky. 'It's here,' she told Adam excitedly. 'The train's here!'

Standing their cups beside a bench, the two of them moved closer to the edge of the night-dark platform, where the train was already beginning to pull in.

As it chugged to a halt, the steam rose and all the doors opened. People spilled out and it was hard to distinguish them through the billowing clouds. 'Where is she?' Lucy strained her eyes, searching for Vicky. 'Oh Adam, what if she changed her mind at the last minute?'

Philosophical as ever, Adam calmed her fears. 'If she has, then there is nothing we can do about it.'

People thronged past and soon there was no one left. The station seemed suddenly eerie.

'Look there!' Adam pointed to the figure climbing out of the train. 'Is that her, do you think?'

They watched as the passenger stepped down to the platform. As the slim figure of a woman came out of the night, it was like watching a ghost materialising from the past.

'It must be her.' Lucy's heart was in her mouth. 'It has to be Vicky Davidson.'

CHAPTER FOURTEEN

FEELING ANXIOUS NOW that her journey from Boston to Salford was over, Vicky had lingered on the train a moment longer. She still harboured a measure of resentment towards Lucy, because if she had not sent the letter, then everything would have stayed the same. Now though, her life had changed and there was no going back, and it was a shattering thing.

Pulling herself together, she gathered up her suitcase and got off the train. In the chill night air she caught a glimpse of them, Adam and Lucy, waiting for her as they had promised. She could not mistake them, for those familiar features – though now older like her own – were etched in her memories of the past.

As she walked towards them it was almost as though she had turned back the years and that somewhere nearby, Barney would be waiting to take her in his arms and hold her as before. But no! That wasn't to be. Her heart was like a lead weight inside her. It was all too much . . . too much! She gave an involuntary sob. Never again would Barney embrace her, his heartbeat close to hers.

From the other end of the platform, Lucy watched her approach. Strange, she thought, how she knew it was Vicky straight off. The walk was the same, the petite figure and the way of holding herself – that was the Vicky she knew and remembered.

As Vicky came closer, she passed beneath a platform lamp, and Lucy could see the tears glinting in her old friend's eyes. Her heart leaped, and when she turned round to speak to Adam, he was gone. She glanced about, and there he was, standing over by the gate, sending her strength, sending her love, watching over her like a guardian angel.

Now Vicky was standing before her, and the emotions that ran through Lucy were overwhelming. 'I'm so glad you came,' she said, choked.

Vicky did not – could not – answer. Instead, she stood motionless, her suitcase still clutched in her hand, tears rolling freely down her face as she began to realise at last that she was here, in the company of someone who had been part of her, part of Barney and the family. 'Lucy.' Her voice broke. 'My God, it's Lucy Baker.'

The two widows fell into each other's open arms.

All those long years between, from that fateful day when Vicky and the children sailed away, to this, long-awaited moment, were as nothing now.

When the embraces were over there remained a certain awkwardness. 'There are so many questions,' Vicky said huskily. 'So much I need to know.'

Lucy nodded. 'I understand.' Of course there would be questions, about herself and Barney, about how it was between them. Questions asking why Lucy had not told her earlier; why now, after all this time?

The prospect of all those questions made Lucy deep-down nervous.

But so too was Vicky, who walked beside Lucy as they made for where Adam waited. By then, they were chatting and smiling, but he sensed the undercurrent between them, and wondered if too much had happened for them ever to be friends again.

'Hello, Vicky, my love,' he said warmly, and his arms opened and she went to him.

'It's so good to see you again,' she said, and the barriers between them were no more.

They talked for a few moments, and then they were in the car, driving back to Knudsden House. 'You might want to rest and freshen up before dinner,' Lucy offered. 'I've organised it for eight thirty. You'll meet Ben and Mary then.'

'I'm looking forward to that very much.' Vicky was anxious about the meeting with Mary, but curious all the same. However, before that, there was something else she must do. With no further ado she blurted out: 'Will you take me to see where Barney is?'

Lucy had half-expected this to be Vicky's first request. 'I've already arranged it with Adam,' she explained. 'The churchyard is too far to walk from the house, yet it's only a matter of ten minutes in the car. First though, I thought you might like to catch your breath, offload your suitcase and give us a chance to talk. I thought tomorrow morning might be a good time to go there, but we'll go straight to Barney, if that's what you prefer?'

That had been Vicky's plan, to arrive and go straight to Barney. Now though, she did feel the need to catch her breath, as Lucy suggested. She wanted to see where Barney was laid to rest, and yet she wanted to pretend it had not happened, that somewhere, somehow, he was still alive. 'You're right,' she told Lucy. 'After that long journey, a few hours here or there don't matter.'

'Good! Then that's settled.'

And the two women exchanged a deep look – of shared sorrow and an acknowledgment of the very special bond that united them.

'It will be wonderful, to meet your Mary,' Vicky told Lucy as they settled themselves into the comfortable back seat of the car. 'Although, funnily enough, I'm nervous, too. You said in your letter that she lived with you. Is that still the case?'

Lucy nodded. 'Not for much longer though. She and her fella, Ben Morris, are to be married soon. Mary's had such bad luck with men in the past, but now it seems she's found the right one.' She waved her hand, as though to bring the conversation to a halt. 'Now then, I hope you're hungry. Our Elsie has really gone to town on our supper tonight.'

'Who's your Elsie?' Vicky asked.

'Elsie Langton is the wife of our local blacksmith. She lives in the village and comes to me every day,' Lucy explained. 'It's too big a house for me to manage on my own these days and well, what with Mary's flower-shop being so successful and all, we can just about afford dear Elsie. To be honest, we'd all be lost without her.' Lucy knew she was gabbling on but Vicky seemed genuinely interested.

'She takes care of the household things – cleaning and cooking and suchlike. She's an almighty chatterbox, she's even bossier than me, and at times she can be so infuriating you could happily strangle her,' Lucy chuckled. 'But she's the salt of the earth, honest and hard-working, and totally reliable. She has a heart of gold and excels at everything she does.'

Vicky was impressed. 'She sounds wonderful.'

'Oh, she is! In fact, she's an absolute treasure. You will just love her, I know you will.'

'Does she look after the grounds as well?' Vicky was beginning to wish she had such a paragon back home in Boston.

'She would, if she could get her hands on them. But no, the grounds are Mary's domain. She grows all of our flowers, fruit and veg, plants them herself, digs and hoes, and spends hours out there, weeding and working in all weathers. The lass sells most of it in her shop or at market, and there's still enough left over for the local charities.'

Vicky was thrilled. 'She really must take after her daddy, with such love for the land. Yes, I can tell that she must have green fingers, just like Barney, because even in this wretched weather, it's easy to see how beautifully kept it all is here.'

They were pulling into the drive of Knudsden House by then.

Lucy was delighted by the compliment to her daughter. 'Mary's also got a couple of cows, which she milks by hand,' she added proudly, 'and a dozen hens that lay enough eggs to feed a whole congregation.'

'So, your Elsie is never short of milk or eggs then?'

'Not so's you'd notice, no – though if she's not complaining that she's got too many, she's moaning that she's never got enough. You can't please our Elsie no matter how hard you try.'

As it happened, the very person herself was waiting for them as Adam helped them out of the car.

'You'll be the old friend that Miss Lucy's been going on about from morning to night,' she said, rushing forward, the hand of friendship outstretched. 'I'm Elsie, general dogsbody and hard done by. How d'yer do?'

Before Vicky could get a word in, Elsie was rushing on; 'I expect that one's already blackened me name, saying as how I'm a lazy good-for-nothing who can't cook, can't make a bed without leaving lumpy bits, and doesn't know one end of a yard-broom from the other!'

'Can't keep quiet for a minute at a time, more like!' Lucy laughed. 'Behave yourself. Our guest is starving hungry and tired from the long journey, so be off and keep an eye on our dinner, please.'

Elsie tutted. 'See how she treats me?' she enquired of Vicky. 'Bossing and bullying. Do this, do that.' Rolling her eyes to the clouds, she went inside and locked herself in the kitchen.

Vicky laughed heartily. 'You were right,' she said. 'She is an absolute treasure.'

Adam went on ahead of them. 'I'll put this suitcase in your room,' he told Vicky, 'then I'll make myself scarce for an hour.'

'You don't have to,' Vicky told him.

'I think it might be best,' he answered. Knowing how these two had a lot of catching up to do, he insisted, 'I'll see you both in an hour or so.' And before they could argue, he was quickly gone.

As they walked into the hallway, Vicky looked around at the wood-panelled walls and long casement windows. 'Oh Lucy, this is so lovely!' she exclaimed. 'So full of character. Is this where you and Barney lived together?' There was a wonderfully warm, inviting atmosphere in this house, she thought.

'We lived here, yes,' Lucy replied thoughtfully, 'for the short time we had. Poor Barney was in the last stages of his illness then. I sold the cottage that Mr Maitland kindly gave to me and . . . and Jamie – thanks to you and Barney – and we managed between us to buy this place, as it was very run-down and going cheap. Dear Adam has put his back into restoring it, over the past twenty years.'

'And were you happy, the two of you?'

'As much as we could be, under the circumstances.' Lucy thought that a difficult question to answer.

Resentment rose in Vicky. 'It must have been very hard for you both.' But her voice sounded tight.

'It was. But we lived one day at a time, and somehow we managed to find a deal of joy in every moment.'

Vicky's thoughts were with Barney, and her heart ached. '*I* should have been here,' she burst out. '*I* should have been with him!'

Unsure how to deal with the situation, Lucy spoke her mind. 'I wouldn't blame you if you felt bitter . . . about me and Barney, I mean.'

Vicky's features hardened. 'I am bitter,' she replied hoarsely. 'I'm angry because you didn't think to bring me back earlier.' Her voice rose in a cry of anguish. 'You can have no idea of the heartache and regrets that haunted me . . . haunted all of us and still do!' Turning away, she began pacing the floor. 'And now when it's all too late, I discover that Barney was ill when he sent us away – that he turned to *you* instead of keeping me by his side.' Her eyes alive with suspicion, she swung round. 'It makes me wonder how long the affair had been going on. Tell me, Lucy. Were you lovers right under my nose . . . all the time making a fool of me? Is that it? He had come to need you more than he needed me . . . *even when he was dying?*' The last words came out as a howl.

Horrified, Lucy took a step forward. 'No, Vicky, you're wrong! It was never like that!'

As she reached out to touch her old friend, Vicky began sobbing, all the pent-up emotions let loose in a vehement tirade. 'How can I believe you? You! A woman who took my husband to herself and bore him a child, when all the time none of us knew why he sent us away.' She was almost screaming now. '*You* knew, though, and still you didn't think fit to bring me back. I missed him so much . . . Oh dear God! My Barney, so desperately ill, and me so far away on the other side of the world!'

Burying her face in her hands, she sobbed like a child. And when Lucy reached out, this time she did not flinch. Instead she fell into Lucy's arms and clung to her, until the sobbing eased and her pain was bearable.

Deeply saddened, Lucy continued to hold her. The tears ran freely down her own face and her heart was heavy with sadness.

Eventually, Vicky raised her head and whispered, 'Oh Lucy, I was just hitting out . . . I didn't mean it.'

Lucy nodded. 'I know.'

Vicky took a deep breath. 'It's just that . . . oh, I have so many regrets.'

After a time, when the two of them were seated and quiet, Lucy had a question. 'Did you find at least some measure of contentment with Leonard?'

Vicky did not hesitate. 'Yes, I did. But it was a strange contentment. It took a long time for me to regard him as anything other than a friend. Even then, it was as though there was something else, *someone* else, always there, between us.'

She looked away, her thoughts going deep. 'Even when I was with Leonard, laughing, working, building a home for the children, Barney was always there. Leonard knew it and I knew it, but it was all right, because Barney had sent me away, and Leonard had taken me under his wing . . . taken all of us under his wing.' She paused, her thoughts going back over the years she shared with Leonard.

'We never had a child,' she murmured softly. 'I suppose it was never meant to be.'

Sensing a deeper sadness, Lucy gently reminded her, 'Leonard was a good man and a good and loyal friend to Barney.'

'I know that. But I still can't forgive him for lying to me.'

'It isn't as if he lied outright,' Lucy suggested lamely. 'He just never told you.'

'But don't you see – it's the same thing!'

Lucy hesitated. 'Will you ever forgive him?'

Vicky shook her head. 'Never! I will never forgive or forget, until the day that I die.'

And Lucy bowed her head in shame for her part in Barney's secret sacrifice.

CHAPTER FIFTEEN

WHEN LUCY HAD shown her up to her room, Vicky rested a while, then washed and changed, ready for dinner. Somewhere in Knudsden House, a grandfather clock was striking eight. 'Got to make a good impression,' Vicky said to herself, and she did a slow, dignified twirl in front of the bedroom mirror.

The cream-coloured dress she had brought with her from Boston was well-suited to her slim, upright figure. You don't look too bad for your age, my girl, she thought approvingly. Leaning forward, she wiped the tip of her finger along her lips, evenly spreading more of the light-coloured French lipstick that brought out the colour of her slate-grey eyes. Her hair was swept back and kept in place by a sparkling diamanté clip in the shape of a curled leaf.

Vicky knew how to dress for dinner. It was one of the social niceties that were part and parcel of her marriage to Leonard. Whereas her life with Barney had been simple and easy, her position in Boston as the wife of a land baron moved her in different circles. Her values and principles had never changed, though. Forging a strong family bond and being there when needed had always been her priorities.

Down the landing, Lucy was beginning to panic. Her hair wouldn't go where it was supposed to, and the shoulder-strap on her dress had just snapped as she slipped it over her head. 'Damn and bugger it!' she cursed.

Slinging the dress over the back of a chair, she stood a moment, contemplating what to do. She could wear the white dress, but that didn't seem appropriate somehow, or she could simply put on her brown skirt and blue top . . . no, she couldn't turn up for dinner looking like a school-marm!

Flinging open the wardrobe door, she flicked through the many garments hanging there. 'Why is it I can never do anything right?' she hissed aloud. 'It's nerves,' she decided. 'It's all too much in one day and now I've got an attack of the heeby-jeebies.'

Finally, she settled on the emerald-green dress, the one with little puff sleeves and a pretty lace neckline. When she slithered into it now, she felt just right; the waist sat snugly and the skirt flounced just the teeniest bit. 'Not too frumpy, not too sassy,' she said, sliding her feet into a pair of black slip-on shoes. There was a gas fire in her bedroom, and a good coal one in the sitting room, but all the same she arranged a mohair stole around her shoulders to keep out the draughts.

With the shoes on and the dress in place, she almost tumbled over while attempting to check that the seams on her stockings were straight; next she brushed her hair and rolled it into a halo round her head, while teasing out just the tiniest curl here and there. A touch of rouge and just the smallest brush of mascara and she was ready to face the world. 'Now, if your bones don't ache too much, and you don't fall asleep at nine o'clock, you'll be all right.' Twice she had done that and never been allowed to forget it.

But that was when she had first come out of hospital so that didn't count, or so she told herself. It wasn't old age creeping up fast. It was the after-effects of lying about in a hospital bed. Well, anyway that's what she made herself believe.

At ten minutes past eight she made her way downstairs. Five minutes later, Vicky followed.

As women do, they admired each other's choice of dress, and compliments flew in all directions, all genuine and all accepted graciously. 'Is Mary here?' Vicky was on tenterhooks.

'I'm sure she'll be down in a minute,' Lucy replied. 'According to Elsie, she didn't get back from the sale until an hour ago, though I think she stayed at Ben's a while before she made her way back. She's a considerate young woman. She so wants to meet you, but I know she was thinking to give us more time together.'

Having poured two sherries, Lucy handed one to Vicky. 'She's a wonderful daughter.'

Vicky thanked her for the drink and after taking a sip she asked, 'How long has she known, about me and the family?'

'Not long. A couple of years.'

'So, Mary was kept in the dark too, was she?'

'I'm afraid so.'

'And how did she take it, knowing that she had a whole new family?'

'She welcomed it.'

'Was she bitter, that she had not been told earlier?'

'No. She understood my reasoning. As a matter of fact, it wasn't me who told her. I was ill in bed at the time. It was Adam who decided the time was right to put her in the picture.'

'Adam?' Vicky was surprised. 'Why would he do that?'

'Because he's always believed that she should be told, and as he's been with us since before Mary was born, he's almost like family. He remained Barney's best friend right up to the very end. He came with us to this part of the world. He helped me nurse Barney, and from as far back as she can remember, Mary has loved him like a second father.'

Vicky smiled. 'Adam was always a good man.'

Lucy wholeheartedly agreed. 'And in case you're wondering, there was never anything between us, but he was always there, always helpful and caring, taking responsibility for us. He never forgot you, or the children. In fact, it was Adam who persuaded me to contact you.'

She paused. 'I can understand why Leonard didn't tell you. It was such a hard thing for me to do, breaking my word to Barney, and even now, with you and Leonard split up, I'm not sure I did the right thing.'

Vicky disagreed. 'It *was* the right thing,' she declared. 'I'm here now, and I shall make my peace with Barney – and I can never thank you enough for that.'

'What about the children?' Lucy thought it strange that Vicky had made little mention of Tom, Ronnie and Susie.

Vicky shrugged. 'That's another story,' she muttered, and for now at least, no more was said on the subject.

At half past eight, Mary came downstairs to meet the long-awaited visitor.

Vicky caught sight of her as she came round the bend in the staircase, and her heart leaped as she looked up to see Barney's daughter; with her easy walk and smiling blue eyes, she was the very essence of her father.

And now as she spoke, even the voice had a resonance of Barney. 'Hello, I'm Mary,' she said softly.

Vicky was momentarily lost for words. She looked at this homely, pretty creature, and all she could see was her late husband. With her bobbed fair hair and those lavender-coloured eyes, the resemblance to Barney had shaken Vicky to the core.

Holding out her arms, she invited the girl into an embrace. 'You've no idea how good it is to meet you,' she said, holding Mary at arm's length and gazing into those familiar, smiling eyes. 'You have such a look of your father,' she said, 'and you're so like my Susie, it's uncanny.'

186

Mary told her that she, Vicky, was exactly as *she* had imagined, and that she, too, was glad that they had met at long last.

It was a warm, satisfying exchange and, as they made their way into the dining room, Vicky felt more at peace than she had done for a very long time.

'Oh, so you've decided to show your faces at the table, have you?' Elsie came out of the kitchen like a hurricane. 'There's me slaving away in that kitchen, while you lot drink the sherry and chat the chat. Well, you're here now, thank goodness, so I'll away and bring in the first course.'

'Not so fast, Elsie, my girl!' Lucy called her back. 'Are you hinting that it's all too much for you? Because if you are, I'll start the girl from the village on Monday morning. I've checked her credentials and she has excellent references. She appears to be a hard worker and an honest soul, and if you'll only give her a chance, I'm sure she'll be a godsend to you.'

Elsie was horrified. 'I never asked for no girl. Don't want her, don't need her.'

'I happen to think you do. You're not as young as you used to be. You need someone to fetch and carry. Even Charlie agrees with me.'

'Well, he's wrong, and if yer don't mind me saying, so are you. I don't want no slip of a girl in *my* kitchen.'

'Look, Elsie, you're on edge all the time, losing your temper at the drop of a hat, and you never stop work from morning till night. You've a home of your own and a husband who wants your company from time to time.'

The little woman gave a hearty guffaw. 'I've a husband who sits on his backside in front of the fire every night, and spends his days looking up the horses' rear ends. He hardly notices me unless it's to have a grumble. If I talk, he grunts from behind the newspaper, and as for a sensible conversation, I might as well go down the park and talk to the ducks. Like as not I'd get more response out of 'em.'

'Why don't you just try this girl? That's all I'm asking.'

'You can ask till the cows come home, Miss Lucy, but I'm not listening. Now, if you feel the need to send me packing, that's another thing altogether and there's nothing I can do about that. But if I'm staying, I'll not 'ave no snotty-nosed slip of a thing under my feet all hours of the day.'

To everyone's amusement, just as they thought she'd finished, Elsie got her second wind. 'You've bullied me into trying it twice now, and I've been proved right each time. They're all the same ... couldn't make a cat's bed never mind yours! They don't know how to wash a pot, ask 'em to clean the windows an' they leave smears all over the place, and as for washing the sheets, they come off the bed white and go back grey, or even bright pink as we've already seen from that first useless article you took on!'

'Oh, for goodness' sake!' Lucy feared she was already losing the argument. 'You're impossible! You wear me down, so you do.'

'Oh do I? In that case, stop interfering and we'll all be fine.'

With that she turned on her heel, marched off in a huff and a moment later from somewhere nearby, a door slammed and shook the picture on the wall. 'You've upset her now, Mum,' Mary laughed. 'I'll not get an extra share of Yorkshire pudding after all.'

Vicky thought Elsie was wonderful. 'I want to take her back to America with me,' she chuckled. 'There'd never be a dull moment.'

The meal went well; Elsie had done them proud. The cream of parsnip soup was delicious; the generous cut of best beef took up half the table; there were dishes bursting with vegetables ... chubby Brussels sprouts, winter cabbage and beetroot, sliced and diced and melting in its own juice. There was a bucket-load of misshapen but mouth-watering Yorkshire puds, and several dishes of potatoes in different forms; crispy-roasted, mashed, and the smaller ones simply left whole.

To top it all off, the meat-gravy was superb. 'The best I've ever tasted,' Vicky announced to Elsie's delight; upon which the little woman picked up the gravy-boat and promptly poured another great helping over Vicky's Brussels sprouts. 'Get that down you,' she instructed proudly. 'It'll put hairs on yer chest.'

Having witnessed Elsie's impulsive action, everyone else discreetly covered their meal before she could get to it.

Once they had reached the stage of the bread and butter pudding, the conversation recommenced on a more serious note. 'You haven't mentioned the children much,' Adam remarked, while pouring Vicky another glass of best wine. 'Put me right if I'm poking my nose in, but is there some sort of a problem?'

'Nothing I can't deal with,' she answered.

'A trouble shared is a trouble halved,' he reminded her. 'And don't forget, you're among friends.'

While Vicky was considering his remark, Lucy thought she knew what might be wrong. 'They've taken sides, is that what's troubling you?'

Vicky smiled. 'You always were able to put your finger on the spot,' she said, 'and you're right, Lucy, because that's exactly what they've done. They've ganged up against me, and sided with Leonard.'

She went on to tell them how, 'Like Leonard, Thomas and Susie believe I should let the past go. They claim there is nothing to be gained from raking it all up now. Although they are content to know their father was innocent of the things they were made to believe ... the drinking and

189

womanising, and the way he seemed hellbent on turning us all against him, and now know he was only doing that to protect us, they still think Leonard was right to keep his promise. Well, I don't! I think he should have told me years ago.'

Lucy was saddened but not surprised. 'I suppose if you think about it from their point of view, it's easy to understand why they feel the way they do.'

Vicky shook her head. 'I don't see how they can feel anger at their father; not now they know the truth.'

She looked along the row of faces and tried to explain how she felt. 'Barney did it for us! He made us hate him, but he did it for a reason. He gave up his entire family. He was prepared to live out his days in pain and alone, not for himself, but because he loved us. Whatever they say, it was *us* in the wrong, not Barney. We let our eyes deceive us, instead of realising he would never become the man he wanted us to see. WE LET HIM DOWN!' She nearly burst into tears, but by a massive effort managed to control herself.

'That's one way of looking at it,' Lucy agreed gently. 'The children obviously see it another way. Maybe he did too good a job . . . making them hate him, sending them away from everything they had ever known. Perhaps they saw themselves as the ones who were rejected! And it doesn't matter that Barney made a huge sacrifice for them, because that was his choice, it wasn't theirs. And Barney didn't ask them. He took it on himself to make that momentous decision, and maybe they resent that?' Phew! She'd never really thought that out before, but it all made sense.

Vicky nodded. 'You're right, Lucy. That's exactly how they feel. But I'll never understand their thinking, or their in-gratitude. Because of what Barney did for them, they now have a wonderful life; they want for nothing – and that's all thanks to their poor, suffering dad.'

She appealed to Mary. 'What do you think, love? Do you think I'm being unreasonable in expecting them to love him for what he did, for the life he gave them and the chance to make something of themselves? Shouldn't they be grateful? Shouldn't they feel compassion for what Barney did, out of love for them?'

'I don't know,' Mary answered truthfully. 'He was my father too, and from what I recall of him, he was a wonderful man, kind and loving. He never hurt me, but if he had, I hope it would not have stopped me from loving him. I didn't have him as long as the others; I was not there when all this happened, so I will never have to choose between the father I knew, and the father that hurt them so. If I had been a part of what happened, I can't say how I would feel.'

Vicky turned to the men. 'You've both been very quiet. Can I ask what your thoughts are?'

In his compassion for her, and his fierce loyalty to Barney, Adam graciously declined to give an opinion.

Ben, however, spoke his thoughts. 'I've tried to see it from all viewpoints,' he told her. 'I can see why you had to come here and make your peace with Barney, and I can't even imagine how you must have suffered, especially when Barney made you think he had stopped loving you.'

He paused to get his thoughts in order. 'But I can see it from your children's viewpoint as well. I think, from the minute he hurt you, they were made to grow up fast. They had to shut him out of their lives. They had to protect you, because now there was no one else to do it. It was Barney who, for all the brave reasons in the world, forced them into that position, and knowing why he did it makes them resentful and angry.'

He was loth to say it, but he had to finish. 'Maybe they will never forgive him.'

'Then I will never forgive *them*!'

191

Not wishing to end the conversation on a harsh note, Vicky changed the subject, by directing a question at Ben and Mary. 'So, there's a wedding in the air, is there?'

Mary blushed deep red. 'Ben asked me to marry him and I said yes. We're planning for it to be in early spring next year . . . maybe Easter-time.'

'Oh Mary, that's wonderful!' Vicky drank the remainder of her wine and holding up her glass for Adam to refill, she announced, 'Here's to Mary and Ben, and a wedding next spring!'

Everyone drank to that and Mary told Vicky, 'I want you all to be there, you and Susie and your sons Thomas and Ronnie.' She hesitated. 'And, of course, Mr Maitland.'

Vicky was embarrassed and it showed. 'I don't think Leonard will be there, my darling, and if my children don't have a change of heart, I can't promise they'll be there either.' She put on a bright smile. 'But I will! Hell and high water would not keep me away.'

Lucy had been recalling Vicky's previous conversation, and one thing in particular was puzzling her. 'What about Ronnie?' she asked now.

Vicky seemed puzzled. 'What about him?'

'You mentioned how Thomas and Susie had been angry at the way their father tricked them about his illness . . . making them believe he had turned bad. But you never mentioned Ronnie. You never said how *he* took the news.'

Vicky paused, her heart aching at the way her children had reacted. 'I don't know how Ronnie took the news,' she confessed. 'He simply looked shocked, then he walked out of the house and never came back.'

'What? You mean you haven't spoken to him? You don't know where he is?' Only now did Lucy realise what chaos she had caused by sending that letter. 'Dear God, I'm so sorry.'

'Don't be,' Vicky sighed. 'You have nothing whatsoever to be sorry about.' She gave Lucy an encouraging smile, but then it slipped away as she spoke of her younger son. 'Ronnie has been a bit of a loner since we left these shores. You know he adored Barney, and somehow he's never been able to come to terms with everything. But he'll come round. He'll go away and curl up in some dark corner and he'll take time out to think about it all. He'll be all right. Susie will find him. She always does.'

Adam also recalled how close Ronnie had been to his father; how the two of them would sit on the hill and talk for ages. Thomas was the worker; Ronnie was the thinker, the poet, the one who was more like Barney inside than any of them.

'Maybe, when you get back, Ronnie will be there,' he told her, 'waiting to confide in you. If I remember, he always found it hard to talk to anyone about his feelings – anyone, that is, except Barney.'

Vicky decided to reveal her intentions. 'He'll have to wait a while longer then,' she confided, 'because I'm not going home just yet. In fact, I won't be going home for quite a while. As already arranged with Lucy, I shall be leaving the day after tomorrow. But I won't be going back to South-ampton. Instead, I'll be taking the train to Liverpool. There are places I need to go, people I need to catch up with.'

Mary was curious. 'How long will you stay?'

'Weeks, months, I haven't decided yet.'

Lucy was astounded. 'Won't Leonard be worried? And what about the children? Surely they need you?'

Vicky was adamant. 'Then they will have to be dis-appointed.' Seeing how her news had shocked them all, she explained, 'Since the day they were born, I've been there for them. And so was Barney. We taught them everything, how to respect other people and have compassion. Be honest and hard-working, and always be on hand for family, because family is the most precious gift you will ever know.'

As she went on, her voice shook with emotion. 'Instead of being angry with their father, they should be grateful, but they're not. Somewhere along the way I must have gone wrong, because my children now seem to think everything revolves around *them*. But it doesn't! And now they expect me to share their anger, but I can't. They're being selfish. They aren't considering *my* feelings in this at all. They were not there for me, so I'm afraid I can't be there for them, not this time. They have each other, and I desperately need to spend time alone, to be quiet, and think about the things that were so cruelly snatched from me.'

Seeing how distressed she was becoming, Lucy reached out and laid her hand over Vicky's. 'You must follow your heart,' she said firmly '. . . and let them follow theirs.'

Vicky composed herself. Raising her glass again, she made a new toast: 'To Barney!'

Everyone chinked glasses, and the evening continued on a lighter note.

Vicky spoke of Liverpool and the old haunts, and how wonderful it would be to see Bridget and Dr Lucas, and when Lucy asked if she wanted her and Adam to accompany her, she graciously declined.

After all, she didn't want them to find out the real reason she was going to Liverpool. Dr Lucas had written and told her how the Davidsons' old home was back on the market, to be sold separately with a few acres of land.

She had an appointment to view it. And if she wanted to, she also had the money to buy it.

'Follow your heart' . . . that's what Lucy had said just now. And that was what she must do.

CHAPTER SIXTEEN

THE NEXT MORNING, Vicky awoke refreshed and feeling more like her old self. She and Lucy were waited on at breakfast by an attentive and vociferous Elsie, who proudly boasted of her 'best bacon' and new-made bread. 'You'll not find anything like that in 'Merica,' she told Vicky, who thought it might be more than her life was worth to disagree.

When left alone, the two friends enjoyed their bacon and eggs. They drank the hot tea, and talked of the old life on Overhill Farm in Comberton by Weir, just outside Liverpool. 'I've never stopped missing it,' Vicky confessed. 'Whenever I thought of Barney, I thought of us out in the field, bringing in the harvest, chasing each other in the long grass, or walking through the spinney with the dog.'

Lucy also recalled the good times – ah, there were so many of them! Before they even began on the bad things, she led the conversation away. 'Adam should be here soon.' She glanced up at the clock. She didn't doubt that he would be on time. He always was.

'Can I ask you something, Lucy?'

'Of course, anything.' Assuming it would be something personal about her and Barney, Lucy prepared herself.

'When you went back to see Doctor Lucas, did you go to

visit little Jamie . . . only you never mentioned him in your letters.'

Lucy was taken aback. 'Yes, I did.' Her voice was low.

'And how did it affect you?' Vicky needed to know. 'I'm just wondering if you were as nervous as I am now, with the thought of seeing where Barney's laid to rest. I don't know what to expect of myself. I never imagined anything like this. I never dreamed . . .' She paused. 'Oh look, Lucy, I'm sorry. Please don't be upset. You don't have to answer. It's just that – well, it makes it all so final, don't you think?'

Lucy came to sit beside her. 'It took me a long time to go back,' she confessed. 'I thought that by cutting off contact with everyone, I could fool myself that none of it ever happened. I know now, that you must never deny your past. You have to cling onto it . . . take it with you, because when it comes right down to it, *your past is who you are.* And yes, it did make it all seem so final, but I knew I had to do it, and though I never believed I would ever say this, I'm glad I went back. I'm glad I went to see Jamie. Yes, it hurt. But I feel calmer in myself for having gone through with it.'

Another question, but this time Lucy saw it coming. 'Did they ever catch that maniac, Edward Trent?'

Lucy shuddered. 'As far as I know, they never did.'

'Do you think he's dead?'

'I hope so!'

'What if he's not?'

'What do you mean?'

'I mean, if he's still around, would he ever take it into his head to come after you?'

Lucy had often wondered about that, and she said so now. 'But there is no way he can ever find me, thank God. The only people I left a forwarding address with were Bridget, Amy and the good doctor. I know they would never give out my address, especially not to him.'

'Well, I hope you're right, Lucy. I haven't forgotten how crazy he was, and how besotted with you.' She cautioned herself. 'Oh, just listen to me, frightening you like that. Of course he won't come back! Why would he, after all this time?'

Lucy laughed. 'I'm not the slip of a thing I was back then,' she pointed out. 'If he did come after me, he'd take one look and head for the hills.'

'Give over!' Vicky could still see the loveliness in Lucy; it was a timeless essence that defied age and shone through the years. 'You might have changed a little on the outside, but you're still that special person you always were.'

When she had seen Lucy waiting on the platform last night, she knew straight away that it was the same Lucy, the same good friend with whom she had shared so much. 'You've still got that everlasting twinkle in your eye,' she said with a cheeky wink. 'I'm sure Adam's told you that many a time, has he not?'

'Hmh! You don't miss much, do you? But don't get too excited, because there is nothing between us. We're both too old in the tooth to be acting like love-struck youngsters.'

'All the same, I wouldn't mind betting that he's asked you to marry him. Am I right?'

Lucy had to admit it. 'You haven't lost your nose for a bit of gossip, have you?'

'So, have you said yes?'

'No, I haven't. Nor am I likely to.'

'Why not?'

'I have my reasons.'

Vicky sensed them. 'You're still in love with Barney, aren't you?'

'If I was, would you mind very much?'

'Yes. But I would understand.' Vicky paused. 'You see, I too have never stopped loving Barney. Soon after poor Barney died, Leonard asked me time and again to marry

197

him. My answer was always the same . . . no. But gradually I grew lonely; he wore me down, and I said yes, not because I loved Barney any less, but because I had a family to think of, and besides, Leonard had proven himself to be a caring, gentle man who had somehow wormed his way into my affections. Also, I believed in my heart that it was time to stop pining for Barney . . .' Her voice broke.

'Vicky, if I ask you something, will you promise to be honest with me?'

She promised.

'Would it have been better for all of you, if I hadn't written and told you the truth about Barney?'

Vicky took a moment to consider, but when she answered it was with conviction. 'Lucy, if you never believe anything else, you must believe me when I say this: I'll be forever grateful to you for telling me. I had *a right* to know! That's why I can never forgive Leonard.'

Lucy despaired. 'Never is a very long time.'

Vicky was adamant. 'He took us to America, away from Barney, knowing full well that what Barney was doing to us was all a desperate act, knowing full well how ill Barney was, and how nothing on God's earth would have kept me from my darling's side.'

'Don't be too hard on him, Vicky.'

Lucy too, felt a measure of guilt, for she had known the same as Leonard – more, in fact. And she had not once tried to contact Vicky, so wasn't she as much to blame as Leonard? Yet hadn't they both kept Barney's secret for the same reason? *Because Barney wanted it that way.*

Vicky's voice hardened. 'What Leonard did was wrong! He took me as his wife . . . and *still* he kept his silence, when all the time Barney had sacrificed himself for us, in order to give us good futures in America. What kind of a man could do that?'

'A man who loved you too much to see you suffer over something you could not change.'

Lucy defended Leonard, as though she might be defending herself. 'He thought he was doing the right thing, for Barney, and for you and the children. Leonard is someone who made a promise and kept it, though I'm sure there must have been times when he longed for you to know the truth . . . to be released from the promise he made in good faith to a man he admired above all others. He didn't tell, because he respected Barney's wish – *that you should never be told.*'

When Vicky would not be moved, Lucy persisted. 'You should consider yourself fortunate, Vicky . . . *we both should* . . . because with Barney we knew love of a kind that comes only once in a lifetime. And now you have Leonard, and I have Adam, both good, honest men who would do anything for us. Not many women are so blessed.'

Just then Adam himself tapped on the dining-room door. 'You'll need to wrap up warm,' he warned. 'It's biting cold outside.'

A few moments later, Lucy had collected the coats from the hallway. When the two women were ready, Adam led the way and gently ushered them into the car. 'Here,' he handed them a plaid rug. 'That should help keep you warm.'

Once they were settled, he climbed into the driver's seat, started the engine and in no time at all, was on his way. 'Don't forget we need to call in at the flower-shop,' Lucy reminded him.

'I haven't forgotten,' he replied.

They drove over to Leighton Buzzard, where Rona helped Vicky to select a huge bunch of red roses from those on offer in the family's florist's shop. 'They were always Barney's favourites,' Vicky said sadly, but Lucy already knew; in the last few years of his life, she had learned everything there was to know about Barney.

At the churchyard, Adam parked the car and Lucy led the way. 'The grave is in a beautiful spot,' she said in a hushed voice to Vicky. 'You go ahead. I'll wait in the car. Come back to the path when you're ready.' She paused, then whispered with a lump in her throat: 'I hope you like the words on his stone. Adam and I chose them to speak for all of us.'

Vicky thanked her and they parted company.

'Do you think she'll be all right?' Like Lucy, Adam was concerned.

'She's a strong woman,' Lucy assured him. 'She'll be fine. But she'll want to be on her own for a while.' Lucy knew, more than anyone else, what Vicky must be going through, and her heart went out to her.

From the car, they could see Vicky go down on her knees; they watched her set the flowers before the marble headstone, and they saw her lean forward and read the words:

BARNEY DAVIDSON

1890–1933

A MAN OF COURAGE.
HE MADE THE GREATEST
SACRIFICE OF ALL.

She seemed to be talking, then she bowed her head and clambered to her feet. For what seemed an age she stood still as a statue, her eyes downcast and her hands folded before her.

After a few more moments, she suddenly turned and walked away. She did not look back, nor did she look down. Instead she walked with her head high, dignified in her grief, and calmer of heart for having come here to speak with her beloved Barney.

As she came nearer, the two onlookers could only guess at the turmoil inside her.

'Are you all right?' Lucy hurried to meet her.

'I am now,' Vicky smiled; it was a quiet, serene smile that spoke volumes. 'When I saw the inscription on my Barney's tomb, I felt a great sense of peace and understanding come over me.'

Lucy was amazed at the change in her old friend. Where before she had been nervous and worried, Vicky now seemed to have found a degree of calm, almost as though she really had been talking with Barney, as though all these years she had wanted to tell him how much she loved him, and only now was she able to.

'Come home now,' she said. 'Let's have a nice cup of tea and some of Elsie's shortbread.'

'That would be just what the doctor ordered,' Vicky replied. She gave a long, heartfelt sigh, and told Lucy, 'I came to Bedford with a purpose: to see you and hear your story, to come here to Barney, and to meet the daughter you bore him. I've got through them all, and now I'm ready to get on with the rest of my life.'

As Adam watched them approach, arm-in-arm and talking in earnest, he thought, This is how it should be. Old friends too long parted, back together at last.

It did his heart good to see it.

$\sim$

A day later, in brilliant sunshine, Vicky set off for Liverpool. Ben and Mary said goodbye. 'Don't forget I want you all at the wedding,' Mary reminded her. And Vicky promised only that she would be there.

Lucy and Adam saw her onto the train. How different it seemed from the night when she had arrived. 'Take care of yourself,' Lucy said as they clung on to each other.

'I will,' Vicky promised.

'Let me know how you are, and when you're likely to go back to the family. And remember, you're always welcome here at any time.'

'I will.'

'And please, Vicky, will you think about Leonard? He does love you so.'

Vicky merely smiled, a dismissive smile that told Lucy she was not yet ready to forgive her husband, or her children, for siding against her.

The train arrived, and in minutes she was lost to them, her face looking sad as she waved out of the window.

'TAKE CARE OF YOURSELF!' Lucy's voice rose above the engine noise.

'You too.'

Then she was gone.

'There goes a sad and lonely woman,' Adam remarked as they walked back to the car.

Lucy made no reply. She knew how much in love Barney and Vicky had been, and she could see how that love still burned in Vicky.

It must have been hard, she thought, when instead of sharing her sorrow and compassion for Barney, the others had become angry and bitter, altogether losing sight of what he had lost and they had gained.

In the event, Vicky could not accept what she considered to be a deeply selfish attitude.

'How do you think it will all turn out, with Vicky and the family?' she asked Adam.

'I think it will turn out all right in the end,' he answered thoughtfully. 'I didn't like to say so before, but I believe they were wrong to blame Barney for doing what he did. God only knows, it was a hard enough decision for him to make!

When I remember the state he was in, poor chap. Like Vicky said, they should go down on their knees and be grateful for a man like that! And to you, for taking him in and caring for him as you did.'

Lucy glanced at the man beside her and, not for the first time, she felt the stirrings of real love. 'Let's go home,' she said, and let him escort her to the car, where she took the liberty of sitting in the front. 'What?' she demanded when he stared at her. 'What are you wearing that expression for?'

'You're sitting in the front!'

'What's wrong with that, might I ask?'

'Nothing.'

'Then will you kindly start the car and take me home?'

'Right away, madam.' In a feigned subservient gesture, he tipped his forehead. 'Whatever madam wants.'

As they drove along, the smile got wider.

And though she pretended to be looking out of the window, there was an answering twinkle in Lucy's eye.

She might be more of a tortoise than a hare these days and she had long forgotten what a kiss was. But life wasn't over yet, she thought merrily.

Not by a long chalk!

PART THREE

~

February, 1955

Old Loves and Evil

CHAPTER SEVENTEEN

THE PRISONERS CALLED out as Edward Trent walked to freedom. 'Have a drink on me, Carter!' shouted an old lag in for arson. Cocking a deaf ear, the prison officer escorted Trent along the white-washed corridor towards the huge main gate where he had entered such a long time ago.

'Give the pretty gals a kiss from old Simon,' laughed another. 'And if yer come across Martha Clayton on yer way, tell her she needn't wait for me, 'cause I'm on the lookout for summat fresher and younger, who knows 'ow to treat a fella!'

Edward Trent ignored them all. He had spent years, dodging and diving to keep out of trouble in this godforsaken place, and many was the time when he could easily have sliced off their gormless heads, but he didn't. He had only one thing on his mind, and that was to get out into the big wide world, sooner rather than later.

Somewhere out there was Lucy Baker, and he had to see her. Try as he might, he could not get her out of his mind. As far as he knew, she could be six feet under the turf. But assuming she was still alive, he had to look her in the eyes and find out if he still had the same feelings for her as he did when they were younger. After all, she had been the mother of his only child. He drew heavily on his cigarette, cursing savagely as it stuck to his lip.

Apart from that, he had a score to settle with her. Lucy Baker was the only woman who had ever sent him away – *him*! Edward Trent, who only had to click his fingers and the women would come running.

But then as he recalled, Lucy was different from the others. She had spirit, and wasn't afraid of anything – except maybe losing her precious kid. Oh yes! She was afraid of that; it was the one weakness in her, and like a fool he had thought he could use it against her. How was he to know she would come after him like a she-wolf after her cub; pursuing him until he went crazy.

It was *her* fault that his only son had been killed. Bitch! He gasped as a sudden pain seized his chest. Savagely stubbing out the cigarette beneath his shoe, he pushed onwards to freedom at last.

As the years went on and he grew older and more lonely, Edward Trent had begun to regret so many things. All his life he had pursued women for pleasure, nothing more. He had never experienced the urge to settle down and start a family, had never truly loved a woman – until Lucy came along.

She was the only woman he had ever warmed to; the only one to win his wicked heart, and through arrogance and spite he had foolishly lost her. Then, when he believed he had a chance to make it up and start afresh, he played it all wrong, and managed to turn her against him for good.

All these years she had haunted him, filled his dreams and beckoned to him.

He had to find her. Even if he was repulsed by how the years might have worn her. Was she haggard and bent, or was she still the same Lucy that he had carried with him all these years? He could see her now, laughing with abandon, running barefoot and free like a wild spirit . . . 'catch me if you can' – that was the Lucy he remembered. Like a butterfly on the breeze, with amazing colour and beauty. To his everlasting regret, he had caught her, had her in the brutal palm of his hand, then let her fly away.

Had time stood still for her like it had for him? Would she still hate him for what he had done? Was she even alive, and if so, how would she feel when he turned up? Was it not possible that somehow, the years had mellowed her, and that she might regret having turned him away that night?

Edward Trent raked a shaking hand through his prison haircut. After all, wasn't she as much to blame for the boy's drowning? At least, that was what he had convinced himself of over the years. Jamie . . . James Trent as should have been.

Growling under his breath, he turned to wave at the prison officers. 'Thanks for nothing,' he jeered. The loathing he felt was lit in his eyes.

'The devil go with you, Carter!' The larger of the two stared him out.

'You'll be back,' said his colleague. 'Your sort are never free for long.'

Making an obscene gesture, Trent deliberately sauntered away, and soon lost sight of them. 'Bastards!' Quickening his step he made for the bus that was pulling in at the end of the street.

As he climbed aboard, he had only one thing in mind. I'm on my way, sweetheart, he thought darkly. Who knows, she might even have been waiting for me all this time, just as I've been waiting for her. The thought was unbearably tantalising.

'Where to, mate?' The bus conductor had his hand on the ticket machine.

'The railway station.'

With a turn of the handle, the conductor rolled a ticket and tore it off. 'That'll be tuppence halfpenny.'

Fishing in his pocket, Trent found the coppers and thrust them into the man's palm.

As he walked away, the conductor stole a glimpse back at him. He observed the brooding eyes, the bull-like neck and he felt decidedly uncomfortable. Many times he had picked up ex-convicts newly released. Mostly, they were penitent and easy to talk with. You kind of got an instinct for their real character, and this one was bad. Real bad.

When they arrived at the railway station, Trent made his way straight to the ticket-desk. 'What time's the next train to Liverpool?'

The clerk checked his timetable. 'Hour and a half . . . platform four.'

'How much?'

'Single or return?'

'Single.'

The clerk checked his listings. 'Two shillings.'

Trent scowled. 'Is there nothing cheaper?'

'Nope! Not unless you want to ride in the guard's van, along with the bicycles and chickens.'

'And what will that cost me?'

The clerk patiently checked his listings. 'Sixpence half-penny should do it.'

When his place was bought and the money paid over, Trent asked, 'Where can a man get a drink round these parts?'

'Across the street, turn left . . . you'll find the George and Dragon on your right.' He glanced up at the master clock. 'Eleven thirty. You should find them open and if he isn't, you could always knock on the side door. Tell him Arthur sent you.' Thinking he deserved to be rewarded for such information, he held out his hand.

'Next time,' Trent promised. 'I'll see you right next time.' He went away grinning. The world was still full of fools, he thought.

An hour later, he left the pub and made his way back to the station, where he had to wait another half hour for his train. When it arrived, he climbed aboard and sat himself down in a second-class carriage.

Ten minutes later, the ticket inspector made his rounds. 'Tickets, please.' He tapped his fingers on the back of the seat, while his surly passenger rooted about in his pockets for the ticket.

'There you go, I knew it was there.' Trent held the grubby ticket aloft.

The inspector took one look at it and told the passenger gruffly, 'Are you trying to pull a fast one, chum, because if so, you're out of luck.' He made a gesture with his thumb. 'You'll find the guard's van back there.'

'Eh? What are you talking about?' Claiming ignorance, Trent told the inspector, 'I paid my money and there's my ticket to prove it.' He made a fairly good job of pretending not to know the value of the ticket.

'Don't give me that!' The inspector had dealt with worse passengers than this one, and he was standing for no nonsense. 'You bought a ride in the guard's van and that's where you're headed now,' he said. 'Either by the cuff of your collar, or on your own two feet – which is it to be?'

Under normal circumstances, Trent would have landed him one, but he had no intention of ending up back inside. So, rather than cause a fuss and have the police waiting for him at the other end, he went back to the guard's van, where he crouched on the floor amongst all manner of paraphernalia.

After a torrent of abuse and cursing, he laid out full stretch, and let the dulling effects of his two pints of booze take over.

If it hadn't been for the guard, who was in the process of taking out a passenger's bicycle, Trent might well have slept all the way to Scotland. 'Hey, you!' Giving Trent a gentle push, the man woke him up. 'You're getting off here, aren't you?'

'What?' Bleary-eyed and irritable, Trent glared up at him. 'What's that you say? Speak up, man!'

Instinctively backing off, the guard picked up the bicycle and hoisted it out on to the platform. 'We're at Liverpool Central, sir. If this is your stop, you'd best get yourself off the train right now!'

Panicking, Trent scrambled up. 'Liverpool, you say?' Throwing the baggage out of his way, he grabbed his kitbag and jumped off, pushing and shoving his way through, ignoring the irate passengers disembarking from the carriages around him.

It had been more years than he cared to remember since he had walked the streets of old Liverpool, but it hadn't changed much, he observed, though many of the old shops now had new frontages, and there were smart office blocks rising out of former bombsites. It was still the same old place though, he thought fondly.

Down at the Mersey, he leaned on the railings and watched the ferries coming and going. 'Just like old times,' he sighed. A feeling of contentment washed over him, although his stomach growled with hunger. At least mealtimes were regular in prison; even a plate of slop was better than sod all.

When an old man took rest on a bench nearby, Trent told him, 'I'm back, thank God! Back in Liverpool, where I belong.'

The old fella was amused. 'Been away, have you?'

'You could say that.' Trent was in a good mood. 'But now I'm back, and I've already rediscovered one old sweetheart – my home town – and now I'm off in search of another.'

'Old sweetheart, eh?'

'That's right . . . the prettiest thing you ever did see – older now, much like myself, but I don't mind betting she's still the beguiling creature that slipped through my fingers long ago.'

The old man tipped his hat. 'Age don't matter nothing,' he declared with conviction. 'It's what's inside that counts, the feelings and belonging.'

'My sentiments exactly!' Trent affirmed. 'She might have a few more wrinkles, same as me, and could be she's not as lively as she was but I'll tell you what, matey . . . I'll only have to look into them beautiful eyes and like you say, nothing else will matter.'

'Well, good luck to you.' The old chap ambled away. 'If you catch up with this sweetheart of yourn, don't let her get away this time, or like as not you'll never get another chance.'

'Oh, don't you worry.' That had been Trent's avowed intention these twenty years – to find Lucy and hold onto her, one way or another. Then, seeing the elderly man moving away, he called out: 'Hey! You there . . . Is the Prince Albert public house still open?'

'What, the one on Victoria Street?'

Trent nodded affirmatively. 'That's the one.'

'Well, you're in luck. There've been one or two old pubs closed down, but the Albert is still up and running, or at least it was when I last called in a few nights back.'

Trent gave a whoop of joy. 'Then that's where I'm headed!' He had another question. 'I don't suppose Peter Bentley is still the landlord, is he?'

The old man shook his head. 'Pete retired some years back,' he answered. 'His missus took bad and the work got too much for them, so they retired and bought one of them terraced houses on Gas Street. His eldest son Mike is the landlord now.' He frowned. 'Though I must say he's not a patch on his father . . . stays out most nights gambling. His wife works hard though, bless her heart. They've got a woman living in and helping behind the bar. Between them, the girls manage to make up for Mike's shortcomings. You'll find Pete calls into the pub most days, but he never interferes. He just sits at the bar chatting and lets them get on with it.'

It was enough for Trent to know that the pub was still up and running. 'I might just look him up,' he said. 'Me and Pete Bentley supped many a pint together in the old days.' Patting the old man on the back, he told him, 'Nice meeting you, matey. It's a change to speak to somebody who isn't looking for a fight!'

As the elderly man set off again, he mumbled under his breath: 'Rough sort. I wouldn't mind betting he's just out of gaol. He'll probably get drunk as a skunk and won't be able to find his way to bed, let alone go after an old sweetheart!'

When he got to the Albert, Trent stood for a moment, just soaking in the familiar things; that same worn dip in the pavement outside the door, where the feet of many a thirsty traveller had walked. The street-lamp which still leaned slightly to the left, and the name-sign over the pub door, cracked down one side, and creaking as it swung in the breeze.

Licking his lips at the prospect of that smooth dark liquid running down his throat, he pushed at the door, growing impatient when it remained fast. 'Damn and bugger it!' He pushed again, and when it still wouldn't budge, he banged his two fists on it. 'Come on, open up!'

'Hey!' a voice called from a window above. 'What the devil d'you think yer playing at?'

On looking up, Trent could see a shadowy face behind a fluttering lace curtain. 'I'm a customer,' he yelled. 'Open the blasted door.'

'You're too early – can't you see we're closed? Go on, bugger off!'

Something about the tone of the woman's voice evoked a memory. 'Lizzie? Good God, is that you, Lizzie?' Stepping back to get a better view, he tried to focus on the face behind the glass. 'LIZZIE MONK, IS THAT YOU HIDING BEHIND THE CURTAINS?'

'Who's asking?' The voice sailed out, the face remained hidden.

'It's *me*, you fool! Edward Trent as was.'

'You lying bugger, Eddie were hanged years back . . . an' if he weren't, then he should've been.'

'Look at me, you silly mare!'

Standing well back, he threw out his arms. 'I'm not a ghost. I'm all flesh and blood, you can bet on that!'

Suddenly the window slid up and a woman's face appeared; in her early forties, without lipstick and her long brown hair wild and dishevelled, she made an awesome sight.

Trent was astonished. Some long time back, he and this woman had enjoyed a brief fling, but she had been a young girl then of barely sixteen, while he was over twice her age.

Nothing ever came of it, mainly because her elder sister Patsy took charge and drove a wedge between them. She tried every which way to drive him out of town and even informed their father of the affair. After that there was no real sense in having the girl anyway; her virginity was gone, and so was the fun. So he left.

Besides, by that time, he had already met Lucy.

Lizzie Monk was eager fodder, while Lucy was elusive and unwilling. That only made him more determined to have her; which he did in the end. And he would have her now, just as before, once he had tracked her down. But there was time enough yet. Meanwhile, he would catch his breath and enjoy whatever came his way, including Lizzie.

'Well, as I live and breathe, it really is Lizzie Monk.' He

beckoned to her. 'Come down 'ere, you little darling! I'm gasping for a pint.' With the memories now stirring deep in his groin, he was gasping for something else too, but first he had to see the lay of the land.

Patsy was a loud-mouthed, formidable type – not that Trent was worried about her in particular, but if she was still around, the bitch, she just might cause enough of an uproar to get him sent back inside, and that was not a risk he was prepared to take for any woman, let alone the likes of Lizzie Monk.

The latter appeared downstairs a good ten minutes later, looking more human with her hair brushed loose and her make-up impeccably applied; in fact, she almost looked inviting. 'I honestly thought they'd hanged you long since,' she said, her brown eyes ogling the sight of him. 'My God, but you've kept well.'

She noted the strong arms and the thick muscular neck, and his long coarse hair gave him a youthful look. 'What are you now, Edward Trent? You must be getting on for sixty, but you still have the body of a younger man.'

'Never mind all that, me beauty.' Grabbing hold of her, he swung her round, eagerly anticipating the fun they might have in store. 'You're the first familiar face I've seen in a long time,' he told her, 'and, if you don't mind me saying, Lizzie my darling, you look as lovely as ever.'

Setting her on her feet he took stock of this buxom brown-eyed woman who, despite being in her forties, was only lightly worn round the edges, and still somewhat of a looker.

Laughing, she shook her head in disbelief. 'Eddie Trent, of all people! Where in God's name have you been all these years?' But before he could answer, she put her fingers to her lips, saying, 'No! Don't tell me. You've been locked up, haven't you? My sister Patsy said that's where you'd be – "locked up till he rots away", that's what *she* said.'

His grin became a frown. 'As I recall, your sister never did have a good word to say about me.'

'You can't blame her though, can you? I mean, I was still wet behind the ears when you took advantage of me. For some reason, from the first time she clapped eyes on you, she said you were no good.' Lizzie scowled. 'Come to think of it, she was right too, wasn't she, eh? Once you'd had your fun, you were away like your heels were on fire!'

'Ha! You can thank your sister for that – and your father. Jesus! He was a crazy man.'

'Crazy like you, you mean?' It was all coming back now, how she had suffered at his hands, and still bore the scars to this day.

'What! I'm nothing like him. He were a damned lunatic!' Trent glanced about, wondering if they were being watched.

She answered the question that was crossing his mind. 'No need to be nervous.'

He took umbrage at that. 'You'll never see the day when Edward Trent is nervous. But I have good reason not to get involved in skirmishes and the like.'

'Really? It's never bothered you before.'

'So, why isn't he around?' Lizzie's father was the only person whose strength and temper matched his own. Because of that, Trent held a slight but grudging regard for him. 'Moved out the area, has he?'

'You could say that,' she replied. 'Four years ago, our mammy took ill and didn't get better, and he followed her soon after.'

He was pleased at that. 'Oh. So you're an orphan then?'

She laughed. 'A bit old to be called an orphan, but yes, I suppose that's what I am all right.'

'And your sister?' His intense dislike for Patsy had never gone away. 'Did she leave the same way as the other two?' He wished.

'That's a cruel thing to say!'

He asked again. 'Is she still around?'

'Would it bother you if I said yes?'

'Not particularly, no.'

'Don't give me that,' she teased. 'I know you, and I know you're after bedding me, and you're worried she'll make life difficult for you. That's the truth, isn't it?'

'What makes you think I still fancy you?'

She glanced down. 'Because I can see the bulge in your trousers.'

He laughed out loud. 'How do you know that's not my baccy tin?'

'Hmh! Funny shape for a baccy tin.' She nudged him playfully. 'Come on, then – do you fancy me or what?'

'Mebbe. Mebbe not.' He fancied her like he might fancy a cut of beef. At the moment, *any* warm, red-blooded woman would do, just for the night, until he was satisfied, rested and cleaned up, and ready to face the one real love of his life.

'There's no need to hide and pretend,' she promised. 'I'm a grown woman now, or haven't you noticed?'

'Oh, yes, I've noticed all right.' In fact, all he could see was the considerable size of her firm breast and the bold way she stood, legs astride, as though inviting him inside.

'You never married then?' he smirked. 'Never got over me, eh?'

'Don't kid yourself! I got married a year after you left.'

'Did you now?' Damn and bugger it, he thought. On the one hand there was her sister Patsy, and now a husband to contend with. Bedding Lizzie Monk might not be as straight-forward as he would have liked. 'So, you're happily wed then, eh?'

'We might have been, if the bastard hadn't gone off with some tart from Ackeroyd Street!'

That was more like it, he thought. 'Oh, I'm sorry to hear that.'

'Liar!'

'No, I am really.' He always prided himself on being as good a liar as the next bloke. 'Bet you weren't on your own for long though, eh? A good-looker like yourself?'

'I was for a while,' she answered soulfully. 'Then I hitched up with the landlord from Daisy Street, and life didn't seem so bad after all.'

'Oh, I see.' Disappointment betrayed itself. 'You're not one to waste time, are you?'

'It didn't last long though,' she grumbled. 'All he wanted was a good time. He didn't want to go serious, so I dumped him.'

'So now you're on your own again?' he probed. 'Or is there another man in tow?'

'Well, kinda.'

He cursed under his breath. 'Someone I know, is it?'

She grinned wickedly. 'His name's Edward Trent . . . the only man I ever really loved, but he went away and broke my heart.' She gave him a come-on wink. 'I'm wondering whether he might stay this time?'

Secretly thrilled and giving little away, he answered quietly, 'I'm sure he'll stay, if you was to ask him nicely.' The most satisfying thing in the world was making a woman grovel.

'All right then, will you stay?'

'Only if you keep your sister at bay. I can't be doing with nagging women.' His smile slipped and his eyes grew darker. 'Women like her send me crazy. They make me liable to turn nasty.'

'She won't nag you. If anything, it'll be *me* she has a go at. But don't worry, I'm not that foolish young girl any more. I'm all grown up, and able to take care of myself.' Lizzie looked him in the eye. 'You would do well to remember that.'

Ignoring the hint, he asked guardedly, 'So where does she live, this Harpy of a sister?' He glanced up at the window. 'Not here with you, I hope?'

'Nope.' She leaned closer. 'As you can see, I work here.' Her fingers stroked the back of his neck, making the hair stand on end. 'Mike, the landlord, is away with his wife. They asked me to stay the night to keep an eye on things. I do stay over on the occasional night, and up until recently, I used to live over. But I got taken advantage of, getting caught for extra hours at the bar and nothing in return. So, I took a little house on Dock Lane. It's not much, but my name's on the rent book.'

Dropping her hand to his nether regions she squeezed up to him. 'We could go there later, if you want?' she said, nibbling his ear. 'Mike and his wife are due back about eleven. I can ask the barman to shut the pub, and there'll be no need for me to stay tonight.'

Trent gave her a smile that melted her at the knees. 'You little hussy,' he teased, and thought he might give her a kiss, but decided not to rush things. Make her wait, he thought, make her hungry for it. She's not Lucy, but she'll do for a couple of nights, until I've got my bearings.

Taking hold of her hands he pushed her away. 'Your offer is real tempting and I dare say I'll take you up on it later. But right now, believe it or not, all I want is a long cold drink.'

'A drink it is then.' Surprised and disappointed, she led the way inside to the bar. 'You still haven't told me where you've been all this time.'

'I've been away at sea. That's all you need to know.' The fewer people who knew where he'd been the better, he thought cagily.

'Hmh! I might believe that, but my Patsy wouldn't.'

Her remark made him curious. ' "My Patsy", is it? So, you two get on all right, do you – even after she made it her goal in life to split us up?'

'She looks after me. She always has.'

'Bosses you about, more like!' But Patsy was a stupid cow who didn't deserve a minute more of his time. 'Stop the gabbing, Liz, and get me a drink, will you?'

Hoisting himself onto the stool, Trent watched her moving about behind the bar. 'I'm in no mood for questions, so leave it be, because I'm back now and raring to go,' he said. 'First a few pints, then a hot bath, and after that I wouldn't mind wrapping my arms . . . and legs . . . round a warm female. If you know what I mean.'

He winked meaningfully. 'You don't happen to know of a sexy woman who might be looking for a randy fella to keep her occupied, do you?'

'I expect that has to be me,' she laughed. 'No one else would want a ruffian like you.' Taking down a pint glass from above the bar, she slid it under the beer tap, to release a torrent of froth and ale. 'One pint coming up.'

Making his mouth water, she leaned forward, just far enough for him to see the rise of her voluptuous breasts inside the open neck of her shirt.

She slid the pint of beer towards him, pointing to the crooked bend in her elbow. 'That's thanks to you,' she said, not smiling this time.

'What d'you mean?'

'That day when you ran for it – remember you and Dad got into a terrible fight? I tried to stop you, and got a broken arm for my trouble.'

'I didn't know that.'

'That's because you didn't stop to find out. But I'm not blaming you. All's fair in love and war, isn't that what they say?'

Edward Trent recalled the fight in detail; him and her father, and that witch of a sister who started it all by opening her big mouth. He pushed it to the back of his mind, preferring instead to remember the fun he'd had while he and Lizzie were on the rampage. 'We had a good time though, didn't we, you and me?'

'The best!'

'After all the disappointments you've had with lesser men than me, I hope you haven't forgotten how to please a fella.'

'That's for me to know and you to find out,' she murmured coyly.

When other drinkers started arriving, Trent retired to the corner table. 'Keep the pints coming,' he told her. And she told him he'd be no good to her with Brewer's Droop.

'You've no need to worry on that score,' he promised. 'I have been known to cover three women in one night of non-stop boozing.'

'That I'd like to see.'

'Well, you won't, because I've got eyes only for you,' he lied.

'That's all I need to hear,' and she told him how she couldn't wait to have him all to herself.

In fact, after the bar was closed and he had downed some five pints, Trent was not even halfway drunk. He waited for the bar to close, and he watched while Lizzie helped the portly barman shut up shop, and afterwards he walked her to Dock Lane and took her inside. 'You've been teasing me all night,' he said hoarsely, 'so now let's see what you've really got.'

No sooner were they in the door than he was tearing at her clothes. 'Hey! Watch the new blouse!' Pushing him off, she made him wait while she peeled off the blouse and the skirt, and then her frilly undergarments one after the other, each strip more tantalising than the last.

'My God!' It had been too long since he'd seen a woman stripped to the bone. 'I could eat you,' he growled. 'Every last ounce of you.'

She laughed nervously. 'Then there'd be nothing left for you to love.'

And love her he did, wild and wanton, with the appetite of a man condemned. In the first hour he took her once on the floor and twice in the bed, and then again when he woke from a slightly drunken stupor.

'Ssh! Who's that?' On hearing a noise downstairs, he sat up to listen. 'I could swear I heard a door go ... listen!' There was another clatter, followed by a mouthful of abuse.

Fearful, Lizzie leaped out of bed. Throwing him a dressing-gown, she hissed instructions. 'Get in the back room – quick, dammit!'

He hesitated. 'Who is it? What's wrong?'

'It's Patsy. She has a key. Sometimes she calls round on her way home from the club. She's a cloakroom attendant in a nightclub – works evenings and weekends.'

He couldn't believe his ears. 'What! You mean to tell me that big-mouth sister of yours is downstairs right now? Gawd Almighty, woman, what the devil are you playing at?'

She began to panic. 'Quick! It's best if she doesn't catch us together.' While she talked she quickly dressed. 'You know how she feels about you. She's never forgotten how you used me.'

Suddenly the door burst open and there she was, a wizened figure with small sharp eyes and an even sharper tongue. 'What's all this?' From the slur in her voice it was obvious she was the worse for drink.

Her quick eyes went to Trent, who made no move; instead he stared back defiantly. 'Hello, Patsy, my love,' he growled. 'I'd like to say you've aged well, but you haven't – not like your baby sister here. You see, I've just been admiring her figure – plumper than the last time I saw her, though a pleasant handful all the same. More filled out and soft to the touch,' he gave a nauseating wink, 'if you know what I mean?'

For what seemed an age she looked at him, eyes widening as she began to recognise who he was. 'Edward Trent . . . the baby-snatcher!' The blood drained from her face. 'You bastard! What are *you* doing here?'

Smiling and arrogant, he pointed to their half-naked bodies, 'I should have thought that was obvious.'

Taking him by surprise, she launched herself at him. 'Get out of here! Go on, get out of here now, you no-good filth.' Drawing blood, her nails caught him across the cheekbones. 'It was your fault we lost our dad. You worried him sick with the way you carried on – bedding a girl half your age and laughing in his face when he begged you to leave her alone. And as if that wasn't enough, you beat him half to death before you ran off like the coward you are. Go on! Get away from her, you dirty bastard! She doesn't need your sort.'

'You're drunk as usual.' Lizzie took hold of her. 'Leave him alone! I want him here – I invited him.' Lizzie tried to pull her away but she was no match for her sister's bull-like strength.

Suddenly it was uproar, with Patsy hell-bent on gouging out his eyes, and Trent fighting to get his clothes back on.

'What the devil's going on in there?' From downstairs the front door rattled under a barrage of thumps. 'I'm calling the police! D'you hear me up there? If the noise doesn't stop right now, I'm fetching the bizzies!'

Fearing the police more than anything else, Trent threw Patsy off. 'I'll be back,' he told Lizzie. 'I promise I'll be back.' No drunken slag was running his life, that was for sure.

Outside, he airily told the neighbours who had gathered there, 'It was a row that got out of hand. No need for the police to get involved.' With that, he sauntered off, leaving them nattering amongst themselves. 'Nosy rats!' he muttered angrily. But his anger became uncontrolled rage when he thought of what Patsy had said ... called him 'filth'. Nobody did that to him, let alone a woman.

Fingering the scratches on his face, he licked the blood from his finger. 'Want to kill me, do you?' he smiled. 'Well, I'm sorry to disappoint you, Patsy my love, but you will never see the day.'

At the end of the street he waited until the neighbours had gone back to their holes, then retraced his steps as far as the shop doorway, where he slid inside and stayed hidden in the shadows for what seemed hours. He grew cold and began to shiver, but his determination kept his angry blood warm.

It was two hours later when she came out; he heard her loud, aggressive voice: 'You're not to let him through that door, d'you hear me? He's no good and never will be. If you ask me, he's spent the last twenty years in prison. Pity they didn't hang the no-good layabout! If he comes back, I'll do for him, and then it won't matter any more, because he'll be out of your life for good and all.'

Then she lowered her voice and it was all he could do to hear her. He shifted closer, cringing as she issued instructions.

'Remember how he treated you last time. For pity's sake, our kid, stay away from him. Think what he did – beat our dad senseless, broke your arm, and left not an inch of flesh on your bones that wasn't bruised or bleeding.'

Her voice shook with rage. 'He'd better not come back, that's all I'm saying, or I won't be responsible for my actions.'

As she came up the street it was easy to see from her unsteady gait that she had consumed even more booze while under her sister's roof.

When she passed within inches of him, Trent pressed back into the darkness. He saw her mean profile and the hard set of her mouth. Her shoulders were stooped as though she carried the weight of the world on them, and he hated her with every fibre of his being.

A few minutes later, she was almost run over when a lone taxi driver had to slam on his brakes in order to avoid her swaying figure. 'You silly mare! I nearly ran into you! Stay on the path, why don't you!' He went away, shaking his fist out the window, while she made a rude gesture and told him to, 'Sod off, you useless git!'

All fired up, Trent followed, keeping enough distance between them so she was not able to detect his presence.

As they neared the river, the street-lamps became further apart and the streets grew darker, until now they were so close to the water he could reach down and touch it. The walkways were deserted at this time of night, which suited his plan.

When they descended towards the railings, he got so excited he let his concentration lapse and didn't take enough care where he was walking; the loose stone bounced from under his foot and hit the side of the railings. Startled, Patsy turned round, peering into the darkness. 'Who's there?'

He gave no reply. Instead he remained still as a statue, not daring to move, thankful for the shadows that were thrown in his direction from an isolated nearby street-light.

She stood quite still for a while, her small sharp eyes cutting through the night air, but not seeing him at all.

Muttering under her breath, she went on.

At the end of the walkway, the railings broke where the steps led down. There she stumbled, leaning on the railings before spewing her heart out all down the steps.

Delighted, he took his opportunity.

As he dashed forward, she heard him and turned round, her face open with surprise. 'You!' Wiping the vomit from her mouth she demanded to know what he was doing, sneaking about in the middle of the night. 'If you think you can make me change my mind about you and my sister, you can think again', she slurred, 'because if it's the last thing I do, I'll turn her against you. I won't be satisfied until she hates you as much as I do!'

Her tirade ended in a gasp as he lunged at her with both arms outstretched. One vicious push and her unsteady legs couldn't hold her.

As she went tumbling down the stairs, her head hit the steps, dulling her senses and making her lose all sense of direction. When she ended up in the river, he laughed out loud. 'Not so clever now, are you, eh? Met your match, haven't you?'

He watched as she floundered in the murky waters, her head appearing then disappearing, her eyes staring at him in disbelief each time she surfaced. 'Help!' She found the strength to scream out. 'Somebody help me!'

He looked round. There was nothing to hand, save for a wooden bench nearby. When she wouldn't stop screaming, he wrenched a plank of wood from the seat, waited until she surfaced again and threw it like a spear at her head. There was a muffled thud, a frantic splashing of hands, then silence. Wonderful, calming silence.

He stared into the water, making sure. But no! There was no sign of her at all. However, in the flickering light there appeared to be a patch of darker water on the surface. In the back of his mind he thought it might be her life's blood. Serve her damned well right. The bitch had had it coming.

Christ, he had a headache! Trent took a deep breath, then, smiling to himself, and satisfied with a job well done, he walked away, a lazy, swaggering walk.

As though he had all the time in the world.

CHAPTER EIGHTEEN

SPRING IN Boston, Massachusetts, could be chilly, but today the weather was so exceptionally cold that even the workmen kept stopping in their labours to rub their hands together in an effort to get the blood flowing.

'I reckon all my toes have dropped off.' Born in the far reaches of Scotland, and used to weather extremes, the truck-driver was frantically stamping his feet in order to revive them. 'How much longer before I can be away?'

'Last panel coming down now.'

Having spent these many years working on the spread for Leonard Maitland, the burly foreman was accustomed to being outdoors in all weathers; summer, winter – it made no difference to him. If a job needed doing, it had to be done properly, and dismantling this huge grain-barn was just another task.

'CLEAR AWAY!' When the cry went up, the workmen ran to safety while the mighty crane toppled the one remaining fifty-foot-high panel. The jaws of the crane wrenched the heavy timber from its roots and with the sound of creaks and groans, the timber lurched sideways before falling to the ground, broken and buckled as it dug itself into the soil.

It was then just a matter of sawing the pieces into smaller, more manageable sizes, which were then hoisted onto the back of the truck to be taken away. 'I'm not sorry to see the back of that.' As the dismantled grain-barn was driven away, the foreman stood back to survey the damage. 'I'm surprised it hasn't fallen down before now.'

The old barn had covered a huge area of prime farming land, which was now scarred and torn by the immense weight of falling timber.

'The soil will find its own level in a week or so,' the foreman told his men. 'Meantime, we've a few miles of ditch-dredging to get on with, before the better weather returns.' When that happened, the land would keep them toiling non-stop, until the last harvest was taken.

From the top of the mound, Leonard felt a surge of sadness when he saw the grain-barn topple. 'That barn has been standing longer than I've been alive,' he told his faithful old mongrel, Chappie. 'But it's a fact of life – we all grow old and outlive our usefulness.' That's how he felt now, useless and old.

He was especially vulnerable these days, what with Vicky gone from his life, and the children torn two ways over the recent revelations regarding their father and the sacrifice he made for them. 'Will she ever come back?' he murmured. 'My life is so meaningless, so empty without her.' Not a minute went by when he wasn't thinking of her. He was desperate to go to England and find her, yet afraid in case he only made a bad situation much worse. He hoped and prayed she would come home soon, of her own volition. Because, God help him, he couldn't live without her.

He walked on. Following the bridleway which ran along the perimeter of the fields, he paused a while and raised his gaze to the far-off horizon. 'See that?' he asked the old dog. 'Every square inch of land as far as you can see belongs to me. But it means nothing, not without Vicky by my side.'

'Morning, Mr Maitland!' The young woman on the bicycle

gave him a cheery wave. She passed him every morning on her way to help milk the cows and pack the eggs, and turn her hand to anything else that came along.

'Morning, Jeanie, how's your mom?'

'Better by the day,' she said merrily. 'She said to thank you for the eggs you sent her.'

'You're very welcome, I'm sure.' He gave her a wave and went on his way.

Entering through the stable-yard, he stopped to talk with the groom while Chappie trotted off to meet the other couple of dogs there. 'How's the gelding coming along?' he asked.

'Raring to go,' the young man replied with a grin. 'Come and see for yourself.'

The gelding, Jack, was a favourite of Leonard's; big and strong, it took his weight without hesitation. 'What did the vet say?'

Strolling along beside the boss, the groom told him excitedly, 'Well, as you know, he feared Jack might have to be put down, but this morning, he was really pleased with the way the wound is healing. The swelling has gone down, and the bone is intact. Jack's still limping slightly, but he doesn't seem bothered when he puts his weight forward.'

'Well, that's a blessing, at least.' Leonard was relieved. 'He's a fine horse. It would be a sin and a shame to have had him put down.'

When they got to the stable, the horse heard Leonard's voice and came to look over the door. 'See what I mean?' The groom was thrilled. 'All fired up and ready for action.'

Letting himself into the stable, Leonard asked the gelding to lift its hoof and it did so without fuss. But the minute Leonard bent to examine the wound, it shuffled nervously. 'Woah, boy, I'm not here to hurt you.'

With soothing words he calmed the animal before taking

a good look at the six-inch wound which, as the groom had already explained, was healing nicely. 'Wonderful!' Leonard gently released the limb. 'Good fella,' he said, stroking the softness of the horse's neck. 'You'll soon be out on the bridleways. But you're one lucky Jack! A kick like that would have finished any other horse, but you've come through and I'm proud of you.' He laughed as the horse nuzzled up to him, tickling his hand with the fine hairs around his big, soft nostrils. 'All right, all right. No need to keep thanking me.'

Outside, he discussed the future of the bad-tempered stallion, Duke, that had kicked the younger horse. 'I've never known a horse to go for another one, like he went for Jack. A vicious kick like that could have snapped his leg clean in two!'

'Have you decided what to do with him?' asked the groom.

'I'm thinking of selling him on. I've had two good offers, but the money isn't the priority. It's knowing he'll go to a good home. Duke's been a faithful old fella. It wouldn't be fair to let him go to just anybody because of one jealous moment.'

'So, that's what you think it was, that he was jealous of the young gelding?' The groom wasn't so sure.

Leonard nodded. 'I do think that, yes – mainly because he's never done anything like it before, and it happened only weeks after we brought the gelding in. Besides, Jack did escape into Duke's field, and you know how territorial he can be.'

For some time, the groom had not been happy with the older horse, and he said so now. 'You know, Mr Maitland, how some stallions can turn rogue without warning, and when they do, it's a bad thing.'

'Well, he won't be doing it again, not on this yard,' Leonard declared. 'We've got eight horses here, all of them good, honest animals, and I'm not willing to take risks with any of them.'

He glanced towards the stallion who was at the field gate.

'At the same time, I want the best for him. We've had him a long time and he's never put a foot wrong until now. I'm determined to find him a good home, where he'll be treated properly.'

'So, who have you got in mind?'

'I've arranged for Georgie O'Sullivan, who runs the stables for Abe Devine, to come down and look at Duke later this afternoon.'

The groom was impressed. 'O'Sullivan, eh? If anybody knows a thing or two about horses, it's the Irishman.'

'Right!' Leonard wholeheartedly agreed. 'I have urgent business in Boston, but I've explained everything to Georgie. He knows what he's getting, and he knows I'll stand for no nonsense. So will you be all right to deal with him in my absence?'

'I'll be fine.'

'Good. Then we'll talk later.'

Bidding the groom good day, Leonard strode off, his mind now filled with an idea which, once planted, would not go away.

Inside the house, he fed the dog and while the elderly animal worked its way through a bowl of leftovers, Leonard came to a decision. 'If I can't go and find your mistress, I'll get a private detective in to do the job for me,' he told Chappie. 'I need to know that she's safe and well. If I can satisfy myself on that, at least I won't have to worry quite so much, and I can keep an eye on her from a distance.'

Vicky was the love of Leonard Maitland's life. She meant more to him than anyone or anything. She might not approve of what he was doing, and he hoped she would never find out; but either way, he knew it was the right thing to do, for his peace of mind, and for Vicky's own good.

～

That same evening, Thomas and his wife Sheila dropped in. 'You wanted to talk about that new combine-harvester,' Thomas reminded Leonard. 'Is now a good time?'

As always, his stepfather was pleased to see him. 'Couldn't be better,' he confirmed. 'As you know, I've just acquired another eight hundred acres, so I'm thinking we should trade in the old machine against one of the larger John Deere models.'

Thomas was pleased. 'So you've come round to my way of thinking at last!' he said triumphantly. 'That's good. You won't regret it, Leonard.'

'I'm sure I won't,' Leonard answered. 'But if we're now agreed on going ahead with it, I reckon we should do it now. We've a way to go before harvest, but it'll be here before we know it, so we need to get the deal done before everybody else begins to think along the same lines of trading up to these new, larger combines.'

'I'm all for getting the deal done,' Thomas nodded. 'And while we're on the subject of machinery, we need to rent another grain-wagon, and hire a driver to work it.'

'It that's what we need, then go to it,' Leonard told him. 'Discuss it with the foreman first. But you're right – we don't want to be halfway through harvest and discover that all the good drivers have been snapped up.'

Wearied by all this farming talk, Sheila wandered across the room, where she lingered by Vicky's photograph. 'Have you heard from *her* yet?' she asked casually, a knowing smirk on her face.

Leonard took offence at the tone of her remark. 'Heard from whom?' He knew who she meant all right, but he wanted some measure of respect when she mentioned his wife's name.

Sheila feigned surprise at his question. 'Well, Vicky, of course.'

He stared her out. 'For all I knew, you could have been talking about the cat.'

Shrugging her shoulders, she smiled sweetly. 'I'm sorry, Lenny. I didn't realise you would be so sensitive.'

Sensing an atmosphere building, Thomas intervened. 'Have you heard from Mother?' he asked worriedly. 'Has she been in touch?'

Composing himself, the man took a deep breath. 'No. Not a word, I'm afraid.'

'Hmh!' Sheila made a snorting noise. 'You shouldn't be too surprised,' she said peevishly. '*I'm* not. I mean, when all's said and done, she did leave you high and dry. In fact, she left all of you high and dry. What decent wife or mother would do such a thing? If I were you I wouldn't even *want* to hear from her.'

Leonard retaliated angrily. 'It's just as well that you're not me, then, isn't it?'

With an exaggerated tut, and a sharp click of her heels, his daughter-in-law slammed out of the room. 'She didn't mean all that,' Thomas said wearily but he was beginning to tire of defending her, especially when she seemed to take pleasure in hurting people, himself included.

Leonard was no fool. 'Oh, she meant it,' he assured the younger man. 'But it doesn't matter, because I know your mother will contact me when she's cooled her heels for a while longer.'

'Do you really think so?' If Sheila hadn't been constantly goading him about how shocking it was for a mother to walk out on her family and not even tell them where she was, he might have started wondering whether he and his brother and Susie had been too harsh on her. As it was, he held fast to his belief that Vicky had let them all down badly.

'If you really want the truth', Leonard said quietly, 'I can't say for certain that she *will* ever come back. All I know is

235

that life is unbearable without her. I miss her dreadfully, and I want her home again the sooner the better.'

'So you don't know where she is?'

'Not yet, no,' Leonard said woefully. But he intended to, he thought. However, he wasn't certain whether Thomas would approve of him hiring a detective to find his mother.

'Can I ask you something, Tom?'

'Ask away.'

'Do *you* think I was wrong in not telling her about your father?'

'I honestly don't know.' Thomas had asked himself that same question many times, but as yet he had found no answer. 'I'm not sure about anything any more,' he confided. 'You have always been a man of your word, and you gave your word to our father when he asked you to promise never to tell Mother, or any of us. You kept that promise. How can a man be blamed for that?'

'But that isn't the only reason why you sided with me, is it?' Leonard could understand their bitterness, but he wanted it to end. 'Oh, Tom, how I wish you could forgive your father for not confiding in all of you! He was a very ill man, desperate to ensure you had the chance that was taken from him. You must believe that he loved you all above anything. He wanted his family to embark on a new life; he wanted to be with you all every step of the way but he couldn't – and that was not his fault.'

It all came back to Leonard, the night he found Barney in the woods, curled up in pain, not knowing which way to turn. He was a special man, a special father and husband, and Leonard wanted his family to appreciate that. 'Please, you must try to understand his motives. Don't belittle the awesome sacrifice he made. Make Susie and Ronnie understand why he did what he did. Barney did not tell you about his illness, because he knew you would never leave him. The last thing he wanted was for you all to stay and watch him fade away, in pain, filled with regret because he had stolen your only chance of starting a new life.'

Thomas considered his words, and they made some sense. But the anger in his heart was strong as ever. 'Susie and Ronnie feel the same way I do. We're angry and bitter. We feel we were tricked into letting him down, when all we wanted was the right to be there for him, just as we've always been there for each other.'

His voice trembled with emotion. 'Dad should have told us! We had a right to know . . . to make the sacrifice for him, just as he made it for us. He was dying, and we should have been with him. But he took away that right, and I don't know if I can ever forgive him!'

Leonard despaired. 'If you can't forgive Barney, then how is your mother ever going to forgive *you*?'

'At least she has a choice.'

Thomas's jaw was clenched hard. He looked at Leonard a moment longer, before in a harsh voice he told him, 'I miss her, of course I do. We all love her and want her back. But she has to accept the way we feel. She's already forgiven Father. We probably never will and, like I say, we were robbed of the chance to look after him to the end, to show him how much we loved him and always would. But all that's gone forever – just like him!'

He squared his shoulders. 'So, we've chosen to side with what you did in not telling Mother, because it was all too late by then. But as to forgiving and forgetting how Dad lied and deceived us, sending us away hating him, sick with pain and disgust at what he had done to us . . . to Mum, not knowing how ill he was, that it was only a year or two before he would be gone . . .' The big man was crying now, unashamedly.

As he turned to leave, Leonard asked, 'Have you seen Susie?'

Thomas shook his head. 'She's not back from the fashion show in Paris.'

'And Ronnie?'

'I don't know where he is – off gallivanting somewhere, I expect, as usual. You never know with him, but he'll turn up. He always does.'

'I worry about him,' Leonard admitted. 'He seems to have no purpose in life.'

Thomas gave a wry little smile. 'There you go,' he said. 'What Dad did has affected us all in different ways. I don't sleep well and I'm riddled with guilt at the terrible things I said to my father; Susie throws herself heart and soul into building the business, so she can't remember how it was, and Ronnie . . . !' He rolled his eyes to the ceiling. 'Poor old Ron is so mixed up, I wouldn't know where to start unravelling him!'

Leonard bade him goodnight. 'Think about what I said,' he pleaded. 'Talk with the others. See if you can bring them, and yourself . . . some kind of peace.'

'Goodnight, Leonard. I'll get the ball rolling on that combiner,' Tom sighed. As far as he was concerned, there was nothing for him to talk about with the others.

And so the two men parted company, firm friends, each hurting in different ways, because of one man, and the bittersweet legacy he had left behind.

CHAPTER NINETEEN

T HOUGH SHE HAD come up in the world and was now Bridget's right-hand woman in business, Amy's modest home on Penny Lane reflected her true personality.

Bright and cheerful, with the firegrate burning merrily on a winter's night and filled with flowers in the summertime, the house was a cosy little place. There were pretty pictures hanging on the wall, chubby armchairs and flowery curtains, and a rag rug all colours of the rainbow set in front of the hearth. A gleaming coal-scuttle sat next to a companion set of tongs, poker and a little brush to sweep the fireplace free of ash.

When on this drizzly February morning, Bridget rapped on the door and walked in, it was as if she had strayed into the most glorious summer's day. The warm colours and smell of new-made bread filled her senses. 'Amy? Are you there?' she called.

Following her nose through to the kitchen, she found Amy in her cosy old candlewick dressing-gown holding a toasting-fork to the range fire.

'Would you like some toast?' Amy asked, removing the slice and dropping it on a plate.

Bridget shook her head, then she licked her lips. 'Oh, go on then. Just the one piece.'

Cutting another chunky slice off the loaf, Amy placed that on the fork and held it up to the flames. 'You can make a pot of tea while you're waiting,' she told Bridget. 'And don't make it too strong . . . remember, it's two level spoons of tea-leaves to the pot.'

Bridget pointed to the loaf. 'The smell hit me as soon as I came in,' she said happily. 'That can't be above a few hours old.'

Amy chuckled. 'You're right! Madge next door used to be a baker. Since she gave up work a few weeks back, she bakes every day . . . scones, muffins, bread and cakes of all kind. She gives the stuff away to anybody who wants it; the baker ran out on his rounds a few weeks back, so he bought half a dozen barm-cakes from Madge. Folks liked them so much, the baker and Madge came to an agreement, so now she's baking, and earning as well.'

When the tea was made and four slices of toast cooked to perfection, they sat down to enjoy it. 'What do you want anyway?' Spreading her butter over the toast, Amy licked her fingers when it leaked through the bread and melted all over her plate. She dug into the pot of Gale's runny honey and drizzled it over the butter.

'Well now!' Bridget had taken a bite of her toast and little bits of bread flew out of her mouth as she spoke. 'Sure, that's a nice way to welcome an old friend, I must say.'

Amy chided her. 'Don't talk with your mouth full.' She took a sip of her tea. 'I can't believe it!' she cried. 'You've actually made a decent pot of tea.'

'Of course, and why wouldn't I?'

'You still haven't answered my question.'

Selecting a cheese triangle from the round cardboard box on the table, Bridget spread it on her toast and with a sigh of satisfaction, took another huge bite of her bread. 'Mmm – delicious. What question was that, then?'

Amy groaned. 'You're a mucky heathen, aren't you? Just look at you . . . spitting bread all over the place and butter running down your chin. You're worse than a bairn. I'm thinking I should have got you a bib!'

Bridget snorted. 'Away with ye! I'm really enjoying this. You tell Madge from me, she bakes the best bread I've ever tasted.' She looked at Amy with a frown. 'What's the matter now?'

'There's nothing at all the matter with *me*. All I want to know is, why are you here? It's Saturday, my day off, and you're supposed to be going to the races with your precious Oliver. So, what's gone wrong this time? Fallen out again, have you?'

Bridget rolled her eyes to the ceiling. 'Sure the man will never learn! I don't mind having it off in the back of a cramped car, and I don't even mind rolling about in the long grass with the ants biting my arse. But I told him, I draw the line at being fondled when there's a thousand eyes all looking at us, instead of watching the horses.'

She tutted. 'I might not be the world's most dignified person, but I have not made, and never will make, a spectacle of meself!'

Amy tried hard not to giggle but the laughter broke through and she was obliged to apologise. 'Are you telling me he tried it on at the races, in front of everyone?'

'Bold as ye like, so he was!'

'And you walked out on him?'

'I did, yes.'

'And that's why you're here?'

'It is.'

'So, what do you expect *me* to do about it?'

'I expect you to finish your breakfast and we'll go shopping.' Bridget glanced at the mantelpiece clock. 'You'll have to be quick or the shops will be shut. It's already half past twelve, and you just out of bed, you lazy article!'

They wolfed down their toast and tea, then Bridget put the guard round the fire, and washed the crockery in the sink while Amy went away upstairs to get ready.

An hour later, the two women got off the bus in the centre of Liverpool, with an appetite to shop and purses at the ready.

Two hours after that, weary and spent out, they made their way to Kenyon's, a delightful café which served hot pies, toasted muffins, and lots of other tasty snacks.

'Jaysus, Mary and Joseph!' Dropping her shopping-bags to the floor, Bridget fell into a seat. 'I'm that parched, my tongue is stuck to the roof of me mouth.'

'I don't see how it can be stuck,' Amy quipped. 'It hasn't stopped you from grumbling, has it? You moaned and groaned all the way through town, and you're still at it now.'

Bridget wagged a finger. 'Don't you get clever with me, my girl,' she chided. 'Just be a darlin', why don't ye, and fetch that lazy idle waitress over here . . . Will ye look at what she's up to, the dirty wee devil!'

She drew Amy's attention to the girl behind the counter. 'Filing her nails, so she is . . . and all the food lying uncovered.'

While Bridget ranted on about health and hygiene and 'bone-idle eejits who've forgotten what it's like to do a day's honest work', Amy went to order. 'A pot of tea for two, if you please, nice and hot?' she said politely.

'Do you want anything to eat?' The girl carried on doing her nails. 'We've some teacakes just in, nice and fresh they are.' Having filed her nail sharp enough, she then blew away the residue.

'HEY!' Bridget's voice sailed across the room. 'Don't fetch me none of them iced buns!' she told Amy. 'Sure, the dirty little bugger's just covered them with nail filings.'

The girl looked up, her face contorted in a frown. 'What's she say?'

Preferring a peaceful life, Amy didn't want to get involved, so she smiled sweetly and explained, 'She said she'd love one of your nice fresh teacakes. Me too, if you don't mind.'

The girl put her file in her pocket. 'A pot of tea for two, two teacakes – with butter and jam?'

Amy had visions of the jam clotted with nail-filings. 'No, thank you. Just plain teacakes, and we'll put our own butter on if that's all right.' She intended to examine the butter before it got spread over the teacakes, just in case the girl had been plucking her eyebrows in the kitchen.

When they arrived, the teacakes were fresh as the girl promised, the tea was piping hot, and the butter was clear right through. 'Thank you, that all looks very nice,' Amy told her.

Bridget glared at her, and said nothing.

'That one's a miserable git,' the waitress told her young assistant, scratching her bottom as she spoke. 'What d'you reckon . . . she's lost a pound and found a penny?'

The other girl shook her head. 'Don't know, I'm sure.' Her eyes shifted to the iced buns, all covered in nail filings, and she made a mental note never to eat anything here that wasn't covered or fresh in.

The café soon began to fill up. 'There must be a train just in,' Amy remarked as the customers entered carrying suit-cases and bags, and rolled-up newspapers under their arms.

Two loud, painted dolls who couldn't stop giggling placed their order. 'Two coffees and two o' them iced buns, and be quick about it, 'cause we've a train to catch,' said the taller of the two.

'Pink icing or white?' The waitress had taken an instant dislike to this arrogant pair.

'Pink . . . no, white. No, hang on!' She called to her friend who had sat herself at the table. 'Joyce, what'll you have – pink or white icing?'

'One of each, Sandra, and have you told 'em we've a train to catch?'

'I've told 'em, but they don't seem to be shifting themselves.' Turning to the assistant who was making the tea, the girl snapped, 'Are you deaf or what? I told you we were in a hurry. Get a move on, will you?'

'We're going as fast as we can!' The waitress was losing her temper now.

'Pair of bloody slowcoaches, that's what you are.' Turning to her friend, the one called Sandra sniffed, 'I could bake the cakes and a tray of loaves as well, in the time it's taking this lot to serve us!'

When the assistant saw how her boss was ready to explode, she stepped forward and, placing a large teapot and two cups on a tray on the counter, she reached into the cake section and took out one pink and one white iced bun. 'There you go,' she said. 'That'll be ninepence for the two teas. The iced buns are on the house.'

The girl thought she'd won the day. 'That's more like it,' she declared, fishing ninepence out of her purse and dropping it onto the counter. 'Took your time though, didn't you?'

Taking a huge bite out of the pink iced bun, she put it back on the tray, and carried the whole lot over to where her friend Joyce was sitting. 'You have to put them in their place straight off,' she told her loudly. 'Else the buggers'll walk all over you.'

Behind the counter, the waitress was threatening to take the cost of the buns out of her assistant's wages. 'What on earth did you go and do a thing like that for?' she asked crossly. 'I was just about ready to throw that pair out onto the street.'

'Ah, you don't want to go doing that,' came the sly answer. 'Look how much they're enjoying their buns.' She watched them licking the icing off the buns before greedily wolfing them down. It did her heart good to see it; especially when she had chosen the ones that were positively littered with nail filings.

A few minutes later, the two girls left after swigging down their tea. As they rushed out, a tall, well-built man in his forties stepped aside to let them by. *It was Barney's younger son, Ronnie, looking well and more confident than he had done in a very long time.*

He didn't speak. Instead he merely nodded to the girls as they looked him up and down; a good-looking man was always an attraction to these two, never mind if he was older than themselves.

Having arrived in Liverpool a few weeks back, Ronnie had trudged the streets daily, hoping he might see his mother walking about, or in a shop, or even getting on a bus. So far, he had seen neither hide nor hair of her. But he wasn't about to give up just yet. He had come here with the intention of finding her, and find her he would. And it didn't matter to him how long it took, or whether she would not be too pleased at him coming all this way. None of that mattered. He just needed to know that she was all right. He felt he had treated her badly, but he still believed his father had done wrong in not letting them take care of him in his final illness.

He went straight to the counter. 'I'll have a coffee, please, black and strong,' he said. 'Oh, and could I get a doughnut?'

The waitress served him quickly and when he sauntered over to a table, she ran to the back of the shop where the assistant waitress was washing up. 'There's a Yank come in,' she said, all big-eyed and wondrous. 'Well, he sounded like one of them GIs, but now I come to think, it was a funny kind of accent.'

'Maybe he's Canadian,' the other girl ventured. 'They do sound a lot like each other.'

Having witnessed his entrance and heard him speak, Amy and Bridget had also noticed his accent. 'It doesn't sound like he was born in America,' Amy said, 'but he must have lived there a long time.'

Like the others, she couldn't take her eyes off him, and just then, as though he could sense her looking at him, he turned and smiled pleasantly at her and her heart flipped over. 'Oh dear!' She felt flustered. 'He saw me looking.'

Bridget had never seen Amy blush as bright red as she did now and she said so. 'Fancy him, do you?' she teased. 'Well now, I can't say I blame you. He's a fine-looking fella, so he is. D'you know, darlin', if he wasn't from overseas, I'd say I'd seen him somewhere before. Oh well – I'm getting daft in me old age. Look, why don't you go and ask him to sit over here with us?' There was a twinkle of mischief in her eyes. 'I'm sure he'd jump at the chance.'

In terror of what the Irishwoman would do next, Amy collected her shopping together. 'It's time we left,' she said firmly. 'We've been out too long already.'

'Hey now! Hold your horses.' Bridget picked up her cup and took a sip of her tea, which by now was stone cold. 'Sure I haven't finished my tea yet.'

Taking off his overcoat, Ronnie draped it over the back of the chair. Drinking his coffee in one go, he went up for another. He was in no hurry to leave. He needed to think, to decide what to do. He had borrowed money in Boston and sold what few possessions he had, in order to pay his passage out here, and now there were only a few pounds left. So what he had must be made to last.

On his way back with his coffee, he tripped over Amy's shopping bag, horrified when his coffee spilled all down her coat, 'Aw, gee, I'm sorry!' Grabbing a serviette, he began frantically dabbing at the stain. 'It doesn't look good.'

'It's all right.' Amy gently pushed him off. 'It'll come out at the cleaners – things usually do. And besides, it was my fault. I left my shopping bags right across your path. It's me that should be sorry.'

'No, no!' He wouldn't hear of it, and besides he liked the look of this darling woman, who made little fuss about what to him was a terrible accident that might well cost her a new coat. 'Let me make amends. I'll buy you a coffee, will that do?' He crossed his fingers in front of her. 'And I promise, I won't throw it all over you.'

'No, it's all right, honestly.' In all her life she had never taken to any man the way she had taken to him. It was as though she had known him all her life. It was the eyes, she thought; warm and smiling they were, though he looked kind of sad, as if he had been through some awful trauma.

'Well, if you won't let me buy you coffee today, how about I buy you one Monday? I'll see you here, same time?'

Smiling reassuringly, Amy graciously refused. 'I don't think so, but thank you all the same.' She so much wanted to accept his invitation, but she was unsure. She didn't know him. She didn't know anything about him.

'I understand,' he said, and as the two women were about to leave, he asked, 'You wouldn't know a clean, reasonable place where I could board for a while, would you? Only I'm not long in from the States, and the place I've been staying at is far too expensive. You see, I'll be in Liverpool for some time yet, so I'm thinking, a more modest lodging would suit me better, and perhaps even the chance to do some honest work.'

Bridget interrupted. 'What kind of work?'

'Farmwork would be ideal,' he answered. 'It's what I do best, but I'll turn my hand to anything if needs be.'

Bridget had an idea. 'I'll keep it in mind,' she promised.

'If anything comes up, I'll leave a note with the girl at the counter; providing you ask her whenever you come in.'

'Oh, I will!' Any chance of earning an honest dollar was fine by Ronnie. 'That's very good of you, thank you.'

'I'm not promising anything, mind.'

Meanwhile, Amy had been searching her brain as to where he could stay that would not cripple him financially.

'There's a small, family-run place along Preston New Road,' she told him now. 'It's nothing fancy, but it's clean and reasonable, and they do a great breakfast. There's a sign up: *Belmont's Boarding House.*'

'That sounds just the ticket.' He smiled cheekily. 'And now do I get to know your name? After all, I did spill hot coffee all over you, and ruined your coat into the bargain.'

Not for the first time that day, Amy blushed hotly. 'You didn't ruin my coat,' she protested. 'It really will be fine.' Though she wasn't altogether certain. She smiled shyly. 'Got to go now.'

Ronnie was disappointed. 'Goodbye, ladies – my name is Ronnie, by the way.'

'Mine's Amy,' she answered softly. 'And this is Bridget.'

'How do you do, Bridget and Amy.' As Amy turned to leave, he bent his head to look her in the face; whichever way she turned she could not escape his smiling, searching eyes – nor did she want to. 'Will I see you again then?' he asked hopefully. 'Monday – here, same time?'

Amy hesitated. Oh, she did so want to see him again. But she felt awkward; if she was on her own with him, she wouldn't know what to say, so she chose to refuse. 'Sorry, I can't,' she lied. 'But I hope you get on all right with the lodgings.'

Outside, Amy glanced back into Kenyon's, to see Ronnie looking at her, the disappointment written on his face. She shrugged her shoulders by way of an apology, and when he smiled sadly, she felt a rush of regret. She had not meant to make him sad, for she had already sensed his loneliness.

'Don't you like him?' Bridget demanded.

'Well, yes I do, but –'

'You're a fool, so ye are!' Bridget had seen the magic between Amy and Ron, and she spoke her mind. 'When two people, strangers, spark it off like you two did in there, it is something very special and precious. It only happens once in a lifetime, and you just threw it away, like it was nothing. Tell me, what harm would it have done to see him again? A chat over a cup of tea in a public place! He's hardly likely to murder you in front of that nosy pair of articles, is he now?'

'No. Don't suppose so.' The very same thoughts had been running through Amy's mind.

'So what in God's name are you afraid of?'

'It isn't that I'm afraid,' Amy assured her, 'it's just that, well, you know how tongue-tied I get with strange men. I wouldn't know what to say. I might open my mouth and he'd run out of the door as if his pants were on fire.'

'He didn't run just now.'

'Forget it, Bridget. I'm just not easy around men. I never have been.'

'Ah, sure, that's only because ye don't give yourself time to get to know them.'

They walked on for a while, when suddenly Bridget gave a shout. 'Jaysus! Now look what you've made me do!' she exclaimed. 'I was so enchanted with the pair of youse, I've left my purse on the table, so I have.'

Amy was horrified. 'Wait here. I'll run back and get it for you.'

'No. You watch the shopping bags. It won't take me but a minute or two.'

When Bridget came in the door, Ronnie was just leaving. 'Hello again.' Looking over her shoulder he searched the street for Amy.

'She's not with me,' Bridget explained. 'Look, I'll have to

be quick. I came back to tell you something.' Seeing the two waitresses stretching their necks, she kept her voice to a whisper. 'It's about Amy.'

'What about her?'

'She'll see you, like you said – Monday afternoon, same time.'

His face beamed with delight. 'Is that so?'

'Yes, but not here. There's a tearooms on the corner of George Street. That's where she'll be.'

She made a quick exit, with some parting advice. 'Be gentle with her. She's always been a bit on the shy side where men are concerned.'

'She'll be safe enough with me. Oh, and thank you . . .' He only now realised that he had been so intent on discovering Amy's name, he had completely forgotten that of her companion.

'Bridget,' she prompted, not at all offended, but secretly amused.

'Well, thank you, Bridget.'

Making her way back to Amy, who was sitting on a shop wall, Bridget suddenly remembered. Fumbling about in her coat pocket, she took out her purse and holding it up, feigned a gasp of relief. 'Got it!' she cried. 'Sure the little divil was right where I left it.'

'Did you see him?' Amy asked.

'I did.'

'And did he mention me?'

'Ah sure, why on earth should he mention you, after you turned him down the way ye did?'

Amy didn't answer. Glancing back, she saw the American leaving the café and was already regretting her hasty decision not to see him again.

As they clambered onto the bus, Bridget said, 'What an eejit I am.'

'What's wrong?'

'The two-piece.'

'What two-piece?'

'The one we saw in Able's window. I meant to go back for it, but I forgot. Never mind, there'll be another time, and when I get to try it on, ye can tell me what you think.'

Amy nodded, not really listening because her mind was back there, with *him*.

'That's settled then.' Bridget congratulated herself. 'We'll pop back on Monday. We'll get the appointments all set up in the morning, and leave instructions with Jackie. Then we'll take a few hours off in the afternoon. Is that all right, Amy? Does that suit you?'

Still not altogether listening, Amy nodded. 'Whatever you say, Bridget,' she answered irritably. 'Whatever you say.'

~

On Monday morning, Bridget had everything organised in half the time it normally took. 'Right then, Jackie.' She presented the woman with a wad of paperwork. 'It's all in there, everything in order. All you have to do is make sure it all goes as written. Oh, and tell Maureen to wear her business suit for the convention. We can't have her attending a formal function in the low-cut dress she wore last time.' She frowned. 'I put her on a warning, so she should know the score. Make sure anyway . . . check her out. I'm beginning to doubt her judgement of late.'

She had a few more instructions before she left. 'Tell Annie to wear her new dress for tonight's Law Society dinner. It's likely there will be people there who attended the previous one last month, and they might notice if she wears the black one again.'

With everything taken care of, she marched into Amy's office. 'Time to go,' she said.

Amy groaned. 'Can't we go tomorrow or Wednesday? I've all these to take care of yet.' She pointed to the thick leather ledger on her desk. 'There are calls coming in left right and centre, and I'm still only halfway through next week's appointments.'

'Leave it to Jackie. I've just briefed her. She knows what's urgent, and what can be dealt with another day.' Bridget gave her a nudge. 'Come on. Time we were out of here.'

'Oh Bridget, must I?'

Ten minutes later, the two of them were in a taxi, headed for town.

They went straight to Able's shop on the High Street, where Bridget made a show of trying on the two-piece. 'Well, what do you think?' She did a few twirls for Amy's benefit.

'It looks good on you.' Amy thought the dark green fitted jacket and long fussy skirt sat well on her employer's curvaceous figure.

'Can I return it if I change my mind?' Bridget asked the shop-assistant.

'Of course.'

So she bought it. Forty-five bob – not too bad. It was well cut and fully lined. 'Maybe I can buy some shoes to go with it,' she suggested, and she and Amy set off for another tour round the shops.

Keeping an eye on the time, Bridget steered Amy down George Street. When they drew alongside the tearooms, she suddenly developed a thirst. 'Shall we take time out for a cuppa?' she asked.

'All right, but then we'll get your shoes. I need to get back,' Amy fretted. 'I've got piles of work waiting.'

Bridget led the way in. She looked around, but *he* wasn't there.

'Just a cuppa is it, Bridget?' Amy asked.

'Thanks, love – yes, just a cuppa.' She checked her watch.

Five minutes to go. Hurry up, Ron! she thought. I won't be able to fool her for much longer.

Amy had just brought the tea over and they were sitting talking when Bridget saw him come in. 'Well, I never!' Feigning astonishment, she leaped out of her chair and called him over. 'Ron! How lovely to see you again.'

He came over, his eyes glued to Amy. 'Hello again, Amy.'

Amazed that he remembered her name, she nodded. 'Hello,' she said shyly. When he looked at her like that, the hairs on the back of her neck tingled, and she could hardly breathe.

'Is it all right if I sit with you?' He sensed her nervousness and thought it best to take things slowly. He liked her so much, the last thing he wanted was to frighten her off.

'I'll get you a black coffee,' Bridget recalled he was drinking before. 'You sit down.'

At the counter she turned round to see the two of them quietly talking; Amy was obviously nervous, but seeming to warm to his natural and easy manner. 'Oh Amy, me darlin' . . . I do hope he's the one,' she murmured.

It would do her old heart good, to see Amy settled with someone who would look after her and love her the way she deserved to be loved.

Placing the coffee cup on the table, she looked out of the window and exclaimed, 'Good grief! Look there, it's Robert Clark. I've been trying to get hold of him for ages.' Apologising, she told Amy and Ronnie, 'I'll have to go. Sure, I don't want to lose sight of him.'

When Amy started to get up, Bridget pushed her down. 'No! You stay me darlin'. I'll have a quick word with Robert, then I'll get back. Enjoy your drinks, the both of you, there's no rush.'

With that, she hurried away. After hiding round the corner for a few minutes, she sneaked back to peer through the window; delighted to see the two of them still talking, and Amy seeming much easier in his company.

She went away, well pleased with herself. 'Oh Amy, my darlin',' she gave a merry little skip. 'Sure, I've a feeling this is the start of something good.'

~

It was two hours later and growing dark, when Ronnie walked Amy to the nearest taxi-rank. On the way, they heard the street-vendor calling out the headlines in the evening paper: 'Woman fished out of the river . . . police suspect foul play.'

Amy commented, 'Murdered! God, that's awful.'

Ronnie told her not to worry. 'Because from now on, I'll be looking after you . . . that is, if you'll let me?'

'I can look after myself,' Amy answered.

'So you don't need me, is that what you're saying?'

She looked up, a smile of contentment on her face. 'No, that is not what I'm saying. Actually, it would be really nice to have someone who cares about me.' All the same, she cautioned him, 'But we hardly know each other, so let's just take it as it comes, eh?'

'Okay. If that's what you want.'

After a while he felt her hand slide into his, and he was thrilled. His every instinct told him that Amy was the woman he had been waiting for, and suddenly, his life had a purpose.

When they got to the first taxi, the driver was reading the *Echo* by the light of a flickering street-lamp. 'Nasty business,' he said, holding up the newspaper. 'Some poor woman was pushed into the Mersey and drowned. According to this, she had been well and truly battered into the bargain. They don't say exactly, but there's a lunatic out there on the loose, that's for sure.'

Ronnie reprimanded him. 'I'm not sure the lady needs to hear all that,' he said.

'Oh sorry, mate.' Folding the newspaper, the driver turned the key in the ignition. 'Where to, miss?' he asked.

Ron saw Amy safely inside the cab. 'I'd feel much better if you'd let me see you all the way home,' he suggested worriedly.

Amy gave no answer, but when she patted the seat beside her, he lost no time climbing in. Amy gave her home address in Penny Lane, and the taxi set off. 'If you don't mind me saying, I think you're doing the right thing in seeing your lady home,' the driver offered. 'I mean, for all we know, the murderer might be on the lookout for his next victim.'

'That's enough!' Ronnie leaned forward. 'I'll thank you not to alarm the good lady here. Wherever your lunatic is, and whatever he's about to do next, I don't imagine he's likely to ever touch *our* lives, do you?'

'You never know,' came the wry answer. 'You never know.'

~

As it happened, he was right, and Ronnie was wrong.

Because at that very moment, the 'lunatic' who had drowned Patsy Monk was lurking not too far away, more determined than ever to track down and find Lucy Baker.

CHAPTER TWENTY

B Y LATE EVENING, the news of Patsy Monk's murder was being discussed all over Liverpool.

In her home, not too far from where Ronnie and Amy had got into the taxi, Lizzie Monk was like a caged animal, pacing up and down, afraid and distressed. She thought of Edward Trent, but no, he might have a wicked mouth on him, and he didn't like Patsy, but he would never have murdered her.

Calling her to sit down, the Inspector asked more questions: When had Lizzie last seen Patsy? Was there anybody who bore her sister a grudge?

'Think carefully,' he urged. 'We're looking for a vicious killer. Is there anything you can recall about her friends . . . any small, seemingly insignificant thing?'

'No!' Patsy took to pacing the floor again. 'I've already answered all your questions. For God's sake, why don't you leave me alone?'

The Inspector observed how exhausted and distressed she was; he glanced at his young colleague who shook his head, and he decided enough was enough, at least for now.

So far, he had no reason to believe that Lizzie was involved in any way with the tragedy of her sister, Patsy.

'Very well, that should do for now. We'll leave you in

peace,' he told Lizzie. 'But I might have to call in again, so don't go too far away. Meantime, if you can think of anything, anything at all . . .'

'I don't know anything,' she answered wearily. 'I've told you all I know.'

'Would you like a WPC to stay with you for a while?' he asked. 'I can arrange that if needed.'

'No. I'll be all right. I'm better on my own.'

After they were gone, she watched out the window while they climbed into the Black Maria and drove off, the headlights making weird moving circles on the road ahead. 'Good shuts to you!' They wouldn't leave her alone. Why did they keep coming back? It was all too much.

Yanking the curtains together, she went to the cabinet and took out a bottle of whisky and a glass. She poured herself a tot and carried it to the fireplace, her sorry gaze following the leaping flames as they vaporised up the chimney. 'Trent, you bastard! If it was you who hurt her, I swear to God, I'll swing for you!'

Taking a gulp of the spirit, she coughed and cursed and took another sip, which she then spat into the fire – jerking backwards when the alcohol sent the flames into a flurry.

She thought of her sister, floundering in the water, maybe even calling for her, and her heart broke. She took to pacing again, then poured herself another drop of whisky and carefully drank of it; somehow the pain seeming to ease. But not the reality. Somebody had murdered Patsy. Was it somebody she had known and fallen out with? After all, it had to be said, Patsy had a spiteful tongue at times. Who could have killed her? And why?

'Did you do it, Eddie?' She pressed her face through the curtains and looked down at the street. 'Did you kill my sister?'

She took another swig of the drink. 'Where are you? Out with some other poor unsuspecting woman?'

In a wild fit she threw the glass across the room. It smashed into the wall, then lay in shards on the floor, the liquid seeping into the carpet.

Sobbing, poor Lizzie fell into the chair and covered her face with her trembling hands. 'I'm sorry, Patsy,' she cried out. 'God help me, I'm so, so sorry.'

~

The news had spread far and wide; people talked of it in the streets, in their homes huddled round the wireless, and in the pubs across Liverpool. But some people had still not heard about the woman who had been fished out of the river. These included workers on night-shift, who were only now getting out of their beds, the desperately ill, or the drunks who had been womanising since earlier that day. Among the latter group was Edward Trent. After picking a couple of pockets he had a few quid stashed in his wallet and was feeling on top of the world.

'See you another time, sweetie.' He stumbled out of the terraced house, gave the woman inside one last, slobbery kiss and a quick fumble, then made his way along the darkened streets, chuckling and congratulating himself. You've still got it, matey! he thought proudly. Ain't nothing in a skirt can resist *you.*

He came to a sudden halt. Narrowing his bloodshot eyes, he peered at the headlines on the paper-stand:

LOCAL WOMAN FOUND DROWNED.
POLICE CONFIRM MURDERER
STILL AT LARGE.

Horrified, his mind filled with the sequence of events that night. He saw Patsy struggling in the water, pleading for him to help her. He recalled the way he had wrenched the plank from the seat and smashed it into her head in a drunken frenzy of rage.

And he was terrified.

Making straight for Dock Lane, he constantly glanced about, more nervous than he had ever been in his life.

Lizzie saw him coming, that burly familiar figure, swaggering and stumbling as he headed for safety. Taking him by surprise, she flung open the door and lunged at him.

'Did you do it?' she screamed. 'Did you kill her, you bastard?' Sobbing and broken, she clawed at his face until, grabbing her by the wrists, he thrust her backwards into the room.

'Shut your mouth, you stupid cow!' He kicked the door shut. 'Want to get me hanged, do you, yelling that sort of stuff to all and sundry?' Sobered by the reality of it all, he pushed her against the wall. 'You don't really believe I killed her, do you?'

'I don't know what to believe,' she choked. 'The police won't leave me alone.' She gabbled on, 'I told them I don't know anything, but they keep coming back . . .'

He threw her into the chair. 'Stop your whining, woman. Tell me exactly what they said.'

She told him how the Inspector had asked her to report anything she might think of that would help track down the killer. 'You didn't hurt Patsy, did you?' she begged. 'Tell me it wasn't you.'

He turned on the charm. 'Of course I didn't hurt her.' Taking Lizzie into his arms, he rocked her backwards and forwards. 'I didn't like her, you know that much . . .' An awful thought struck him. 'You didn't tell the police that we fought, me and your sister – you didn't tell them that, did you?'

'No.' She hadn't said anything because, whatever he was, she still loved him, God help her. But if he *had* murdered Patsy, then that would be a different tale. 'I don't want to believe it was you,' she confessed tearfully, 'but I know how much you hated her. Eddie, I don't know who or what to believe. My head is pounding so hard, I feel I'm going insane.'

'Ssh.' He kissed the top of her head. 'Like I said, I didn't care much for Patsy, no use pretending I did, but what in God's name makes you think I could do a thing like that to her? Drowning her like you would a diseased rat . . . smashing her head in when she was pleading for help. What kind of a monster would I be if I'd done a terrible thing like that, eh?'

He felt her stiffen in his arms, and knew straight away what he had done. 'Slipped up there, didn't I?' he asked cunningly. 'So, you didn't know that part of it, eh?'

When she tried to loosen herself from his hold, he held on even tighter. 'Silly me!' he laughed. 'Letting my tongue run away with me.'

'YOU!' From somewhere she found the strength to free herself. 'YOU KILLED HER . . . *like that?*'

His words made a picture in her mind, and it drove her crazy. Sorrow became rage; she started battering at him with her fists, screaming at him, wanting to hurt him like he had hurt Patsy.

Like a mad thing he turned on her, hitting out with bunched fists, sending her crashing into furniture, snatching her up and knocking her down again, until bloodied and battered, she lay on the floor, her nose split, her front teeth gone and her eyes swelling out of her head.

He looked down on her and laughed contemptuously. And when the laughter stopped, he issued a grim warning. 'If I find you've opened your trap to the police or anyone else – *ever* – I'll be back to finish you off . . . just like I finished your sister.' He had no pity or compassion. *'Do you hear me?'*

Her hands up as though to protect herself, she moved her head in acknowledgement. Blood trickled out of her mouth.

'Good girl.' He grabbed her purse and emptied it, leaving a few shillings. 'There's enough there to get you right away from here – the sooner the better, if you know what I mean?'

He next went to the kitchen, where he stuffed his face with food before leaving. 'Don't forget what I said, Lizzie girl,' he said chillingly. 'One word, and you know what will happen.'

Fearing for her life, she lay still as he went out the door, remaining that way for what seemed an age; she heard the clock chime the passing hours. Drifting in and out of con-sciousness, she wasn't sure of time or place, or even if she was still alive.

After a time she crawled to the chair and pulled herself up. Going on unsteady legs to the bathroom, she washed and changed and patched herself up the best she could.

Returning to the bedroom, she took the small suitcase out of the wardrobe, packed a few things and left.

She didn't know where she might go, or how she would manage once she got there. All she knew was, if she stayed he would be back. If she talked he would find her and kill her, just as he had killed her sister, Patsy.

And so she left, as silently and quickly as her injuries would allow.

Because just as Patsy predicted, Edward Trent had ruined her life, yet again.

CHAPTER TWENTY-ONE

'CLEAR OFF, YOU filthy devil!' The burly proprietor of a butcher's shop in a little parade a few streets away from Dock Lane, opened his door to find Edward Trent sprawled across the porch and lying in his own vomit. 'Go on, get off with you. I don't want the likes of you on my premises!'

When Trent made no movement, the butcher gave him a vicious prod with the brush-end of his broom. 'Go on, you drunken bugger . . . GERROUT OF 'ERE!'

Opening one eye, Trent rolled over in his vomit and clambered up. 'What the 'ell's wrong with *you?*' His bloodshot eyes met the look of disgust on the other man's face. 'Can't a poor bloke lie his head down for the night, without being poked and prodded awake?'

The big man gave him another shove with his broom. 'Bugger off . . . or you'll feel the sharp end where the sun don't shine.'

'Who the devil d'you think you're talking to, eh?' Trent squared up to retaliate, until he saw the other man's massive, muscular neck. On better days he would not have thought twice about going for the throat, but feeling drained by a night of booze, violence and fornication, he had neither wish nor energy to tangle fists, especially with a man the size of an ox. 'All right, all right! Hold your horses.' He coughed and spat. 'Give me a minute to pull meself together.'

'Pull yourself together somewheres else.' With a mighty shove, the butcher sent him flying backwards, where he fell in a heap on the pavement. 'If I see you round these parts again, it'll be more than a broom-end that comes at you! It'll be a bloody great meat-cleaver!'

Still grumbling and cursing, he went back inside, returning a moment later with a bucket of water, which he slung over the vomit and Trent as well. 'That should wash the stink off you!'

Laughing, he went back inside and slammed the door, leaving Trent hobbling down the street, with water dripping from his every angle.

Heading for a public convenience, he relieved himself and afterwards swilled his hands and face at the sink. He flattened his hair with the palms of his hands, straightened the collar of his shirt and tidied himself up for his next port of call. 'It's your long-lost lover-boy, Lucy darlin',' he crooned to himself in the mirror. 'Up to now I ain't been able to pin you down, but I will, my pretty. Come rain or shine, I'll not give up till I find you.'

Trent had made a trip out to Overhill Farm the day before, to check out the lie of the land. It had been a blow to hear from the village tobacconist that Lucy had moved south many years ago; the man who sold him his packet of baccy seemed to imply there'd been some scandal, but Trent couldn't take it in. One of his headaches was starting up, and the proximity of the river where his son had drowned made a rushing noise go through his head, like the sound of the water on that terrible night. He had had to leave the shop in a hurry.

Maybe Lucy had come back, he thought. Back to Liverpool where she belonged. But where would she go? The thought struck him like a flash of lightning. *To the Irish-woman's house, that's where.*

His next stop was Bridget's old house, the brothel at 23, Viaduct Street.

He banged on the door, until a young girl emerged.

'Can I help you?' she asked politely.

'I want to speak with Bridget,' he growled. 'Tell her I'm looking to find an old friend, and I reckon she's the one to help me.'

Frowning, the girl began to close the door. 'No one called Bridget lives here.'

Trent thrust his foot forward and jammed the door. 'I don't believe you.' He bent his head to her. 'You'd best go and get her,' he threatened. ''Cause if you don't, I might just force my way in. So you'd best shift yerself and do what I say.'

Growing afraid, the girl continued to argue. 'I told you there's no one here of that name. Now please go away!' Again she tried to close the door and again he stopped her, until she called out for help. 'Daddy!' Her voice sailed through the house. 'Dad, it's a man and he won't go away.'

On hearing heavy footsteps come down the stairs, Trent decided to leg it. The man might report him to the police and have him arrested – and then who knew what might happen.

Snatching the girl by the lapels, he told her gruffly, 'If I find out you've been lying to me, I swear I'll be back to punish you.' Although from her demeanour he had a sneaking suspicion she might be telling the truth and if so, that was a real setback in his search for Lucy.

As he ran away, he could hear the girl sobbing, then the man shouting as he ran in full pursuit, 'HEY YOU! COME BACK HERE!'

At the bottom of the street, Trent turned to see the man

gaining ground, so he darted into the ironmonger's and when he saw his pursuer run past the shop, he made a cautious exit, afterwards cutting down an alley and getting away, out of sight.

A short time later, having retreated to a public house in search of ale, he was seated by the window downing pint after pint. 'I'll find her, you see if I don't!' he told anyone who would listen. 'She'll not get away from me this time.'

Bleary-eyed and incoherent, with no one taking any notice of his ramblings, he took to gazing out the window. *And that was when he saw her walk by, a tall woman with a bold step and a pretty face. A woman who stirred a memory deep down inside him.*

She was older than he remembered, but there was something about her – the walk, the profile – something that he recognised from years gone by.

Then it came to him: she bore a distinct resemblance to Vicky Davidson, the wife of Barney and a dear friend to Lucy. He had been told in the village that Vicky and her family had left England and emigrated to America – so what could she be doing here?

Growing excited, he followed the woman, becoming more and more convinced that she was Vicky Davidson.

Unaware that she was being watched, Vicky went into the estate agent's office down the road and seated herself on a chair set before a desk. 'Is it all ready?' she asked the young man seated opposite.

He greeted her with a smile. 'It's all done,' he informed her. 'The house is yours, for twelve hundred pounds.' He handed her the key, together with an envelope. 'Congratulations, Mrs Maitland.'

With his hands in his pockets, and his cap pulled down well over his eyes, Edward Trent strolled into the shop and meandered about as though he was in no particular hurry, examining the For Sale details pinned up on the wall. And when the young man promised to be with him shortly, he merely nodded and looked away, and no one was any the wiser about his true intentions, though he had been slightly thrown to hear the woman being addressed as Mrs Maitland.

'You're the first person I've ever had who's come in to buy back a house they lived in many years ago,' the young man was saying to Vicky. 'You must have loved it very much.'

'Oh we did.' Vicky cast her mind back over the years to those happy days in the little farmhouse, when her three bairns were born, and her beloved Barney had been with her. They had not had a care in the world. Paradise lost, indeed.

None of this felt real to her. It was as though she had stepped back into a time that was so long gone, it might never have existed. And yet it had, for it was stored right there – in her heart, her mind and in her soul. Secure in her deepest memories.

From that first moment when she had returned to this part of her world, she instinctively felt as though she belonged. The poor, war-damaged streets of Liverpool had welcomed her like an old friend. Despite the passage of the years, its character had not changed all that much, and even the very air smelled the same – thick and salty from the Mersey, alive with the essence of people and life. This was her world, this had been the true magic in her life; Liverpool, Overhill Farm, and her precious family.

'How long did you live at the farmhouse?' The young man sensed how she had slipped into her memories and he was intrigued.

Vicky smiled apologetically. 'Sorry, I was miles away. It seems a lifetime ago that we lived there,' she answered. 'My husband Barney and I had our three children in that same house. We lived in it, worked the land around it and were very content.' She said wistfully, 'In fact, the years in that lovely place were the happiest of my entire life.'

'And now you're moving back in?'

Taking the envelope, she stood up. 'That's the idea, yes.'

'With your husband, Barney?'

Deeply moved, she merely shook her head, then said quietly, 'I really must be going now.'

'You do know the house needs a deal of work?' The young agent wanted to sound businesslike.

'Yes, I'm aware of that,' she answered confidently. 'I've already arranged for a builder to renovate some of the original features that have fallen into disrepair, and I've spoken with a decorator and such. I'm assured they can complete the work within a month. Meantime, I intend to stay at the hotel, though very soon, I shall be going down south for at least a week, as the daughter of my old friend Lucy is getting married.'

'Something else to look forward to then?'

'It certainly is. We go back a lot of years, me and Lucy Baker.' She held out her hand to him. 'Thank you so much for all your hard work.'

Before she left, Edward Trent sneaked out of the shop, moving quickly to where he could easily follow her while she could not see him. So! His eyes darkened. Lucy had a daughter, did she? Didn't take her long to get over the death of their own bairn, did it, before she was opening her legs to some other man!

A wedding? He spat on the ground. 'We shall have to see about that, won't we?'

He followed Vicky out of the town centre and on towards the boulevard, where she appeared to be heading for a bus. Suddenly, taking him by surprise, she hailed a passing taxi and was quickly driven away.

'Damn and bugger it!' Trent cursed. Quickly, he made his way back to the estate agent.

The young man was busy with some paperwork when

Trent entered. He looked up and recognised the unsavoury character who'd been hanging around before. His heart sank; he had a bad feeling about this one. 'How can I help?' he asked politely.

Trent lost no time. 'The woman who was in here just now, the one who bought back her old house. Which hotel is she staying in?'

'I beg your pardon?' The young man's initial suspicion strengthened. 'I'm afraid I can't give out confidential information.' Snatching up Vicky's case-file, he slipped it into the filing cabinet and locked it, placing the key into the top drawer of his desk. 'Now, if you have no other business, I'd very much like to get on with my work.' He gestured to his overcrowded desk.

For a moment the two men eyed each other, until Trent wisely decided to leave. However, he had a plan, which he fully intended carrying out soonever the coast was clear.

Later that evening, after forcing an easy entry from the back of the shop, he went straight for the desk drawer, took out the key and opened the cabinet. Skimming through the file, he found everything he needed to know.

Carefully he replaced the file, returned the key to the drawer, and left the shop the same way he had arrived, leaving everything as he found it. After all, the last thing he wanted was for the police to be alerted; particularly since they were still actively searching for the 'monster' who had murdered Patsy Monk. Trent wished now that he'd finished off that stupid bitch Lizzie, too. She'd better keep her trap shut or he'd be along to shut it for her . . .

A wave of giddiness swept over him and he clung to the doorframe for a long moment. Then it passed. Making good his escape, he smiled to himself. 'Handy place, prison,' he chuckled. 'Full of men who know every trick of the trade.'

Not too far away, seated in his car outside Vicky's hotel,

the American private detective was still keeping watch over her.

Taking the opportunity to fill out his surveillance notes for Leonard Maitland, he wrote down his report, at the same time deciding to send a cable to warn him about the other man who watched her.

Your wife paid a further visit to the land agent that I mentioned in my recent despatch. I'm not certain as to what transpired there, but as you know from my previous reports, she had paid numerous visits to a farmhouse at Comberton-by-Weir, both in the presence of the agent and on her own. She also consulted builders and other tradesmen, who consequently joined her on her visits to the house.

Most days she either goes out to the farmhouse or walks the shops in Liverpool; some days she stands by the docks, just watching. She then makes her way back to the hotel, where she remains until emerging the next day, sometimes early, sometimes later, but always on her own.

Before ending this report, I think I should draw your attention to the fact that today, a certain rough-looking man showed a decidedly unhealthy interest in Mrs Maitland. He appeared to follow her to the agent's office, and afterwards he trailed her to the boulevard where she took a taxi back to the hotel.

Would you like me to find out more about this man, should he show his face again? I am sending you a cable that will arrive before this letter, and will await your instructions.

Meantime, rest assured I will be diligent in my discreet observation of your good wife.

There! This report would be on its way to his client in no time at all. And if he wasn't very much mistaken, Mr Maitland would want him to watch that ruffian. Calling up Edward Trent's image, the detective shook his head woefully. 'The guy was up to no good – that much was obvious.'

~

When the cable was delivered to Leonard's office, he tore it open, fearing the worst.

'Are you ready for coffee now, Mr Maitland?' Marybelle, his typist, inched open his office door, visibly surprised when Leonard dismissed her instantly. 'Leave me be, girl!' he snapped. 'I'll let you know when I'm ready to be disturbed!'

Po-faced, the girl returned to her desk outside his office. 'Whatever's wrong with him? He's real grumpy this morning,' she told the woman at the other typewriter.

The woman looked up knowingly. 'Did the mailman bring him a letter from England?'

'No, but he got a cable. Why?'

'That's the reason why he is so touchy, then. I don't know anything about the cable, but he has the letters regularly, as you'd know if you'd been here longer. When he reads them he likes to be alone, with no interruption.'

'Who are they from?' the junior asked curiously.

'If I knew that, I might tell you.'

'Is it to do with his wife, only I heard someone saying how she'd gone off to England and nobody knew if she was ever coming back.'

'If you want to keep your job, honey, you'd best shut your ears to idle gossip.'

'Hmh!' The girl shrugged impatiently. 'I only asked.'

'And I'm only saying, the least you know the better.'

A short time later Leonard rushed out of his office. 'I won't be back today,' he told the woman. 'Call the house tonight if there are any urgent matters to be dealt with.

Meantime, inform Taylor Crompton that the price of grain remains the same; and that if he wants a delivery, he pays top dollar for top-class harvest. If he dithers, call Bambridge and offer it to him. At least he's a regular customer who knows a good crop when he sees it.'

The woman saw how flushed he was, and her concern was genuine. 'Are you feeling okay, sir?'

'No, I'm not.' He took a deep, invigorating breath. 'I have just received a cable that might mean me going to England. I have urgent calls to make, which will be best served in the privacy of my home.'

He issued a few more instructions before enquiring where his son Thomas might be at that moment in time.

'I believe he went to the Southlands,' the stenographer said. 'There seems to be a problem there.'

'Contact him, will you,' he said. 'Get him to come out to the house straight away. Tell him it's urgent!' With that he made a hasty departure.

'The poor guy looks flustered.' Marybelle was intrigued. 'Do you think the cable carried bad news?'

The older woman pointed to the girl's ledger. 'You just get on with the orders, young lady, and leave Mr Maitland's business to Mr Maitland.' She got out of her seat. 'I'll be a few minutes,' she advised. 'I need to catch Jim. He's taking out a few samples of that new seed for Thomas to look at. If I hurry, I might just catch him before he leaves.'

As it happened, she did catch him in time. 'You're to ask Thomas to make his way immediately to the house,' she informed him. 'His pa needs to see him straight away. It's very urgent.'

Jim told her he would deliver the message, and he did.

~

'What's it about?' Deep inside the workings of a massive truck, sleeves rolled up and covered in oil, Thomas was none too pleased to be summoned away. 'I'm in the middle of trying to get this darned machine to work. It cost the company an arm and a leg, and now it's given up the ghost for the third time. I've got a man from the manufacturer on the way, so I can't leave right now.'

'I'm only passing on a message,' Jim protested. 'The boss wants you up at the house and it's urgent. That's all I know.'

Thomas gave a long, weary sigh. 'Jacob!' Calling his right-hand man over, he said, 'It looks like I'll have to leave this to you. When the engineer comes, don't let him swan off without taking a proper look, and don't let him sweet-talk you, either. Like I said, this machine is a rogue. No ifs or buts, Jake. They're to take it back today if possible or tomorrow at the latest, and supply us with a full refund. I want it replaced with one that actually works.'

'They won't agree to a full refund,' Jacob argued. 'You know how tough they are.'

'Not half as tough as I can be! If they won't cooperate, you can tell him from me, their name will stink throughout the farming community, and their business will fall through the floor overnight. Okay?'

Jacob grinned. 'Okay, boss. You got it!'

Wiping away as much of the grease and muck as he could, Thomas leaped onto his motorbike and was away across the fields like the wind. 'He'll never get this machine replaced, not with a full refund!' one of the men exclaimed. 'Not when he already squeezed them down to their knees on the price.'

'Oh, they'll replace it all right, *and* with a full refund.' Jacob was confident. 'They know when he says he'll make their name stink, that's exactly what he'll do.'

'What d'yer reckon the old man wants?'

'Search me.' Like his workmate, he glanced towards

Thomas's speeding vehicle. 'There seems to be some sort of panic on, that's for sure.'

~

Kicking his boots off at the door, Thomas found his step-father in the drawing room, pacing back and forth like a caged lion. 'What's wrong? What's the urgency?' he asked.

Leonard looked at him for a brief moment, at this big, hardworking man who had grown to be like his own son. 'We need to talk,' he said quietly. 'It's about your mother.'

Thomas stepped forward. 'What about her?'

His face drained of colour. 'Has something happened? She's not hurt, is she?'

Leonard shook his head. 'No, no, son. She's not hurt.' He paused before adding, 'At least, I hope not.'

'What's that supposed to mean?' Thomas stared at him. 'I think you'd best explain. Why am I here? What is it that you so desperately needed to tell me, that you had to drag me away from my work?'

Leonard took a deep breath. 'As you know, your mother went to England, to your father's –'

'I know why she went,' Thomas interrupted, 'and I think there have been enough discussions on that particular issue. I happen to believe Dad was wrong not to tell us how ill he was.'

'I understand,' Leonard answered quietly. 'I know how you feel, and I have to respect that.'

'No, you *don't* know how I feel ... how we *all* feel! We should have seen him through what must have been the worst, loneliest time of his life, and he sent us away. Did he think we were so selfish that we'd resent having to stay by his side and help him? Did he really think we weren't strong enough to cope with it all?'

His voice began to shake with emotion. 'No, Leonard! We all believe he should have given us the choice of leaving or staying. He took that choice away, and we can't forgive him for it. Mother doesn't agree – she never will. So, if she prefers to be with him now, when it's too late and there is nothing we can do, then so be it. That's her choice.'

'Listen to me!' Squaring himself, Leonard stopped Thomas in full, vehement flow. 'Your mother is hurting too. Look, I felt the same, all those years ago. I tried hard to persuade your father that he was doing wrong in sending you all away. But now I think I understand, and maybe I was wrong in condemning his actions. I can't imagine how he must have felt, watching his entire family sail away from him, after he had put himself through what must have been torment . . . drinking himself stupid, fighting and cavorting with street-women, all to make you think he was not worth the saving. When all the while, he was so desperately ill. He did that, yes, and there are those who will always blame him for it.'

He had never lost the image of Barney curled up under the tree, a sorry, broken man. 'In all honesty, could any one of us do what he did? Could we torture ourselves like he did, and all for the ones we love? Look, Tom, maybe it isn't for us to judge his actions, brave or foolish though they might have been. What he did, he did for you – *all* of you. And for the rest of your life, you must never forget that!'

Thomas was taken aback. 'But you sided with us! You said we should try to forget, and carry on with our lives. You did your best to stop Mother returning to England. You said there was nothing to be gained from it, that it would only cause more pain.'

'You're right, I did,' Leonard admitted. 'But only because I didn't want her hurt any more. But now, I'm afraid I may have lost your mother forever, and all because I promised

Barney that I would never tell her the truth. I kept my word, but she found out anyway, through Lucy. Now your mother has turned away from me, Thomas. All I hope is that she can find it in her heart to forgive me, the same way I hope you, your brother, and Susie can find it in your heart to forgive your father.'

'Never!' Thomas was adamant.

'Don't say that,' Leonard implored him. 'We can't change the way things were, all those years ago. We did what we thought was for the best; maybe it was, maybe it wasn't. And maybe we will never know.'

He paused. 'There's something else you need to know,' he revealed. 'I've booked a flight to London. I must go to your mother straight away. I'm afraid she might be in danger.'

Thomas was visibly startled. 'What do you mean, in danger?'

Leonard explained. 'Do you recall how we told you of a man by the name of Edward Trent, the same man who came to Lucy's cottage at Overhill Farm and caused the death of little Jamie?'

'Yes, but didn't Edward Trent disappear without trace? Wasn't it rumoured that he'd been hanged for some other crime?' Tom well remembered little Jamie; he and the others had loved playing with the little lad. He had been like a part of their own family, and dark days had followed his death by drowning.

'Nobody ever knew for sure. But now, there appears to be some ruffian following your mother when she goes about her business. From the description, I suspect it might be him.'

Thomas was surprised. 'How do you know all this?'

'Your mother is hurting badly, Thomas. I've been so worried about her that I hired a private detective to keep a watchful eye on her. I receive a report twice a week.' Taking the cable from his pocket he handed it to Thomas. 'This arrived earlier today.'

Thomas read it through quickly. When he had finished, he handed it back to Leonard and in a quiet voice, asked, 'When do you leave?'

'I have booked a flight to London with a private airline; the plane leaves this afternoon at four.'

'Book another seat. I'm coming with you.'

Smiling with relief, Leonard patted him on the back. 'Good man. I was hoping you might say that.' God willing, this could be the first step towards reuniting his family.

Before Tom went off to arrange things, Leonard asked him, 'Is there any word from Susie?'

Thomas shook his head. 'Not recently. Since Mother left, she's thrown herself into her work. The last letter I had from her, she was in New York drumming up business.'

'And Ronnie – have you heard from him?'

Thomas shook his head. 'Nope.'

'I've been wondering . . .'

'What?'

'Well, since no one seems to know of his whereabouts, do you think he might have gone to England, to look for his mother?'

'It wouldn't surprise me.' Thomas grinned suddenly. 'In fact, he might be the ruffian that's following her.'

That brought an answering smile to Leonard's face. 'Could be.' The smile slipped away. 'But somehow I don't think so.'

With that disturbing thought in mind, the two men prepared for their journey.

Leonard fearing for Vicky's safety.

Thomas wondering who the ruffian was that showed such an interest in his mother.

PART FOUR

March, 1955

The Wedding

CHAPTER TWENTY-TWO

IN SALFORD, ELSIE Langton watched her grandson from the kitchen window. 'Just look at him,' she tutted, hands on hips. 'Anybody would think he was a child of ten, instead of a man of twenty-two.'

Charlie was of the same mind. 'Gawd Almighty!' He shook his head, rolled his eyes and sighed. 'It's no wonder his mum's chucked him out on his ear. What I want to know is, why should we offer him a roof over his head? He won't work, he lolls around in the garden kicking that damned football about, and if you so much as ask him to help dig the allotment, he carries on alarming. I thought his National Service would have sorted him out, but no. He's about as much use as Andy flippin' Pandy, or Looby Loo, come to that.'

A third voice intervened. 'He's not really lazy. He's bored, that's all.' Ben's daughter Abbie was staying with her father until after the wedding. Having taken to Elsie and Charlie, and having made acquaintance with their grandson Stuart, she often called round to say hello.

'What d'yer mean, he's bored?' Elsie demanded. 'There's enough work round here to keep him occupied. He's not bored, he's downright idle, and if he doesn't buck his ideas up, he'll find himself out on his ear.'

'That's right!' Charlie could never abide with time-wasters, and said so. 'I've worked all my life, man and boy, and even now when I should have my feet up and resting, I'm breaking my back down at the smithy.'

Elsie smiled fondly. 'You love it,' she reminded him. 'You wouldn't be doing it if you didn't.'

'That's not the point, is it?' he commented with a grunt. 'All I'm saying is this: every man has to work for a living, or he's not worth salt.'

'And what about every *woman?*' his wife demanded.

'What's that ye say?' He cupped his earlobe.

Elsie raised her voice. 'YOU SAID EVERY MAN IIAS TO WORK FOR A LIVING, AND I ASKED, ''WHAT ABOUT EVERY WOMAN?'' OR IS IT NOT WORK, WHAT I DO UP AT THE HOUSE?'

Charlie laughed. 'Oh, it's looking for a fight now, is it?'

'If you want one, yes.'

'Oh love, I'm sorry. O' course you work hard, I know you do. It was a slip o' the tongue, that's all.'

'Well, you'd best not let it happen again, or I'll not bother cooking you a meal for a while. Soon teach you a lesson, that would.'

Having got used to their banter, Abbie offered to have a word with Stuart. 'He's not happy doing nothing,' she said in his defence. 'It's just that he doesn't yet know what to do with his life. He's . . . well, he's still contemplating.'

Charlie raised his eyebrows. 'Well, I'll be blowed! Contemplating, is it? If he doesn't soon get off his backside and pay his way here, he can bugger off and contemplate somewhere else, where they'll feed and lodge him for nothing.'

Elsie was not quite so harsh. 'Oh, give over, Charlie, the girl is right. Anyway, I thought you were off to pull up a few o' them cabbages for me? And don't worry about Stuart. Once he's made up his mind as to what he really wants out of life, he'll be right as rain.'

Charlie cupped his earlobe. 'Gonna rain, you say?' He glanced out the window. 'Best get yer washing in then, hadn't yer?'

'YES, AN' YOU'D BEST GET YOUR HEARING AID IN, YOU SILLY OLD SOD!'

Whereupon Charlie scurried out of the room. 'Why didn't yer tell me afore?' he groaned. 'I left the blessed thing out on the garden bench. If it rains as you say, it'll be ruined and no mistake.'

When he left the room, Elsie told Abbie softly, 'He's dead crafty, you know. He doesn't want to pull up the cabbages, so he pretends not to hear.' She put her finger to her lips, and winked. 'Just listen.'

She raised her voice very slightly. 'Good grief, is that a ten-bob note on Charlie's chair? It can't belong to him as he said he were broke, so it must be mine.'

'It's *mine*, yer thieving old divil!' Rushing into the room, Charlie looked shame-faced on finding he'd been tricked and rushed out again. 'Steal the fillings out of a man's teeth, she would,' he grumbled. 'I've always said it: yer can't trust no woman, not even yer own wife.'

While Charlie was outside, Elsie took a moment to speak with Abbie. She had come to like her a lot, as Abbie was a sensible young woman. 'Are you all set for being bridesmaid to your daddy and Mary?' she asked. 'Have you got your dress all ready and waiting?'

She thought Abbie would make a lovely bridesmaid. With her long dark hair and big black eyes, she was a striking little thing.

'Not yet, no.' Abbie was a trifle nervous. 'I'm going out with Lucy and Vicky this afternoon. They're taking me shopping for my dress, and all the bits and pieces.'

'Leaving it late, aren't you?' Elsie was the type who liked everything to be in place weeks before an event. 'I mean, if the dress needs altering, they'll not have much time. It's only four days to the wedding. Before you know it, Easter Saturday will be on us and it'll be too late to start worrying about dresses and such then, won't it, eh?'

Abbie was convinced everything would be all right. 'We visited so many shops in Bedford, I've lost count,' she said. 'There's only two more to visit now, so I've got to get it today, or you're right. It will be too late.'

Elsie sighed. 'It's already too late for Stuart,' she worried. 'Rona and I have nagged at him, threatened him and pleaded till we're blue in the face, and *still* he's made no effort to get himself a decent suit and shirt. If he doesn't get it soon, I've told him, he won't be welcome at the church.' She set her mouth hard. 'I'm not having him show us all up, and that's that!'

Abbie got to thinking. 'Has he got any money?'

'Enough. You know that his dad died a few year ago, and Rona, poor lass, has always given him as much as she could. We help out, too. His grandad might grumble and argue, but he thinks a lot of the lad. He had him helping out at the smithy and gave him a few pounds so he could get some clothes for the wedding, but he still hasn't been anywhere to find any – not that I know of anyway.'

'Would you like me to have a word with him?' Like Charlie, Abbie too had a soft spot for Stuart. 'He might listen to me where he won't listen to you.'

'Yes, why not give it a go. If you think you can make him smarten up, nobody would be more grateful than me and Charlie.'

'Right then!'

A few minutes later, Abbie had run out to where Stuart was kicking the ball. She chased after it and snatching it up, held it tight. 'I want you to come out with me tomorrow morning – will you do that?' she asked.

Stuart launched himself at her, trying to grab the ball though not very successfully. 'Grandma's been on at you, has she?' he asked with a cheeky grin. 'Don't tell me . . . if I don't get myself some decent clothes I'll not be allowed in the church, and I'll shame them by not being there. Am I right?'

'Yes, so will you let me take you shopping tomorrow morning?'

'No. Whatever would folks think if I turned up at some poncey shop with you telling me what to buy?'

Abbie observed this fair-haired young man, with his sky-blue eyes and physique to be proud of. 'They'd think you were a lucky man, to have me looking after you.'

He smiled. 'Thank you, but I'll get my own clothes.'

'I bet you've spent the money and daren't tell your grandad.'

'Then you'd lose your bet!' Digging into his pocket, he took out the money Charlie had paid him. 'It's all here, every penny.'

'So why haven't you bought some decent clothes for the wedding then?' When he didn't answer, she guessed, 'You don't know what to buy, do you?'

'Not really, no,' he confessed. 'I'm not used to getting all trussed up like a joint ready for the oven.'

'I could help, if you'll let me?'

'No!'

'Aw, go on. I promise it won't be too painful.'

'I said NO!'

'No shopping, no ball.' With that she ran off, the ball under her arm and Stuart in full pursuit.

Going at a run he threw himself at her in a tackle, bringing her down. Laughing, she threw the ball into the lake. 'You'll have to swim for it now,' she said, smiling up into his eyes and thinking what a handsome bloke he was.

He made no reply. Instead, he looked into those big dark eyes and he was lost. 'You're a devil-woman,' he teased.

'And you're a coward ... won't even come shopping to please Elsie and Charlie.' She felt the warmth of his smile and when he kissed her, it took her by surprise. At first she lay there, arms wide, then she wrapped them round his neck and right there, in that wonderful moment, she fell hopelessly in love.

Some time later, Elsie saw them approach, hand-in-hand, talking and laughing. With the ball under his arm, Stuart was dripping wet, and shivering in the cold March air. 'Look at that!' Coming up behind his wife, Charlie was open-mouthed. 'Well, I never!'

Elsie stared at him. 'What are you on about?'

'The lad ... look at him.' He pointed to Stuart. 'Can't y'see he's soaked to the skin? That little bugger ... she's only gone an' pushed him in the lake. Well, I never!'

Shaking her head, Elsie walked away. 'Roll on Saturday,' she groaned. 'Let's get this wedding over and done with, afore somebody else gets pushed in the lake!'

'Does that mean me?' Charlie thought he wouldn't put it past her.

'If yer like,' she laughed.

'I should hope you'll have a word with that young madam ... pushing our grandson into the lake, indeed!'

'Oh I will,' she replied. 'I most definitely will.' She had seen the way they gazed into each other's eyes, and she was thrilled.

'I wouldn't mind betting she's talked him into going shopping with her,' she remarked.

'Never!' Charlie thought it most unlikely.

'Trust me,' Elsie said. 'I might be a bit old in the tooth, but I still know a thing or two, Charlie, me darlin'.'

And what she thought she knew, was that their grandson and Ben's daughter were attracted to each other.

And she was proud as punch.

Charlie, however, had no idea of what was going on. Rummaging in the dresser-drawer, he asked, 'Where did you put my best tie?'

'Well, you'll not find it screwed up in the drawer, that's for sure! I've ironed it.'

'Oh yes, and where is it then?'

'Upstairs, hanging in the wardrobe.'

'An' where've you put me best shirt?'

'Hanging in the wardrobe with your tie.'

He would have gone on, but Elsie intervened. 'Your tie is with your shirt and your shirt is with your Sunday suit. Your shoes are all polished and shining. They're in the wardrobe, all together, and I don't want you moving them. I know what you're like, and I will not have you panicking on the morning. You already know they all fit, and so all you have to do on the morning is to get washed, shave off your whiskers, and get dressed like the handsome fella I wed . . . Gawd help me!'

Charlie wagged a finger. 'It'll not be me panicking on the morning, you'll see.'

'Oh yes, an' who will it be then, eh?' Going into the kitchen, Elsie took a tray out of the oven, filling the house with the warm smell of fresh-baked bread.

Charlie followed her. 'In my experience, something always goes wrong with weddings.'

'Not this time,' his wife assured him. 'It's been planned right down to the last tiny detail. Ben and Mary's wedding will go like a dream.'

'Yes, well – that remains to be seen.'

~

Many miles north, up in Liverpool, things were already starting to go wrong.

Edward Trent had waited and watched while Vicky went about her business. He followed her to the solicitor's office; he trailed her when she was shopping for hats, and he had gone back and forth to the farmhouse when she met with builders and the like. And on every occasion he was both discreet and cunning, invisible as the wind, but present all the same.

Today, wearied with the waiting and eager for her to make her way to Lucy, he took up his position in the public house opposite the hotel where she was staying. He ordered what he considered to be a well-earned pint, and settled back to enjoy it.

Today he had a feeling in his gut that she would be making her way to Lucy. He mustn't lose her. Not now. Not when he had resisted the temptation to waylay the woman and knock Lucy's address out of her by brute force.

So far, he had avoided any direct confrontation with Vicky – not because he didn't want to hurt or frighten her, but because if he caused a furore, she or someone else was bound to call the police.

So he wisely decided to play a waiting game, and today when he was almost at his wits' end, he was certain his patience was about to pay off.

Across the street and out of sight, Leonard was talking with the private detective. 'He's in there.' Pointing to the public house, the detective explained, 'I arrived here about seven, and he was already here, walking up and down the street until the pub opened.'

'And have you managed to find out anything about him?'

The other man shook his head. 'Not much, I'm afraid. He covers his tracks well. All I know is that he's some kind of vagabond. He never gives his name and never gets into trouble. He's a dark horse, that's for sure.' He issued a warning. 'If I were you, I wouldn't approach him on your own. Matter of fact, with him having followed your good wife and all, I think you should call the cops.'

'There's time enough for that,' Leonard replied thoughtfully. 'Once the police get involved, he'll clam up. His sort always do. I need to know what he wants with my Vicky.'

With his jaw set hard and his stepson by his side, Leonard made his way towards the public house. 'Leave it to me,' he told Thomas. 'We're just two men looking to quench our thirst, okay?'

Thomas nodded. 'What I'd like to do is take him by the scruff of his filthy neck and shake the truth out of him.'

'Not yet. We don't want to frighten him off.'

Inside the pub, Trent was downing his third pint when they came up behind him. 'I'd like a word with you.' Closing him in on one side, Leonard gestured for Thomas to keep close to the left, effectively blocking any escape route.

'Who the hell are you?' Wide-eyed with fear, Trent looked from one to the other. 'What d'yer want from me? I ain't got no money, if that's what yer after!' Scrambling from the stool, he found himself hemmed in.

'What can I get you gents?' The landlord was a weasel type, with sharp beady eyes. 'Two pints, is it?'

Thomas was about to refuse, but Leonard replied with a smile, 'That'll be fine, yes. Two pints of best bitter, if you please.'

'Coming right up, sir!' He went away to the other end of the bar.

'You!' Taking hold of Trent's arm, Leonard gestured to the far table in the corner. 'Over there . . . NOW!'

'What's yer game, eh? Who are you?' Discreetly escorted across the room, Trent was scared out of his wits; it was one thing beating up a helpless woman, but being faced with two big blokes like this was an unnerving experience.

'Shut up, and keep walking!' Thomas wanted only half an excuse to lay him flat. 'We've a few questions to ask, and if you know what's good for you, you'd better have the answers!'

'Sit down.' Leonard approached the table. 'We won't be disturbed here, so now you can tell me why you've been following my wife all over Liverpool.'

'Your wife?' Trent was filled with dread. 'You must be crazy!' Realising he was in deep trouble, he began struggling. 'You've got the wrong bloke,' he protested. 'I know nothing about your wife.'

As they began shuffling him into the chair, he shouted out, 'Landlord! Hey, landlord, these thugs mean to do me over!'

Already on his way with the beers, the little weasel stopped in his tracks. Looking suspiciously from one to the other, he sensed there might be trouble. 'What the devil's going on here?'

While Leonard was assuring the little man that he had no need to worry, Trent took the moment to break loose.

Thomas went after him, but was stopped in his tracks when Trent picked up a chair and smashed it over his head.

'Hey! I want you out of here – all of you. NOW!' Slamming the beer down on the table, the landlord threatened to dial 999 unless they cleared out.

With Trent already away down the street and Thomas reeling from the blow, there was little choice.

From his safe vantage point in the hired car, the private detective had seen it all. 'Get in!' he shouted as they emerged from the pub. 'We'd best get after him.'

They drove in the direction Trent had fled, but there was no sign of him. They scoured the area relentlessly, but in the end had to give up. 'Like I said, he's a real cunning guy,' remarked the detective. 'It's no use looking any more. We won't find him, not now.'

Disheartened, the two men made their way back to their hotel.

Later, when they were washed and changed, with Thomas having bathed and treated the gash across his forehead, Leonard told him how the next phase of their journey, to visit Vicky at her own hotel, was going to be the most formidable for him. 'I don't know how your mother will react when she sees us,' he remarked nervously as they climbed into a taxi. 'I hope she's had time to reflect on things. My one desire is to put things right between the family.'

Thomas shook his head. 'I wouldn't count on it,' he said heavily. 'You know how stubborn Mom can be.'

He was right, because when Vicky opened her hotel-room door to them, her face fell. 'If you've come to try and make me change my mind, you've wasted your time, the pair of you.' But she let them in all the same. 'How did you know where I was?' she asked, hugging Thomas but keeping her distance from Leonard.

Leonard had only ever kept a truth from her once, and that was when he had given his word to Barney. This time he thought it best to tell the truth. 'I had you watched.'

'You did *what?*' She never imagined he would do such a thing.

'I had to,' he confessed. 'I was going crazy, not knowing where you were or whether you were all right. When you still didn't get in touch, I called in a private detective, just to keep a watchful eye on you, that's all. Just so I knew you were safe.'

Vicky was none too pleased. 'Did you think I wasn't capable of taking care of myself?' she snapped. 'I came here to be among friends, and I'm perfectly safe, thank you!'

'No. It wasn't like that at all,' he replied. 'I . . . we . . . needed to know that you were safe.' He had missed her so much, he had nearly gone mad. He wondered whether he would ever get her back: it seemed to him that, here in Liverpool, she was reunited with her beloved Barney, even more strongly than before.

'Oh, did you now?' she said crossly. 'So you sent a dirty, scruffy-looking detective to follow me every step I took. Oh, he was clever, or he thought he was, but I saw him, always a step behind, watching every move I made. I thought it was some old tramp after money.'

Shocked at her description, Leonard thought it safer to tell her. 'That was not the private detective,' he told her. 'He is a smart-looking professional.'

'What do you mean? If it wasn't him, who was it then?'

Thomas answered. 'We don't really know. The detective wrote to Leonard to warn him about that particular fella, and that's why we're here, Mom, to try and find out who he is, and why he's following you. We're worried about your safety.'

Vicky was suspicious. 'Really? Are you sure about that, or is this all a devious plan to make me come home? Because if it is, you're in for a disappointment.' She looked angrily from one to the other. 'You, Thomas, because you turned against your own father. Poor Barney! Not one of you children could see the enormity of the sacrifice he made for you – for all of us!'

Her voice shook with emotion as she turned her attention to the older man. 'As for you, Leonard, how can I forgive you? I will never understand how you could have been with me all those years, sharing my life, my days and nights, with the knowledge that you had taken me from Barney. You should be ashamed. You saw how ill he was; you knew he was putting on an act, draining his energy in doing things to turn us against him, when all the time he must have been crying out for us to help him, to be with him.'

When suddenly she was crying bitter tears, Leonard took a step forward. 'Please don't torture yourself,' he pleaded. 'It was what he wanted, you have to believe that.'

'Please, Mother.' Thomas intervened with his own plea. 'Can't we resolve our differences? Don't let it split the family forever.'

Looking up with tear-filled eyes, Vicky asked softly, 'Will you forgive your father for turning us away?'

Thomas shook his head. 'I can't. I just can't. I'm so sorry.'

Looking from one to the other, she said calmly, 'I'd like you to go now. I'm here for Barney, and I'm here for Lucy. You don't need me, any of you. You must all take comfort from each other.'

Leonard could not believe she was turning them away, but as Thomas had already pointed out, his mother had a strong stubborn streak, and besides, she was still deeply shaken by what had happened to Barney. It would take a long time for her to come to terms with that, if she ever did.

'All right, my dear, we'll leave you now,' he said gently, his love for her evident in every word and gesture. 'But we won't be too far away.' Slipping his fingers into the breast pocket of his jacket, he took out a card and laid it on the sideboard. 'That's the name of the hotel where we're staying. Please, Vicky, think about what's happening here. Think about the family. This isn't what Barney intended, you must realise that.'

He looked her in the eye. 'And you're wrong in what you said just now,' he promised in a low voice. 'Because we all love, and need you.'

There was a moment, one brief heartbeat, when her resolve almost melted. Then she thought of Barney and her heart hardened. 'Please go now,' she repeated, and then she turned away.

After she had closed the door against them, she stood with her back to it for what seemed an age, questioning herself. Was she being selfish? Her head told her yes, her heart told her different.

For now though, all she could think of was Barney, that small solitary figure, left alone and terminally ill as they went out of his life forever. Dear God, how lonely and desolate he must have felt. She and the children had gone away, confused and hurt, despising him. But he never stopped loving them. Lucy had told her, 'Barney talked about you, right up to the day he lost his fight to live.'

Falling onto the sofa, she closed her eyes and let the tears flow. 'You were my first love,' she said brokenly. 'My first and last.' Though she had been with Leonard for an age, and she had deep feelings for him, it was never the same passionate, all-consuming love she had felt with Barney. Leonard knew that. And of course, he understood.

CHAPTER TWENTY-THREE

'OH MUM, DON'T fuss so much!' Mary had stood until her legs ached and now she was ready to sit down. 'What on earth are you doing?' she asked Lucy. 'All I asked you to do was snip off a wayward thread.'

'Stand still, child!' Lucy waved her scissors about. 'If you keep fidgeting, you'll make me cut a chunk out of your dress, never mind the thread!' She snipped once, then twice and now she was satisfied.

'There were tag-ends hanging all round the hem,' she explained. 'I shall have words with that dressmaker when I next see her. I shouldn't be getting down on my old knees, not at my age,' she added. 'They're already creaking and groaning as it is.'

Elsie tutted. 'It's your own fault,' she said. 'I did offer to do it, but oh no! You had to do the job yourself, so if yer don't mind me saying, it serves you right if yer old bones ache.'

From the far end of the room came an offer none of them could refuse. 'It's a tipple of the good stuff ye need,' Bridget informed them merrily. 'That'll stop the old bones aching, so it will.'

'Good idea!' Scrambling up with a groan or two, Lucy stepped back to see her handiwork. 'That's better,' she told Mary. 'A job well done, though I say so myself.'

They each had a glass of 'what the doctor ordered', and taking another long look at her daughter in her wedding gown, Lucy was close to tears. 'You look so beautiful,' she said brokenly.

'Aye, so she does!' Bridget nodded. 'And when the groom claps eyes on her he'll be knocked out, so he will.'

Mary's dress was simple but lovely. Straight and slim, with pretty puffed sleeves and a sweetheart neckline, it suited her beautifully. The veil was figured in delicate lace, with a deep scalloped train that fell to just below the hem of the dress. Her hair was caught up in a mother-of-pearl comb which belonged to Lucy, and altogether she made a stunning figure.

Proud Amy was maid of honour, and Abbie was bridesmaid; both dressed in long flowing dresses of blue, with posies of pink silk roses and matching silk roses in their hair. 'Youse look a picture, so you do!' Bridget was already three sheets to the wind.

'Stay off the booze, now, Bridget,' Lucy warned. 'Or we'll be carrying you down the aisle.'

Looking proud and glamorous, all the women had turned out in their new outfits: Lucy, Vicky, Elsie, Bridget – all the good women, except for Vicky's daughter, Susie. Her absence on such a day had been a huge disappointment to Lucy and Vicky, though they made little of it, because this was Mary's day.

Vicky had joined in the excited preparations and no one knew how bittersweet were her thoughts. Her own children were not here. The bride was Barney's other daughter, borne by Lucy out of a union with her husband. Had they loved as she and Barney had done? And when Mary was born, small and helpless, did Lucy and Barney feel the same way she and Barney did when their own daughter was born?

Envy and regret tinged her thoughts, and she was ashamed.

Barney had turned to Lucy for comfort, and a kind of love had grown between them. For that she should be thankful. Mary was a lovely girl, Barney's flesh and blood, and today, the biggest day of her life, she was getting wed to Ben. For the moment, little else mattered.

'I hope Charlie is taking good care of the bridegroom,' Elsie declared. '"Go straight to the church", I told him. I hope he was listening, 'cause he's a silly old bugger at times. One time, he lost our old dog on the way to the vet's; he slipped his lead, ran off, and didn't come home for days.'

Bridget sniggered. 'And what happened to the dog?'

Along with the others, Elsie squealed with laughter. 'He found Charlie an' brought him home, o' course!' she said, and the place was in uproar.

'Where's Adam?' Frantic, Lucy looked about. 'I hope he hasn't forgotten he's walking Mary down the aisle.'

'I'm here.' Appearing at the door, Adam looked the part in his dark suit and white shirt dressed with a smart tie. 'Are we ready then?'

Lucy had it all organised. 'The rest of us are all ready to leave, so we'll be away now and will be waiting for you at the church. Give it ten minutes and then you and Mary will follow in the front car. Bridesmaids go in the second car.'

And so they set off as planned.

Having kept herself busy since early light, Lucy suddenly found the occasion overwhelming. Making her excuses, she hurried away upstairs. 'You all go ahead,' she told the others. 'I'll be down in a minute. I've forgotten to collect a hankie.' She smiled tearfully. 'You know how mothers cry at weddings,' she joked.

Her eyes met those of Vicky, who was looking at her with a sincere gaze, as if to say, 'It's all right, Lucy, I understand.' Because didn't she also have those very same feelings, about

Mary, and Barney, and hadn't she come to love Lucy all over again?

Lucy nodded, and made her escape. She was glad Vicky was here, so very glad.

Upstairs, she watched through the window as the others made their way down the path, Elsie organising them all in her inimitable manner, and the others looking up to her, following every instruction. 'Oh Barney, my precious darling . . .' Lucy glanced up at a shifting sky. 'Can you see what's happening? Vicky is here to see your daughter marry. We're friends, Barney, just like always.'

Gulping back the threatening tears, she made her way out to the others. 'Here I am,' she announced with a grin. 'Now let's be off, before we're all late for the big event.'

And so they set off as planned.

~

When Lucy and the women arrived at the church, everyone was there, all gathered outside waiting for the bride. 'Oh Lucy! I'm nervous as a kitten.' Stuart had made his grandparents so proud when he agreed to be best man. 'I keep thinking I've lost the ring and everything.'

'Nonsense!' Lucy was having none of that. 'You'll be fine. Just keep a clear head, that's all you need to do.'

Already the church was close to full with neighbours and well-wishers, as well as those who loved a wedding regardless of whose it was.

Now, at the sound of the organ music striking up, Charlie suggested they should all get inside. 'Else the bride will be in there afore we are.' Feeling important because, after all, he'd been put in charge of the groom, he led the way inside.

As Vicky and Lucy settled themselves in place, Lucy saw

Ben turn to glance at the door. She caught his gaze and smiled encouragingly, and he smiled back, albeit nervously.

Vicky turned to see her son, Ronnie, just a short distance behind, and her heart jumped with surprise – and a deep maternal affection. 'I hope you'll go to him afterwards,' Lucy whispered. 'Oh Vicky, I do so wish you could make your peace with them.'

Suddenly there were others making their way into the church.

'It's Leonard!' Vicky leaned towards Lucy. 'They're all here . . . Leonard's brought Susie and Thomas. Look!' Tears poured down her face as her beloved family trooped into the church, proving their love, and their solidarity. Never had her heart felt fuller. Nor Barney so close to them all. Light poured through the stained-glass windows, and a huge burden rolled from Vicky's shoulders.

As Lucy turned to look, the organ thundered into life, and the majestic chords of The Wedding March rolled out . . . Everyone stood and as the bride went down the aisle, there were gasps of delight and admiration from all sides.

Ben turned and his soft shy smile said it all. Here was his love coming to wed him, his life and his joy.

And, as the service got underway and eventually the rings were exchanged, that love and joy was written on both their faces.

Lucy and Vicky had opted to stand together, and for a moment there were no words whispered between them, though their hearts spoke volumes. At one point, when Ben placed the ring on Mary's finger, Vicky took hold of Lucy's hand and the smile they exchanged said it all.

In that special moment, when Mary and Ben returned down the aisle as man and wife, it was as though Barney walked beside his daughter. With soft, tearful eyes, Mary glanced to Lucy and Lucy smiled encouragingly. They both felt his presence and were comforted. Old sorrows had been put to rest now, and the years between were as nothing.

Outside, the photographs were taken and everyone clapped, and then it was time to leave for the wedding reception.

~

Having driven the long journey down to South Bedfordshire in a stolen car, Edward Trent left the churchyard after the guests, following the wedding party from a discreet distance.

He had recognised Lucy straight away: the eyes, the way she held herself when she walked, the voice, the laughter. Through the greying hair and the laugh-lines, she was still the same woman. The mother of his son. The virgin whom he had deflowered. The woman he should have married. The light, to his darkness.

He wanted her. He needed her.

He glanced at the hand-gun beside him.

A lightning flash seared his brain, and he gasped with the pain of it but the thought drumming through his mind kept him going.

One way or another, he meant to have her.

~

He chose his moment well.

The guests were all inside the hotel, drinks in hand and waiting to be called take their seats at the tables.

Lucy was walking alone in the garden, deep in thought as she strolled the walkways. She was thinking of Mary and Barney, and how proud of their daughter he would have been.

Sitting on the swing, she gave vent to her emotion as the tears ran silently down her face.

That was the moment he decided to intrude.

Having parked the car round the corner and out of sight, he had been lurking behind the fountain. Now, though, seeing Lucy alone, he could not believe his good fortune.

'Well, isn't this cosy, eh?' Taking Lucy by surprise, he stepped forward from his hiding-place. 'Just the two of us.'

Lucy was shocked to the roots. 'YOU!' Clambering to her feet, she looked at Trent in disbelief. Her heart was hammering with shock, and with revulsion. 'I thought you'd be long dead by now,' she whispered. 'I hoped you were. I prayed you were.'

He laughed. 'Sorry to disappoint you. As you can see, my lovely, I'm very much alive.'

Catching sight of the gun in his hand, Lucy instinctively stepped back. 'What do you want? Why are you here?'

'I'm here for you, Lucy.' Darting forward, he grabbed hold of her. 'Oh no, my darling.' Pressing the gun into her side, he whispered in her ear, 'You mustn't scream. I don't want to have to shoot you. Not when I've been through so much trouble to find you.'

Keeping a tight hold on her, he began dragging her towards the car.

'Just keep quiet and do as you're told, and there'll be no trouble. I mean, you wouldn't want anyone to get hurt, would you? Not today of all days. Barney's daughter getting wed, eh?' Jabbing her with the gun, he made her wince. 'I can't believe you let him give you a child. It turns my stomach!' The pain was drumming again, maddening him. Then it was gone.

Suddenly he was quietly charming. 'We'll go somewhere quiet, you and me . . . talk about old times. Make plans. Oh Lucy, my lovely, I can't tell you how many times I thought of this day when I was locked away. Y'see, I've never stopped wanting you. Oh, I've had other women, young and not so young, but they've never made me feel the way you do. I'm worried, because I have to make sure you never get too close to this Adam. He seems to have your favour, and we can't allow that, can we now? Oh no! No, my lovely, you and me belong together . . . for always. But we need to talk first. To decide what to do.'

Lucy kept her silence, because she now realised that he was totally insane. Any minute now, he might burst in on the wedding party and shoot everyone in sight. She was mortally afraid. It was cold, so cold in the garden, and she began to shiver.

Having come out to look for her, Adam saw her in the distance, and was puzzled. Who was she with? Certainly, it was not one of the wedding party. 'Lucy!' he called out, surprised when she did not turn.

Behind him, Leonard sauntered up with a glass of champagne in his hand. 'Is something wrong?' he asked.

Adam shook his head. 'I think there might be.' He began to walk down towards the edge of the gardens.

Concerned, Leonard went with him.

'Lucy, are you all right?' Adam called.

With her arm twisted behind her back and Trent trying to keep the gun on her and open the car door at the same time, Lucy began struggling to escape.

Seeing this, and with Leonard shouting that it was the man who had been following Vicky, the two older men made a lunge for Trent. In the ensuing confusion, Edward Trent pointed the gun at them, Lucy was thrown aside, and as she went down she managed to pull on his leg, enough to unbalance him.

That was when the two men darted forward. Caught in this trap, Trent was like a madman. While Adam tried to get the gun from him, Trent smacked him with a vicious blow on the side of his head. As he fell, Leonard went for Trent, the gun discharged itself and Leonard fell to the ground, where he lay still and silent, seemingly lifeless.

'Jaysus, Mary and Joseph! They've killed him!' Bridget had appeared, and her appalling cry rang through the air. Scurrying into his car, Trent made a dash for it.

He was heading for the open road when two police cars rammed him. Blinded by the persistent pain in his temples, he felt so terribly weary, he tried to reach for his gun but his strength was ebbing fast. Quickly now the police moved in.

'You left a trail of unhappy people behind you,' the officer said as he handcuffed him. 'Stealing cars, breaking into offices and causing trouble in the public house. We have a lot of questions needing answers – and so do our friends in Liverpool,' he stated. 'There's the woman who says you beat her up. She also says you killed her sister. And now we've got attempted murder. Well now, that should be enough to be going on with, don't you think? It'll be the gallows for you this time, chummy.' Snapping shut the handcuffs, he threw Trent unceremoniously into one of the police cars.

～

Behind them, the ambulance took Leonard away, with Vicky beside him and his family following.

'Don't you die on me, Leonard Maitland.' Vicky's tears fell on his quiet face.

He didn't hear her.

He had no sense of her nearness.

The guests watched him being taken away. 'Dear God, let him be all right.' Lucy was still shaking, her mind in turmoil. 'Edward Trent said we had things to talk about, and then we'd be together forever.'

She felt desperately afraid for Leonard. Poor Vicky was in a terrible state. 'We must go to the hospital,' she said to Adam.

Then, with Adam's arms around her, she felt safer and more at peace than she had been for a long time. 'I'm sorry,' she whispered. 'Sorry for everything. It's all my fault.' It frightened her to realise how any one of them might have been killed.

'No, Mother, it isn't.' Mary too, was shaken, but deeply thankful that Lucy was safe.

'Leonard . . . and Vicky,' Lucy murmured again. 'We must go to them.'

Adam looked at Mary, as though seeking her approval. 'Please take her,' the new bride told him. 'We'll wait for news.' There was little else they could do.

$\sim$

It had been touch and go.

With the bullet lodged in his chest, Leonard had undergone dangerous surgery to remove it.

A fortnight later, Vicky having spent every possible moment at his bedside, Leonard finally turned the corner to recovery.

'I love you,' Vicky told him on this bright April morning.

'And are we forgiven?' he asked weakly.

Vicky nodded. 'You were right and I was wrong. It was what Barney wanted. I understand that now.'

$\sim$

On a glorious day in mid summer, Lucy made her usual visit to St Andrew's churchyard. She knelt by Barney's little cross and she told him everything that had happened.

'At last, our hearts are settled and we're able to get on with our lives,' she said. 'Abbie and Stuart are already planning a future together, as are Ronnie and Amy. Vicky and the rest of the family have resolved their differences and have returned to America, though of course we'll always keep in touch and hope to see each other again before too long.'

She laid her posy of flowers on the grave and as she arranged them she carried on talking, though somewhat shyly. 'Adam has asked me again to marry him, and this time, I've said yes. We're getting old now, Barney, and we need each other. He's a good man, as you know. I do love him, but not in the same way I loved you. I will always love you, deep in my soul. That's where you will always be, my Barney. I can never change that, nor would I want to. Vicky and I have reached our journey's end now, and we are reconciled. We both love you, oh so much, and we will never forget you. Our four children will love and honour you always. Goodbye, my darling. Goodbye.'

Suddenly a small voice spoke from beside her. 'Is your Barney in Heaven?' The little girl was blonde-haired and blue-eyed, with the look of an angel.

Lucy smiled. 'I hope so, yes.'

'That's where my grandad is,' came the reply. 'He was very special, my grandad. Was your Barney very special too?'

Lucy took the girl by the hand and walked her back to where her mother was waiting. 'Yes,' she whispered. 'My Barney was very special.'

With a smile, she handed her back to her mother, and walked on.

Mary met her, and escorting her to the gate she said, 'I've got something to tell you, Mother.'

'Have you, dear? And what's that then?'

'Ben and I . . . we're having a baby.'

Filled with emotion, Lucy turned to look at her. 'A baby!' The tears fell and suddenly the two of them were embracing. 'Oh Mary, my love, congratulations!' She glanced back at Barney. 'Did you hear that, my darling?' she asked him silently. 'Your daughter is going to make you a grandad.'

They strolled on, talking and laughing, and feeling so incredibly happy. 'A grandchild,' Lucy sang. 'Oh Mary, your daddy would have been so happy.'

'He is,' Mary said. 'Look!' She pointed to the skies. 'Do you think he's given his approval?'

Filled with wonder, Lucy looked up to see the most beautiful rainbow!

~·

Six months later, Mary gave birth to a sturdy little boy. They named him after his grandad, for he was strong in character, brave in heart. He was a fine boy, with his grandfather's blood flowing through him. In the years that followed, Barney would have been proud of his grandson.

Here was a special man in the making.

Another Barney.

Read on for a bonus edition of

Josephine Cox's
Chatterbox

with puzzles, recipes and more!

To my dear readers...

I hope you are all healthy and much loved.
By this time, you will probably have read
the very special story about Lucy and her
family that make up *The Journey* and
Journey's End, which I wrote ten years ago.
I hope you have enjoyed this unique edition
that we have put together as a gift, either for
yourself (which you're allowed to do every
once in a while, you know!) or as a keepsake
for someone you love.

I know how generous you are from the letters
that you send to me, which I love to receive.
Please forgive me if sometimes I'm a little
slower at replying than you might like; I will
always write back to you eventually! I'm sure
you understand that sometimes the days aren't
long enough for me to do everything I would
like to do - isn't that the same for us all?
But I really do treasure the letters that you

send me – many of you are kind enough
to tell me how much you enjoy my books,
and you often come to me with stories
of your own lives as well. These are your
gifts to me, and I am eternally grateful for
each and every one.

God bless, stay well and much love from me,

Josephine Cox

Why not make
a very special meal
for the ones you
love using these
delicious recipes?

RUSTIC SALMON PÂTÉ

I love a delicious pâté, and none more so than this one, which is made up of both fresh and smoked salmon and lots of grated fresh nutmeg, all brought together with, of course, lovely salty butter.

Serves 4-6 as a starter

85g (3¼oz) skinned smoked salmon, cut into 1cm (½in) dice

85g (3¼oz) skinned fresh salmon, cut into 1cm (½in) dice

3 tsp chopped dill

3 tsp chopped capers

1 tbsp lemon juice

pinch of salt

twist of black pepper

¼ tsp freshly grated nutmeg

1 clove of garlic, peeled and finely grated or crushed

50g (2oz) crème fraiche

50g (2oz) cream cheese

Put both the salmons with 1 tablespoon of water in a small saucepan with a tight-fitting lid on a low heat and cook for a few minutes until the fish has changed colour the whole way through, making sure not to let it burn.

Mash the fish with a fork, then mix together with all the remaining ingredients. Taste and check the seasoning. Serve on crusty toast.

Recipes taken from Coast by Rachel Allen, which is published by HarperCollins

LAMB SHANKS BRAISED IN RED ALE

I love how beer transforms in flavour when cooked. The gentle, toasted, malty twang of a red ale turns into something very mellow and deep when simmering away for a couple of hours with delicious meaty lamb shanks.

Serves 4 as a main course

4 lamb shanks

salt and freshly ground black pepper

400g (14oz) red onions, peeled and cut into wedges through the core

100g (3½oz) celery, trimmed and cut at an angle into 1cm (½in) chunks

8 cloves of garlic, peeled and sliced

2 tbsp chopped sage

250ml (9fl oz) red beer or ale

500ml (18fl oz) light lamb or chicken stock

1 tbsp tomato puree

Recipes taken from Coast by Rachel Allen, which is published by HarperCollins

Preheat the oven to 150°C (300°F) gas mark 2.

Trim some fat from the shanks and render it on a medium heat in a pot big enough to take the four shanks. Season the shanks with salt and pepper.

Turn the heat up to high and fry the lamb shanks in the pot until golden on all sides. You might need to brown them two at a time. Remove the shanks, leaving any fat behind, then fry the onions, celery and garlic for a few minutes and season again.

Return the shanks to the pot with the sage, beer or ale, stock and tomato puree. Bring to the boil, then cover with a lid and cook in the oven for 2½-3 hours until the meat is succulent and almost falling off the bone.

Serve on a bed of roast garlic mash or plain mashed potatoes with plenty of the braising liquid.

Recipes taken from Coast by Rachel Allen, which is published by HarperCollins

QUICK CHOCOLATE MOUSSE

This is, without doubt, my go-to dessert to whip up in five minutes. Delicious served with simply a few raspberries sitting on top, or softly whipped cream and a sweet sticky toffee sauce.

Serves 4

120g (4¼oz) dark chocolate, chopped or in chips

120ml (4fl oz) double or regular cream

2 eggs

finely grated zest of 1 small orange (optional)

1-2 tbsp Irish whiskey (optional)

Put the chocolate in a heatproof bowl. In a pan on a high heat, bring the cream to the boil, then pour it over the chocolate and stir to melt.

Separate the eggs and beat the egg yolks into the melted chocolate. You can add the orange zest or whiskey with the egg yolks, if you wish.

In a separate, clean, grease-free bowl, whisk the egg whites until just holding a stiff peak, then carefully fold them into the chocolate.

Spoon into individual bowls or glasses and place in the fridge for at least 1 ½ hours to set.

Recipes taken from Coast by Rachel Allen, which is published by HarperCollins

Get stuck into some
FIENDISH PUZZLES

WORD WHEEL CHALLENGE

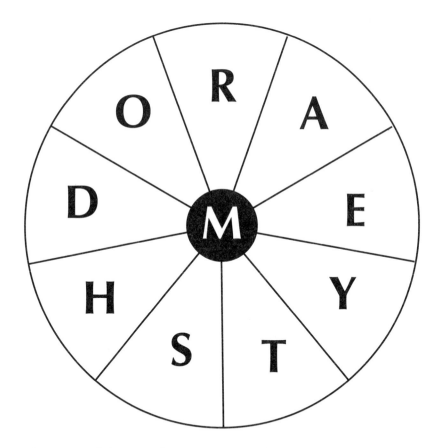

The aim of this challenge is to make as many words as you can, using the letters in the word wheel only once each.

There's also a 9-letter word hiding – can you work out what it is?

A Mother's Gift Word Search

We've created a very special Mother's Day-themed word search for you to complete. Can you find all words in the list below?

CARD
CHILDREN
CHOCOLATE
DAUGHTER

FLOWERS
GRATEFUL
MARCH
MATERNAL
MOTHER

PRESENT
SON
SPRING
SUNDAY

S	N	U	S	L	C	Y	W	J	A	W	S	L	G	N
P	O	R	E	T	H	G	U	A	D	U	D	R	T	E
R	S	Z	I	Y	O	L	Z	K	N	D	A	R	P	R
I	K	S	J	T	C	S	A	D	W	T	Z	S	R	D
N	P	N	O	X	O	P	A	N	E	U	R	B	O	L
G	I	R	E	B	L	Y	O	F	R	E	U	T	C	I
N	E	Y	N	M	A	M	U	X	W	E	H	Z	O	H
I	G	N	W	Z	T	L	O	O	W	I	T	U	M	C
D	S	Z	O	Z	E	B	L	T	X	D	K	A	L	X
F	R	O	G	Z	O	F	V	T	H	C	R	A	M	T
Q	Q	A	G	O	L	X	Q	F	N	E	V	W	Y	H
V	E	L	C	T	W	C	I	B	C	C	R	T	Y	I
A	G	S	I	I	Z	C	W	A	A	U	L	I	C	W
X	I	I	U	M	V	O	F	B	Q	P	T	B	Z	X
Q	N	S	S	P	R	E	S	E	N	T	R	O	N	Y

SuJOku

				2				
					5	1		
6		8		1	3			
7	8					9		
	1					4		
				5		3		8
	3		7		1			
		6			9	8		3
4		5	3	8		7		6

Can you complete the Sudoku grid above?

The aim is to fill in all of the empty squares so that the numbers 1 to 9 appear only once in each row, column, and 3x3 box.

Get ready for a
BRAND NEW
Josephine Cox novel in 2017

Keep an eye on Jo's Facebook
page and website, or look out
for the next edition of Chatterbox
for more details.

Join Jo Online

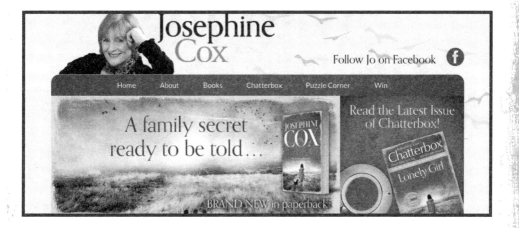
www.josephinecox.com

Visit Jo's beautiful new website
to read the latest news from Jo,
download extra puzzle pages
and enter exclusive competitions!

Keep up to date with Jo